CHILDREN OF MADNESS

JARRETT BRANDON EARLY

For my daughter Alex Beam—who has all the best qualities of Ash, Ditto,
Sammi, Hana, and (especially) Fincher Bugg

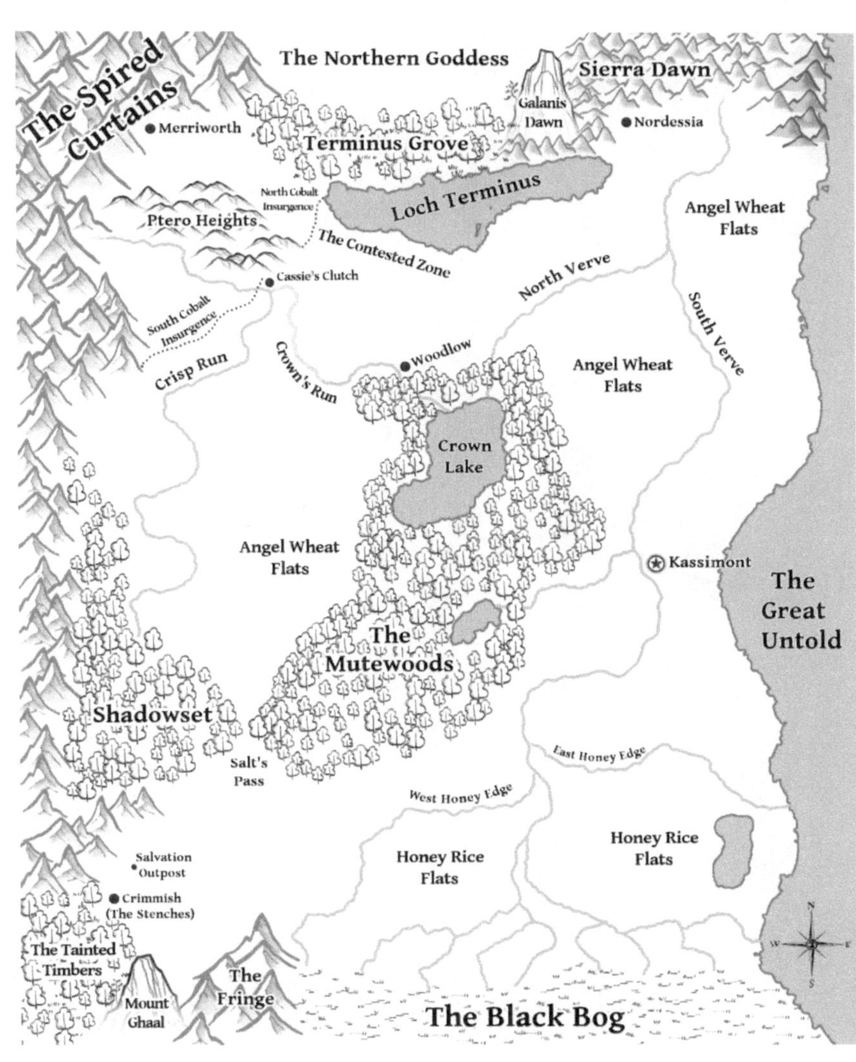

The Spired Curtains
The Northern Goddess
Sierra Dawn
Merriworth
Galanis Dawn
Nordessia
Terminus Grove
North Cobalt Insurgence
Loch Terminus
Angel Wheat Flats
Ptero Heights
The Contested Zone
North Verve
South Verve
South Cobalt Insurgence
Cassie's Clutch
Crisp Run
Crown's Run
Woodlow
Angel Wheat Flats
Crown Lake
Angel Wheat Flats
Kassimont
The Great Untold
The Mutewoods
Shadowset
East Honey Edge
Salt's Pass
West Honey Edge
Salvation Outpost
Honey Rice Flats
Honey Rice Flats
Crimmish (The Stenches)
The Tainted Timbers
The Fringe
Mount Ghaal
The Black Bog
N
W E
S

PROLOGUE

"Eight days! Eight days now!" roared Imperator Kasspar Rayne from the throne room as he paced frantically across the immaculate tiled floor. "Eight days since the Centennial Star appeared in the sky. And what word do we have of the Supreme Helices? Nothing!"

Imperatrix Kassidy Rayne, standing on the castle balcony looking out toward the Great Untold, shot a look at Chancellor Sologar Crimm before rolling her striking blue eyes.

"He's nothing if not passionate, my Lady," quipped Crimm.

"Do not mistake passion for desperation, Sologar. For once, my husband's desperation is well-placed. We know not how much longer the Rose Comet will remain above us. Or more importantly, when or where the Snail-Gods will honor us with their divine presence."

"They always appear, my Lady. And they have yet to let us down over the last half of the millennium. They will provide us with what we need to lift this shroud from the land."

Kassidy scoffed. "Oh, they will offer a solution, to be sure. But to us? Perhaps the Divine Pentad has already come to Quaan. And if so, who's to say that we find them first? From what I can gather from the historic records, the God-Snails care little for politics, meaning they care little for the Titian Empire. Their gift in the wrong hands—an ambitious governor or, even worse, the Sluggs—could bring down the walls of this castle and our celebrated reign."

"We will find them, my Lady. The God-Snails' gift will be ours to control, once again."

"I wish I could share in your optimism, Sologar. Something feels off this time. Kasspar senses it, too. My husband may be unsophisticated in many areas of state, but I have learned to trust his intuition against my more logical inclinations."

The sound of a chalice slamming against the stone wall brought the pair back to the throne room.

Kassidy sighed. "He's drinking too much. Again."

Sologar placed a pale, ringed hand on her silk-covered shoulder. "The Imperator has much to bear, my Lady."

"We all do, Sologar. That is no excuse."

Kassidy and Sologar grimaced in unison as the Imperator tripped and fell hard to the throne room floor. High Captain Gorman Graff, ever vigilant in his rust-colored uniform, was there in a flash, helping his leader back to his feet.

"Please, my Lord, have a seat and try to relax. I have put forth all of the empire's resources toward locating the Supreme Helices. They will be found."

A grating, high-pitched voice cut through the throne room from its entrance. "They may already have been."

All the occupants of the room turned to find Lieutenant Benson Kruger just inside the throne room, a wolfish grin pasted on his narrow, rodent-like face. Kassidy and Sologar rushed in from the balcony.

Captain Graff assisted Imperator Rayne back into his throne before speaking. "Lieutenant Kruger, I hope you have some good news for us."

"I do not." The wolfish grin grew wider. "I have the best of news. A farmer to the North saw the falling of the Pentad."

The throne room exploded into chatter as Kasspar leaned forward anxiously on his gilded seat of power. "And where is this farmer?" demanded Kasspar, his bloodshot eyes on the edge of mania.

Kruger waited for a moment before responding. Captain Graff snorted derisively, understanding that his attention-seeking underling wanted to build suspense, relish in self-importance.

Finally, Kruger acquiesced to this enraptured audience. "I have brought him to you, Sire. He is here, just outside this door."

"Bring him to me at once," said Kasspar, his knuckles white on the golden arm rests.

"Of course, your highness. But please know, the farmer witnessed the divine fall eight nights ago. Like the good Titian that he is, he immediately told the local magistrate, luckily one loyal to the empire, and was instantaneously whisked away to Kassimont. We have been relaying him here ever since. Three imperial horses died in the effort."

"What's your point, Kruger?" asked Graff, ever annoyed by his unscrupulous subordinate.

Kruger's grinning mask fell for a moment before it was quickly replaced. "My point, *High Captain* Graff, is that the poor simpleton hasn't slept in eight days. I simply wanted to warn my liege that he may be a bit unfocused, a bit scattered. I may be able to fill in the blanks where his farmer brain cannot."

"Enough," cried Kasspar. "Good work, Lieutenant. Send him in before I have everyone flogged!"

Kruger threw Graff a challenging look. "Of course, Your Highness."

Benson Kruger pulled open one of the throne room's large double doors. Standing meekly in the opening, dirty hands wringing before him, was the farmer, head down as if the secrets of the universe were spelled out on his worn boots.

"Go stand before your Imperator," shouted Kruger. Graff thought it unnecessarily harsh and commanding.

The small, grime-covered man shuffled over to stand before Imperator Kasspar Rayne, seated several feet above on the dais.

"What is your name, loyal subject?" inquired Kasspar softly. Imperatrix Kassidy smiled to herself. Despite her husband's many weaknesses, she always admired his ability to speak effectively to the common folk, something she was never able to lower herself to do.

Although the little man lifted his head, he did not meet the Imperator's light brown gaze. "My name is Clancy. Clancy Boyd, my Lord."

"I hear you reside in the North, Farmer Boyd. Where exactly?"

"I live in Nordessia, my Lord. But I am no farmer. I raise Blacknose along the mountains' edge."

Captain Graff turned angrily to Kruger, who shrugged and mouthed, *close enough.*

"Blacknose? That is a type of sheep, is it not?"

"You are correct, my Lord."

"An admirable profession. Roast mutton is one of my favorites. And I hear Blacknose meat is among the most tender. I would love to try one from your flock."

Boyd smiled broadly and finally managed to look upon Imperator Rayne. "You honor me, my Lord." Again, Kassidy silently congratulated Kasspar for one of his few talents.

"No, it is *you* who honor *me*, citizen Boyd. You have an important message for me, do you not?"

Boyd's wringing hands began to move faster. "I do. Or, at least, I think I do. I'm not sure how to explain what I saw."

Imperatrix Rayne gritted her teeth, wanting to throttle the filthy man for his slow wit. Luckily, Kasspar had more patience.

"Take your time, Shepherd Boyd. Just tell me the when and where of the matter. Ignore everyone else in this room. You are only speaking to me. And I like you already." Kasspar's kind words had an immediate effect as Boyd's posture slackened ever so slightly.

"I forget how long ago it was…"

"Eight nights?"

"Yes, that could be right. I haven't slept in days so…"

"Please continue."

"Of course, my Lord. I was tending to my sheep, and it was early. They like to get a move on several hours before Paragon rises over the horizon. As I pushed the flock higher into the mountains where dally weed—their favorite—grows in giant bunches, I saw something strange against the black sky."

Kasspar's red eyes flashed. "What did you see, Shepherd Boyd?"

"Five red streaks, my Lord. Falling toward Quaan from the great starry nothingness above."

"Where did they land, Shepherd Boyd?"

"I can't be sure, my Lord, but it was a goodly distance away. I would think on the other side of Sierra Dawn."

A look of panic crossed the delicately manicured face of the Imperator. "What direction precisely, Boyd?"

"I can't be sure, my Lord."

"Try!"

Clancy Boyd jumped at the change in his imperator's tone. His eyes once more found his weathered boots.

"Answer your liege," cried Benson Kruger.

"I, I, I'm not sure, my Lord," Boyd stammered in his terror. "Let's see, I was heading straight up the Dawn because I know of a good patch of dally weed several hundred feet up. The red streaks were just ahead and to my left. Which means it must have landed to the northeast."

"Was it more north or east?" The desperation was beginning to seep through Kasspar's faux cool exterior.

"To the east, my Lord?"

"Are you sure?" A pause. "Are you sure?!"

"I am, I am, I am, my Lord."

"Not east, but northeast?"

"Yes, my Lord."

"And you're sure? You weren't smoking any of that rummy weed that I hear shepherds like to partake in?"

"Never, sire! Well, perhaps when I was younger, but not in many, many turns of Paragon. In fact—"

"Enough." Boyd stopped mid-sentence. "Tell me what happened after you witnessed this unusual occurrence."

"I abandoned my flock and ran down from the mountain, my Lord. I immediately informed Governor Merritt. And let me tell you, he was none too happy that I awoke him at such an hour. In fact, he…"

"Did you tell anyone else, Shepherd Boyd? Anyone at all? A wife? A friend? A stranger on the hillside?"

"None, my Lord. I swear on my life. I know not what I saw, but I knew it was beyond a simple shepherd like me."

Kasspar sat back on his throne, simultaneously more at ease and more disturbed. "You did well, Shepherd Boyd. The Titian Empire owes you a great debt. Get some much-deserved rest. Lieutenant Kruger! Make sure that Shepherd Clancy Boyd is not only monetarily rewarded but is given an escort of honor back to Nordessia. He has perhaps ensured that the Titian Empire continues for another hundred years."

While Boyd's dirty face cracked into a wide smile, Benson Kruger's appeared to have sucked in something sour. As Boyd bowed and made his way back to the throne room entrance, Captain Graff, Chancellor Crimm, and several other advisors approached Kasspar, speaking in hushed tones.

Shepherd Boyd passed gleefully through the massive open door. Benson Kruger moved to follow but was stopped by a soft hand on his arm.

"A word, Lieutenant Kruger," said Imperatrix Rayne, her eyes dancing conspiratorially.

The wolfish grin reappeared. "Of course, my Lady. How can I be of service?"

"How sure are we of the farmer's discretion?"

"From what I have gathered, he had neither the time nor inclination nor opportunity to inform any others of what he saw."

"And moving forward?"

Kruger smiled dangerously. "I am no oracle, my Lady."

"Then you cannot know?"

"Know what exactly, my Lady?"

"Know that this farmer won't take the reward that you give him and spend it at the first pub he comes across, raining chips upon any sweet face that brushes across his lap and bragging about how the

Imperator told him that he saved the Empire by seeing five heavenly bodies falling to Quaan. It wouldn't take much for that story to spread. For it to be heard by the wrong ears."

Kruger's teeth began to show. "It wouldn't take much at all, my Lady."

"Perhaps it's better that this story remains here, amongst those that can be trusted."

"The road out of Kassimont can be treacherous, my Lady. I will do my best to protect our valued citizen. But accidents *do* happen."

"Yes. Perhaps it's best that they do."

Kruger bowed deeply. "Your wish is my command, my Lady."

"There was no command, Lieutenant."

"Of course not, my Lady. There never is."

Imperator Rayne pressed his fingers to his temples, a pained look on his face. Kassidy returned from her conversation with Kruger and threw a concerned glance toward Sologar Crimm.

"Is this… shepherd to be trusted?" asked the Imperator to his gathered council.

"I detected no lies from the man, my husband. Of course, I didn't detect much in the way of brains, either."

A Titian guard rushed forward and whispered something into the Chancellor's ear.

"Apparently," said Sologar, "the man's story did not change over the course of his journey south. And he has had no intoxicants in that time. If it is a lie, he believes it."

Kasspar ceased his massaging. "Then let us assume that he is both truthful and correct. My knowledge of Quaan's geography is not what it once was, but am I right to conclude that the God-Snails are in the one location in which we do not want them?"

"I share in your worry, husband. If the farmer was correct, the Supreme Helices have landed in the Northern Goddess. The only worse outcome would be if they had made landfall within the Cobalt Insurgence. Then all would surely be lost."

"Is it not already?" snapped Kasspar, more roughly than he had intended. He took a breath. "Excuse my tone, my love, but our messiah sits, ready to deliver us from this shadow that has enveloped our land, on the other side of Terminus Grove. Our Lord might as well be across the Spired Curtains or beyond the Black Bog. Alas, even if the Divine Pentad was in the grips of the Sluggs, at least we could fight for control of their gift. At least it would be within reach. One cannot fight that which one cannot see or touch or hear, which is exactly what the toxic fumes of Terminus Grove bring. I fear all is lost."

The Imperatrix used all her willpower to avoid rolling her eyes again. Her husband had an unusually soft heart for a ruler, and that often led to a weak resolve, a quitter's mentality. She needed to nip this in the bud before it spread.

"Nothing is impossible, my Imperator," said Kassidy, determined to right the ship. "This is but an obstacle, although a massive one. Perhaps the God-Snails are testing us. Perhaps this gift will be the grandest of all, one that will cement the Titian Empire for hundreds of years to come. But great reward will require great sacrifice. Maybe God wants us to work for His gift this time."

"Work, sure," complained Kasspar. "I am never one above tough labor." A few of the guards shared looks. "But this is not a test that one can pass. This is a tease, a promise doomed to never be fulfilled. Oh, how my father would laugh if he could see me now. Oh, how he would relish in my ultimate failure." A pause. "Chancellor Crimm, you are unusually quiet. Are dire troubles facing the kingdom not your domain?" There was a challenge in the Imperator's words.

Sologar Crimm remained silent for several beats, his eyes closed and his hands steepled before him. Eventually, his dark green eyes appeared and a small smirk twitched within the slight man's carefully maintained goatee.

"Apologies, my liege, but I was pondering our situation. It is both unique and dire, requiring an equally unusual solution."

"Spit it out, Crimm," said Captain Graff, his disdain for the Chancellor evident. Jade eyes shot daggers at the Captain before they quickly cooled over.

"Forgive the Captain, Sologar," offered Kasspar, although he was clearly amused by his loyal soldier's distaste for not only Sologar, but the long line of Crimm advisors. "If you have such a solution, we're all ears, including Captain Graff here."

Sologar Crimm smoothed down his immaculate silk robes, obviously annoyed that his revelation had been interrupted.

"*As I was saying*, my Lord, such a vexing problem will need a unique, almost preposterous solution."

"And you have one in mind?"

"I do, my Lord."

"Then speak it. Please."

Sologar Crimm began to pace around the throne room, making sure all eyes were on him before he began. Captain Graff's calloused hand tightened on the pommel of his well-worn sword.

"What is it about Terminus Grove that makes it so impenetrable? So impassable?"

"You mean other than it being behind the Cobalt Insurgence?" asked Captain Graff flatly, confident this was not what Sologar was hinting at.

To his credit, the Chancellor brushed off the attempt to disturb his flow.

"Yes, Captain Graff. Other than the politics of the region."

"It is toxic," offered Kasspar. "The air is thick with poison."

"Of course, you are correct, my Lord. And what causes such conditions?"

This time it was the Imperatrix who responded. "The flora. Many of the plants within the grove emit gasses that burn lungs, pollute minds, and infect various organs. Many say that you go mad long before you drop dead in Terminus Grove."

"An accurate statement, my Lady. But go back further. What was the genesis of Terminus Grove? And Loch Terminus, to that end."

"Galanis Dawn?"

Chancellor Crimm's face lit up, adding theater for the moment. "That's right, my Imperator! Now, what exactly did Galanis Dawn's eruption do?"

Kassidy Rayne's beautiful head cocked to the side, sending her bejeweled earrings and hair ornaments to clink together like wind chimes. Pieces began to fall into place.

"Galanis Dawn's eruption sent magma and toxic ash to settle to the south and west of the great spire. Ultimately, this altered the soil and gave rise to the dangerous flora that now blocks our path to the Messiah."

Crimm bowed to the Imperatrix. "As always, I am but a small servant in the shadow of my Lady's greatness."

"What are you getting at, Chancellor?" asked Kasspar, growing tired of the dramatics.

Sologar stepped toward the dais. "Where has a similar situation occurred?"

Kassidy's too-blue eyes grew wide. "Mount Ghaal!"

Crimm held up a ringed finger. "Yes! Correct again, my Lady. Mount Ghaal erupted around the same time as Galanis Dawn. And what now sits at the feet of that sleeping giant?"

This time, even Captain Graff was unable to help himself. "The Tainted Timbers."

Sologar grinned slyly. "Right you are, Captain Graff. The Tainted Timbers. Home to the Reaper Vines whose noxious fumes made possible the growth of the Moonflower, the God-Snails' last gift to humanity. Do you see how this all ties in?! Oh, the Supreme Helices are testing us, to be sure. And I think I have cracked the code. Or, at least the first code."

A silence fell over the throne room. Kassidy Rayne smirked but waited for another to break the spell.

High Captain Graff, never one for inaction, spoke first. "Okay, but I still don't understand. What do the Tainted Timbers have to do with dealing with Terminus Grove?"

Sologar and Kassidy locked eyes. "The Timbers? Nothing. The people who call the Timbers home? Everything."

Graff's lined face scrunched together. "You mean the Stenches?"

Sologar Crimm's eyes narrowed. "It is called Crimmish, Captain. It has always been named Crimmish."

Graff chuckled to himself, reminded that the Stenches had been founded by one of Sologar's forebears, an ambitious advisor who founded the town as a penal colony for those deemed enemies of the crown. Unfortunately, the name was quickly lost to the more popular moniker, the Stenches, attributed to the toxic gas emitted by the forest's Reaper Vines.

"My apologies, Chancellor."

"An unintended error, I'm sure. But, as I was saying, it is the people of Crimmish who may be the key to solving this most pressing of issues."

Kasspar leaned forward, his light brown eyes gleaming. "You have my attention, Sologar. Please continue."

"Thank you, my Lord. Why are the people of Crimmish so vital to Quaan?"

The Imperatrix answered once more. "They harvest Moon Tears, from which Salvation is concocted."

"Exactly, my Lady! After generations of living along the Timbers, trekking within to harvest the Moon Tears that helped us overcome the Bloat, the people of Crimmish have developed an immunity to various toxins and poisons. If they can survive the Tainted Timbers, what's to say that they will not survive Terminus Grove?"

One of the guards along the throne room wall loudly cleared his throat. Only Captain Graff noticed.

"Something on your mind, soldier?"

The young man hesitated but stepped forward. "What the Chancellor says is not entirely true, my Captain."

Sologar's eyes blazed with rage. Graff enjoyed the moment.

"What is your name, soldier?"

"Second Lieutenant Tobias Vale, sir."

"And what, exactly, is incorrect about the Chancellor's words?"

"Well, sir, nothing is exactly incorrect."

"Then why are you speaking, man?!"

The young soldier's unusual yellow eyes went wide, and he looked as if he'd rather be fighting a Ghost Puma. "It's just that… one of my assignments is to regularly visit Salvation Post and collect the harvested Moon Tears…"

"And?"

"Well, sir, I've ascertained quite a bit over the course of my many trips."

"And what have you ascertained, soldier?"

"Well, for one, they aren't immune to the tainted air, sir. They're simply resistant to it, especially when they are younger. That's why all the harvesters are children. They have to stop late into their teens, or they'll drop dead just as surely as you or I will. Even then, the damage has been done. Adults in the Stenches…" Sologar overtly fingered the dagger at his side. "Apologies, Chancellor. Adults in Crimmish typically die in their mid to late thirties from the toxic buildup in their brains. The locals call it the Maddening."

"Anything else, soldier?"

"That's all I know, Captain."

"Thank you for your insights. Return to your post." Second Lieutenant Vale let out a sigh of relief and returned his back to the wall, accepting subtle nods from his fellow guards. "So, where does that put us, Chancellor?"

Sologar began to pace once more, his ringed fingers combing his pointed goatee. After several moments, he stopped. "Perhaps in a better position than before, Captain." Sologar addressed Kasspar and Kassidy. "My Lord and Lady, may I have some time… alone."

Kasspar and Kassidy looked to each other before the Imperator nodded reluctantly. "Clear the room! Only the Imperatrix and Chancellor Crimm are to remain!"

High Captain Graff appeared put out but enacted the order. "You heard the Imperator! Clear the room!" After all the guards and attendants had exited, Graff turned to Kasspar. "I'm just outside if you need me, Lord."

"Thank you, Gorman."

Graff shot Sologar a warning as he passed. Crimm returned it with a smile. Soon, only the three remained.

"We are alone now. Speak freely, Chancellor."

"Of course, my Imperator. This new information not only does not alter my plans, it cements them."

"How so?" asked Kassidy.

"Children do not ask why. Children do as they're told. Children have no political inclinations. Children are motivated by sweet candy and sweeter words, and not getting smacked in the back of the head. Children can be trusted to carry out orders. Because children cannot imagine the benefits of being distrustful."

"And so..."

"And so, my Lady, we will have the children of Crimmish carry out this most important of duties. After all, does the old adage not state that *God can be found in the eyes of a child*?"

Kasspar and Kassidy's eyes met. The Imperator voiced his concern first.

"Chancellor Crimm, this seems like too momentous of a task to be left up to children."

"Or, my Lord, is it too momentous of a task to be left in the hands of scheming men?"

Kassidy cut in. "There is much to consider, Sologar. Crimmish is far to the southwest. Have you considered how the children will cross Quaan unscathed? How they will penetrate the Cobalt Insurgence before entering Terminus Grove? How they will understand the necessity of returning the Pentad Gift to its rightful owner—Imperator Rayne—upon completion? There are many moving parts to ensure that this bizarre plan comes together. How do you intend to address these issues?"

Chancellor Sologar Crimm flashed a toothy smile as he combed his silken regalia with ringed fingers. "I have some thoughts, my Lady."

"You always do, don't you, Sologar?"

Crimm simply bowed in return.

~

High Captain Gorman Graff waited impatiently outside the throne room, wondering what poison Chancellor Crimm was dripping into Imperator Rayne's receptive ears. The other guards chatted quietly amongst themselves, unsure of the where the next few weeks would take them. Captain Graff found Tobias Vale within the group.

"Second Lieutenant Vale. You've made the trip to the Stenches several times, correct?"

The young man jumped to attention, unused to being addressed by the High Captain of the Titian Empire. "Correct, sir. At least half a dozen."

"And how long does the trip take you each way?"

"Around eleven rises of Paragon, Captain. Longer if we stop at one of the settlements along the Mutewoods." Vale hesitated. "Several have been declared Spirit Zones along the Kassimedes Thoroughfare."

"Expensive girls but worth every chip," stated one guard, who laughed then fell silent when Graff's grey eyes fell upon him.

Vale cleared his throat. "With cases of the Bloat still dropping, need for Salvation has decreased significantly, meaning we have been able to take our time, as of late."

"Well, that certainly won't be this trip, Second Lieutenant. If you had to, what's the fastest you and a team could reach the Stenches?"

Vale thought for a moment, doing calculations in his head. "I suppose if we really pushed ourselves and the horses, a team could reach the Stenches in nine days, sir."

"Good to know, soldier. Stay close. I don't care how bright the Five Sisters get in the night sky, I have a feeling you'll have new orders before Ommori Prime fades into dawn."

"Of course, my Captain."

The doors to the throne room burst open. Captain Graff's mouth turned down within his gray beard as he was greeted by the visage of Chancellor Crimm.

"Captain Graff. Your presence is requested."

Graff nodded, motioned for Tobias Vale to stay put, and moved into the throne room, Crimm slamming the door shut behind him. He spoke as he approached the dais.

"Ready, as my Lord commands."

Kasspar Rayne took a long swig of wine from his recovered golden chalice before speaking. "My loyal High Captain Graff. Time is of the essence, unfortunately, so forgive me if I don't mince words. I have heard Chancellor Crimm's plan, and it seems a solid one. To be honest, it seems the only option we have, so we are all going to have to pull together to make it work."

"Understood, my Imperator."

"We need a team to travel to the Stench… to Crimmish. Once there, they are to secure the best harvesters that godforsaken place has to offer and guide them north to Terminus Grove. Hopefully, the harvesters' resistance to toxins will allow them to pass through the Grove relatively unscathed. Once clear, they will make contact with the Divine Pentad, receive humanity's centennial gift, and deliver it to the Titian Empire. Questions?"

Captain Graff looked as if he had spent the past hour downing Honey Rice Wine. Chancellor Crimm almost chuckled aloud.

"Many, sire."

"Let loose then, Captain. Time is a luxury we do not possess."

Graff took a beat to compose himself. "These… harvesters? They are children, are they not?"

"They are."

"Can we ask children to embark on such a dangerous journey?"

Kasspar took another large gulp of wine. "We all must do our part, Captain. For the greater good."

Sologar Crimm cut in. "The children of Crimmish are used to danger, Captain. I dare say that they won't encounter much on their travels any worse than what can be found in the Tainted Timbers."

Graff's scarred face twisted as he considered the plan. "Okay, let's say that a team does get the children…"

"The harvesters, Captain," corrected Kassidy Rayne from the side.

"... Does get the harvesters north. The entrance to Terminus Grove is not only through the Contested Zone but is behind the Cobalt Insurgence line."

"Chancellor Crimm has already thought of that," replied Kasspar, his eyes starting to dull from the strong wine.

Crimm took the baton. "The Titian Army will launch an all-out offensive, catching the Sluggs off-guard. We only need to gain a bit of ground, just enough so that the harvesters can slip in behind them and gain access to Terminus Grove. We don't need to hold the position for any length of time."

Captain Graff's head spun, quickly losing count of the number of holes in Sologar Crimm's hasty plan. The Imperatrix's voice sliced in from beside him.

"This is not a conversation, Captain Graff. Nor is it a strategy session. These are orders."

Kasspar held a bejeweled hand up, begging his wife for some patience with the grizzled vet. "Captain, we know this is a lot to take in. But things are happening quickly, things that could upend the empire as we know it. Unfortunately, in this case, the time for discussion is something we simply cannot afford."

Captain Graff gathered himself. "Very well, your Eminence. I will have Second Lieutenant Tobias Vale take a squadron and leave at Paragon's first light. I will..."

"Uhh, Captain Graff," interrupted the Chancellor, "you don't seem to understand. This mission is of the greatest import to the future of the Titian Empire. Which means that we need the empire's greatest champion to lead the effort."

"You want *me* to collect the children?"

Kassidy raised a manicured finger at Crimm and answered for him. "We want you to collect and guard perhaps the most vital resource Quaan has known, aside from the actual gifts of the God-Snails themselves. A mission befitting your rank, I would think."

Graff bowed slightly to the Imperatrix. "Of course it is, my Lady. But readying the men for the Cobalt push seems more in line with my skills. Perhaps Lieutenant Kruger could..."

"Gorman." Kasspar Rayne's dull eyes cleared for a moment, focused intently on Captain Graff. "Kruger is a valued Titian asset, but let's not kid ourselves. He is a wolf that always chooses blood over diplomacy. I'm not sure he's the best choice to gain the trust of children."

"And I am?"

"Despite your giant beard, lined face, and jagged scars, you have a good heart, Gorman. We all see that and appreciate it." Crimm smoothed his goatee. "Children see more than most adults. At least, they see what truly matters. You will gain their trust, which will be essential for such a dangerous journey."

Captain Graff let out a long breath. Despite a life of accepting unwanted orders, it never got any easier.

"Then I am honored to be selected for such a vital task, my Lord. I will gather the harvesters and bring them back up the Kassimedes. We will meet up with the army once we cross North Verve and…"

"That won't be possible, I'm afraid," said Crimm.

"And why is that?"

"Have you not been listening, Captain?" asked the Chancellor, his voice thick with annoyance and a touch of glee. *Time is of the essence.* Every day that we do not reach the Supreme Helices is a day that they could be found by another. Or worse, another day that they could leave, abandoning us to this cursed wave of melancholy that is infecting the land. No, no, the Kassimedes is not an option, I'm afraid. The fastest route from Crimmish to Terminus Grove is due north, through Salt's Pass and across the Angel Wheat Flats."

Captain Graff looked as if he had been doused with icy water. "You want me to take… children… through some of the most disputed territory in all of Quaan?"

"No," replied Crimm. "I want you to shuttle an invaluable asset to a designated area in time to save the empire to which you have sworn allegiance! Does that phrasing ease your troubled mind?"

Graff looked to Imperator Rayne, worried that he might throttle the perfumed Chancellor. "My Lord, there are rumors that the Sluggs have skirted the Spired Curtains and retain hidden outposts in Shadowset. Salt's Pass could be dangerous."

Although Sologar Crimm responded, Graff refused to look his way. "Our spies have seen no movement within Shadowset nor along the Angel Wheat Flats. Once you're through the Pass, simply hug the Mutewoods. You'll reach Crown's Run and Woodlow before you know it."

"Sire, regardless of reported movement or not, I am inclined to believe that there are Sluggs around Shadowset. And if this is the case, a Titian squadron will draw their attention almost immediately. It will be hard to keep the children safe if it comes to swords."

Again, Crimm spoke. "Which is why you will not have a squadron, Captain."

Graff's grey eyes finally found Crimm. "Come again?"

"No squadron, Captain. You are precisely correct about the dangers inherent in bringing a significant guard. We all agree that this will need to be a stealth mission. What did we say, my Lord? No more than twelve men? And leave your colors at Kassimont. That way, even if there *are* Sluggs, and even if they *do* see you, they will think you nothing more than a small trading party. Certainly not worth exposing their positions for. Positions I believe them not to have."

Graff's hand flexed on his pommel. "No men. No colors. A group of children. Anything else? Would you have me complete this mission in the nude?"

"If you think it will help," snipped Crimm, and Kassidy spoke to relieve the tension.

"I hope now you see why this requires a man of your stature, High Captain Graff. There is no other that we would entrust with such an assignment. The Titian Empire is in your capable hands."

Graff nodded solemnly. "And if we make it to Woodlow?"

Kasspar spoke through wine-stained teeth. "Lieutenant Kruger will have prepared and moved the army into position north of the town. He will have men waiting for you at Woodlow. From there, you will reclaim command and use whatever means necessary to get the harvesters into Terminus Grove. Regarding how to retrieve the harvesters and deliver the God-Snails' gift, I leave that in your veteran hands."

Graff took in the Imperator's words and steeled himself. "I will do my best, my Lord. For you and for the empire. But I have one more concern."

"Give it voice, Gorman."

"These harvesters… these children. How can we trust them to help us?" Graff shot a look at the Chancellor. "The Empire has not exactly been kind to their people, regardless of the sins of their forebears. Why would such outcasts care to help those who have relegated them to a toxic corner of the land?"

"You have a keen mind, Captain," stated Kassidy Rayne. "You will make a formidable politician after your retirement. You are correct, of course. Why would they save those who have cast them aside? They wouldn't."

"My Lady?"

"I said they wouldn't. And we would be in great error to think that they would. But Chancellor Crimm, to no surprise, has a vested interest in Crimmish and keeps up with news of the horrid place. He informs me that the residents are, if nothing else, unfathomably loyal to each other. Them against the world and all that. So let us feed into that. The Bloat has all but vanished in Quaan, rendering Moon Tears less and less valuable. Crimmish is starting to feel the pinch as prices plummet. Therefore, we will make them an offer they cannot refuse. We will significantly reduce our requirement of Moon Tears, lessening their trips into the Timbers, while quadrupling the current rate. Additionally, we will send a team of Kassimont's greatest physicians, alchemists, and apothecaries to Crimmish. We will continue these regular visits until a cure to the Maddening is found. Chancellor Crimm tells me that this is perhaps the largest concern facing these people. Hope where there was none before is the greatest currency in the universe. This is what we will present to them."

"And if the Bloat returns?" countered Graff.

Crimm chuckled from the side. "There are always enemies of the Empire who need internment. We could have Crimmish's numbers tripled within one complete cycle of Ommori Prime."

"And these promises will be honored?" asked Graff.

Kassidy Rayne smirked. "To the best of the Empire's ability."

Gorman Graff's face twisted, and he stopped short of spitting onto the polished marble floor. He looked to the Imperator and Imperatrix, avoiding the Chancellor. "Then I am off. I will take Second Lieutenant Vale with me and ten others. We should be able to reach the Stenches near the end of the ninth Paragon."

"You have eight days, Captain," retorted Crimm with a gleam in his dark eyes. "Switch horses at every available town. We will provide you with an official Imperial Decree. Take what you need... more than you need."

"Very well. Eight days." Gorman Graff bowed to Kasspar and Kassidy. "Can someone please inform my wife that duty has called and that I am not sure when I will return?"

"It will be done, Captain," snapped the Chancellor.

"Someone else, perhaps," said Graff as Crimm began to finger his dagger.

"I will let Hilly know personally, Gorman," stated Kasspar gently. "And will let her know the criticalness of your service. You will leave a proud woman behind."

A smile reappeared within Captain Graff's grey beard. "Thank you, my Imperator."

"No, thank you, Gorman. When this mission is complete, a lucrative and much-deserved retirement is in order."

Graff nodded in appreciation. "My Liege." The Captain exited the throne room, shouting orders as soon as he hit the tapestried hallway.

Chancellor Sologar Crimm stared at the entrance door long after it had closed.

"I hate having to trust that old man. I know you care for him, my Lord, so if he fails, I will be happy to give the order. His head above Kassimont's walls will show all the severe ramifications of failure."

Kasspar Rayne laughed before finishing off his wine. "It is *your* plan, Sologar. If Captain Graff fails, *your* head will decorate the gates of Kassimont long before his."

Chancellor Crimm grimaced and looked to Imperatrix Rayne, his usual partner in crime, for moral support. He looked deep into her too-blue eyes that danced with intrigue.

But no support was to be found.

PART I

THE CHEESE-EYES OF THE STENCHES

1

THE SOUR FLOWER GANG—A NAME THAT STICKS

"My arm is tingling," said Ash, and the other four children instinctively glanced at the dark-skinned girl. More specifically, they looked just beyond the stump that ended the girl's left arm, slightly above where her elbow should have been. They all knew that it didn't make sense, that a phantom limb shouldn't be able to detect the proximity of a Moonflower. They knew this. And yet, they also knew not to question this strange phenomenon, especially when it had proven accurate time and time again.

"Then let's keep pushing," offered Fincher.

Ditto looked around nervously. Despite his massive size for a twelve-year-old, the boy remained the group's most cautious member. But one would be gravely mistaken to confuse Ditto's prudence for cowardice. Many a bully had found that out the hard way.

"We're already deep into the Timbers."

"You want to go back empty-handed again, Ditto?" challenged Fincher.

"You know I don't. But the shadows are getting thicker. And where there are dark shadows there are Ghost Pumas."

"Group vote?" asked Fincher, his smirk revealing that he already knew the final tally.

Ditto sighed heavily. "Fine."

Fincher's smirk widened into the genuine smile that was usually found on the eleven-year-old's handsome, pale face. "Ash?"

"Let's push on. Sorry, Ditto."

"Sammi?"

The thin girl pushed her round glasses higher up onto her nose. "I'm with my sister." Despite being the second-youngest of the crew, Sammi was by far the most intelligent. Only her devotion to her older, more reckless sister could cloud her judgement.

Fincher quietly clapped his hands together. "That's all we need."

Ditto shook his head. "Everyone's opinion should be heard, even if the vote is decided."

Fincher rolled his eyes, hazel within the yellow sclera that marked all in the Stenches. "Always a stickler for the rules, Ditto. Hana?"

The almond-eyed girl, both the group's youngest and smallest, jumped at her name. Her black-on-yellow eyes scanned the colorless landscape of the Tainted Timbers, dark wood surrounded by endless greyness, as if storm clouds of soot had released themselves upon the world.

"I'm scared."

"You're always scared, Hana," said Ash gently.

"I know. So, it won't hurt to keep going."

"Ditto?"

"You win, Fincher. But can we at least try to keep it down?"

"I can. But you're the farking oaf who plows through the forest like Old Man Toots after a handle of rotgut."

The other three children laughed, and even Ditto had to chuckled at the image of the Stenches' most amusing drunkard. "I'll do my best. Lead the way, Ash."

Ash took the lead as the group moved deep into the Tainted Timbers. Fincher lost track of the number of Reaper Vines they passed, that most toxic of plants that poisoned the air and gave the Tainted Timbers their infamous name. Despite making jokes, the quintet did grow more quiet as they continued to penetrate the dismal woods.

Finally, Ash held up her right hand and the group pulled in tight. "It's throbbing. We're close," she whispered. "Everyone look around."

The children fanned out, and it wasn't long before a whistle cut through the relative quiet. They hurried over to the source.

Sammi pushed her glasses up once more and pointed near the base of a smoke pine. There, rooted against the colorless tree, as they always did, was a Moonflower. The round blossom swirled with hues of blue, lavender, and indigo, a beacon of color against a drab backdrop.

The group drew closer to the Moonflower.

"It's grown high," remarked Sammi as she studied the glowing flower. "This one will probably be gone within a few more phases of Ommori Prime."

"Then let's get all we can from her," said Ash, looking toward Hana.

"I'll do my best," stated the seven-year-old.

Fincher searched all around the Moonflower. "Does anyone see it?"

"I don't. But it's gotta be in that hollow just above the flower," replied Ash.

Fincher took in several deep breaths.

"What are you so nervous about?" asked Ash. "Ditto has the hard part."

"Yeah, but it's my farking face on the line."

"Some scars could be an improvement," teased Sammi.

"Yeah, yeah, yeah. Let's just get this over with. Ditto, you in position?"

Ditto had moved to the side of the smoke pine. He stared intently into the blackness of the hollow. "I'm ready."

Fincher looked to his large friend, eyes pleading. "Don't miss. Please don't farking miss."

Ditto refused to take his green-on-yellow eyes from the hollow. "I won't."

Fincher let out several more breaths for good measure as the others slowly backed away. "Alright. I'm going in." Ash removed a knife from her waistband and held it at the ready.

Fincher inched up to the Moonflower, his feet shuffling across the forest floor. The blossom pulsed before him, hurting his eyes with its brightness. He stepped closer and held his breath. Closer. Closer.

A blur leapt from the smoke pine's hollow, moving straight for Fincher's vulnerable face. His hazel eyes slammed shut, and he prepared for a bite that would take half his face with it. Luckily, no strike landed, and only the thud of meat on meat could be heard.

Fincher slowly opened his eyes and was greeted by the slit-like pupils, giant maw, and dripping fangs of a Moon Adder, the white snakes that acted as necessary guardians for the Moonflowers.

While the other four children let out a collective sigh of relief, Ditto's muscles remained tensed as he held the serpent in the air, having intercepted the creature mid-strike. Ditto kept one hand around the Moon Adder's throat while he grasped its thick body with his other hand and slowly removed it from the hollow.

"I've got her. Isn't she a beauty?"

While Fincher couldn't deny the elegance of the snake's glimmering white scales, he wasn't ready to throw his attacker a compliment. "Yeah, a real stunner. Maybe bring her with us and you can take her to the Sisters under Paragon Dance?"

"Can't be worse than that horse-face you took last year," quipped Ash, and the other three filled the air with laughter.

Fincher held up his hands defensively. "Reba Bugg is a wonderful girl with unfortunate teeth, I'll have you know."

"Didn't she try to bite you when you got caught eyeballing Stella Bugg?" asked Sammi between laughs.

"Sounds like she and this Moon Adder have more in common than you'd like to admit," joked Ditto, and the group exploded.

Fincher surrendered. "Yeah, yeah, laugh it up, chuckleheads. But we'll see who ends up dancing with Stella Bugg."

Ash wiped tears from her eyes with the back of her lone hand and spoke through labored breaths. "Hana has a better shot of getting with Stella than you, Fincher."

"Well, good for her," shot back Fincher. He turned to Hana. "Aren't you the popular one, *Miss* Hana. Care to show us how you got so popular? You're up."

Hana nodded and stepped toward the Moonflower. The Moon Adder writhed in Ditto's hands, but the large boy held tight. Hana caressed the blossom with a thin, alabaster finger. Despite the group's tendency toward raucous laughter, all four fell quiet when Hana was about to sing.

Fincher's breath caught when the first gentle notes escaped the young girl's lips, as it always did. Her voice, although soft, carried throughout the Tainted Timbers, as if the forest thirsted for something beautiful, something the opposite of grey.

Sammi wiped a tear as the song came out in a language that none of them understood. Hana's ancestors came from high in the Spired Curtains, just north of Shadowset, and although songs had been passed down, the meanings of words were lost to time and sorrow.

Even the Moon Adder ceased its thrashing, caught up in the enchantment that was Hana Bugg's voice. The Moonflower, too, was not immune to her musical charms. Its pulsing quickened, and the blossom began to swell. As it did, Sammi retrieved a glass vial from her pouch and held it just beneath the flower. Moments later, the Moonflower started to contract, releasing a syrupy white substance from its stomata. The Moon Tears ran down the face of the Moonflower, collected at the bottommost point, and began to drip into the waiting vial. The drip became a small stream, and the first container was quickly filled. Sammi deftly switched out vials, handing the full one to Fincher, who topped it with a cork stopper.

"Wow, this one is gonna be filled, too," whispered Sammi under Hana's song. "You got another one, Fincher? Hurry."

Fincher scrambled in his bag but offered only a shrug. Ash moved in quickly, pushing the boy aside and presenting her sister with a third vial. The third vial's contents climbed halfway up the glass before the stream became a drip once more. A few beats later, it became obvious that no more was to come.

Seeing that the Moonflower had finished its "crying," Ash put her hand against Hana's small back, letting the girl know that she could stop. Hana, who always sang with her eyes closed, let the final note drift out before looking at her handiwork.

Muffled applause broke out from the group.

"Great work, Hana," said Fincher, giving the sensitive girl an appreciative shoulder squeeze.

"Almost three full vials," remarked Sammi, corking and placing them all into a specially padded area of her pouch. "That's a new record."

"Everyone's gonna be delighted with you, Hana."

Hana looked down at her tiny feet. "Thanks, Ash. Thanks, everyone."

"Uhh, if you all don't mind," cut in Ditto, the Moon Adder once again aggressive in his hands, "can I toss this thing aside now?"

"Yeah, but send it far enough away that it won't double back on you," answered Ash. "And be gentle with it!"

"So, sending it against the nearest ash oak is out of the question?"

Ash shot Ditto with a serious look. "You know it is, Ditto. This Adder might find and protect the next Moonflower that we harvest. Otherwise, it will be devoured by the critters before we ever have the chance."

"Yeah, yeah, I know. It's just that y'all aren't the ones that have to catch the stupid things. One wrong move, and I'm a goner."

"No," corrected Fincher. "One wrong move and *I'm* a goner. It's my farking face that the thing goes after."

"Well, nobody faults it for that," joked Ash, and the five all shared in a quick laugh. "Ditto, gentle please."

"Yeah, yeah," said Ditto, already stepping carefully farther into the Timbers. "Your wish is my command." He returned a minute later. "All done. I dropped it on a nice, soft bed of sponge moss. Bugger still snapped at me."

"So, we're good?" asked Fincher, and the group all nodded in assent. "Then, there goes another successful mission of the Sour Flower Gang! The absolute best harvester team in Crimmish!"

Most chuckled, but Ash rolled her brown-on-yellow eyes. "Sour Flower Gang? Fincher, you know I hate that stupid name."

Fincher flashed a wide smile, delighted that his selected handle annoyed the oldest of the group. "It's a good name and you farking know it. It's got meaning, rhyme, and is syllabically correct."

Sammi's pushed up her glasses. "*Syllabically, correct?*"

Fincher held up fingers as he spoke. "Sow-wer flow-wer gang. See! It all fits."

"It's also stupid," argued Ash. "Sour because everyone thinks we stink? Because of our stupid eyes and the stupid smells the stupid Reaper Vines put out? I don't like people saying we stink. And I don't like to be reminded that they think that way."

Fincher held up his hands in surrender but pressed on. "I get it, Ash. I really do. But we all know it's unfair. And mean. And, yes, stupid. So let's farking own it and take away the only joke they have. If we're able to call ourselves sour, what could they possibly say to hurt us?"

"Lots of things."

"Maybe if they had farking brains. You're giving them too much credit."

"Well, I still think the name sucks!"

Fincher and Ash stared at each other for a moment. And while there was a challenge there, no animosity could be felt.

"Group vote?"

"Fine."

Fincher's mischievous grin returned. "Ditto?"

Ditto gave one of his patented shrugs. "Fine with me. As good as any other dumb name. Honestly, I still don't know why harvester crews even need—"

"That's one for me," declared Fincher. "Hana?"

"Whatever you all want," she said shyly.

"You gotta vote, Hana. Or else this *group vote* thing doesn't work."

"Okay, Fincher. I like sour things. To me, it's one of the best tastes around. Reminds me of my mother's cooking. She loves to use tart ice berries in our food."

Ash tried to be gentle with the group's Moon Voice. "Sour tastes are quite different from sour smells, Hana."

"Semantics! Semantics," cried Fincher. "Another vote for me. Sammi, care to bring us home?"

Sammi giggled under her older sister's threatening stare. "Sorry, Ash, I think it's kinda funny. And I like the way it sounds. And he's right about the syllable thing." She pushed her glasses up once more. "As intellectuals, we care about these things."

Ash's face twisted from the playful betrayal. "Oh, you're an intellectual now? Well, riddle me this, *little* sis, how are you gonna remain an intellectual when I—"

"It's near unanimous," declared Fincher. "We are the Sour Flower Gang, and we have once again conquered the Tainted Timbers and brought home the bacon. Let us return and collect our kudos! And, for me alone, perhaps a soft kiss from one Stella Bugg. Let's ride!"

Fincher, Hana, and Sammi took off back through the forest, cutting a straight line for Crimmish. After they had gone a few dozen feet, Ash moved to follow but was stopped by a strong hand on her stump. Ditto leaned into her, and her heart jumped more than she wanted to admit.

"Keep an eye out," whispered Ditto, looking around the shadowy forest canopy. "Fincher's celebrating, but we're not home yet."

～

Fincher led the way, growing loud as the children drew closer to Crimmish.

"Sour Flower Gang don't give a what! Coming back with Moon Tears to kick the Bloat's butt!"

"Shh," admonished Sammi. "Ditto said we need to stay quiet."

"He *did* say that, my dear intellectual. But that was back *there,* and we are up *here.* We're near home now; nothing to worry about, my bespectacled friend."

Sammi pushed up her glasses and looked around as she walked.

Hana remained close to her side and Ash trailed some distance away. Ditto wasn't to be found. Sammi called out to her sister.

"Shanti! Where's Ditto?"

"I told you," Ash answered angrily, "it's *Ash* now, not Shanti! And I don't know where Ditto is. He probably had to go pee. Which I'm going to have to do if we don't hurry it up. In fact—"

Ash's words were cut short as something passed over the group in the forest canopy. The four children spun as one, just in time to witness a dark mass fall from the smoke pines and land heavily twenty feet behind the lagging Ash.

The Ghost Puma, two-hundred pounds of rippling muscle under a thick, black coat, did not growl as it began to slowly stalk forward. Instead, it simply opened its mouth, revealing razor-sharp teeth as its jade eyes became brighter with excitement.

"Fark, fark, fark," cursed Fincher as he moved into action. "Hana, Sammi, get behind me. Ash, can you start walking backwards to me? Ash? Ash!"

Unfortunately, the normally unflappable girl was frozen with fear as the Ghost Puma stepped forward on padded, clawed paws. Ash trembled and tears ran down her dark cheeks as her phantom limb began to throb, the horrible memory of her last Ghost Puma encounter two years ago flooding to the surface.

Fincher recognized his friend's terror. "Okay, Ash, stay there. I'm coming to you." Fincher removed a long hunter's knife from his belt as he slowly made his way back, careful not to startle the approaching cat. "Okay, Ash, I'm almost there. I'll need you to—"

The Ghost Puma sprung forward with impossible speed, creating an obsidian blur in the grey air. Ash cried out and closed her eyes as the flying beast torpedoed ahead, fangs and claws leading the way.

Just as the Ghost Puma was about to reach Ash, another form sprang from the undergrowth and slammed into the lunging cat, driving the beast to the side to collide hard against the thick trunk of a smoke pine.

Ditto thrust his knee forward as hard as he could as he landed atop the devilish feline, forcing a strange sound from the monster as several of its ribs shattered.

The Ghost Puma continued to wail as it thrashed about beneath Ditto, its snapping jaws narrowly missing the boy's exposed arms. Its claws, however, did not miss, and the right front claw ripped down the top of Ditto's forearm. The large boy screamed and gave way, allowing the Ghost Puma to right itself and go on the attack.

The massive cat pushed off the smoke pine, driving Ditto to the ground. Ditto, however, a veteran of dozens of brawls despite his young age, used the momentum against the hunter, pressing his feet against the Ghost Puma's chest and leg-pressing it up and over as he fell to his back.

The Ghost Puma flipped through the air but unsurprisingly landed softly on its paws. It spun back immediately to face Ditto, its jade eyes flaring with bloodlust, and moved to strike once more.

Again, the Ghost Puma was thwarted as another pale blur rammed into it. This time it was Fincher, his knife leading the way, driving the blade deep into the thick side of the onyx killer. The Ghost Puma roared and tossed Fincher aside, sending the boy flying into the nearest thicket. The Puma coughed up a wad of blood, shook its black head, and started to follow the boy into the bushes. The delay was all that Ditto needed as he dove back into action, landing hard on the Puma's back.

Ditto's arms wrapped around the feline's thick neck and the boy's impressive strength, aided greatly by gravity, pulled the Ghost Puma to the ground. The breath was driven from Ditto's lungs as the Puma's back rolled onto the boy. Ditto held on for dear life beneath the jade-eyed demon as it clawed the air and twisted. Soon, it would complete its turn and have Ditto pinned to the ground, its jaws wrapped around the boy's throat.

But the Sour Flower Gang had other plans.

Before the Ghost Puma could complete its spin, Sammi darted forward and stabbed down three times, sending her small dagger into the beast's chest before back-pedaling away. The Puma turned its head to face this new threat and was rewarded with more wounds as tiny

Hana came in from the other side and slid her own blade between the creature's ribs one, two, three, four times.

Ditto, feeling the Ghost Puma begin to fade, used what little energy he had remaining to tighten his grip, locking the cat in place. With a great and unsurprising shout, Fincher escaped the thicket and leapt into the air. He dropped from the sky like an arrow, coming down on the Ghost Puma's chest and thrusting his hunter's knife through the heart of the forest's apex predator.

Fincher hugged the Puma's chest closely for several seconds, sandwiching it between himself and poor Ditto until the cat's too-sharp claws stopped raking the air.

When he was sure the Puma was dead, Fincher slid off, pushed the carcass off Ditto, and helped his friend to his feet.

"And *that* is how you kill a farking Ghost Puma," exclaimed Fincher, his hazel eyes wild with excitement.

Ditto shook his head and carefully fingered the deep cuts on his arm. "No, *that* is why you don't go traipsing through the Tainted Timbers like a traveling troubadour troupe."

Fincher waved him away. "Ahh, that farking thing would have been clocking us no matter, even if we were as silent as honey wheat mice. That's not the takeaway here."

Sammi came over with strips of cloth and started bandaging Ditto's wounds. "And what is the takeaway, Fincher?"

Fincher's grin widened. "Isn't it obvious? The takeaway is that you don't mess with the Sour Flower Gang!" The boy raised his head to the shadowed canopy. "Do you hear me, you rotten forest," he called out. "You mess with the Sour Flower Gang, you get farking got!"

"Shut up, Fincher," said Ditto between grimaces as Sammi continued to dress his cuts. "We're lucky it was an adolescent. A full-grown cat would have ripped us to shreds."

"No way! Tell me any other crew who could have done what we just did? None of them! We're the best. We all played our part and were farking awesome. I wouldn't put it past us to—"

"Fincher." Hana's soft voice brought the boisterous boy up short. "Look."

Fincher followed Hana's eyes and found that Ash had remained frozen throughout the whole ordeal. The girl continued to tremble, her eyes locked forward to where the Ghost Puma once stood.

"Fark!" Fincher ran over and threw his arms around Ash, pulling her in tight. "It's okay, Ash. It's all over now. We won. It can't hurt you now." She continued to shake against his body.

"Move!" Ditto's words were not a request as the large boy took Fincher's place. As soon as he was in place, Ash melted into his arms, tears pouring forth in massive heaves.

"What am I, chopped bog rat meat?" asked Fincher.

"Shut up, Fincher," snapped Sammi as she joined them.

After several minutes, Ash finally began to settle. She separated from Ditto and offered a heartfelt nod. "Sorry. Sorry, everyone."

"Nonsense," offered Fincher, "you were integral to the kill."

Ash laughed and wiped away the last of her tears. "As what? Bait?"

"That's right! Impossible to catch a farking Ghost Puma without bait. It's just too bad your arm doesn't detect Pumas the way it does Moonflowers."

"Shut up, Fincher," cried Sammi, Ditto, and even Hana in unison.

"Just an observation," said Fincher defensively. "Now, if everyone's done being downcast, can we please get a move on. I'm returning to Crimmish with a dead Ghost Puma and three vials of Moon Tears. I expect a champion's return and many rewards, including a farking kiss from one Stella Bugg."

"Your reward sounds like her nightmare," shot Ditto, but Fincher simply waved him away.

"Women are attracted to wealth and power. And I happen to be bringing representations of each. Now, again, let's get moving."

"I can't," Ash said from the side, her body angled away from the others.

"Well, of course you can. You just have to—"

"I said I can't, Fincher!"

"Why not?"

Ash reluctantly turned back, revealing a giant wet spot covering the crotch and legs of her pants. Tears began to well up once more. "I told you I had to go. And when I saw that, that, thing… I don't know, I guess…"

"It's okay. It's okay," comforted Ditto. "Likely no one will even be able to tell."

"The heck they won't, Ditto! Most of them already hate me. I can't stand to show my face like this."

Fincher stepped forward and untied the rope holding up his pants. They dropped to the ground, showing off ragged underpants beneath. He collected the trousers and handed them to Ash.

"Here, put these on. I'm the only one close to your size. We throw yours in my pack and wash them later."

Ash wiped the lone tear that fell. "But what will you wear?"

Fincher's wide smile returned. "Me? I'm wearing the greatest outfit of all—the mantle of Ghost Puma slayer!"

"I think Ditto did most of the heavy lifting," said Sammi, holding back laughter.

"Semantics! Semantics!"

"I'm not sure you know what that means," stated the group's intellectual through giggles.

"It means, my four-eyed friend, that all eyes will be on yours truly when we make our triumphant return, which is exactly how I like it! Now, in addition to a Ghost Puma and Moon Tears, I will be offering a third gift." Fincher shook his hips for emphasis and the other four children collapsed in laughter.

"I don't think that's much of a gift, Fincher," said Hana, shocking the others with a rare jibe.

Fincher glared at Hana but was secretly proud of the young girl's insult. "We'll let Stella Bugg be the judge of that."

The Sour Flower Gang finally cleared the Tainted Timbers. Fincher, Ditto, and Ash groaned as they pulled the dead Ghost Puma along on a sled that Sammi had hastily crafted with rope, Reaper Vines, and branches using her uncanny knotting and building abilities.

As they cleared the final smoke pines, Fincher looked to the South, as he always did, to view Mount Ghaal, the dead volcano that soared into the sky and hung heavy over Crimmish like an angry, watchful god. It was Mount Ghaal's eruption that had poisoned the soil of the forest below, making conditions such that only grim flora like smoke pines and worse, Reaper Vines, could thrive. Ironically, the noxious vapors that Reaper Vines released created the perfect, and only, environment in which Moonflowers could grow.

Sometimes, in his darker moments, Fincher wished that Mount Ghaal would erupt again, ending the cycle of poverty and madness that defined Crimmish. But the usually optimistic boy always shook these thoughts loose, reminding himself that the work they did was important—no, vital—to countless lives across Quaan.

Without the children of Crimmish, there would be no harvesting of Moon Tears. Without Moon Tears, there would be no creation of Salvation, the only compound known to cure the Bloat, that most evil of plagues that oozed forth from the Black Bog over a hundred years ago.

Fincher locked onto this fact, bathed in it when he began to feel that his home was more *Stenches* than *Crimmish*. It made him feel proud. And Fincher liked to feel proud.

"How much farther?" asked Ash, her head down with effort.

"Almost there; just a bit farther," answered Ditto, who barely looked to have broken a sweat although his wounds had bled through his dressing.

"I'll run ahead and get some others to help," said Sammi before dashing off.

"Some intellectual," complained her sister Ash. "We could have used that idea a thousand paces ago."

"Ignore the pain," offered Fincher as the trio continued to pull. "Think of Stella Bugg waiting for us at the end of our journey. Perhaps she'll throw on a special dress for me."

"That doesn't help us one bit," shot back Ash.

"Oh yeah? Ditto?"

"Sorry, Fincher. Not my type."

Ash's heart jumped again. She blamed it on the exertion of the pull.

A short time later, as the group approached the edge of town, Sammi returned with a group of adults. Among them were Crimmish mayor Dann Bugg, the parents of Sammi, Ash, and Hana, and Fincher's father.

"Ho there! You five never cease to surprise," shouted Fincher's father Gill as the group neared, and the trio dropped their ropes.

Fincher's usual wide grin made an appearance. "You know that the Sour Flower Gang never returns empty-handed!"

"Who?" asked Mayor Bugg.

"I told you that stupid name wouldn't stick," whispered Ash to Fincher.

"Give it time. It's a good name," he answered back quietly before yelling to the incoming group of adults. "Us! The Sour Flower Gang! Crimmish's best harvester crew. You'd do well to remember our name, Mayor, especially given the treats that we've brought."

Fincher's dad laughed aloud as the parents of Sammi, Ash, and Hana ran forward to bury their daughters in deep hugs. Gill Bugg gave his son Fincher a paternal slap on the shoulder.

"Wait till you see what we have, Da," said Fincher.

"Doesn't matter, son," replied Gill. "We're just glad that you are all back. You can't imagine the fear that we endure when you lot head off into those cursed woods. But you will."

"Oh, but look at what they *have* brought back, Gill," exclaimed a wide-eyed Mayor Bugg. "I haven't seen a Ghost Puma bagged since I was a child. Back then, the group that brought it back returned three less than they started with."

"Ditto did the heavy work," stated Sammi, much to the chagrin of Fincher. "Although we all did our part," she added when she noticed her friend's disappointment at his lack of credit. Ash turned away at her sister's words.

Ditto shrugged in embarrassment. "It's just a juvenile."

"Nonsense," insisted Dann Bugg. "This is a real cause for celebration. This cat will provide some much-needed meat, especially with how lean it's been recently. And that coat will make a nice blanket for some lucky family."

"It should go to Ditto and his dad," said Ash. "Look at his arm."

"Thanks, but it's nothing," replied Ditto, hiding the red-stained bandages of his arm. "It should go to the Widow Till. She lost her husband and both children in the fire. She has nothing. She could use something good in her life."

Although Fincher, like everyone, wanted the Ghost Puma pelt, no one could argue with Ditto's logic and heart. Till Bugg had lost everything when some kids from Salvation Outpost had started a fire on her porch as a callous prank that quickly spiraled out of control.

Mayor Bugg nodded his agreement. "A good call, Ditto. You'd make a fine mayor."

"That's not all we have," said Fincher, looking to wrench a little attention back. "Three full vials of Moon Tears. Show him, Hana."

The small girl dug through her pouch and carefully removed the three glass containers of Moon Tears. She handed them gently to the mayor, who looked upon them as if he held wine diamonds from the base of Galanis Dawn.

"How remarkable. I've never seen so much from one harvest."

"That's Hana's doing," said Ash, and Fincher once again looked stricken.

"Hey! It was *my* face that was offered up as a sacrifice to the Moon Adder," he protested.

"Then we're lucky it took the bait. Stella Bugg never would have," joked Gill Bugg, and everyone roared in laughter.

"Da! You're supposed to be on *my* side!"

"Sorry, son. You left yourself open to that one."

Fincher relented and joined in the fun. "Yes, I guess I did. Well played."

Mayor Bugg was still staring into the glittering white substance of the Moon Tears. "It's a shame that prices have plummeted as of late. Otherwise, this could have really given us some breathing room."

A silence fell over the group. The children looked to each other but kept their questions to themselves.

Ash and Sammi's father Taff finally broke the spell. "Well, these children look like they could use a hot bath, a warm meal, and some rest. Let's get them home."

"Yes, yes, of course," stammered Mayor Bugg. "Where are my manners? You children head back to your homes with your parents. The rest of us will take this Ghost Puma to Carver Rett. We'll divvy up the meat, giving your families the usual founder's cut, and make sure that Widow Till gets the fur. Hopefully, it will help shield her against cold memories."

The children, along with their parents, began to walk back toward Crimmish. Fincher looked back at the Ghost Puma, desperate for one last look at his crew's great triumph. Mayor Bugg noticed and called out to the boy.

"And don't worry, Fincher. I'll make sure everyone knows that these wonderful gifts were supplied by the, uhh... Sour Flower Gang!"

Fincher's smile exploded on his face. He leaned into Ash as he marched forward. "See! I told you it would stick!"

Ash simply rolled her brown-on-yellow eyes and hugged her ma closer.

Ditto, bringing up the rear, gently tugged on Sammi's arm, pulling her away from her parents. Hana, wedged between her parents, secretively eavesdropped.

"Sammi, my da didn't want to come?"

Sammi's eyes grew wet behind her thick glass lenses. "I'm sorry, Ditto. My da said that he's been sequestered back at the house. For his own protection. And others."

"Already?"

Sammi couldn't find the words, so simply nodded. "You want me to tell the others?"

Ditto put on a brave face. "No, please don't. This should be a happy moment. We don't have enough of those."

"You sure? We can help, Ditto."

Ditto softly pushed his small friend back into the waiting arms of her ma, Jazz Bugg. "Not this time, Sammi. Not this time."

~

Fincher and Gill Bugg hiked through the wet clay of Crimmish toward their house. With Crimmish's location at the base of the Spired Curtains, any precipitation brought incessant flooding, leaving the town a constant muddy mess. When they reached home, a modest, single-room dwelling, similar to most in the town, made from scrap planks and dried clay that filled in wide gaps in the exterior, Fincher sighed as he always did. Given that smoke pine was near impossible to cut, the residents of Crimmish had to make do with what could be traded for, found, or recycled.

Although he was thankful for what he had, Fincher couldn't help but believe that he deserved better. His da deserved better. And his beloved ma Gwynn Bugg certainly deserved better. The fact that he was unable to give her more before she succumbed to the Maddening relentlessly tore at Fincher's heart.

Fincher entered the sparsely furnished house, hung his pouch on a nail by the door, leaned his hunter's knife against the wall, and collapsed into his little bed that sat beneath the building's lone window.

Gill smiled, delighted to have his son home, and moved to the back, where he collected wood from against the back wall and began to place it within the stone-lined fireplace.

"Relax, son. I'll get a fire going and start a soup. I gathered some Sweet Tooth Truffles while you were gone and even managed to trade for some spire elk meat."

Fincher sat up. "Spire elk! Jeez, Da, what did that cost you?"

Gill waved his son away. "Don't you worry about it. Nothing's too good for a son of mine, especially one that heads up the infamous Sour Flower Gang."

Fincher sat up even higher, his grin threatening to cleave his small face in half. "You really like the name?"

"Of course. It's got rhyme and really sticks."

"I farking knew it," Fincher said under his breath as he fell back into his hay-covered bed. A few moments passed. "Da?"

"Yes, son," said Gill as he worked to light the fireplace.

"What was that about the price of Moon Tears falling?"

Gill Bugg hesitated for a second before returning to his work. In short order, a small fire was growing within the stone hearth. "Don't worry too much about it, Fincher. It's just that Salvation has proven to work almost too well. The Bloat is pretty much under control, although a few cases continue to bubble up from the Honey Rice Flats. With reduced demand comes reduced prices. Simple economics, really."

"But Moon Tears are how we survive, Da. Without Quaan needing Salvation, what can we trade with? What can we possibly offer the outside world?"

Gill placed a pot full of water over the fire. "You kids don't need to concern yourselves with that kind of stuff. You let us adults worry about such things."

"I just don't want things to be the way I heard they used to be," said Fincher, his voice growing weaker. "We have so little, as is. Not that I'm complaining."

Gill threw some meat that he had already prepared into the heating water with a splash. "We're survivors, son. Crimmish was founded before the Bloat, before Moonflowers, and, despite having nothing to offer, our people still endured. We were given a death sentence but defied everyone—especially those rotten Crimms—by living on. The Bloat and the subsequent Moonflowers gave us an opportunity to improve our positions. Even if Moon Tears become worthless, which I highly doubt, we'll find another way to make it. It's just what our people do." Gill added the Sweet Tooth Truffles to the pot. "Now tell me, leader of the *Sour* Flower Gang, would you like me to add some ice berries to the stew? Hana's father gave me some, although I have no idea how he got them." Gill Bugg finally turned back to his son. "You know, he may have…"

Gill stopped short, noticing Fincher was fast asleep on his bed, the boy's shallow snores highlighting how exhausted he truly was. Gill walked over to his son, removed the boy's tattered boots, and threw a blanket over his small form. He kissed Fincher on the head and wiped a tear that had found purchase in the corner of his eye.

"Never mind, my son. You sleep and dream. Dream of beautiful girls that put Stella Bugg to shame. And of magnificent worlds far removed from this horror that is the Stenches. Because I fear that I will never be able to show them to you."

Gill Bugg returned to his stew. "I'm going to add the ice berries," he said to himself. "We have to relish what little we are given, even when it's sour."

~

Hana's parents, Kenn and Joon Bugg, put away the girl's travel kit and helped her change into more comfortable clothes. Although this was a joyous occasion, they couldn't help but notice that a sadness had fallen over their young daughter.

Joon pulled Hana's straight, black hair into a neat bun before spinning the girl around to face her.

"What's troubling you, my darling? You're home, you're safe, and you've made the entire town extremely proud with your success. This should be a time for smiles."

Hana looked down and studied the stained blanket that covered her pine needle bed before looking up with shrink-wrapped almond eyes. "I heard Sammi tell Ditto that his da was sequestered."

Joon's face then fell, just like her daughter's. Kenn had to pause his chopping of vegetables in the corner to wipe a tear that had splashed onto the makeshift table. He resumed. "Durn mud onions always get me."

"Ma, how much longer does he have?"

Joon stroked her daughter's cheek. "I'm sorry, my love. He doesn't have long at all now. Link Bugg is deep into the Maddening. If someone doesn't do something soon, Link will do it to himself. Or someone else."

Kenn wiped away another droplet. "Link Bugg was a great man. The best man I ever knew. We should all aim to be more like him."

"You talk about him as if he's already gone," shot Hana.

Kenn's chopping increased in speed. He didn't look up from his onions. "You're right, sweetie. It's just…"

Joon saved her husband. "Hana, we all know that this is the way things go in Crimmish. Some are luckier than others, get more time to cherish their families. More time to say goodbye."

Hana finally broke down. She spoke through massive sobs. "I hate the Maddening. I hate this place."

Joon and Kenn shared a look before mother spoke to daughter. "Hey, hey, don't say that. Hate the Maddening, but don't hate this place. This is our home. Your home. And we don't have much, but we have each other. Nowhere else in Quaan would offer you the relationships that you have here. Nowhere else would you have friends like Fincher and Sammi and Ash. Friends like Ditto. In Crimmish, we treasure things that really matter. And it's not fancy homes and shiny bracelets."

Hana nodded. "Poor Ditto. What can I do to help him?"

Joon smiled at her daughter's kind heart. "The most impactful gifts are simple things. Free things. Give Ditto friendship, understanding, and support. And, most of all, love. You all know how to do that for each other already." Joon wiped the last of Hana's tears and a few of her own. She straightened the girl's pajamas. "Now, Da's preparing a real feast. You must be famished. Would you like to sing a song while we wait?"

Hana finally smiled. "Sing with me?"

"Of course, my love."

Hana and Joon began to sing, and the melody floated around the room like medicinal vapors. Kenn wiped a final splash. And his chopping once again slowed.

~

Ditto's stomach cramped as he turned the corner, and his small home came into view. Not only had a board been hammered across the door, but Zedd Bugg sat guard outside. Zedd offered a sympathetic nod to Ditto as the boy approached.

"Is it bad?" asked Ditto, skipping the usual pleasantries.

"It's not good, lad."

"Can I see him?"

"Of course. I'll remove the board." Zedd turned and pried the scrap lumber away from the front door. Obstacle removed, he waved Ditto forward. Ditto's hand paused for a moment on the handle. "Ditto." The boy and Zedd's met eyes. "I'm sorry."

Ditto pushed in and closed the door behind him. The inside was dim as the home's only window had also been partially boarded up. Ditto left his belongings near the door and stared toward the back of his small house.

A large shadow stood facing the rear wall. Ditto stepped closer and saw that Link Bugg was shaking, his forehead pressed against the rough wood.

"Da? Da, it's me. I'm home. Our harvest was a big success. Not only did we get Moon Tears, but I was able to bag a Ghost Puma. It was an adolescent, but still... I think you'd be proud."

Link spoke through clenched teeth. "Always p... p.. proud of you... son."

Ditto felt tears begin to form but forced them back. "Da, what can I do?" He moved forward and placed his hand against Link's broad back.

"M... m... my brain. It... it... it itches. C... can you... can you scratch it?"

The dam broke and tears flowed from Ditto's soft green eyes. "I'm sorry, Da. I can't."

"Oh. That's okay, s... son. I... can... do it."

Without warning, Link slammed his head against the wall, leaving a crimson stain on the planking. Ditto jumped back in surprise, and Link banged his head again before the boy could react, leaving even more blood on the wall and painting the man's face red. Ditto leapt upon his father, wrapping his arms around the giant man in an attempt to pull him away from the back wall.

Unfortunately, Link Bugg, Crimmish's largest resident, proved too strong and easily tossed his son to the floor as he continued to bash his skull against the hard wood.

"Da! Please stop! Da," cried Ditto from the floor as Link continued to headbutt, spraying blood across the wall. "Da!"

"Itchy! So… itchy," Link could be heard saying between impacts.

"Da!" Ditto scrambled to his feet, but before he could reach his father, one last crack echoed through the home and Link stumbled backward. He stood there for a moment, and a dumb grin could be seen through the mask of blood.

"That's better," said Link Bugg, before collapsing into a pile on the ground.

Ditto dropped alongside his unconscious father and held him tight, deep sobs shaking both large boy and giant man.

"I'm sorry, Da. I'm so sorry," Ditto kept repeating as he rocked them both back and forth on the grit-covered floor.

Ditto cried for his father. But he also cried for himself. For he knew that the worst was yet to come.

~

"Shanti, you've barely touched your food," observed Taff Bugg. "I thought mountain hare was your favorite. Your ma went out of her way to get it for you."

"Ash."

"What's that?"

"I've told you a million times, Da. My name's Ash now, not Shanti."

Taff looked to his wife Jazz for support. She didn't disappoint. "We know, sweetie, it's just that you'll have your whole life to be called Ash. Can't we enjoy *Shanti* while you're still young?"

Ash pushed her food around without eating it. She spoke without looking up. "We use our one-syllable names when we're no longer kids. I haven't felt like a kid since my arm got taken. It just makes sense."

Taff and Jazz exchanged concerned looks. Sammi helped them out through bites of stew.

"She's upset about Ditto's da. We all are."

Ash shot her younger sister with a look of anger. "Well, it hasn't seemed to affect your appetite!"

Sammi slammed down her spoon. "That's not fair! And fark you! All our hearts hurt for Ditto!"

"Girls! Enough! And Sammi! Such language?!"

"Sorry, Da," exclaimed Sammi. "But just because she doesn't eat means she cares more? Fark that!"

"Language," screamed Jazz Bugg.

"Sorry, Ma."

Taff Bugg took a deep breath and exhaled slowly. "It's okay. Everyone, it's okay." He patted his wife's hands. "This is certainly unfortunate timing. And your ma and me are very sorry about your friend Ditto. Link Bugg has helped us through some tough times. He's helped everyone in Crimmish, truth be told. But we all have our time, and our families and friends must meet it with courage and empathy. And action, most of all. Ditto knows what needs to be done. He's the spitting image of his old man."

Ash pushed more food around. "May I be excused?"

Taff started to say more, but Jazz's dark hand on his arm held him back.

"Of course, sweetie. Get some rest. You've earned it. You all have."

Ash stood up. "Oh, I'll get some sleep. But poor Ditto won't!" With that, Ash slammed her fork down on her plate, ran to her bed, and buried herself in blankets. Crying could be heard beneath the layers of wool.

Jazz watched the heaving pile of covers for a moment before turning her attention to the younger of her two daughters. "How are you doing, kiddo?"

Sammi shrugged as she shoveled rabbit into her mouth. She spoke around bites of meat and potato. "My heart hurts for Ditto, Ma. But unlike Shanti, my heart's not connected to my stomach."

"It's Ash," came an angry, muffled voice from the nearest bed.

"Well, that's good," said Taff, pushing Ash's plate towards Sammi. "Here, have Shanti's portion. Let's not let it go to waste."

Sammi pushed her own empty plate aside and began to dig into Ash's leftovers. "Plus, I'm not the one who's in love with him."

Taff's face twisted in confusion. "What was that?"

Sammi shrugged. "Nothing." She took Ash's plate in her hands. "I'm gonna finish this outside. There's a new colony of syrup ants next to the porch and I want to watch them."

As Sammi exited, Taff turned to Jazz and whispered, "What did she say? What about Shanti loving Ditto? She means platonically, right?"

"I don't know, Taff."

"As friends, right?"

"Leave it alone, husband."

"Right?"

~

Ditto sat with Link Bugg all night, ignoring the man's shouts of brain itch and grimacing every time his massive father's thrashing threatened to rip the ropes that held him tight in a reinforced chair. Luckily, Ditto was able to complete the ties before his father gained consciousness. They certainly weren't as pretty as Sammi's knots, but they held.

Ditto spoke to his father well into the night, sharing his deepest thoughts and desires while telling Link how much he meant to him. Every now and then, the violent head movements would cease, eyes would clear, and Link Bugg would manage to say something unrelated to itches and scratches and brains. It was always the same.

"I love you, son."

As Paragon began to rise over the horizon, Link finally succumbed to exhaustion, and his damaged head fell into his chest. Ditto rose from his chair, kissed the top of his da's head, and exited the house.

As his eyes adjusted to the morning light, Ditto saw that he wasn't alone. Fincher, Ash, Sammi, and even Hana were waiting outside, all sitting cross-legged on the dirt. They rose upon seeing their friend.

"How long have you all been here?" asked Ditto, the tears in his eyes in stark contrast to the appreciative smile on his face.

"Not sure. A couple hours maybe," answered Fincher. "How are you holding up, Ditto?"

Ditto walked to his friends. "Ahh, you know. It is what it is. Part of life in the Stenches, isn't it?"

No one responded, but all nodded solemnly.

Sammi put her hand on her big friend's big shoulder. "Is there anything we can do, Ditto? My da said he can help if you can't go through with it. Said he owed Link Bugg a lot."

"My da said the same thing," offered Fincher.

"Mine, too," added Hana.

Ditto wiped some wetness from his face. "Thanks, you all. Truly. But I need to do this. We've said our goodbyes. There's nothing left to do now." Ditto drew circles in the dirt with his boot. "Well, just one more thing, I suppose."

Fincher stepped forward, stood on his tiptoes, and pressed his forehead against Ditto's. "Want me to come in with you? I will."

Ditto slapped his smaller friend's shoulders. "And take all the credit? No way." The friends all shared in a somber laugh. "Okay, then. Be back in a minute."

Ditto turned to leave but was stopped by Ash's lone hand on his bicep. She pulled him in and kissed him on the cheek. "We'll be out here waiting."

"Thank you, Ash."

The group watched as Ditto returned to his house. On his way in, he collected the large dagger that leaned against the building and closed the door behind him.

Several minutes passed. And then several more.

Eventually, the door sprung open, and Ditto stepped out. Despite his size, the boy looked deflated, as if he had left a big chunk of himself back in the home. While Ditto's dagger dripped with blood, his face looked devoid of it, replaced by a pale veil of sadness. He tossed the blade aside and stumbled to his friends, who rushed forward and buried him in a massive hug.

And there the Sour Flower Gang remained for dozens of minutes, dispersing Ditto's grief while sharing their collective strength. They rubbed backs, squeezed hands, and wiped tears, only separating when every eye was dry, and the color had returned to Ditto's face.

Finally, Ditto nodded to each of his friends in turn and they began to walk arm-in-arm to Mayor Bugg's, who would arrange to have Link's body collected and prepared.

Ditto looked to his left and his right as he walked, and although he was experiencing anguish beyond words, he was not hopeless. A small smile formed as he marched forward with his Sour Flower Gang.

Ditto Bugg was parentless. But he was far from alone.

2

A CRUEL PROPOSAL FROM KASSIMONT

High Captain Gorman Graff arrived to Salvation Outpost on horseback late into the night. It was bright, as Ommori Prime and her four sister satellites were all full in the evening sky, shining their quintet of beacons down upon the land of Quaan.

Always one to keep his promise, Captain Graff had arrived to the small trading town exactly eight turns of Paragon from when he departed. It was a difficult trip for both soldiers and horses, one without rest and with meals on the saddle. To keep up morale, Graff promised that all accompanying soldiers would receive an adjournment of twenty Paragons at the successful completion of their journey.

Making things worse, without their Titian fatigues and armor, bandits saw them as potential targets. Graff lost one soldier over three skirmishes that could have been avoided had he been allowed to at least bring his colors along for the ride.

The thought of unnecessarily losing a soldier, especially when he only had eleven, boiled Graff's blood and caused him to lose a wad of spit onto the town's dirt-covered ground.

"So, this is Salvation Outpost," said Captain Graff to no one in particular.

"Looks like an absolutely shite hole," remarked Second Lieutenant Heleena Dell as she smoothed back her short red hair.

"It is," agreed Second Lieutenant Tobias Vale. "They're a prickly bunch, which is ironic given that their whole town only exists to host outsiders looking to trade. They're especially hostile to those coming from the Stenches. Which, again, makes no sense. This place wouldn't even have been erected if it wasn't for Moon Tears. But they're too stupid to see it."

"Mountain trash," concluded Dell.

"Mountain trash," agreed Vale.

"Nevertheless," stated Captain Graff, "they will accommodate us. And quickly. And if I have to crack some heads to get it done, so be it. We are under Imperial orders and will not play games with Spire Rubes." Vale and Dell chuckled at the antiquated term. "I don't care that it's late. Start knocking on doors. I want everyone with a hot meal and a bed within the hour or I start swelling eyes. Understood?"

"Crystal, sir," answered Lieutenant Vale.

"Good. We'll head out at first light to the Stenches. They say it's a half-day trip, so make sure the horses are fed and watered." Grumbling broke out amongst the soldiers. "I hear the buzzing of insects. Voice your concerns or close your mouths!"

Voices from the back reached Graff.

"Uhh, isn't the place toxic, sir?"

"Yeah, no offense, sir, but I'm not trying to poison my lungs. What kind of soldier would I be with bad lungs?"

"I heard you can catch the Maddening within a few minutes."

"Enough," roared Captain Graff. "My senile old housekeeper has more guts than most of you."

"Maybe because she's senile."

Graff's eyes went wide. "Who said that?! Make your voice known!" No one came forward. "Just as I thought. Now I'm almost glad we left our colors at Kassimont. Save the Empire the embarrassment of this group. Lieutenant Vale, please educate these brave cowards."

Tobias Vale spun his horse to face the other soldiers. "The Stenches are on the edge of the Tainted Timbers, not *in* them. While the sprays of the Reaper Vines reach them, it is not in any concentrated form. You won't be affected in a few minutes, hours, or even days. The Maddening comes from prolonged, year-long exposure to the fumes."

The soldiers shared unconvinced looks as their mounts stepped nervously beneath them. Lieutenant Vale noticed and leaned into Captain Graff.

"You know, sir, the Stenches are unused to visitors. All business is usually conducted through Salvation Outpost. Perhaps only a few of us should make the trip, deliver the message. I mean, if we need to earn their trust, maybe a group of edgy, exhausted soldiers isn't the way."

Captain Graff mulled over his subordinate's words before sighing deeply. "I don't like your logic, Lieutenant, but I can't argue with it. Plus..." Graff raised his voice to be heard. "... I've seen more spine in a bowl of flushing jellyfish soup!" Graff collected himself. "Very well. Listen up! Second Lieutenants Vale and Dell will accompany me to the Stenches at first light. The rest of you get some rest and stay out of trouble. You should be more than recovered by the time we set off in two days. Which means I don't want to hear any more whining and complaining! Is that understood!?"

"Yes, Captain," came the collective, relieved cry from the soldiers.

"Good. Because one group of children to babysit is more than enough."

"Well, look who it is—the *Needsa Shower Gang*," said a laughing Brando Bugg as Sammi, Ash, and Fincher collected dried smoke pine branches on the edge of town.

"I thought it was the *Dour Coward Gang*," joined in Renton Bugg as the other three lackeys giggled from behind.

"Still like the name?" asked Ash to Fincher.

"Mockery is the sincerest form of flattery," asserted Fincher smugly.

"I think you have that wrong," said Sammi as she continued her work.

"Still, you can't say that it didn't stick." Fincher called out to the rival harvester crew passing through. "And what, pray tell, is the name of your group, Renton?"

"We are the Plucky Gents," cried out Renton with pride.

Sammi, Ash, and Fincher's faces all twisted before they broke out into laughter.

"What's so funny?" demanded Brando as he grabbed the axe handle tucked into his belt.

"Oh, nothing," responded Fincher, "except that name really stinks."

"No way," shouted Renton. "*Plucky* as in brave. And *plucky* as in we *pluck* Moon Tears from the Timbers. It's smart! It's smart and you're jealous!"

"Jealous of what?" asked Ash.

"Jealous that we don't allow weak girls in our crew. Especially one-armed ones!"

Having heard enough, Ash picked up the nearest thick branch and strode toward Renton Bugg. As Sammi attempted to pull her back, Fincher issued a retort.

"You're right! The *Sucky Gents* has a nice ring to it!"

"It's *plucky*, you motherless whelp," screamed Renton. That comment stung, but Fincher didn't let it show. "And put a leash on your armless dog before I set Whyllo on her."

With that, black-mohawked Whyllo Bugg stepped forward, the biggest boy in all of the harvester crews. Although Ditto would eventually be bigger, Whyllo was three years older and at least two stone heavier.

Ash stopped her advance. "If Ditto was here…"

"But he's not, is he? You may be tough, but don't forget what you are. Just a one-armed *girl*."

"He's a hard guy to like," commented Fincher to his friends, and Sammi almost lost her composure.

"Let's get out of here, gents," said Renton to his crew before turning back to Fincher. "We're off for the Timbers in two days and are gonna top anything the *Diarrhea Gang* has ever done!"

"Well, that one wasn't even clever," muttered Fincher, before responding with, "You mean to tell me, *plucky* Renton, that you all are going to fill three vials of Moon Tears and then bag a farking Ghost Puma?"

"It was a baby Puma, Fincher! You know that! We all know that!"

"Then I look forward to seeing the grown one that you bring back. That is, if you're a *gent* of your word."

Renton searched for a comeback but found none. "Fark you, Fincher. And fark your whole stanking gang. Let's go, guys."

With those parting words, Renton Bugg led his crew away to prepare for their future excursion into the Tainted Timbers. When they were out of sight, Ash finally tossed her branch onto the pile and resumed work.

"You know," she said as she went to collect more wood, "the Plucky Gents *is* a pretty good name." She waited a beat. "It really sticks."

"Oh, fark off," cried Fincher, sending Sammi into a fit of laughter.

Edd Bugg stormed into the Mayor's office, interrupting his lunch of roast hill rat.

"Mayor, Mayor, Mayor," he said between deep breaths.

"My god, man, catch your breath. What is it that could be so dire?"

Edd, also known as Simple Edd, inhaled deeply before continuing. "Riders are approaching. Probably in town by now."

"How many?"

"Only three that I saw."

"From where?"

"No idea. Look like traders."

"Why would a trader come into town instead of waiting at Salvation Outpost?" Edd simply shrugged. Mayor Bugg tossed his rat aside and grabbed his mayoral jacket. "You're a wealth of information, Edd. Gather the Committee, and let us meet these guests properly.

Just because we rarely receive visitors doesn't mean that we've forgotten decorum."

"You want me to go now?"

Dann Bugg rolled his eyes. "Yes, man, now!" The Mayor's words sent Simple Edd off. Dann moved over to the mirror hanging on his office wall and started taming wild eyebrows and combing unkempt hair. After a few minutes of primping, he smiled at his reflection and readied himself for whatever might come.

For visitors to Crimmish only brought one of two things – trouble, or opportunity.

The Crimmish Committee assembled within minutes and greeted the trio of riders just inside the town's open front gates. Along with Fincher's father Gill, Ash and Sammi's parents Taff and Jazz Bugg, and Hana's mother Joon, were among the other adults that comprised the seven-person ruling council.

At the front of this group was Mayor Dann Bugg, his purple jacket standing out against its drab surroundings.

"Greetings, greetings. Greetings and salutations, brave guests. I am Dann Bugg, mayor of this fine town of Crimmish," welcomed the Mayor warmly. Unfortunately, none of the three riders reacted, except for the red-haired female who lifted her shirt up over her nose. "And what do we owe the pleasure of your company? Interested in goods? We have several unique pelts and many dried fruits that can only be found at the southern base of the Spired Curtains."

"That's not why we're here, Mayor," replied Captain Graff from atop his horse.

"No worries, no worries at all. We have much more to offer and are open to many trade items in return. Perhaps I can interest you in some hill rat jerky?"

Tobias Vale's nose turned up in disgust.

"It's much tastier than it sounds; I promise you," stated Mayor Bugg defensively. "In fact, if you dip it in—"

"I meant, we're not here for your goods, Mayor," proclaimed Captain Graff.

Dann Bugg's hand slowly drifted to the blade kept at his waist, just as the hands of Gill, Taff, Jazz, and Joon slid to their own weapons. "Then what are you here for?"

"Your children," answered Second Lieutenant Dell callously, and Captain Graff shot her with a look that ensured she remained quiet for the remainder of the conversation.

"Apologies for my subordinate," said Graff, returning to the Committee. "She's too young to know the power of words. Especially the wrong ones." Graff cleared his throat. "We are not traders. We are soldiers of the Titian Empire. My name is High Captain Gorman Graff and these are Second Lieutenants Tobias Vale and Heleena Dell. We have been sent here on a mission of the utmost importance and urgency directly from His Majesty, Imperator Kasspar Rayne." The gathered villagers all gasped in a mix of surprise, fear, and curiosity. Graff gave them a moment to digest this new information before dropping his key line. "The Empire desperately needs your help."

More chatter. Finally, Mayor Bugg stepped forward. "Strong words. Do you have any proof of their veracity?"

Graff reached into his pocket, retrieved the Imperial decree, and handed it down to Dann Bugg. The Mayor looked over the calligraphy, ran his fingers across the wax imprint, and even held the thick paper up to Paragon to discover an Imperial watermark. He then carefully rolled the decree back up and delivered it back to Captain Graff.

Mayor Bugg turned back to the Committee, a frightened, almost doleful look upon his fleshy face. "It appears legitimate."

Gill Bugg was the first to speak up. "You said something about children. Why do you need our children?"

Captain Graff fidgeted uncomfortably and cursed Sologar Crimm. He was no ambassador, nor negotiator. Gorman Graff was a soldier, nothing more, nothing less. These matters were beyond his pay grade and his abilities.

"It's not that we need your children," Graff tried to clarify. "We need your harvesters."

"But those *are* our children," shot back Joon Bugg.

"That's right," agreed Ash and Sammi's father Taff in unison.

"And you *can't* have them! I don't care what the Empire needs!" Taff declared.

It was at this most inopportune of times that Second Lieutenant Tobias Vale decided to offer his two chips. "We don't *need* your permission, good sir. The Imperial decree states that we can take whatever it is that we require. And we require—"

"That will be enough, Lieutenant Vale," barked Captain Graff, not only silencing his Second Lieutenant, but everyone else within earshot. Graff calmed himself. "Mayor, is there somewhere that we can talk more privately? I promise that this issue is much more nuanced than it appears. And potentially much more lucrative for you and your constituency."

Dann Bugg pulled on his mayoral jacket. "I have no constituency. We aren't divided in Crimmish."

"My error. Let me rephrase. Much more lucrative for all the people of Crimmish."

Mayor Bugg looked back to the committee of seven and nodded.

"There will be no meeting unless we involve the Crimmish Committee. You may represent an inequitable empire, but I do not."

Captain Graff had a hard time suppressing his smile, silently admitting that he liked what he saw so far from the people of Crimmish. He had yet to detect the greed that permeated towns up and down Quaan.

"Invite anyone you deem necessary," declared Graff as he dismounted and tossed his reins to Heleena Dell. He addressed Tobias Vale. "You two can stay here and watch the horses since you're worthless in a sensitive discussion." Graff approached Dann Bugg. "Lead the way, Mayor?"

Dann spoke to both Captain Graff and the Crimmish Committee. "Let's convene in the meeting hall, shall we?" Everyone nodded and made their way to Crimmish's largest building.

Captain Graff hooked the Mayor's arm as they walked and leaned in. "Any chance I can try some of that jerky?"

Mayor Bugg smiled. "Of course, Captain. But I have to warn you. Once you acquire a taste for hill rat, you'll trade away your own mother to get more."

"How about two idiots on horseback?"

High Captain Gorman Graff had faced down charging Cobalt armies with a smattering of soldiers. He had been cornered alone by a gang of Titian dissenters. He had engaged in fisticuffs with one of the Titans of Crown Lake. Captain Graff had kept his chin up and heart controlled under all matter of dire conditions.

But he was having a hard time matching the angry looks of the Crimmish Committee, many of whom were probably parents of harvester children.

Mayor Bugg had given Graff one end of the long table, and he took the other. In between, men and women glared at Graff, and the Captain wondered how many fingered knives under the table. He didn't blame them one bit.

After awkward introductions, the Mayor fell silent, letting the room stew in its own tension. Gill Bugg was the first to break the spell.

"So, you want to take some of our kids?"

Graff wrung his hands. This was proving harder than hunting bog boars.

"Like I said, I don't *want* to take your children. No one does. Unfortunately, the Empire *needs* the unique... characteristics of your harvesters."

Jazz Bugg cut in. "You mean, the same Empire that banished us here to toil away in poisonous air?! For *crimes* that none of us committed?!"

"For crimes that your ancestors committed," corrected Graff. "Treason is the greatest of offenses, lest we not forget."

"*You* called it treason," said Taff Bugg.

"I wasn't alive then."

"*Your* Empire, then."

"It is yours, as well, good sir."

"Sure doesn't feel like it."

"Then perhaps my offer today can help fix that."

A look of confusion crossed over Taff's face and spread to the rest of the Crimmish Committee. Finally, Mayor Bugg decided to chime in.

"I think we're getting a bit off track. Captain Graff, you cannot expect us to be all smiles and guffaws. As of right now, we know nothing more than that you want to take away some of our children. Perhaps you can tell us what's really going on? You mentioned an offer. We would like to hear that. But first, I think we would like to have a bit of context." Dann Bugg paused and leaned forward on the table, putting all the strength he could muster into the next questions. "What is going on, Captain? Why do you need our children?"

Gorman Graff continued to wring his scarred hands. He was directly instructed by Chancellor Sologar Crimm not to mention anything about the God-Snails or the true purpose of the journey. *The Empire demands it of them. That's all that those mud-dwellers need to know!* As Graff looked around at these proud people—these mothers and fathers, these survivors—the Chancellor's words rang empty.

Fark Sologar, decided Graff. If the people of Crimmish were going to trust him with their children, they deserved to know why. All of it.

Gorman Graff's hands ceased their wringing.

"What do you all know about the Supreme Helices?" A heaviness descended upon the gathering room.

"You mean the God-Snails?" asked Joon.

"I do."

The table looked around in a mix of confusion, curiosity, and fear bordering on horror. Mayor Bugg answered for the group.

"We know what most know, I suppose. The God-Snails come down in dire times of need and offer gifts to humanity. The earliest that I recall was hundreds of years ago, when they caused the twin eruptions of Galanis Dawn and Mount Ghaal. This led to the Reshaping, which allowed water to flow down from the mountains and create rivers for our parched land. Next, we were given the Legacy Seeds and Kernels to combat the Great Famine. Our Honey Rice and Angel Wheat are direct offshoots of those gifts."

"Go on," prompted Captain Graff.

"Let's see, most recently… and most relevant to those here today, we were granted the cure to the Bloat in the form of Moonflowers, which, to our knowledge, only grow in the Tainted Timbers. As far as I know, the God-Snails have not blessed us with their presence since, which I suppose is a good thing. How did I do?"

"Very well, Mayor Bugg. Surprisingly well, in fact. Few in Quaan know the history of the Divine Pentad in such detail."

Mayor Bugg smiled in satisfaction. "We don't only trade for chips and goods, Captain. We also trade for information, that most valuable of resources."

"Sounds like you have made some good deals," offered Graff. "There are only a few details that you are missing. First, the Supreme Helices don't visit randomly, they arrive every hundred years on the Centennial Star, also known as the Sky Rose. Perhaps you've seen the red comet in the sky as of late."

"I saw such a thing several Paragons ago when I was fetching water from the stream before dawn," said Jazz. "It was beautiful, but I paid it little mind. We have too many things to worry about in Crimmish to let our minds drift to the cosmos."

"Understood, ma'am. But that was certainly it. It's much easier to view the Sky Rose the further north you go."

"Everything is easier the further north you go," spat another of the Committee, and Graff could only nod in agreement.

"In any case, that brings me to the second detail that the Mayor missed. The Centennial Star has arrived and, thus, so have the God-Snails. Our saviors are here now, as we speak."

Shocked silence gripped the table. Gill Bugg was the first to recover.

"To save us from what? I have heard of nothing dire in Quaan beyond the ongoing war with the Cobalts."

Captain Graff cleared his throat. "Yes, that may be due to your... location... tucked away here as you are. But just because we aren't experiencing drought or famine or plague doesn't mean that the Titian Empire isn't in great need. There is something strange and awful that has been sweeping across the land over the past few seasons."

"What is it?" asked Joon Bugg.

Graff paused for a moment to collect his thoughts. "Our scholars call it the Gloomtide. It started far to the Northeast and began fanning out to all the cities, towns, and villages—no one seems to be spared."

"But *what* is it?" reiterated Joon.

Graff let out a long breath. "Truth be told, we really don't know. It is a kind of despair that is infecting young and old, rich and poor. Production across the board—farming, metalworking, textile creation —has plummeted as suicides have risen to unfathomable heights. There are stories of mothers wandering into the wilderness in the dead of night. Of fathers filling their pockets with stones before wading into the nearest lake or river. Of teenagers refusing to eat until they waste away to nothing. I have visited some of the towns beset by this invisible monster, and never before have I felt such help-lessness.

"With famine or plague, we can pinpoint the culprit and recognize the solution, even if that solution is hard or impossible to come by. But with this..." Graff's mind drifted to a bitter memory. "How do you combat that which you can't understand? I tell you this now. After the horrors I have recently witnessed, I would rather take my chances with a Bog Behemoth... in my skivvies, than have to fight off the Gloomtide."

Another long silence followed the Captain's words. Graff bore the scars of a hundred battles and had the demeanor of someone who had made friends with death. To hear the fear in his voice unnerved everyone in the gathering room.

"How is the Empire planning on dealing with this?" dared the Mayor.

Graff laughed sardonically. "Plans? We have no plans, no answers. We are counting on a miracle, which is exactly what the God-Snails are known to provide at times like these. If we cannot reach the Divine Pentad, I fear all will be lost."

Faces fell as the direness of the situation took hold. But the sounds of twisted laughter brought chins back up. The others looked over as Taff Bugg chuckled in strange glee.

"You find humor in something I said, sir?" demanded Captain Graff.

Taff's maniacal laughter slowed. "I did, indeed, Captain. This horrible, terrible, nightmarish condition of which you speak—this Gloomtide—sounds no worse than what the people of Crimmish have lived with for generations. Your Gloomtide is no worse than our Maddening. You simply care more about those who are just now becoming afflicted. I'm sorry, Captain, but fark you and fark the Empire. You banished us down here, where our minds would slowly be ravaged by Reaper Vine fumes, and have had us harvest, in dangers you cannot imagine, the cure for the Bloat, saving an ungrateful population from its previous plague. And now you ask us to do it again? Fark you, Captain."

The Crimmish Committee all tensed, preparing for an explosion from the head of the Titian Army. Instead of widening with rage, however, Gorman Graff's grey eyes softened. He leaned forward on the table.

"Of course, you are correct, dear sir. Your people have been dealt a raw hand and the Titian Empire has no right asking you for more. Your efforts saved us from the worst plague in the history of Quaan once. How can we ask a second time?" A pause. "But we are. And let me tell you why you should care." Another pause. "Because you *have* endured. Because you *have* experienced the Maddening. You know the heartbreak that accompanies such an ailment. Now, imagine all of Quaan in the grips of a similar disease. The rest of Quaan does not have the strength found in Crimmish. They will fold under the weight. Civilization, as we know it, will come to an end."

"Maybe misery loves company," offered Jazz Bugg.

"It often does," agreed Graff. "But I do not think it does here in Crimmish, which eats misery for breakfast, lunch, and dinner. But please, correct me if I'm wrong."

No retort came. Instead, the conversation came full circle with Gill Bugg's next words.

"You still haven't told us why you need our children. We have so little here. Family and friends mean everything. More than those in Kassimont could ever understand."

Graff simply nodded. "Fair enough, good sir. And I will tell you truthfully. I respect you all too much to present lies. I told you that the God-Snails have arrived on Quaan. This is the good news."

"And the bad news?" asked Jazz Bugg.

"The bad news is where they have landed. I have it under good authority that the Supreme Helices have made landfall in the Northern Goddess." The Crimmish Committee looked around confusedly. "It is a massive steppe littered with hills and tucked away between the Spired Curtains and Sierra Dawn. Unfortunately, these flatlands are guarded by mountains to either side and something much worse below."

Mayor Bugg's brow creased in thought. Finally, he asked, "Loch Terminus?"

"Yes, good geographical knowledge," congratulated Captain Graff. "Our Imperator could take note. Loch Terminus, which is known to be filled with acidic water that burns holes in ship hulls and is home to all nature of nightmarish denizens of unbelievable size, takes up more than half of the southern border to the Northern Goddess. The remainder is taken up by thick forest called Terminus Grove."

"They share a name," pointed out Joon.

"They do indeed, madame," replied the Captain. "Because they share some regrettable qualities. Which brings us to our interest in your harvesters. Your children." Graff let that sink in for a moment. "Like your Tainted Timbers, Terminus Grove absorbed the brunt of ash and soot and toxic gases upon the eruption of Galanis Dawn. Like your Tainted Timbers, this toxified the ground and made it so that only certain flora could grow there. Of note, Reaper Vines."

"Another Tainted Timbers," commented Gill Bugg. "Well, I'll be durned."

"Indeed. Any man or woman or soldier trying to pass through Terminus Grove will be dead within the day. The good people of Crimmish, however, have developed a natural resistance to Reaper Vines, have you not? As I am told, this is especially true for those yet to reach full adulthood. Is that not why you send your children into the Timbers to fetch Moon Tears? What would happen if one of you were to enter the Tainted Timbers?"

Taff sighed deeply and answered for the group. "At our ages, we would probably swell up like any outsider if we drew too close to a Reaper. And even if we were to return from the forest, exposure to that concentration of Reaper fumes would dramatically hasten the Maddening."

"Exactly. Thank you for your confirmation, dear sir. With conditions comparable to the Tainted Timbers, we believe that children from Crimmish could easily pass through Terminus Grove. Once on the other side, they would locate the God-Snails, receive their gift, and deliver it to Titian representatives—namely, me—thereby ridding the world of the Gloomtide and saving humanity once again."

"There's one problem, Captain," stated Taff Bugg.

"Give it voice, good sir."

"We don't represent humanity, and it doesn't represent us. Humanity shunned us. They call where we live *the Stenches* and let their kids call our kids *Cheese-Eyes*. We have no kinship with them. We collect Moon Tears because they are worth far more than anything else in trade. Not because we care that some aristocrat's wife is about to be ripped apart from the Bloat. You ask us to hand over that which we hold most dear to save those who would not spit on us were we to catch fire. You seem an honorable man. An honorable man making a ridiculous request. I bid you good day, Captain."

At that, the Crimmish Committee all rose as one and moved to exit the gathering hall. Captain Graff smiled to himself before speaking loudly.

"I said the same thing, sir! Which is why I was authorized to make the following offer. Please! Hear my offer!"

Taff Bugg scoffed. "What offer? An offer that would justify us risking our children?!"

Gorman Graff shrugged mysteriously. "Perhaps... Yes, I think it would. Hear me out?"

The Crimmish Committee looked to each other, skepticism painted on each of their faces. They wanted nothing more than to send this agent of the evil Empire away. To spit in his face and curse him for his gall. They wanted to do these things. But instead they sat.

"You heard me correctly," reiterated Captain Graff. The Empire will halve its requirement of Moon Tears while quintupling the price it currently pays. You'll make as much, if not more, than in previous years, and your children will have to make far fewer treks into the Tainted Timbers. Less work, more pay—at a guaranteed rate!" Graff was only authorized to quadruple the current rate, but he took his little wins against the Imperial bureaucracy where he could get them.

"Our people got by long before Moonflowers even came to the Tainted Timbers, Captain Graff," asserted Gill Bugg. "Still lots of things we can pull out of the Timbers and pluck off the land to trade. We can survive Moon Tear demand fluctuations."

"But what about something you can't survive? Like the Maddening?"

Graff watched as faces clouded over, as steely demeanors started to show thick cracks. The people of Crimmish were a sturdy folk, resilient and adaptable. But even they had difficulty in facing the invisible scythe that hung heavy over all of their heads.

Mayor Bugg spoke for the Committee. "The Maddening is our curse to bear. It is the weighty, unending consequence of our ancestral missteps. We serve as an example to others who would consider crossing the Empire—*your* Empire, Captain."

"But what if you no longer had to bear it?"

Shocked, fearful looks greeted Captain Graff. The veteran soldier knew those looks only too well. They were the faces of a people terrified of hope, that most dangerous of emotions. Graff himself wore that same face five years ago, when he was promised retirement and finally dared to dream of life spent with his wife on his country farm instead of days filled with blood and mayhem and the screams of young soldiers.

When his retirement was stripped away days later by Sologar Crimm, citing an uprising to the North, Graff learned firsthand the pain of hope. It hurt worse and cut deeper than any enemy blade he had ever encountered.

He dared to hope once more, though. High Captain Gorman Graff hoped that what he was offering the people of Crimmish was real and not some trickery of the perfumed and bejeweled.

"What do you mean by that?" demanded Taff Bugg, his dark hands gripping the edge of the table. "Speak plainly, Captain! Please."

"In addition to the increased price of Moon Tears alongside decreased demand, I have also been authorized, directly by the Imperator himself, to make this promise. Provide the harvesters we need for this mission of critical importance, and the Titian Empire will send its greatest physicians, alchemists, and apothecaries to Crimmish to research, study, and, ultimately, create a cure for the Maddening." There was no response. Captain Graff knew that he had them. "Of course, this will not happen overnight. But the Imperatrix Kassidy Rayne personally swore that waves of Quaan's greatest minds, even the Royal Physician Lantiss Timms, would visit Crimmish until the Maddening was nothing more than a horrible memory of the past."

"You'll have to excuse us if we are dubious, Captain," said Joon.

"I don't blame you one bit."

"Then, why should we trust you?"

"You shouldn't, Miss Bugg. But what you should trust is that the

Empire will do whatever it takes to survive, to toss aside the shroud of the Gloomtide. And to do that, the Empire needs representatives it can trust to reach the Supreme Helices and receive their divine gift. You can't trust the Empire, but you can trust it to save itself. They… we need your children right now. You may never again have the Empire over a barrel as you do today. Please, I beg you, grab this opportunity while you can. Before they conjure another solution that cuts you out completely."

A long silence followed the Captain's speech. He launched into his closing argument.

"It is clear to me how much family means to you. How much community means to this town. Imagine living long enough to watch your children grow into men and women. Long enough to bounce your grandchildren on your knees." Graff waited for dramatic effect. "Imagine a life where your children did not have to watch as you descend into madness. A life where your children's final memory of you wasn't you bashing your brains out with a rock. A life where your children were not responsible for putting their parents out of their misery. Can you imagine?"

Several of those in attendance wiped tears from their yellow eyes.

"How many would you need? What would they have to do?" asked Jazz.

"No more than half a dozen or so," replied Graff. "As you can see, we are traveling light and not donning our Titian colors. It should be a peaceful, quiet trip north through Salt's Pass and then the Angel Wheat Flats. We should reach Terminus Grove without much difficulty. And, from what I hear, other than the noxious air, to which your children should be resilient, Terminus Grove is fairly innocuous. Certainly nothing in there as dangerous as your Ghost Pumas."

"I've heard that the Sluggs have traveled south and now maintain positions in Shadowset," stated Mayor Bugg. "Why not go east around Kassimont?"

"Time is of the essence, Mayor. We know not how long the God-Snails will wait for us to make contact. We must move swiftly. This will not only get us the divine gift faster, but it will ensure your children get home sooner."

"And the Sluggs?"

Captain Graff hesitated before answering. "Our most current intel suggests that there is no Cobalt presence in Shadowset or anywhere outside of the Insurgence Line, for that matter. Word of Sluggs creeping down from the North is hearsay, nothing more."

The Crimmish Committee looked around uncomfortably, as if they were being asked to choose between fighting a Bog Behemoth or a swarm of Hellion Wasps. "You'll understand if we need to discuss this more. In private," offered Dann Bugg.

"Of course," replied Captain Graff, rising to his feet with a grunt. "I'll return tomorrow just before Paragon is at its height. If your answer is affirmative, please have the harvesters ready to travel. Again, time is of the essence."

"Regardless, we would like to thank you for the kindness, and honesty, that you have shown here today, Captain Graff," offered the Mayor. "It's nice to be treated like a fellow human. We so rarely are."

Gorman Graff bowed slightly at the compliment. "I am a lifelong soldier. Nothing more, nothing less. I respect survival beyond anything. Except loyalty. Good luck with your decision."

"Captain Graff," said the Mayor, "stop by the shop with the blue sign in front on your way out. Tell Lynn Bugg to give you as much hill rat jerky as you can carry. And have her put it on my tab. A gift for your humanity. And honesty."

Graff nodded in appreciation and left feeling deflated, slightly less of a man. For although Gorman Graff had tried his best to remain truthful with the Crimmish Committee, his candor had come to an end several minutes ago.

When he promised their children a safe journey north.

The Sour Flower Gang met up shortly after Mayor Bugg had, along with the Crimmish Committee, addressed the town, informing them of the Empire's strange request. After some prodding from the towns-folk, Mayor Bugg also eventually revealed the finer details of the offer, including a potential cure for the Maddening. The villagers, adults and children alike, stumbled from the meeting as if drunk on too much honey rice wine.

Fincher, as usual, initiated the discussion. "What the fark were they talking about? More chips? A cure for the Maddening? What do we need to do for such a prize? Travel up north? For what?"

"And why do they need us kids?" added Sammi.

"Yeah, why do we have to agree to the job before we know what it is? This seems like a setup," said Ash.

"Fark yeah, it is," agreed Fincher.

There was a brief break in the conversation before…

"I'm going."

Everyone turned as one to Ditto, who stood with his broad chest out, an unfamiliar look in his normally placid eyes.

"Say again," said Fincher, confused.

"I said that I'm going."

"But why?" demanded Ash, and there was a slight tremble in her voice.

Ditto delivered his typical shrug. "Three reasons, really. First, I'm alone now. My parents are both gone, as is my duty to the town to end their suffering. I am without a family."

"We're your family, Ditto," stated Ash, the tremble growing.

"Of course, you are. But you know what I mean." Only Fincher and Sammi nodded. "Second, if there's something I can do that could possibly lead to ending the Maddening, I have to do it. I don't want any of you to have to go through what I've gone through." Ditto looked to Fincher. "Again."

Sammi pushed her glasses higher on her nose. "You know it's probably a lie, Ditto. You know the Empire is rich in empty promises."

"I know, Sammi. But it's more hope than we've ever had. I can deal with betrayal. I can't go on knowing I could have done something, but chose to believe in the worst of people."

"And the third reason, Ditto?" prompted Fincher.

A small smile crept onto the large boy's face. "It's a bit more selfish. I want to see the world. We've never even been to Salvation Outpost. All we know is Crimmish and the Tainted Timbers, which try to kill us every time we enter."

"And which always succeeds in the end," added Fincher.

"Exactly! This is an opportunity to escape the Stenches, to see the entirety of Quaan. How many from Crimmish can say they've seen Shadowset, or Crown's Run, or Ptero Heights?" The Sour Flower Gang fell silent. Ditto continued. "I'm not speaking for the crew. This is my decision and my decision alone. You all have much more to lose. Much more to live for. I don't expect you to follow me."

Everyone's head dropped. Fincher stared for a while at the wet clay at his feet. When his eyes rose, he saw buildings made of recycled bits of lumber. Past the homes, he saw a black and grey forest teeming with danger. Fincher wanted to, for once, look up and see vibrant green. He wanted to see the wind create soft ripples across the Angel Wheat Flats. He needed to see more of this world.

"Fark that."

Ditto's face scrunched up. "What was that?"

"I said fark that, Deetarik Bugg. The Sour Flower Gang rides together or not at all. I'm only speaking for myself, but I'm in."

"But your da—"

Fincher waved away Ditto's protest. "Gill Bugg hungers for adventure more than anyone. My da will understand."

"We're going, too," blurted Ash, as if she was trying to get the words out before she had a chance to wrangle them back in. Sammi's brown eyes went wide behind her glasses.

Ditto stumbled over his words. "But… Jazz and Taff… they'll never let you—"

"You let *me* deal with them." A pause. "I'm not as tough as I seem. There's lots I'm scared of in this world. But none is as terrifying as seeing Ma and Da fight the Maddening. If this… mission… can prevent that, I have to do it. Sis?"

"I'm with you, always, big sister."

"Except about the name *Sour Flower Gang*."

Sammi giggled. "Yes. Except about *that*."

As usual, some had forgotten about the youngest member of their crew. Ditto went to Hana now, kneeling before the small girl.

"Hana, you should stay here. Your parents only have you. And you still have a lot of time to spend with them. You stay here and watch out for all of our parents… for all of us who won't remain."

"No." The girl looked up with moist, black-on-yellow eyes.

"But, Hana—"

"I said no!" The group all jumped a bit, unused to such force from their youngest member. "We're a harvester crew, the Sour Flower Gang, and we do the most dangerous tasks possible—together. My Ma and Da will be brokenhearted, but they will be whether we go or not. In Crimmish, everyone ends up brokenhearted. If you all are going… I'm going, too."

"Then that farking settles it," said Fincher will a wide smile on his face. "The Sour Flower Gang is going to roll north!"

"But what if others want to volunteer?" asked Sammi.

"Fark them!"

~

"Fark you!"

Unsurprisingly, the voice belonged to Renton Bugg, representing the Plucky Gents. The collected town of Crimmish, gathered in the square before dinner, all turned to face the angry youth.

"That's right, fark *you*," reiterated Renton. "We, the Plucky Gents, also volunteer for the mission."

Fincher winced, hoping that they had it in the bag, that no other harvester crew would volunteer for the unsettling, secretive assignment.

"We're by far the most accomplished harvester crew," declared Fincher to the crowd.

"By what metric?"

"By every metric!"

"You mean seniority?"

Those words made Fincher grimace even worse. Although one couldn't deny that the Sour Flower Gang was the best at harvesting Moon Tears, Renton's crew was older and had been making treks into the Tainted Timbers literal years before them. It's the one hand the older boy had to play, and he'd played it to perfection.

Mayor Bugg held up his hands, hoping to bring order to the discussion. "Now, now, it's always nice to have *too many* volunteers. It's what we call a *good problem*. Perhaps we can take the eldest from each crew and—"

"No!"

"Never!"

"Fark that!"

"Fark you!"

The Mayor's hands dropped immediately. The idea to merge two crews obviously would not work. "A town-wide vote, perhaps?"

"Oh, for fark's sake!"

"Let them figure it out!"

"Let the parents decide!"

Gill Bugg stepped forward. "Now, I think all of us have discussed this with our children and have granted consent." He looked to Joon and Kenn, Jazz and Taff, and the parents of the other harvester crew. All nodded. "The children, whoever they are, will embark on a journey filled with challenges. Let this be their first to figure out on their own."

All the adults seemed to come to agreement, delighted to have the ultimate decision stripped away.

Renton Bugg smiled darkly as an idea popped into his head. "Champion's Challenge," he called out. "Our best versus their best! Winning team goes on the adventure!"

Fincher looked to Ditto, who would surely represent the Sour Flower Gang. The large boy gave his approval.

"Accepted!"

The residents broke out into excited chatter, and a space was cleared in the town square. As a circle of onlookers formed, Whyllo

Bugg, his black mohawk leading, stepped into the middle and began stretching his thick muscles.

Ash and Fincher leaned into Ditto.

"He's not going to fight fair, Ditto," said a concerned Ash.

"She's right," agreed Fincher. "Dirt in the eyes, headbutts, it's all an option. Whyllo doesn't discriminate in a fight."

Ditto looked down to his friends, and there was a dark twinkle in his too-green eyes. "My da was the champion of champions when he was only a few years older than me. He passed down a few tricks... and something more tangible. Just watch the other members of the Plucky Gents. I'll take care of Whyllo."

"Done," stated Fincher. There was nothing more that needed to be said.

Ditto marched into the circle to great applause, standing before the larger Whyllo. The two big boys stared each other down.

"Don't do this, Ditto. I'm going to hurt you."

"I'm used to that, Whyllo. You're going to have to do better."

"I'll farking cave your head in if I have to. Don't make me do it."

"Deal. Leave now, and you won't have to."

"Farking punk. You and your crew never know when to back down. You can't win."

"I've never claimed to be smart, Whyllo. We have Sammi for that."

Whyllo looked over to Sammi, and a smirk perched itself on his thick lips. "Maybe *I'll* have Sammi once our business is concluded. I think she would like—"

Whyllo never got the chance to complete his grotesque sentence as Ditto's fist smashed against his cheek, sending him reeling backwards. Ditto followed it up with several other hooks and jabs, many of which found Whyllo's face and neck. Eventually, however, the massive fifteen-year-old got his large hands up as protection, allowing him an opportunity to recover.

His initial assault concluded, Ditto took several steps back, his fists balled up at his shoulders. Whyllo wiped his face and took a moment to look upon the crimson liquid that now stained his hand. He spit a red loogie to the muddy ground.

"That was your shot. And you blew it. Time to eat shite. You better hope they're able to pull me off you."

Whyllo waded in throwing wide-arcing haymakers. Ditto was able to duck and dodge the first two, but caught the third blow with his shoulder, sending a numbing shockwave down his left arm. When Whyllo's next punch came in, a right hook, Ditto was unable to raise his arm and ate it cleanly with his jaw.

Ditto spun to the ground and remained there unmoving.

"Ditto," cried out Ash as Whyllo moved forward and kicked the boy in the side with a thick boot, launching him into the crowd.

Ditto landed amidst the spectators with a grunt and rolled. As he did, Fincher watched as his friend dug into his pocket and brought his right hand tight into his chest.

Whyllo raised his meaty hands in triumph, screaming to all in attendance.

"It's not over yet, Master Whyllo," said Mayor Bugg as Ditto stumbled to his feet, his left fist up but his right kept down by his side.

"Finish him, Whyllo," called Renton, and the large boy stalked toward the obviously woozy Ditto. Seeing that his younger adversary had little to offer in the way of resistance, Whyllo swatted away a weak straight left and grabbed Ditto by the throat with his own left hand. As he held Ditto steady, Whyllo raised his right fist and cocked it back for the knockout blow.

"Don't worry," he told Ditto, "I'll write Ash and Sammi when I'm gone on my adventure. And I'll accept any gifts of appreciation they offer when I return and cure their parents of the Maddening. In fact, maybe I'll take those gifts in advance. Tonight maybe. I'll let you watch if you—"

Ditto's seemingly distant eyes snapped into focus. Before Whyllo could react to the sudden shift, Ditto's left hand shot up, grabbed Whyllo by his collar, and wrenched him to the side. As he did this, Ditto's right hand swept up, an object clinging to his fist, and came down in an angle that was impossible to block. Driven by rage, Ditto's fist slammed into Whyllo's jaw, taking the boy off his feet to strike the ground back-first, driving the air from his lungs.

Ditto wasted no time, springing ahead to land hard atop the larger boy and rain blow after blow upon the giant teen. A fountain of blood spewed from Whyllo's face as Ditto continued his assault.

"Fark this," declared Renton as he drew a blade and entered the circle. A wad of dirt found his eyes, compliments of Sammi, as Ash finished the job, wrapping her good arm across the boy's throat and choking him out.

Brando Bugg also brought out a dagger and charged forward. He was stopped when Hana stealthily tripped him from within the crowd and Fincher ended up on his back, knocking him unconscious with a vicious strike using the hilt of his hunter's knife.

The remaining Plucky Gents began to move, but were halted by a shrieking whistle. Everyone, including Ditto, paused the melee and looked up to find the Mayor with two fingers between his lips. He removed them before speaking.

"A good showing for both groups. But it is decided. The..." He looked to the side to confer with Gill Bugg. "Sour Flower Gang is declared the winner and will leave with High Captain Gorman Graff tomorrow. Could someone please see to Whyllo's wounds? And I guess Brando's, as well? Ditto, do you need attention?"

Ditto rose from the unconscious Whyllo. "I'm all right, Mayor," declared the boy, although he was obviously nursing some bruised ribs.

"Then, you and the rest of your harvester crew can join us in the gathering hall. We have the additional details of your mission. The rest of you, please enjoy your supper."

As the crowd dispersed, Renton and his friends went to retrieve the fallen Whyllo. Ash ran over and hooked Ditto's arm over her shoulder, helping him to the gathering hall. As she did, Fincher removed the bloody object from Ditto's right hand. He inspected the strange implement.

"What the fark is this, Ditto?"

Ditto looked down and laughed. "From my Da. It's the top of a tunnel fox skull with four finger holes drilled through. You can swing with all your might with this thing on your hand and not break your knuckles."

"Cheeky bastard," said Fincher admiringly, before catching himself and understanding the weight of his words. "Oh, sorry, Ditto, I just meant—"

Ditto smiled through bloody lips. "It's okay. An accurate term now, I suppose. In any case, my da won this one for us."

"To Link Bugg," shouted Fincher, and the other members of the crew echoed his words. Ditto's red smiled widened.

Soon, the Sour Flower Gang found themselves in the gathering hall facing Mayor Bugg and the Crimmish Committee, many of whom were their parents. They were given water and mountain rat jerky before the meeting officially began. Finally, Dann Bugg spoke.

"You all have proven yourselves to be brave. And because much of your bravery stems from a desire to help us, the aging population of Crimmish, we think it only fair that you know the true purpose for your trip to the north."

"Moonflowers found in another area," offered Sammi.

"Another rarity for us to harvest," guessed Ditto.

"Someone needs killing," surmised Ash.

The Mayor looked around the room, making deliberate eye contact with each child. "What do you all know of the God-Snails?"

"Oh, fark us," declared Fincher.

Gill Bugg crammed some of his own belongings into Fincher's knapsack. "Take my toothpick and rain hat. I already resoled your boots so they should be good to go. Did you already pack extra socks?"

"I told you already that I did, Da."

"Okay, okay, just making sure, son. I'm throwing an extra bar of butter soap in there, as well. Make sure you wash up. They already think we smell bad; no reason to lend that awful rumor any credence. Don't forget to pack extra socks."

"I already did, Da."

Gill smiled and gently tossed the sack onto the bed. "Good." He sat down next to his son. "You know, of course I'm sad to see you go, but I'm also excited for you. All I ever wanted was for you to experience life outside of this muddy prison. And now you'll get that chance. I couldn't be happier for you. Or prouder of the boy you've become."

Fincher fought back emotions. "I had a good teacher, Da. Two good teachers."

Gill's head dropped a bit. "Yes, I wish your ma could have seen this…" He quickly returned from a dark place. "Anyway, we're both proud and excited. I can't wait to hear all about your adventures when you return."

"Return and bring a cure to the Maddening."

"Yes, yes. That, too. But you don't worry about that. Soak in all that Quaan has to offer. Take mental pictures for all of us who will never be able to venture out. We want to share in your journey. We'll taste freedom through all of you." A pause. "Did you remember to pack extra socks? You have to take care of your feet, you know."

Fincher's stomach threatened to expel the jerky he had recently eaten. His heart began to pound in his chest.

"I packed extra socks, Da."

"Good. You're going to need those." Gill Bugg rose from the bed. "I'm going to visit some of the neighbors and see if they have anything of use for your adventure. You going to turn in early?"

"Sure. But I think I'm going to watch Paragon set one last time. Not sure how long before I see its last rays against the mountain again."

"Sounds good, son. See you in a bit." Gill moved toward the front door and stopped at the threshold. He turned back to Fincher.

"I just remembered. Make sure you take extra socks."

Ditto found Fincher sitting alone on a massive stump, staring out at Mount Ghaal as Paragon began to fall below the Tainted Timbers.

Already, Ommori Prime and her four sisters were clear in the darkening sky.

Ditto made sure to approach loudly so as not to frighten his friend who seemed lost in thought. Also, stealth was not exactly the large boy's strong suit.

"I was looking for you. Want some company?" There was no response. "I understand if you want to be alone."

Fincher appeared to shake himself from a waking dream. "No, I could use some company." Ditto dropped next to his good friend. He could sense Fincher's unease. "How'd you find me?"

Ditto chuckled. "You're always staring at Mount Ghaal, whether in good times or bad. I just figured out where to get the best view."

Fincher simply nodded. "You need something?"

"Nah, just came by to give you this." Ditto handed Fincher a large tooth tied neatly to a piece of black cord. "It's one of the fangs from the Ghost Puma we killed. I visited Carver Rett and was able to get five of them. Of course, I had to have Sammi make them into pendants." He held up his meaty hands. "It's not like these things can tie a knot."

"But they can throw one heck of a punch."

"Yeah, well… at least I'm good for something."

Fincher ran his fingers over the Ghost Puma tooth. He pulled it in close to admire the tight, clean knot that Sammi had tied. "Thank you, Ditto. I'll treasure it."

"Yeah, well, thanks for saving my life."

Fincher looked over confusedly. "What are you talking about?"

"That Puma had me in a bad place before you leapt in."

"Ditto, you saved us *all*. Especially, Ash. You've saved us all countless times."

Ditto shrunk from the compliment. "Well, maybe we all saved each other. In any case, I thought we all could use a constant reminder."

"A reminder of what, Ditto?"

"That nothing can stop us if we stick together."

Fincher's hazel eyes returned to the tooth and found that it had additional meaning. "Thanks, again, Ditto. I'll treasure it."

Ditto shifted uncomfortably. "Carver Rett tried to trade me for the fur, durn fool, but I made sure Widow Till received it. I also got the bladder for Sammi."

"What the fark does she want that for?"

Ditto shrugged his broad shoulders. "Said she wants to pack some Reaper Vines for the trip."

"What the fark for?"

Another shrug. "No idea. But Sammi's always steps ahead, isn't she? If we run into trouble, it'll be her brains, not my hands, that get us out of it."

Fincher continued to stare at the pendant. "I think it's gonna take us all to get through this one."

Ditto could no longer hold his tongue. "What's the matter, Fincher? I would have thought that you, more than anyone, would be excited for this trip. You look like you're saying goodbye forever."

Fincher turned the tooth in his hands. "It's my da. He's repeating himself… forgetting stuff."

Ditto's shoulders fell. "Oh… How long?"

Fincher's voice started to crack. "Just today. But I know the beginning when I see it, Ditto."

Ditto put an arm around his smaller friend. "So, it just started. We'll be back before he's in it too deep."

"Will we? Or will he not even know me when I return?" Tears had begun to fall from Fincher, reflecting the light of the Five Sisters as they dropped to the muddy ground. They boy finally looked up at Ditto with wet, pleading eyes. "I'm not strong like you, Ditto. I don't know if I can do it. How could I?"

Fincher buried his head against his friend, who began to slowly rock back and forth. Ditto's first words were more to himself than to Fincher. "You'd be surprised what you can do when you face a nightmare… But this is stupid, Fincher. We're gonna be back in plenty of time. Your da is gonna remember you and throw his arms around you when he sees you. Then the doctors will start coming and, before you know it, the Maddening will be a dark thing of the past. We're gonna change Crimmish forever, for the better. Then Stella Bugg will have no choice but to fall madly in love with you."

Fincher laughed between cries. "That would be something, huh."

"How does Sammi say it? It's an inevitability."

Fincher finally pulled back and wiped his face. "Thanks, Ditto."

Ditto smiled in return before his face grew serious. "And listen, worst case scenario, if the time comes, and you can't do it… I'll do it for you."

Fincher couldn't find the words, so he simply patted Ditto's thick cheek. "Every member of the Sour Flower Gang is great. But you're the best of us, Ditto. You really are."

Ditto playfully pushed his friend's hand away. "Nah, I'm just the dumbest." He rose from the stump. "Now, get up and wish Mount Ghaal a good one. You ain't saying *goodbye*, you're saying *see ya later*."

Fincher did as he was told. As soon as he stood, he placed the pendant over his neck. He felt more confident as soon the tooth was tucked away, as if some of the strength of the Ghost Puma had entered through his chest.

That distinguishable smile reappeared on Fincher's face. "You're right, Ditto." He turned to Mount Ghaal. "See ya, ya stupid mountain. When I return, you won't crack the top hundred wondrous things I've seen." Back to Ditto. "I'm gonna head back, spend some time with my da."

"Don't stay up too late. We've got the adventure of a lifetime to start tomorrow." Ditto's green eyes flashed excitedly. "And gods to find."

"And cures to earn."

"Exactly."

The boys began the long walk back to Crimmish. Ditto suddenly turned to Fincher.

"Oh, I almost forgot. I saw your da as I was leaving the house. He wanted me to remind you to pack extra socks. Said it was important."

"Of course he did." And just like that, Fincher's smile lost a little luster.

3

THE TURDS OF SALVATION OUTPOST

High Captain Gorman Graff studied the five small children before him. Well, four small children, for the fifth was massive for a boy of twelve. When his old eyes fell on the two youngest girls, he noticed that the sacks they wore threatened to swallow them.

"So, this is them? Your *best* harvester crew? I have to admit, I thought they'd be a little older. Maybe it would be best to replace the two youngest with—"

"No!"

Captain Graff spun to the hazel-eyed boy who'd made the comment. Graff was taken aback, not only because he was unused to being challenged, but because there was surprising resolve behind that declaration. He moved to the boy.

"What did you say, young man?"

"With all due respect, Captain, I said no. We're the Sour Flower Gang, and we're the best harvester crew in Crimmish. Don't judge us on our ages. We work well together, we understand our roles, and we're dedicated to each other. You take us all, or you can explain to your Imperator why you returned empty-handed."

While half the people of Crimmish covered their faces in embarrassment and fear, Gill Bugg couldn't hide his prideful smile.

Captain Graff stared down the boy for several beats before he, too, cracked, and white teeth appeared within his grey beard. "You've got backbone, son. I like that. And loyalty to boot. Fair enough. These are our five harvesters, and I'll shut up about it. Say your goodbyes, and I'll meet you at the edge of town."

With that, Captain Graff moved off, stopping only to chat briefly with Mayor Bugg before making his way to where his horses waited.

As Ditto took the time to check everyone's bags, Fincher, Ash, Sammi, and Hana bid farewell to their parents. As the girls were getting buried in hugs and kisses, Fincher and his father simply stood, Gill's hands on his son's shoulders.

"Your ma would be so proud."

"I know, Da. You said already."

"It's worth saying again. Did you pack extra socks?"

"I did, Da."

"Good. Good. That's very important. Now, you listen to Captain Graff; he seems like a good fellow and he's made promises to us parents that I believe. As far as everyone else goes... fark them. Don't trust anyone, and never turn your back. Quaan is full of snakes. Luckily, you and the gang have experience in handling those, don't you?"

"We do, Da."

Gill knelt to face his son. "I know Ditto's the strongest, Ash is the bravest, Sammi's the smartest, and Hana's the sweetest of the group, but you're the leader, Fincher. You're the soul. They're gonna look to you when things get hairy, when things don't go to plan. Do whatever it takes to get you all home. And if it comes to it, fark the God-Snails and fark Quaan. You five are worth more than a thousand empires and a hundred gods."

"I will, Da. And, please, you take care of yourself, too."

Gill patted his son's cheek. "Don't you worry about your old man. I've also faced a Ghost Puma and lived to tell the tale." Tears began to well up in the man's eyes. "I want to hear about all your adventures when you get back. Every detail, I don't care how minor. I'll see the world through you, Fincher."

"I promise, Da."

Gill Bugg took Fincher into his arms and squeezed him hard. "I love you, son," he said into his ear before releasing him. "Now, run along. You have a world to experience."

Fincher almost said more, but the words caught in his throat, and he swallowed them back. In the end, a simple, "Yes, sir," was all that he could muster.

As Fincher walked through the crowd of townsfolk, accepting both well wishes and dirty looks from rival harvester crews, a delicate form jumped out to block his path.

Stella Bugg looked stunning in her stained yellow dress. Her amber eyes sparkled in the sun, and Fincher found that his legs could no longer move.

"So, you're off, I guess? I'm scared for you but also a bit jealous. Are you ready for your big adventure?"

Fincher tried to respond, but his mind was a tangle. Ditto slapped him hard on the back and leaned in as he passed, carrying everyone's bags in addition to his own. "This is where you say, yes."

"Yeah, yes. Yes!"

Stella stepped closer. "Bring me back something cool?"

Fincher stumbled over his words. "Yeah, sure, of course. The best. Only the best."

"Great. Don't forget about us. Here's something to make sure you remember."

Stella placed a soft kiss on Fincher's cheek. She smelled like cinnamon and vanilla. As Fincher's face grew red, a smiled appeared that almost cleaved his face in two.

Stella went on her way and Fincher stood dumbly for a moment, deaf to the laughter of onlookers. Only a set of narrow, hate-filled dark eyes sitting above a too-large set of brownish teeth brought him crashing back down to reality. Fincher shook off the spell and shrugged helplessly as Reba Bugg made a slashing gesture across her throat.

Perhaps his return home wouldn't be celebrated by all.

Luckily, Ash and Sammi swept Fincher up as they moved forward.

Ash shot Reba with a threatening look to ensure that the smitten girl didn't try anything crazy.

"You sure have a way with the girls, Fincher," said a giggling Sammi.

"I didn't *do* anything," said Fincher defensively.

"That's what they all say, sis," countered Ash, and soon the trio was clear of the gathered villagers.

At Crimmish's entrance waited Ditto and Hana. There was also High Captain Graff and two soldiers, all on horseback, and three riderless horses.

"Is this everyone, then," asked Graff, and Ditto answered in the affirmative. "Great. Well, then, let's get the pleasantries out of the way. You already know me, High Captain Gorman Graff. Behind me are Second Lieutenants Tobias Vale and Heleena Dell." The man with sandy-blond hair and yellow eyes and the red-headed woman nodded in turn. "You do what we say, when we say, and you'll be protected. It's our task to get you up north and back safely. And we take our job very seriously. Isn't that right?"

"Yes, Captain," both responded.

"Now, let's have your names."

The children took turns.

"Finchius Bugg."

"Deetarik Bugg."

"Ashanti Bugg."

"Sammira Bugg."

"Hanako Bugg."

The woman with short red hair burst into laughter. "Are you all relations? I can really see the similarities."

Second Lieutenant Vale responded before any of the children could.

"Family names are stripped away when you're sentenced to the Stenches. Everyone is given the common name of Bugg."

"Fitting, I think," quipped Heleena Dell.

"That's enough out of you, Dell," roared Captain Graff.

Tobias Vale, a veteran of numerous trips to Crimmish, continued. "Those fancy first names are just the names they're given at birth. A sort of rebellion against their designated, shared surnames. Their names are shortened once they start walking and again when they're too old to continue entering the Timbers, probably around eighteen. That's why all the adults you met, Captain, had single-syllable first names. I think they try to make themselves smaller prior to succumbing to the Maddening."

"You know, we could probably explain it better than this goof," said Fincher as he helped Hana with her pack and began putting on his own. Most would be offended by such a conversation taking place around them, but the children of Crimmish were used to disrespectful commentary.

"What are your *real* names?" demanded Vale from above. "The ones you want us to call you by."

"You can call me Fincher. This is Ash and Sammi. They *are* of relation, dear woman." Lieutenant Dell frowned atop her horse. "And this is Ditto and Hana. I hope you'll not only remember our names, but show us some respect. Because, from what I hear, we're the only hope you all have of not rotting away from the farking Gloomtide."

The female soldier started to form a retort, but Captain Graff's laughter cut her off.

"Oh, how I like this group already. You heard the lad, Dell. And you, too, Vale. Make sure the others hear the boy's message and respond accordingly when we reach Salvation Outpost." Graff thought for a moment and turned to Ash. "You, girl. Ash, correct?"

"That's right, Captain."

"You're not even close to eighteen. Why the one syllable?"

Ash held up the stump of her left arm. "A Ghost Puma didn't just take my arm."

Grey eyes met brown-on-yellow and held for several beats. "Fair enough. I know as well as any how physical wounds can fundamentally alter our spirits." Graff motioned to the riderless mounts. "I brought three horses and am glad that I did. The two sisters can share one, Fincher and… Hana?" The small girl nodded. "You two can ride together on another. Ditto, lad, you're as big as some soldiers I've fought alongside. You can go at it alone on the third. Sound good?"

The children each gave a thumbs up. Fincher boosted Ash and Sammi onto one horse, jumped onto his, and accepted Hana when Ditto lifted her up. Captain Graff watched silently and admired the way the children worked together. Indeed, it looked like he may have landed the right harvester crew, after all.

When everyone was seated and their packs were secured safely to their mounts, Graff finally spoke.

"Nice work. Before you know it, you'll be back with your loved ones and celebrated as heroes. Now let's be off. I want to reach Salvation Outpost before dark. Sour Flower Gang, keep up and stay close behind us."

With that, High Captain Graff squeezed his legs together, sending his horse sprinting ahead. Vale and Dell followed, but not before the woman threw Fincher another dangerous look.

"She seems to have taken a liking to you," joked Ditto.

"You sure have a way with the girls, Fincher," repeated Sammi, and the group descended into hysteria as their well-trained mounts began to give chase.

"At least he remembered the name the Sour Flower Gang," offered Hana, seated in front of Fincher.

"Yep. I told you it would farking stick!"

"Hey! Cheese-Eyes! Go back to the Stenches, Cheese-Eyes!"

"I can smell them from here!"

"Everyone can smell them! Their brains are rotting away!"

Slanderous words and guffawing flew at the Sour Flower Gang before the first lumps of horse dung did. Luckily, the youngsters of Salvation Outpost had terrible aim, so only a couple of attempts had to be actively dodged. When Captain Graff, lost in his own thoughts, finally realized what was going on, he threatened the abusers with tar and feathering, chasing the cowards off.

They had reached Salvation Outpost just before Paragon fell below the horizon. Once well inside the town limits, Graff dismounted and tossed his reigns to a waiting soldier. Vale and Dell followed suit.

Ditto dropped from his horse and then moved to help Ash and Sammi, stepping carefully to avoid the various excrements and trash that littered the muddy ground.

"And they call *us* gross," commented Ash.

"Farking inbreds," said Fincher as he slid down and then caught Hana in his arms.

Graff turned back to the children. "You all rode unexpectedly well."

Ditto answered. "We have a few horses in Crimmish that are shared by the community. Everyone gets their turn and learns how to ride."

"It seems more and more that others could take a note from your little community."

Ditto accepted the compliment with a nod.

Graff continued. "I was going to have each of you ride with a soldier, but I think we can keep things the way they are. You'll probably be more comfortable with that arrangement."

"We will, Captain," agreed Fincher.

"Well, then, consider these three animals yours for the duration. It's best for the horses to form a bond with their riders."

Hana shrieked a little, excited to have a horse to call her very own, even if only for a while.

Ditto began to remove his bag but was stopped by Captain Graff.

"Just leave your bags. I'm sorry, children, but I intend to head out tonight, just after dinner." Graff addressed the soldiers taking the reins. "Get these horses fed, watered, and massaged. We didn't push them too hard today, so they should have some juice left. Watch the children's bags while you're at it. If anything comes up missing, you'll be the ones I blame. Understood?"

"Yes, Captain," the four soldiers responded.

"Good, now when's chow being served?"

One of the soldiers, a small woman with streaks of grey in her long black hair, responded. "It's being served as we speak, Captain. Over there in the dining hall. We've already eaten, so the others are sitting down for second shift. The Outposters are a grotesque bunch, but they're giving us space. Which reminds me, the town's head, Controller Bitkiss, wants a word with you. Something about *earned compensation*. The little rat kept talking about the market value of things like soap and angel bread and honey rice. And even water. Two more minutes of his moaning, and I would have cut him ear to ear."

Graff sighed deeply, and, for the first time, Fincher noticed the advanced age of the veteran warrior.

"Thank you, Sergeant Cattell. Both for the information and for not dissecting that human worm. I have enough on my plate as it is."

Sergeant Vera Cattell placed a fist over her heart in salute. "Of course, my Captain."

"You all, take the horses. Second Lieutenant Vale, come with me. I'll need your assistance in obtaining the additional supplies we'll need for the trip and in keeping me from throttling Controller Bitkiss. Dell, take the children to the dining hall, and make sure that they're fed." Graff turned back to the kids. "I'm sorry to push you so hard on the first night. But, as I mentioned, time is of the essence. If moving on tonight is too much, tell me now."

The Sour Flower Gang all looked to each other and exchanged thoughts without speaking. Fincher responded for the group. "With all due respect, Captain, our treks into the Tainted Timbers are much more taxing than a simple horseback ride. And we'd be fine moving on from Salvation Outpost as soon as possible. I don't know if you've noticed, but it's infested with farking Spire Rubes."

At that, Gorman Graff released uproarious laughter. The soldiers actually stepped back in surprise, for rarely had they heard their hardened Captain express himself in such a way.

After a moment, Graff wiped his eyes and collected himself. "Forgive me, but I thought I was the only one left alive who remembered that term. Noted and noted, young Fincher. Enjoy your meals.

I'm afraid I won't have much of an appetite after negotiating with Controller Bitkiss."

~

The Outpost servers slammed a plate down before each child, spilling some of the stew onto the filthy table.

"Sorry, we ain't got no cheese, Cheese-Eyes," said one particularly pockmarked teen.

"It appears you don't have any soap either, poor girl," Fincher snapped back. "We have plenty in Crimmish. Ash, the young woman to my right with the perfect skin, could even show you how to use it."

One could almost hear the gears turn in the Outposter's head as she searched desperately for a comeback. She found none.

"Your kind should never be let outta the Stenches. You'll infect us all with the Maddening."

"Don't worry, my dear, you have nothing to fear. You have to have a brain for the Maddening to take hold."

The mean girl stormed off as the Sour Flower Gang broke out in giggles. It was short-lived, however, as they noticed the other soldiers seated at their table staring them down. The group quieted.

Sammi and Ash pushed their stews in circles, questioning every lump they found. Ditto dug in, tossing massive spoonfuls into his mouth. Ash looked horrified.

"Ditto," she whispered, "you know they probably spit in the food... at the very least."

Ditto paused for a second, then shrugged. "I've eaten way worse than spit when lost in the Timbers. In fact, we *all* have. Plus, I'm really hungry. It's been a long day already."

The group let Ditto's words digest. He was right. They slowly started eating, moving faster when nothing abnormal appeared within the thick broth. Hana gave hers to Ditto.

"I'll just eat some jerky on the ride," the small girl stated. "Ditto needs it more than me."

Ditto accepted the food and the children ate in peace. It didn't last.

"They say that you pukes from the Stenches go crazy, start thrashing about and bashing your brains in. That gonna happen on this trip?"

Fincher looked up from his stew and found that it was one of the soldiers speaking, a particularly nasty looking fellow with a shaved head and brownish-orange face tattoos. Fincher looked over to Second Lieutenant Dell for some support, but the fiery-haired woman simply smirked in her seat.

"Ahh, shut up, Doakes," demanded the large, black-skinned soldier sitting across from him.

"Nah, fark that, Boone! I need to know if one of these little yellow-eyed twists is gonna go bonkers on us. I'll be ready to crush their heads with the nearest rock if that's the case."

"Better not let Captain Graff hear you talking like that, Doakes," said Heleena Dell through a wicked smile. "The boss has taken quite a shine to these runts. He actually thinks we need them."

"Fine," responded the bald Doakes. "He could at least let us tie them up, keep 'em on leashes or something."

"I'd like to keep that chocolate, one-armed girl on a leash," added a thin, mustached man that resembled a gully weasel.

"If Feenk gets *her*, then I want the young, tiny-eyed one," declared a burly, bearded man who sported a bulbous nose and too-few teeth.

"No need to argue," said Specialist Grady Feenk. "Do the math, Neers, there's plenty to go around."

"Enough!" cried Corporal Mac Boone, slamming his fist onto the table. "They're just children!"

"Hey, if you want the girl with glasses, just say so, Boone. I certainly don't mind letting you cut through the bush ahead of me."

Ditto's arm began to shake with rage. Ash placed her lone hand over his to calm him as Fincher addressed the soldiers.

"What's the problem, gentlemen?" he asked, purposefully leaving out Second Lieutenant Dell. "Upset that a group of children—children from the Stenches, to be exact—has to be brought in to save your butts? Did you tell your wives and girlfriends that you were insuffi-cient, that you were helpless to stop the Gloomtide? Please, send a message along to them. Tell them not to worry, that *real* men and women, the Sour Flower Gang, have appeared to fix that which you could not." He turned to Dell and Feenk. "Fear not, I was not talking to you two. For I cannot imagine that there's anyone—man, woman, dog, cat, or parasite—waiting at home for either of you."

Feenk shot to his feet in a rage. "You cheeky little twat! If they just let us burn down farking Terminus Grove, we wouldn't need you mouthy shites at all! In fact, let me find out that—"

"Awfully chatty, Feenk!" Grady Feenk slunk to his seat, beady eyes blazing, as Captain Graff entered the dining hall. "I assume you were offering your undying loyalty and protection to our valued quintet here. Because if you were doing anything else, I'm afraid I may have to introduce my thumbs to the inside of your skull."

"Of course not, Captain. Just making small talk."

"Good! Then you must be done eating. Go help the others with the horses. In fact, all of you go help with the horses. We leave shortly." All of the soldiers got up and moved for the dining hall entrance. "Lieutenant Dell! A word."

Heleena Dell waited at the head of the table, her chin high and defiant. Graff watched as the last soldier exited before delivering a massive backhand that sent Dell flying across the room to land with a heavy thud on the dirt floor. The Outposters sniggered at the woman's punishment.

"Get up," roared Graff, "and get out!" Dell scrambled to her feet on unsteady legs and stumbled to the door. "Consider that a warning, Dell. You don't help protect these children, and the Imperator, himself, will not be able to protect you from me." Graff ran a shaking hand over his face and beard before addressing the kids. "My apologies for any harsh words that you heard. We have been traveling hard for many Paragons and have only begun our quest. Their anger is misplaced. Give it time; they'll come around." Graff fingered the stew left in Dell's bowl and screwed up his face. "I think I'll just eat some mountain rat jerky on the road. Mayor Bugg was right; I'm gonna be in dire straits when we run out." He faced the children once more.

"Take your time finishing your meals. We'll be outside when you're ready."

When Graff left, the Sour Flower Gang conversed quietly amongst themselves.

"Jeez, these are who's supposed to protect us?" said Ash. "They're as bad as any bandits or Sluggs we'll meet along the way."

"Listen," said Fincher, "my da told me to be wary, and he's already being proven correct. Other than Captain Graff and maybe Lieutenant Vale, I say we don't trust anyone."

"Especially any adult," added Hana.

"Where does that leave us?" dared Sammi.

"It leaves us relying on ourselves. It leaves us leaning on each other to get through this. It leaves us with the Sour Flower Gang and no one else. The way it's always been and the way it's always gonna be. What do you say?"

"Let's do it," exclaimed Ash, and they all rose from their seats.

Except for Ditto, who was still eating Hana's stew. "Hold up, I wanna finish." He ate a few more spoonfuls before speaking between bites. "Yeah. They definitely spit in this."

The retreat from Salvation Outpost went somewhat uneventfully. Controller Bitkiss *did* continue buzzing around Captain Graff like a field skeeter, and the youngsters of Outpost *did* come out to yell obscenities at the Sour Flower Gang.

High Captain Graff did his best to ignore the leech that was the Controller, and the children pretended not to hear the jeers from the Outposters. Eventually, everyone was mounted and began to march out of Salvation Outpost, even as the Controller and the town's unruly youth followed, carrying on with their verbal assaults.

"You don't seem to comprehend, Captain," said Controller Bitkiss from below, "that we've incurred tremendous costs from this little stop of yours."

"And you've been properly recompensed," stated Graff, his patience wearing thin.

"For the goods, yes," Bitkiss went on. "But what about the intangibles?"

"What intangibles?" demanded Second Lieutenant Vale, his yellow eyes narrowing.

The Controller's mind spun with possibility. Finally, his dull little orbs went wide. "The dining hall! Yes! You brought those dirty little Stenchfolk into our normally pristine eating area. Who knows what kinds of germs they brought in? And the Maddening! They may have brought the Maddening along with them. We'll need to toss every-thing and start anew. That's not cheap, Captain, I'll have you know."

Captain Graff rolled his grey eyes as he continued to ride out. "So, you're looking for extra, beyond what the crown deems fair?"

"I'm looking for what I deserve, Captain! Nothing more and nothing less! I deserve—"

As if on cue, a massive wad of horse dung struck the Controller in the face, much of it disappearing into the little man's open mouth. Bitkiss immediately doubled over and began retching onto the dirt.

"There's what you farking deserve, *Butt Kiss*," cried Fincher, the empty, rudimentary sling that Sammi quickly crafted minutes ago hanging limply from his right hand.

Two more great heaps of poop flew from slings in the hands of Ditto and Sammi, both of them finding home in the face of a screaming Outpost teen. The pair fell to the ground, scrambling to remove the excrement from their faces, mouths, and eyes.

The horses slowly began to trot, leaving Salvation Outpost behind.

"It's been a real farking pleasure," cried out Fincher. "I always heard that Spire Rubes were shite, but I didn't know they were being literal! Enjoy wallowing in your shite, you farking mountain trash! We're off to see sights you could never dream to behold!"

Screams of anger and curses followed the group into the deepening night. Captain Graff was unable to control his laughter for the first fifteen minutes, and several of the other soldiers, including Sergeant

Cattell, Corporal Boone, and, of course, Second Lieutenant Vale, tossed the children appreciative nods and bows. Even the horrifying Doakes couldn't help but chuckle at the exploits of the Sour Flower Gang.

Fincher threw a wink to each of his friends. It was good to finally earn a little respect.

Even if it was for chucking turds.

The Titian retinue galloped along deep into the night. Captain Graff and Second Lieutenant Heleena Dale led the way, followed by five soldiers spread out wide. Next came the Sour Flower Gang on their three steeds. Second Lieutenant Tobias Vale and three others brought up the rear, protecting the group from any potential sneak attacks from behind.

Fincher let Hana lean back against him to sleep, holding the girl tight to make sure she didn't slip off their horse, which Hana had named *Windsong*. He looked over to find Ash doing the same for Sammi. Ditto kept looking over, no doubt wondering how he could help and ease someone's burden.

Just as Fincher's eyes were growing heavy and the saddle was beginning to cut painfully into his groin, Captain Graff pulled back on the reins of his steed and brought the group to a halt.

Gorman Graff twisted his horse around and addressed everyone.

"Paragon rises in about five hours. We've made great progress this evening. Let's make camp along that grove up ahead. You all decide who's getting firewood, setting up camp, and establishing a perimeter. We don't have to leave at first light, but close to it. Settle the shifts amongst yourselves. I want at least four up and alert at all times. Clear?"

"Yes, Captain," came the united call.

Despite the Sour Flower Gang's poor initial interactions with many of the Titian guard, they could not dispute the soldiers' speed, efficiency, and talent when it came to divvying up tasks, executing orders, and setting up camp. In what seemed like the blink of an eye, campfires were raging, water from a nearby stream was boiling, and meat was roasting over makeshift spits.

The children, unused to being catered to, jumped to help. After a while, it became clear to the soldiers that the children were not only not getting in the way, but were proving a legitimate help. Several commented on the quality of Sammi's knots, the impressive strength of Ditto, and the sheer amount of chores that Ash could accomplish with only one arm.

Soon, horses were cared for, bellies were full, bedrolls were laid out, and sentries were posted. Just as the children were laying down, Ditto marched up to Captain Graff, who was speaking quietly with Vale, Doakes, Boone, and Cattell.

"Captain," said the large boy, "happy to take a shift, if needed. I don't have a sword but I have a good knife and know how to use it. And my eyes may be yellowed, but they're good and can see well in the dark."

Graff looked to the others, who simply smiled and shook their heads. Doakes even laughed aloud before letting loose a wad of fire-leaf onto the grassy ground.

"You're a good lad, Ditto. You're all good, in fact," said the Captain. "You've all given me less trouble and pulled more weight than any group of adult merchants I've ever had the displeasure of escorting. And we appreciate it. But you go on to sleep. You've probably been up earlier than any of us, and have ridden more leagues than anyone save myself, Vale, and Dell. You've earned your rest."

"Farking right," added Mac Boone with a smile on his face.

Even Doakes offered support. "Piss off, kid. You've done your fair share."

"A good showing," agreed Vale.

Ditto simply nodded, unsure of what to do with the strange compliments. "Very well. But don't hesitate to wake any of us if you need us. We're not helpless."

"Noted. Will do, laddie," said Graff. "And thanks."

∽

They rode hard the next day, stopping only for bathroom breaks and to water the horses. As Paragon once more began its descent behind the western Spires, massive trees could be seen in the distance, spreading out to the left and right.

Captain Graff called for a stop.

"We'll rest here for the evening. I know there's light left, but I want everyone fully rested and alert when we enter Salt's Pass tomorrow. If my calculations are correct, we'll get there mid-morning, keeping us in the shadows of the Mutewoods. I don't want Paragon directly over-head, blinding us to whatever may be hiding in Shadowset. Plus, we've all been going hard. An extended stay will do all of us a world of good."

Similar to the past evening, the Titians launched into their tasks. The Sour Flower Gang, now understanding what needed to be done, raced to help. Ditto chopped down small trees and split wood for various purposes. Fincher and Ash collected firewood. And Sammi crafted several contraptions to optimize the cooking process. Meanwhile, Hana went around brushing and feeding all the horses, paying special attention to *Windsong*.

Like before, the soldiers were impressed by the work ethic and capability of the Sour Flower Gang. Few, if any, derogatory words continued to come their way.

But other risks remained.

As Hana ran a soft comb over *Windsong*'s auburn hair, a rough hand brushed along her small back. She jumped at the unwanted touch and spun around to find Specialist Jarvis Neers presenting her with a toothless smile through his unkempt beard. Hana's delicate nose twitched at the offensive smell that emanated from Neers's round, hairy body.

"You have a soft touch with the horses," whispered Neers, leaning forward to put his grime-covered face closer to Hana's. "We could all use a soft touch. I could touch you so softly, you couldn't help but purr. Then you could touch me, and I would—"

"Please go away," said Hana, her almond eyes filling with panic.

"Go where? We're here for the long night, little girl, and all of my tasks are done. We have a long trip ahead of us, with no time for stops. That means, just like we often eat on the road, I'll need to drain myself with what's provided. Come now, you may even grow to like it. Come on, give us a kiss, and see how we taste."

Hana was frozen with fear. Neers moved in to lick the young girl's pale face. Just as his tongue was about to make contact, a heavy boot slammed into the side of his face, sending the Specialist reeling to the side.

Sergeant Vera Cattell didn't say anything as she passed by Hana. Instead, she simply stalked toward the fallen Neers. As Cattell approached, she raised her boot again, dropping it onto the large man's bloody face. Up and down her boot went, cracking bone and slicing open flesh with each stomp. Eventually, the Sergeant stopped, and Neers was left a crimson mess on the green grass.

When she was done, Cattell straightened her civilian clothes, calmed her breath, and returned to what she was doing. She spoke to Hana as she passed.

"Now you see why that pig is missing so many teeth. He won't bother you again."

Although shocked by the violent display and even more terrifying sexual advance, Hana went back to brushing the horses, keeping an eye on the mound of flesh that was Specialist Jarvis Neers. Luckily, over the next thirty minutes, he did not stir.

After a hearty meal, the Sour Flower Gang and accompanying soldiers sat around the fires, digesting silently. While the children's silence was from tiredness, the soldiers' was from something else entirely. For they knew that once they were through Salt's Pass, the possibility of encountering Sluggs grew exponentially the farther north they ventured.

Everyone in the circle stared into the fires, as if each searched for something distinct and personal in the red, orange, and yellow flames. Everyone but Neers, that is, for both of his eyes were swollen shut, leaving him to feel around for his bowl, spoon, and bedroll.

Several minutes of shared soundlessness passed before Captain Graff finally broke the spell.

"Feenk! You have the voice of a dying dwarf mule but you play a mean tortoise lute. Play for us!"

"Of course, Captain." The weaselly Feenk dug through his bag for a moment before retrieving the small stringed instrument. He tested each note before nodding to himself. Then he began to play.

The sounds that came from the little soldier forced the heads of the children to twist in confusion, for there was no reason that such a melody should come from the same man who spewed such perversity from his mouth.

The other soldiers must have grown accustomed to Feenk's playing because many simply started small tasks such as sharpening blades, mending boots, and repairing holes in garments as they listened. Captain Graff leaned back against his bedroll and closed his eyes, allowing the drifting, melancholy notes of the tortoise lute to carry him to his retirement farm, where his beloved Hilly awaited him.

Hands ceased their movements and Graff sprung up, however, when Hana started singing, her small voice swelling and growing in power as it melded with the sounds of Grady Feenk's lute.

Hana's voice traveled across the campground, grabbing everyone in earshot by the soul and drawing them in, bringing some dangerously close to the fires. Some eyes went wide and others slammed shut as they were assaulted by feelings and memories, dreams and fears, surges of emotions carried on waves of melody. Hana sang in a language that none understood, and yet, somehow, her words rang painfully true and horrifyingly honest, forcing the listeners to confront their deepest desires and regrets.

On and on the unusual pairing played and sang, forcing many, even the hateful Second Lieutenant Dell and intimidating Corporal Doakes, to wipe wetness from their faces.

After what felt like an eternity, Hana's voice faded away as the tortoise lute's notes grew lighter and lighter, eventually leaving only the crackling of the cook fires to fill the silence. Once more, dumb, spellbound faces merely stared ahead.

"And that," said Fincher, slicing through the spell like a sharp blade against a taut string, "is why we're the best harvester crew in Crimmish."

The boy's words shook others from their reverie.

"It's true, then?" asked Tobias Vale. "You really do have to sing to the Moonflower to collect Moon Tears?"

"You don't have to," answered Ash. "But we learned long ago that without singing, you'll only be able to collect a small amount—maybe a few droplets' worth. Enough to make a few batches of Salvation, but not nearly enough to cure the Bloat on a large scale. Now, all harvester crews carry a Moon Voice. Ours just happens to be the best."

"By far," added Ditto, squeezing Hana's shoulders as a big brother would.

Gorman Graff let out another bellowing laugh. "Well, I think it's great! Just great! To think that such a massive treasure could be concealed in such a small chest. For a moment, I actually thought I was on the hill overlooking my white pear orchard, drinking cool ciders with my wife as the wind sent her hair out to be caught by the last rays of a dying Paragon. Thank you, Hana."

"I was bathing in the cool waters of North Verve with my girlfriend who passed away six seasons ago," said Sergeant Cattell, her cloak stained with tears.

"My daughter." All turned to face Corporal Boone. "I'm away so much I sometimes forget her smile. I saw it just now. And I'll never forget it."

Even Heleena Dell shared her experience. "My father was a Titian soldier, a hero during the first Slugg War. He died when I was very little. I reconnected with him just now. He hugged me and said that he was proud of me." She swung her red-topped head toward the Sour Flower Gang. "Anyone that can offer such a gift is worth protecting." She rose to her feet. "I'll join the first watch."

"Quite right, Lieutenant Dell," declared Captain Graff. "Everyone get on something. You're either standing guard on first shift, sharpening blades for tomorrow, or sleeping. Nothing more. Children, grab your rolls and come this way. Please."

As everyone began either leaving or setting out bedrolls, Jarvis Neers spoke to those around him.

"What in the Black Bog was everyone seeing? I can't see shite through these swollen eyes, and my ears are still ringing. Fill me in, Doakes."

Doakes, with a new appreciation for Hana Bugg, looked at this fellow soldier in a new, less positive light.

"You ain't missed nothing, Neers." He leaned into the large man's ear. "And if you ever so much as talk to that little girl again, I'll remove that fat tongue of yours from your farking gob."

Doakes stalked away, leaving behind a blind, confused Neers.

"What the fark did I do?" Neers asked. But no one stayed close enough to the man to answer.

Captain Graff had found a nice, flat area for the children to lay out their bedrolls.

"You children mind if I sleep over here? I've got scouts on all four sides, but you never can be too sure." Graff's grey eyes kept looking to the North, where Shadowset and the Mutewoods came together in a kiss.

"Of course, Captain," responded Fincher. "Good to have you."

Gorman Graff groaned as he settled down onto his bedroll. It was the sound of a man well past his prime, a man whose painful accomplishments deserved a permanent holiday.

For several silent minutes, the Sour Flower Gang and High Captain Gorman Graff looked up at Quaan's five moons, watching how the shadow of the world was just beginning to creep across the largest of the sisters.

"Do you have any children, Captain Graff?" asked Ash, laying on her back. Graff took a moment to respond.

"No, afraid that I don't. Hilly—that's my wife—and I tried many times, but it just wasn't in the cards for us. Had a few close calls, but, in the end, the powers that be called them all home. Each one wore on poor Hilly something awful. Eventually, we had to just stop trying and start focusing on each other. I was afraid that I wouldn't be enough for her, but she's a remarkable woman. It's a terrible life, being married to a soldier, always having to share your husband or wife with the Empire. But she's stronger than I could ever claim to be, so she makes it work. I definitely got the better end of the deal there."

"For what it's worth, I think you both got a pretty good deal, Captain," said Sammi.

"Yeah, well..." Graff and the children continued to stare up at Quaan's moons. "Do you all know the legend of the Five Sisters?" They all answered in the negative. "Yeah, few do anymore. Would you like to hear it? If you're too tired, I—"

"Please, Captain," interrupted Ditto. "I've always wondered where the name came from." All the others agreed.

"Very well." Graff cleared his throat and began. "Long, long ago, the Grand Maker, responsible for all that you see above you, started to tire of creating. He began to weaken and became increasingly frightened of the vastness that He had conjured. The role of Maker was growing too much for Him, and He feared that another God would usurp Him. He needed others to share in His burden, to help Him ward off threats. Therefore, He decided to make something for Himself. He decided to create a family of His very own.

"But this desire did not spring from love but, rather, from fear and exhaustion and a need to hold on to what was His. He did not want to create equals but minor Gods that would be beholden to Him, to do His bidding.

"With these opposite thoughts driving His work—family and paranoia, love and fear—the Grand Maker drew into existence five daughters—the Five Sisters. But His making did not go according to plan.

"In His holding back, in His fear of making an equal, the Grand Maker shaped five beings of what He considered poor quality. His shame in His own work was only matched by the disgust He felt for his new family. With these unusual feelings of inadequacy and humiliation, the Grand Maker tossed His children aside in a fit of rage, banishing them to the empty, featureless land of Quaan, where they would waste away to be forgotten by time and, most of all, the Maker Himself.

"The Five Sisters fell to Quaan and wept for millennia. Ommori, the eldest sister, could only feel. She rubbed her hands across the land but felt nothing. Nori, the next in line, could only see. She swept her gaze up and down, from left to right, but found nothing. Tori, the smallest of the group, could only hear. But, try as she might, the one sound that she picked up was the weeping of her sisters. Kori had just her nose to follow, but she detected only the familiar odors of her sisters when she turned her head to and fro. Finally, there was Ori, whose tongue wanted more than anything to feel new sensations and flavors. But she discovered none.

"The Sisters huddled together for warmth and safety, crying for the father who'd abandoned them and the dire predicament in which they found themselves. Ultimately, it was Ommori who had enough first and decided to act.

"Ommori reached out to each of her sisters and placed a gentle kiss on each of their foreheads. Although they could not feel the kiss, they felt her love and grew emboldened. Ommori then crawled across the flat landscape, carefully feeling her way along. Strange compulsions began to strike, so she started pinching the land here, molding it there. She bit her nails and used the hard pieces to create the mountains. She ripped out chunks of hair and made forests. She thumbed giant divots in the ground and ran a finger across the world. Within these depressions, she placed the tears that she had collected from her sisters. Ommori grabbed up tiny pieces of material and formed birds, fish, deer, all manner of creatures.

"Soon, featureless Quaan was anything but, full of mountains and forests, lakes and rivers. Nori's eyes took in the new landscape and her own compulsions began to appear. Nori painted the forests a bright shade of emerald green. She made the mountains brown and the frozen tears atop them white. The lakes and streams she made a vibrant blue, so much so that it actually pained her sensitive orbs. Nori gave the birds a potpourri of colors, made the fish shimmer under the water, and granted each animal their own personal coat of paint.

"Tori, although she could only sense it, was excited by her sister's work and jumped in. She conjured the wind as the soundtrack to the burgeoning land, helping the trees find their sound when it tickled their leaves. She gave the rivers a voice, as she did the birds and the sheep and the pigs.

"Kori was next, and she doused the forests in delightful perfumes. She gave each flower a distinct smell, and made sure to distinguish the odors of the mountains from those of the woodlands and lakes.

"Ori was the last. She filled the trees with sweet-tasting fruit and ensured that water drank from the mountain streams had an unrivaled crispness. Ori gave the meat of each animal its own flavor, including the massive variety of fish found in Quaan's waters.

"When the Sisters were finished, they held each other once more, putting their heads together and mentally sharing what each felt, saw, heard, smelled, and tasted. Soon, each had a complete picture of their collective creation. Once more, they wept, but it was no longer fear causing the tears, it was a profound joy in crafting something even their father could not dream. Their tears pooled and formed the Great Untold, locking Quaan away from potential foes.

"There, the Five Sisters stayed for many millennia, working together to experience rich, full lives. And they found happiness.

"The Grand Maker, cold yet curious, checked in on His creations, wondering if they had finally perished on that desolate world on which He had abandoned them, ending His shame. Imagine His shock by what He found.

"Instead of nothingness, He discovered unencumbered life. Instead of flat land, He found mountains and rivers and lakes and forests. Instead of the grey landscape which He crafted, He encountered shades of green and blue and red and yellow. Instead of silence, He heard beautiful notes from the wind and the rivers and the birds. Instead of the smell of stale, odorless air, he detected sweetness from the flowers, the musk of countless animals, and the salty scent of an ocean that should not have existed. Instead of the bland world He had last tasted, He found a potpourri of flavors, from fruits of all shapes and sizes to animals that ran and swam and flew. Instead of five corpses, He found five daughters, helping each other not only to survive, but to thrive and to create.

"Oh, how the Grand Maker's shame returned ten thousand-fold. But it was quickly replaced by something else entirely... pride. He looked upon His daughters with new eyes, a new perspective. In trying to create His inferior, the Grand Maker had molded something else entirely, something greater than He could ever hope to become. Something with power, but also heart.

"The Grand Maker dropped to Quaan and swept His daughters into His arms, begging for their understanding, begging for their forgiveness. The Five Sisters should have scolded their father. They should have cast Him aside as He had to them. But they did not.

"The Five Sisters placed their heads against their father's and welcomed Him to their land, one that was formed from necessity—yes—and fear—yes—but also universe-swallowing love. Love for each other and—yes, love—for the father who only knew power and control and shame and fear.

"The Grand Maker was so moved by the unconditional love of His daughters, He welcomed them back to take their rightful places in the cosmos where He dwelled. But they rejected His offer. Not because of anger or spite, but because of the love that they had for the world they had created. The Grand Maker, unused to being rebuffed, was initially enraged. But the softness and empathy of his daughters had rubbed off, and He came up with a Grand compromise.

"The Five Sisters, led by the bold Ommori, now to be called Ommori Prime, were granted positions in the cosmos circling their beloved land of Quaan. From atop their divine perch, they would watch their world grow and mature. They would smile and laugh as great things transpired below. They would cry and scream when catastrophe and blight struck the land. Then they would truly understand the burden of a Grand Maker.

"As a last gift, or perhaps it was more of a test, the Grand Maker placed humans into this new world. The Grand Maker kissed each of His daughters and chuckled as He left Quaan, knowing that He had burdened them with a chaotic element that would test the sisters' patience, love, sympathy, and restraint.

"They say that, in olden times, the Five Sisters remained full year-round, beaming their lighted love onto all of us. As we disappointed them time and time again, they grew weary like their father, tired of fixing our messes and having their affections thrown back at them. They started to take reprieve, which is how the moon cycles came into being. Now, we are only worthy of a handful of nights of their full love per season. Soon, perhaps we will no longer have even that...

"And *that* is the story of the Five Sisters."

The end of Gorman Graff's tale was met with a muted response. The veteran sat up on his bedroll and found four sleeping, innocent faces, lost in the worlds of dreams and nightmares. He truly hoped that they were in the former.

"Great story, Captain," came a voice from the fifth bedroll.

"Fincher. You made it all the way through. I feared my tale had bored all of you to sleep."

"Don't take it personal, Captain. It was a grand story and masterfully told. But we've had an exhausting time of it these past ten Paragons."

Graff reclined back against his pack. "You're still up, son."

"Yeah, well, I don't find much rest in sleep, sir. For us in Crimmish, there's always a waking nightmare up ahead, whether it be for our parents or ourselves. But these nightmares somehow get even worse in our dreams."

"I see. I'm sorry, son."

"It's okay, Captain."

"Did you get anything from the story, Fincher?"

"I'm not sure, Captain. What do you get from it?"

"Before? Not much, truth be told. I just fancied it as an old legend, a good yarn for putting children and soldiers to sleep." Graff lifted his head. "And it seems to have worked," he said, and chuckled softly. "But now, I see parallels that I cannot unsee."

"What kind of parallels, Captain?"

"To you, Fincher. To the Sour Flower Gang. Don't you see? You *are* the Five Sisters. Individually, you aren't much, but *together*, as a cohesive group, you are truly a force, something that can weave magic into the air and harvest that which others cannot. And, unfortunately, like the Five Sisters, you have been tasked with saving humanity."

"Captain?"

"Yes, Fincher?"

"Do you think humanity is worth saving?"

Graff grimaced. It was too heavy of a question for such a light child. The grizzled warrior wanted to lie, but found that he could not. "I don't know, son. But I have to try. My mother would have wanted me to try. What about your mother?"

"She's gone, sir."

Graff grimaced again but pushed on. "But would she have wanted you to try?"

"She would have, sir."

"Then, there we are."

"There we are."

"Get some sleep, son. I'll wake you if you seem to be having a bad dream."

"Thanks, Captain."

Gorman Graff slid down but did not close his eyes. Instead, he stared up at the Five Sisters and couldn't help but picture the faces of the Crimmish children within each of Quaan's moons. Gorman and Hilly never had a child of their own. They were never granted that most glorious of divine gifts. But if they did, Graff hoped that they would have been anything like the five children that he currently shepherded north. *Was humanity worth saving?* Probably not. And it sure as shite wasn't worth the life of even one of the children that currently slept near the old soldier.

Graff forced his eyes closed but a small voice opened them once more.

"Captain?"

"You should try to sleep, Fincher."

"One last question?"

"Go ahead."

"Sour Flower Gang. You think it's a good name?"

Captain Graff stifled a laugh beneath his thick grey beard. "I do. It really sticks."

"Thanks, Captain. I knew you were a man of class."

"You, too, Fincher. All of you."

4

GOODBYES AT SALT'S PASS

Captain Graff brought the group to a halt and stared ahead. Several hundred yards before him was Salt's Pass, a gap separating the mammoth forests of Shadowset and the Mutewoods. Graff's grey eyes studied both sides, but Shadowset, in particular, for any signs of movement. He found none.

Second Lieutenant Tobias Vale rode up to meet his superior.

"Danger, Captain?"

"None that I see."

"Good."

"That doesn't mean it isn't there." Graff's mind swam with a hundred possibilities, few of them positive. He turned in his saddle to see the five Crimmish children among his soldiers. They were his responsibility. And even the threat of death wouldn't prevent him from protecting them.

"Toby," whispered Graff, and Vale leaned in his saddle to hear the old captain. "If something happens in the Pass, if you sense that we're outnumbered, fight your way out and ride to Kassimont. Tell the Imperator, and only the Imperator, what you saw. He will guide you on what to do next."

"But, Captain, there has been no word of Sluggs in—"

"I know what's been heard and not heard, Vale. But I also know to trust when the hairs on my arms stand on end."

"Then, perhaps we should go around. Or cut through the Mutewoods, even."

Graff shook his head. "No, that worm Crimm was right about one thing. Time is of the essence. If we don't reach Terminus Grove in short order, the Supreme Helices may return to the Heavens, leaving us to deal with the Gloomtide alone—a war we cannot win. Going around will double our journey and there is no clear path through the Mutewoods. Plus, I have heard too many tales of horror from within that awful place to risk it with children. I may not like it, but this is the only way."

"I'm sorry, Captain, but I will not abandon my regiment. I will—"

"You will do as you're told, *Second Lieutenant*. This is a direct order, so you can leave behind all those notions of loyalty and dying a soldier's death right here, right now. Do I make myself clear?" Vale did not answer as he struggled internally. "Vale?!"

The young Lieutenant jumped. "Yes. Yes, Captain. I understand."

"Good lad. Keep this between us. No use in spooking the others, especially if there's nothing to be found up ahead. Now, back to your position. I'll take the lead."

"Yes, Captain." Tobias Vale began to turn back but was stopped.

"And Toby?"

"Captain?"

"If the worst does come to pass... stop by my house before seeing Imperator Rayne. Tell Hilly that I love her and that I'm sorry. Tell her... that I died protecting the children we should have had. Tell her that she would have been proud. And that I'll see her on the other side."

"Captain?"

"Will you do it or not, man?!"

"It would be my honor, my Captain."

"Good lad."

～

A sense of foreboding overcame Fincher and the other children as the group slowly began to trot through the deep shadows of Salt's Pass.

To their right was the Mutewoods, a place of natural beauty and abundance. But also the setting for a thousand terrible stories, each more gruesome than the last. Bark-skinned cannibals, lake-dwelling leviathans, and brain-feasting parasites were the stars of these tales, and even if only ten percent of the accounts were to be believed, the Mutewoods was no place to visit—unless one had a death wish.

To the left was Shadowset, cloaked in blackness. With tall, thick trees creating an impenetrable canopy, the forest needed no tales of woe to garner fear and respect. Little word came out of Shadowset, making that world ever the more frightening.

As the Sour Flower Gang looked into the darkness of that mysterious place, they imagined a hundred sets of red eyes staring back at them from the shadows, their owners praying that the children would step foot into that lightless trap.

Yes, thought Fincher as they pushed ahead, *Salt's Pass certainly seemed the best course to set.*

Birds chirped and small animals scurried through the underbrush to either side of the group. Although it was supposed to be clear, Salt's Pass was littered with recently downed trees and the skeletal remains of numerous former travelers.

"Looks like the Empire could toss a few chips toward the upkeep of this passage," commented Corporal Boone.

"You're right, Corporal," agreed Graff. "But much is being spent to combat the Gloomtide. During times like these, necessary tasks often go ignored. You should have heard the stories my grandfather used to tell me of the Bloat. This was before Salvation had wrangled it under control. We became little more than animals back then. Consider yourselves lucky. All of you. For now."

Vera Cattell leaned into Boone. "Sheesh, any other words of encouragement from the Captain?"

"Silence!"

Everyone tugged on the reins of their horses as Captain Graff studied the scene before him. Several truly massive trees had been felled from the Mutewoods and now lay sprawled across the pass. To go around them would force the riders closer to Shadowset and the invisible threats that resided within.

Second Lieutenant Heleena Dell urged her horse forward, stopping level with Captain Graff. "See something, Captain?" asked Dell as she wiped her brow with a bright yellow handkerchief.

Graff didn't remove his eyes from the pass. "No. But that doesn't mean something isn't there. Stay close to my right, Dell. Have everyone else flank out as wide as they can, children in the middle. Protect them at all costs."

"It will be done, Captain."

"Good. Then, let's go. There's no time to live or die like the present."

Heleena Dell turned and quietly delivered orders as Graff removed his sword from its scabbard. The metallic ring of other blades being freed followed soon after. The Sour Flower Gang mirrored their guides, taking out daggers and knives. Soon, the group was marching ahead once more, all eyes scanning both tree lines for signs of ambush.

Captain Graff slowly began moving to the left to round the downed trees. As commanded, Second Lieutenant Dell kept to his right, continually wiping her sweaty forehead with bright yellow cloth.

After a few minutes, Graff slipped through the narrow alley between Shadowset and the massive fallen trunks that greatly narrowed Salt's Pass. Nothing stirred as Graff pushed on. No movement at all could be seen in the shadows that separated pass from forest, known from unknown. Gorman Graff breathed a sigh of relief as he passed the toppled impediment, finally willing to believe that the rumors he'd heard were, in fact, untrue.

His comfort was short-lived.

Motion, not along the ground but high within the trees of Shadowset, caught Graff's attention. A collection of night rooks tore out from Shadowset, their black wings beating as they moved briefly across the Paragon-lit sky before diving into the protective dimness of the Mutewoods.

Graff studied where the birds had exited their natural home. Night rooks didn't scare easily and rarely entered the brightness of day without good reason. Graff's grey eyes went wide as more activity was perceived up in the dark trees.

"Back," roared Captain Graff, just as the twang of a crossbow being released reached his ears.

With a quickness well beyond someone of his advanced years, Graff jerked left while bringing his sword up and across, narrowly deflecting the bolt as it reached for his face. Instead, the arrow moved on, sinking itself in the throat of Second Lieutenant Dell. The woman's blue eyes bulged as she reached up, yellow kerchief still in hand, and ripped the dart from her neck, releasing a fountain of blood that immediately stained the ground beside her horse.

More twangs filled the air as a dozen crossbows were fired from high in the Shadowset trees. Most missed their targets, but a few found home in the arms, chests, and thighs of the Titian soldiers, eliciting screams from each that was struck.

"In the trees! They're in the farking trees," cried out Corporal Doakes as he pulled a bolt from his bicep. Another round of shots arced down from above, these aimed at the Titian horses, sending the mounts into a bucking fury as their thick skins were penetrated by the sharp projectiles.

Cattell, Neers, Feenk, and a few others were thrown to the ground as men and women appeared as if by magic around them, pouring out of holes covered with branches and needles along Shadowset. Atop the giant fallen trees, more attackers appeared, perfectly camouflaged with soot-covered faces and cloaks covered in loose leaves.

In short order, the Titian entourage was surrounded by more than thirty assailants, with even more rappelling down from the branches of Shadowset to join their ambushing counterparts.

With *Windsong* anxiously dancing beneath them and arrows soaring past their heads, Fincher decided to dismount, pulling Hana down with him. As he did, the boy looked to the South and made out

Second Lieutenant Vale in the distance, galloping away to safety. *Coward*, thought Fincher as he returned his attention to his friends.

Ditto had followed Fincher's lead, leaping from his horse and sprinting over to help Ash and Sammi down from their terrified steed. When all of the children were safely on the ground, they put their backs together, pushing Hana to the center, and held their weapons at the ready. Fortunately, their now-bucking horses remained where they were, creating a defacto wall for the kids to hide behind.

Elsewhere, things were not going as well.

Ahead, Mac Boone faced off against three assailants, many wearing blue-dyed slips of cloth around their heads, arms, and waists. He removed the hand of one with a deft feint followed by a lightning-fast backswing. Boone caught another in the shoulder with a straight thrust and would have finished the man off if not for the female attacker on his opposite side, who plowed forward and ran a slim rapier through the exposed ribs of the honorable Titian.

Despite their grotesque behaviors, Specialists Feenk and Neers fought valiantly in the rear. Jarvis Neers, barely seeing through the slits in his swollen eyes, caved in a man's chest with his giant mace and then destroyed the knee of another before a knife soared in from the fracas and buried itself in the barrel-shaped Titian's chest. Although dying, the toothless Neers still managed to tackle an assassin rushing at Feenk. Once on top, the bearded man slammed his forehead into the face of the attacker repeatedly, leaving a crater where there were once cheeks, nose, and eyes, not stopping until the cavity began to fill with blood. Then Specialist Jarvis Neers fell forward, his own corpse joining the one below it.

Specialist Grady Feenk floated in and out of battle like a wraith, dipping and dodging without directly engaging. Feenk sliced the calcaneal tendon of a woman moving toward Sammi and then went on to slip a small blade into the right ear of a man standing above a downed Titian, readying a killing blow.

Back and forth, side to side, Feenk waded in and out of the skirmish, wreaking havoc wherever he went, delivering three mortal wounds for every minor cut he received. Finally, however, luck caught up with Grady Feenk as an axe was flung from a giant, blue-clad assailant, catching the specialist squarely in the back and propelling the small man forward.

Sammi cried out in horror as Feenk's body slid to a stop next to her feet, and a crimson lake started to pool around her. Ash, ever protective of her sister, yanked Sammi to the right, switching places with her. The one-armed girl then reached down, wrenching the axe from Feenk's back, and hurled it with all her might. The axe spun head over handle through the air until its sharp edge found skull, neatly splitting the head of the ogre who had felled Grady Feenk— ironically, the weapon's original owner.

The terrifying Elliot Doakes, one arm now useless, still managed to cut down four attackers before a series of arrows was released upon the man, dropping the fearsome Titian to his knees with a half dozen wooden shafts protruding from his large chest. Doakes let out one last roar of defiance as a handsome, clean-dressed man wielding a gleaming, blue-pommeled sword skillfully removed Doakes' tattooed head from his body.

As Titians died, the attacker numbers grew increasingly over-whelming. Sergeant Vera Cattell fought especially valiantly, saving her Captain on more than one occasion before a halberd snuck in from the side as the woman was engaged with another female warrior. The halberd's spike took Cattell in the upper chest, puncturing her right lung. As the metal twisted within the sergeant, Cattell's opponent seized on the opening, running her shortsword into the wailing woman's open mouth and forcing its sharp point through the back of her head.

Fincher spun his hazel eyes back and forth, dodging bolts, blocking random attacks, and pushing the group away from a stam-peding horse when necessary.

Everywhere Fincher looked, screams and blood were the precur-sors to empty eyes. The Titians battled bravely, but the numbers and positioning were proving too much to overcome. Eventually, as the chaos of conflict began to subside, and the dust started to settle, a clearer picture of their dire predicament took hold.

Gone were Cattell and Boone, Doakes and Feenk. Even Tobias Vale, although not deceased, was missing, the coward having abandoned the group at the first sign of danger. From what Fincher could immediately see, the Sour Flower Gang, ten of the Titian horses, and a host of assassins were all that remained in Salt's Pass.

Fortunately, a familiar, enraged voice from up ahead showed that to be incorrect.

"Come on then, you hatchet men! You fight a coward's fight, now die a coward's death!" The Sour Flower Gang all turned as one to watch as Captain Gorman Graff stood defiantly in the middle of a massive group of attackers, his famous broadsword cocked back and at the ready. "Attacking simple travelers accompanying children? How dare you!"

The handsome man who decapitated Doakes stepped forward, fearlessly entering the clearing that encircled the captain.

"Enough!" The man's powerful, light-turquoise eyes swept across the gathered assassins. "It's over! Put your weapons away."

"But, sir," came a complaint from the blue-ribboned group.

"I said enough!" Blades immediately went to scabbards and crossbows were lowered at the man's words. "That's better." Turquoise eyes returned to Graff. "Let's not pretend to be someone we are not…. High Captain Graff. Your reputation precedes you, as does your description. I don't know about you, but I would like to drop the surprises and the pretense. And let us have a conversation—man to man."

Graff spat onto the blood-covered ground. "That's easy for you to say. It's not your people lying dead around you."

"Actually," replied the handsome man, "there are more of my loyal men and women lying dead around us than yours. But I understand your point. And I empathize. I truly do."

Graff's grey eyes looked around desperately, as if he had forgotten something of severe importance. "The children! Where are the children!? I swear on my life, if any of them have been harmed, I will—"

"They are fine, Captain Graff," interrupted the assassin leader. "They are right over there. In fact..." He shouted over the group surrounding the Titian. "Let the children join Captain Graff!"

The throng of attackers cleared, allowing the Sour Flower Gang to finally unite with the Captain. Graff looked over each child, locking onto a gash over Ditto's eyebrow and a small cut on Sammi's cheek. He wiped blood from the girl's dark face before spinning back to face the attractive leader.

"Is this what you call *fine?*! Cowards, the lot of you!"

The blue-clad soldiers reached for their weapons, but the turquoise-eyed man discreetly held up his hands, freezing everyone's movement.

"We apologize, Captain Graff. It certainly was not our intention to harm any children. I am glad to see that there is no permanent injury." A pause. "Do you know who I am?"

"You're a rat. A rat that scurries about in the shadows of trees."

The leader chuckled. "I'll take that. I've been called far worse. My name is Byronn Paxxis. Commander Byronn Paxxis, to be exact. Head of the Cobalt Army."

"You're a Slugg. You're all Sluggs!"

"True. But have you heard of me?"

Graff's rage began to burn itself out. "I have. You're a good soldier, better strategist, and fair leader from what I gather. It's too bad you're also a seditionist and playing for the wrong team."

Commander Paxxis bowed to Graff. "You honor me with your words, Captain Graff. I have long admired you. We met once on the battlefield, you know?"

"I do not."

"Yes, well, I was much younger—just a grunt, really. I was under the orders of Commander Paalo Cheeb."

"Paalo Cheeb was arrogant and impetuous. Two qualities of a bad leader."

"For the record, he was an arsehole to boot. But you wielded your knowledge of Cheeb with such cunning, I had to admire it. We were entrenched between Ptero Heights and North Crisp Run. It would have taken all the might of Quaan to remove us. But you sent a small force north, with yourself at the head, to attack. In short order, it was clear that you were outmatched, so you fled back south. Commander Cheeb, showing hubris and selfish desire, ordered our entire regiment to chase you down and bring back your head. He said that the Titian Empire could not survive without Gorman Graff leading its armies. But, really, I think he just wanted credit for your death.

"Anyway, we all followed you down and past the southern tip of Ptero Heights, where the vast majority of your forces waited. They poured forth from the hills like an avalanche of violence, quickly pinning us against Crisp Run, which was especially deep and fast given that we were in the middle of the Warming, another variable that you accounted for and we did not.

"We were routed. But that's not where my respect for you comes from, Captain Graff. Once the battle was over, you took some prisoners. But many of us—those under twenty years of age—you set free, allowing us to return north. I'll never forget what you said. *I'll not hold children accountable for the faults and missteps of their elders.* I thought, for sure, I was to die that day. Instead, I learned the most valuable of lessons." Paxxis paused once again before continuing. "I heard much later that you got into real trouble for letting us leave that day. Is that true?"

Graff waited a moment before responding. "It is. I lost a Captain's Star and a half-year's wages. For *conduct detrimental to the Empire.*"

"And did you regret your actions?"

"Never once."

"And that is what makes you great. And worthy of my admiration."

Gorman Graff, never one to want the focus on himself, shifted subjects. "Have you been waiting in Shadowset all this time, just hoping that a prime target would come your way?"

"Not at all, Captain. We have several strategic positions throughout Shadowset." Graff spat onto the ground, imagining Sologar Crimm's face in the blood-stained dirt. "But, in this case, we were tipped off." Commander Paxxis looked around questioningly. "Where is our inside man? Let him be known and join us in victory."

"Here, Commander," came a voice from the side. Everyone looked over to find a weathered Cobalt veteran kneeling at the body of Second Lieutenant Heleena Dell. He lifted a bloody yellow handkerchief from the corpse. "This is her. This was the signal that the spy was to use, telling us to attack."

"Then, why is she dead?" demanded Paxxis.

"She ate the projectile meant for me," answered Graff. "And now I'm glad she did. My ability to read people is obviously waning with my increased years."

"Don't blame yourself, Captain," consoled the Commander. "You would be absolutely shocked by the number of Cobalts hidden within Titian ranks. Your Empire is dying. It has been for a long time; its demise hastened by greed, cruelty, and dishonesty. Do you really think the Gloomtide just appeared? Or is it the Chestnuts finally receiving their just desserts?" Paxxis turned to his soldiers. "A pity about the woman. She has simultaneously delivered the greatest gift to the Cobalts and the most grievous wound to the Titians." He returned to Graff. "What was her name, if you don't mind me asking?"

"Heleena Dell," said Captain Graff as if he was trying to remove poison from his lips. "The Titian Empire will forever curse her name."

"And we shall celebrate it." Byronn Paxxis called over his shoulder. "Saari Zahlee?!"

The tallest, most striking woman Fincher had ever seen stepped forward, her light golden eyes standing out against tan skin and jet-black hair. "Here, sir."

"There you are, Captain. What was the entirety of Miss Dell's correspondence?"

Captain Zahlee dug through a pouch at her hip and retrieved a small letter. "It's in code, sir, so forgive me if I stumble."

"Forgiven."

"The first part of the message is about High Captain Graff, that he was departing that very evening on an urgent mission for the Imperator, and that he would most likely be traveling through Salt's Pass ten to fifteen Paragons from the date on the note. It says that this will be the best chance to remove the wily Captain from the game board."

"You made fantastic time, Captain Graff. We barely got into position before you started through the Pass. One day earlier and we would have missed you. Anything else, Captain Zahlee?"

"Yes, Commander. It says that the group Captain Graff leads holds a secret of the greatest importance, both to the Cobalts and Quaan, at large. But she says that it is too sensitive to commit to paper, lest the carrier pigeon be captured and the message fall into the wrong hands. She says that she will fill us in when the Titian group is eliminated."

"Well, that ain't gonna happen," came a gruff voice from the back.

"Why wouldn't she just tell us?" wondered Captain Zahlee aloud.

"She was just being prudent," answered Paxxis. "Not only would it be a little sweetener to ensure that we acted on her tip, but a withheld secret could also provide insurance for her safety. And give her some additional bargaining power when it came time for rewards. Heleena Dell may have been a loyal Cobalt in disguise, but a spy is a spy and never to be fully trusted."

"Hear, hear," agreed Graff.

Commander Paxxis swung back to Graff. "Care to share the big secret, Captain Graff? For old times' sake?"

Graff laughed bitterly. "The big secret is that I'm no more than a lapdog these days. A lapdog with no real power. I get sent on small, impulsive missions that keep me out of the way and prevent me from infecting the minds of the younger officers."

"Infecting them how?"

"You know, by teaching things like compassion and empathy."

Commander Paxxis nodded sadly. "Yes, Captain, I can see that. So clearly can I see that. And your mission this time?"

Graff shrugged heavily. "There was rumor of an unusual apothecary who brought rare ingredients from the Spired Mountains and had a potential cure for the Gloomtide. This apothecary was supposed to have set up shop in Cassie's Clutch. I was to find him and bring him back, willingness not necessary."

"And the children?"

Graff waved them away. "They are nothing. A favor for an old friend that has nothing to do with the mission. I saw an opportunity to complete two tasks at once and took it."

"Care to share this favor with an old friend?"

"I do not."

An uncomfortable silence fell between the two leaders. "Very well," said Byronn Paxxis. "We will make sure they are sent back from whence they came with ample supplies. Unfortunately, we will have to detain you, Captain Graff, for obvious reasons. But please know that you will be treated with the utmost respect and provided comfortable lodgings behind the Cobalt Line. And if you come around to helping us with intel and even strategy, there will be rewards awaiting you. Significant rewards."

"No," stated Gorman Graff flatly.

"I understand. Loyalty and habit are hard things to break. I will not push you. But you *are* coming with us, Captain Graff."

"I am not."

"This is not a discussion. You have no other option, Captain."

"Champion's Duel."

Commander Paxxis's face fell and his shoulders slumped, making the handsome warrior age ten years in seconds. "Don't do this, Captain."

"Champion's Duel."

"We can tie and bound you, if we must, Captain Graff. I have no desire to see you thrown over the saddle of a horse like an unruly heiress being brought back to her wealthy parents. But if you leave us with no choice…"

Gorman Graff's grey eyes flared with anger. "Are you a coward, Commander?"

Now it was Paxxis's turquoise eyes that raged to life. "You know I am not."

"I know nothing but what I see before me—a leader refusing a just challenge from an equal. What would you call that person?"

"I would call him level-headed, especially when there is nothing to be gained from the challenge."

"Is there nothing to gain from slaying the long-time head of your bitter enemy's army?"

"Nothing more than what is already gained from your capture."

"But you haven't captured me, yet."

"Semantics, Captain Graff."

"Not to me." Graff raised his voice to be heard by all within earshot. "I am Gorman Graff, High Captain of the Titian Empire. I have been in over one hundred legitimate battles and three times that many smaller skirmishes. I have been cut by blades, pierced by arrows, and thrown aside by hammer and cudgel, alike. But never once have I ran from a fight. And never once have I been taken hostage. Never!" The Sluggs standing near the Captain took several steps back. "I have the respect of my men and my country. And you *say* I have yours, as well, Commander Paxxis."

"You *do*, Captain Graff."

"Then *show* me. If you want to show me respect, then respect me! Accept my challenge. I'm too old and too tired to cope with the weight of dishonor."

Byronn Paxxis was clearly running out of arguments. "But Captain—"

"Champion's Duel! If I win, you allow the children and I to continue on our journey north."

"You will not win, Captain. And not because of skill. I am simply younger, stronger, and faster. Therefore, I don't find this to be—"

"You owe me your life, Byronn Paxxis." The Commander's mouth snapped shut. "You said so yourself. You incurred a debt long ago, and I'm calling it due for collection."

Paxxis's blond-haired head fell, and he spoke to the ground. "Very well, High Captain. I so wish it could be another way, but I understand. I was foolish to hope that we could form some of kind of friendship away from all of this death."

Graff's weathered face softened. "This is Quaan, Commander Paxxis. You'll need to grow accustomed to constant disappointment. Now ready your sword, sir."

Captain Zahlee leaned into Commander Paxxis. "This is madness,

Commander. Just give the word, I beg of you. We will have this grizzled vet bound and gagged in short order. He'll come around to being a prisoner. They all do."

Paxxis shook his head. "Not this one, Saari. This one is from another time, another world, where change does not exist. He is the last of his breed, and we must honor his wishes."

"But Commander—"

"Durn it, Captain, are you questioning my judgment as your leader?!"

Captain Zahlee looked as if she had taken a knife to the gut. "Of course not!"

"Then back up and form a circle. All of you! Hear me! High Captain Gorman Graff has called for a Champion's Duel and I, Commander Byronn Paxxis, have accepted. There will be no interference from any here today. There will be no stopping until one can't continue or is dead. Do you hear me?!"

"Yes, Commander," came the unified cry from the Cobalts.

At that, Commander Paxxis drew his sword, a beautiful blade with a white hilt and blue pommel. Captain Graff knelt in the dirt, his sword tip down, touching his own brownish pommel to his lined forehead. A gentle breeze cut through Salt's Pass, sending Graff's grey hair into the air.

Fincher thought it was the most majestic anyone had ever looked.

When Graff stood, he turned to face the Sour Flower Gang. His grey eyes took them all in, and he nodded to each in turn before finally stopping at Fincher.

"I'm sorry that you have to witness this, children. But I know that you've all seen worse in your short lives. I'm sorry for that, too. Let this be a lesson. No one can take your dignity from you. You can only give it away freely, and that is one thing to never do. Death is a better alternative. And lastly, we all must finish what we start, no matter the pain that must be endured. Do you understand me?"

"Yes, Captain Graff," responded the children together.

"Good. You have each other. That's more than most in this cursed land. Do not take that for granted. Together, you can move worlds."

"Just like the Five Sisters, Captain," said Fincher, his voice wavering.

"Yes. Just like that. Good lad."

Gorman Graff turned back to Byronn Paxxis. "Are you ready, sir?"

"I am, Captain."

"Good, then let us—" Graff didn't finish his sentence, instead shooting forward like a Moon Adder, his famous sword leading the way.

Paxxis was caught off-guard, and only his insanely fast reaction allowed him to turn aside the thrust before the tip of metal found his chest. Paxxis pushed the strike to his left as he stepped to his right. He brought his own sword back up and around, but it was intercepted by Graff, who showcased his own surprising speed.

Fincher's face scrunched in pain as his hands were squeezed by Sammi on one side and Hana on the other. To his right, Ditto and Ash held each other tightly, both worried for the old man who had become a close friend in such a short time.

As a unit, the Sour Flower Gang watched as the two leaders battled in the long shadows of Salt's Pass. While Paxxis was easily the quicker of the two, Graff proved the more experienced, his sword always in the best position to parry a blow or offer a unique strike from a difficult angle. In fact, it was Gorman Graff who drew first blood, deftly sliding his broadsword up and over Paxxis's falchion to dig deep into the Commander's left shoulder.

Paxxis bellowed and quickly backed up several paces. To their credit, none of the Cobalts stepped forward to interfere. Fincher noticed, however, that although Commander Paxxis was the only one bleeding, it was Captain Graff who was beginning to breathe heavily.

Paxxis saw this, too, and waded back in, determined to take advantage of his youthful stamina. The clang of metal on metal filled the Pass as the two respected warriors launched blow after blow and countered with parries, sweeps, blocks, and dodges. Blood now showed on both men as each had found small gaps in the other's defenses.

As the minutes passed, both soldiers began to slow, but it was

Graff's movements that were most obviously affected. Even sloppy attacks from Paxxis were beginning to sneak through and find home in Graff's sides, and thighs, and arms. The men separated once more.

Grey eyes found their turquoise counterparts as both men stood across from each other, only respect and sadness being silently offered.

Gorman Graff, the decorated veteran of a hundred battles, knew that time was as much his foe as Byronn Paxxis. With that understanding, he prepped himself for one last offensive, digging his right foot into the ground. With a last roar of defiance, Captain Graff pushed forward, swinging his broadsword low before pirouetting and sweeping it high.

Commander Paxxis, seeing the blitz for what it was, accepted a shallow cut to his upper thigh and pushed ahead, dropping below the arching high attack and running his falchion across the exposed gut of Graff.

Paxxis continued forward and spun around when he reached the edge of the fighting circle. The length of his sword was covered in blood, as was the left hand of Captain Graff, who was pressing against his abdomen to prevent his guts from spilling out.

"It is over, Captain Graff. Please, I beg of you, concede, and I will have one of our medics stitch you up. You have upheld your honor and fought valiantly. There is nothing more to prove but plenty of life yet to live."

Graff studied his hand as blood ran from his fingers to stain the ground beneath him. All the blood that he had shed in his decades of service to the crown appeared from the dark recesses of his memory, young men and women dead at his feet, killed for nothing more than wearing the wrong color or following the orders of those whose nails were never darkened with dirt.

Yes, thought High Captain Gorman Graff, *this is a fitting end for one who has brought so much pain upon the world.*

"Children," cried Graff. "Finish what you start! Not for *them*! But for *you*! For each other!" Graff leapt forward, his broadsword out wide, leaving Commander Paxxis with no choice.

The tip of Byronn Paxxis's falchion tore into Graff's chest and exited his back. Paxxis grimaced as he caught the revered High Captain in his arms, for Graff had not even brought his broadsword around for a legitimate blow.

His faced pressed against the Commander's chest, Gorman Graff began to breathlessly speak.

"I'm sorry, Hilly. I'm so sorry. I just... I could never say no... could I? But we... we still had each... other... I miss you... already."

By the time Commander Paxxis gently lowered Graff to the ground, the High Captain was already dead, his grey eyes closed forever.

As Paxxis stumbled away from the body, nursing a half-dozen wounds, the Sour Flower Gang approached and knelt by their fallen friend. Heads bowed and tiny hands went to Graff's chest. In the silence that followed, Hana's powerful voice came to life, singing a song in which no words were known but all feelings were understood. It was an ancient song of goodbye, filled with sadness and appreciation and a hope for something beyond this life. It was a sentiment that the Sour Flower Gang knew all too well.

When Hana finished, the children stood and found that more than a few Cobalt cheeks were wet with tears, including those of Commander Byronn Paxxis, who limped forward to meet them.

"A fitting farewell for a man of such high moral fabric. He had a wife?"

"He did," answered Fincher.

"Then, I will see that his body is returned to her." Paxxis spoke to the Cobalts. "Select four among you. Wrap this hero in cloth, strip off your colors, and take his body to Miller's Bluff, the small village to the southeast of here, just along the border of the Mutewoods. Pay whatever you need to ensure their discretion and to see his body safely delivered to Kassimont. Make them understand with your blades if you must. Find us at our southern Shadowset base when you finish."

"But sir—" came a voice from the group.

"There will be no discussion. I'm confident that Gorman Graff would have done the same for me. Captain Zahlee?"

"I will see that it is done, Commander," said the powerful woman.

"Good. For the rest of us, back into Shadowset. Already we have been out in the open too long."

"What about the children, Commander?" asked a large man who was missing his left ear.

"Bring them. But be gentle. They are not our enemy." Paxxis turned to face the Sour Flower Gang. "Captain Graff would not admit it, but I think there is more to your story. I will know the truth of it." The Commander moved to leave but returned to the children. "As I hope you can see, I try to be a fair, honorable man. But I ask you not to test me. Nothing turns the kind-hearted into a villain faster than dishonesty."

Paxxis disappeared into his soldiers, calling out orders and clapping shoulders as he passed.

Fincher, Ash, Ditto, Sammi, and Hana stood in a circle, sharing thoughts with their eyes. The one man outside of Crimmish who they could trust was gone, leaving them with many more questions than answers about the status of their quest. The children found each other's hands and shoulders and waists, drawing strength from one another before moving forward as group.

"Remember," whispered Ash as they were whisked away by Cobalt soldiers, "*trust no adults.*"

"Words to live by," echoed Ditto.

"Farking right," agreed Fincher, and the Sour Flower Gang vanished into the dark unknown of Shadowset.

5

HOSPITABLE SLUGGS AND THE LADY OF SHADOWSET

After several hours of marching through the lightless forest known as Shadowset, the Sour Flower Gang, along with their Cobalt captors, reached one of the Slugg outposts hidden within the shadow-filled foliage. It was a massive encampment dotted with several large, more permanent buildings nestled between ancient giant mountain oaks and pines.

The group was greeted with a hero's welcome, as their return surely meant that the clandestine operation was a success. Hands were shaken and shoulders excitedly grabbed as the men and women made their way through the camp. One man with short, bleached hair approached.

"Where is he? I have to see this Captain Graff with my own eyes. All the stories surely cannot be true."

Merrik Quell, one of the Cobalts walking alongside Commander Paxxis, motioned the short-haired man to calm down with his questions. As he did, Paxxis moved on from the group, a frown etched upon his relatively youthful face.

"What did I say?" asked the bleached man known as Bellows.

Captain Quell, the regiment's other captain along with Saari

Zahlee, responded. "We did not bring back High Captain Gorman Graff."

"What? Then the mission was a failure?"

"It was not. Gorman Graff is off the game board. Just not in the way we had hoped."

"Then, he fell in battle," guessed Corporal Bellows.

"No," responded Quell. "Champion's Duel."

Bellows' eyes went wide. "You're farking kidding me. Wow, I would like to have seen that. From Commander Paxxis's limp, it must have been a real back and forth."

Merrik Quell thought for a moment before answering. "It was the most beautiful display of skill, heart, and honor that I have ever seen. A truly wondrous duel. You can tell the others that."

Bellows' faced cracked into a smile of pride for his beloved Commander. "What did you do with the Captain's body?"

"Commander Paxxis saw that it was returned to Graff's wife in Kassimont."

Bellows' smile fell a bit. "Was that smart?"

"Perhaps not. But it was the right thing to do. And if we start cutting corners on things like rightness, then we're no better than the durn Chestnuts."

"Fair enough. Who are the kids?"

"They were with Captain Graff. Said he was simply doing a friend a favor by letting them tag along, but Commander Paxxis thinks that there's more to it."

Bellows nodded. "We should get to the bottom of it. I wouldn't put it past Chestnuts to use children for deadly purpose."

"Agreed. The Commander intends to do that very thing this evening. But first, I think he needs to… Mourn might be too strong a word. He took the life of a man he respected greatly today. In single battle, no less. Tell the others to give the Commander some peace and quiet for the next couple of hours. He'll come back and join us when he's ready."

Bellows nodded once more. "I will make sure he goes unbothered."

"Good. And see that these children are given proper lodgings, hot food, and cold spring water. Although we know not what they are, for now they are our guests and nothing less. Make sure they are treated with respect. Gorman Graff seemed to hold a soft spot for them, which means that Commander Paxxis does so, as well. Anyone who values their appendages should mind their manners; I don't care how long they've been stuck in these infernal woods."

"Yes, sir," said Bellows simply before moving to relay Captain Quell's orders.

"Oh, and Corporal Bellows," stated Quell, stopping the soldier in his tracks. "The children seem to be good-natured and obedient, as far as I can tell. But they're also smart as whips and work together remarkably well. Add to the fact that we just killed their adored guide and we could have a recipe for attempted escape."

"Excuse me," cut in Ash," we're right here, you know."

"Yeah, we can hear everything. Really showing your farking cards, Quell," added Fincher.

Captain Quell spun to face the children. "Good. I want you to know that I know that you all are an intelligent and potentially dangerous bunch. And I want you to know that I'm letting others know this fact so that any ideas of taking flight through Shadowset can end here and now."

Ditto leaned into Fincher. "Is he talking in riddles? I'm terrible at those. I have no idea what he's saying."

"He's saying that we're too smart for our own good," said Sammi, absently tying two short pieces of rope she'd found into a complex knot.

Fincher built onto Sammi's words. "And that, if not properly watched, we may farking take over this whole Slugg encampment with our wit and cunning."

Quell's face twisted. "Well, that's not really what I was—"

"Ditto, I'm hungry," interrupted Hana, pulling on the large boy's shirt.

"Glad we have that settled," stated Fincher. "Now, if you'll point us in the direction of our rooms, or tents, or reserved spaces on the ground, we'd be most grateful. It's been a long few days for us kids, and we're exhausted and parched, with farking empty bellies, to boot. And don't worry about us running off. How could five children ever survive the terrors of a place like Shadowset? Why, we'd be farking monster food inside a day if not for the protection of true warriors such as yourselves."

Ash and Sammi giggled as Ditto simply rolled his eyes at Fincher's words, which were dripping with sarcasm. Hana once again complained about her stomach.

Quell started to say something but stopped. He restarted. "Will someone please show our guests to their quarters."

Without further word, a female Cobalt with a sweeping mohawk ushered the Sour Flower Gang off as Fincher immediately struck up a conversation peppered with curses.

After watching them disappear into the mass of soldiers, Captain Quell turned back to Corporal Bellows.

"See what I mean?"

Bellows nodded. "I'll double the sentries."

Despite the death of High Captain Graff and being taken as unwilling *guests*, the children had to admit that they were treated well by the Cobalts. After being given plenty of refreshing spring water and a delicious meal of roasted sharp-tailed grouse, the Sour Flower Gang was afforded a large tent in which to store their packs and a clearing away from the soldiers to settle in around their own personal fire.

As shadow began to fall into actual night, Fincher and the gang stretched out on their bedrolls, staring up at the starless canopy above. Around them, stationed at regular intervals, were a half-dozen guards standing silently. Fincher rolled onto his stomach to count each one just beyond the perimeter of the fire's light.

"More than one farking guard for each of us," commented Fincher. "Should we feel flattered?"

"You should, Master Fincher," said Byronn Paxxis as he stepped into the light and took a seat between the children. "It means that I sense real value in your collective and—"

"The Sour Flower Gang," stated Fincher.

"Come again?"

"We're called the Sour Flower Gang."

"And why is that?"

"Long farking story. Just know that that's who we are."

Paxxis chuckled to himself. "Very well. I sense real value in the Sour Flower Gang, although I have no idea of your true worth. Perhaps you can all help me with that." Only the crackling of the campfire filled the tense silence. Paxxis went on. "I want you all to know that I took no pleasure in the death of Gorman Graff. Quite the contrary, it has been an extremely difficult day for me. He was a personal hero of mine, regardless of the color that he chose to drape himself in. But High Captain Graff served an empire no longer worthy of his loyalty and a world too dim for his brightness. In the end, all he had left was his honor, and he refused to sacrifice that even for his own life. I didn't think I could possibly respect him more, but today I stand corrected."

Fincher and Sammi wiped tears while Ash and Hana sniffled loudly. Ditto simply stared silently into the fire. Corporal Quell stepped out of the dark night and joined the group, stopping to stand just behind Paxxis as the Commander continued.

"So, when a man relied on by an Empire is sent on a secret mission without his Titian colors and accompanied by only a few soldiers, I tend to have suspicions."

"Captain Graff told you what he was tasked with," said Ash.

"He did," assented Paxxis. "And I, in no way, mean to besmirch the good Captain's name. But I don't think he was being truthful with me, which would make sense if he was trying to protect a more prime objective. Or the role of a group of children in said objective." A heaviness fell over the clearing. "Now, who wants to tell me what's really going on here?" The heaviness quickly grew suffocating for the children. Then it got worse. "Does this have anything to do with the Rose Comet?"

"What do you mean?" asked Ash, a bit too nervously for Fincher's liking.

Commander Paxxis leaned forward and swept his bluish gaze left and right, looking each child in the eyes, one by one. "The Rose Comet. The Centennial Star. I know you haven't missed it. It was in the sky for many nights. Was that the impetus for Graff's mission?" Paxxis lowered his voice a bit, but a twinge of desperation replaced the volume. "Have they found the God-Snails? Is that what this is about?"

"Impossible, sir," answered Captain Zahlee, who had just returned from transporting Graff's body. The imposing woman joined her fellow captain, playfully slapping Quell on the backside as she did. "If the Chestnuts knew where the Supreme Helices were, they would send their entire army to secure the area, not a small, ragtag group."

"But they were not ragtag, were they Captain Quell," retorted Paxxis.

Quell sighed heavily, not wanting to get between his boss and his love. "No, they were quite skilled, Commander. Although we won the battle, we lost twice as many soldiers. Only our initial ambush and significant numbers advantage ensured our victory."

"So, not ragtag at all?"

Quell could feel Zahlee's golden eyes boring into the side of his head. He would pay for his words later, when the two were alone. "Not ragtag at all, sir."

"So, an important mission then?"

"I would think so, sir." Quell's side ate a sharp elbow from Zahlee.

Fincher's breath came quicker and quicker as the sharp-witted Commander started to piece the full story together.

Paxxis's turquoise eyes grew increasingly penetrative. "An important mission requiring the participation of children from Crimmish?" Paxxis laughed at the kids' shocked faces. "What? Do you think that your yellow eyes are invisible to us? Or that we do not know what those lemon orbs denote? Do not worry, the Cobalts feel for your people more than you could ever imagine. Most of those banished to Crimmish were done so, correctly or incorrectly, for aiding or supporting the Cobalt Insurgence. We mourn your people in many of our songs and poems. Your treatment is a constant reminder of what awaits us should we prove unsuccessful against the tyranny of the Titian Empire." Paxxis paused to let this new information sink in. After a moment, he asked, "Now, what could the Titian Empire need with a group of Crimmish kids, if not to help them find the Divine Pentad?"

Fincher looked around and could see his friends each panicking in their own quiet way. And while Sammi was the smartest of the bunch, she was utter shite at lying, demonstrated by her small hands working furiously at the knot between them. Fincher knew that he needed to step up. If he could stare at Reba Bugg's horse face and convincingly tell her that she was the prettiest girl in Quaan, then he could get one over on the kind Byronn Paxxis.

"You farking got us, Commander," said Fincher, drawing all eyes to him. "At least, you partially farking got us."

Paxxis's blue eyes narrowed. "Go on."

Fincher's cunning mind spun like a top. "We *were* brought on for a special mission. Requested specifically by the Imperator and Chancellor, no less. Although *requested* is probably much too kind a word."

Paxxis leaned forward, and light from the campfire danced across his handsome face. "A special mission to find the God-Snails? Then you know where they are?"

Fincher's hazel eyes shot over to Ash, who shook her head ever so slightly.

"I'm sorry to disappoint you, Commander. A special mission? Yes. But I... we... know nothing about the God-Snails. If the Imperator knew where they had landed, the entire army would be heading there now. I think Captain Zahlee is right about that."

Paxxis's face twisted in disbelief. "What other special mission could be so important as to need High Captain Gorman Graff in disguise chaperoning a group of children from Crimmish?"

"Captain Graff gave you a partial truth. The mission doesn't have to do with the God-Snails, but rather the Gloomtide."

"Go on."

"You know Terminus Grove?"

"Young man, Terminus Grove serves as the northern border of Cobalt land. Of course, we know it. And better than any Chestnut."

"Sorry, Commander. We obviously don't get out much. Apparently, there is a rumor—I have no idea how credible it is—that there are strangely unique flowers there, some which may have major medicinal qualities."

"Meaning?"

Fincher shrugged. "Meaning the Imperator is desperate. The Gloomtide is spreading quickly across Titian territory. Mothers are abandoning their babies. Husbands are burning down their homes while their families sleep inside. One boy named Renton apparently chopped off his own tiny dangler in a fit of inconsolable woe."

Fincher realized that he may have gone too far as Ditto, Ash, and Sammi began choking back laughter at the expense of their old adversary. Their eyes bulged as they tried their best not to give away the lie. Fincher went on.

"Anyway, I think you get my point. The Imperator has a real farking problem on his hands, and it's only getting worse. He'll latch onto any old rumor if its potential truth could lead to a Gloomtide cure."

"I don't understand where you all come in."

"Tell me this, Commander. Why don't you enter Terminus Grove?"

"The air is poisonous. To enter the forest is…" The pieces clicked into place in Byronn Paxxis's mind. "Of course. You all harvest Moonflowers in the Tainted Forest. Is that supposed to give you some kind of immunity to the toxic air of Terminus Grove?"

Fincher shrugged once more. "I guess that's how it's supposed to work. And immunity is probably too strong a word. Sammi?"

"Resistance is the correct word," said the girl as she pushed her glasses higher up on her nose.

"Yeah, that's it," agreed Fincher. "Terminus Grove's shite air is supposed to come mainly from Reaper Vines, same as the Timbers. I guess they figure we won't immediately drop dead like everyone else, giving us time to collect whatever weird specimens their apothecaries want. They're hoping to find something that can cure or, at least, slow the Gloomtide."

"Just like Moonflowers led to Salvation."

"Exactly, Commander."

Byronn Paxxis thought for a moment. "What if there's other toxins in the air of Terminus Grove? Toxins that you don't have a… resistance to?"

Fincher offered one last shrug. "Then, I guess we'll drop dead as surely as any of you."

Paxxis looked to both Zahlee and Quell before returning to Fincher. "Why are you all doing this, Master Fincher?"

"What do you mean, Commander?"

"I mean, the Chestnuts have banished your people, left you to toil away in a land that poisons your brain and kills your kinfolk. Why help them?"

"Well, the Imperator doesn't really *ask* for things, now does he, Commander?"

"That's bellywash, Master Fincher. There isn't much the Imperator could do to you. Very few would dare come into Crimmish with fears of the air. And the youngest of you could always take shelter in the Timbers, where none could reach you. You had a choice." A pause. "Has the Gloomtide reached Crimmish?"

Fincher laughed bitterly. "We deal with the Maddening on a daily basis, Commander. In comparison, the farking Gloomtide looks like a chest cold."

"Then why help them?"

"Maybe they offered us something."

"What could they possibly offer you?"

"An end."

"An end to what?"

"An end to the Madness, Commander."

That caught the handsome warrior off-guard. "Please explain."

"Captain Graff said that Imperator Rayne promised to send his best physicians, apothecaries, and alchemists to Crimmish, for as long as it takes, to find a cure to the Maddening."

"*If* you find a cure for the Gloomtide?"

"They said the deal was for supplying them with odd plants, herbs, and flowers from Terminus Grove. Nothing more."

"And you believed them?"

"I believed Captain Graff."

That comment put Paxxis back on his heels. To his credit, the young leader recovered quickly. "Captain Graff was a man of honor. He believed in things like a person's word. You and I know better. Your people know better. So, I ask you again. You actually believed them?"

As Fincher searched for a valid response, Ditto cut in.

"Have you ever watched your mother or father bash their heads against the wall until blood leaks from their eyes, nose, and mouth, Commander? Have you witnessed a loved one cave in their skull only to smile dumbly after, for they had finally found relief from Brain-Itch?"

"I admit that I have not, Master Ditto."

"Then you don't know the power of possibility, no matter how remote, when it comes to ending the Madness."

Paxxis digested Ditto's words. Fincher watched as Captain Zahlee wiped something from her eye.

"You're right, Master Ditto. I obviously do not. And I apologize for my ignorance. Hope is a dangerous thing. But a world without it isn't worth living in."

Fincher jumped back in. "But that's not the only reason, Commander." Paxxis motioned for the boy to continue. "You're right; there's no love lost when it comes to the people of Crimmish and the Titian Empire. Truth be told, we don't consider ourselves part of the Empire, and we barely consider ourselves the same race of humanity as the rest of Quaan. Our minds may be sick, but our hearts are more pure. Of this, I'm sure. Of this, we *all* are sure. Despite what the world has done to us, we don't wish ill upon them. We know the pain of the Maddening. We don't want anyone else to experience such suffering, whether that be in the form of the Gloomtide or any other farking malady. So, if us traveling to Terminus Grove can save Quaan from such an ailment, we cannot refuse."

At this, Byronn Paxxis had no response. Instead, he let silence fill the circular space alongside flickering firelight. Finally, he nodded sadly and rose with a grunt, the wounds from his duel with Captain Graff still obviously paining him greatly. When Paxxis had found his balance, he stared down at the children, taking each one in.

"I think Quaan would be a much better place if it took a page from the people of Crimmish. And that goes for Cobalts as well as Chestnuts. You've lived difficult lives for ones of such youth. For that, I'm sorry on behalf of all the adults in the world. But you've persevered with a grace that we should all hope to emulate. Sleep well, my new friends." Paxxis began speaking to the surrounding sentries. "Bring the children more food and water. And see if you can't scare up some sweets for them. After that, retire to your quarters. They need no watching."

Just as Paxxis began to turn to leave, Fincher offered one last comment.

"Commander."

"Yes, Master Fincher?"

"We have our share of Danglin' Andys in Crimmish, too. We're not saints."

Laughter broke out amongst the soldiers. Paxxis simply smiled. "Could've fooled me."

Commander Paxxis walked into the night, followed by Captains Quell and Zahlee. The surrounding sentries also dispersed, eager to follow their leader's orders. As soon as they were alone, the Sour Flower Gang huddled up.

"Wow, wow, wow, Fincher," whispered Ash excitedly. "What a lie! What a beautiful, twisted lie."

"You really outdid yourself," agreed Ditto.

"I really like Commander Paxxis," offered Hana meekly.

"Me too, Hana," agreed Fincher. "Do you guys think I did the right thing by lying to the Commander?"

"Never trust adults, right?" asked Sammi.

"Never," said Ash.

"Never," echoed Ditto.

"Okay, then," conceded Fincher. "Let's wait and see where this takes us."

"And see if they actually bring us some sweets," said Sammi, her voice on the edge of hysteria from the idea of candy, a rare delicacy in Crimmish.

"She's *your* problem if they do, Ash," stated Ditto, recognizing the wildness in the brilliant girl's eyes, even behind those bottle-like lenses.

"The heck she is, *Master* Ditto. I'll make sure her bedroll is next to yours tonight. Good luck discussing the mysteries of the cosmos with her until Paragon-break." Ash stood, dragging Sammi and Hana up with her. "Come on, girls. Let's take a bathroom break before our snacks fit-for-a-king arrive."

As soon as the girls were out of earshot, Ditto leaned into Fincher.

"Tell me, Fincher. What was harder? Lying to the Commander or lying to Reba Bugg to grab her plump rear."

Fincher waved Ditto away. "That's easy. The Commander didn't have horse breath to contend with. Lying to him was child's play."

Ditto laughed. "So, the Reba Bugg lie still takes the crown."

"No. That would be telling my ma that she would make it through the Maddening."

Ditto's sweet face fell. "Oh, of course. Sorry, Fincher."

Fincher clapped his large friend on the shoulder. "Nothing you haven't had to do yourself. Two times."

Ditto nodded lamentably. "I guess in Crimmish, we all become liars sooner or later." Ditto rose and offered his hand to his smaller companion. "But our hearts are in the right place; aren't they, Fincher? We can't say the same about the other liars of Quaan, can we?"

Fincher accepted the powerful hand. "Farking right, Ditto. Farking right."

~

The Sour Flower Gang woke to find the Cobalt outpost a hub of activity. Everywhere they looked soldiers were sharpening blades, collecting items into travel bags, and securing packs onto horses.

After being brought a wonderful breakfast consisting of whistling duck eggs and dried caramel carp, and devouring it in minutes, the children followed suit, preparing themselves for another inevitable day of travel. Just as their packs were closed and hoisted onto their small backs, Commander Paxxis approached with Captains Quell and Zahlee in tow.

"Up and packed, I see," commented Paxxis. "Well done. You would make a fine addition to any army." Paxxis purposely met eyes with Ash, Sammi, and Hana. "All of you."

"We saw everyone getting ready, Commander," said Fincher. "Where're we heading?"

Paxxis shared a strange look with Quell and Zahlee. "Listen, I need to speak with you all frankly. We have… spoken in detail about your situation. Unfortunately, we cannot allow you to continue on your quest for the Chestnuts. It may seem cruel, but the Gloomtide has proven a significant strategic advantage to the Cobalt cause. We have made more progress in this last year than in the past ten combined, ever since High Captain Graff sent us scattering along the Spired Curtains."

"Then, what is everyone packing for?" asked Ash, a hint of anger in the fiery girl's voice.

"Our work is done here, Mistress Ash. We came here to sever Gorman Graff from the Titian forces. And although I wish—oh, how I wish—that it could have been accomplished another way, Captain Graff no longer heads the Chestnut army. The hearts and minds of their military forces is now gone. The Titians are vulnerable. We must return to our stronghold in the northwest and prepare for an all-out assault. When the stagg is hobbled you must rush forward, not bide your time. Even a wound such as Captain Graff's absence will heal. Now is the time to act."

"So, you are abandoning us?" inquired Hana, fear evident in the shy girl's words. "Here in this dark place?"

"Nonsense," exclaimed Paxxis, as if offended by the suggestion. "We are abandoning this outpost, not you… for now. It has served its purpose. You all are to return to Crimmish to rejoin your families and community."

"With all due respect, Commander," said Fincher, "the journey here was long and full of potential dangers no doubt kept at bay by our rough-looking entourage. We'll be farking food if we travel there alone."

"Of course, you will, Master Fincher. Which is why you won't be traveling there alone. A few soldiers and I will be taking you to someone who can ensure your safe passage back to Crimmish." Paxxis turned to his captains. "Finish the preparations and leave as soon as possible. Don't wait for me. I'll catch up soon enough."

Quell and Zahlee nodded and dispersed, barking orders as they did.

Paxxis returned to the children. "Now then, just let me know when you are ready to depart. We have your horses already fed and watered."

"We're ready now, Commander," stated Ash.

"Good! I wish my regiments had such fires under them! Then, let us depart at once. Follow me to your horses."

"Uh, where are we going, Commander?" asked Ditto, speaking for the group.

"Are we heading back to the Pass?" added Ash.

"We are not."

Sammi pushed her glasses up. "Then, where are we going?"

"Deeper, Mistress Sammi. Deeper into Shadowset."

The children's faces contorted in confusion.

"Deeper into Shadowset?" questioned Fincher. "I heard there's nothing there but predators and prey in the deep forest."

Byronn Paxxis chuckled at the punchline to a joke that only he heard. "You're correct, Master Fincher. It is mainly predators and prey in the darkness of Shadowset. But there's one thing you don't know."

"And what is that?" demanded Ash.

"I'm taking you to Shadowset's apex predator. And she's the one who will make sure you get home safely." The Sour Flower Gang looked to each doubtfully. "Now, let's ride!"

The nine horses, including *Windsong*, gingerly made their way west, keeping to a small natural trail created most likely by forest staggs and the plethora of animals hunting the majestic creatures.

Three Cobalt soldiers led the way, followed by the children and Commander Paxxis. Two more tough-looking warriors trailed the group, preventing a rear ambush.

Despite the darkness of the forest, there was great beauty to be seen. Shadowset was not all browns and greys and blacks like the Tainted Timbers. Colorful flowers, bioluminescent insects, and graceful, bright green plants filled the dim landscape. Everywhere one looked, lizards skittered, small mammals raced for insects, and thick bushes shook with a foreign beast hiding within.

Byronn Paxxis spoke as they rode, apparently unafraid of the movements sensed within every deep shadow.

"Do you know why the Titians call us Sluggs?" he posed to the Crimmish youths.

"I suppose because they want to be rid of you," answered Sammi.

Paxxis snickered. "Yes, I suppose that is one reason, but an ancillary one. The real reason is much lazier. It's because of our colors—cobalt. The only common creature in Quaan with a similar complexion is the Azure Slugg. Therefore, their simple minds put together the simple connection and we became known as Sluggs, those humble gastropods at which most turn up their noses. But this only shows their ignorance of Quaan."

Ash swatted a bug from her face, accidentally hitting Sammi in the back of her head in the process. "Oh, sorry, Sammi."

"Careful," chided Sammi, rubbing her head. "How does this show their ignorance, Commander?"

"Great question, Mistress Sammi. First, Azure Sluggs are critical to the Quaan ecosystem, part of its natural balance. In addition to providing nourishment to an array of animals, many of which are needed to control pest populations, Azure Sluggs also help remove decaying material from the world."

"Seems like a farking stretch, Commander."

"Maybe, Master Fincher. But hear my next point. What are sluggs but snails without a shell? Without a home? We Cobalts consider ourselves the true children of the God-Snails. A people kept from securing a home. The Chestnuts claim we are insurgents. They call us a plague upon Quaan and declare us criminals. But, in that same breath, they compare us to the gods that they so depend on to save them from their recurring sins. They embolden us with every insult, the fools!"

Fincher, Ash, and Ditto locked eyes and shrugged. The Commander was making a strong case. And he wasn't finished.

"Do you know why we call them Chestnuts?"

"I assume because of the Empire's color," responded Sammi.

"Which is?"

"Uhh, Titian."

"Describe it to me, Mistress Sammi."

"It is a brownish-red, I suppose."

"Exactly! It is the color of chestnuts, which are only good when roasted in a fire, when their composition is completely changed. But, more fittingly, titian is also the color of rust, which truly describes the Empire's rule. It is old and outdated and pockmarked. It is ripe for the breaking, a tool no longer fit to serve its purpose. It is decaying before our eyes. And what eats decaying matter?"

"Azure Sluggs," answered Hana excitedly.

"That's right, Mistress Hana! I see your intellect is only matched by your singing voice. Sluggs? They honor us with that slight. And dig their own graves in the process."

Commander Paxxis's turquoise eyes widened as a large, multicol-ored bird flew overhead, eventually coming to rest upon a low-hanging tree limb that crossed the trail ahead. Once it had landed, the bird began to let loose a booming yet melodic song.

"Halt," cried Paxxis, bringing everyone to a sudden stop. "The Quilted Raven is here!"

The Cobalt contingent looked around nervously as the giant bird continued to sing, its tune seeming a direct accusation. Commander Paxxis waited several minutes before he spoke again. When he did, it was in a loud voice.

"Alicia Salt! Do not fire that famous longbow of yours! It is I, Byronn Paxxis! I have an offer for you! And many chips to go along with it!"

After a few tense beats, the tree branches to the left of the group started shaking, far above the heads of the mounted Cobalts.

Eventually, a beautiful woman appeared between the parted pines, her silver hair in a tight ponytail as she delicately balanced dozens of feet above the ground. Tight, sinewy muscles were evident beneath dark, tight-fitting clothing that seamlessly blended into the canopy above. A massive longbow was pulled back, arrow notched, as glowing silver eyes studied the group beneath.

"Byronn Paxxis. I have already granted you use of my forest. What more could you possibly need of me? Answer quickly as my arm is already growing weak."

This was an obvious lie as it looked as if the woman could hold that pose for the duration of Paragon.

Paxxis shook his head in disbelief. "Alicia! Why must we go through this every time?"

"Because every time we talk you want another outpost established in *my* forest. That's why!"

Paxxis held up his hands in surrender. "Fair enough. But not this time. In fact, our business has concluded here for now and we will be leaving you to your beloved Shadowset. With much heavier pockets, I may add!"

"Then, why are you here? If I don't care for your reason then I will press my lips together and release a whistle that will attract every muscle-bear within earshot. They are especially active and hungry this time of year."

"Alicia," begged Paxxis, "please take a closer look at our group. Do you not see the children amongst us? I have a simple task for you. One that comes with a significant payday. Can we come to your compound and talk about it? The darkness of Shadowset is no place for negotiation, especially for younglings."

Alicia Salt's bright silver eyes took in each of the children. Slowly her bow began to ease back into its neutral position.

"Very well, Byronn. But come with a good price. I'm in no mood for negotiation. The Silver Stagg was sighted several Paragons ago, and you are keeping me from my hunt. I don't need to tell you the seriousness of such an interruption."

"You do not, Alicia."

"Good. At least there's something that you understand. Move forward. When you reach the fork up ahead, make sure you take the righthand path. I know this seems counterintuitive, but I have set an elaborate trap along the other trail. One that even your lead riders wouldn't be able to detect." Alicia smirked. "Or maybe I got the two confused. I guess we'll find out together. See you at Salt House. Or not."

Alicia Salt offered a toothy grin before disappearing into the foliage behind her. Seconds later, the Quilted Raven let out one last cry before it, too, took to the sky and vanished into the shadows.

"Talk about a tough girl to like," said Fincher, inviting laughter from Ash, Sammi, and several accompanying Cobalts.

"Don't worry, children," offered Commander Paxxis, "Alicia Salt may have a tough exterior, but I suspect there is a creamy center somewhere beneath that protective shell."

"You *suspect*," asked Fincher.

"Yes… well… I've yet to crack the code myself, Master Fincher. Regardless of how many chips I spend." Commander Paxxis seemed to have spoken the last part to himself. He addressed the kids again. "Anyway, it takes a unique disposition to live in shadow, surrounded by beasts in waiting. She'll warm to you children, just as we all have.

And you'll warm to her." Back to himself. "I hope." Once more the children. "Let's be off. Best not to keep such a woman waiting."

The group lurched forward, all eyes pointed to the darkness around them.

"What a scary woman," said Hana to Fincher as the pair were propelled forward by *Windsong*.

"I think she was magnificent," said Ditto absently, a dumb smile pasted on his face as his mind raced ahead, imagining Alicia Salt's calloused hands on his thick neck.

Ash's brown eyes flashed angrily. "She's a forest frump," she spat so quietly that only Sammi could hear her.

Seated in front of her sister, Sammi giggled loudly, recognizing the source of Ash's sudden rage. Shortly after, the bespectacled girl's lower back ate a sharp elbow, forcing out a loud groan.

"Any other comments?" demanded Ash.

There were none. But Sammi's knowing grin remained all the same.

Salt House was a beautifully constructed mansion, made from dark, thick lumber that looked impossible to crack. The entire Salt Compound, complete with various buildings for butchering, tanning, storing, and, yes, salting, sat hidden deep within Shadowset. Unlike the dark forest, however, Salt House was bathed in light as a massive circle of trees had been felled to make room for the family's spread. It was truly a beacon of light in an otherwise frighteningly dim world. Needless to say, the children loved it.

The interior of Salt House was even more impressive than its exterior. Comfortable-looking antique furniture faced the roaring fires of one of the largest hearths ever built. Down the center of the cavernous main room was a giant dining table, large enough for a banquet.

On the walls, instead of fancy tapestries, were the heads of hundreds of animals. Antlered staggs, roaring muscle-bears, and sharp-beaked birds of prey were interspersed with dozens of species unrecognizable to not only the children, but even the worldly Cobalt soldiers.

As he stared open-mouthed at the literal cornucopia of bizarre fauna, Fincher noticed there was a noticeable blank space on the wall above the hearth, strange since it was the obvious focal point of the room.

Alicia Salt sat easily at the head of the banquet table when the Cobalts began filtering into Salt House.

"I left water out for your horses," Alicia said offhandedly as she petted the Quilted Raven perched on her arm.

"We saw," responded Paxxis. "You have our thanks."

"Oh, I better have more than that, Byronn." She motioned toward the table. "Please. Sit down and tell me how richly you're about to reward me." Paxxis sighed heavily before directing his five soldiers and the Sour Flower Gang to take their seats. No matter how many successful transactions they executed together, Alicia Salt never made it easy.

"You're much too handsome to frown like that, Byronn. Don't worry, I know what will cheer you up." Alicia clapped her hands loudly and the door to one of the side rooms—probably the kitchen— burst open. An elderly couple entered the main hall, pulling a wooden cart along with them. Atop the cart was a wide silver dish heaped high with smoked meats while the shelf below was filled with dishes and silverware.

The elderly couple brought the cart alongside the banquet table, placed the silver serving dish upon it, and deftly distributed ceramic plates and polished cutlery.

When they had concluded, Alicia spoke.

"Thank you, Tess and Earl. Now, let's see if my theory holds true that full bellies beget loose purse strings."

"We'll get waters for everyone, Miss Alicia," said the old woman. "And mead?"

"I don't see why not, Tess. Perhaps some mead will lessen the shock of the price tag I place upon my services."

Paxxis's frown deepened but, true to the silver-haired woman's words, all but disappeared once roast meat literally melted on his tongue.

The group ate in silence for several minutes, too busy shoveling delicious food into their mouths to speak.

"What is this with the orange bark?" asked one of the Cobalt soldiers. "I've never had its equal."

"You wouldn't believe me if I told you," was that all Alicia would offer. Her cryptic answer did not slow the eating frenzy. Soon, mead and meat went down in equal parts, except for the kids, who were left with waters.

When there was no roasted meat left to consume and the cups of mead had been filled several times over, Alicia Salt finally spoke again.

"So, tell me, Byronn. What is it that you need from me this time? And remember, I may be no fan of the Chestnuts, but neither am I one of your Sluggs."

"As you have told me on every occasion, Alicia."

"Just making sure that you remember, Byronn."

Fincher looked over to find Ditto staring at Alicia Salt, meat grease covering his face. Ash angrily shoved a cloth napkin into his hands, and he absently wiped his mouth, cheeks, and chin.

"It is a small task, Alicia. But one I am happy to compensate you more than fairly for completing."

"I wait with bated breath, Byronn."

"These children. I need you to travel with them back to Crimmish."

"The Stenches? Why would I want to visit such a terrible place?"

"Because I'm paying you."

"All the chips in the world won't cover the costs of the Maddening, Byronn."

"You know that's not how it works, Alicia."

"Maybe I do and maybe I don't, Byronn. Maybe an additional fee will offset those concerns."

Paxxis exhaled deeply. "Fine, Alicia."

"And who are these younglings? Why are they here? And why aren't you taking them back yourselves?"

"I guess chips don't cover discretion."

"They cover mine, not yours. And they certainly don't satiate my curiosity, which has no price."

Commander Paxxis took his time before responding. "Very well. I guess you're in no position to be running off to the Chestnuts. We recently set a trap for High Captain Gorman Graff. A successful trap."

Alicia sat up in her chair. "You captured Captain Graff?"

Paxxis fidgeted uncomfortably with his fork. "I wish. The old man refused to go the easy way."

"Which is why you're limping, I take it."

"You take it correctly."

Now it was Alicia's turn to think for a moment. "Gorman Graff was a good man. My father often spoke glowingly of him. But he was a good man tied to a bad government. Still, he will be missed."

"Yes, he will be," agreed Paxxis. "Most of all by the Chestnut army. But that's neither here nor there. When we ambushed the good Captain, he was traveling in secret with a small group of soldiers. These children were also among that group."

Alicia swung her silver eyes to the kids. "What reason could they possibly have for being with a disguised Gorman Graff?"

Commander Paxxis shrugged. "He originally claimed that he was simply doing a favor for an old friend."

"I'm not sure that favors exist in modern Quaan, Byronn."

"Agreed. Which is why we had a nice chat last night. Turns out, the Empire wanted to use these younglings to enter Terminus Grove and bring back samples to see if any medicines could be derived to counter the Gloomtide."

"Ahh, there it is," said Alicia. "Of course, there was selfish intent behind the plan. Favor, my arse."

"Yes, well, there is no longer a need for them to travel north. In fact, as you know, the Gloomtide has proven greatly beneficial to Cobalt efforts. The last thing we need right now is a cure."

Alicia's silver eyes flashed. "My, my, *Commander*. I didn't know you had this kind of callousness in you. What else is hiding behind those soft blue eyes of yours?"

"The Titian Empire has been siphoning life from Quaan since long before the Gloomtide came to being. It is a nightmare of their own creation. Let them sleep with it for a while longer."

Alicia stroked the head of her Quilted Raven once more. "And why can't some of your fighters return the children to the Stenches?"

"We prefer to call it Crimmish," cut in Ash bitterly. "That *is* its name, after all."

Alicia smiled, as if enjoying the girl's pluckiness. "Forgive me, Mistress. Crimmish."

Paxxis leaned forward on the banquet table. "Removing Gorman Graff from the equation has set many things in motion and created new opportunities to strike. We must return to Merriworth posthaste to prepare for the Cobalt Crush. This could be our last, and best, chance to topple the Rayne dynasty."

Alicia Salt considered the Commander's words. "And the children are potty trained?"

"Better than your farking bird, I would imagine," snapped Fincher.

Alicia's head spun to face Fincher. "This *bird* is a highly trained Quilted Raven, the most intelligent of the avians and worth more than all your lives combined." The colorful bird let out a melodic tune. Alicia stroked its beak. "Don't worry, Rashii, their brains are small and full of the Maddening. Their words have no meaning."

"Alicia," exclaimed Paxxis, enraged by the woman's cold comments.

"Why?! Why, Byronn? Why should I dedicate many Paragons to taking these children back to their poisoned homes?"

Instead of answering, Commander Paxxis simply tossed a swollen leather pouch onto the banquet table. The many chips within clinked loudly as they struck the dark-stained wood.

Alicia's silver eyes went wide at the size of the bag. "You could have just led with that, Byronn."

"Then, we have an agreement?"

"We do." Alicia scooped up the bag of chips and bounced it in her right hand. Her smiled grew as she realized the number of chips it would take to create such a weight.

Commander Paxxis stood, and the five other Cobalts followed. "Then, our business is concluded. You never cease to surprise me, Alicia, with both your greed and your total lack of care for anything beyond yourself."

Alicia grinned wickedly. "If you're trying to get into my pants, Commander Paxxis, you're going about it exactly the right way."

Paxxis waved the woman away angrily and collected his belongings. Once fully outfitted, he knelt before the kids, who remained seated at the large table. His turquoise eyes took them all in.

"Alicia Salt can be a real cranny, but she's the best at what she does and will keep you safe."

"I'm right here, Byronn." Paxxis ignored her.

"Do as she tells you, and you'll be home before you know it. I'm sure your parents will be delighted to have you back long before they'd anticipated." Ditto winced at the comment. "It has been an honor and privilege to accompany you all, even for a short time. I truly wish our paths could have crossed under more positive circumstances. You have my word, when the Titian Empire falls, Crimmish will be freed."

"Don't make promises you can't keep, Byronn!" He ignored Alicia once more.

"You have my word."

With that, Commander Byronn Paxxis, flanked by his five Cobalt underlings, made their way for the large double doors leading out to the rest of the Salt Compound. When he reached the exit, Paxxis spun back to face the impressive woman.

"If I ever find out that these younglings didn't make it back to Crimmish, I'll be back, Alicia. And I'll be carrying blades, not sacks of chips, when I do."

"Don't threaten me with a good time, Byronn. And don't worry that pretty head of yours. The younglings will get where they need to be."

"The Sour Flower Gang," said Paxxis.

"What's that?"

"They like to be called the Sour Flower Gang."

Fincher spun to Ash and mouthed the words, *See?! Sticks!*

"And why are they called that, Byronn?"

"They have mouths, lips, and, most of all, voices, Alicia. Maybe you should ask them yourself." The Cobalts exited Salt House, leaving the silver-haired woman alone with the Crimmish youth.

"You know," stated Alicia after several beats, "he really is too handsome to be so serious all the time. Don't you agree?"

"Absolutely," said Ditto dreamily, just before the stump of an arm struck him in the ribs, driving air from his lungs.

Little more was said after Commander Paxxis left for the long journey back north. Alicia Salt excused herself, stating that she had chores that needed attending, but not before giving the children permission to explore Salt Compound. She only presented one bit of advice.

"When Paragon falls behind the Spired Curtains, be here shortly after for supper. Tess and Earl may look like old, gentle souls, but they don't tolerate tardiness and can turn quite nasty if they feel unappreciated. Understand?"

"Yes, Mistress," responded Ditto, and Ash rolled her brown-on-yellow eyes before leaving.

The Salt Compound proved endless fun for the children. Several clear streams ran out of the dark forest to cross the spaces between buildings. Hana laughed aloud as she peered within the crystal waters, finding them full of moonbow trout. Elsewhere, miniature stone deer stepped carefully into the compound to feast on plump indigo berries that sat heavy in the bushes bordering the tanning house.

The children frolicked all afternoon, relishing in the rare opportunity to forget about the Maddening, the Gloomtide, Terminus Grove, and anything else that overburdened young minds. For an afternoon, they were not Harvesters, nor Cheese-Eyes, nor the sole providers of a sick community.

Fincher, Ash, Sammi, Ditto, and Hana were simply kids. And that felt pretty farking good.

~

"Well, if it isn't the Sour Flower Gang, right on time," said Alicia Salt as the children entered Salt House for dinner.

"You remembered the name," exclaimed Fincher, beaming with pride. "It's a good one, isn't it?"

Alicia shrugged noncommittally. "Could be better, could be worse. It does stick, I suppose."

Ash refused to look over as Fincher attempted to send her an *I-told-you-so* look.

The children sat down at the banquet table, where plates had already been set out alongside mugs of cool water. Alicia studied the kids as she sipped honey rice wine from a goblet.

"Tess and Earl will be bringing the food in shortly. Did you all have fun today?"

"Very much so," answered Fincher. "Our home isn't nearly as… green. Or full of life. It was a nice break from the shite." Ash kicked Fincher under the table. "Uhh… sorry for the curse, Miss Salt."

"I'm not your mom, boy. I'm not any of your mothers. Speak freely while here. I sure the fark will." Alicia looked to Ditto. "What about you? You don't talk much, do you, big boy?"

Ditto stammered for a response but found none. Fincher came to his friend's rescue.

"Ditto's more a deep thinker. And right now, I think he's overwhelmed by the… beauty of this place." Fincher barely got the last words out, trying hard not to burst into laughter. The others joined him in giggling—except Ash.

They sat in silence for a few minutes more, with Alicia emptying her goblet before filling it again from a large silver pitcher. As everyone waited for dinner, Fincher's eyes drifted across the wooden walls of Salt House, taking in the various trophy heads. He hadn't noticed it before, but nestled between two massive muscle-bear heads was a portrait of a serious-looking man. He had thick white hair and a matching white mustache that hung to his lower jaw. And while piercing black eyes seemed to look through Fincher from high above, that was not the man's most striking characteristic. On his upper left cheek was a perfect hole that seemed to disappear into the man's head, upgrading the painting from intimidating to downright frightening.

Fincher couldn't help himself. "Who the fark is that?"

Alicia didn't need to turn in her seat to know to whom the boy was referring.

"That is Albert Salt. My father."

"He looks very…" Fincher searched for the right work, one that wouldn't offend Alicia.

"Stern," Sammi cut in for him. "He looks very stern, Miss Salt. Was he?"

Alicia chuckled into her rice wine. "That would be one way to describe him."

"What happened to his face?" asked Fincher, and ate another kick from under the table.

"Oh, the cheek? A stagg Father was hunting burst out from the brush next to him and drove one of its antlers through his face. If he was… stern before the accident, he became downright nasty after it." Alicia's silver eyes began to unfocus, as if her mind was drifting back in time. "But Father did his best, I suppose. I mean, he didn't ask for the love of his life—my mother—to be taken from him at such a young age. He thought we were safe from the Bloat, tucked away in Shadowset, as we were. But it managed to find us. Well, one of us, at least. Watching her body swell and crack day after day must have been unbearable for him. I'm lucky I was too young to register it."

"That's awful," said Hana. "I'm sorry that happened to you, Miss Salt."

"Like I said, it happened to Father much more than to me. He turned cold after her death. Of course, it didn't help that she died before giving him what he wanted more than anything in life—a son." Alicia upended her goblet and filled it again. She gestured around the room. "I mean, how could a daughter possibly continue to fill the dining hall with trophies, or keep Salt's Pass clear? How could a woman properly carry on the Salt name? The Salt legacy? By the end, no matter what I did, Father determined that I could not. And this made his final months particularly dark, both for him and I."

"So, what did you do?" asked Ash.

Alicia's eyes snapped back into focus. "I decided to live life to spite him. I became the greatest hunter in the history of Quaan, better than he could have ever wished to become. These heads you see all around you, these are *my* kills, every one of them. Slowly but surely, I replaced all of his trophies with my own. A muscle-bear ten stone heavier than the one he downed. A ridge fox with longer teeth and a thicker pelt than any he had ever seen. A luna bat with a wingspan wide enough to block out the Five Sisters! I bested all of his records, and, yet, when people talk about the Salts, my name comes in at a distant third."

Fincher's gaze once more fell to the roaring hearth. "What about that empty space over the hearth?"

A look of surprise quickly crossed the beautiful woman's face. "Very observant, Master Fincher. *That* is for my final prize, the one that will earn me ultimate victory over the ghost that haunts me."

"What will go there?"

Alicia's visage grew serious, and for a moment she resembled the stony-faced man on the canvas above her. "That is where I will place the head of the Silver Stagg. It is said to be the only one of its kind. It is said to be immortal. It is said to be invincible. But that's only because no one can get close enough to shoot it. I will prove everyone wrong and take my rightful place at the head of the Salt line."

Sammi sipped water without looking at her mug, so entranced was she by Alicia's tale. "Did your father hunt the Silver Stagg?"

"Of course, he did. It was his dream, as well. And he came close, durned close, to bagging the animal. During his closest encounter, the Silver Stagg betrayed its true intelligence, doubling back to go on the offensive. It tore out of hiding and ran a glimmering antler through Father's face. Little did the magical creature know that it was setting off a chain reaction of events that would transform a young girl into an even more formidable foe."

Alicia had begun to drift away again. This time, she caught herself and shook loose the uncomfortable memories.

"Anyway, enough about the past, younglings. Let's talk about the immediate future. Tess and Earl will have the food ready soon. Have your fill. I'll make sure that they wrap up some jerky for breakfast and the journey tomorrow. We'll leave at the break of Paragon. I expect to have you back in the… in Crimmish by lunch of the third day." The children began to look at each other nervously. "What? Am I missing something?"

"Go on, tell her," urged Sammi to Fincher.

"Why me?"

"Because you're the self-proclaimed *voice* of the group, dummy," shot back Ash.

"Okay, okay. Sheesh, keep your cranny covers on." Fincher looked to Alicia, hesitation etched on his young face. "We're not going back to Crimmish. At least, not yet."

"Come again?"

"We're not going back to Crimmish."

"I heard you the first time. I was inquiring as to the reason, Master Fincher."

"We're going to continue our journey north. We want to finish what we started. We weren't traveling to Terminus Grove because the Titian Empire told us to. I mean, what more can they possibly do to us?"

"They always find something, Master Fincher."

"Nevertheless, that's not why we were doing it. We were doing it because they promised us a possible end to the Maddening."

"Empires lie more than the greatest of Quaan's raconteurs. I would be careful with such promises, Master Fincher. They lead to false hope, a very dangerous thing."

"You didn't let me finish, Miss Salt. We were doing it for a potential cure to the Maddening. But we were *also* doing it because the Gloomtide is the closest thing that the world outside of Crimmish will experience to the Maddening. And no matter how much we may resent what they've done to us, we don't wish this kind of suffering upon anyone. If there's a chance that we can help stop it, we must try."

Alicia finished another goblet of honey rice wine. "How very honorable of you all. I wish you all the best."

Fincher looked to his friends, and they all shared in the confusion. "You mean, you're not going to try to stop us?"

Alicia laughed as she filled her goblet a final time, emptying the contents of the silver pitcher. "Of course not, dear boy. I was hired as your guide, not your jailer. Byronn Paxxis purchased my *willingness* to accompany you, not my enforcement of your return to Crimmish. Truth be told, I had no wish to visit the Stenches... no offense."

"None taken," snapped Ash, although offense had clearly been taken.

"But, more than that, *Mistress Ash*, I really do find what you're doing to be somewhat noble. By all means, cure the Gloomtide for Kasspar Rayne. Just don't expect credit and rewards for what you do."

Fincher sat up excitedly. "So, you'll guide us north, instead?"

Alicia Salt collapsed into a fit of laughter. When she finally recovered, "Oh, that's not happening, dear, dear boy."

"But you were paid—paid handsomely—to *guide* us!"

"To guide you to the Stenches, not north through the Cobalt Insurgence, past Titian spies, and across the path of every category of highwayman, slaver, and murderer. You want to go to Crimmish, we leave at first light. Other than that, my hands are clean. I have given you food, shelter, and even some recreation. I have been more accommodating to you five than any previous visitor to Salt House. But my hospitality ends tomorrow morning. North or south, the choice is yours. But you *will* be exiting my compound shortly after waking."

A collective look of fear gripped the Sour Flower Gang, except for Ditto, who still looked as if he might ask for Alicia's hand in marriage. They leaned in and began to whisper desperately to each other. In an attempt to better hear Fincher from across the banquet table, Sammi pushed forward onto the table. As she did, something slipped out from beneath her shirt. Alicia Salt took notice.

"What is that?!"

"What's what?" asked Fincher.

"*That,*" responded Alicia, pointing to Sammi, who was now halfway across the wooden divide. "Girl! Come here, now! Please."

Sammi reluctantly did as she was told, moving hesitantly toward the woman whose wide silver eyes were locked on the young girl's chest.

As soon as she was within reach, Alicia gingerly grabbed the item dangling from Sammi's neck. She turned it carefully in her calloused palm, studying every pit, every stain.

"And what, pray tell, might this be, Mistress Sammi?"

"It's a Ghost Puma tooth, Miss Salt."

"And how did you find such an item?"

"She didn't *find* it. We *killed* it," corrected Fincher.

"Impossible. Ghost Pumas are said to be second only to the Silver Stagg in their difficulty to hunt."

"Well, hunt it we did," boasted Fincher.

"Ditto did most of the work," said Ash.

"Fallacious," declared Fincher. "But that's irrelevant. Show her, you all."

As one, the children removed the Ghost Puma teeth from beneath their shirts, leaving them to dangle from the black chords around their necks.

Alicia Salt looked in disbelief at the collection of Ghost Puma teeth. One could be found by accident. But all of these fangs together, and apparently from the same animal, only supported the younglings' assertion.

"How? How could children fell such a beast?"

"Why do you think Crimmish selected us for this task, Miss Salt?" asked Fincher before answering. "It's because we're the Sour Flower Gang. We're the best Harvesters that the town has ever produced. We know each other's strengths and weaknesses, execute game plans to perfection, and work together like the farking Kassimont Orchestra."

"You've never heard the Kassimont Orchestra, Fincher," chided Ash.

"But I can imagine, can't I? Anyway, you wanted to know how we did it? You're looking at the Sour Flower Gang. *That's* how we did it."

Sammi rolled her eyes beneath her glasses, forcing a giggle from Hana. Alicia Salt, however, was not laughing in the least. Quite the contrary, her mind seemed to be spinning in a million different directions, each more enticing than the last.

Alicia looked at Sammi Bugg with a newfound respect. "Thank you, Mistress Sammi. Please return to your seat. Tess and Earl will be out any moment now."

As Sammi sat down, Alicia tried to refill her goblet, forgetting that the silver pitcher was already empty. Leaning back in her chair, the huntress carefully studied the children seated before her, a dark smirk forming on her thin lips.

When the tension grew to climax, Alicia spoke. "Well, Master Fincher, it looks like you might have that guide north, after all."

Fincher replied after recovering from his shock. "I do? I mean, I'm glad, but why the sudden change of heart?"

"Because I'm finally seeing the Sour Flower Gang for what you truly are. And what you can do for me."

Just then, the large doors to the kitchen were rammed open by the wheeled service table. Tess and Earl appeared behind it, pushing the smoking, aromatic meats toward the Salt House proprietor and her guests.

"And what can we do for you, Miss Salt?"

Tess and Earl started placing various dishes on the banquet table.

"First, you can eat, and eat well. Build up your energy. For tomorrow, the real work begins."

Fincher looked around for support but was only met with perplexed faces. "What real work? What would you have us do, Miss Salt?"

"The Sour Flower Gang is going to help me kill the Silver Stagg, Master Fincher, the one beast that got the best of Albert Salt. The one beast standing between me and my legacy. The one beast that can exorcise the ghost that haunts me in this house of judgment."

Fincher thought for a moment. "The farking Silver Stagg, huh?"

Alicia stabbed a slab of meat with her knife. "The farking Silver Stagg."

6

THE FARKING SILVER STAGG

True to her word, Alicia Salt wanted to get started the very next morning. When the children entered Salt House for breakfast after a restful night in one of the three guest houses, they found that half of the banquet table was covered in a mixture of forest maps, ropes, and unusual trapping mechanisms.

Alicia bounced around the main room, energized by the mere thought of capturing her longstanding foil. Rashii stared down from the rafters, taking everything in with eyes too smart for a bird. The Sour Flower Gang was nearly right next to the woman before she noticed them, so lost was she in her thoughts of the hunt.

"Oh, children, there you are! You startled me. But don't worry, I never startle when on a hunt, especially *this* hunt. Don't worry about all this stuff right now; I'll walk you through it after breakfast, which should be—"

Tess burst through the kitchen door and held it open for Earl, who had a tray full of meat, egg, and cheese sandwiches between his old hands.

"... ready now," said Alicia, concluding her sentence. "I hope you don't mind, but I asked Tess and Earl to keep it simple this morning. I don't know about you, but I find myself without appetite."

"Uh, we can eat," said Fincher, speaking for the group who cared little about the upcoming hunt.

"Yes, yes, of course, you can. Sit. Sit!"

Fincher looked to Ash and Sammi and each understood what the other was thinking. *Alicia Salt is manic and on the verge of losing it.*

Everyone sat, and the breakfast sandwiches were distributed. Alicia did not touch hers. Instead, her silver eyes drifted to the empty space above the hearth before returning to the younglings devouring their food at her table.

"Mistress Ash, if I may be so bold, how did you lose that arm of yours?" Ash looked up from her breakfast, a surprised look on her dark face. Most people went out of their way to ignore the stump of her left arm. "I apologize if the question is inappropriate. I am a forest girl, always have been, always will be. We speak plainly and voice questions as soon as they enter our minds."

Ash put down the remainder of her sandwich. "No, I don't mind, Miss Salt. It's just that most in Crimmish know the story already, and those who don't are too uncomfortable to ask."

"And do you think that would be different if you were a boy?"

"I think so."

"Me too. Well, as you can see, I am not encumbered by such emotions. Feel free to tell me to go fark myself if it's too painful."

Ash laughed. Despite immediately disliking the forest frump for catching the green eyes of Ditto, she had to admit that there were things to like about the mysterious woman.

"Not at all. We—"

"The Sour Flower Gang," interjected Fincher with his usual impish smile.

"Thank you, Fincher," said Ash, rolling her brown eyes. "The Sour Flower Gang was on a harvest a couple of years ago—"

Alicia shot upright in her seat. "A couple of years ago?! How old were you? Three?" She pointed at Hana. "And was this one even alive?!"

"This was just before Hana joined the crew, when we were a group of four. We were trying hard to prove ourselves and ventured too deep into the Timbers looking for Moonflowers. One second, I was searching through the grey brush, the next, a Ghost Puma had my arm."

Alicia's mouth fell open. "A Ghost Puma attacked you?! How on Quaan did you survive?"

Ash nodded across the table. "Ditto saved me." Fincher loudly cleared his throat. "And Fincher. When the Puma took hold, I didn't feel scared. I didn't feel pain."

"You felt rage," stated Alicia.

"Yes. I felt rage. I pummeled its head with my right fist with all my might. I'm not silly enough to think I hurt it, but I'm sure I surprised it. It's the apex predator of the Tainted Timbers and not used to prey fighting back. It loosened its jaws just a bit, and, when it did, Ditto came flying in from the side, freeing my arm from the cat. This was crazy because Ditto was only half the size that he is today." Ash glanced at Ditto with a strange look. "But still he managed to push the Ghost Puma away from me. And he took a grievous blow for his efforts. Show her, Ditto."

Ditto rose from his seat and lifted up his shirt. Four thick red scars ran from his left shoulder across his chest.

"Very impressive, Master Ditto," commented Alicia, and Ditto wobbled where he stood.

"My da always said that I had thick bones. That's why the bugger couldn't get through my breast plate," said Ditto, beaming.

Ash started to look annoyed. "Okay, you can put your shirt down now, Ditto." The large boy sat, but the dumb grin remained on his face. "The Ghost Puma tossed Ditto aside. And just as it was about to pounce on me, Fincher threw a knife from behind a tree and caught the beast in the eye. It shrieked and took off into the shadows."

"For the record, I wasn't *behind* a tree, I was strategically using it for leverage for the throw," clarified Fincher unconvincingly.

"It was a heck of a throw, Fincher," said Ash, her voice full of nothing but appreciation.

Fincher smiled knowingly at his friend. "One in a million shot."

Alicia seemed enthralled by the story. "What happened next? How did you make it back to Crimmish?"

Ash shrugged. "Step by step, I guess. My sister tied a tourniquet around my arm to stifle the bleeding and keep the poison at bay. Fincher bandaged up Ditto best he could. And, slowly, we made our way back. I passed out at one point, so Sammi rigged something to help Ditto and Fincher pull me across the forest floor. Predators could be heard on all three sides, trailing us the entire journey back. It was the most scared I've ever been."

"Farking right," agreed Fincher.

"Yep," added Sammi.

Alicia sat back in her seat. "Well, that certainly is a tale. Thank you, Mistress Ash. I know that was a traumatic event, but remember this. We are defined by the scars that we *do* have, not the ones that we don't. Those without scars are those who haven't lived life, whether those scars reside above or below the surface."

"See, Ditto, no need to hide those gross scars of yours," joked Fincher, trying to bring some levity to the room.

"Shut up, Fincher," said Sammi and Ash in unison.

"What did I say?" demanded Fincher, feigning ignorance.

"Enough!" Alicia's words quieted the children. "I see now what the Sour Flower Gang really represents. Partnership. Love. Dedication. Fearlessness. This is exactly what is needed to bag the Silver Stagg. Are we all fed?" The kids nodded. "Good, then let's begin. Everyone up!"

The children rose. Ditto scooped up the rest of Hana's sandwich that the small girl couldn't finish. Alicia moved down to the far end of the banquet table, where planning materials for the hunt had been laid out.

"Master Fincher, shall you and I start with a general conversation concerning strategy?"

"Why would you ask me?"

Alicia looked confused. "Aren't you the head of this operation?"

"My dear lady, I am the personality, the charm, the—"

"Mouth. He's the mouth," said Ash, but there was no malice in her words, only affection.

"Well, that's simplifying it a bit, Ash. But my one-armed friend here is correct. I am the voice of the Sour Flower Gang, not the farking brain."

"Then, who should I be speaking with?"

"That would be Sammi, our resident genius."

Alicia looked to Sammi. "Really? Is this true, girl? Are you the one responsible for the group's stratagems?"

Sammi looked down and pushed her glasses up at the same time. She spoke to her feet. "I guess I am, Miss Salt."

"Well, now, color me impressed." Alicia took note of the girl's apparent shyness. "It's hard to keep so much brains *and* beauty in such a tight package, isn't it, Mistress Sammi?" The young girl looked up, her bright smile almost taking over her face. "Shall we get to work? Would you like to see what I have so far?"

"Absolutely," said Sammi as she marched toward the far end of the banquet table.

"And Master Ditto?"

"Yes?" stammered the big boy.

"No scars are gross. Some may tease you about them, but women will always flock to a man's scars. Just as men flock to mine." Alicia lifted her shirt above her taut stomach, revealing a jagged purple line running the width of her slim body. "Scars are a physical representation of our past. Never run from them. Or those that judge you for them." She dropped her shirt. "And that doubly goes for you, Mistress Ash."

Alicia turned to face the banquet table and began pointing things out to Sammi.

"Well, that was nice of her," said Hana to Ash, who appeared not to listen. Instead, she was staring at Ditto, who looked ready to collapse under the weight of seeing Alicia Salt's naked navel.

"Yeah. Nice for a forest frump."

～

As Fincher, Ash, Ditto, and Hana played around Salt Compound, Sammi and Alicia worked on a plan to finally bag the elusive Silver Stagg.

"What in the world is this?" asked Alicia, admiring a complex knot that Sammi had tied in one of the many ropes scattered across the banquet table.

"I call that one the Jazz Noose. I named it after how my ma said she ensnared my da with her famous fermented flower crab noodles." Sammi laughed lightly. "Little did he know that it was the only thing she knew how to cook back then."

"It looks overly complicated. How does it differ from any other loop knot?"

Sammi took the rope from Alicia to better demonstrate. "Believe it or not, despite the added crossovers, this knot slips closed with the slightest touch. Even the most timid-stepped animal will cause the noose to close on their paw. Or this case, hoof."

"Why not go with a simpler version?"

"Easy. The one thing these knots are susceptible to is slack. Most intelligent animals, as soon as they feel the rope, will kick up and out like lightning. This usually loosens most strangle knots just enough to free themselves. The Jazz Noose isn't affected by slack. It will not only remain taut, but will actually tighten when the animal tries to kick free."

Alicia's silver eyes seem to shine as she studied the complicated loops. "Tremendous."

Sammi continued. "And here's something even better. Although it looks intricate, the knot is actually much simpler than it appears. This means that it can be effectively created even with the thicker ropes necessary for larger quarry. Take, for instance, the Silver Stagg."

"So, you think one of these… Jazz Nooses, would be best to ensnare the creature?"

Sammi pushed up her glasses as she thought it over. "No. I think *three* Jazz Nooses would be best. You said that the Silver Stagg is smart?"

"I would put its intellect over half the population of Quaan."

"That's not saying much, Miss Salt."

"No, I don't suppose it is, Mistress Sammi. But trust me when I say that it's smart."

Sammi nodded. "I believe you. And I bet it thinks *us* dumb."

"That wouldn't surprise me. I certainly haven't given it any reason to think otherwise."

"Good. We'll use that. I say we place three Jazz Nooses consecutively. One hidden as you might with any other animal. The second hidden even better, as if you were trapping a rare creature. The third Jazz Noose—the one that will catch the Silver Stagg—that is the one that we will conceal as if trying to capture an omniscient god. The Stagg will see the first trap and roll its eyes. It will sense the second and step lightly over it. But it won't see the final ensnarement coming. That will be our chance."

Alicia Salt's too-white teeth began to show. "I love it."

"I can also rig something, a hanging log or set of sharpened limbs, to fall upon the animal, once triggered."

"No."

Sammi's face twisted in confusion. "What do you mean, no?"

"I mean that I want nothing triggered to kill the Silver Stagg. It must be my own arrow, fired from my own longbow and by my own hand, that fells the beast. Father will be watching, and I cannot give him a reason to diminish my accomplishment."

Although the perplexed look remained, Sammi nodded. "Very well. But if the Silver Stagg is as powerful as you say it is, even the thickest rope will only hold it for a short time. We'll need something to entrap it further, or at least slow it without killing it, allowing you to get close enough to fire the finishing blow."

"Do you have any ideas, Mistress Sammi?"

"Maybe. Hand me my pack, please."

Alicia reached over and grasped Sammi's pack from the empty chair on her right. As she passed it along, a dried pouch fell onto the table, it's bottom sewn shut and its top tied with leather bindings.

"What's in here?" asked Alicia.

Sammi quickly snatched the unusual container off the table and returned it to her travel bag. "That's nothing of relevance, Miss Salt." The girl then searched through the contents of her pack before removing a thick notebook. She flipped through several pages before finally landing on a particular sketch. "Here," she said, thrusting the book at Alicia.

The huntress stared at the diagram for a long time, marveling at its sophistication and ingenuity. "It's tremendous, Mistress Sammi, but will it work? Have you tried it?"

Sammi shook her head in the negative. "I've never actually built it. But it works in my mind. And most things that work in my mind work in real life. At least, the mechanical things do."

Alicia couldn't take her eyes from the plans. "How long would it take you to construct this?"

Sammi considered the question. "Depends. I'll need bindings, spools, a variety of straight wooden poles—giant cane bamboo would work well—and a few massive pieces of thick leather."

"I have all of these things. And more."

"Then, I can have it built within two days."

Alicia's silver eyes shot up to regard the bespectacled girl. "Surely, you're joking?"

"No, Miss Salt. I work fast. It's the only way I know how."

Alicia was drawn back to the strange sketch. "How wonderful."

Sammi cleared her throat. "But, Miss Salt, we'll still need a way to drive the Silver Stagg into the trap."

Alicia excitedly handed the notebook back to Sammi. "Ahh, now that's where I come in." She began to collect and organize maps on the table. "There is not one speck of this forest that Rashii and I have not visited, documented, and mapped out. I know where the Silver Stagg likes to forage, where it likes to gather water, and the trails it tends to stick to. Where do you want to begin?"

Sammi looked at the collection of maps as if they were written in the dead language of the Spired Curtain hill tribes. "Uh, that's not really my area, Miss Salt."

"What do you mean?"

"If you want to know about strategically utilizing the topographical makeup of a particular hunting ground, then Ash and Ditto really need to be brought into the conversation."

"So, they're really the brawn to your brains?"

"That's fairly accurate."

Alicia turned to fully face Sammi. "So, if you're the brains, and Ash and Ditto are the brawn, what does that make Fincher? That boy does a lot of talking for not bringing much to the table."

In this case, Sammi didn't need time to offer a retort. "Fincher provides us with sunlight, even during the darkest of times." There was a sharp edge to the girl's words, as if she was challenging the seasoned huntress to disagree with her.

Alicia actually found herself backing up a step from the glare that appeared behind the thick lenses. When what Sammi was really saying had sunk in, Alicia could only offer a small smile to the brilliant youngling.

"Yes, I suppose that it is a valuable addition."

Unsurprisingly, Sammi did not relent. "You have no idea. In a place like Crimmish, someone like Fincher Bugg is worth a thousand stupid Silver Staggs."

Alicia surrendered. "Fair enough. Then perhaps we should bring them all in for the brainstorming."

Sammi pushed her glasses farther up her nose. "Yes, ma'am. I'll go fetch them."

Alicia Salt watched as Sammi exited Salt House. And while she was still roused by the idea of, at long last, achieving her familial dream, there was a twinge of sadness.

Alicia Salt had lived a solitary life for many years, dedicating herself to hunting, trading, and building the Salt legacy—all while proving her father wrong. Alicia Salt needed no one, only the comforting rush of serotonin that came with achievement.

But witnessing the loyalty, commitment, and honest care that emanated from the friendship of the self-proclaimed Sour Flower Gang, Alicia Salt was forced to admit that she felt many voids in her life. And while the Silver Stagg's head hanging over her hearth would certainly fill one of those cavities, it may only serve to better highlight the empty spaces that she had been adept at ignoring these past focused years.

Rashii, Alicia's longtime companion, released a melodic tune from the rafters, reminding her of his presence, as if sensing her loneliness. Alicia looked up and nodded in thanks, although she didn't feel very grateful.

Rashii was smart, perhaps the smartest animal in all of Quaan. But he was still a dumb bird.

And Alicia was beginning to realize what had been sacrificed to maintain the Salt name. She was seeing, for the first time, that the Silver Stagg might not be enough. That she wanted an unconditional friend like Sammi. That she wanted a lover to glance at her the way Ash looked at Ditto. That she may, indeed, want a sweet daughter who very much resembled Hana.

Alicia Salt would use the Sour Flower Gang. She would make sure she got what she wanted from the children of the Stenches. But had to admit that she would also get much more.

And that terrified the otherwise fearless huntress.

The next few hours were spent pouring over forest maps. Some ideas were enthusiastically agreed upon, others were angrily countered. The children quickly discovered that the Silver Stagg was no simple prey. It was intelligent and cunning, with senses heightened well beyond any other creature in Quaan. In some instances, the Silver Stagg could also be quite vicious. It's glimmering antlers, with tips sharper than any Titian pike, not only almost killed Albert Salt, but had claimed the lives of more than twenty hunters over the past one hundred years. Alicia even claimed to have found countless muscle-bear and cave wolf carcasses over the years, many with puncture wounds in their chests, bellies, and sides.

Despite their youth, Alicia had to admit that the Sour Flower Gang were real forest folk. They understood, better than most, the movements of animals along trails, the strategic importance of waterways, and the instinctive reactions of frightened animals.

Given the Silver Stagg's supernatural talent for escaping capture and sniffing out traps, any plan would need to be complex, multi-faceted, and innovative, with several optional endgames, each dictated by the Stagg's decision-making.

Luckily, the children were more than up to the task. They brainstormed and bickered, created and destroyed, started and stopped. When Alicia asked if they wanted to stop for lunch, the younglings waved her away.

"We sometimes go days in the Timbers without eating," said Fincher. "There're more monsters than just Ghost Pumas in there. And many would love a meal of packed lunches and a dessert of human meat."

The unusual alliance worked into the early evening. Just before Tess and Earl were about to bring out supper, everyone stepped back from the banquet table and admired their work.

Gone were the piles of maps and sketches and knotted ropes. Instead, there now rested a single map with a single path highlighted that split, leading to three separate potential destinations. Detailed notes were made at each node containing multiple if-then statements. One unique sketch was placed at each of the three trap points.

"Well," said Alicia to the group, "I think it's pretty farking marvelous. What do you all think?"

"It should work," commented Sammi.

"It *will* work," added Ash.

Fincher stared at the plans and nodded. "Unless the Stagg sprouts wings from her arse and flies away, we'll bag her."

Alicia looked at the boy, a confused look pasted on her handsome face. "Why do you think that the Silver Stagg is a female? Typically, only male staggs are able to grow antlers, Master Fincher."

Fincher's hazel eyes flashed with mischief. "Anything playing this hard to get for this long has to be female, Miss Salt."

Alicia stared hard at the boy for a moment before her hard facade collapsed into a fit of laughter. The other children followed suit.

"Is that what you keep telling yourself, Fincher?" joked Ash between laughs. "That Stella Bugg is *playing* hard to get? Maybe for *you*, she's just hard to get, plain and simple."

"No way," the boy protested. "Did you see the way she looked at me when she saw me off? There was passion in her eyes!"

"Passion alright," continued Ash. "Passion for what you might bring her back from your journey!"

Fincher lifted his small chin in defiance. "Passion is still passion, my dear girl. And it was directed at me, regardless of its source. I can work with that."

Ditto decided to chime in. "But, can you work with that with Reba Bugg breathing down your neck?"

"I'm afraid of a lot of things in this world, my dear Ditto, but Reba Bugg is not on the list." Fincher paused for effect and the group quieted. "It's at the top of it!"

Fincher, Ash, Ditto, and Hana descended into fits of hysterics as Alicia and Sammi smiled widely at the edge of the group. Alicia spun to face Sammi.

"Sunlight, huh?"

"You see it now, Miss Salt?"

"Yes, Mistress Sammi. I farking see it."

Alicia Salt did indeed see the sunlight that Fincher Bugg brought to the world. It illuminated the close friendships that he had, the family he had created in the worst of situations. And it made her own world seem all the more dim.

The next morning, after a hearty breakfast, preparations for the Great Hunt began. Tasks were divvied up among everyone, with even Tess and Earl receiving a few additional duties. Ditto and Ash would collect the needed timber for three complicated traps. Sammi would prepare for the assembly of her creations, using Fincher as her verbose assistant, tying complex knots in ropes of various lengths and thicknesses. Alicia would go out after lunch to prep the landing locations for Sammi's contraptions.

With nothing of note for Hana to do until the Great Hunt, she took it upon herself to wash everyone's travel clothes, politely refusing Tess's offer to help. Alicia didn't hesitate in throwing a few of her own delicates into the pile of laundry before directing the girl. She knelt down beside Hana and took the child's shoulders in her tough hands. There was a particularly warm look in the huntress's eyes.

"You see the stream that kisses the western edge of Salt Compound?" Hana nodded. "Follow it into Shadowset for maybe fifteen minutes. It will eventually cut to the right. As it does, the stream will widen and grow shallow. The bank on the eastern side will begin to run almost even with the clear water. Soft, springy moss will appear, making for the perfect place to rest. The area is surrounded by beautiful flowers as thick streaks of light are able to touch down from above. It's one of the few places in Shadowset to allow this. Gentle animals will appear as if by magic from the shadows to partake of the cool water. There is no better place to wash clothes and relax than here, Hana. I hope you enjoy it as much as I have over the years."

"Will I be safe there?"

"Absolutely. But just in case, I'm sending Rashii along with you. He can sense the slightest disturbance in the forest. If he squawks loudly, and I don't mean his usual sweet notes, just leave the clothes and walk back here. Every creature in Shadowset knows not to step foot near Salt Compound."

"Okay, Miss Salt. I can't wait."

Alicia rose. "Then off you go. When you return, I want to hear your favorite thing about the trip."

Hana flashed a smile. "Oh, I already know what my favorite part will be."

Alicia's head cocked to the side. "And what will that be, pray tell?"

"Being able to do something nice for my friends."

Hana moved to collect the dirty clothing, soap, and washboard she would need to complete her task. As she walked away, Alicia's mouth turned down. At every step, the Sour Flower Gang made Alicia question her life choices. And wonder about things for which she already, deep down, had painful answers.

~

Hana raised her face to the thick canopy above, catching the rays of Paragon that snuck down to kiss her soft cheek. She giggled lightly as tiny tadpoles gathered in the stream to tickle bare feet that she kept submerged in the cool water. Looking around, Hana marveled at the colorful blossoms that dotted both banks and the prismatic insects that traveled from flower to flower, ensuring continuation of the floral portrait.

A melodic tune forced Hana's head up and around, and she glimpsed Rashii through thick branches, watching over the young child while also admiring the view.

Hana tossed a wink at the bird before repositioning herself to kneel on the soft moss at the water's edge. She moved the washboard into place, took the soap in her hand, and dragged the basket of clothes closer. Soon, Hana was lost to the rhythmic sounds of cloth against metal, the gentle hum of water on rock, and the crisp notes of bird chatter.

As she tossed one clean garment aside and collected another, a song began to form within Hana, one she could no longer keep inside.

Closing her eyes, as usual, Hana slowly began to release a soft song inspired by the beauty surrounding her. The enchanting melody carried across the stream. It ran up and down into the relative darkness of Shadowset as if traveling on invisible currents. It climbed high into the tress, floating through forest limbs as if intended for the ears of the Five Sisters.

As Hana's voice grew in strength and volume, Rashii's head bobbed back and forth on his neck before he silently flew off, leaving the girl alone. Other creatures found themselves unable to do the same.

Small fish dared to swim up to the bank, if only to sense a fraction of the music being created in the world of air. The cornucopia of birds nestled in the neighboring trees ceased their own musical endeavors, for they could not compete with the sounds from the tiny human below. Even the work-driven insects halted mid-journey from one blossom to another, stopping on the nearest leaf to hear the powerful sounds echoing through their little slice of forest. Long-eared hares, star-nosed hedgehogs, and redback squirrels, despite being potential meals for countless predators, could not help but shuffle out from the hidden protection of tree hollows, burrows, and root mazes.

Continuing her seductive tune, Hana tossed another cleaned garment aside and opened her almond eyes to find another.

Hana's voice caught in her throat, and her eyes went wide as a glimmering creature had appeared and stood several feet away up the mossy bank. Now, it was Hana's turn to be bewitched as the Silver Stagg stared curiously at the human songbird. Within its white eyes swam flecks of bright silver, and its white coat of fur was peppered with starlight that reflected Paragon's rays in a spectrum of color. Atop its beautiful head sat antlers larger than Hana could have ever imagined. They were clear, as if crafted from pure crystal, and caught the light like the rumored necklaces of Imperatrix Kassidy Rayne that were said to be worth more than most villages.

With the music paused, the Silver Stagg snorted angrily and began to turn away. Hana, desperate to spend more time with the majestic animal, dove back into her song, now putting her full heart and soul into the melody.

The Silver Stagg returned and began to slowly approach Hana, as if its will was no longer its own. As it drew closer, the Stagg lowered its head, careful that its deadly antlers fell to either side of the vulnerable child. Hana, in turn, dropped the clothes in her grasp and held out a small hand.

As Hana reached forward, the Silver Stagg moved to meet her. Soon, her fingertips brushed against the animal's impossibly soft snout. All the creatures in the vicinity looked on, spellbound, as human and Silver Stagg connected for the very first time.

Continuing her melody, Hana locked eyes with the Silver Stagg and gasped, pulling back her hand.

Exiting her body, Hana was drawn into a maelstrom of silver flecks. Through the portal she flew, and, within the Silver Stagg, she saw the miracle of the cosmos as she soared past the Five Sisters and through the unimaginable beauty of gas giants, stopping only to take in the majesty of a spiral galaxy creating and spitting out stars in equal measure.

On Hana traveled, to the very edge of the universe, where a pulsing energy awaited her. It bathed her in euphoric light, washing away fear and putting her troubled young soul at ease. Hana smiled at the energy and, although it had no face, she knew that it smiled in return.

Hana opened her eyes to find herself back at the stream's edge, still facing the Silver Stagg, even though her song had faded. She grinned brightly at the magical animal.

"Thank you," she whispered, wondering how she could ever repay such an experience. "Want some more pets?" Hana put her hand out again, and the Stagg started to lower its head once more. Hana's mouth widened into a giant grin.

Just as Hana was about to make contact with the Silver Stagg, she was forced back as a fountain of blood struck her face and stained her white teeth. Falling onto her backside, Hana quickly wiped the gore from her face to find the Silver Stagg thrashing back and forth, the shaft of an arrow protruding from its left eye.

In sharp contrast to the enchanting notes of Hana, the Silver Stagg's cries sounded like the wails of a thousand dying children. It shook its increasingly blood-covered head, working in vain to free the sharp barb from its brain, its howls cutting into Hana worse than any blade ever could.

Amidst its fit of pain, the Silver Stagg froze for a moment, its remaining white eye fixed solely on Hana Bugg. The silver flecks within spun in a tight circle, forming an iris that aimed its judgmental gaze directly at the young girl.

Just as Hana was about to collapse under the weight of that look, something tore out from the shadowy forest, tearing past in a blur.

Alicia Salt slammed into the Silver Stagg, knocking it over into the shallow water. As she did, Alicia brought a massive hunting knife around and plunged it into the noble animal, drawing out more guttural screams. Over and over again, Alicia ripped into white fur with sharp metal, painting the Stagg and herself in coats of thick crimson.

After nearly a dozen strikes, the Silver Stagg finally ceased its movement and moaning. Alicia lifted herself from the corpse, her hands shaking so violently that she could no longer maintain hold of the hunting knife. The blade fell to the water below, the blood from the metal running off to join the red liquid pouring out from the Stagg's body. The viscous fluid took off on the stream's currents, stretching away to stain the once-clear water.

Once her shaking had subsided, a slice of white appeared within the bloody mask of Alicia Salt's face. After taking in a deep breath, Alicia released a primal scream, sending all of the birds, insects, and critters in attendance scattering.

"I did it," she called out to the forest. "Do you hear me, Father?! I farking did it! Me! Your *daughter* Alicia! I did what the great Albert Salt could not! I have killed the Silver Stagg! I am the Salt to be remembered now! Me!"

After that liberation of emotion, Alicia seemed to return to the scene at hand. She noticed, as if for the first time, the small child shaking on the bank of the stream.

"Hana, you beautiful, beautiful girl. I owe it all to you." Rashii let out a tune from above. Alicia looked up. "I haven't forgotten your role, my dearest friend. You'll get triple the fish this evening. No! Quadruple!" Rashii flapped his wings happily. Alice returned to Hana. She swung a bloody arm to the dead Silver Stagg. "This is your kill as much as mine, Hana. I'll make sure that your contributions are recorded in the many songs that are sure to come. How does it feel to be a part of legend?"

Hana bent over and retched into the stream. Her vomit melded with the blood of the Silver Stagg and floated away, further tainting the glassy waters.

"Yes," said Alicia with a satisfied smirk. "The weight of legend can be a sour pill to swallow. But once you get used to it, it becomes sweeter than candy."

Hana puked once more. This time it wasn't from Alicia Salt's words. It was from the realization of what she had done.

~

"She's stopped crying, but hasn't started talking yet," said Ash as she exited the guest house where Hana continued her self-isolation.

The little girl was inconsolable when she had come out of the woods covered in blood two days ago. As the Sour Flower Gang rushed to help their friend, the story of what had transpired quickly became obvious. Although Hana found herself unable to speak, Alicia Salt entered Salt Compound sometime later, guiding a quite-deceased Silver Stagg down the stream, using the cool water as a conveyance, before pulling her trophy onto land and across the clearing with the help of a large wheeled cart that could tip down level to the ground.

Alicia did not talk as she loaded up the Stagg and pushed the cart toward the Butchery.

"Hunt's over," was all that Alicia said as she passed the four children holding their despondent, gore-covered companion. "In the end, a much simpler plan was all that was needed. A simple plan and a voice that could touch the heart of the Silver Stagg."

"She didn't farking ask to be part of that plan," snapped Fincher, enraged to see Hana so upset.

"We rarely volunteer for life's plans, Master Fincher. Most often, we are rolled into them. A key lesson for you all."

Fincher began to shout back, but the huntress had already passed and seemed to have no intention of turning back or engaging in more banter. Instead, she opened the large doors of the Butchery and pushed her prize inside. When the doors slammed shut, Salt Compound grew quiet, with only the heavy sobs of Hana to be heard.

Even the wind and birds had gone silent, as if mourning a great loss.

Two days later, and still the sounds of Shadowset seemed less than before, as if the volume of the forest had been turned down. As Hana continued to wallow in her solitary anguish, the rest of the children had tried to stay busy, hunting small game and fish and drying the meat for the long voyage north.

Alicia Salt had barely made an appearance over that time. She moved from the Butchery to the Tannery and could be seen stretching and hanging white fur over a small fire late in the night. Ditto and Ash watched as the huntress's shadow played across the orange and red hues of the controlled fire pit, making her seem more witch than woman.

"Forest frump," snickered Ash as she turned to go to bed, leaving only Ditto to watch the nocturnal activities.

Finally, on the evening of the third day, Tess found the children shortly before Paragon started its descent below the Spired Curtains.

"Full supper in Salt House, children. Please be there at the usual time," requested the old woman. She hesitated for a moment. "Will Mistress Hana be joining us?"

"She's doing better," answered Ash. "Not talking but doing better. And she needs to eat. I'll make sure she's there."

Tess looked as if she was going to say something but, in the end, simply nodded before shuffling away.

Just as the housekeeper left, the door to the guest house swung open and Hana slipped out into the early evening. The girl's slim shoulders were hunched, as if she were bearing the weight of the world, and her black-on-yellow eyes stared ahead as if gazing upon a horrific future. Fincher, Ash, Sammi, and Ditto ran to her.

Ditto buried Hana in a massive bearhug as Ash stroked her back and Sammi spoke.

"Good to see you up and around, Hana," said Sammi carefully. "We've all missed you so very much."

"We're not the farking Sour Flower Gang without you," added Fincher brightly.

When Ditto eventually released Hana, Ash knelt down and put her dark hands upon the tiny girl's shoulders. She spoke softly.

"Hana, it wasn't your fault. You didn't do anything wrong. And, anyway, we were all *planning* to do it. It was going to get done with or without you."

"But it didn't," mumbled Hana inaudibly.

"What's that, sweetie?"

"But it didn't get done without me," repeated Hana, this time more loudly.

"But it would have."

"You don't understand." The other children looked to each other.

"What don't we understand, Hana?" asked Ditto.

"I killed something beautiful."

"You didn't kill anything," clarified Sammi.

Hana shook her head defiantly, sending her black hair swinging. "Doesn't matter. I'll be judged just the same."

Sammi pushed up her glasses. "Animals are killed every day, Hana. By humans and by each other."

"This wasn't an animal."

"Sure, it was. It was a—"

"No!" The unusual outburst put Hana's companions on their heels. "You don't understand! I looked in the Silver Stagg's eyes! I saw what was inside!"

Fincher leaned forward. "What was inside, Hana?"

Hana's eyes shot up, and her blacks found Fincher's hazels. For the first time, she was focused.

"The universe. The universe was inside the Silver Stagg."

"How can that farking be?"

"Because it wasn't a Silver Stagg. It was a god. It was a beautiful god of Quaan, and I helped kill it!"

The other children waited for more crying to follow, but none came. It was as if the young girl was arguing that Paragon would come up tomorrow, so convinced of her words she sounded.

Ash discreetly held up a hand for the others to see. "Let's just agree to disagree. It's been days since you've eaten, poor thing. You probably don't know what's up from down. Miss Tess and Mister Earl are serving dinner in Salt House in a bit. Let's get some food in you and a few sweets. Then, maybe you can sing for us around the fire tonight. We all miss your voice more than you can imagine."

"I'm done singing. I'll never do it again."

"Don't say that, Hana."

"It's true."

"Give it some time. You'll come around."

"If you say so."

Ash looked to her friends with concern. Perhaps this event had scarred Hana deeper than they thought. Perhaps it would be a long road back, worrying, since they were already facing a long road ahead.

"I *do* say so. And I've yet to steer you wrong." Ash turned to the others. "Let's wash up in the stream for supper. I don't want to hear Miss Tess comment on my fingernails again."

The others nodded and marched to the closest stream cutting through Salt Compound. As Hana had not been out working or playing during the day, she remained behind. Fincher stayed with her.

"You're scaring them, Hana."

"I don't mean to, Fincher."

"This is no way to start a long journey north."

"Tell me something I don't know."

"Then, maybe you can pretend, even if just for me, that it's not all gloom and doom. We're the Sour Flower Gang, and we need you. We need the *old* you."

Hana paused but nodded in agreement. "I'll try, Fincher."

Fincher's tight face relaxed, and he delivered a brotherly hug that elicited a pained groan. "See! You're sounding farking better already. Take it from me; you fake something long enough, and you'll begin to believe it. Then, it will become fact."

"Okay, Fincher."

"Durned right! Every day that passes, this will be farther behind you, until one day you won't be able to see it anymore. I haven't got there yet with Reba Bugg's smelly, horsey kiss, but, one day, I will be free of that toothsome memory."

Fincher was hoping for fit of laughter from the small girl, which usually followed jokes about Reba Bugg. But none came.

Instead, she said, "It's not the past that I'm worried about, Fincher. It's the future."

"And why's that?"

"Because I'm cursed. I'm cursed, and my end will not be a gentle one."

"I don't believe in curses, Hana."

"Yes, you do. All of us in Crimmish believe in curses."

"Fair enough. But I don't believe in this one."

"You don't have to. Prince Kasstin Rayne didn't believe in Bog Behemoths, but that didn't stop one from swallowing him whole."

Fincher winced but recovered quickly and put an arm around his friend. "Well, I'm quite sure that you aren't going to be swallowed whole, Hana."

"I agree. I don't think I'm going to be that lucky."

The head of the Silver Stagg greeted the Sour Flower Gang as they entered Salt House. Just as Fincher had suspected, it hung over the home's roaring fire, a centerpiece if there ever was one.

Hana's black eyes went wide as she was confronted with her greatest sin. Gone were the god's silver-flecked white eyes. In their place were two black marbles that looked out coldly onto the great room. The crystalline antlers had also changed. No longer were they crystalline, soaking in light to reflect a spectrum of color into the dimness of Quaan. With the Silver Stagg's death, the antlers had gone opaque and were now simply a dull white, looking very much like common bone.

In short, gone was the majesty and godliness of the Silver Stagg. What now sat above the giant hearth looked like nothing more than a run-of-the-mill albino stagg—rare but not special.

Hana took a small amount of comfort in this.

Ash, seeing Hana staring at the newly mounted trophy, whisked her young friend around the banquet table and seated her on the far side where she wouldn't have to look upon the recent tragedy.

As the children took their seats, they noticed the table was covered in a literal potpourri of grilled, roasted, and smoked meats along with several plates of seasoned sickle potatoes and tendersweet carrots.

"Oh no, are we late?" asked Sammi worriedly.

"You are not, Mistress Sammi," said Tess from the corner of the room, where she had been patiently waiting. " Earl and I decided to set the table early this evening. But, I appreciate your concern. Miss Alicia will be joining us shortly. She asked that you go ahead and start without her."

As Tess spun away to reenter the kitchen, Ditto began to dig in as the others stared at the mountains of meat. The large boy put a fair amount of each onto his plate, pausing only at an especially unusual dish. Unlike the other offerings, the lone platter made of crystal-veined black marble sat in stark contrast to the other dishes, holding only a few long pieces of grilled meat.

Ditto cocked his head to the side before grabbing a piece with his thick hand and placing it gently into his mouth. His green-on-yellow eyes closed as the meat literally melted on his tongue. Ditto could feel his pulse quicken and his insides warm as he swallowed. The large boy always felt strong, but, at this moment, he felt as if he could wrangle a fully grown Ghost Puma with his bare hands.

"How is it?" asked Fincher, seeing his friend's slackened face.

"It's the greatest thing I've ever tasted," stated Ditto, his voice heavy with astonishment.

"I want to try some," said Fincher and Ash simultaneously, and both reached toward the black platter.

"Don't," said Hana simply, bringing their hands to a halt. Fincher and Ash stared at Hana mid-reach. The Sour Flower Gang, as a unit, froze.

A voice from the front doors finally broke the spell, sending Fincher and Ash back into their seats.

"Good! I didn't want you to wait for me," said Alicia Salt cheerily as she entered Salt House and took her usual seat at the head of the banquet table. Without hesitation, she filled her goblet from the pitcher of wine next to her and took it down in one massive swig. She repeated the act once more with blue-stained hands and let out a great belch before returning to her guests.

"Forgive me, I've been working *very* hard these past few days."

"I can see that," said Fincher, nodding to the Silver Stagg head directly across from him. "I thought those took weeks to mount."

Alicia offered a small smirk before refilling her goblet again. Instead of drinking, however, she held up her stained hands.

"For anyone else on Quaan, it would have. Father invented a new process for tanning and taxidermy, using proprietary chemicals found only in the plants of Shadowset. Plants that only reside at the intersection of Shadowset and the Spired Curtains, no less. Very difficult to collect and even harder to synthesize. Anyway, it allows me to cut weeks into days, given that I work around the clock. Which I did."

Alicia tossed a wink to Ditto, but the large boy, once smitten by the fit, handsome huntress, stared back blankly in return. Alicia's actions, without being purposely cruel, had hurt one of Ditto's closest friends. The large boy didn't take kindly to that, and it cooled any feelings he might have had for the tough woman.

Ash took note and fought hard to hide her grin.

"Was it worth it?"

Alicia turned to view Fincher curiously. "What was that, Master Fincher?"

"Was it worth it, Miss Salt? All the years that you've spent hunting and worrying and stressing and running from family ghosts? The head's up there now. Was it worth it?"

The question forced the huntress back in her seat, for it was a question that she, too, was struggling with, although she aimed to never show it.

"Of course, it was, Master Fincher," said Alicia defiantly. "I have already sent messenger doves across Quaan, where word will reach the world's greatest hunters, troubadours, and bards. Soon, songs will be written about my achievement, and I will live forever, outliving even the great Albert Salt."

Fincher noticed that although Alicia was speaking to all of the children, her gaze seemed to purposefully skip Hana, who was again staring ahead into the future.

Fincher looked up to the trophy once more. "All of this for a head."

"Nonsense," snapped Alicia Salt. "The head is merely proof of my might. The meat of the Silver Stagg will be dried and sent across Quaan, where I will sell it for a fortune five times the size of what Father accumulated over a lifetime. In fact, some will even be sent to Imperator and Imperatrix Rayne, saving me a ransom in taxes and preventing their sharp eyes from looking too closely upon my comings and goings. Legend *and* fortune! Is that not enough for you, Master Fincher?"

"The meat's *that* special?" asked Ash doubtfully.

Alicia's thin lips broke into a smile. "You tell me, Mistress Ash. I have had some placed upon the table for you all to try. You'll find it in the black onyx dish. Tonight, you all will literally dine like kings!"

The children looked to Hana, who appeared ready to empty her stomach. Luckily, the girl's stomach had nothing in it.

Sammi forcefully elbowed Ditto in the side. The large boy grunted.

"I didn't know," he stammered defensively. "How was I to know?"

"Why do you have to stuff yourself so fast?" shot back Ash in an angry whisper from the other side of the table.

"I. Was. Hungry," was all that Ditto could offer.

Fincher looked around and decided to take charge.

"We appreciate your generosity, Miss Salt. But, in light of recent events, we're going to pass on the offer. One of us didn't care for Silver Stagg blood—not one bit—so the rest of us are also gonna steer clear."

Anger flashed in the icy blue eyes of Alicia Salt. "Very well. I should have known better than to present a once-in-a-lifetime experi-ence to a bunch of Stenchlings. I've obviously lived in the woods too long, Master Fincher, confusing filth for royalty."

Alicia shot up, loudly pushing her chair back. She turned to leave.

"You're not gonna stay for dinner?" asked Fincher, taken aback.

"I found that I've lost my appetite, Master Fincher. That often happens when you discover another's spittle on your face. Good evening to you all."

The furious woman marched toward the stairway leading to her retirement chambers. The Sour Flower Gang shared worried glances before Fincher jumped in again.

"Uh, Miss Salt, about our agreement—"

"Yes, yes, yes," the huntress cut in, stopping at the base of the stairs. "Regardless of you all thinking me terrible and horrible and no good, I'm a woman of my word. And despite you having no purposeful hand in my achievement, I'll keep to our bargain and take you north. We'll leave after lunch tomorrow, if that suits you high-minded children."

Fincher looked around helplessly. "That would be fine, ma'am."

"So happy to hear it! Tess!" The old woman slipped out from the kitchen, wringing her worn hands nervously.

"Here, Miss Alicia."

"Good! Please remove the Silver Stagg meat from the table and have it dried and shipped to Linnscomb. I'm sure the Count and Countess there will appreciate it more than some mud-dwellers. I'll have handwritten notes for each shipment ready by morning."

Tess looked like she wanted to offer a retort, but she was a wily veteran who knew her place and had an impeccable sense of timing. "Of course, Miss Alicia."

"Then, it's settled. Enjoy my food and drink, *esteemed guests*," said Alicia as she trounced up the stairs, not once looking back at the banquet table.

Tess came to collect the Silver Stagg meat, and the children spoke among themselves.

"Fark, you think she's really that upset about the stupid meat?" asked Fincher aloud as Tess reached in to pick up the onyx platter.

"Miss Alicia's upset about a million things, Master Fincher," answered Tess as she collected the platter and held it close to her chest. "But I very much doubt that *this* meat counts among them. Now, you children enjoy the rest of your meal. If you think Miss

Alicia is mad, just wait until I come back and see these plates still full of food."

As Tess spun to leave, all the children save Hana dove in, delighted to be rid of the tainted Silver Stagg meat. Ash took the liberty of placing a heavy helping of vegetables on Hana's plate, avoiding the meats altogether for the traumatized young girl.

Between mouthfuls of food, Ditto looked to Hana and his face fell a bit.

"I'm really sorry, Hana. I didn't know. Honest, I didn't know. I never would have eaten it if I had known. You know me when I get around food. I lose my mind."

Hana raised her eyes and tried to smile at her big friend. "It's okay, Ditto. It's too late, but it's okay. You didn't know."

"Too late for what, Hana?" asked Ditto.

"Everything."

~

Alicia Salt finally came down from her bedroom after breakfast the next morning. There was an evident spring in the huntress's step as she handed Earl a mound of letters for the various lucky recipients of Silver Stagg meat before gliding over to the banquet table. Alicia seemed fifty pounds lighter, as if there was a great weight that she'd somehow managed to leave behind in the sleeping quarters above.

"Good morning, children. I trust that you all had your fill this morning." They all nodded in agreement, save Hana. "Fantastic! We have the first of many long days staring us in the eye, so you'll all need plenty of energy. I want to be away from Salt Compound as soon as the lunch table is cleared, which makes now the time for packing."

"What do you want us to do, Miss Alicia?" asked Sammi.

"Yes! Good! I like the initiative. Let's start with you all grabbing your packs and bringing them here. Let's see what we're working with and what needs to be added to our supplies. We'll need to travel light, but that doesn't mean that we need to go without." The younglings simply stared, shocked by the sudden change in the woman who had been so angry just the night before. "Are you hearing me? Let's go!"

The Sour Flower Gang leapt up from their seats and sprang into action, with even Hana putting aside her trauma for the necessary greater good.

As soon as the children had exited Salt House, Alicia collapsed into her seat at the head of the banquet table, exhausted. The huntress had tossed and turned all night, a deep sense of dread preventing her from any real rest. The little sleep she did have was beset with nightmares.

In her dreams, all of the animals that she had killed over the years chased her naked through a field of flowers, the Silver Stagg leading their charge. And although she had never seen them in person, Alicia knew the white bulbs to be those of Moonflowers.

As Alicia ran, muscle-bears and staggs and winged foxes hot on her heels, thick-bodied vipers struck at her exposed calves as she dashed past, their fangs tearing deep holes in her flesh.

The Sour Flower Gang watched silently from a hillock to the huntress's left, drinking tea from cups that were being constantly refilled by Albert Salt. The old man, never one to smile, grinned ear to ear as he approached each child and carefully emptied the contents of his porcelain, topping off their drinks as quickly as they could consume them.

Alicia, still sprinting for her life, screamed as another Moon Adder sprung out from the undergrowth, this one just barely missing her thick thigh. Her father, turning at the sound, met his daughter's eyes with his own and nodded in encouragement, a small action of support that was unheard of in their past relationship.

Alicia Salt returned her father's nod and redoubled her efforts, slowly putting distance between herself and her pursuers. Soon, there was no Silver Stagg, nor animal attackers, nor striking serpents. There was only Alicia Salt and the Moonflowers, which grew brighter and brighter until—

Alicia woke with a start, panting and covered in sweat, as if she had truly been running for her life. She swung her bare legs over the edge of the bed, smoothed down her wet hair, and wept. But, for once, these were not tears of sadness or regret. They were tears of relief.

For Alicia Salt knew what needed to be done to right the many wrongs of her life, to finally cast aside the specter of Albert Salt.

Alicia Salt needed to take a band of children north, playing a pivotal role in their adventure, assisting their lofty goal of discovering a cure for the Gloomtide.

By healing Quaan, Alicia Salt would heal herself. Or die trying. Either way, she would finally escape the trap which had ensnared her life. Either way, she would no longer have to stare at that portrait of Albert Salt and wonder what could have been.

All children's packs had been laid out on the banquet table. Alicia Salt moved from one to the next, slowly removing and declaring its contents as Earl, sitting off to the side, recorded them in his notebook.

"Where did you get so much smoked meat?" inquired Alicia as she took out bags of dried fish and rabbit from Ash's bag and added it to the jerky she found in Ditto's travel sack.

"We stayed busy while you were tending to your trophy," answered Fincher. "Hunting is much harder around Crimmish, so we wanted to take advantage of your well-stocked surroundings."

Alicia cocked her head to the side. "Didn't trust that I would supply you with enough food for the journey?"

"We don't trust anyone outside of Crimmish, Miss Salt. No offense."

Alicia turned back to the packs. "None taken. Hold tight to that rule and you lot may see your twenties." As she spoke, Alicia began to empty Sammi's pack, which had a variety of small contraptions and bundles of rope and twine alongside her own collection of smoked meat and jerky. "What was this again?" asked Alicia as she removed the balloon-like container that was sewn shut at one end and tied off with leather lashings on the other. The huntress began to undo the bindings.

"No! Don't," shouted Sammi, surprising Alicia enough that the woman dropped the fleshy balloon to the table.

Alicia spun back to Sammi. "What is it?"

Sammi pushed her glasses farther up her nose. "It's a Ghost Puma stomach."

Alicia carefully picked up the organ and brought it closer for inspection. "Really? Fascinating. But why the panic? Is the stomach toxic?"

Sammi replied. "The stomach isn't toxic at all. In fact, once treated and dried, it doesn't even have a smell. And it remains super supple, meaning it will take years before it starts to crack, making it the perfect vessel."

"Then why startle me?"

"It's not the stomach that I'm worried about, Miss Salt. It's what's inside. And I'm not worried about *us*. I'm concerned for *you*."

"What's inside?"

"Reaper Vines."

Alicia immediately tossed the Ghost Puma stomach to the table, looking as if she had just found out that a branch she was holding was actually a venomous snake. She desperately wiped her hands on her breeches.

"Reaper Vines! Why would you pack such a thing, child?!"

Sammi shrugged while Fincher and Ash giggled. "Never know when they'll come in handy, I suppose. Better have them and not need them than the other way around, right?"

"Just keep them far away from me," stated Alicia, her voice shaking a bit as she side-eyed the stomach. "And put a proper knot in those bindings!"

"It is a proper knot, Miss Salt."

"I don't recognize it."

"That's because I invented it." Fincher could be heard laughing in the background.

"Something funny, Master Fincher?" Fincher held up his hands in mock surrender. "Good. Then, let's see what's in your bag, shall we?

Give me a heads up if there's any drawings of naked ladies in there, will you?"

The Sour Flower Gang quickly turned on one of their own, with Ash digging an elbow into Fincher's ribs.

Fincher spoke above the good-natured ribbing. "I'll have you all know that I don't need farking drawings." The boy pointed to his head. "Everything I need to see of Stella Bugg is right up here."

"Stella Bugg? Or Reba Bugg?" asked Hana.

"Yeah, check that bag for hidden compartments," demanded Ash. "I'm sure there's a drawing of Reba Bugg in there somewhere!"

The children roared, and even Hana couldn't help but laugh. Alicia Salt found herself joining in, admitting that she, too, was not immune to the charms of this unique friendship.

"Wrong, wrong, wrong," cried Fincher, working desperately to defend himself. "I have only a small notepad in there, nowhere near the real estate needed for Reba Bugg's horse teeth!"

The Sour Flower Gang exploded, and a series of dull barbs and retorts crossed between the young friends. After Alicia had recovered, she returned to Fincher's travel bag.

"Master Fincher? Why on Quaan would you have so many socks in here?"

The mirth abruptly came to a screeching halt.

7

A GROTESQUE AWAKENING IN THE MUTEWOODS

Sologar Crimm watched as the Imperator Kasspar Rayne stumbled drunkenly around the throne room, snapping at anyone foolish enough to put themselves in the way of his crooked path.

Eventually, after catching himself from falling to the floor several times, the Imperator made his way out to the castle balcony, where he leaned heavily against the stone wall and stared out upon Kassimont with bleary, water-filled eyes.

"He's taking it worse than I could have imagined," commented Crimm from his usual perch next to the Imperatrix, nervously wringing his too-soft hands.

"He's responded to the news with the appropriate amount of distress," the Imperatrix snapped back, her striking blue eyes flashing angrily. "Unfortunately, it appears as though I can't say the same about you, Chancellor."

"We all digest poor tidings in our way, my Lady. I mean, we can't all seek refuge at the bottom of a goblet. Who would that leave to pick up the pieces?"

"As usual, it would leave me, Sologar." Crimm began to form a response but thought better of it and simply nodded his acquiescence. "Let's talk this out."

"Of course, my Lady."

"That young soldier... What was his name again?"

"Second Lieutenant Tobias Vale, my Lady."

"Yes, him. He said that they were beset by Sluggs when attempting to traverse Salt's Pass."

Crimm ran a hand along his perfectly trimmed goatee. "When this is all done, he should be hung for his cowardice. Who abandons his High Captain during a mission of the greatest import?"

Kassidy Rayne shook her head. "No, I believe him when he said he was commanded by Graff to return to Kassimont. Just as I believe that they were facing an overwhelming number of Sluggs. Just as I believe that *your* intel, Chancellor, was incorrect. Wasn't it you who claimed that the Cobalts had failed to make their way south into Shadowset?"

Although Crimm shrugged nonchalantly, his wringing hands betrayed the brave facade. The small man knew that he was traveling on the thinnest of ice. "There *were* reports, of course, my Lady. But is time not of the absolute essence? Is there not a chance that that God-Snails could return to the Rose Comet at any moment?" The Imperatrix was unable to argue the point. "I did what I did for the mission. I did what I did for the Empire. I did what I did for the Imperator. I did what I did for *you*!"

A manicured, heavily jeweled hand went up. "Enough, enough, Sologar. This is not the time for blame and punishment. Although there may be plenty to go around later." Crimm shrank a bit at the veiled threat. "Now, back to what that young soldier said."

Crimm forced his hands to separate, placing them at the side of his chancellor's robes. "He said it was an obvious trap, that the Sluggs were waiting for them."

"What else? What about before the ambush?"

"Let me see... He said that the children were very capable, very determined, and very loyal to each other and their home. He said—"

"*That*," cut in the Imperatrix excitedly. "That will be our hope. Unfortunately, it is all we have."

Crimm's dark green eyes narrowed in confusion. "I don't understand."

"Of course you don't. Which is why my *throne* is placed higher than your *chair*. Let me explain—"

"Explain what," asked the Imperator as he returned from the balcony. Surprisingly, the Imperator's eyes seemed clearer, as if he had discovered something in the city torchlights far below. As if he had found some inner resolve in the momentary solitude.

The Imperatrix and Chancellor simultaneously straightened their silken clothes, as if they had been caught in a compromising position.

"I was just telling the Chancellor that there is still hope," answered Kassidy as the Imperator climbed back onto his throne. Kasspar reached once more for his goblet of wine, which was never allowed to remain empty, but restrained himself, turning his attention fully to his wife.

"And what hope might that be?" inquired Kasspar doubtfully.

Kassidy Rayne steeled herself, putting all the strength she could muster into her words. "The children, my husband."

"Go on."

"The young officer—"

"Second Lieutenant Tobias Vale," jumped in the Chancellor, desperate to add value.

"Thank you, Chancellor," said the Imperatrix coldly before continuing. "Lieutenant Vale stated that the children of Crimmish were most impressive, showcasing commitment and capabilities far exceeding their ages and station."

"And how does this aid our plight," demanded Kasspar, his kingly demeanor far removed from the emotional drunkard he was only minutes before.

The Imperatrix took her time, selecting her words carefully. "Because there is a chance that the children stay the course, determined to complete the mission for their families and friends. After all, we promised them the greatest gift of all, did we not?"

"The Sluggs attacked them!" screamed the Imperator, sending both his wife and the Chancellor backpedaling from the throne.

"They no doubt slaughtered High Captain Graff and all the other Titians—"

"There was no mention of Graff's demise, my Lord," interrupted Crimm foolishly as Kassidy rolled her too-blue eyes.

"You fool!" roared Kasspar. "Do you think Gorman, my most loyal soldier, would ever let himself be taken hostage?! Do you think his pride would allow for such an insult?! Or is your mind too weak to comprehend such heart?!"

"My Lord! I, I, I just meant—"

"Oh, shut up, Sologar," interjected Kassidy, saving the stammering Chancellor. "Of course, you are right, my husband. Please continue."

"Where was I?"

"The slaughter of the High Captain and his entourage."

"Yes, of course," the Imperator went on. "These loathsome Sluggs clearly set this trap to murder our people. Those that embark on a journey of assassination have no morals."

Crimm covered his mouth with a pale hand to hide a smirk. After all, how many times had the Chancellor orchestrated the "accidental" death of a political dissenter, usually under orders from the husband-and-wife duo standing before him.

"What are you saying, my husband?"

"I'm saying that the children are dead, no doubt! Or worse, they are prisoners of the Sluggs and have spilled the proverbial beans, giving the Cobalts the exact location of the Supreme Helices! All is lost! I will be known as the Imperator who was unable to accept the Gift of the Pentad! The Rayne who lost the Empire!"

The Imperatrix and Chancellor exchanged concerned looks. And while Kassidy wanted to dismiss her husband's despondency, deep down she knew that he was right. There was little to hold onto. But the strong-willed woman had topped seemingly insurmountable walls using the tiniest of handholds before. She could do it once more.

"Allow me to offer another scenario, my husband?" Kasspar waved his wife on. "The Sluggs are weak. They have been for years now, since Captain Graff pushed them back into their holes beyond Ptero Heights. Their new leadership is soft, unwilling to stain their hands with the dirty deeds needed to build an empire. There is a reason that they have made little progress. There is a reason that they stagnate and rot in their capital of Merriworth. There is a reason why they have not attacked, even as we bend under the weight of the Gloomtide."

"And that is?" prompted Kasspar.

Kassidy's blue eyes flashed. "They are simply too nice."

The Imperator's brow furrowed as he sat back on his ornate throne. "You're telling me, my dear wife, that my enemies, who just recently butchered my High Captain, are *too nice?*"

"I am, my love."

"Go on."

"Over the years, the Cobalts have made consistently poor strategic decisions to save the lives of both Sluggs and Titians, alike. Theirs is a war of justice, a war dictated by perceived right and wrong. Which is why they will never win. And why we still have a chance."

"Continue."

"It is my belief that the Sluggs got what they wanted in their removal of High Captain Graff from the game board. I'm sure that they dispatched the other Titian soldiers. But I'm equally confident that they let the children of the Stenches go free."

Kasspar Rayne leaned forward. "Why?"

Kassidy shrugged lightly. "Just a hunch. But a strong one. And when have my hunches been proven incorrect?"

The shadow of a smile appeared on Kasspar Rayne's face. "Very rarely, my heart. But wouldn't the children have been forced to reveal their true purpose? What reason could they give for traveling with the High Captain of the Titian Army?"

The Imperatrix thought over her husband's questions for a moment, shooting a nasty glance at the Chancellor when it looked like the dainty man might speak up before her. Finally—"Crimmish is far removed from the rest of Quaan. I doubt that they know much about the Cobalts or their politics. I would assume that they would fear the Sluggs, and this fear would lead to mistrust. This mistrust would ensure the children's silence, at least in regards to their overall mission. It is we, after all, who promised to cure them of the Maddening. Not the Sluggs."

Kasspar rubbed his jaw in thought. "And why were they in the company of the Titian Empire's most powerful officer?"

For once, Kassidy was at a loss. "I regret that I do not know, my husband. But the young officer did mention that the children were exceptionally quick-witted. Perhaps they were able to offer up a believable explanation."

"That's asking a lot from a group of mice from Quaan's gutter, don't you think?"

A lacquered nail tapped against beautiful red lips. "Perhaps. But are not mice amongst the greatest of survivors? They thrive in a world where everything wants to eat them."

The Imperator considered his wife's words. "So, what do you propose?"

Kassidy's chin went high. The impressive woman had been waiting for this question. "I propose that we continue the mission under the following assumptions. First, that the Sluggs simply released the children after claiming their real trophy, which was High Captain Graff. Second, that the children, committed to saving Crimmish from the Maddening, continued their journey after being cut loose by the Cobalts. Third, that the children, given that they are as competent as they are purported to be, will be able to claw their way north, whether via the Spearway or through the Angel Wheat Flats."

"And what would you have me command?"

"Send word to Benson Kruger, who is already leading your northern armies. Let him know that the children will now be alone and could approach anywhere along Crown's Run. Have him set patrols from Woodlow all the way to Cassie's Clutch. When he locates the younglings, we will be back on course with the God-Snails in reach."

"But without the greatest warrior that the Titian Empire has ever known," remarked the Imperator sadly.

"Well, yes. But still..."

Kasspar Rayne slunk in his throne, as if the past few moments of concentration had sapped him of his limited strength. He threw a lazy hand out toward his wife. "I trust in you, my wife. I am without your hope, but my faith in you and your intelligence is enough to keep me going. Dispatch a few trusted riders to deliver the message to Kruger. And let us pray that these children are as impressive—and loyal—as they've been described."

Kassidy and Sologar bowed in unison. "My Imperator!"

As soon as the Imperatrix and Chancellor had moved away from Kasspar Rayne, the Imperator's shoulders sank more as he reached for his goblet of wine.

"Well done, my Lady," whispered Sologar conspiratorially. "I will see that your orders are followed to the tee." He quickly glanced at the Imperator, who was softly sobbing into his wine, and snickered. "You offer him a light in the darkness, and he responds with tears. You are truly the backbone of this Empire, my Lady."

"No more out of you, Sologar. What makes my husband a great leader is that he cares. Too much? Perhaps. But that is why his people love him. He's just lost his best friend, maybe the only true friend he's ever known. It's lonely at the top, Sologar, so you grow to love those very few that you can trust."

Crimm looked dismissively at the grieving king. "But still…"

Now it was Kassidy Rayne's turn to offer a contemptuous look, this one aimed at her Chancellor. "You don't have many friends, do you Sologar?"

The little man feigned insult. "My Imperatrix, I consider you and the Imperator to be the greatest of friends and hope you feel the same."

Kassidy Rayne delivered a wicked laugh that forced the smug advisor's smile to vanish. "Oh, Sologar, you are too much. You are not a friend. You are the pet snake that we keep to clean out the rats, complete with forked tongue and dead eyes. And like any pet, you'd do well to avoid biting the hand that feeds you. Are we understood?"

Sologar Crimm bowed to Kassidy Rayne, bending much lower than he did for the woman's husband. When he rose—"Of course, my Lady. These fangs are yours to use as you see fit."

"Good boy. Now, off you go. There are still pieces for me to collect. And a bruised heart for me to mend as only I can."

Crimm turned to go. As he did, Kassidy watched her husband down another goblet of honey rice wine and slump further.

"Sologar!" The Chancellor paused and turned back to his Imperatrix. "Where is that young officer with the yellow eyes?"

Crimm's mouth turned down. "You mean Tobias Vale?"

"Yes, that's him. Is he still around?"

The Chancellor shifted from one foot to the other. "He is not, my Lady. The Imperator was in no condition to do it, so the young man went to inform Hilly Graff of her husband's fall."

Kassidy nodded disappointedly. "A pity. I would have had him share my bed this evening. I'm afraid that Kasspar will be sleeping on his throne again."

Sologar slid forward like a serpent. "I could offer myself in his stead, my Lady."

The Imperatrix released a cackle that echoed throughout the throne room. "Oh, I'm afraid that won't be possible, Sologar. You see, I don't share myself with dead men."

"A dead man, am I?"

"At the moment? Yes. This plan was yours. The poor intel that drove this plan was yours. If the Gloomtide takes our world, all blame will be yours."

Crimm thought for a moment, looking as if he had eaten something rotten. "But a dead man can be resurrected, can he not?"

Kassidy's blue eyes flashed. "It is rare. But not impossible."

The Chancellor's frown transformed into a naughty smirk. "Then we can chat again? When I am once more in the good graces of the living?"

"Doubtful. But not impossible."

"You're taking us *where*?! That wasn't part of the farking deal," cried

Fincher as he peeked out from Shadowset and into Salt's Pass, eyeing the equally terrifying forest beyond.

Alicia Salt shot back. "Deal? I believe our *deal*, Master Fincher, was for me to guide you all north. We never agreed to a particular path or, come to think of it, even how *far* north I would be taking you. Truth be told, I haven't decided how high into Quaan I'm really willing to go, so you'd best keep yourselves on my good side."

"Yeah, but the farking Mutewoods?!"

"It's safer, Master Fincher."

Fincher nodded toward the dark woods directly across from where the group currently stood. "How's *that* safer?!"

Alicia let out a sigh. She truly hoped that she wouldn't have to explain every decision to these younglings. If so, this was going to be a painful journey, indeed!

"Do you know what lies along the Spearway, Master Fincher? Any of you?" Alicia took their silence for ignorance. "Then, let me educate you. The Spearway extends from Salt's Pass all the way to Cassie's Clutch."

"What's Cassie's Clutch?" asked Ash.

"It's a place to steer far clear of, Mistress Ash. In fact, everyone would do well to avoid that horrid place entirely. But back to the Spearway. That stretch of road is the worst in all of Quaan, home to a steady collection of highwaymen, bandits, slavers, rapists, murderers, and worse."

"Farking heck," whispered Fincher to Ditto. "What could be worse than that list? A farking family of Bog Behemoths?"

If Alicia heard Fincher, she ignored the boy and went on. "Not to mention, I think you witnessed firsthand how far the Cobalts have extended their reach. Do not doubt that the Spearway will also have Slugg and Chestnut eyes on it at all times. And please know that most soldiers are *not* like the sweet-faced Commander Paxxis. My job is to guide you all north, not reach the upper territories with a collection of small bodybags."

"But the Mutewoods?" said Sammi doubtfully.

"And why not?" Alicia's tone revealed that she was losing patience and growing offended. "I think you all forget who you're being led by. I am Alicia Salt, the uncrowned Lady of Shadowset and Quaan's greatest hunter. I have made home with parts of the dark forest that make men shiver. I am a master of the wooded plains and feel more comfortable under leafed canopies than the famed Tusk Whalers do on the Great Untold." The five small faces didn't look convinced. Alicia's hard face softened. "Look, there is nothing in the Mutewoods that I haven't crossed in Shadowset. In fact, Shadowset is far more remote and known to be home to vastly more dangerous creatures. With my bow and sword, and Rashii keeping watch for us—" The Quilted Raven let out a tune from the limbs high above. "—there's absolutely nothing to fear. We'll keep a modest pace and, with luck, will enjoy a quiet jaunt through some beautiful scenery. How does that sound? I can assure you that we'll receive neither quiet nor beauty along the Spearway."

The Sour Flower Gang looked around, as usual exchanging complete ideas in single glances, before nodding to each other and then to Alicia Salt.

"Good. Then let's be off. Enjoy this quick shot of Paragon. Although the Mutewoods are not nearly as dark as Shadowset, we'll still be traveling mainly in shade, something your bodies will appreciate in a few days."

Alicia Salt, with the Sour Flower Gang in tow, stepped out of Shadowset and into the Paragon-filled light of Salt's Pass. With Rashii relishing the brief moment of open air overhead, the children slowly crossed the empty expanse between forests, their small heads swiveling back and forth, expecting soldiers to once again appear as if by magic.

While blades and arrows failed to present themselves, the children were, nonetheless, reminded of a painful memory. Despite the passage of time, blood stains still marked the dirt where Cobalt descended upon Titian, with one particularly darkened patch representing where High Captain Gorman Graff fell.

The younglings stared at the spot as they marched ahead and could almost make out the protective Captain laying there, urging them to finish what they'd started, begging them to save Quaan, even though the world certainly didn't deserve their sacrifice. Their *sacrifices*.

"He's in a better place," said Alicia simply, breaking the spell in which the children found themselves caught. "We should all be so lucky. Come on, now. Double time. I'm enjoying Paragon as much as you, but we're still exposed out here."

In short order, everyone found themselves again surrounded by dimness. This time, however, they were under the cover of the Mutewoods. And while Shadowset was cloaked in mystery, the Mutewoods had a thousand tales told about it, with more being horrific than enchanting, although both kinds were certainly shared in taverns and story houses across Quaan.

Rashii called out from somewhere ahead.

"Sounds like the path forward is clear," stated Alicia as she moved deeper into the forest. "Stay behind me. I know it doesn't appear so, but we're on a natural trail. If we stay on this for a while, we'll no doubt find water and a place to put up for the night."

"How do you know it's clear?" asked the ever-curious Sammi. "How does Rashii tell you?"

"Good question, Mistress Sammi," answered Alicia as she pushed on, slicing through branches and anything else that protruded onto the small trail. "And something you all should probably know. One squawk from Rashii means that the way ahead is clear. Two squawks means that there is danger, but nothing I can't handle. I can discreetly check out the situation and decide whether I want to engage or simply avoid the situation altogether."

"And three squawks?" asked Ditto.

Alicia stopped and turned to face the children. "Three squawks from Rashii means that there is imminent danger all around us. That there is no choice but to ready our weapons and fight."

The weight of the huntress's words brought an extended silence that only Fincher could eventually shatter.

"Have you ever heard three squawks, Miss Salt?"

"Twice, Master Fincher. And I have the ugly scars to prove it. It is a sound I hope to never hear again." Alicia said no more, spinning back to resume her chopping and advancing, leaving the children speech-less. Well, almost speechless.

"Farking heck!"

~

The following three days and subsequent evenings were uneventful in the most beautiful and enjoyable way. Paragons were spent with Alicia Salt plowing ahead through the Mutewoods, showing the Sour Flower Gang how to read trails, identify sounds of the forest, and locate edible berries and root vegetables. And although the children were already fine hunters, Alicia educated them on more advanced trap-ping and bow hunting techniques. Her lessons paid off quickly, with Ditto using her wondrous bow to fell a fat king quail mid-flight as it soared across the trail high in the canopy above.

As Paragon fell, Alicia Salt introduced alternative shelters that could be tossed up and taken down within a score of minutes. She also demonstrated different methods of cooking meat, especially the forest fowl that was proving so abundant in the Mutewoods.

At night, with the apparently always-alert Rashii perched high above, only one person was needed to take watch. Alicia always took the first watch, sleeping only for a few hours before relieving Fincher or Ash or Ditto.

The children slept well. They ate well. They were learning valuable skills. Nothing they couldn't handle sprang from the wooded dark-ness to rip soft flesh from hard bone. Things were going well, alarm-ingly well for residents of the Stenches. And then…

"This way," said Ash, but it sounded more question than statement.

"Are you asking me or telling me, Mistress Ash?" demanded the huntress.

Ash thought for a moment before nodding her head determinedly. "I'm telling you. *This* way."

Alicia smiled brightly. She was starting to do that more and more as the younglings started applying what they learned from the woman's many unending lessons.

"Then, by all means, lead the way."

Ash turned to her left and advanced, slicing random vegetation that laid in her path as she did. Alicia, who had begun allowing others to sniff out the barely detectable trails, followed along with the others.

Ash hadn't gone ten steps, however, when she jumped, almost dropping her blade, as a great cracking sound exploded from somewhere above the forest canopy and shook the ground on which they walked. Everyone looked up reflexively, and even Rashii seemed startled, the Quilted Raven descending quickly to draw closer to Alicia.

In seconds, another booming sound echoed throughout the forest, and the dim surroundings grew dimmer still. A chilly breeze joined the once-pleasant air, and the thick limbs above the Sour Flower Gang began to sway and moan, slightly at first but increasing by the moment.

When the initial shock wore off, the children as one spun to face their guide.

Alicia did not meet their concerned looks, instead sweeping her gaze up, looking into the spaces between the natural awning to spy the weather above. When she finally lowered her unusual silver eyes, there was something there that the children noted. It was less than worry, but greater than minor concern.

"It's going to rain." Alicia corrected herself. "It's going to rain a shite load. We need to move. Fast."

Alicia exploded into action, moving off from the trail to the right, where the ground slowly seemed to rise. After several minutes, the huntress found what she was looking for, an impossibly massive tree with a trunk that would take twelve grown men holding hands to encompass it. Thick roots emerged from the ground in places, offering shoulder-height "walls" of protection in certain areas.

"This is it," Alicia said excitedly as she rushed to the tree. Above, the drumming of water on leaf could be heard, the storm having commenced. Alicia ran her hand along the tree's rough bark. "This is a Monarch Brown, found throughout the Mutewoods. We're lucky one was so close. This will make a fine place to hole up." She spun to the children. "We have to act quickly. The canopy will keep the rain at bay for a while. But when those leaves eventually fill, a literal waterfall will be dumped on our heads, bringing all kinds of nastiness with it. Do you understand?"

"We do," the children answered as one.

"Good. Ditto, you go and chop down eight—no, make it ten—thick branches about *yay* thick."

"How long do you want them?" asked the large boy.

"Good question. Six my height and six Hana's height. Here, take my axe and off with you!" Alicia tossed her axe to Ditto, who caught it deftly before disappearing into the forest. "Ash, follow Ditto and drag those branches back here as he cuts them and looks for more." Ash nodded and ran to follow Ditto. "Fincher, I'll need many more thinner branches of the same length. Lots of them. And if you find any good low-hanging limbs with thick pines on them, bring those, too." Fincher offered a salute and took off as the first drops of rain began to penetrate the forest and find their way to the ground. "My sweet Hana, I heard the unmistakable sounds of a stream coming from *that* direction. Please go there and collect as much clay moss as you can fit in your bag—just dump its contents out here. Rashii will accompany you to make sure you find both the stream and your way back. Can you do this?"

Despite Hana's refusal to speak with Alicia Salt, the young girl was a product of Crimmish, where things that needed to be done were taken care of, regardless of personal feelings, relationships, or grudges. Only survival mattered at the end of the day.

"Yes, Miss Salt."

"Then off with you. You'll need to make several trips." Alicia delivered a series of whistles into the air, and Rashii squawked once in response. "Rashii is with you."

Once Hana had dumped her travel sack and sprinted out of sight, another small voice cut through the fast-deafening sounds of heavy rain.

"What about me, Miss Salt?"

Silver eyes found brown-on-yellow. "Sammi, my dear, you'll play the most important part." Alicia ran her foot back and forth to clear the leaf litter before kneeling in the newly revealed dirt. "Join me, please."

Sammi slid in next to the huntress and watched as the Lady of Shadowset drew designs into the soft ground, nodding her understanding as she did.

"Well, what do you think?" Sammi studied the drawing. "Mistress Sammi, this looks to be the storm of the season. You need to tell me if you see any area for improvement!"

Sammi was startled by both Alicia's urgency and her insistence on the young girl's opinion. She pushed her glasses up as she thought. "What are the chances of the Monarch Brown catching fire?"

"From our little campfire? Impossible. Not only is the Monarch's bark thick and hard, but it will soon be wet as rainwater runs down it. Why?"

"In that case, I would keep an opening between the Monarch and the covering, allowing for smoke to run up and out. So close to the tree, most of the water will run along the trunk and won't find the opening."

Alicia stood. "A fine alteration. We'll make it so." The silver-eyed woman grabbed one of her two bags and dumped its contents, revealing a collection of thin, tough rope. "As the others bring back the wood we need, you sharpen the ends and give them to me. I'll pound the major poles into the ground, position the others, and then you'll bound them together with one of those fantastic knots of yours."

"You got it, Miss Salt."

"Good." Alicia spun to leave.

"Where are you going?" asked Sammi. "No one's brought anything back yet."

The huntress unsheathed her sword as she spoke. "I have to go pray before the Monarch Brown and ask its forgiveness for what's about to happen."

Sammi's brow furrowed in confusion above her round glasses. "What's about to happen?"

Alicia hefted the large sword. "I'm about to carve two deep fissures into one of the oldest trees in Quaan. I've destroyed enough natural beauty over the years, as Mistress Hana will be sure to point out. It's time to start asking permission first. Or at least apologizing ahead of time."

"Do you think it really matters, Miss Salt?"

"Maybe not. But I think it matters that I'm trying to be better."

Alicia turned back to the Monarch Brown and knelt at its base in prayer.

"Fair enough, Miss Salt," said Sammi Bugg. "It's never too later to turn things around. If not, what the heck are we all doing out here?"

Sammi may as well have been talking to herself, for the pounding of rain swallowed the young girl's words.

Oceans of water fell upon the Mutewoods that night and continued through the following Paragon. New rivulets began to run throughout the forest, breaking free from swollen creeks, streams, and lakes. Thunder consistently shook the drenched ground, and the sharp crack of trees could be heard sometime later from where lightning had touched down and weakened ancient wood. Critters of all shapes and sizes tore across the brush, desperate to seek safety, wherever possible.

The Sour Flower Gang and their guide Alicia Salt, however, remained fairly comfortable, tucked beneath their makeshift shelter that was topped with clay moss, then pines, then flowery leaves. High up as they were against the Monarch Brown, nestled between massive roots that sprang from the ground to either side, rainwater simply rushed around them, touching neither fire nor bedroll nor pack.

Most of the smoke from the campfire escaped through the small gap between the shelter roof and the trunk of the Monarch Brown. Even better, it drifted up to spread across the menagerie of life that was waiting out the storm in the broad limbs of the massive tree. Every few minutes, a thud could be heard, denoting that something small had fallen onto the shelter roof. When Ditto went to investigate, he reported that all manner of frogs, lizards, and insects were dropping down from above, shocked by the smoke.

This made for a literal smorgasbord for Rashii, who hopped across broad-leafed branches, devouring the tastiest looking organisms. When he had his fill, Rashii started collecting the frogs and lizards, holding two and three at a time in his mouth as he flew into the shelter and gently deposited his gift before Alicia. He would then release a musical note and exit to capture more—or eat again.

Alicia, delighted to dine on fresh meat and save their jerky for more dire circumstances, immediately went to work, cleanly chopping off the heads of the reptiles and amphibians before skewering them on sharpened sticks and laying them over the fire to cook. The huntress was even more delighted when all the children joined in, reminding her, yet again, that these were not typical younglings. These kids were made of much sterner stuff.

All during the rainstorm, the Sour Flower Gang laughed and joked, taking advantage of every opportunity to deliver some good-natured teasing, especially to Fincher, who seemed everyone's favorite target.

Alicia couldn't help but giggle as she listened. And she couldn't believe that this Reba Bugg's teeth could possibly be as large as they were rumored to be. It simply wasn't conceivable.

When they weren't clowning, the children were eating or taking turns sleeping, one always resting their head in the lap of another who was keeping watch. The huntress watched as Ash laid down on Ditto but only pretended to rest. The small smile that refused the leave the girl's lips was a dead giveaway. Alicia eventually tore her silver eyes from the pair, for something about their quiet closeness stirred long-buried feelings in the Lady of Shadowset.

As Paragon drew to a close, the torrential downpour transitioned into a steady rain, void of thunder and lightning.

Ditto fed the fire once more in preparation for night, using much of the remaining wood that was collected before the worst of the storm and kept relatively dry under the shelter. As he did, Fincher stared out into the darkening forest, looking on as thick ropes of rainwater fell from cupped leaves high above.

"You ever seen a storm like this, Miss Salt? That lasted this long, I mean?"

Alicia thought for a moment. "No, I don't think I have, Master Fincher. I mean, storms this strong hit Shadowset all the time, but they usually pass within a few hours, at the most. By the time they reach us, the fronts have usually smashed against the Spired Curtains, dumping most of their liquid into the mountains that feed the rivers that, in turn, feed Quaan. But *this* violent for *this* long? Can't say that I recall. Maybe when I was a girl, but that was so long ago…"

"Ahh, that's donkey shite," said Fincher. "You're not that old."

"And how would you know?"

"I got a ma and da, don't I?" An uncomfortable tension fell over the group. Fincher, however, worked quickly to dispel it. "What I mean is that you're still a pretty woman. Prettier than any in Crimmish, to be sure."

"Thanks, Master Fincher," said Alicia, but there was little appreciation in her tone for being compared to contemporaries in the harshest territory in all the land.

"I know that Ditto thinks so," offered Sammi Bugg as she grinned devilishly, having delivered the perfect barb at the perfect time. For her efforts, she received a frown from Ditto and a hard punch from her older sister.

Ash smiled triumphantly as Sammi groaned, rubbing her throbbing shoulder. "Fincher's an idiot, but he's right, you know. I saw how Commander Paxxis's men, and even some of the women, looked at you. There was more than respect in their eyes." The next words pained Ash, but she spoke them anyway. "You're quite striking."

Alicia seemed genuinely surprised. "Really? I thought everyone simply feared one of my arrows through their chests."

"I wouldn't farking discount that, too," offered Fincher and was promptly hushed by Sammi.

"It's not that," asserted Ash, shooting Fincher a look before returning to their guide. "Brains and brawn along with beauty can have that effect on people."

Alicia Salt averted her silver eyes, obviously uncomfortable. "I appreciate that, Mistress Ash, but I don't feel beautiful."

Ash considered the huntress's words. "Well, have you done anything lately to feel beautiful?"

"What do you mean *done anything*? Like what?"

"Like this," replied Ash, pointing to her tightly braided hair. "Whenever my sister or I are feeling bad—ugly even…" Ash's brown-on-yellow eyes flashed quickly toward Ditto before she continued. "…we do each other's hair. Or our ma does it for us."

"Yeah, Jazz Bugg is the best in Crimmish," added Fincher absently between bites of an especially large barbecued frog.

"My hair," pondered Alicia aloud. "I've never done anything but pull it back."

"You made it that wonderful silver to match your eyes," stated Sammi.

Alicia laughed hollowly. "My eyes aren't naturally silver, Mistress Sammi. And I'll let you in on a little secret. Most of my silver hair actually *is*."

Sammi pressed on. "Regardless, it's stunning. You should do something with it. And not for potential suitors. For yourself."

"Maybe…"

Ash met her sister's eyes, and they nodded in unison. "Not maybe. Now."

The sisters sprang into action, digging through their respective packs to retrieve brushes, combs, and clips. Overriding the huntress's weak protests, Ash and Sammi began to brush and comb silver hair, parting it in some places and clipping it in others.

After a while, Alicia Salt stopped her feigned disinterest, closing her eyes and relishing in the feeling of hands on her head. Alicia's mother had died during childbirth, something her father had never let her forget, and the closest Albert Salt had ever gotten to brushing his daughter's hair was when he threw delousing powder on her after terra lice were found on the girl's favorite pet.

With a crackling fire and gentle rain serving as the perfect auditory backdrop, Alicia Salt simply smiled and let the Bugg Sisters express affection in a way that only females could.

Easing into the feel of human connection, Alicia finally opened her eyes, looking on as Ditto sharpened blades and Fincher applied a salve to some fairly recent scars on his friend's arms. Once complete, Fincher returned to his cooking duties, lancing a tree frog and two crested geckos before placing the meat sticks above the fire on a makeshift skewer rack.

"That's not too tight, is it?" asked Ash from behind.

"Not at all, Mistress Ash. But, thank you for asking."

Alicia continued to take in the scene, reminding herself to never forget this moment, this brief time in her life when she felt part of something larger, something more important than the Salt legacy.

Rashii stole Alicia from her musings as the Quilted Raven returned, placed something gingerly on the ground, and squawked twice before exiting as quickly as he had appeared. Alicia's silver eyes went wide as a small black salamander with webbed toes and a long, rounded tail scampered across the ground before being scooped up by Fincher.

"I think we can fit this one on the skewer. The others haven't been cooking too long."

"Master Fincher! No!"

Fincher froze, as did Ditto and Hana, and the two sets of hands working furiously behind the huntress. Alicia embarrassedly cleared her throat.

"I'm sorry, but you can't eat that. What you have in your hand is a Trigon Newt, a very rare creature, indeed. They are usually found in water, but the forest flooding must have swept it away from its natural habitat."

Fincher studied the salamander in his hand. 'What's so special about it?"

"It's the most poisonous creature in all of Quaan."

"Farking heck," exclaimed Fincher, dropping the Trigon Newt to the dirt before shaking his hand in the air. "Am I gonna die now?!"

Alicia couldn't help but laugh. "Not at all. Unless you had pierced it with that stick of yours. It's their blood that's poisonous, not their skin or saliva or excrement."

"Good to know," said Fincher sourly, wiping his hand vigorously on his pants. "And better to know before I farking picked it up."

Alicia laughed again. "Your hunger proved faster than my voice, Master Fincher." At that, more laughter filled the air from behind the huntress as hands got back to work on silver hair.

"How do you know it's a Trigon Newt?" asked Hana, the young girl leaning forward to watch the small amphibian as it darted back and forth, unsure of its path.

"See the red triangle atop its black head?" Hana nodded. "Trigon Newt."

"With that kind of toxicity, shouldn't it have a more ominous name," complained Fincher, now rubbing his hand along the dirt ground.

"It used to be known as the Death Newt, Master Fincher. Is that better?"

"It farking is! It should still be called that. The old timers knew best how to name something. If a critter's gonna kill you, let it be known in the farking name!"

Alicia waved Fincher away. "Anyway, like I said, the poison is in the blood—a last resort, if you will. In the olden times, they were captured by the thousands, maybe tens of thousands. The newts were cut open and their blood was spread onto spear tips, arrow heads, and blade edges. Very effective. Too effective. That's why there are so very few today."

Hana's black-on-yellow eyes remained on the undeniably cute Trigon Newt. "So, it can't hurt me?"

"It cannot, Mistress Hana."

"Can I keep it?"

"Can you make sure that nothing cuts into it or squishes it?"

"Sure, I can. I have the perfect front pocket for it. And I'll line it with extra cloth. And maybe even make a bed out of soft moss."

"Are you farking kidding me? A farking *Death Newt?*"

Ditto discreetly motioned his boisterous friend to shut up, understanding that this was a way for Alicia Salt to start making things right with Hana Bugg.

Alicia ignored Fincher's outburst. "Then, he is yours, Mistress Hana. Keep him safe and away from your skin if there is even a chance that he may be cut."

"Thank you," squealed the young girl as she gently scooped up the Trigon Newt. "I will call you Triggy. Don't worry, Triggy, I'm going to take good care of you."

Hana placed the Trigon Newt into her front shirt pocket. Triggy spun around a bit before settling in and poking his head out over the top. Ditto chuckled before collecting a dead birch fly from the ground and handing it to Hana. The young girl held it out to her new friend, who snatched up the snack with an impossibly long tongue for one its size. Hana giggled with delight.

"He likes me! And he really likes his new home!"

Alicia smiled warmly. "Of course, he does."

Ash's voice broke out from behind the Lady of Shadowset. "But, does Miss Salt like her new hair?"

Alicia picked up her sword, pulled it free from its scabbard, and looked upon her reflection in the shiny metal. Her breath caught as a woman of great allure stared back at her. A massive braid ran over the top of her head with two smaller braids to each side. They all joined at the back in the most beautiful pattern which now hung over the huntress's right shoulder.

"Well, what do you think?" repeated Sammi.

"I think I've never felt so pretty. Nor so lucky. Thank you both."

Later, after yet another meal of tree meat, the children laid in their bedrolls and listened joyfully as Hana spoke in length to her new friend Triggy. Although Hana still refused to sing, hearing their young friend's happy voice again was music enough to the Sour Flower Gang's ears.

Soon enough, everyone was fast asleep under the shelter and its protection from the now-drizzling rain. Everyone save Alicia Salt, who decided to keep watch the entire night, allowing the children to save their energies for Paragon's march through the Mutewoods.

As Alicia watched the children rest, a strange thought entered, unwelcome and impossible to ignore. Alicia Salt had been on many great adventures, had lived the lives of any ten men and twenty women. She had explored every inch of Shadowset and had gone deeper into the Spired Curtains than anyone alive. She had hunted and killed Quaan's mightiest animals save the Ghost Puma and Bog Behemoth. She was the only human to ever bag the magical Silver Stagg. She was the daughter of the famous Albert Salt and was known throughout the land as the Lady of Shadowset, second only to Kassimont royalty.

These things were facts. And yet, when Alicia Salt looked back at her decades of achievement and experience, one truth became painfully clear.

She had never been more content, more at ease with herself, more happy than being stuck in the rain these past days with the Sour Flower Gang.

Her mind began to race with possibility. Perhaps they didn't have to return to the unavoidable death that was Crimmish. Perhaps they would be open to living in another woods, one free of Reaper Vines and Moon Adders. Perhaps they would like their own beds in a guest house all their own. Perhaps Salt Compound was the perfect place for five children to grow up safe and healthy. Perhaps a long shot dream could be made real.

Perhaps there was still hope for Alicia Salt.

"What a farking mess."

Ditto nodded in agreement. "It's more ocean than forest. Have you ever seen anything like this, Miss Salt?"

Alicia Salt did not immediately answer Ditto's question. Instead, she swung her silver eyes back and forth, surveying the scene before her. Finally, she responded.

"Seen it? Yes, a few times in my life. I can count them on one hand. They are called vernal pools. Tried to journey through one? Never."

Ahead of the group, it appeared as if the Mutewoods sprouted from a massive lake that extended in all directions as far as the eye could see. Still water sat heavy on the saturated ground.

"Should we wait it out?" asked Ash.

"Yeah, it could dry up in a day or two," said Sammi.

Alicia was shaking her head before the girl finished her sentence. "While not Shadowset, the Mutewoods are also a land of shadows. With that much water and minimal Paragon poking through, this watery wasteland won't go away for weeks."

Triggy popped its head out from Hana's shirt pocket. She rubbed its head before speaking. "Can we go around?"

Alicia looked left and right. "We could, Mistress Hana, but I'm not sure how far this vernal pool extends. We could lose several days trying to bypass it."

"Days we don't farking have."

"Is Terminus Grove going somewhere, Master Fincher?"

All eyes went to Fincher as the boy stumbled for a believable reason for the rush. Luckily, Alicia saved him from offering a half-baked lie.

"Never mind. I don't want to be in this forest any longer than I have to. They may seem the same to you all, but this forest is a far cry from my lovely Shadowset. I know these woods, but just as a passing acquaintance. We are not friends, and I do not doubt that she will stab me in the back the first chance she gets. We will go through."

"We're gonna get soaked," complained Sammi.

"Not necessarily. Look." Alicia pointed to a network of long, winding trails of forest floor that jutted up from the dark water. "Those high points are where rivulets run through the Mutewoods during typical rains, depositing loose dirt and soil to either side. If we stay atop those, with any luck we'll stay fairly dry and get through this swamp before Paragon falls."

"Looks farking sketchy," commented Fincher.

"Or we could hole up and wait for the water to evaporate. Best case scenario, we'll be back on the move in a week. What do you think, Master Fincher?"

Fincher stared out across the foreboding vernal pool and sighed deeply. "Let's farking go."

～

Rashii flew from limb to limb overhead, letting out single squawks to declare the path ahead clear of danger. As the Quilted Raven did, Alicia Salt and the Sour Flower Gang walked single-file along the loose ground that rose up above the swampy vernal pool.

Although there were occasions where the group had to leap from one high pathway to the next, invariably submerging a foot in the process, for the most part, it appeared that the huntress's gamble was paying off. They were making good progress and remaining generally dry. Looking into the distance, the network of dry paths seemed to continue without interruption.

As Paragon ascended to its height, rays of light increased in strength and number, warming the cool air and raising spirits.

A few hours later, water slowly started to give way to dry land, in some places allowing the children to walk two abreast.

"Tell me about Crimmish," said Alicia as she marched forward at the head of the line. "I've never been closer than Salvation Outpost, which I found to be a rotten little town full of rotten little people."

The children hesitated in responding, the divided feelings about their home evident. Unsurprisingly, it was Fincher who ultimately answered.

"It's the best collection of people in all of Quaan. But the location could be farking better."

The children giggled, and even Alicia found herself laughing at the precocious boy.

"Then, tell me, Master Fincher, what—"

The Quilted Raven cut in loudly overhead. One squawk followed by another. And then a third.

Alicia's longbow appeared in her hands as if by magic, an arrow already notched. Her silver eyes shot back and forth and her braided silver hair swung to and fro as her head swiveled on her neck.

"No, no, no," she recited but was only met with silence.

The Sour Flower Gang followed the huntress's lead, drawing their weapons and holding them at the ready. Everyone froze in place.

"Maybe Rashii is wrong," offered Sammi weakly.

"He's never wrong," snapped Alicia. "He's either early or late."

"Well, which farking is it?"

Alicia remained silent as she studied the trees and the canopy overhead. But the harder she looked, the less she saw.

"There," cried Hana, thrusting her small dagger down at the water to the group's left.

Bubbles could be seen rising to the surface of the once-placid vernal pool. They began small, like the head on freshly poured mead, before transforming into massive spheres that exploded on the surface.

"We need to farking go!"

"Too late," stated Alicia simply as the Quilted Raven cried out desperately in threes.

All around the group, the water churned, as if the ground itself was releasing great exhalations. And then it stopped.

"Something's moving under the water," whispered Ash to Ditto. The large boy nodded, confirming what everyone else was also seeing —large waves running across the opaque surface. Still, there remained nothing to see. Until—

"What. The. Fark?"

In the near distance, something finally broke free from the water and began to slowly rise from the swamp. Brown and green, slimy and decaying, it looked like a thick root reaching for the heavens. Three feet became six, which soon became nine. As the first root finally stopped, others rose to join it, appearing on all sides of the younglings. Soon, the group was surrounded by a garden of rotten-ness, a grotesque stench filling the air.

Alicia spoke under her breath. "Everyone be quiet. Start to shuffle forward. Whatever you do—"

Hana's piercing scream filled the Mutewoods as giant all-white eyes popped open on each of the gently swaying roots. Then, the creatures' true forms began to take shape.

Gangly arms separated from slimy bodies. They swung through the air with too-long fingers tipped with blade-like nails. Giant, elongated, pointed heads lifted from dripping chests, oversized white eyes wide over gaping mouths filled with jagged, pointed teeth. Loud, ear-splitting shrieks sprang from cavernous maws that looked as if they could swallow half of Ditto in one bite.

"Hungeee," cried one monster in the distance.

"Hungeee!"

"Hungeee!"

"Hungeee!"

Alicia Salt let loose with her longbow, sending an arrow directly between the ovular white eyes of the nearest swamp creature. The arrow passed neatly through the brown head, and a fluorescent yellow ooze poured forth from the hole and dripped into the open mouth and down along the impossibly long chin.

The monster wavered back and forth for a moment before collapsing forward. But instead of disappearing into the muck, it slammed its long arms into the water and began hand-walking toward the group.

"Hungeee," screeched the horrors as one as they all dropped to their hands and began frantically advancing on their prey.

"Father, help me," Alicia said to herself before calling out to the Sour Flower Gang. "Children! Run! Run for all you're worth!"

"That's what I farking said!"

Alicia launched several more arrows as the children passed her on the winding path, Ditto taking up the lead. Seeing her bolts having little effect, she slung the longbow back over her shoulder and unsheathed her shortsword just as a fiend reached the group and thrust its twisted hand toward Hana.

Alicia's blade swept down, removing the creature's arm at the elbow. It screamed in defiance, but Alicia's next swing removed the bottom half of its too-long jaw. A river of bright yellow gore flowed from the wounded monster, which was soon pounced upon by its disgusting kin, who stopped momentarily to rip their brethren apart, shoveling pieces of arm and head and chest into their eager mouths.

"Hungeee!"

Ditto pushed forward, snapping pointy elbows with well-placed kicks, removing long fingers with slicing strikes, and exploding white eyeballs with accurate thrusts.

Sammi followed closely behind Ditto, her older sister and Hana close on her heels. Fincher and Alicia brought up the rear, the huntress taking one side while the Crimmish boy defended the other.

Despite their size, strength, and terrifying appearance, the monsters were clumsy like newborn fawns, unable to get their heads and bodies to work in unison. Driven by an all-encompassing hunger, the devils attacked sloppily, ignoring their size, strength, and numerical advantages.

Had they been a bit more organized, a tad more thoughtful, a smidge more skillful, the sextet of humans would have been dead in minutes.

Still, damage was done. Ditto yowled in pain as a filthy nail raked across his face. Ash winced as a giant hand grabbed tripped her up, tweaking her knee. And Fincher cried out as the tip of his left pinky finger was bitten off by a snapping, dripping mouth.

Still the group slowly progressed ahead. Ditto called out from the front.

"There's an island of dry land to my right!"

"Make for it," responded Alicia as she tore through the throat of an advancing root monster. "We can't keep fighting like this!"

Ditto was joined by Ash, and they redoubled their efforts, cutting a swath through the raging swamp fiends. Within a few chaotic minutes, all of the Sour Flower Gang and Alicia Salt had reached the island, the center of which was dominated by a typically massive Monarch Brown.

As the group huddled together, weapons facing outward, Sammi backed away and dug through her bag. In a few beats, she had soaked an extra garment in an oily compound that she carried, wrapped it around the end of a thick branch, and lit it using some stone and flint.

"Here," Sammi shouted, giving the torch to Alicia. The huntress swung the fire back and forth, forcing several of the dripping monstrosities to back away.

"This won't last long," lamented the silver-haired woman.

"Then, what do we farking do?!"

"I don't know, Master Fincher! Just keep fighting!"

"Hungeee!"

"Hungeee!"

"They're going around!"

"They're gonna surround us!"

"There're more coming!"

As the horrific scene unfolded, Hana began to back away, her feet soon hitting the thick roots of the Monarch Brown. Her black eyes and young mind searched desperately for an escape but found none. Just as hopelessness took hold, an unfamiliar voice reached Hana.

"In trouble you are, you are, I'd say."

Startled, Hana looked down to find a boy squatting between the large roots of the giant tree.

Hana dropped to her knees. The boy looked to be around Ditto's age, although that's where the similarities ended. A bowl of snowy white hair sat upon a too-pale face. The boy was skeletal, wearing dirty clothes that looked three sizes too large. His light pink eyes vibrated in their sockets, and when the boy licked his thin lips, a black tongue came out from behind pointed teeth.

"Of course, we're in trouble," said Hana, barely keeping the terror from her voice. "Can you help? Where did you come from?"

Pink eyes oscillated faster as the black tongue darted out once more. "Elsewhere is where I come from, somewhere else."

"How did you get here?" Hana demanded, losing patience.

The dirty boy quickly glanced behind him. "Tunnel is the way in, is the way out. Of course, the tunnel to elsewhere."

Hana's almond eyes went wide. "There's a tunnel back there?!"

"Tunnel to elsewhere. Yes, of course."

"Can we use it? We need to get out of here. Fast!"

The dirty boy thought for moment before his pointed teeth appeared in a strange smile.

"Yes, come to elsewhere. Stay here, and you'll be meat for the Marsh Ghouls. The Marsh Ghouls are always hungry, always wanting meat, only meat. They care about meat."

"Ditto, come now, please," called out Hana. Ditto carved a deep cut into the forehead of an encroaching Marsh Ghoul and sprinted over.

"What do we have here?"

"A way out," replied Hana.

"And who is this?"

At that, the dirty boy slipped out from beneath the Monarch roots and stood. In addition to his other unusual features, the boy was missing the bottom half of his right arm.

"Dooley Hamm's my name and that's what people call me, Dooley Hamm. I have a tunnel, I like tunnels."

Ditto's face twisted, unable to hide his immediate distaste for this new character.

"What the heck is going on?" asked Ash as she joined the group.

"There's a tunnel under this Monarch Brown," answered Hana. "A way out."

"I don't like it," said Ditto.

"What don't you like about it?" demanded Ash.

"I don't like *him*."

Ash's brown eyes immediately fell on the boy's missing arm. "Well, Ditto, if you have another escape plan in mind, then voice it. If not, this boy's our only chance."

"Dooley's this boy's name, his name's Dooley Hamm. I have a tunnel to elsewhere, it goes to elsewhere."

Ditto shot Ash a look, but the one-armed girl ignored him. "Can we use your tunnel, Dooley?"

Dooley's pink eyes shook. "Yes, but quick. It must be quick. The Marsh Ghouls want meat, and this island is full of meat, sweet meat for their empty stomachs which crave meat."

Ash didn't hesitate. "Fincher! Sammi! Miss Salt! We found a way out!"

Fincher raced over, pulling Sammi with him. "Are you farking serious? Oh, what luck! What farking luck! What are we waiting for?!"

Alicia's torch finally winked out and the huntress quickly backpedaled in the face of an oncoming rush of Marsh Ghouls.

"They're coming from all angles now!" Alicia's silver eyes found Dooley Hamm. "Who the fark is this?"

"This is Dooley Hamm. He likes tunnels," responded Ditto, unable to keep the sarcasm from his voice.

"Well, I don't give a fark who he is. If there's a tunnel back, there you all go through it. Now!"

Alicia's command sent everyone in motion. Ditto pushed Dooley Hamm down into the hole between the Monarch roots. "Lead the way!"

Dooley said something inaudible and was immediately followed by Ash and Sammi. Ditto nodded to Hana, who also climbed down into the hole, before turning to Fincher.

"Go ahead," said Fincher. "Miss Salt and I will be right behind you. Stay with the girls. I don't like the look of that pink-eyed little shite." Ditto nodded once more and dove into the hole.

Fincher's face dropped when he looked back up. The island was now swarming with Marsh Ghouls, with four surrounding Alicia Salt and several others coming around from behind the Monarch Brown.

"Miss Salt," Fincher cried out as the huntress cut her shortsword back and forth through the air. "Wait there, I'll come to you!"

"Don't you dare, Master Fincher!" The power in the huntress's voice stopped Fincher cold. As she sliced off the pointed top of a Marsh Ghoul head, Alicia deftly slid the longbow and her quiver of arrows from her shoulder. Without looking, she tossed them to Fincher. "Now, get out of here!"

"I'm not leaving you!"

"The fark you aren't! This is the end of the road for me, Master Fincher, but just the beginning of yours. You take that longbow north with you." Alicia's blade carved into the knobby shoulder of one swamp fiend as another raked its razor-like nails across her back. She screamed out as the rear of her shirt was immediately stained crimson. Pivoting on the ball of her foot, Alicia spun like a top, gleaming metal leading the way. Her shortsword passed neatly through the head of the attacking Marsh Ghoul, sending a geyser of neon yellow into the air. The huntress laughed maniacally.

"Miss Salt, come with me! There's still time!"

"Sweet boy, if you don't go this instant then I'm going to run you through myself for being the stupidest boy alive!" Just as he was about to turn to go, Fincher's hazel eyes met Alicia Salt's silver orbs. "Thank you for letting me know what family felt like, even if only for a moment. Now go, go, go!"

Fincher dove into the hole just as a clawed hand reached for his exposed throat. The boy crawled into the small tunnel at the base of the Monarch Brown and turned back one last time.

Alicia Salt was calling out to the Mutewoods as her blade danced majestically before her. "Do you see me, Father?! Can you see my heart now?! Can you appreciate my bravery?! Will you welcome me with open arms?!"

As Alicia fought and yelled, the largest Marsh Ghoul Fincher had seen slid onto the island from the dark water. It rose up to its full height of twelve feet, balancing on the gnarled remains of what may have once been legs. Alicia saw it too late and could only offer a curse in the creature's direction as it fell upon the huntress, consuming her head and shoulders in a single massive bite.

Blood spurted as other Marsh Ghouls dove forward, fighting for the woman's precious meat.

Tears streamed down Fincher's face as he repositioned the longbow and scampered down the tunnel to safety.

As Fincher put some distance between himself and the grisly scene, only two things could be heard—the continual shrieks of "hungeee," and the hopeless squawks of Rashii the Quilted Raven, who was already mourning the death of Alicia Salt, the one and only Lady of Shadowset.

8

THE MUTED HOME OF MATILDA HAMM

"Oh, thank the Five Sisters! We thought you were in trouble for sure," said Ash in a panic when Fincher finally caught up with Dooley Hamm and his friends. Ash and Hana were holding small lanterns they had pulled from their packs and lit, bathing the tunnel in an eerie glow.

After descending for dozens of feet, the tunnel had both leveled off and opened up, allowing even Ditto to walk upright, albeit with a slight hunch. Sammi was the first to notice the wetness on Fincher's pink cheeks.

"Is Miss Salt behind you?" asked the bespectacled girl, but her quavering voice exposed that she already knew the answer.

Fincher wiped his face and repositioned the longbow. "Miss Salt is gone. She stayed back to make sure we got away."

There was a long moment of quiet as water filled the eyes of Ditto, Ash, and Sammi. Always the strongest of the bunch, Ash recovered first, hugging each friend in turn before breaking the silence.

"Then, let's honor her sacrifice by getting away." Sammi cleaned her glasses and nodded at her sister's suggestion. "Dooley, how much farther until we're in the clear?"

Dooley Hamm spoke from the shadows up ahead, only his vibrating pink eyes showing in the darkness.

"There are several exits for exiting, if you want to exit, but best if we keep going. The tunnels are for taking us elsewhere, and we want that elsewhere to be outside the marsh where the Marsh Ghouls dwell."

The Sour Flower Gang shared confused looks.

"So, how much further is that, Dooley?" asked Ash.

"A ways to get there, to get elsewhere, that elsewhere where the Ghouls cannot come."

Ash sighed at Dooley Hamm's non-specific answer. "Very well. Then, let's get moving. Lead the way, Dooley."

Dooley's pink eyes disappeared as he turned and began moving forward, speaking as he did. "These tunnels will let us tunnel away to elsewhere, away from the Marsh Ghouls. Elsewhere, closer to Meemaw, closer to…"

Dooley's voice faded as he rounded a tunnel corner.

"What did he say?" asked Ditto.

"Doesn't matter," said Ash. "Hurry up and follow. The last thing we need to do is get lost down here."

"I don't like him, Ash."

"Why, Ditto? Because he's different?"

"Not different. Because he's strange, Ash."

Ash held up the stub of her left arm. "Well, I'm strange, too. Maybe that's why you don't like me."

"That's not at all what I mean."

"I know what you mean."

"Ash, wait!"

Ash had already moved to follow Dooley Hamm, and Ditto hurried forward to keep up.

"What the fark was that about?"

Sammi pushed up her glasses. "I'm the one who can't see, but I swear boys are the most blind." The young girl chased Ditto into the darkness.

"What the fark did I say?!" Fincher noticed that he and Hana were alone. Unlike the others, Hana's eyes and cheeks did not glisten with moisture. "You okay, Hana?"

"I'm all right, Fincher."

"Aren't you upset about Miss Salt? It's fine to cry, you know."

"I know, Fincher, but I already said goodbye to Miss Salt."

"When?"

"Before we left Shadowset. I said goodbye to all of us."

Fincher's face scrunched in confusion. "Why would you do that, Hana?"

The young girl shrugged. "I like to be ready for the inevitable. We'd better not let them get too far ahead of us."

Hana spun and sprinted down the tunnel, taking the last of the light with her, leaving Fincher in the dark—in more ways than one.

For several hours, the Sour Flower Gang progressed through the surprisingly vast network of tunnels that ran under this part of the Mutewoods. Dooley Hamm led the way with supreme confidence, turning left here, right there. In certain areas, he would break off from a main tunnel, forcing everyone to crawl for a while before intersecting another large shaft.

The entire time, the unusual pink-eyed boy spoke to himself, repeatedly mentioning "elsewhere" and "Meemaw." After a while, the Sour Flower Gang managed to tune out Dooley's odd ramblings, paying him no more mind than the sounds of torrential rain the day before.

Just as the weight of the dirt above the children started to feel overwhelmingly suffocating, the tunnel began to ascend. A few minutes later, and the Sour Flower Gang was breathing fresh air for the first time in hours.

"It's okay, we're elsewhere, somewhere else where the Ghouls can't come," said Dooley proudly when Ditto hesitated exiting the tunnel. When the large boy finally did, he took a look around before calling back down.

"He's right. It all looks clear. The forest floor is dry here. Come on out."

"Farking right, let's get a move on, then," said Fincher from his position in the back. "I don't need to be surrounded by so much farking dirt again until I'm dead."

The Mutewoods were already beginning to dim by the time everyone crawled out of the tunnel. Similar to the tunnel through which they escaped the Marsh Ghouls, the one from which they now exited was beneath a Monarch Brown.

Sammi helped Ash and Hana place their lanterns back into their packs as Ditto looked around, keeping an especially keen eye on Dooley Hamm.

"We'd better make camp for the night," said the massive boy. "I don't know about you all, but I can't imagine taking many more steps today."

"Agreed."

"Farking right."

"Yes."

Only Dooley Hamm seemed put off by this suggestion, and he voiced his displeasure.

"But, but, we're not to the elsewhere yet, not yet. The elsewhere is elsewhere, and that is not here."

Ditto looked around once more before responding. "Well, Dooley, it seems that we've made it past the reach of those swamp creatures. That's good enough for me right now. We've had a trying day full of hiking and fighting and running and crawling. And death."

"So?"

"So, we're tired, Dooley. And we may not be at your *elsewhere*, but we're *elsewhere enough* for me." Ditto turned to the others. "Hana, you want to start clearing an area for camp? Ash, come with me to collect firewood? Sammi, get a fire pit ready?"

Everyone quietly agreed and jumped to their tasks. As they did, Fincher slid over to Ditto.

"I noticed you didn't give me a farking job, my friend."

Ditto looked down at Fincher with his green eyes shining. "Watch Dooley Hamm. I don't trust him."

"You don't trust him, or you don't like the way he looks?"

"You sound like Ash. When have you ever known me to dislike someone?"

Fincher conceded. "Never, my friend."

"Then watch him?"

"Of course."

"Good. We'll be back shortly."

As Fincher watched Dooley Hamm, who sat down angrily on a nearly fallen tree, whispering under his breath, Ditto and Ash walked on, blades in hands to collect wood for the upcoming evening.

"Why don't you like him?" asked Ash when they were out of earshot.

"Who?"

"Don't be daft, Ditto. You know who. Dooley Hamm. You know, the boy who saved us from certain death."

Ditto thought for a second before answering. "I don't know. Something about him bothers me. A lot."

"Is it his missing arm?"

"You know that's not what it is."

"Do I?"

Ditto spun back to face Ash. "Look, the boy talks to himself, has teeth like a river eel, and speaks in riddles. We don't know him. And what we do know is beyond weird."

"He saved our lives."

"To what end?"

Ash paused for moment, as if considering her words, before continuing. "Do you know what losing a limb is like, Ditto?"

"You know I don't, Ash."

"It… changes you. It changes the way you see the world. It changes how others see you."

"What are you trying to say, Ash?"

"I'm saying, there are reasons why Dooley is odd. I'm saying, why don't you cut that boy some slack. Or maybe you only do that for people with two arms."

"Ash, I don't—" Ditto never got to complete his thought as Ash had already stormed away in a huff. Confused and tired, the large boy simply started chopping away at a small tree to his left. It was so green that he wasn't even sure it would burn. But he felt the need to chop something.

After a meal of dried jerky meat, of which Dooley Hamm had none, the Sour Flower Gang sat around the small fire, exhausted beyond the point of sleep. As Hana fed Triggy small insects she had plucked from a nearby spiderweb, Sammi practiced her complex knots while Ditto and Fincher sharpened their weapons. Ash remained unnaturally quiet.

Dooley Hamm stared into the campfire, his pink eyes shaking as he muttered to himself.

Fincher, unaccustomed to such heavy silence, couldn't help but break the spell.

"Dooley, I heard you call those creatures back there *Marsh Ghouls*. What the fark are they?"

Dooley looked across the fire at Fincher. "Bad words shouldn't be used, especially when they're bad. Especially when you can get punished for them. Bad words, that is."

Fincher smiled at the too-thin boy. "Apologies, Dooley. I'm a known potty mouth but will work hard to improve. Now tell me about the Marsh Ghouls?"

Dooley licked his lips with a black tongue. "Bad people, a long time ago, is what they were, these Ghouls." Dooley's pink eyes jumped back and forth, and the boy showed his sharp teeth in an unnerving grin upon realizing he had the full attention of the Sour Flower Gang. "They worshipped the other god, the one Meemaw says to never say. So, I don't say it. They danced to evil songs, evil song dancing, and used magic in the forest. The black magic of the forest is the magic that they used. They killed animals for the other god, and maybe things bigger than animals, maybe animals that could talk were killed. They killed and killed and killed, killing, for the other god, trying to live forever. By living forever they could never die and would live forever. Like the other god. Then they would *be* other gods and people would dance and kill for them."

Despite Dooley's unusual, circular way of speaking, the bony boy had the Sour Flower Gang entranced.

"What happened to them, Dooley?" asked Sammi, her brown eyes large behind her glasses.

Dooley shot another dark grin. "The other god made them live forever. They wanted to live forever, so the other god did it for them, made them forever. But the other god is naughty, much more naughty than Dooley, a real naughty. The other god made them more forest than people, people who were now half-people, half-tree. The other god sank them into the forest, the ground is where they went, and their new skin would pull food from the dirt. But it was never enough, this dirt food, and never could they feel full, always hungry they were, with bellies that screamed for more, never enough. Their mouths grew longer and longer, hunger screams pulling down faces, always hungry. Their screams even started to bother the other god, the other god usually loved a good scream, but this was too much. The other god put them to sleep, a no-good sleep where nightmares of endless hunger chased away any memory of them being people, people they were no more."

Dooley Hamm paused for dramatic effect, his pink eyes racing in his head as the others listened with rapt attention.

"Thousands of years they sleep, a bad sleep they have. Never seen, they are forgotten, no one remembers them, they are forever no one. But every now then..." The children leaned forward. "Every now and then such a rain comes, a real rain, an ocean of rain, some say from the other god, it comes and water dives deep enough to touch the forever people. The cold water wakes them from their sleep, a bad no-good sleep, and they are able to climb through the wet dirt, swimming through dirt, and finally reach air, fresh, fresh air. When they awaken, when they get the fresh, fresh air, they remember their hunger, so, so hungry, and that's all they know, their hunger. They eat, eat, eat, they eat all they can. They eat birds, bugs, critters, yes critters. They eat talking animals, their favorite are the talking animals, the talking animals remind them of something, but they cannot remember. Their hunger is too much, so hungry, so that's all they know. After the water begins to go away, they also must go away, back to sleeping, back to bad, bad dreaming, back to the ground. Where they can live forever. Just as they wanted. Just as the other god made happen."

When Dooley finished his bizarre tale, for a long time the only sound to be heard was the crackling of the small fire. Finally...

"Farking Marsh Ghouls, huh? Dooley, how often do the Marsh Ghouls wake up?"

Dooley simply shrugged, a movement that made his bony shoulders protrude even more from his dirty, ripped shirt. "Only when the big rains come, when the rains are the biggest."

Ash cut in. "Have you ever seen a Marsh Ghoul before today, Dooley?"

"Me? No, I've never seen a Marsh Ghoul before, just seen stories in my head, my head had stories about them."

Ditto appeared skeptical. "What were you doing out there, Dooley?" He ignored the dirty look that Ash sent his way. "And what are all these tunnels under the forest? Did you make them yourself?"

Dooley flashed his sharp teeth once more. "The Hamms are tunnelers, always been tunnelers. My Peepaw was a tunneler, and his Peepaw a tunneler. But Dooley's the best tunneler, he made tunnels never-before seen, connected tunnels to other tunnels, made tunnels to other areas of the forest..." Dooley licked his lips. "... to other villages."

"Why the tunnels, Dooley?" asked Sammi.

"Tunnels are great, they are the best, such a good road. Tunnels are safe, they can sneak past danger, past eyes, past many eyes. Tunnels help me creep, I like to creep, moving around like a ghost, I like ghosts."

"What were you doing out there today, Dooley?" Ditto asked again.

"I never seen such rain, such a rain in the forest. I knew if the Marsh Ghouls were ever to wake, they would wake today, for today I knew there would be a marsh, a marsh for the ghouls."

Fincher looked horrified. "So, you went out of your way to see a farking Marsh Ghoul?"

Dooley's pink eyes focused on Fincher. "Not out of my way, nothing's out of my way, my way is every way, in every tunnel. I know where water likes to go, where marshes may form, where ghouls may come. And I was right, I knew I was going to be right, and I was."

Sammi chimed in. "Weren't you scared, Dooley? I mean, those Marsh Ghouls are the scariest thing I've ever seen. And I've seen a lot."

"We all have," added Ash.

"Right, sis. We all have. And Alicia Salt was the toughest, bravest hunter in all of Quaan. And she was terrified. May she rest in peace forever. Weren't you scared, Dooley?"

Dooley Hamm looked into the fire, his pink eyes vibrating faster than usual. "There's scarier things than Marsh Ghouls, things more scary, things most scary."

"You mean in Quaan?" asked Sammi.

"I mean in the forest, in this forest, in the Mutewoods, that is."

"Fark me, what could possibly be scarier than a farking Marsh Ghoul?!"

"You shouldn't use bad words, words that are bad. Bad words can get you in trouble, and trouble is not good." On the topic of what was worse than a Marsh Ghoul, Dooley Hamm said no more.

"Well, I sure as shite ain't gonna sleep well tonight," said Fincher, only partially joking.

"But we have to try," countered Ash, clearing the ground around her little sister with her right arm before Sammi spread out her bedroll. The others followed suit. Dooley continued staring into the fire.

"Don't you need to rest, Dooley?" asked Ash.

"I don't like to sleep, sleep is no good. There're monsters in the sleep, and no tunnels in my brain, I like to hide in tunnels, tunnels are safe."

"Well, I'm sorry to hear that, Dooley. But we're exhausted. Could you keep watch?"

The thin boy licked his thin lips. "I can watch, I always watch. Watching is what I do best. Second best."

Ditto stood, thumbing the blade at his hip. "I'll stand watch. You all get some rest."

"Dooley said that he can stay up," said Ash. "And you're exhausted too, Ditto. You need sleep."

"I'm fine," snapped Ditto, more severely than he intended. He immediately softened. "I mean, I'm too wound up to sleep. You all rest. I'll go collect some more wood for the fire."

Ditto moved off but knelt down as he passed Fincher, who was also readying his bedroll. They spoke in whispers.

"I don't like this kid. And I don't care that he saved our butts."

Fincher looked up at his large friend. "What don't you farking like, Ditto? The constant licking of lips? The bizarro way of talking? The farking pink, shaky eyes?"

"Then we're in agreement? Ash doesn't seem to agree."

"Girls' hearts are softer than ours. Which is wonderful when they're right."

"But when they're wrong?"

"Not so farking good."

"Then we're in agreement?"

"We are. You take the first watch, like you said. Wake me in a few hours. You're no good to any of us half-asleep."

"Done. Don't fall asleep until I return with the wood."

"And you don't forget to wake me for my half of the farking watch."

"Done." Ditto rose and disappeared into the Mutewoods to gather more kindling for the small fire.

Fincher spread out his bedroll and laid atop it. He looked over to find that Ash, Sammi, and Hana were already fast asleep, hopefully dreaming of something other than Marsh Ghouls and Silver Staggs. And while Dooley Hamm still stared into the small fire, every now and then his pink eyes found their way to Fincher's sleeping friends.

And he would lick his thin lips.

~

Ditto called out from his position at the rear of the group. "Dooley, do you know where you're going? You know we're trying to head north, right?"

Dooley grumbled from the front of the group, Ash and Sammi walking just behind the strange boy.

"Yes, yes, elsewhere is where we're going, heading to elsewhere, that's where we need to be. That's where you'll get what you need, what we all need."

Ditto threw up his arms, decidedly exhausted from Dooley Hamm's verbal chaos.

Fincher looked up through the thick canopy of the Mutewoods and spotted Paragon. "For what it's worth, Ditto, it *does* appear that we're moving north."

"Where's this little twist taking us?"

"I don't farking know. But remember that this little twist saved our lives. Without him, we'd all be in the bellies of Marsh Ghouls, sharing the same fate as Alicia Salt, may she rest in peace."

"You think I don't know that?!" Ditto's unusual anger sent Fincher back on his heels. "You think that doesn't make it worse?"

"I guess it does. But what do you want to do about it, Ditto?"

The large boy looked to be at a loss. "Just stay sharp. And if I make a move, you back me up. I don't like this kid."

"You've never disliked anyone, Ditto. Even those that hate us."

"Doesn't that make this all the more concerning?"

"It does."

"Then stay sharp?"

"Of course."

There was a much different conversation taking place at the head of the line as the group wove its way through the Mutewoods.

"How long have you lived in the Mutewoods, Dooley?" asked Ash.

"My life is the forest, I'm born into it, the forest."

"And you love it?"

Dooley seemed unsure how to answer. "I am it, and it is me. I don't know love; I only know the forest. And the things in the forest, the good things, and the bad things."

"What are the bad things, Dooley?"

"Many bad things. Many, many, many. Bad things, that is."

Ash hesitated but ended up voicing the question that was really on the tip of her lips. "How did you lose your arm, Dooley? Was it one of the bad things?"

Dooley seemed unbothered, so focused was he on the journey ahead of him. "Oh, yes, the bad things took my arm, my favorite arm. I did my best digging with the arm that they took, made the best tunnels, great tunnels for hiding and sneaking."

"Why did they take your arm, Dooley?"

"They were hungry, weren't they? Always hungry, like a Marsh Ghoul but different. That's why I wanted to see a Marsh Ghoul, the only things with more hunger than the bad things, I had to see if they really are that hungry. They are."

Ash looked down at the stump of her own arm as she walked and felt a weird kinship with Dooley Hamm. Who else, especially a perfectly fit boy like Ditto, could ever understand the feeling of losing an essential part of yourself, a part critical for survival? A part needed for fully caressing the face of a loved one. Who could love someone who couldn't cup your face in their hands, couldn't adequately pull you in for a kiss?

"We have a lot in common, Dooley. As you can see, my arm was also taken. Taken by a hungry Ghost Puma. I know what it feels like to have your favorite arm taken."

"Was that your digging arm, the arm that you did your best digging with?"

Ash thought for a moment. "No, but it did other things that I loved. Other things that I dearly miss." A pause. "I'm sorry you lost your arm, Dooley."

Ash went to put her right arm around the skeletal boy. As soon as her dark skin touched his pointy shoulders, the boy jerked forward as if a branding iron had landed on his too-pale skin. Dooley didn't turn around, but he did increase his pace.

"We aren't far now, from elsewhere, that is. Elsewhere is up ahead, that's where I'm taking you, elsewhere."

In the back of the group, Ditto's head cocked, and the large boy's brow furrowed. He stopped and pulled Fincher to a halt along with him.

"Fincher, do you hear that?"

Fincher listened for several seconds. "I don't hear a farking thing."

"Exactly."

"What do you mean?"

"I mean listen! Do. You. Hear. Anything?"

Fincher humored his obviously bothered friend. Then, his brow also furrowed in confusion.

"Farking heck, I don't hear shite. I mean, I don't hear *anything*."

"Exactly. No birds. No insects. No rustling through the under-brush. Nothing."

"It *is* called the Mutewoods, Ditto."

Ditto shook his blond-haired head. "Woods are woods, Fincher. And they're never mute. Unless."

"Unless what?"

"Unless something is killing everything. And I mean *everything*."

"That doesn't seem possible, Ditto."

"Maybe not in Crimmish. And maybe not in Shadowset. But what about elsewhere?"

"Where?"

"Elsewhere. Like where Dooley Hamm is taking us."

Fincher thought for a moment, continuing to listen to nothing-ness. "Fark me." He pulled out his hunting knife. "Let's catch up to the others."

Five minutes later, Dooley Hamm grew even more animated as he led the Sour Flower Gang into a small forest village, one of the hundred or so rumored to be scattered about deep in the Mutewoods.

The village was serene and quaint, with thatch-roofed buildings dotting the clearing. Some were made of river stones while others were constructed purely out of wood. A musical stream ran along the eastern portion of the village, neatly carving it in two, with a moss-covered stone bridge connecting both sides.

The village seemed magical. It also seemed abandoned.

"Is this your village, Dooley? It's lovely," remarked Ash, who could only dream of growing up surrounded by such beauty.

"It's a village but not my village. Meemaw and me live away from the village but not far from the village, this village."

Sammi looked around before speaking. "Where is everyone, Dooley?"

Dooley Hamm didn't bother lifting his pink eyes as he increased his speed across the village. "Gone. Left or gone, gone or left, they went someplace else, someplace that isn't elsewhere."

Ditto leaned into Fincher as they took up the rear, their blades at the ready. "This place looks well cared for."

Fincher nodded. "Yep. If it's been abandoned, it hasn't been that way farking long."

"Abandoned? Or something worse?"

"Farking heck, you're full of cheery theories today."

"Just stay ready."

Fincher called up ahead. "Hey, if this place is farking empty, shouldn't we take a look around, see if there's anything that can help us on our journey? You know, the long farking journey that we're on."

Dooley Hamm growled from the front of the line but kept moving forward. "There's nothing here for you, nothing at all, unless you want to take ghosts with you, there's plenty of ghosts to take, if you want them."

Fincher and Ditto shared a look and Hana whispered something to Triggy. Fincher called out once more.

"But a quick look wouldn't hurt, would it, Dooley?"

Dooley mumbled something under his breath before answering over his shoulder.

"Meemaw has many things for you, when we get to elsewhere, you'll have all you want in elsewhere, when we get there. Meemaw has it for you, it's all with Meemaw."

"You mean Meemaw has food and supplies for us? Does she have much to spare?"

"Sure, sure, sure, sure," replied Dooley, more to himself than to Fincher.

On the too-skinny, too-pale boy walked, taking the Sour Flower Gang out of the picturesque village full of picturesque cottages and back into the wildness of the Mutewoods.

This time, however, the group traveled along a well-worn path that passed several lone cabins and bungalows, each looking as empty as the village they recently left behind.

At an intersection in the path, Dooley Hamm turned right, his walk transitioning into a manic skip, his footsteps clearly heard against the backdrop of silence. Soon after, the forest opened up, revealing an isolated wooden cottage with smoke billowing forth from its stone chimney. A small sign staked into the ground next to the door read *The Hamms' Welcome All*.

Dooley Hamm excitedly spun on the balls of his feet to face the Sour Flower Gang, his skeletal arm spread wide in welcome.

"This is elsewhere, elsewhere is where we are, where we finally made it, the home of Matilda and Dooley Hamm, me and Meemaw."

Ash was the first to comment. "This is your home, Dooley? It looks really nice."

"Yeah, if you like farking cemeteries," said Fincher so only Ditto could hear.

Dooley's pink eyes moved faster than ever before. "Yes, yes, my home. Well, it is really Meemaw's home, but Meemaw and me are the same, are we not, Meemaw and me. Come, come, come, she's waiting to meet you, to see you all, to offer lots of gifts and food, yes, yes, there will be food, lots of food. Come, come, come."

Dooley showed his sharp teeth once more and spun back to his home, anxiously making his way to the front door. The Sour Flower Gang, all but Ash, looked to each other doubtfully.

"What's the problem?" Ash asked angrily. "Are we too good, too well-provisioned for some decent hospitality?"

"I don't like it," Ditto stated flatly.

"As you've made perfectly clear, Ditto. But let me point something out." Ash lifted her right index finger into the air, as she often did when really upset. "This boy saved us from the Marsh Ghouls. He whisked us away from imminent death and the deadly vernal pools using tunnels that he and his family dug themselves. He has brought us further north, the direction we need to go, and has now taken us to his home, where we will get some proper rest, proper food, and proper shelter. And all you lot can do is doubt and hate and sneer? I thought we were better than that. I thought we were different from everyone else in Quaan. But maybe we aren't."

As everyone remained stunned by Ash's outburst, Fincher tried to speak for the group.

"It's not that, Ash. It's—"

"Oh, I *know* what it is," Ash snapped back. "Someone different equals someone strange equals someone bad. Well, then, I guess I'm bad, too! So, I'm going to enjoy the kind deed that someone is trying to do for us. The rest of you can stay out here for all I care!"

Ash Bugg stormed off to follow Dooley Hamm, who was now waiting impatiently at the door to his home.

"Farking shite, what's gotten into her?"

"Don't be daft, Fincher," said Sammi, as if that answered all questions. "I'm going with my sister. I'm not sure if she's right or wrong, but we're family. *We're all* family."

As Sammi moved to follow her older sibling, Fincher turned to Ditto and Hana.

"Well, she farking has me with that one. We go?"

Ditto looked down at his friend. "Of course, we go. Hana, you stay behind me."

Dooley offered another toothy grin as the Sour Flower Gang gathered at the front door.

"Meemaw's gonna be so excited, excited she'll be, so happy to see kids, she always says I need to bring her more kids, kids for dinner. Come, come, come."

As Dooley opened the front door, a wave of warmness struck the children, offering a nice reprieve from the chilly forest air. Dooley stepped forward and ushered the others in, Ash the first, Ditto the last.

Surprisingly, at least to all but Ash, the cottage seemed perfectly cozy. Two beds, one much large than the other, sat to the right as the group entered. A comparably large hearth with a roaring fire within was located to the children's left, about halfway down the length of the home. A dining table, much bigger than necessary for two people, dominated the center of the single-roomed house, an oversized chair at its head. A small kitchen occupied the back righthand corner of the cottage. The fattest woman the Sour Flower Gang had ever seen stood barefoot and silent against the wooden counter, staring blankly out of the small window that peered out into the forest beyond. Massive rolls of impossibly white skin appeared around a too-tight dress, veins and capillaries clear under the nearly transparent surface.

"Is that you, Dooley, my boy?!"

"It's me Meemaw, Dooley, your son, Dooley." Pink eyes turned to the group. "Meemaw doesn't see too well anymore, but she's good at other stuff, so good, too good, but not seeing, not with eyes, at least."

"What have you brought Meemaw, Dooley, my boy?" The round woman sniffed the air. "Have you brought Meemaw guests? Guests for a feast? I do love a feast, Dooley, my boy."

"I have, Meemaw. I brought some children, children that were lost in the forest, the forest almost got them, it did, you know the forest, always getting people."

Meemaw continued to stare out the window. "Oh, I know how terrible the forest can be, Dooley, my boy. No one knows more than me how awful it can be. That's why it's so important to take care of guests in this dark place, to have feasts when you can. Dooley, my boy, have our guests seated, make them comfortable."

"Are you coming over, Meemaw, over to the table, where the feast will take place?"

"Of course, Dooley, my boy. But let me prepare myself. I don't move around as well as I once could."

Dooley swung his one arm out toward the long dining table.

"Please, please. Long walks need long rests, and rests should be in chairs or beds, but first chairs. Have a seat, seats are good, they're for resting."

Ash didn't hesitate in taking a seat and shot the rest of the group with a dark look when they did. Sammi sat down next, followed by Fincher and Hana. Ditto remained standing.

"Ditto," Ash cried out angrily, and the large boy begrudgingly sat down at the far end of the table.

Meemaw spoke again without turning around. "Dooley, my boy, why don't you go into the storage shed and get us some meat. It isn't a feast without meat, is it, my boy?"

Dooley's sharp teeth shone in the firelight. "No, Meemaw, it's not a feast without meat, meat is needed for a feast, there is no feast without meat. I'll go now, get the meat, the meat for the feast, the meat we've been waiting for."

"Good. Go now, Dooley, my boy."

Dooley exited the cottage. When the door closed, Fincher thought he heard a *click*, but perhaps it was nothing.

The Sour Flower Gang took off their packs and settled into their seats, looking at each other questioningly when the obese woman known as Meemaw kept staring out the window, saying nothing more to her guests.

Suddenly, Meemaw reached for a large pot sitting on the counter and pulled it in close. The woman's large body convulsed, creating waves in her fat rolls, until she leaned forward and began to vomit. The younglings' faces screwed in disgust as a torrent of small bones found the bottom of the metal container with a loud, rapid-fire *clang*. Letting out a sigh of relief, Meemaw calmly took the now-full pot and emptied it onto the floor to her left, where its contents joined more bones piled high in the corner.

After several uncomfortable beats, Meemaw turned and made her way toward her oversized chair. The unusually fat woman moved in short, jerky motions, as if she was a marionette in one of Quaan's famed traveling puppet shows. Dumb grin pasted on her swollen, veiny face, Meemaw loudly scooted out the giant chair before collapsing into it. All of the children winced, thinking the wooden legs would surely explode under the extreme weight. But they held.

"Now, tell me, where're you lot from? You don't smell familiar, now do you?"

The children would have answered, would have had no problem answering, except for Meemaw's eyes. Like Dooley's, Meemaw's eyes oscillated rapidly in their sockets. Unlike Dooley's pink orbs, Meemaw's eyes were white, and even the pupils were clouded over with a thick membrane.

"Since when has it been polite not to answer a host's question, especially when that host is prepping for a feast?" said Meemaw into the uneasy quiet.

"Sorry, ma'am," answered Ash. "We've had a frightful time of it the past day or so, which I'm afraid may have affected our manners, which are usually very solid."

Meemaw giggled, her white eyes racing back and forth. "Oh, I understand, child. Change can come quick, yes it can. Surroundings change, predicaments change. People change. But we make the best of what we have, don't we now?"

"Yes, ma'am."

"Good. Now, tell me. You all smell different. Where are you from? Not anywhere around here, I suppose. No, no, we would remember a smell like this."

Fincher looked to Ditto and mouthed a word. "*We?*"

Ash, however, went along with the strange interrogation.

"No, we're from Crimmish, ma'am. Far from the Mutewoods."

The white eyes stopped moving. "Crimmish? You mean the Stenches?"

"We prefer the actual name—Crimmish, ma'am."

Meemaw's white eyes returned to their shaking. "Crimmish. The

Stenches." The massive woman seemed to be speaking to herself. "Poisonous? They could be. Or perhaps the toxic air made their meat more tender, more juicy, more succulent. Perhaps they are a delicacy. Like the crippler eels of Crown Lake. Oh, how we always wanted to try those. Perhaps this is the same. Of course, we could handle this. We can handle any meat. It is but meat. We are the eaters."

Fincher and Ditto's hands returned to their hilts as Ash spoke.

"Excuse me, ma'am, but who are your talking to? We're right here. And what is this meat that you're talking about? The meat that Dooley's bringing in from the shed?"

Meemaw's nostrils flared as her head began dancing in the air. "No, no, no, no. Dooley's already brought the meat. The meat is here already."

Ash looked around, fear starting to show on her face. "Where?"

Meemaw's head and white eyes stopped moving and finally focused on the Sour Flower Gang. "Here."

"Farking heck! Look at her," exclaimed Fincher, just as the others also took note.

Meemaw's too-white skin began to ripple just beneath the surface, as if dormant rivers there had begun to swell from the recent rains. But, it soon became painfully clear that it wasn't rivers or veins or capillaries that were rising from within the fat woman. It was something much more horrifying.

From the corners of Meemaw's cloudy eyes, thin worms began to emerge. They swung to and fro, as if testing the air for particles of meat, for the location of the nearest child.

As one, the younglings shot back from the dining table, Sammi and Hana scooting their chairs backwards so suddenly that they tipped over and fell to their backs. Ash was with them in an instant, pulling them to their feet and behind her with her one arm.

"Where are you going?" asked Meemaw. "The feast is just beginning. And you're the guests of honor. You can't have a festwthothgst..."

As Meemaw spoke, a thick worm, as big around as Hana's arm, slithered out from the back of the fat woman's throat, its eyeless head swinging slowly back and forth in the air. Suddenly, it grew rigid, pointing directly at the three girls, and opened its mouth, revealing row upon row of razor-like teeth. A terrifying, unnatural shriek emerged from that horrible mouth, filling the small cottage with horrendous sounds.

"Oh, fark this," declared Fincher, jumping up from his seat and sprinting to the door. "Fark, fark, farking fark," the boy yelled as the door would not budge, having been locked from the outside. "Farking Dooley! Let us out, you little shite!"

Loud giggling could be heard just behind the door. "Welcome to elsewhere, where the feasts are many, where you are the feasts, and the feasts are meat!"

Ditto was already up, knife in hand, pulling Ash and Sammi and Hana behind him, the long dining table separating the children from the worm-infested woman.

Meemaw laughed around the worm protruding from her mouth. As she did, hundreds of other worms, thin like thread, exited the woman's ears and escaped through pores in her forehead and neck and arms and chest.

"Move any closer and I'll cut you," declared Ditto, his knife out before him.

The thick worm disappeared back down into Meemaw's throat, allowing the obese monstrosity to speak once more.

"Will you now, boy? Tell me this. How will you cut me when I plan on devouring both of your arms? But don't worry, boy, I'll stop there. Then, you can watch as Dooley and I eat your friends. One by one. Your cries will be my dinner music, your screams my digestive. I will—"

Meemaw didn't get the chance to finish as Ditto ran forward and sliced his blade through the air, neatly carving a line across the woman's swollen face. Ditto made to strike again but was forced back when a torrent of worms poured out of the deep cut, making a slithering pool on the wooden floor where his feet once stood.

Meemaw released a wicked laugh. "Stupid, stupid boy. You are not fighting *me*. You are fighting *we*, and *we* are hungry, *we* are starving. *We* are forever!"

The massive woman then leapt from her seat with impossible speed, sending the wooden chair to shatter against the back wall. Worms reached out greedily from her eyes and ears and neck and chest as she advanced on Ditto and the girls, her movements now more akin to a dancer than a puppet.

"Now, then, who wants to feed us first? The young one perhaps? Yes, we think the young one will have the sweetest meat. We think—"

Fincher, having given up on the locked door, flew in from the opposite side, his hunting knife leading the way. The boy plunged his blade into Meemaw's side, easily tearing through her thin white dress, getting in several deep thrusts before the woman spun on him in a flash, sending him across the cottage with a meaty backhand.

Fincher spun over both beds and landed with a grunt in the corner, where he remained unmoving.

Ash, never one to hide behind anyone, rolled over the dining table and drew her own knife, flanking Meemaw, who was now squaring off with Ditto once more. As she did, Sammi and Hana retreated toward the front door, keeping the wooden obstacle between them and the worm-woman.

Meemaw, seeing how the children were using the table against her, screamed out in rage before dropping a heavy arm onto the wooden top, smashing it into several large chunks. She then kicked out, launching one of the front corners soaring through the air. Sammi released a yelp as she dropped to her stomach, the wooden projectile barely missing the girl's head as it smashed against the front wall in an explosion of splinters.

Ditto and Ash simultaneously moved in behind Meemaw's kick, both slashing down and across, carving fissures into the woman's thick skin. Unfortunately, both recoiled in horror as not blood, but twin waterfalls of white worms fell from the wounds.

Meemaw cackled.

"Now you see, my fine, sweet-smelling children? There is no escape. There is only meat. You are meat. You are *our* meat!"

A knife flew in behind Meemaw's words, sinking itself deep into the woman's fat neck. While Ditto turned to see Hana's small arm outstretched, Ash darted forward, burying her own blade in the side of Meemaw's head.

Meemaw's white eyes rolled back, but only momentarily. The woman recovered in an instant, spinning in a blur to grasp Ash by the shoulders, locking the girl in place. Without missing a beat, Meemaw pulled Ash in as her worm-filled head shot forward, slamming her too-pale forehead into the girl's dark cheek.

"No," Ditto called out as Ash dropped to the floor unconscious, the piles of worms unraveling as they made their way toward the potential new host.

As Ditto faced off with Meemaw, Ash's body on the floor between them, Sammi wasted no time in collecting the children's packs and tossing them toward the barred front door before rushing over to kneel before the fire, grabbing some of the extra kindling beside the hearth as she did.

Keeping his green eyes on Meemaw, who swayed before him like a hooded field viper, Ditto reached down and pulled Ash to temporary safety. The one-armed girl moaned as he did, beginning to come around.

"Get behind me," demanded Ditto, and Ash responded, crawling desperately to get away from both Meemaw and the approaching worms.

Meemaw licked her lips. As she did, more white worms wiggled freed from the corners of her mouth. They fell out onto the floor as she spoke, the small knife still lodged in her fat throat bouncing along with her words.

"Silly boy! There is no escape. You can only serve something larger, just as those villagers did. Just as my Dooley did. The Worm is the future of Quaan. The Worm is the other god! I see that now. Oh, how do I see it now. And we must all make our sacrifice. For you, it will be your meat. Now, give it to me! Give me your meat!"

Meemaw pounced on Ditto, and even the quick boy was too slow to dodge the lightning attack. Meemaw's left hand caught Ditto's right wrist before he could attack with his blade, and her right hand found the boy's throat. Immediately, Ditto's green eyes began to bulge as he was lifted from his feet.

Meemaw pulled Ditto in close, a wicked, open-mouthed grin revealing a black tongue. The worms around her eyes and mouth reached for Ditto and the boy slammed shut his eyes. The horror was too much to bear.

Just as the nearest worm was about to make contact, Meemaw recoiled a bit and Ditto dared to look.

Hanging from Meemaw's back was tiny, sweet Hana. The girl's thin right arm was draped across the giant woman's shoulder as she plunged her small dagger, retrieved from their host's fat neck, again and again into Meemaw's back.

Meemaw screamed out, more in rage than pain, and hurled Ditto angrily across the cottage. The large boy flew with such velocity that the front door exploded upon impact, the boy tumbling into the outside clearing.

With hands now free, Meemaw reached back and grabbed Hana by her long, black hair. As the young girl shrieked, Meemaw ripped her over her fat shoulder and seized both of Hana's shoulders, locking the girl in place, her tiny feet desperately kicking the air.

Hana's almond eyes went wide as Meemaw opened her mouth, freeing the arm-thick white worm once more. It slithered out from its host's throat and hung in the space between Meemaw and Hana. After waving in the air for a moment, it let out an excited, high-pitched screech. Hana released a shriek to match it.

Outside, Ditto found that his breath had been driven from his lungs. As he was fighting to recover, a dark form fell over him, all bones and teeth and nails.

Dooley Hamm's sharp teeth dove for Ditto's throat, but the large boy was able to slide his forearm up and across the skeletal boy's neck, halting his attack and locking the two boys nose-to-nose.

Dooley sneered from above. "Meat doesn't fight back, it can't fight back, it's meat. Meat must be eaten, must let us eat it, it's meat. The Worm must eat, the other god must eat the world, to make it a Worm world. Let me feed my worm, *the* Worm. You must let me, let me, you must."

Dooley fought like a feral spire tomcat, teeth and the nails of a lone hand looking for anything to strike.

But Ditto was bigger. And stronger. And now much more enraged. And with only one arm, Dooley Hamm didn't stand a chance.

Ditto bellowed in fury, easily rolling the two combatants to his left, with the large boy ending up atop his smaller foe. Up and down went Ditto's heavy right fist, slamming into Dooley's cheek, mouth, eye, and jaw. Sharp teeth flew to the woodland ground as a pink eye swelled shut. Soon, the thrashing boy went limp, and Ditto fell to the side, his head still ringing from careening through the thick barrier.

The large boy rose quickly, intending to help his friends, but the world spun around him, and he fell to the ground once more.

Back inside, tears ran down Hana's cheeks as the mouth-worm, *the* Worm, inched closer. As it did, Triggy ran free from Hana's front pocket, disturbed by the commotion and its new friend's cries of terror.

The Trigon Newt dashed up the girl's shirt and made its way to her right shoulder. The quick movement caught the attention of the mouth-worm, which struck out like a Moon Adder, consuming Triggy in a flash. Hana cried out for her amphibian friend, but her mouth promptly shut as the worm came back around, sniffing the air for a way in. It slid forward once more. Then stopped.

Black lines began to form along the skin of the white mouth-worm, and it hissed before retreating into Meemaw's throat. The fat host moved to say something, but her words were swallowed as black, veiny lines erupted under the skin of her face, shoulders, arms, and hands.

A shadow of confusion crossed Meemaw's swollen face as she released Hana, who dropped to the floor and crab-walked backward as fast as she could.

A small voice, full of venom and power, came in from the side of the cottage, demanding the bloated host's attention.

"What's the matter, Meemaw?" asked Sammi Bugg, a flaming stick held in each dark hand. Fire reflected in Sammi's round glasses, causing the girl to resemble a demon of judgment. "You've never tried a Trigon Newt, I see. Well, enjoy it. Because it'll be the last meal you ever eat. Here's your dessert."

As the final word left her mouth, Sammi tossed the flaming kindling at Meemaw. Despite the thick black lines that were beginning to crisscross her skin, the woman managed to dodge both flaming branches. Instead, they hit the ground of the cottage and quickly spread, running along the floorboards and up the dry, wooden walls.

Meemaw roared as flames leapt up around her and the black lines thickened, stretching the surface of her already tight skin.

"There is no escape from the Worm! The other god must be fed, must be nourished, must be worshipped! For He is God! Feed him!"

Meemaw rushed for Sammi, who now appeared locked up in fear. But midway through her assault, Meemaw was pushed back as an arrow slammed into her forehead. She reached up with a shaky, blackening hand and snapped the shaft off at its base, but another bolt followed, exploding a white eye and releasing more worms, now black, to fall listlessly to the floor below.

"Get out of here," commanded Fincher as he notched another arrow from the bedded area of the home. The boy cocked back Alicia Salt's longbow as far as he could and sent another dart streaking across the room. This one struck Meemaw in the chest and forced her back into the now-raging fire behind her.

The fat woman let out an unnatural howl as the flames took hold, starting with her stained white dress before crawling along her skin. Whether it was Meemaw or the Worm making the sound, the children would never know.

Ditto appeared in the demolished doorway and ran forward to collect Hana, who was still paralyzed with fear on the floor.

"Get her out of here," cried Fincher as he sent arrow after arrow into the engulfed Meemaw. "Get them all farking out of here!"

Ditto didn't hesitate, tossing Hana through the opening before gathering everyone's packs and calling back to Sammi and Ash, who had finally recovered enough to join her sister.

"I've got everything! Let's go!" The sisters didn't move. "Let's go," Ditto repeated.

Ash and Sammi Bugg refused to respond. Instead, they both stalked forward, flaming sticks in hand, and lit the dining table. Its dry top instantly danced with flames, ensuring Meemaw had no escape.

The sisters, with blank looks on youthful faces, then finally exited the cottage, hefting their packs as they did.

Fincher and Ditto slid over to guard the door, longbow and hunting knife in their respective hands. The two boys looked on with shock as Meemaw stood before them, covered in fire.

The mouth-worm swung back and forth, screeching as it tried in vain to put out the fires consuming it. Threadlike worms, some white but most black, poured out from Meemaw's eyes and mouth, as well as the various open wounds inflicted by the Sour Flower Gang.

Meemaw shook uncontrollably for several seconds before freezing in place. Just as her movements stopped, a massive worm, at least a foot in diameter, exploded from Meemaw's too-extended stomach. It flopped loudly onto the engulfed table, covered in gore and flame, and writhed back and forth, squealing curses in a language that none understood.

"I think that's enough of this farking place," said Fincher, covering his mouth as he gagged.

"Agreed," replied Ditto, and both boys backed out of the cottage, their weapons still at the ready.

Ash, Sammi, and Hana were waiting outside, blades held out in shaking hands. As one, the Sour Flower Gang faced the cottage of horror as fire overtook it.

Bone-chilling, alien cries emanated from within, promising retribution of the darkest sort. And then they went quiet. And all was silent again, except for the crackling of heat on wood.

Fincher spoke without removing his hazel eyes from the inferno. "Where's that farking bastard Dooley?"

Ditto answered, also refusing to look away from the burning home of the Worm. "I gave him a pretty good beating, which is better than he deserved. I left him on the ground there."

"There's no one here, Ditto," said Sammi. "Just some of the worst-looking teeth I've ever seen."

"Fark," exclaimed Fincher. "The little shite could be anywhere."

"Not anytime soon," maintained Ditto. "I messed him up really bad."

"You should have finished the farking job."

"I had other things on my mind, Fincher! Like saving your butt!"

"My arse was fine, Ditto. In fact, it was better than—"

"Stop arguing," cut in Sammi. "Look."

The engulfed cottage collapsed in on itself, leaving only a mound of heat and fire and coals to denote where the Worm of Quaan had once called home.

"Let's get a move on," continued Sammi. "The farther away we can be from this cursed place before Paragon falls, the better."

"Finally, something I can agree with," said Fincher as he shouldered both Alicia Salt's longbow and his pack. "What a farking day."

After it was apparent that nothing would be slithering forth from the burnt cottage, Ditto finally sheathed his own blade and silently collected his belongings.

"These God-Snails better be worth it," was all that the large boy offered as he moved around the cottage, looking for a path to take him and his friends far, far away.

"Gods never farking are," stated Fincher flatly as he followed his friend, Sammi Bugg in tow.

Ash and Hana continued to stare into the roaring fire that once was Matilda and Dooley Hamm's home. Ash looked down at her younger friend and spoke with a voice that broke with sadness.

"I'm so sorry, Hana. This was all my fault. The boys knew Dooley was no good, but I wanted to believe. I wanted to believe that someone so different can still be good. I wanted to believe that someone missing so much could still offer something. I wanted to believe that someone like me not only existed but was capable of helping others. But I guess I was wrong. Oh, the Five Sisters, how I was wrong."

Hana looked up with soft eyes and took Ash's hand in hers. "You don't get it, do you, Ash?" The older girl's head cocked in confusion. "You didn't cause this. I did."

"But, Hana, how could you—"

"The Silver Stagg. I still must pay for the Silver Stagg. And none of you are safe around me until I do."

"But, Hana, that's ridiculous. This was all my doing. I'm the one who entrusted that little twist Dooley and I'm the one who—"

Hana held up a small hand. "I know what I did, Ash. And I know what must be done to me. But that doesn't mean that you all must suffer, as well. You should leave me here. Don't let me hurt the mission. There's too much at stake, too many lives still worth saving."

Ash knelt and swallowed her young friend in a one-armed hug. "Oh, Hana. You're one of us. An irreplaceable member of the Sour Flower Gang. We'll never leave you. We love you." Ash rose. "Now, let's catch up to the others. The sooner we can forget this dark place, the better our future will look."

Ash started to follow Fincher, Ditto, and her sister, but was stopped by a soft voice.

"I'm so sorry, Ash."

Ash offered a genuine smile to her friend. "I'm the one who needs to shoulder the blame here, Hana. Not you. There's nothing to be sorry for. Now, let's go."

Ash turned back and began to walk around the fiery home of Matilda and Dooley Hamm.

"Oh, but there is," Hana said quietly to the back of Ash. "Not only for what I've done. But for what will happen because of me. And a million sorries will never be enough."

~

Soon after leaving the Hamm cottage behind, sounds began to return to the forest. Although welcomed, each sound brought on a wince, a jump, a flinch. The Mutewoods had already revealed two sets of nightmares. How many more could the dark woods contain?

The children walked north in silence for hours, each processing the horrors they had endured over the past two days. At one point, sharp-eyed Hana spotted something off the trail, covered in leaves and dirt.

"What's this?" asked the girl as she wiped the flat object clean. The others leaned in and sighed heavily at what was revealed.

"Fark me."

It was large wooden sign, the words etched upon it done with care and precision. It was a sign meant to be seen. They were words meant to be read.

Turn Back! The Worm has returned to the Mutewoods. Matilda Hamm is the Worm! Turn Back! There is no hope.

"And how do you suppose this sign got to be here, buried under dirt and leaf," asked Ditto, but everyone already knew the answer.

Ash thought aloud. "I wonder how many signs there were. How many are now hidden from view?"

"This Dooley Hamm is a farking hard kid to like. Let's keep moving."

They continued even as the shadows began to deepen, denoting the fall of Paragon and the upcoming rise of the Five Sisters.

Sammi tripped over a root that ran across the small animal path on which the Sour Flower Gang walked. Luckily, Ditto was there to catch her before the girl fell to the ground.

"Okay, I think we've gone far enough," said Fincher. "We can barely farking see."

"Sammi can barely see even when Paragon's out," shot back Ash, and the children laughed a bit for the first time in what felt like an eternity.

Fincher continued after offering an appreciative nod to Ash. "Still, none of us are any good with farking twisted ankles or broken wrists. We need to set up camp."

"No way I sleep," said Sammi.

"Me either," agreed Hana.

"Sleep isn't the point," countered Fincher. "I may never sleep again thanks to the shite we've just seen. The point is to rest our muscles, properly tend to our wounds, and not farking snap our legs in the dark. What do you say?"

While the idea of closing their eyes was terrifying, the group could not disagree with Fincher's logic. They all shrugged in acquiescence, and the younglings moved off, each knowing their role and responsibility.

As they always did.

In no time at all, the Sour Flower Gang sat around a small campfire once more, injuries tended and wrapped, passing around jerky that no one felt like eating. They ate without speaking, their eyes darting into the surrounding Mutewoods. Every now and then, larger movement could be heard amidst the sounds of minor critters scampering around in the undergrowth.

Ditto was the one to give voice to everyone's worries.

"It's Dooley Hamm. He's been tracking us for the past couple of hours."

"You've known?" asked Ash, much more accusatory than she intended.

Ditto shrugged. "Didn't see the need to frighten anyone. We're all on high alert anyway."

"I didn't hear or see anything," said Fincher.

"And you're some great tracker?" asked Ash sarcastically.

"I know a farking creepo when I meet one."

Ash's face fell as Fincher's barb landed. Fincher looked away, upset at himself for hurting his dear friend. Ditto stepped back in before things could escalate.

"It's hard to make him out. I think he's taken to his tunnels. The little twist just pops out to make sure that he's still following us." Ditto looked to Fincher. "I actually never heard him." Back to the group. "I just happened to look to my right a while ago and caught a glimpse of him diving back under a Monarch Brown. He's stealthy, I'll give him that."

Sammi spoke without looking up from the fire. "You have to be to hunt and kill almost everything in a given area. And to send everything else left alive running."

"So, what do we do?" asked Ash, recovered from Fincher's words.

"Fark him," replied Fincher. "Dooley's a coward. He won't do anything."

"Well, I'm certainly not going to sleep knowing Dooley's out there," said Sammi.

"Chances are we weren't going to sleep anyway, sis."

Ditto pulled out his hunting knife and began to sharpen it. "You all should try to rest anyway, even if it doesn't result in sleep. We still have a long way to go to get through this forest, and who knows what awaits us in the coming days."

"I'll keep watch with you," said Fincher.

"The heck you will," snapped back Ash. "This is my mess, as you've said in so many words. I'll stay up with Ditto."

Fincher started to argue, but a look from Sammi behind the girl's round glasses held his tongue. He nodded reluctantly.

Fincher, Sammi, and Hana laid down on the forest floor, heads on packs and blades within reach. None of them bothered to lay out their bedrolls. As Ditto and Ash sat on logs on opposite sides of the encampment, weapons in hands and staring out into the Mutewoods, three sets of eyes stared up into the black canopy, refusing to close. Refusing to let the nightmares back in.

Sometime later, it could have been ten minutes or an hour, a voice reached out from the darkness, tickling the collective fear of the Sour Flower Gang. It floated in like a ghost, impossible to defend. And although the voice was familiar, it sounded different through missing teeth and a swollen face.

"Meemaw was my everything, everything to me was my Meemaw. You took her from me, burned her like a Shadowset witch, something she was not, Meemaw was never a witch."

At Dooley's words, Ditto and Ash sprung to their feet. The others rolled over quickly, kneeling with knives at the ready.

After several minutes of quiet, Dooley's voice came in from another angle, another part of the forest. Closer.

"Meemaw gave me everything, everything she gave, and I gave her whatever she needed. When she needed a snack, I gave what I could. I gave her squirrels and rabbits and foxes and birds, all of the creatures that I could catch." There was another long silence before Dooley spoke again, now farther away. "When the creatures were gone and Meemaw still hungered, I gave her more, I gave her what I could, what meat I could find. I started with little Mary Adlen, and, oh, how Meemaw enjoyed her, I've never seen Meemaw so happy, happier than I've ever seen her. I liked when Meemaw was happy, when she was happy, she was at her best. I kept bringing her meats, meats that made her happy, meats that made her full, even if for only a bit."

The children's heads swiveled back and forth as they looked for Dooley in the shadows. Their heads cocked as they listened for the pink-eyed boy's footsteps. But no sign of Dooley could be found. Only his voice gave him away, now coming in from the opposite direction.

"When the meats were gone and Meemaw still wanted meats, what could I do? What could I do? The village was empty, all had left the village, and the creatures were gone, they had left our corner of the forest. What could I do? Meemaw's hunger knew no end, and my love for her knew no end, and her love for me knew no end. But she cried, oh, how she cried, always crying for meat, meat that I could not give her. So, you know what I did, what I did for Meemaw, for my love of my Meemaw?" Another silence.

"I think I know where this farking story is going. And it ain't a love story like I'm used to."

"It actually seems pretty close to you and Reba Bugg," said Sammi, attempting in vain to cut the tension.

Dooley's monologue returned several long minutes later, sounding closer than ever.

"I let Meemaw pick an arm, an arm that could give her meat. Oh, how I hoped that she would pick the other arm, the arm that wasn't the best at digging, that was the arm I hoped she would pick. But my favorite arm, the good digging arm, it had more muscle, more meat, and that was the one Meemaw wanted, the one that would make her the most happy. That's the one I gave her…"

Dooley Hamm trailed off.

Eventually, when it became clear that the macabre story had ended, the Sour Flower Gang settled back onto their packs and logs. They stared wide-eyed into the trees and the canopy, hoping that their little bodies would continue to heal with only rest, for sleep was not an option.

After a while, Fincher looked back to find Ditto shaking with anger, his now-sharp knife bouncing on his knee.

"Just let me know if you want some relief, Ditto. No one's sleeping anyway."

The large boy responded without looking over. "The only thing I want is for Dooley Hamm to burst out of those cursed woods and into this camp. I want him to try it. I've never wanted anything more in my life. I've never wanted blood on my hands until now." Ditto finally looked down at his friend. "I don't like this feeling, Fincher."

Fincher fought for the right words. "Yeah, it doesn't suit you. But we still appreciate you for it. Ditto?"

"Yeah."

"Thanks."

"For what?"

"For protecting us."

Ditto scoffed. "It seems that I'm a terrible protector."

"Maybe. But you're ours, and we love you."

Ditto's green eyes returned to forest as he wiped a tear. "Thanks, Fincher."

"Give me a holler if you need help introducing Dooley to your knife."

"I can manage. Of at least that much, I'm sure."

Three things happened as the Five Sisters hung heavy over the Mutewoods. None of the Sour Flower Gang spoke. None of the Sour Flower Gang slept. And Dooley Hamm failed to make another appearance.

9

BERSERKERS, BURIALS, AND BADDIES

"I miss Triggy."

Ash looked down at her young friend as they marched north through the Mutewoods. "I know you do, Hana. But Triggy gave his life to save all of us. His death was more meaningful than most."

"We should all be so lucky," added Ditto at the lead.

"Yeah, there's no meaning in dying due to the farking Maddening. But Triggy? Now there's death to be farking proud of."

"I suppose," said Hana sadly. "But, I still miss him."

Ditto spoke, hacking at some branches that were blocking the animal path as he did. "Have you heard of the Wellspring, Hana?"

The young girl shook her head, sending her dark ponytail back and forth.

"My ma told me about it… when she first started to forget things. She said that when all living things die—plants, animals, people—it's just their physical forms that expire. The energy that really makes them alive never goes away. Instead, it flies up, past the Five Sisters and Paragon, past all the other stars, and returns to the Wellspring, where all the energy of the universe is kept and eventually recycled by the God-Snails. But it takes millions of years to recycle this energy, meaning that Triggy will be there when you finally pass on, as will I and Fincher and Sammi and Ash. And your ma and da. And my ma and da…" Ditto's voice began to quiver. He cleared his throat. "Anyway, what I mean to say is that you'll see Triggy again. And then you can thank him properly. We all can."

Hana didn't respond for a while and simply followed Ditto's lead through the forest. Then, "You really believe that, Ditto?"

The large boy turned back, his green-on-yellow eyes meeting Hana's, and he smiled warmly. "I do. My ma wouldn't lie to me."

Hana returned a smile of her own and wiped her cheeks with her sleeve. "I believe her, too. Thanks, Ditto."

"Don't mention it, squirt."

Ditto and Hana moved forward once more through the woods, the others following behind.

Fincher, Ash, and Sammi shared a knowing look.

"Farking guy always knows the perfect thing to say."

"Yes, he does," agreed Sammi.

"And he always means it," added Ash. "That's why he's the best."

Ash moved to catch up to the leading pair as Fincher and Sammi glanced to each other and smirked.

Later that afternoon, when Paragon was no longer overhead, a flash of color passed above the children, forcing them all to duck for cover. Their worry was short-lived, however, when Ash giggled and pointed her lone index finger to a branch just ahead.

"Look who finally found us," she said, and all eyes followed her line to the bright-colored bird that rested on the nearest Monarch Brown. The Quilted Raven released a loud squawk, and everyone let out relieved laughs.

"Rashii! How did he find us?" asked Hana.

"What do you mean?" replied Ditto cheerily. "Rashii's the partner of Quaan's greatest tracker and huntress. Of course, he was going to find us. It was just a matter of time. Isn't that right, Rashii?"

Another squawk filled the forest air.

"Finally, some farking good news. It's great to have you back, Rashii."

"We missed you, Rashii. And your eyes in the sky," remarked Sammi.

"You can say that again, sis."

"See," said Fincher. "Things are already getting better. Rashii's back. We're making good progress. I think we finally left the shite behind us. Isn't that right, Rashii?"

This time, the Quilted Raven did not answer.

"Shite! Shite! Shite! Shite," exclaimed Fincher under his breath from the front of the line the next day, waving the rest of the Sour Flower Gang down as he did.

"What is it?" asked Ash as she took a knee on the leafy ground.

Fincher pointed ahead and to the group's left. "Look."

The younglings had been ascending slowly for the past couple hours and were now looking down a steep decline to the forest floor beneath them. There, three creatures lounged, their light grey fur easily standing out against the background of brown and green.

Sammi shuffled forward. "What are they?"

Fincher's hazel eyes studied the scene below, where the trio of animals had begun to wrestle with each other. Although they pounced around on all fours, every now and then one of them would rise up on two thick legs, showcasing their full height of five feet, taller than both Hana and Sammi.

White spikes of bone escaped their grey fur and ran from the top of the creatures' heads down their broad backs. Their front paws were tipped with the longest claws Fincher had ever seen, and the boy had seen Ghost Pumas up close.

Fincher whispered back to Sammi and the gang. "Berserkers."

"What?"

"Berserker bears. My da told me about them."

"Impossible!" fired back Ditto quietly. "They're only supposed to live in the Spired Curtains. Only along Shadowset, to be exact."

Fincher turned to face his big friend. "You think humans are the only things that can use Salt's Pass? They must have crossed over into the Mutewoods."

"Why?" asked Sammi.

"Do I look like a farking bear? I'm sure they had their reasons."

Ash continued to stare down as she spoke under her breath. "And you're sure that's what these are?"

Instead of answering, Fincher simply said one word. "Ditto?"

Green eyes moved from the trio of bears to Ash. "They certainly fit the description."

"Are they friendly?"

"They're called farking *Berserkers*."

Ash swatted Fincher with a dark hand. "But what does that mean?"

"It means that they go farking crazy when they feel threatened. They're supposed to be all muscle and rage."

"They don't seem that scary."

"Oh, yeah? You see those claws of theirs? They're tipped in poison. You know why?"

"To poison you?" Ash snapped back.

Fincher rolled his eyes. "Yes, to poison you. But not to kill you. Oh, no, that wouldn't be near horrible enough. The poison simply paralyzes you. Do you know why?"

Ash shrugged.

"Because Berserkers like to eat their prey while they're still alive. In fact, they won't eat anything that isn't still breathing. They're the opposite of scavengers."

"Okay, okay, I get it," Ash relented.

"I thought they'd be bigger," stated Ditto as he returned to studying the Berserkers. "I heard that they were ten feet and more."

Fincher thought for a moment. "Yeah, well, you know how stories go. Ten feet sounds a lot farking more interesting than five."

"Well, they weren't exaggerating about the claws."

Fincher sighed deeply. "No. No, they weren't."

Sammi pushed her glasses farther up her nose. "So, what do we do?"

Fincher looked to his left and his right. "I guess we need to find a way around."

"Why can't they smell us?" asked Ash.

Ditto responded before Fincher had the chance, holding up a wet finger as he did. "Feel the wind. We're downwind from them. For now."

"Which is why we need to move fast," agreed Fincher before looking up at Rashii perched above the children. He called out quietly to the bird. "And where was the heads up, Rashii? Forget your farking job without Miss Salt here?"

"Don't talk to him like that," scolded Hana, and Ash and Sammi swatted Fincher at the same time to back up their young friend.

"Okay, okay, sorry. Sheesh. I hope one day to get as much support as that farking bird." Everyone grinned as they always did when Fincher got worked up. "But, we still need to move fast. Agreed?"

The group nodded as one.

Fincher went on. "Let's drop our packs and investigate. Sammi and I will go to the left and see if there's another trail down. Ditto and Ash, do the same to the right. We'll make a ruckus through the trees and undergrowth if we can't find an alternative path. I don't know about you all, but being eaten alive sounds like the runny shites."

Packs were removed from shoulders and laid gently upon the ground. The pairs went off, down the trail a bit and then to opposite sides, leaving Hana to watch over the bags.

Several minutes later, a whistle resembling birdsong but unmistakably Ash reached the others' ears. They all returned and met where they had split from the trail, Hana still standing guard above them.

Ditto gave a thumbs up. "We found another trail, actually larger and cleaner than this one. Should keep us quiet."

"Where does it go?" asked Sammi.

"It goes east for a ways and then northeast down the hill, which is less steep farther that way. Anyway, it will keep us moving forward while taking us far from the Berserkers."

"Good. Let's get our packs and farking—"

Squawk! Squawk! Squawk!

A look of terror passed among the children as heads shot toward the Berserkers, who remained where they were, unbothered by the Quilted Raven.

"Hana," screamed Sammi, no longer caring about the man-eating bears at the bottom of the hill.

The group spun back just as Dooley Hamm fell upon Hana from behind. The small girl shrieked in pain as the pale boy appeared out of shadow and sank his dirty, pointy teeth into her neck.

The younglings sprung forward as one, blades in hands, and ran up the trail as fast as they could. As they did, Dooley ripped his head back, sending a geyser of Hana's blood into the air, licking his thin lips as he did. The young girl dropped, small hands covering a giant wound, while Dooley jumped to the side, giggling in bloodlust.

Ditto ran past Hana, knowing that Sammi would see to her, and chased after the pink-eyed boy. Fincher scooped up Alicia Salt's longbow and joined in the hunt. Sammi slid next to her fallen friend, her glasses nearly tumbling from her face as she did, and placed her own hand over the hole in Hana's neck.

"Bandages," called out Sammi desperately and looked over when she saw no immediate response. Ash stood frozen, her eyes large as she took on the blood-soaked ground. "Ash! Ash!" The one-armed girl finally looked to her sister. Sammi spoke more softly. "Bandages. Now."

Ash dove into the nearest pack, removing some strips of white cloth and handing them to Sammi, who began wrapping the wound as if she were a veteran war medic.

Away from that chaotic scene, another unfolded. Dooley Hamm laughed as a he quickly dipped behind a tree, an arrow burying itself in the trunk as he did.

"Thank you for the snack, what a snack it was, just what I needed to heal, to heal from the big boy's hits, but this snack will help."

"Get over here," demanded Ditto, "and let me finish what I started, Dooley."

"No, no. No, no. The start was no good, but the finish will be grand, a grand finish and a full belly. Full of your friends. Full of you, large boy."

Fincher snuck around the tree, but Dooley was already gone.

"Where the fark is the little shite?!"

Ditto shook his head and called out over his shoulder. "Ash! Stay ready!"

"You don't have to tell me," the tough girl called back, standing overtop Sammi and Hana, knife in hand. "And I hope the little bastard comes!"

The rare cuss word from Ash gave Fincher an idea.

"Yeah, show yourself you *bastard*, Dooley! Or should I call you a farking *orphan*?! No ma and no da? Sounds like a farking orphan to me! You're an orphan because you're a shite little twist, Dooley! No one likes you! No one loves you! Meemaw let the worms in to get away from you! Meemaw—"

Dooley leapt out of shadow, the sharp nails of his lone hand leading the way. Despite the suddenness of his attack, however, Fincher was ready for him.

Fincher brought Alicia Salt's longbow down and across, catching the boy in the face mid-air and sending him somersaulting across the forest floor. Ditto sprinted toward the downed boy, ready to kill.

Dooley recovered impossibly fast, scooping up a handful of soil and hurling it into Ditto's green eyes just as his hunting knife went up to strike.

Ditto shouted as his left hand went to his damaged eyes, but he swung anyway, his blade catching nothing but air as Dooley rolled to the side and jumped to his feet. Vibrating eyes went wide, and Dooley took off running.

"Fark! He's heading for the Monarch Brown, Ditto! Another farking tunnel, I'm sure."

As Ditto tried to clear his eyes, Fincher gave chase, notching an arrow as he did. Unfortunately, Fincher Bugg was no Alicia Salt, and bolt after bolt missed its moving mark. Dooley reached the base of the

Monarch Brown unscathed. He turned back to Fincher before leaping into one of his beloved tunnels.

"Don't be sad, sad isn't the thing to be. I'll return shortly, and an empty belly I'll have, a belly with no meat in it, but you'll have the meat that I want, the meat that I need, the meat that I'll—"

A roar snatched Dooley's words from his mouth as something raced around the Monarch Brown and rose up, higher and higher. Five feet became seven which became ten and then twelve.

"The farking momma," said Fincher to himself as Dooley dove headfirst toward his hole at the base of the Monarch.

But the momma Berserker was faster.

Impossibly long, impossibly sharp claws clipped Dooley's back, just enough that the boy went twisting and turning to land hard on the thick roots of the mammoth tree.

Fincher held his breath, waiting for the boy to spring back up. But Dooley remained unmoved.

As Ditto, eyes now clear, and Fincher slowly backed away from the twelve-foot beast, the momma Berserker easily lifted Dooley with a clawed paw and tossed the boy onto flatter ground. Dooley Hamm rolled to a stop on his back, his head facing Ditto and Fincher. Pink-eyes remained open, vibrating very slowly now.

Fincher and Ditto continued to carefully back away until they reached Ash, Sammi, and the injured Hana.

Ditto spoke without looking away from the apex predator. "Everyone collect your things. We need to be away from this place."

"She can't move," said Sammi from her knees.

"Then I'll carry her. But we have to go now."

Sammi began to say something, but instead tied another knot around Hana's wound and jumped up to gather her pack, as did everyone else.

The momma Berserker released a strange, guttural sound into the air, and the three now-obviously Berserker cubs ran past the Sour Flower Gang to join their mother.

Another guttural sound and the trio of cubs dove into Dooley, two taking hold of the boy's legs as the third bit into his stomach. A loud *crunch* echoed across the forest as a tibia was snapped followed by the popping of a fibula on the other leg.

Packs went to backs, Alicia's longbow found Fincher's shoulder, and Ditto cradled Hana Bugg in his arms.

The third Berserker cub shuffled backward, taking Dooley's entrails in its mouth with it. Little white worms could be seen swimming in the blood that began to pool around Dooley.

The children stared as the worms were lapped up by the cubs, a surprising accoutrement to the regular meat and blood.

The momma Berserker, taking note of the Sour Flower Gang as if for the first time, roared into the air, sending every creature in the vicinity, including Rashii, scampering or flying away.

"I think that's our farking cue to leave."

"Agreed," came the reply as one.

Ditto, Hana in his arms, ran down the trail first, followed by Sammi, then Ash.

Fincher started to turn to leave but hesitated. He watched for a moment as the cubs continued to feed, their grunts and moans denoting pure joy as the momma Berserker looked on protectively.

Fincher's hazel eyes crept up the boy's bloody body, from half-consumed legs to cavernous belly, until he reached Dooley's face. The boy's pink eyes no longer vibrated, so fully paralyzed they were from the Berserker poison, but neither were they dead.

Light still shone behind the pinkness and an unusual, almost imperceptible smile was pasted on the boy's thin lips as worms, part of Meemaw, entered the Berserker cubs to live again in another host.

Fincher spun away and followed his friends, leaving Dooley Hamm behind—alive but eaten.

"We have to stop," implored Sammi as the group moved north with all haste. "I have to see to her wound!"

A roar flew through the Mutewoods, chasing after the Sour Flower Gang.

"That's her telling us that we're not farking far enough away!"

"Agreed," said Ditto, Hana bouncing in his arms as he spoke. "We have to keep going."

Sammi didn't argue, but the girl did continue preparing new bandages in her hands as they continued to travel. Finally…

"Ditto! Please! I need to see to her!"

Ditto looked to Fincher, who nodded, not having heard the sounds of the momma Berserker for at least ten minutes. The large boy immediately dropped to his knees, placing Hana gently on the ground before him.

Sammi was there in an instant, pushing Ditto away. She removed the old bandages, which were now stained a deep crimson. As she did, a fountain of blood escaped the wound, striking her in the face and coating her round glasses.

"I can't see! Someone hold these clean bandages onto the wound!"

Ash was there before anyone else, her hand pressing the clean dressing into the hole at Hana's neck. Once her glasses were wiped clear, Sammi took over once more.

"Hana, look at us! You're going to be all right. Okay? I need you to know that. You're going to be all right."

Hana slowly opened her black, almond eyes. "It had to be this way. The Silver Stagg had to be avenged. I'm sorry you all have to see it."

"Fark that! There's nothing to see, Hana. Just you getting better and us going to meet the durn God-Snails. Now, no more crazy talk!"

Hana continued to speak from the ground. "Ditto?"

The large boy pushed his way forward. "I'm here, Hana."

"I'm sorry, Ditto."

"There's nothing to be sorry for, sweet girl. Especially you. You never have anything to be sorry for."

"Not this time, Ditto."

"Enough of that talk! Just lay there and Sammi will fix you up."

"Ditto?"

"I'm here, Hana."

"Do you really believe what you said about the Wellspring?"

The girl's question, as did the entire terrible scene, caught Ditto off-guard. "I… I don't know, Hana. I don't know what I believe."

"You should. Believe about the Wellspring, that is. I saw it, Ditto. I saw it in the eyes of the Silver Stagg. That's why I'm not afraid, Ditto."

"You're not afraid because there's nothing to be afraid of," responded Fincher when Ditto could not. "You'll be up and singing in no time."

Hana offered up a smile from below. "Not this time, Fincher. This time I'm going home. Back to the Wellspring. It's really not much of a punishment…"

Hana's words grew quieter as she spoke.

"No, no, no," repeated Ditto, as if his denial could stop the inevitable.

"Tell Ma and Da I'll see them later. I'll see you all later…" The girl's black eyes drew to a close.

"The fark you will! Hana, wake up! We still have a long way to go, and we need you, you durn fool! Wake up!"

Sammi removed her glasses and wiped her face. "She's not sleeping, Fincher."

"Then, what's she farking doing?!"

"She's gone. Our Hana's gone."

Everyone fell to the ground, as if their strings to the heavens had been cut. Seven hands went to Hana Bugg as tears flowed down faces. From above, Rashii squawked, not in warning but in mourning.

Minutes turned into an hour before the younglings were able to recover and rise to their feet.

"We need to bury her," stated Sammi, always one to return to the task at hand first.

"No!"

"She needs a proper burial, Ditto!"

"That's not what I mean! I mean not here! She needs somewhere beautiful, like her."

"She's gone, Ditto."

"I don't care!"

Fincher, Ash, and Sammi leaned back, unaccustomed to such outbursts from their usually even-keeled friend.

"It's fine," cut in Fincher. "It's fine. We'll find the perfect place for her. Okay, Ditto?"

The large boy nodded as he wiped the moisture from his cheeks. "I'll carry her as far as I need to."

Sammi almost said something, but Fincher held up a hand. "You got it, Ditto. I'll grab both your packs. Let's find a place before night falls."

The children walked in silence for several more hours. Every now and then, someone would point out a possible location, only to have it shot down by Ditto.

Eventually, the large boy found something he liked, stating simply, "Here."

A loud, musical forest stream had crept out from the west and ran parallel to the trail. To the right, a hillock broke free from the ground and rose up several dozen feet. Ditto began to scale the incline without further word. The others followed their grieving friend.

Ditto was panting heavily by the time he crested the forest mound, which was topped by a circular collection of wildflowers. Below, the Mutewoods spread out in all its shadowy beauty, and the air was thick with the gentle sounds of the stream that ran just beneath.

"What do you think?" asked Ditto, although he already knew the answer.

"It's perfect, Ditto," said Ash. "She'll love it here."

The large boy nodded sadly and softly placed Hana's body onto a grouping of wildflowers. Fincher knelt down and carefully removed the Ghost Puma pendant from around the girl's neck. It was stained with her blood.

"I'll make sure that Kenn and Joon get this," he said as he placed the tooth in his pack.

Without words, the four children all began to dig into the soil with their hands, not wanting to dull the edges of their weapons.

An hour later, Hana Bugg's body was returned to Quaan, her spirit already well on its way to the Wellspring.

Fincher, Ash, Ditto, and Sammi stood around the mound topped with colorful petals in mournful silence, each saying goodbye to their young friend in their own way.

As Paragon fell again, it was Fincher who finally voiced his thoughts.

"And, so, the Sour Flower Gang is no more. The world's greatest Moon Voice has returned to her rightful place in the stars."

"It's my fault," said Sammi, pushing her glasses up her runny nose. "I couldn't stop the bleeding."

"Fark that, Sammi. It's mine. I never should have left her alone in the Mutewoods. I really thought that little twist had stopped following us."

"No, Fincher," stated Ditto flatly, "I had Dooley under me, beaten to a pulp. I was too cowardly to finish the job. And now my friend is dead."

"Shut up, all of you!" Ash's anger made all the others jump. "You all know that Hana's death is on me. Me and my stupid trust in Dooley freaking Hamm. You can all stop pretending. I know what I've done."

"Look, I think we all can agree that there's plenty of blame to go around," asserted Sammi. "But Hana's gone, and we're still here. And we have a job to do. Not just for us, but for all the people of Quaan."

"Fark the people of Quaan."

"Fine, just for us, then."

This seemed to rally the children from their despair.

"Aye, just for us," echoed Ditto.

"Yeah, just for us," echoed Ash.

"Farking right. Just for us."

Sammi hefted her pack. "Then, we keep pushing?"

The others nodded and grabbed their packs, Ditto adding Hana's to his own. After kneeling to kiss the mound where their friend lay, the children carefully made their way down the steep hill.

Fincher, as he was wont to do, turned back one last time. More than the others, Fincher understood that he was leaving behind more than simply Hana Bugg. He was leaving behind the Sour Flower Gang.

He was leaving behind the idea that nothing could bring harm to him and his friends, as long as they stayed together and true to each other.

Fincher Bugg was leaving behind the belief that good would always triumph over evil, that their mission was fated to be successful. Fincher Bugg was leaving a part of himself on that hillock overlooking the Mutewoods.

He just prayed that it wasn't the best of himself that he was leaving behind. And that the worst was not yet to come.

The next two days proved rather uneventful, offering the children a much-needed break from the madness of their journey. Sleep, although filled with dreams of beasts and worms and assassins, came at night, providing their small bodies a chance to heal and recover, although their spirits remained heavily bruised.

Fincher's skill with Alicia Salt's longbow was improving, with the boy dropping a fat woodland turkey at the end of the first day.

With bellies stretched full and a bit more distance between the younglings and the loss of their friend, days were slowly growing brighter, even under the thick canopy of the Mutewoods.

Every now and then, Rashii would squawk—one time, thank the Five Sisters—from up ahead, denoting that the pathway before them was clear of danger.

Just as Paragon was beginning to rise on the third day, something unexpected happened.

The stagg trail on which the children had been traveling for the better part of a day emptied onto an actual road that was running through the Mutewoods. Although nothing like the Spearway or the Kassimedes Thoroughfare, it was still a manmade construct, stamped down with gravel and bearing evidence of regular use.

The Mutetrack, as the children would go on to call it, ran from east to west, but could also be seen offering a northern option not far down to the younglings' right.

The now-quartet stood for a moment on the stagg trail, pondering their next move.

"I thought the whole point was to avoid major roads," stated Ash.

Sammi took the break from walking to clean her glasses on her shirt. "Yes, but I would hardly call this a major road. It's more of a traveling lane, a track."

"That's right, sis—a *traveling* lane. Meaning that there are *travelers*. I thought we were trying to avoid those."

Fincher cut in. "Any more than farking Marsh Ghouls and Berserkers?"

"And the Worm," threw in Ditto.

Ash sighed deeply. "No, I suppose not. So, what do we say? Vote?"

"Vote," everyone said together.

"Sis?"

Sammi returned her glasses to her face and looked in all directions, always wanting full information before making a decision. "We were supremely unlucky our first few days in the Mutewoods and have just recently found another smooth time of it. The percentages still aren't in our favor in terms of trekking through the woods. I say we take this Mutetrack."

"Agreed," said Fincher immediately, not waiting for his turn. "I've seen enough of the farking Mutewoods to last me a lifetime. The Mutetrack is a welcome sight."

Sammi turned to Ash. "What are your thoughts, sis?"

Ash took some time. "I feel like we've handled the worst of the Mutewoods. What else could this place, this natural world, possibly throw at us? But the Mutetrack is the world of men. And I don't think we've even begun to see the horrors that they can bring."

"The heck we haven't, Ash. In case you didn't notice, we live in the farking Stenches!"

Sammi thought her sister would yell back at Fincher, but she didn't. And that bothered Sammi all the more.

"I think that there's probably a lot worse that they have to offer than Crimmish, Fincher."

Ash's words hit like a punch to the gut. Sammi turned to the large boy.

"Ditto?"

Fincher looked over at his friend and, for the first, recognized that a change had taken place. Ditto stood taller, tighter, his large frame coiled as if ready to strike. Gone was the surrounding easiness, the looseness of demeanor, that made Ditto so uniquely special. This probably would have vanished with age, anyway, but Fincher was hoping for a few more years with the carefree version of his friend. Now, a serious look had settled on the boy's face. And it didn't look to be leaving anytime soon.

"There's nothing left that frightens me. I've lost almost everything. There're only three things that I care about now. And those might not matter if we don't get north fast. I say we take the Mutetrack. And all the danger that it may bring."

A heaviness settled over the group as others started to pick up what Fincher had already discovered. Their large friend, the great protector, had changed. And not necessarily for the better.

Ash, who looked the most saddened by this revelation, still managed to speak first.

"Then it's settled. Goodbye forest trails and hello Mutetrack. North?"

"North," everyone agreed.

The children, for the first time in what seemed an eternity, stepped out of the wilderness of the Mutewoods and into the world of man. Only time would tell which was more nightmarish.

It didn't take long for the world of man to show its inhospitality.

The Quilted Raven squawked once, then again from up ahead, around a sharp bend in the Mutetrack. Luckily, a third signal from Rashii did not come.

"Fark me. Someone's waiting for us."

"Some*one* or some*thing*," inquired Sammi, and none could even begin to formulate a guess, not after what had been witnessed since entering these cursed woods.

"Both sound shite," said Fincher. "Go around? Back into the forest?"

"No." Three heads turned to face Ditto, whose answer seemed to leave no room for discussion or vote.

Fincher decided to bite. "And why not?"

The green-on-yellow eyes that ran from hazel to black had something different within them, an anger at the world that wasn't there three days before.

"Because I'm not running anymore. I'm not hiding. I'm not *going around*. Going around has cost us days we don't have and the life of a dear friend that we'll never get back. Whatever's up ahead, I'm going through it. I'm done letting life just *happen* to us. It never tips in our favor. I aim to put my finger on the scale and change our luck." Ditto was speaking to himself as much as the others, and he finally seemed to take notice. "Of course, that's just my opinion. If a vote's in order, then let's take it."

"I don't need one," said Ash. "If you want to go forward, Ditto, then I go with you. I hope you can do something with a girl with one good arm."

"It's never not been enough, Ash."

Fincher and Sammi shared a look, the whisper of a smile, and shrugged at the same time.

"No farking vote this time, Ditto. You go. We follow. Knives out?"

"No," declared the large boy emphatically. "Let them underestimate us. It's the greatest weapon we have."

For once, the three consecutive squawks from Rashii did not send the children into a panic. Instead, they continued along the Mutetrack as if they didn't have a care in the world. Blades remained in belts and Alicia Salt's longbow stayed slung over Fincher Bugg's shoulder.

The forest shook along both sides of the Mutetrack as grizzled highwaymen stormed out from the left and right, just ahead of the children. Another exited the forest behind the quartet, smiling wickedly while bouncing a heavy club in his hands.

"Well, well, what do we have here?" asked the cutthroat to the right, showcasing his brown teeth as he spoke.

All three of the men wore dirty breeches and ripped vests that revealed tattooed arms and chests. The man to the children's left was missing an eye while the spokesman of the trio seemed without a large chunk of his skull, courtesy of a well-placed sword strike, no doubt. The club-wielding bandit closing in from behind looked to be without major injury, perhaps due to him being significantly younger than his fellow robbers.

The man who originally addressed the children continued to speak as all three advanced on their targets.

"Four lovelies, each more lovely than the last," he remarked under his dented head. "Is that what you see, Marvin?"

"It is, indeed," answered Marvin from the left, twirling a nasty-looking hatchet in his hand as he did. "Two strapping boy lovelies to be sold into slavery—"

"They'll fetch good money in Cassie's Clutch," interrupted the young man from the back.

"That's what I was going to say, Lee, you twat! But maybe I'll sell you instead since you're always in such a rush. They love twats like you in—"

"Enough! Both of you!"

"Sorry, Ray."

"Yeah, sorry, boss."

Ray rubbed a dirty hand over his scarred head. "Finish what you were saying, Marvin."

Marvin grinned, showing more gaps than teeth in his mouth. "I was saying two lovely boys for the slavers. And two more-than-lovely girls for us, Ray. I'd say we've just hit the jackpot. Oh, but the fun the five of us are gonna have." Marvin aimed his next words at Ditto and Fincher. "Sorry, lads, but seven's a crowd, so you'll have to just look on from the sidelines."

"Maybe they'll learn a thing or two," added Lee, and Marvin rolled his eyes.

"Anyway," cut in Ray before his co-conspirators could start arguing once more, "the point is that you four are our property now. Now, I know you don't like this, but it's really your best option. Better to be valued property than discarded meat."

Something in that word—*meat*—triggered Ditto, who stood a little taller, his chin out a bit more. The large boy took a careful step forward, his hands still clear of his weapon.

"We don't want any trouble, misters. We know when we're outmatched by our betters."

"I've heard of taking candy from babies, but never babies just giving over their candy," commented Lee from the rear, disgust heavy in his voice.

"Yeah, I was hoping for a bit more than yer giving, kid," stated Marvin. "But, I guess they don't make men like they used to."

Ray snickered in agreement. "Just as well, I suppose. Keeps us from having to damage the goods." He shot a look at Ash and Sammi. "Especially the girly goods."

"I bet they taste like caramel," shouted out Lee from behind.

"You've never tasted caramel, you twat," countered Marvin.

"Yeah, but I can imagine! And I'm gonna know soon enough. Very soon enough. I can smell what I'm looking for from here!"

As the idiotic trio kept up their banter, Ditto slowly walked forward, his hands out easily to his sides, offering no threat to the confident highwaymen.

Ray watched as Ditto approached, fingering the weathered sword still sheathed at his side. He licked his too-dry lips before speaking again.

"My eyes aren't what they used to be, living in this durn dark forest. But now that you're closer, I see that you're a hunky boy, aren't you? Perhaps I'll make an exception for you, hunky boy. Maybe we can have a little fun, after all. Before I sell you to highest bidder, that is. Maybe I'll let you—"

Ditto spun in a blur, drawing his hunting knife and running it across Ray's exposed belly in one clean motion. When the large boy finally ended his spin, all seven characters on the Mutetrack stared at each other in silent confusion.

That is, until Ray's entrails poured out of the deep cut in his stomach and made a loud *splat* onto the gravelly road. Then, everything came unpaused.

"You little shite," screamed Ray as he clutched at his intestines with both hands. "I'm gonna—"

Ray's words were cut off, however, as Ditto lunged forward, planting his knife with a *thud* between the cutthroat's eyes.

As Ditto struck, Marvin's one eye went wide and the bandit hollered in rage, raising his hatchet overhead as he did. In two strides he was upon Ditto, whose own blade was now buried deep in Ray's skull, leaving the boy completely vulnerable.

Something stayed Marvin's hand, however, just as he meant to bring his small axe down onto Ditto's blond-haired head. The highwayman looked down in confusion as the shaft of an arrow now peeked out from his chest, vibrating in the cool forest air.

"What the fark?" asked Marvin before two more bolts found new homes in his throat and side. The hatchet hit the Mutetrack a few seconds before its owner's body.

Lee called out to his companions, hefted his club high, and ran forward to avenge them, his rage squarely pointed at Ditto and Fincher.

Big mistake.

Ash's lone arm shot out as the younger bandit passed, cutting a neat line in the side of Lee's neck, sending a fountain of blood into the air.

Sammi wasted no time in backing up her sister, sidestepping around the man and sending her own knife into his back once, twice, thrice.

Lee paused in the middle of the Mutetrack, confusion painted on his dumb face. "What the fark?" he said with a watery voice before face-planting onto the gravel, leaving a crimson mark to pool around him.

Ditto calmly ripped his blade from Ray's forehead and slid it back under his belt before scooping up Marvin's wicked hatchet and placing the new weapon along the opposite side of his waist.

Fincher retrieved his arrows from Marvin's body, wiping the gore from their tips onto the dead man's clothes before returning them to his quiver.

Ash and Sammi silently ran through Lee's pockets, collecting what little chips there were to take and adding them to their own purses. They also found some dried meat, which they wrapped with their own rations.

When they had all completed their tasks, the children met back at the center of the Mutetrack, nodding to each other as they came together.

"No more victims, I guess," said Ash.

"No more," agreed Ditto.

"Bury the bodies?"

"Fark them. And fark their bodies. Any problems with that?" The other three shook their heads. "Then we keep it moving?" All nodded.

Ash and Sammi moved on ahead, creeping north along the Mutetrack, both sets of brown eyes scanning the edges of the rudimentary road, leaving Fincher and Ditto alone.

Fincher watched as Ditto tried in vain to wipe the dried crimson onto his trousers.

"You got blood on your hands?"

Ditto looked up with green-on-yellow eyes. "I do."

"It suits you better now."

"Is that a good thing, Fincher?"

Fincher sighed heavily and clapped his large, kind friend on the back. "It's a necessary thing, I'm afraid. Not just for you, but for all of us. The world wants to fark us? Then, we fark them first. And we do it without hesitation."

"For us?"

Fincher smiled. "That's right. For us. And no one else."

Ditto's eyes went wide as he looked past Ash and Sammi, who had stopped in their tracks up ahead, to a group that was heading south along the Mutetrack, inevitably toward the younglings.

Despite the distance, one thing was clear. These were not normal men. They were giants. And not in the way that a big man was referred to as a giant. But in the way that a true colossus of legend was called a giant.

Ditto looked down at his suddenly puny-looking hunting knife and hatchet. "But, in some cases, maybe a little hesitation is called for. Wouldn't you agree?"

Fincher watched as the six figures drew closer, seeming more enormous with each step they took.

"Farking right, Ditto. Farking right."

PART II

THE BLOODLESS TITANS OF LAKE CROWN

10

ALSO KNOWN AS VATTASSAV

Ash shielded her eyes from Paragon with her lone hand. She squinted, as if unable to believe what she was seeing.

"Do we have to stand and fight?" she asked, nervously fingering her dagger as she did.

"Fark that. Do you see the size of those... *things?*"

"Maybe it's an optical illusion. You know, caused by heat off the Mutetrack or something."

"It's not," Sammi stated flatly. "They're literal giants."

"Then we run?"

"Maybe we don't have to do either." Ditto pointed up, and the group raised their heads to find Rashii resting lazily in a tree along the gravelly road. "Either he's suddenly gone blind, or Rashii knows something we don't."

Sammi lowered her face and pushed her glasses back up her nose. "Wait and find out?"

"I guess so, sis. Ditto?"

"Agreed. Fincher? Is this where hesitancy is the greater form of valor?"

"I farking hope so."

The children didn't have to wait long for the towering sextet to reach them. As the giants approached, more than their eight-foot heights began to stand out.

Despite there being a clear mix of four men and two women, the similarities between individuals were striking, with each having long amber hair, wide-set eyes of the brightest orange, and a variety of colorful rings through their ears. Red tattoos of unique design covered the whitest skin ever seen next to Dooley Hamm's. But while Dooley's was a sickly, ghostly white, the skin of these colossuses looked healthy and nutrient rich. This too-white skin was pulled tight over bulging muscles that looked able to bend the world. Or a child, at the very least.

Although large and frightening and powerful, the men and women who strode toward the younglings were also beautiful under their oversized conical hats fashioned from fresh forest leaves. They walked softly in stagg-skin moccasins that complemented loose breeches and tight-fitting vests. All six wore massive axes at their hips made of a strange material.

The group of giants stopped several feet from the children. The man in front, who also wore a thick amber mustache, was the first to speak.

His brow furrowed in confusion. "This is who has been pestering our trade mates and upending shipments? They look truly unimposing."

Another male voice came in from the back. "Not unimposing. Truly tiny."

"I think they are children, Victiss," said a woman from the right whose long hair came down in tight braids.

"How would you know, Tallia?" asked the male from the back. Fincher leaned over to see that the man was clean-shaven and sported a dark red scar across his left cheek.

The woman responded over her bare shoulder. "Because they're *small*, Vochus, you fool!"

"They are *all* small! *All* the Soul-burned." This brought laughter from the others.

"Quiet," demanded Victiss, and the group quickly fell silent. The man's orange eyes took in all four of the kids. "Are you children?"

"We are," answered Fincher.

"And you have been interfering with our shipments?"

Fincher looked to the others before responding. "We have not."

"Are you sure? The penalty for lying is the same as the penalty for stealing, which is death, although you can expect it fast and painless."

"We didn't mess with your farking shipments. And I don't farking lie."

"Unless it's telling Reba Bugg that she's beautiful," retorted Sammi, who was already laughing before she could even get the joke out. Fincher glanced over with a look of shock.

"Even now, Sammi? Farking heck!"

"Sorry, Fincher, I couldn't help myself."

Ash jumped in. "Yeah, you did kind of set yourself up for that one, Fincher. I mean, how many times did you tell that horse-face—"

"I *told* you! It's not a horse *face*. It's just horse *teeth*! When we get back—"

"Silence!" Victiss's booming voice caused all the kids to jump. The giant turned to the woman known as Tallia. "They are definitely children. And not the highwaymen that we seek. I'd recognize that prattle anywhere."

Fincher stepped forward, determined to show that he was not afraid, although his cracking voice betrayed him a bit.

"If it's highwaymen you're farking looking for, take a peek behind us. We left three of them to rot under Paragon."

Victiss nodded to Tallia, and she and another male, this one with long amber sideburns and a small diamond tattoo on his chin, sprinted ahead on long legs.

As the two quartets stared at each other, Fincher Bugg couldn't help himself.

"Looking for cutthroats, are you?"

Victiss looked down at the boy. "We are."

"Cutting into your profits, are they?"

"They are."

"So, how much?"

"How much, what?"

"How much are you going to give us for doing your farking job for you?"

"Fincher," the other three yelled as one, convinced that their loud-mouthed friend had just doomed them all.

To his credit, Victiss did not rise to the bait. Instead, he simply smiled at the precocious boy. Moments later, the giant pair returned.

"Well?" prompted the giant leader.

Tallia looked upon the children as if for the first time. "Three bodies back there. They appear to be the men we were looking for."

The other giant chimed in. "They are cut to pieces. One has a pile of his insides next to him. Another is full of arrows. The third looks to have been—"

Victiss interrupted. "I get the picture, Vimos."

Vimos continued. "There is no way that these… *children*… did this."

In a flash, Fincher had unshouldered Alicia's Salt's longbow and drawn it back with an arrow already notched, pointing squarely at Vimos.

"Care to farking rethink that?"

After a tense few seconds, the pressure was released as deep laughter emanated from Victiss. When he had a chance to catch his breath, the giant leader spoke.

"Oh, but fair play. We always say not to judge a lake pike's fight by its size. I hope Vimos has finally learned that lesson." More raucous laughter followed, this time from all the giants—except for Vimos. Victiss addressed Fincher, who still had Vimos in his crosshairs. "Young sir, please lower your weapon. Your point has been made. And taken. You children have nothing to fear from us. In fact, as you stated, you have done us a tremendous service. We were traveling down the artifice of this road, away from our beloved lake, to rid this avenue—"

"We call it the Mutetrack," cut in Sammi.

Victiss mulled over the word. "The *Mutetrack*. Well, I must say, that's much more clever than what we've been calling it. Do you mind if I steal it?"

Sammi looked around shyly. "I don't."

"Then, that's twice that we owe you. One for disposing of those vagabonds and another for giving this pile of gravel a proper name. I must admit that naming is not my people's strongest suit."

When Victiss had concluded, Tallia spoke. "What are we to do with the bodies?"

Victiss's orange eyes glided over the younglings. "Is there a reason that you did not give the dead a proper burial?"

Fincher answered for the group. "Because fark them. They wanted to enslave Ditto and me and do even worse to Ash and Sammi."

"Understood. That is what highwaymen do. But is it still not custom for you to bury your dead?"

"Not if we say fark them. Let the carrion have a big lunch."

Victiss looked around to his fellow giants. "It never ceases to amaze me how different our races actually are."

"What races?" asked Fincher. "You're just a big shite. No different from us."

Victiss smirked to himself. "Perhaps. We will bury the dead." Fincher started to argue, but Victiss beat him to it. "Not to honor them in any way, Young... Fincher, was it? But because we are the Ommori, the Moon Folk, the Forest People. Also known as the Titans elsewhere in Quaan. In burying these foolish humans, we will be nourishing our forest, providing essential nutrients for the next batch of life. Do you all have any qualms regarding my decision?"

Fincher started to speak again but ate a sharp elbow from Ash that held his tongue.

"We have no qualms, Mister Victiss," replied the one-armed girl.

Victiss's orange eyes found the stub of the girl's left arm, but he made no comment. "Thank you, young miss." Back to his giant group. "Tabitha! Viverius! Join Vimos in returning the bodies to the forest. Bury them close to a Monarch Brown. Our old girls need the nourishment."

Tabitha and Viverius jumped to follow orders.

"Why me?" complained Vimos.

Victiss smiled broadly, showcasing teeth studded with multicol-ored jewels. "Because you owe me."

Vimos appeared perplexed. "Owe you for what?"

"For saving your life. Young Fincher here had you dead to rights."

The other giants giggled as the sideburn-wearing Vimos looked ready to explode.

Before Vimos could even formulate a retort, Victiss had turned his attention back to the group formerly known as the Sour Flower Gang. "Where are you heading, my young friends?"

"North," responded Ash.

"North, where?" inquired Victiss.

The gang looked to each, unsure of how much to divulge to these giant strangers.

"Just north for now."

Victiss grinned. "My own children give similarly vague answers under my questioning. Very well. Now that you have done our work for us, we are also heading north. May we accompany you? Perhaps we can learn about each other and discover more parallels than our differing statures would have us believe."

While simply nodding felt sufficient for the rest of the group, Fincher felt compelled to talk.

"I can think of worse escorts than a group of giants."

"We are not escorts, young Fincher. Nor are we giants. We are the Ommori, the Moon Folk, the Forest People. We—"

"Just lead the way, you big fark."

The children had to walk double-time to keep up with the long strides of Victiss and his team, despite the giants' doing their best to slow the pace. The perspectives of the younglings were less than ideal, with their heads coming to just above the waists of their fellow travelers.

While Fincher, Ditto, and Ash were comfortable in letting the giants initiate conversation, Sammi and her curious, too-sharp mind would not let her many questions go unanswered. The young girl spoke between the breaths of her power walk.

"You called yourselves the Ommori. You mean like Ommori Prime of the Five Sisters?"

Victiss looked down from above. He responded from within the shadow that his large hat cast.

"That is correct, Youngtress..."

"Sammi."

"Youngtress Sammi. As I was telling Young Fincher, we are the Moon Folk. Also known as the Forest People and the Titans."

"Heard you the first two times," Fincher muttered under his breath, and this time it was Ditto who delivered an elbow, drawing a grunt from the boy. Ditto followed up by immediately putting an arm around his friend.

Victiss swallowed a laugh and continued. "We did not name ourselves the Ommori; it was one given to us long ago because our skin was said to be so white and reflective that it would shine brightly even in the darkness of night. I can assure you that this is not true, but as we hold the Five Sisters in such high regard, we did not object to the label. In fact, we embraced it."

"Why?" asked Ash.

"Good question, Youngtress..."

"Ash."

Victiss touched a long finger to the front of his hat. "Youngtress Ash. Before adopting the name of the Ommori, we called ourselves the Forest People. We worshipped Quaan, the wondrous nature of Quaan, to be exact, and still do. This includes our beloved Five Sisters, for without them Quaan would be something else entirely, nothing like the world that we know it as." Victiss rubbed his amber mustache absently. "Tell me, younglings, do you know the tale of the Five Sisters?"

"We do," responded Sammi.

"Really?" There was real surprise in the deep voice. "I have found very few outside of the Moon Folk who do."

Ash wiped the corner of her eye. "We had a good teacher who

recounted the tale to us in full. It's a beautiful story."

Victiss went on. "That's wonderful to hear. I always fear that the world outside of our forest forgets itself. Although I must make a slight correction, Youngtress Ash. It is not a story. It is a history. It is our shared history."

Ash nodded out of respect for the man's conviction in his beliefs.

"How'd you all get so farking big?"

As the eyes of Ash, Sammi, and Ditto rolled, Victiss, Tallia, and the other Ommori looked to each and laughed.

"A fair question, Young Fincher. Although I could almost ask your friend, Young…"

"Ditto, sir."

"I could almost ask Young Ditto the same thing." Ditto smiled with rare pride. "We have always kept separate from the others of Quaan, keeping ourselves close to the land. And there is no more beautiful land in all of Quaan than Vattassav, which you probably know better as the Mutewoods. We live off of the land and try to give back as much as we can to Vattassav."

Sammi's mind spun like a top. "Is that why your skin is so white? Because you spend all your time in the shadow of the Mutewoods… uhh, I mean Vattassav?"

"She's a quick one," remarked Tallia from the side.

"That is correct, Youngtress Sammi. For thousands of years, our people kept to the relative darkness of these woods, where we found food and shelter and purpose, but little of Paragon. I'd say we made a fair trade."

"That doesn't explain why you're so farking big."

Victiss chuckled once more. Despite the boy's mouth, there was an innocence, honesty, and gall (with a little stupidity thrown in) that the giant leader could not help but like.

"That's a tale for another day, Young Fincher."

Sammi jumped in once more. "Forgive our friend. There are no side paths from his brain to his mouth. It is one of the many reasons that we love him."

"And feed him a steady supply of elbows," added Ash. Fincher shrugged helplessly.

Sammi continued. "But, I think what Fincher is getting at is that your… distinct… characteristics lead us to believe that you have enjoyed significant isolation over many, many years."

"That would be a correct assumption, Youngtress Sammi."

Sammi hesitated. "But how?"

"What do you mean?"

Another hesitation. "How have you not been conquered? Absorbed by the various empires that have risen and fallen? Assimilated into the rest of Quaan? The Titians and the Cobalts are separate groups waging war for Quaan, but the individual members of each look identical. It is only the colors they wear that differentiate them. The Ommori, however…"

"Yeah, what she said. That is *exactly* what I was getting at," said Fincher rather unconvincingly.

Victiss dropped his head again, this time with a new appreciation for the bespectacled girl beneath him. "How old are you, youngtress?"

"Nine."

"How marvelous. As to your insightful question, you are correct. Although we have not purposely sequestered ourselves, we *have* stayed true to our home, stayed true to Vattassav. And, as to how we have managed to remain independent? As your Young Fincher would put it, we are *big farks.*"

Ommori and child alike howled at Victiss's successful attempt at humor. When everyone finally settled down, the giant leader continued.

"Truth be told, there were attempts for hundreds upon hundreds of years to subjugate our people, to conquer this land, to rape Vattassav of its riches. But we were bigger, and stronger, and our purpose was more pure. Wave after wave of enemy entered this ancient forest and few exited with their lives. Eventually, it became cheaper for the outside empires to simply partner with us than try to eliminate us."

"Strange how chips can force the evil to play righteous cards."

"Well said, Young Ditto. Well said. And given that Vattassav has many necessary goods—from meats to minerals to lumber to medicines—not found anywhere else in Quaan, it's in the best interests of the powers-that-be to keep up positive relations, despite how much they obviously despise and fear us."

Fincher switched his longbow from one shoulder to the other. "And so, living here alone, away from the rest of Quaan, made you big and white with funky eyes?"

"Fincher!"

Victiss held up a massive hand. "It is quite all right, Youngtress Ash." Back to Fincher. "Yes, Young Fincher, that is why we differ in appearance." Victiss's head cocked to the side. "But, I see that our eyes are not the only ones that are different. I have never seen such yellow before. Could it be that you younglings, too, have grown up in an isolated part of Quaan?" The children looked to each other, and silence filled the Mutetrack. "Apologies if that is a sensitive question. I meant no offense."

"Crimmish," said Fincher. "We're from Crimmish."

Victiss's face twisted in confusion. "Crimmish. Crimmish. Why do I recognize that name and, yet do not know it?"

Vochus responded from the side. "It's the Stenches."

Victiss's amber eyes went wide. "Oh! The Stenches."

"We prefer Crimmish. That's the real farking name."

"Of course, Young Fincher. Crimmish, it is. At the base of the Spired Curtains, correct? Near Mount Ghaal?"

"That's right," said Ash.

"They straddle the Tainted Timbers," added Vochus, and the scar across his face danced as the giant spoke.

"Is that what gives your eyes that wonderful yellow hue?"

"It is," answered Ash again, unwilling to give Fincher the opportunity to offend their intimidating entourage. But muting her friend was easier said than done.

"It's the farking poisonous air, to be exact. And most don't find it wonderful, us included. Those outside the town call us *Cheese-Eyes* and torment us at every turn. So, how's that shite wonderful?"

Victiss took several long strides before speaking again. "I'm sorry to hear that. It seems that I was right, after all. We have much in common once one looks past these physical shells. The Chestnuts hate us but cannot live without the goods we supply. The Chestnuts have banished your people to the farthest corner of Quaan, and yet, was it not the people of the... of Crimmish who harvested the Moonflowers necessary to create Salvation? Was it not the people of Crimmish who brought an end to the Bloat? Two peoples, so hated despite being so necessary. Yes, we have much more in common than it would initially appear."

The children, surprised by the giant leader's insightfulness, continued to speed walk in silence, unsure of what to reveal to this seemingly good-natured monster.

When none of the younglings offered a response, Victiss pushed for what he really wanted to know. What he felt that he needed to know.

"Well, I guess that is enough with the formalities. Would anyone like to tell me what four children from Crimmish are doing in the middle of Vattassav alone, trekking north into a snake pit of danger, marching toward a certain death?" The kids kept walking. No one, not even Fincher, was willing to supply an answer. Finally, Victiss shrugged his tattooed shoulders. "Very well. If you feel the need to protect your secrets, then I will respect that. The Ommori have many of our own that we are unwilling to share. Let us enjoy simply enjoy the majesty of Vattassav.

A short time later, just as Paragon was starting to descend, the Mutetrack ran directly into the largest gate the children of Crimmish would ever encounter. Every bit of twenty feet high and made of thick logs, the gate, although now closed, looked like it would swing inward on both sides. An equally impressive palisade ran east and west from the gate, quickly disappearing into the thickness of the Mutewoods.

When the eclectic group was several dozen feet from the gate, Victiss spun on a moccasin to face the children.

"It has been an absolute pleasure, younglings. But this is where we must part. I thank you again for ridding... the Mutetrack... of those miscreants. Every time you kill a living creature, a piece of you also dies. So, I thank you for saving that piece of me."

Fincher looked confusedly at the others and received perplexed glances back.

"Why can't we keep going with you, Mister Victiss?"

Amber eyes met the boy's hazel-on-yellow. "Because we do not let strangers into our home, Young Fincher. And although you children seem truly lovely, I know not why you are in Vattassav, why you are traveling north, and what you hope to accomplish at the end of this obvious quest. I do not begrudge you your secrets, but I cannot let you see ours without understanding yours. Trust, like this avenue, must be two ways, Young Fincher."

Fincher chewed on his lip as he considered how much to disclose. Ash rubbed the stump of her arm, which always grew itchy when difficult decisions needed to be made. Sammi pushed her glasses farther up her nose. Surprisingly, it was Ditto who bailed out the group.

"We were brought into the Mutewoods, into... Vattassav by the Lady of Shadowset."

The unexpected news put Victiss back on his stagg-skin moccasins. "The Lady of Shadowset? You mean Alicia Salt?"

"You know her?"

"Of course, we know her! Alicia Salt is the closest thing to an Ommori without actually being one of the Moon Folk. In her younger days, she would travel here often to trade in both goods and gossip. Since Albert Salt's passing, her visits have become more sporadic, but the huntress is *always* welcome in our home."

"Well, what about us?" cut in Fincher. "You know, friend of a friend and all that."

The giants looked to each other doubtfully. Tallia spoke as Victiss was still collecting his thoughts.

"You mean to tell us that Alicia Salt guided you all into Vattassav?"

Ditto nodded. "That's correct."

Tallia laughed and shook her head, sending her long amber braids swinging. "I can't believe it. I am friends with Alicia Salt, and she would rather fight a Bog Behemoth with her bare hands than escort a group of younglings north, away from her beloved Shadowset."

Fincher started to say something, but Sammi's hand on his arm stopped him. When the young girl looked at Fincher from behind her round glasses, the boy knew exactly what she was thinking—best not to admit to any role in the killing of the Silver Stagg, especially to a group who call themselves the *Forest People*.

Fincher nodded subtly to show that he understood before jumping in. "She was paid a heavy bag of chips to do so. Also, I think she took a shine to us. And no one can farking blame her for that."

Tallia seemed unconvinced. "So, she was your paid guide?"

"She was our friend," corrected Sammi.

"Then, where is Alicia? She would not let a job go unfinished. And, although I never knew her to like children, nor do I think that she would abandon them in the woods."

The faces of the four younglings fell moments before their heads followed.

Tallia repeated her question, this time with more urgency. "Where is Alicia Salt?"

"She fell," responded Ash, her brown-on-yellow eyes still squarely on the gravel beneath her. "She's gone. She died protecting us."

"Impossible." Tallia turned to Victiss. "There is nothing in any of the forests of Quaan that Alicia Salt cannot handle."

Victiss seemed torn. "Vattassav holds mysteries that even the Ommori have not solved, Tallia. Those thinking that they have seen everything are often the first to die at the hands of the unknown." Victiss addressed the children. "But, still, your word is not enough, I am afraid. Not enough to jeopardize our home."

Just then, a loud squawk from above sent every amber eye up. Against a backdrop of perfect blue, Rashii hovered in the sky for several seconds before dropping to land perfectly upon Sammi's shoulder. There, the bird let out another squawk, as if attempting to address the giant leader's doubt.

"Tallia, is that what I think it is?"

The female giant studied the bird before responding. "It is, Victiss. That is the Quilted Raven, avian companion to Alicia Salt."

"His name is Rashii," said Sammi as she fed the bird a small piece of jerky from her shirt pocket.

Tallia's white face dropped a bit. "Yes. Rashii. That *is* his name. Then, it is true?"

"I'm afraid farking so."

"The Quilted Raven seems to have taken a liking to you all," stated Victiss, watching as Rashii ate happily, perched on Sammi without a care in the world.

"He's our friend," said Sammi.

"As was farking Alicia Salt."

Victiss turned his attention to Fincher as the boy's voice broke with emotion. His amber eyes fell on the longbow that was slung over the boy's shoulder. Tallia leaned in and whispered into the giant leader's colorfully studded ear.

"Young Fincher, that would not happen to be Alicia Salt's longbow, would it?"

"It is."

"May I see it?"

Fincher hesitated before handing over the weapon. Victiss and Tallia studied the bow, looking closely at its top where the string wrapped around wood. Tallia said something quietly to Victiss, and the mustached Ommori nodded.

"The Salt insignia has been etched into the wood here. There is no mistaking it. How did you come by the Lady of Shadowset's longbow?"

"Miss Salt gave it to me, just before she fell. She said to take this north but had no time to say more." The boy wiped a tear. "So, I farking did."

Victiss glanced over at Tallia, who was wiping her own tears from a pale cheek. The giant leader released a great sigh.

"And so, you did." He handed the longbow back to Fincher. "As you said, Young Fincher, a friend of Alicia Salt's is a friend of ours. And you lot were obviously friends of the Lady of Shadowset. I will learn more of her passing, and we will honor her in a way fitting her station, fitting the essential role that she played as a fellow guardian of the natural world. Alicia Salt was not Ommori, but she was a child of the forest, through and through. She will be remembered as such."

Sammi gave Rashii one more piece of jerky before cleaning her glasses on her shirt. "Then, we can accompany you?"

Victiss's smile highlighted his gem-covered teeth once more. "It would be our great honor, Youngtress Sammi." Victiss bellowed over his shoulder. "Crownkeepers! It is Victiss Three and crew! Open the Crowngate, I beg you!"

Several seconds passed before the mammoth gates began to swing inward. Victiss's amber eyes flashed in the dimming light of Paragon as he matched looks with each of the children. "Can you all keep a secret?"

"Isn't it obvious that we farking can?"

Victiss chuckled. "Yes. You all can obviously keep a *secret* to yourselves. But what about a *secret world*?" There was no response, only the confused stares of younglings. "Come. Let us find out."

Yellow-tinged eyes went wide as Fincher, Ash, Ditto, and Sammi Bugg moved deeper into the mysterious world of the Moon Folk.

At first, the forest within the Crowngate seemed no different than what existed outside of its high walls. As Paragon continued its inevitable departure, however, the woods fell into shadow. And Vattassav awoke.

Interspersed with the Monarch Browns and other typical Mutewoods flora were unusual shrubs that had been trimmed and shaped into five round balls, one atop the other. These manicured bushes were planted strategically, lining the cobbled path on which the children now walked and spreading out into Vattassav in regular intervals.

As the Five Sisters revealed themselves overhead, so too did the six-foot shrubs. Small white blossoms exited green casings within each of the five balls, opening themselves up to the night air and emitting a white glow. With thousands of small bioluminescent flowers in each shrub, Vattassav was quickly bathed in soft light—by the Five Sisters from above and these magnificent bushes far below.

Victiss noticed the younglings' wonderment and grinned. "We call them Astars. They light Vattassav so that we are not so reliant on fire, which can be the great enemy of the woodlands. We still use fires for cooking and, on occasion, warmth, but the Astars allow us to minimize their usage and risks. What do you think?"

"They're glorious," commented Sammi, awe thick in her child voice. "How do they work?"

Victiss laughed. "How does Paragon work? How do the stars work? Such questions are not for us to answer. They offer illumination in darkness and we, in turn, make sure that they are well-fed, watered, and cared for. That is what Vattassav is about, living *with* the land, not *on* it. And certainly not *owning* it. Do we take from it? Yes. But we also work to give back, to ensure that it's just as lovely a hundred years from now, when our grandsons and granddaughters are leading the Ommori."

As the group advanced north, more of the Forest People could be seen, some transporting items, others tending to Astars and other flora, and many more simply lounging in massive hammocks that swung lazily between trees. They each held up their right hand, palm out, in greeting as Victiss and the other giants passed.

Soon, Ommori homes could be seen. One had to look carefully to find them, as they blended in perfectly with the surrounding forest. More often than not, they leaned against a Monarch Brown, using its trunk for support, and had several Astars planted outside of the home.

After a while, Monarch Browns seemed less prevalent, giving way to shelters of lean-to and teepee design that also matched the woodland backdrop. These grew increasingly common until the children felt that they must be in the closest thing to what the Ommori could call a *town*.

Tallia and Vochus eventually fell away. As they did, Victiss spoke over his too-white shoulder, which now seemed to also glow under the light of the Five Sisters and Astars. The red tattoos that adorned his arms also shone in the relative dimness, as if finally releasing Paragon's rays that had been absorbed all day.

"We are almost there."

"And where would that farking be?"

"You will see, Young Fincher. You will see."

It was only a few minutes later when the forest opened up to nothingness, as if there was a line of demarcation that the trees dared not cross. Undergrowth, leaves, and pine needles gave way to flat, rocky ground. The sounds of the forest—birds and insects and nocturnal creatures—gave way to the lapping of water, an impossible amount of water.

As the Crimmish youth walked forward, their jaws fell again, which was becoming habit in this new, secret world.

"Well? What do you think?" asked Victiss, although the colossus already knew the answer.

Ash's brown-on-yellow eyes watched as the light of the Five Sisters reflected on water—so much water—more water than she ever thought possible. Waist-high waves rolled in from the darkness, audibly kissing the land and leaving a collection of foam and tiny shells in its wake.

"What is this?" pondered the one-armed girl, more to the heavens than to anyone around her. "I'm not as smart as my sister, but I thought the Great Untold was much farther east. And yet..."

"This is not the Great Untold. It is Crown Lake, Youngtress Ash. It is the heart of Vattassav. The heart of the Ommori."

The children stood shoulder to shoulder, slack-jawed, staring out over water that extended out infinitely in three directions. Crown Lake was an impossibility, especially to those from Crimmish, where life was defined by limits and dangers and timelines, not the endless possibility that was currently laid bare before them.

It was finally Fincher who said what was on all their minds.

"Can we go in?"

Sammi leaned in and whispered loudly. "Maybe it's sacred to them."

Victiss chuckled. "It *is* sacred, Youngtress Sammi. But not like that. You all are free to go in. Just don't venture out past your chests. There are creatures in those waters that could swallow each of you whole. Could swallow *me* whole, truth be told."

Victiss had not even completed his last sentence when packs were dropped, weapons laid atop them, and clothes kicked off, leaving the kids in their undergarments.

The younglings then hooked arms at the elbows and waded into the shimmering waters of Crown Lake, giggling as children should.

Victiss found a large boulder at the water's edge and lowered his massive body onto it, shifting his axe as he did. Amber eyes watched as the children of Crimmish splashed each other. Ditto dove under the surface, coming up with a fist-sized conch shell that sparkled under the Five Sisters. The boy immediately gave the shell, which would actually fetch a significant price in the outside world, to Ash, whose smile upon receiving the gift brightened the lake by several more degrees.

Victiss offered his own grin, thinking of the events of the day. The giant leader had exited the Crowngate with a heavy heart, thinking that he would have to end several lives. Instead of death, however, Victiss had found something much more agreeable—the innocence and fascination of youth—two things that were becoming increasingly easy for him to forget, especially now that his own children continued to sprout and mature.

Victiss leaned back against the rock, determined to enjoy the show before him.

Back in the water, breaths grew labored as the younglings wrestled and played, swam and dove. Before long, the kids found themselves bobbing amongst the waves in silence, watching as the light of the Five Sisters danced across the rippling tides.

Ditto wiped water from his face. "Hana would have loved this."

Sammi nodded. "She would have loved it the most."

"The farking song she would have sung after seeing this, after experiencing this. I can't even imagine."

"I can," countered Ash.

"Me, too, sis."

"Me, too."

Fincher smoothed back his cinnamon hair. "Yeah, I guess I can, too." A long pause. "Farking heck. Look at us! Four Cheese-Eyes from the Stenches, swimming in the magical waters of Crown Lake, a place most of the losers who spit at us don't even know exists."

Another pause before Ditto spoke.

"I'm glad you all are here to experience it with me. Even this wondrous place would have no value without good friends to share it with."

"Me, too, Ditto."

"Yeah, me, too."

The children stared out into the great unknown of Crown Lake, watching as a family of large fishlike creatures sprung out from the water and sailed through the evening air in perfect arches before diving back into the darkness.

Sammi dipped her glasses into the lake before putting them back on.

"But, I'd still give this all up to have Hana back. I'd give it up in a second. I'd have stayed in Crimmish forever if it meant growing up next to my friend."

"Me, too, sis."

"Me, too, Sammi."

"Farking right."

~

After a delicious meal of grilled fish, the former Sour Flower Gang sat on their bedrolls around a small fire outside of a lean-to that acted as a guest housing. Although Victiss's own home was down Crown Lake a ways, the giant offered to stay with the children for the night. The group sat in satiated silence, listening to the crackle of the fire and the lapping of the lake's waves, which was taking place not fifty feet from their current shelter.

Victiss sat cross-legged next to the fire, sharpening his multi-hued axe with a black stone. He talked as he ran the rock up and down the edge of his weapon.

"You never told me how Alicia Salt came to fall." When there was no response, Victiss went on. "I am especially surprised that the huntress found her end in the forest. The Lady of Shadowset was as much at home among the trees as the Elder Whale is beneath the surface of Crown Lake." Again, the giant leader was only met with silence. Victiss gently placed his axe next to him. "Remember what I told you about trust being a two-way avenue? I have shown you the truth of our world. At least, some of it. I will now hear the truth of your journey."

"It was Marsh Ghouls," said Ash, keeping her brown eyes on the fire.

"Yeah, farking Marsh Ghouls."

Victiss shot perplexed looks to the children. "Marsh Ghouls? Trust me when I tell you that I know every inch of Vattassav and every creature that roams this land. I have never heard of a *Marsh Ghoul*."

Fincher tossed a small branch into the fire. "You know, a farking Marsh Ghoul. Nasty, tree-like creatures that appear after a heavy rain. Shooting up from a forest swamp, or vernal pool, as Miss Salt called it."

Victiss leaned forward. "Vernal pool?"

"You know, from all the farking rain a few Paragons ago."

Victiss kicked at the campfire with a stagg-skin boot. "I should have known…"

"Known what?"

"I don't know where you got the term Marsh Ghouls from, but we have another name for them. We call them the Famished. Nothing was ever enough for them in life, and now nothing will ever be enough for them in that terrible limbo in which they currently exist." Victiss kicked the fire again. "The Ommori have not heard of a Famished awakening in many, many years. Although, I must admit that our communications with the humans of the Mutewoods has grown increasingly infrequent over time." Victiss's amber eyes turned toward the children, and firelight danced within them. "The Famished are called such because there is never enough; they will never be satiated. So, how in Quaan did you children manage to escape?"

When Fincher did not speak, Ash took up the story. "We were… saved… by a boy. A boy who had dug tunnels throughout that part of the Mutewoods. Miss Salt bravely fought off the Marsh Ghouls… uh, the Famished… giving us the time needed to dive into one of the boy's tunnels and escape."

"And where is this boy? He sounds like a hero."

Ash rubbed the stump of her arm without looking up. "He was anything but."

"He was a farking twisted shite, is what he was. Farking Dooley Hamm."

Victiss watched closely as eyes grew moist and tiny rivers ran down soft cheeks. The giant leader rose and moved closer to the lean-to, sitting down cross-legged again just in front of the kids of Crimmish.

"I know it hurts, but tell me about it. Please."

It was Sammi Bugg who was eventually able to put aside feelings of rage, sadness, and guilt to tell the grotesque tale of Matilda and Dooley Hamm. Picking up from where her older sister left off, Sammi recounted how Dooley had led the five—

"Wait, there were five of you," interrupted Victiss. "Where is your fifth?" The giant immediately regretted the question. "I apologize. Please go on."

Sammi continued, describing how Dooley Hamm led the children with the promise of help, the promise of assistance from Meemaw. How they passed through an abandoned village before reaching the isolated cottage that Meemaw and Dooley called home.

The young girl showcased steely resolve in recalling the worst of the visit. How the Worm and its young, using Meemaw as their puppet, fell upon the children. How—

Victiss interjected again. "We Ommori know of this parasite. We call it Borggos the Lurker or Borggos the Many. Or, to echo you younglings, Borggos the Worm."

"What is it?" asked Ditto.

"We do not know, Young Ditto. We only know that it has plagued southern Vattassav for as long as the Ommori have been here. The monster might go back as far as the Famished. For all we know, it was their black magic and the power of the Other God that created the cursed thing. Borggos has been dispatched more times than I can remember, but it always returns. We call it the *Many* for good reason. It only takes one of its progenies to survive for Borggos to find a host and rise again. And woe to any community that finds Borggos lurking within it." Victiss shook, as if forcing himself from a waking night-mare. "But I brought your story to halt again, and I am sorry for that. Please, go on."

Sammi nodded. She spoke about how the kids, then still the Sour Flower Gang, bravely worked together to survive and battle their way free from the house of horrors. How they burned down the building with the Worm inside. How Dooley Hamm got away. How they marched north with the pink-eyed boy trailing them. How, just as they finally thought that the one-armed boy had fallen away, they encountered a trio of Berserkers and looked for ways around the predators. How they left Hana behind to watch over their packs. How—

Even Sammi Bugg had to pause as the memory of sweet Hana's end proved too much to bear. The young girl removed her glasses and wiped her eyes, her small chest heaving with emotion.

Fincher placed a hand on his friend's back and offered a nod. She had gotten the story far enough on her own.

Fincher picked up the sad tale and told Victiss how Dooley Hamm had appeared out of the shadows to attack Hana. How the Berserker mother showed up to finish Dooley Hamm, consuming the boy alive along with her cubs. How white worms ran from the boy's open wounds and seeped into the forest floor.

"Borggos the Many," commented Victiss without pausing the story.

Fincher, now with hazel eyes full of water and glistening cheeks, went on, speaking about how Ditto had carried their deceased friend to the most beautiful spot they could find in the Mutewoods. How they buried her and said goodbye. How the end of the Sour Flower Gang meant an end to their childhood. How they were now in things only for themselves, only for their families, only for the people of Crimmish.

Although Fincher used much more colorful language.

Fincher concluded the tale with their encounter on the Mutetrack, using the cutthroats' incorrect evaluation of the children's abilities against them. How they will no longer hesitate to strike first, kill first —and discover notions like intent later.

When Fincher was finished, the giant leader and the younglings sat around in silence. After appropriate time was given for their loss, Victiss addressed the boy.

"With this newfound perspective, why did you not attack us when we approached you, Young Fincher?"

"Well, you were all farking big, now weren't you? Like, really big. But don't think Ditto and I didn't talk it through."

"Hesitation seemed the smartest approach at the time," added Ditto, and Victiss roared in laughter.

"Oh, and I am happy that you did. You younglings survived the Famished, killed Borggos the Lurker, escaped a Berserker attack, and slayed three notorious bandits. I am not sure that I would have liked our chances against such formidable foes!"

Fincher, Ash, Ditto, and Sammi Bugg all forced out giggles, a much-needed reprieve from the darkness of their account. Although they knew that Victiss was attempting to cheer them up, they appreciated the giant's effort and allowed it to happen.

Victiss clapped his massive white hands together. "Enough! Where are my manners? You all have been through an ordeal and have answered enough questions for tonight. The others can wait for Paragon. Sleep, my new friends, and know that you are completely safe under the Five Sisters for the first time in a while. For you are now under the protection of the Ommori, and *that* is something we do not take lightly. Sleep and think only of the good times with your dear friend Hana. Sleep and know that tomorrow you will see things beyond your wildest dreams. For although this part of Vattassav and

Crown Lake are enchanting at night, they are absolutely breathtaking under the brightness of Paragon."

The children, too exhausted to argue, literally collapsed onto their bedrolls, light snoring emanating from each in short order.

Victiss took in the sleeping younglings with amber eyes, unsure of what their arrival meant or foretold. Their story was beyond unbelievable, except that the giant leader believed them. Victiss now understood how Fincher, Ash, Ditto, and Sammi Bugg had gotten to Crown Lake. Shortly after the rise of Paragon, he meant to answer a much more important question—*why* were four children of Crimmish now in Vattassav?

Victiss threw another small log onto the fire and laid back on his own large bedroll. He did not close his wide-set eyes, however, for even with his size and strength, Victiss was afraid of what he might discover that next Paragon. And what it might mean for not only the Ommori, but for Quaan at large.

11

LIVYATANS AND OTHER SECRETS OF
CROWN LAKE

Despite Victiss's words the previous night, the kids from Crimmish were still astonished by what they found when they finally awoke.

Where the starlight blooms of the Astars had retreated for Paragon, they were replaced with massive indigo blossoms that released the sweetest of scents into the forest air.

Many animals, seemingly unafraid of the Ommori, skittered, pranced, and played in the open. One particularly spirited tangerine fox ran through Ash's legs before jumping into Sammi's open arms, burying the girl in kisses before springing away into the forest.

And although the forest was—in Victiss's words—enchanting, especially with all the normal threats of the Mutewoods now absent, it was Crown Lake that proved truly magical.

Paragon's rays glistened off the surface of the water, with waves sending shots of daytime starlight into the fresh, moist air. Creatures never before seen nor imagined leapt from the water at regular intervals, pausing in the air so long that a quick artist may be able to render their likeness in paint on canvass.

Crown Lake stretched out further than the eye could reach in every direction. If the children did not know better, they would have wagered all the chips they had that this was, in fact, not a lake but the Great Untold, that endless body of water that marked the eastern limit of Quaan.

Above Crown Lake, an equally impressive show played out, with dozens of bird species soaring low over the glimmering water, diving beneath the waves in search of breakfast. While they all were impressive, one kind flew above the rest, both literally and figuratively. With an extra-long bill and massive throat pouch, the mammoth waterbird would shoot into the water from on high like one of Alicia Salt's arrows, more often than not resurfacing with a beakful of fish as liquid ran off its impossibly multicolored coat of feathers.

Victiss caught the children reacting to one such fowl's massive haul and chuckled to himself.

"That is the Gemmed Pelican," the giant leader said as he reached the younglings, who were pointing and shouting at the water's edge. "It is a spiritual animal to the Ommori and one that we never hunt or kill. If there is a danger to or within Crown Lake, they will be the first to know and will signal the rest of Vattassav." Rashii the Quilted Raven, never far from the kids, squawked loudly from a tree branch. Victiss looked up and laughed. "Yes, just like you, my friend! Do not think we have forgotten your value to Alicia Salt or these children!" Rashii squawked again, apparently satiated by the recognition.

Victiss gave the kids a few more minutes to appreciate the view before saying, "Come. Let us have breakfast. Crown Lake and the beauty that surrounds it are not going anywhere."

After another delicious meal of grilled fish that none of the Crimmish kids could recognize, Victiss gathered the children, despite their obvious desires to explore more of the Ommori's world.

"I will release you into the wilds of Vattassav in short order, my young friends. But there are still questions that require answers."

"Farking heck, Mister Victiss. Didn't we give you enough last night? We poured our farking hearts out!"

"You did, Young Fincher, and I could not be more appreciative. But that was a tale as to *how* you got here. I am still in the dark about *why* you all are here. In Vattassav."

The children shot subtle glances toward each other, communicating in a language only they could understand. Victiss could feel them sharing ideas and strategies through mere closeness.

"I want you to know that you will not be in any trouble, no matter what you tell me. I consider you friends of the Moon Folk. If I did not, you would never have gotten past the Crowngate. But, your appearance in Vattassav is, needless to say, strange and may forebode much. As one of the leaders and guardians of this place, I *need* to know."

Ash, Ditto, and Sammi all looked to Fincher, who usually served as the group's spokesman, whether selected by the group or himself. Fincher brushed a spot of dirt from his pants, buying some time. In the end, although he liked and, surprisingly, trusted his new giant friend, the boy followed the strict law set by the Sour Flower Gang when they were still a full entity—never trust adults. Giant or not, be damned.

"Do you know who we are, Mister Victiss?"

Victiss's too-white face looked confused under his wide hat, but he decided to play along. "You are children of Crimmish, also known as the Stenches, although I understand why you would reject that unkind label."

"Correct. But that is not all we are. We are harvesters, the best farking crew of harvesters that Crimmish has ever seen. We go into the Tainted Timbers, where Ghost Pumas and Reaper Vines and Moon Adders make their home, and we collect Moon Tears from the Moonflower, which are used to create Salvation, the only known cure for the Bloat."

Victiss stepped forward suddenly, forcing the children back, and bowed deeply. He talked as he rose.

"I had no idea that I was in the presence of actual heroes. The world of Quaan owes you more than can ever be repaid."

"Yeah, well, it has a farking shite way of showing it."

"Yes, Young Fincher, it often does. But *I* thank you. If you will..."

"Well, Crimmish isn't called the Stenches because it stinks—that's a common and farking mean misnomer—but because its air is toxic from the Reaper Vines. Living right next to that farking poisonous air, we've developed an..."

"Immunity?"

Fincher and the others all released a bitter laugh. "I farking wish. But let's not get into that. I want to hold on to that delicious fish I just ate. Anyway, let's say that we've developed a *resistance* to the poison. What would kill you in a few minutes takes us decades."

"But it still gets us in the end," said Ash sadly.

Ditto chimed in absently. "Yes... it does..."

Victiss seemed at a loss for words. "I am... so... sorry."

Fincher waved the giant leader away. "Not the farking point. Do you know of the Gloomtide?"

"Of course, Young Fincher. Although it began north of Kassimont, the affliction has washed across Quaan and now affects most of the cities and towns with which we trade."

"Yeah, well, the geniuses in Kassimont think that there might be a cure in Terminus Grove."

"And what leads them to believe this?"

Fincher shrugged. "You know, a farking cure for the Bloat in the Tainted Timbers must mean a farking cure for the Gloomtide in Terminus Grove. Two fairly untouched ecosystems that none can enter must have plants and medicines never before seen. Shite that can save their unworthy arses."

Victiss thought for a moment before speaking. "And they think that you all, with your resistance to the poisons of the Tainted Timbers, will also be resistant to the toxic air of Terminus Grove?"

Fincher picked up a flat rock and sent it skimming across Crown Lake. "You got it, Mister Victiss."

"Do they have any proof of this?"

"Farking. None."

Ash jumped in. "They say that Terminus Grove also has Reaper Vines, and that's why the air is bad. At least, that's their guess."

Victiss seemed troubled by the news. Looking around for something to occupy his too-large hands, the giant ended up leaning against a tree, sharpening his strange multi-hued axe. He ran a dark stone along his weapon's edge, unable to raise his amber eyes to meet those of the kids from Crimmish.

"Why?"

"Why, what?" asked Fincher.

"I know of Crimmish, of the Stenches, of how they made pariahs of your people. Now, I find out they have sentenced you all to an early death. I'm sure you did what you did with the Moonflowers to survive. But I ask you now…" Victiss looked up from his axe. "Why help them? The same rapers of Quaan that cursed your people are the same that would overtake ours if we gave them but a moment's chance. Why not let the Gloomtide have them?"

Sammi pushed her glasses up. "Because they made a promise."

"What could they possibly promise you, Youngtress Sammi?"

"That they would try to save our mas and pas, at least those that are still with us."

"And how do they suppose to accomplish that?"

When Sammi had no answer, Ditto entered the conversation.

"The Titian Empire said that they would send Quaan's best physicians to Crimmish to find a cure to the Maddening, the disease that afflicts our people. They said that they would keep sending them until the Maddening was no more."

"And you believe them, Young Ditto?"

Ditto shrugged his large shoulders. "It doesn't really matter, now, does it?"

"I do not understand your meaning."

Ditto ran a hand through his hair before responding. "I mean, we're gonna do it anyway, aren't we?"

"And why is that?"

"Because we don't want others to go through what we go through. There is nothing worse than watching a loved one succumb to the Maddening. Losing someone to the Gloomtide sounds comparable. No one should have to experience that."

"Even those that have cast you aside, Young Ditto?"

"Even them. Matching another's indifference doesn't make you better. Being better makes you better."

"Farking right."

Victiss took a moment to look out onto Crown Lake, taking in the beauty of his home. When his amber eyes returned to the children of Crimmish, he gazed upon the younglings with a newfound respect, something the giant thought he could never bestow upon any of the Soul-burned.

"And, so, you all are to travel to Terminus Grove. Then what?"

Sammi jumped back into the mix. "We're to bring back as many samples as possible, hoping that a remedy to the Gloomtide hides within our collection." The young girl looked away as she spoke, growing uncomfortable with lying to the friendly colossus.

"I see," was all Victiss said for a long while. Then, "I want you all to enjoy Vattassav this fair Paragon. Our land is your land, so go as you please. I am one of the seven leaders of Vattassav, known as the Heptorii. Several others are currently visiting the banks of Crown Lake not far from here. I must confer with them on several issues. You are inside the Crowngate, so everyone will treat you as one of our own. I'll come find you later, before the fall of Paragon. Soak in Vattassav, the only portion of untouched Quaan, just as the Five Sisters left it for us."

With that, Victiss strode down the shores of the lake on long legs and was out of sight in short order.

Ash looked around. "So… what do we do now?"

Fincher began to pull at his shirt. "I don't know about you all, but I'm going back in that farking water."

Ash, Ditto, and Sammi nodded, giggling as they removed their own clothes, relishing in the opportunity to, for a few hours at least, remember that they were, in fact, children. And not saviors of the world.

A full Paragon of swimming, climbing, wrestling, singing, hiking, and dancing followed. Most of the other Ommori were just as kind as Victiss, with a few nasty looks thrown the kids' way every now and then, something to which those of the Stenches were practically immune.

One striking giantess named Tufferia, whose long amber hair was braided and tied up in two massive buns that covered her ears, invited the gang into her lean-to, where she served them creamy fish soup, the best meal any of the children could ever recall.

Another giant named Vannys took Ditto and Ash high up a Monarch Brown using steps that had been carefully inserted into the tree's thick bark. From a round observation platform that had been neatly built into the top of the tree several hundred feet up, Ditto and Ash looked down upon not only Crown Lake, but the entirety of the Mutewoods. Looking south, the forest appeared serene and unsoiled, offering no hints as to some of the horrors that hid below the thick canopy.

As Ditto stood against the railing, watching schools of fish jump from the water by the thousands with choreography rivaling the Kassimont Toe Dancers, Ash joined him, eventually laying her head against the large boy's shoulder. Ditto looked down and put an arm around his friend to fight off the chill air. At least, that's what he told himself.

"I wish Hana was here to see the forest like this, Ditto."

"Me, too, Ash. Me, too."

Below, Fincher and Sammi fished off the banks of Crown Lake, using poles loaned to them by Taana, a giantess with red tattoos that covered her face without hiding any of her beauty. She disassembled the fishing poles and restrung them using only half their lengths, allowing the smaller humans to cast more easily.

Within a few minutes, Sammi squealed with glee as she reeled in what proved to be a two-foot-long fat-lipped bass, a rare fish that Taana claimed not only brought good luck, but an even better dinner.

"Hana would have loved this," remarked Sammi as she baited her now-empty hook, her catch safely stashed away in a wicker container.

"Yeah, but she would have farking moaned about hurting the fish."

Sammi laughed. "Yes, she would have."

"But, she still would have eaten the farking stew. When Hana was hungry, there was no one who could put more away."

"Well, Ditto…"

"Oh, yeah, farking Ditto, for sure."

"I miss her something terrible, Fincher."

"Me, too, Sammi. Me, too."

True to his word, Victiss returned just as Paragon retreated behind the western horizon. After congratulating Sammi on her catch and commenting on the aroma of the bass meat being grilled, Victiss sat down cross-legged the other side of the fire.

A short time later, the fat-lipped bass was served over beds of honey rice. Just as everyone was about to dig in, Tufferia appeared and offered the group a freshly baked loaf of angel wheat bread with homemade butter made from snow ram milk, a true delicacy. Although Tufferia waved away Victiss's invitation to stay, a look passed between the two Ommori that went noticed by Ash and Sammi and completely unrecognized by Fincher and Ditto.

Victiss smiled as the children devoured the food, acutely aware that they were probably unused to such variety in their meals. When plates made from large, polished clam shells were scraped clean, Victiss finally addressed the group.

"I have spoken with three others of the Heptorii. We are all in agreement. You are not like the others that we refer to as the Soul-burned. We want you to know that you are welcome to stay in Vattassav as long as you wish. In fact, we would welcome you all to join us here permanently, make new homes here around the majesty that is Crown Lake." Victiss's offer was met with silence. "Apologies, but I thought this news would come with more excitement. Very few outsiders have ever been given such an honor."

The quartet of younglings glanced to each other before Fincher spoke.

"But, what about our mission?"

Victiss tossed his clam-plate to the side. "Forget it. You owe the Titian Empire nothing. It is *they*, in fact, who should owe you. They have condemned your families to death and, in the same breath, ask that you save theirs. I do not see the logic in this. They will never save your people. As soon as they have what they want, you will be cast away once more. Their promises are as empty as their hearts, and their words hold no more weight than the husks of their souls." Victiss took the time to look each child in the eye. "You four, however, are something more. I suspected it when I met you, but now I am sure of it. You do not deserve the fate that they have resigned you to, but they certainly deserve the one that they have drawn from themselves. Alicia Salt, a great woman and friend of the forest, has already died needlessly. Do not follow in her footsteps. There is a life for you here, fuller than you could have ever imagined."

Victiss said no more, letting the proposition hang in the air. The children all put their plates down and nervously wiped their small hands on their pants and shirts. Ash, rubbing the nob of her arm, nodded at Fincher, who responded.

"It's not that we're not appreciative, Mister Victiss. We are. And it's not that we don't farking understanding what you're offering here. We do. But we made a promise to try to end the Gloomtide. And, in Crimmish, you're only as good as your word. Without it, you're useless to yourself and to the town. Without it, you're just what everyone else says you are—dirty, diseased Cheese-Eyes."

"No one will call you that here, Young Fincher."

"I know. We know. But what about the Gloomtide? Are we to pretend not to know what will happen outside of Vattassav?"

"They don't care what happens in Crimmish, now do they?"

"No, sir. No, they don't. But we ain't them, even if they think themselves better than us." Fincher thought something over. "Mister Victiss, aren't you afraid of the Gloomtide? What happens when it finally comes to Vattassav?"

"That will not happen, Young Fincher?"

"How can you be so farking sure?"

"Because I know."

"How?"

Victiss did not answer for a long while. His wide-set amber eyes shot to and fro, as if the giant were contemplating something important. He finally shrugged to himself, as if silently saying *fark it*, and leaned forward.

"Do you know how the Ommori got so big, Young Fincher?"

Sammi interjected. "I thought we talked about this. Isolation."

Victiss nodded. "That is true, Youngtress Sammi, but only part of the equation. There is a fish that makes its home in Crown Lake, a fish that is not found anywhere else in all of Quaan. It is called the Prism Gaar, and its meat has unique properties."

Sammi pushed up her glasses as she scooted forward and spoke in a whisper. "What kind of properties?"

Victiss smiled, and his bejeweled teeth shone in the firelight. "The kind that make you big. The kind that make you strong. The kind that make you immune to certain maladies."

"Like what?" asked Ash.

"Like the Bloat, Youngtress Ash. While the rest of Quaan saw themselves swell like balloons until their skin ripped open and yellow pus leaked from every orifice, the Ommori went about life as usual, with not a single member of the Moon Folk succumbing to the disease. For hundreds upon hundreds of years now, Ommori families gather on the seventh rise of the Five Sisters during the Cooling and on special occasions during the year to consume meals of Prism Gaar. We owe everything to this godly fish, from our size and strength to our complete immunity from outside ailments. So, you see, we do not fear the Gloomtide, any more than we feared the Bloat and countless other maladies that accosted Quaan before it, requiring salvation by the Supreme Helices."

The gang stared into the campfire, unsure how to digest this new turn of events, this new proposal that had so many positives to counteract very few negatives.

Ditto finally spoke into the fire without raising his green eyes. "That ain't us, Mister Victiss. We're not the Sour Flower Gang anymore, but we're not *not* the Sour Flower Gang, either. And the Sour Flower Gang never turns its back on a friend or a duty. Most of this world is mean and heartless and angry and sad, but there's good in it, too. I... we have to believe that. What we're doing is bigger than us, even bigger than the families that we're trying to save back in Crimmish. I need to see it through. But that's just me. I go where my friends go. Vote?"

"Vote," agreed Fincher, Ash, and Sammi in unison. Ditto nodded at Ash.

"Thank you so very much for the generous offer, Mister Victiss, but we've come too far to call it quits now. We've sacrificed too much. My vote is to see it through, as well. Sis?"

Sammi pushed up her glasses. "Hana didn't die so that we could live it up on the shores of Crown Lake while Kenn and Joon Bugg await an arrival that will never come. And neither did Miss Salt."

"And don't forget about Taff and Jazz," added Ditto.

"That's right. I vote to see it through. Fincher?"

The precocious boy stood up and walked to the shore, picking up a flat rock as he did. Fincher sent the stone skipping into the darkness of the encroaching night and watched his handiwork with wonder before turning back to the group.

"The world thinks us shite. But from shite grows the most beautiful flowers, the most bountiful food. The world thinks us lesser, and yet, they come to us to save them. If we don't, we'll just be proving them right—and fark that. And fark them." Fincher's eyes found Victiss's. "There's no better revenge than a life well-lived. Except to gift those who once hated you, those now looking into the abyss, lives well-lived. How will the world react, knowing that a group of Cheese-Eyes from the Stenches saved them?"

"They may never admit it, Young Fincher. They may never thank you. Many may never know."

"But we'll know. And that's enough for me. I vote we see it through." Fincher then surprised everyone by kneeling before Victiss. "And I say this will full understanding of what you have offered us here today. And full farking appreciation. I have never been more grateful."

"Nor I," echoed Ditto, kneeling before the giant leader.

"Nor I," repeated Sammi and Ash in succession as they dropped to their knees.

Victiss sighed deeply before shaking his head, unable to keep the grin from his pale face.

"Rise, please. Although your decision saddens me, I have never been prouder to call a group of humans friends."

The children each rose and sat back around the fire. Sammi removed her collection of knots from her pack and began twisting as she spoke.

"So, you're not angry with us, Mister Victiss?"

"Youngtress Sammi, I could never begrudge someone for following their heart, as you younglings most certainly do. It is the opposite of anger that I feel. It is respect. And that is something the Ommori do not give out lightly."

Each person went about their own work around the fire—Sammi practicing her knots, Ditto sharpening his blade, Fincher fletching Alicia's arrows, and Ash rubbing ointment on her stump. Victiss took it all in, hopeful that he would be able to experience many more evenings with this unique group of younglings.

Finally, the giant's curiosity got the best of him.

"The Sour Flower Gang, you said?"

Fincher smiled brightly. "Yeah, what do you think?"

Victiss rolled the phrase around in his mind several times. "I like it. It really sticks."

"Farking right, it does."

"Where are we going?" asked Ash as she and the gang followed Victiss early the next Paragon.

The giant answered without turning around. "You all are going north, so we are going to help get you there."

Fincher kicked at a rock as they walked along the shoreline. "Too bad we gotta go all the way around this this durn lake."

Victiss called over his shoulder again. "Oh, we are going a much faster way, Young Fincher. And much more exciting."

The children looked to each other as the giant leader offered no further explanation. Luckily, things became clear soon after as the group approached a wide dock that ran far into Crown Lake. Victiss easily stepped up on the dock then turned around to pull the children up.

Ditto lifted Sammi and Ash into Victiss's reaching hands and then moved toward Fincher.

"Don't even think about it, Ditto. Can't have people thinking I'm some damsel in distress needing assistance. I have a reputation to uphold."

"I think that crumbled when you cried in front of everyone after Stella Bugg chose Hylinn over you for the final dance at last year's Moon Tear Festival," joked Sammi, and the others laughed. Even Victiss couldn't help but join in.

Fincher's hazel eyes went wide in faux shock. "Fallacious! Fallacious on all accounts!"

"We all saw you, Fincher," said Ash matter-of-factly.

"Ahh, you saw *me* but not the cause of said tears! I happened to have been standing near Widow Till's food stand as she was making her famous mud onion pies. It was the onions that brought out my tears, not Stella Bugg's poor choice of dance partner." Sammi and Ash looked down from the dock doubtfully. Fincher spun to his large friend desperately, making a strange face as he spoke. "Isn't that right, Ditto?"

"Uhh, yeah, that sounds right. That whole area was heavy with onion fumes. I had to step away myself to keep from crying."

"See! I have been farking absolved!" Sammi and Ash rolled their eyes simultaneously before marching further down the dock.

Fincher clapped Ditto on the shoulder. "Thanks for the support there." Fincher waited until the girls' attentions were fully on Crown Lake. "Now, maybe just a little boost."

Ditto put out his knee and Fincher stepped from it and into the hands of Victiss. Soon, all the children were on the massive pier. The white-skinned colossus took the lead once more, advancing the younglings further out into Crown Lake.

As they reached the end of the dock, several strange boats could be seen moored to either side, some with large masts rising from their centers.

Victiss passed these by, opting to stop at the vessel at the very end —what appeared to be two immense, sharply pointed canoes connected in the middle by three thick poles that ran horizontal. From this central connecting structure and the points of the two canoes, thick ropes extended forward and met in a thick braid that dropped off and disappeared into the water below.

Another Ommori, this one with blue tattoos that sat in stark contrast to everyone else's red, lounged in a large, shell-shaped chair that was built into the pier, drinking a pale purple liquid from a clear mug. Leaning next to the blue-inked Ommori was a ten-foot tube of brass that flared out on both ends.

Victiss extended an arm out to the lounging Forest Child. "This is Valimoos. He is one of the Vattalirr—the Lake Talkers. There are always seven Vattalirrs among the Ommori—no more, no less. It is a position of great honor."

Valimoos released a great belch, seemingly unmoved by Victiss's grand introduction. Victiss rolled his amber eyes.

"Anyway, Valimoos is going to help initiate our cross-lake voyage." Victiss turned to address the half-drunk Lake Talker, whose eyes were starting to close. The giant leader kicked angrily at Valimoos's relaxation chair, cracking the wood and threatening to send the entire structure into the cold water below. Valimoos's eyes shot open.

"Okay, okay, okay. Relax, Victiss."

"We have need of travel. And a sleeping Lake Talker is no good to us."

"Of course, you do. And do not dare judge me, Victiss Seven. You know not the boredom of sitting here all Paragon, conversing with none but the water creatures."

"Many would give their right arms to have your gift!" Victiss caught himself and turned to Ash. "Apologies, Youngtress. I meant no offense."

"None taken. You can't have my right arm—I really need that one

—but my left one is all yours if you can find it somewhere in the Tainted Timbers."

"Probably smells like shite by now."

"Fincher," cried Sammi as Ditto punched the boy in the shoulder.

Victiss chuckled again at the younglings' antics and returned to Valimoos. "Anyway, you are awake now. We require conveyance to Ori One." Victiss glanced back at the gang. "That is the northwest corner of Crown Lake."

"Speed?" asked the Lake Talker as he began to rouse himself from his reverie.

A mischievous smile broke out below Victiss's amber mustache. "Oh, let us go fast. As fast as possible."

"Very well," replied Valimoos tiredly as he rose to his feet and snatched up the unusual instrument next to him. "Go ahead and get those… what are they then?"

"These are children, Valimoos. Human children."

Valimoos shot an amused look at the younglings. "Better tell them to hold on tight. They are about the same sizes as reef manatees. A favorite of the megamouth sharks."

"The what?" asked Sammi nervously.

"He is just trying to scare you," said Victiss as he waved the Lake Talker away. "Let us get seated in the Glisser as Valimoos does his work."

Victiss helped each child into the large seats of the vessel called a *Glisser*. As he strapped each in with rope ties, Valimoos dropped one of the belled ends of his strange instrument into the waters of Crown Lake, allowing it to submerge several feet. When Victiss finally took his seat at the front of the Glisser, Valimoos nodded, and a serene look passed across the Lake Talker's face.

Fincher, Ash, Ditto, and Sammi watched as Valimoos began to call into the other end of the instrument—they would later discover that it was called a *Linkiss Tube*—in a language that none could understand, even Victiss.

Grunts, groans, and shrieks emanated from the Lake Talker, sounds that seemed impossible from anything even resembling the human form. When Valimoos finished, he removed the belled end from his mouth and placed it to his ear, where he listened to something no one else could hear. Valimoos nodded at times, and even smiled at others, before responding into the end of the Linkiss Tube. Finally -

"He will be here shortly. And he is upset that you interrupted his pursuit of an especially in-heat cow." Valimoos paused for dramatic effect. "You better buckle in tight. I got the distinct impression that he wants to get this over with quick."

The Lake Talker fell back into his comfortable chair, retrieved his mug, and took two giant swigs of purple liquid.

"What now?" asked Fincher.

"You will see very soon, Young Fincher." A moment later, he added, "In fact, you will see right now. Please look ahead."

The children's mouths all collectively fell open as the largest creature any of them had ever seen or imagined breached the surface of Crown Lake. Looking to be every bit of one hundred feet in length, the aquatic beast had a bulbous head, dark skin, and a wide mouth filled with rows of large, pointed teeth that looked able to swallow several Ommori whole, or a dozen human children.

Victiss's jeweled teeth shone brightly under Paragon rays no longer blocked by the Vattassav canopy. "Younglings, I am delighted to introduce you to one of the Livyatan, also known as the Elder Whales. The Ommori and the Livyatan have long maintained a strong symbiotic relationship on Crown Lake. We take care of certain... threats to their survival, and they, in turn, aid us in traveling across the vastness of this great body of water."

With its head now above the water, the great eye of the Elder Whale, as wide as Ditto was tall, took in the human children on the Glisser. The Livyatan blinked, and a geyser shot from its blowhole, sending water dozens of feet into the air where it caught rays of Paragon and reflected them back in a prismatic show.

Victiss's smile faded. "He knows we have younglings on board?"

Valimoos grinned as he further settled into his seat. "He does."

"Then, he knows not to be too crazy?"

Valimoos took another big swig. "Tell him yourself! Oops! Too late."

Victiss spun and noticed that the Elder Whale had already disappeared beneath the surface of the water. He twisted back to the gang.

"Hold on! For the Five Sisters, hold on!"

Fincher looked around. "What do you mean? It looks like he's—"

The boy's words were abruptly cut short as the Glisser shot forward as if launched from Alicia Salt's longbow. The children were thrust back in their oversized seats as the shoreline quickly shrunk then vanished from view.

When the acceleration halted and the speed, which was beyond comprehension, began to normalize, Victiss turned around in his seat, another big smile evident on the giant's white face.

"What do you think?" he shouted over the lapping water.

Fincher fumbled at his ropes for a minutes before freeing himself and standing. The boy called back as he stared down at the lake rushing past beneath him. "It's fantastic!"

Victiss's amber eyes bulged. "Young Fincher! Please return to your seat! It is not safe to—"

The giant's words were cut off as Ditto, Sammi, and even Ash (with her one hand) undid their bindings and stood to fully absorb the show that was playing out around them.

Victiss began to argue, but then reminded himself that this was a group from the Stenches, who survived both the Famished, Borggos the Many, and Berserkers. They could handle a little speed.

Instead, Victiss ran two fingers across his mustache and laughed. The giant laughed as he hadn't since his own younglings were actually young. Instead of looking forward, as one was ought to do when traveling, Victiss kept his amber eyes to the rear, for the passengers on this journey were much more interesting than the destination.

Fincher, Ash, Ditto, and Sammi hooted and hollered, screamed and yelped, shouted and giggled, as they stood on the Glisser, flying across Crown Lake. They pointed as a pod of spinner dolphins swam beside them for a while, jumping and twisting in the air before their slim bodies needled back into the water. They called out in feigned fear as a school of colorful flying fish used the Glisser as an apparatus, launching themselves from the lake to soar over the speeding vessel, one catching Fincher on the side of the boy's head.

"Farking fish don't know their environment," complained Fincher as he rubbed his temple, much to the delight of the others.

Every now and then, the Elder Whale that was pulling them rose to the surface for air, shooting up a curtain of water that the Glisser passed through, thoroughly soaking everyone on board.

"He's doing that on farking purpose! I know it!"

"What are you going to do about it, Fincher?" demanded Sammi through laughs.

"Tell him to farking meet me back on land, where things are more equal. Then we'll see what's what!"

As if understanding the mouthy boy's words, the Livyatan shot another pillar of water into the air, but this one was much shorter, much more condensed. It arched perfectly through the air, over the ducking heads of Victiss and Ash, to slam into Fincher, who would have gone overboard if it wasn't for Ditto's strong hand on his shirt.

Everyone roared in laughter as Fincher coughed up lake water and shook his head free of the onslaught.

"Still want a fair fight, Young Fincher?!"

Fincher blew snot rockets from each nostril. "Tell him I'll allow him to keep his dignity! Just this once!"

"Look!"

Sammi's alert forced everyone, including Victiss, to look up, where more than two dozen giant, colorful birds, six to each side, flanked the Glisser. Between the two groups of six, Rashii the Quilted Raven flew, somehow protected from what could have been one of the smaller bird's natural predators.

Victiss looked up and howled in delight, letting his oversized hat fall to the Glisser floor. "The Gemmed Pelicans favor your journey, younglings! It appears that fate is on your side! It is a great Paragon, indeed, when the great birds unite to back an effort!"

"Can they fly us to Terminus Grove?!"

"Well, no, Young Fincher. But—"

"Then just another farking well wish!"

Victiss had no words with which to respond to the boy, so he simply turned around and enjoyed the remainder of the trip, knowing that the Ommori, too, probably had little to offer their new friends.

Instead, the giant and his four acquaintances raced across Crown Lake, enjoying the tranquility, the color, and the peace of their surroundings, all knowing that this would not last beyond the borders of Vattassav, which is exactly where the younglings were heading—alone and without the strength of giants to protect them.

But this understanding made the rapid trip across Crown Lake all the more memorable. All the more appreciated.

At one point, one of the famed Gemmed Pelicans dove down and intercepted a flying fish just above the Glisser. It snatched the prey clean out of the air and took off towards the shore, Paragon glimmering off its multicolored coat.

Fincher poked Sammi, who sat just in front on him.

"How's that for a show?"

The bespectacled girl spun back, smiling wider than Fincher had ever seen her.

"That's farking amazing."

Fincher had no response to his young friend. For she had already delivered the perfectly worded answer.

After several hours that seemed to have passed infinitely faster, the Elder Whale released the Glisser, sending the vessel gliding to another pier in the far northwest corner of Crown Lake.

The Livyatan rose to the surface one last time, its giant eye taking in the children before sending a final stream of water into the air.

"He said that your screams and laughs made this journey one he will not forget. He said that he wishes you well, wherever your journey takes you," said another of the Vattalirr who was listening through his Linkiss Tube at the end of the dock. The blue-tattooed giant put down his instrument as he knelt to help the younglings out of the Glisser. He stopped Victiss as the giant leader stepped onto the pier. "And he said that *you* owe him for such a long trip during prime mating season. Said he lost a…" The Vattalirr searched for the right word. "… particularly fertile cow. Or something like that."

Victiss chuckled lightly. "Thanks for the message, Vergess. I will put something very fine together for that one."

"Wharlsinbrottush is the closest pronunciation to his name."

"Good. I know who to request when delivering his prize. Thank you, again."

The Vattalirr, this one seemingly much more into his job than Valimoos, nodded and reclined back in his chair, his amber eyes continually scanning the waters as he listened intently with his Linkiss Tube.

"Come, children, this way," declared Victiss, leading the gang off the pier and down a small path that rounded north. As they walked, curiosity again got the best of Sammi.

"Mister Victiss, can I ask you a question?"

"You can ask me anything, Youngtress Sammi. Any of you can. Within Vattassav, there are no secrets."

"Why do the Elder Whales do what you want? I can't imagine that was an easy task for him, pulling us across Crown Lake."

"Yeah, if I were him, I'd have told you to fark right off."

"Fincher!" came the expected cry from everyone.

"It is fine," cut in Victiss, trying to avoid further squabbling from the kids. "And you are both correct. The Livyatan are the true kings of Crown Lake, and we are no more their masters than we are masters of the Monarch Browns or the Five Sisters, for that matter."

"Then, why do they help you?" asked Ditto.

Victiss mulled over the question for a moment. "Because we are friends, the oldest of friends. And friends help each other."

Ash repositioned the pack on her back before speaking. "We see how they help you. But how do the Ommori help them?"

"Several ways, Youngtress Ash. The most obvious way is that we are the protectors of Crown Lake. Without the Ommori, the humans of Quaan would have ransacked Vattassav and Crown Lake long ago.

The Livyatan would have been massacred for their meat and blubber and oil. And anything else deemed valuable. The Elder Whales know this. They have conversed with their cousins who venture up and down Crown's Run and North Verve. They know only too well how the world of man infringes upon the natural world."

Sammi pushed up her glasses as she walked. "What are the non-obvious ways?"

"The Livyatan are without natural predators, but that does not mean that they are immune to the threats of Crown Lake. Unusual seasons can create toxic red algae blooms that change the acidity of the lake water. Various non-native parasites can find their way into Crown Lake from the rivers and rivulets that run into it. No creature is large enough to threaten an Elder Whale. But what about those too small for them to combat? Those that latch on by the hundreds, by the thousands. Just as one man from Quaan cannot harm Vattassav, ten thousand tiny parasites, chopping away and slowly draining its life force, can ruin what the Five Sisters gave their all to create. We Ommori have given our word to keep the waters of Crown Lake pure and to do what we can against foreign invaders, whether they be of the worm, fish, plant, or human variety."

Fincher tripped over a wild root but was caught by Ditto. "Well, when you put it that way, it sounds like you lot actually got the shite end of the bargain!"

Victiss answered without turning around. "Like I said, we are *friends*, Young Fincher. Does the Sour Flower Gang keep track among yourselves of who has done what for who?"

Victiss's words, namely him using the Sour Flower Gang term, immediately brought a heaviness to the conversation that the giant never intended, although he certainly sensed it.

"I meant... when you were..."

Luckily, Fincher stepped in to save the Ommori.

"We know what you mean, Mister Victiss. And, no, we certainly did not. And currently do not. So, your point is well-taken."

Victiss twisted to offer Fincher a thankful nod, but the giant leader knew that the damage had already been done. As the mustached

Moon Folk member continued to lead the younglings, he felt another pang of sadness. *None so young and innocent should bear such open wounds that can be set afire by benign words. None with shoulders so slight should bear such weight.*

Victiss thought long and hard for the proper words to restore the children's excitement and embolden them for the meeting to come. But rousing words were his wife's specialty and an area in which Victiss was hopelessly deficient. In the end, he settled on something short and ineffective.

"Not much further now. We are almost there."

The largest structure the children of Crimmish had seen in all the Mutewoods slowly came into view between the Monarch Browns and pine varietals and groupings of bamboo. Despite its size, it appeared to be born from the forest, as if Vattassav had formed around it and not the other way around. As if it was always here, even before the woods that surrounded it.

"Younglings, welcome to Vattasseer. If there was a capital of Vattassav, which there is not, this would be it. Here is where the Heptorii gather to make important decisions. Here is where the Primirri resides, the wisest and most respected of all the Ommori. It is she that sees what others, even the Heptorii, cannot. Perhaps she can help guide you on your passage north."

The children barely heard what Victiss said, so enchanted were they by Vattasseer, which was encircled by magical ponds filled with bioluminescent creatures and Astars awakening with the falling of Paragon.

Vattasseer was a place of arches, made of pliable bamboo that cast aside any notions of the straight lines that defined the world of man. The palace moved from here to there without any obvious rhyme or reason, mirroring the natural world. If it weren't for the odd bridge and light shining from the numerous windows, one would question their sanity, debating whether they were looking upon a creation or a natural occurrence.

"… and that is why it is important, I think, that you speak with Thyccaria the Prime. If there is a way to hasten or smooth your travels, she will discern it."

Fincher shook himself from the otherworldly scene around him and attempted to play off his and his friends' complete ignorance of their guide's words.

"Yeah, yeah. Sounds farking great."

Thyccaria the Prime was everything one would have wanted out of a queen. Tall and muscled and lean, the giantess was covered in clean red tattoos that accentuated every line on her impressive Ommori body. Instead of the usual wide hat, she donned a crown of shiny shells and unusual gems. Instead of moccasins, the giant queen wore nothing on her massive feet, allowing those visiting, stationed far beneath her, full view of her carefully manicured nails decorated with precious jewels.

When she spoke, Thyccaria the Prime's voice echoed powerfully throughout the wooden construct, which caught Sammi Bugg off-guard considering the acoustical nature of the palace.

"Victiss Three. I asked you to bring me a solution to our leecher problem and, instead, you bring me more problems. Account for yourself."

Fincher and the other children could not help but take a step back from the strength of the Ommori queen's words. Luckily, Victiss was without such hesitance. The Heptorii stepped forward confidently.

Victiss's palm went up as he spoke. "Thyccaria the Prime, I have not brought you a solution to the leechers, but I have with me something much more valuable."

"And what is that, Victiss Three?"

The giant leader thought over his words carefully. "Hope. I have brought hope to the Prime."

"Explain yourself, Victiss. And know that I have many to see today. And remember the Soul-burned are usually not on the docket."

Victiss glanced to the children and shot a wink before addressing his queen.

"First and foremost, thank you for seeing us. I know how the stacks of requests continue to pile upon your stout shoulders."

Thyccaria rolled her amber eyes, and only in that moment of normalcy did Fincher finally see how beautiful the giantess was. Thick locks of amber hair cascaded down in ropes, perfectly framing the Ommori queen's angular face that was tastefully accented with red lines.

"What do you want from me, Vicky?"

Fincher burst out laughing, much to the horror of Ditto, Ash, and Sammi. They all shot daggers at the boy with the yellow eyes. Fincher shrugged helplessly.

"I'm farking sorry. But Vicky?! Vicky?! Oh, it's too much."

Victiss only offered a half turn, not wanting to face away from his queen. "It is a term of endearment, Young Fincher. Had you ever been close enough to a girl who was not your friend, perhaps you would understand such an endearment."

Silence. Followed by, "Ohhhh, Fincher! You got crushed," said Ash.

Sammi join in. "Yeah, I thought Stella Bugg did a number on you, but this was… something else. He *smoked* you, Fincher."

Even Ditto joined in. "That one had to hurt, Fincher. Maybe sit the next few minutes out."

Fincher's hazel eyes, open and accusatory, swung to Ditto.

"You, too, Ditto?"

"Sorry, buddy, but you opened yourself up to that one."

Fincher's mouth slammed shut, and his mind raced over the many (less than manly) things he had watched Ditto do, the many times Ditto had wept on his shoulder. What would Ditto do if he released all those moments into the world? In earshot of Ash Bugg? How would Ditto feel then?

Fincher formulated a retaliation, had the weapon readied and cocked back. Then he looked into his friend's green eyes, and the anger washed away like masked-face rat droppings during downpours of the seasonal Warming.

In the end, Fincher simply shrugged in surrender.

"Apologies, Mister Victiss. As you can see, I am the dumbest of our group and need to be reminded of how to act. Although, I think they would agree that without me this would be a poorly, ill-tempered gang, susceptible to melancholy and despair."

Victiss waited for the obvious humorous rebuttal.

"Of course, Fincher," said Ash he heard instead. "Without you we'd be as dry and tasteless as the *Plucky Gents*—all name and no heart. You know we love you."

"You're the propeller in our backsides, Fincher," added Sammi, still giggling from Victiss's barb.

Ditto slapped his friend on the back, sending him forward several steps. "We wouldn't let anyone else speak for us, Fincher. Only you. What else do you need to know, my friend?"

Thyccaria the Prime flashed a smile from her dais on high. Her teeth were even more ornamented than Victiss's. She nodded to her left and one of the servant Ommori dove behind a screen.

"Victiss…" Her widespread amber eyes found Fincher. "Vicky…" Fincher stifled a giggle and Thyccaria hid her mouth behind ringed fingers. When the queen had recovered, she lowered her hand. "I now see why you have brought these human children to me. They are unlike the others of Quaan; it does not take the Primirri to discover that. What would you have of me, in their regard?"

Victiss hesitated for a moment before speaking. "These human children are on a task of extreme importance—to all of Quaan. The need to get north… far north. Obviously, the land outside of Vattassav —and even within—is no place for younglings to be traveling alone."

"And you were hoping for…"

Victiss shuffled from one large foot to the other. "I was hoping there might be some support that we could offer. Perhaps a protected ride with the Tuggers."

"Impossible."

"But Thyccaria, I think that—"

The Prime silenced the giant leader with an upraised hand. She turned to the four small humans gathered beneath her.

"What are your names, younglings?"

Ash nodded at Fincher and the boy stepped forward.

"My name is Finchius Bugg, Miss Thyccaria. And this is Deetarik Bugg, Ashanti Bugg, and Samira Bugg—although we go by Fincher, Ditto, Ash, and Sammi."

The Prime's amber eyes squinted in confusion. "Are you of relation?"

"No, ma'am, we are from Crimmish. We all share the same last name there."

A ringed hand went to the giant queen's beautiful face. "Of course, Crimmish. Yes, I have heard of the atrocities of living there, of what is being done to your people."

Fincher shrugged. "It's not all bad, ma'am."

"And how is that?"

"We have each other."

A tiny smile appeared on the Prime's lips. "And you have traveled alone from Crimmish to here? How? How have you made it this far?"

"Like I said, we have each other. But it hasn't come without losses. Painful losses."

Thyccaria's face softened as she felt the weight of those losses, so palpable was the grief in the air. "I see. And I am sorry." The Prime offered a sympathetic moment of silence before pressing on. "You are traveling north from Crimmish, a place your people are not allowed to leave, on a mission to save Quaan, in some way. Correct so far?"

"Yes, ma'am."

"Then, tell me. Under whose orders are you acting. Certainly not your own. And certainly not those of your elders."

Fincher turned to regard Ash and Sammi, who both simply shrugged helplessly. *Fark it*, he thought.

"No, Miss Thyccaria, it was under the order of the Titian Empire. We were supposed to be escorted north by High Captain Gorman Graff but were attacked by the Cobalts when passing through Salt's

Pass. From there, we were delivered to Miss Alicia Salt, who was to return us to Crimmish."

"Long has the Lady of Shadowset been a friend to the Ommori, although I have not seen her in many years. She is a woman of honor, a woman of her word. Why did she not return you to Crimmish?"

Fincher began to tell the Prime of the deal struck between the Sour Flower Gang and Alicia Salt. Of the Silver Stagg and the unpleasantness that its death caused. Instead, the boy opted for a much simpler explanation.

"Because we asked her to."

The Prime snickered. "You will have to do better than that, young man."

"Well, I can't, ma'am, because that's the truth. We explained our mission to Miss Salt, and she agreed to take us north. She was paid well by the Cobalts to guide us, so guide us she did. But north, not south."

"Wait! The *Cobalts* paid to have you returned to Crimmish? Why? Were you not prisoners? Why would they not simply release you to the wilds? Or dispatch you, even?"

Fincher flashed a smile, putting all his rakish charm into the look. "I guess they took a farking liking to me."

"Fincher!"

Laughter escaped Thyccaria's thick lips once more. "Okay, okay, Young Fincher. Let us assume that I believe you, so far. Where is the Lady of Shadowset?"

Hazel-on-yellow eyes fell to the floor. "She fell protecting us from some Marsh Ghouls."

"Marsh Ghouls?"

Victiss cut in. "The Famished. Alicia Salt and the younglings stumbled into a Famished awakening."

Now, it was Thyccaria's angular face that fell. "How terrible. Poor Alicia. My heart hurts for her. She was one of the few humans that truly understood Quaan, understood and appreciated the gift of the Five Sisters. We will honor her memory at the Conclave of the

Cooling." The other Ommori nodded. Back to Fincher. "How did you all manage to escape?"

"It wasn't easy."

"And how did you manage to survive your trek through southern Vattassav?"

"It wasn't any easier."

"Fair enough. Details can be shared across a fire and not in a room of administration." Thyccaria turned back to Victiss. "You said that their mission was for the benefit of all Quaan. What is it?"

Victiss wrung his giant hands. "They are searching for a cure to the Gloomtide. That terrible affliction that is—"

"I know what the Gloomtide is, Vicky. You think I have not heard the reports of what was seen along the banks of Crown's Run?" Victiss bowed his head in apology. "Why would these younglings be able to find a cure when others cannot? When adults cannot?"

"They will be searching in Terminus Grove."

The Prime's eyes widened in surprise. "That place is pure poison. No one can venture into that cursed place."

"Apparently, these younglings can."

Thyccaria remained quiet for several seconds before realization finally struck. "Because of their proximity to the Tainted Timbers?"

"Yes, my Prime."

"And what I would surmise to be their resistance to toxins in the air?"

"You are too wise, my Prime."

Thyccaria waved the Heptorii's compliment away. "Flattery will get you nowhere, Vicky." She continued to think. "Let me ask you this. You said that their mission—curing the Gloomtide—will help Quaan. Does that include Vattassav? Does that include the Ommori?"

Victiss winced, as if he could see a blow coming. "Well, not directly. But given that—"

"Then there is nothing that we can do, I'm afraid. This is not just a story of healing the sick. This is now a tale of politics, of the Titians and the Cobalts. Did you ever stop to consider that there may be powerful forces looking for these younglings? That their unique...

attributes, could be used as valuable political capital?" Victiss had no response, so the Prime went on. "Our truce with the Titian Empire is a tenuous one. Always has been, always will be. Right now, we stay out of their business, and they stay out of ours. But you know as well as any, *Victiss Three*, that part of our agreement entails only crossing the lands outside of Vattassav in the course of trading agreed-upon items. And only up and down North Verve and Crown's Run. What you are asking me is to risk this fragile peace on something that will not directly benefit our people. This I cannot do. No matter how much I may immediately like these younglings."

"But—"

"Enough! This meeting has already put me behind. These humans can stay in Vattassav as long as they wish, but when they leave here, they will leave alone as soon as the last tree of the forest has been passed. Is that understood?"

"It is, my Prime."

"Good. Then return to me when you have a solution to our leecher problem. You know, the one that *does* directly impact the Ommori."

Fincher leaned into the others. "Farking heck. We survived the Sluggs, the Marsh Ghouls, the Worm, and Berserkers, only to get stonewalled by farking politics?"

Although Fincher whispered to his friends, he could clearly be heard by Victiss standing next to him. The Heptorii's head shot up, as if an idea had shot lightning up his too-long spine.

"My Prime! I request a private meeting to discuss an idea. A proposal, really."

"If it does not have to do with our leecher problem, Vicky, I do not want to hear it. The conversation regarding these younglings has concluded. What is it you want to speak about—our leecher problem or these human children?"

"Both, my Prime. I want to speak of both. And how human and Ommori may help each other. Directly."

A long, heavy silence fell over the throne room. Finally, the Prime relented.

"Everyone out! Youngling and Ommori alike! I will hear this

proposal but will save Vicky the embarrassment of having you all see me put him on his rear should his scheme prove ridiculous."

Victiss stood his ground as the other Ommori began to filter out of the throne area, some ushering the children along as they went.

Fincher turned around to see Victiss standing beneath the imposing Primirri, the giant leader nervously rubbing his amber mustache. He caught up to Ditto.

"I would hate to be that farking guy right now."

Ditto looked back, but the large boy's green eyes only took in the beautiful and decorated Thyccaria, her taut, too-white skin showing around her skimpy Ommori garb.

"I wouldn't mind it."

12

THE EYE OF GOD

It was several hours later when Victiss finally returned to the children, who had already been fed another delicious meal and brought to a lovely lean-to for the duration of the evening. The kind Ommori who had chaperoned the younglings made a large bonfire for the children before retiring for the night, concerned that the small humans might be afraid of the dark.

When Victiss appeared on the edge of the firelight, he was not alone. Behind the Heptorii, cloaked in shadow, were two more massive Ommori, each carrying what appeared to be a massive load, which they carefully set down before touching the light.

The three Ommori did not speak. Instead, they went into the lean-to and carried out a large table from within, bringing it as close to the bonfire as possible without getting burned. The top of the wooden table, coated in a hard, clear substance, danced with reflected firelight.

Victiss stared down at the lounging children and launched in without preamble. "How determined are you to continue your voyage north?"

"Very," said Ash without missing a beat.

"Are you willing to risk it all?"

"We already farking have, Mister Victiss."

"Are you willing to do it again?"

"You're farking right."

Victiss seemed relieved. "Good. Then my efforts over the past few hours have not been in vain. Join me, please."

Fincher, Ditto, Ash, and Sammi all rose and walked over to the table that was now bathed in light. As they did, Victiss motioned to the hulking shadows and the other two Ommori approached, each carrying the end of a long object. They tossed the item onto the table with an audible *splat* and slid out of the way, revealing an eight-foot-long fish with an abnormally long snout and jaw filled with pointy teeth. But it wasn't the size or unusual head of the fish that opened the mouths of the Crimmish kids. It was its scales.

Rays of red, orange, yellow, green, blue, indigo, and violet shot forth from the deceased fish, forcing the children to squint. And though they wanted to shield their eyes or look away, they found that they could not, so entrancing was the light show playing out before them.

Victiss clocked the humans' reactions and smiled, adding light from his own colorful gems to the show. "What do you think?"

"Beautiful farking fish, Mister Victiss."

Victiss swept out his long arm. "This is the Prism Gaar. Next to the Livyatan, it is what the Ommori hold most precious in Crown Lake. The meat of the Prism Gaar is blessed by the Five Sisters. Consuming it has given the Ommori our size and strength. It had given us long life. It has made us immune to ailments like the Bloat. Like the Gloomtide. The Prism Gaar is precious to us, so we consume it sparingly. We are careful not to disrupt its mating patterns or reduce its already limited numbers. The Prism Gaar is one of Vattassav's many secrets that we keep from the world of man. If any ever found out about the magical benefits of this extraordinary fish, it would be hunted to extinction within a season. Of this, I am sure."

"Like the goose who laid the golden eggs," said Sammi, rainbow colors dancing within the frames of her glasses.

"Yes," agreed Victiss. "I am surprised you have heard that tale. Would you believe that it's an Ommori parable, based on the Prism

Gaar? Even we, so in touch with the natural world, almost fished the Prism Gaar to extinction. It was only the wisdom of Primirri Velentiuss Two who prevented us from eliminating our greatest advantage over the world of man. Now, we thoughtfully harvest the Prism Gaar, only consuming once every seven evenings during the Cooling and on special occasions."

Everyone enjoyed the light show for several more minutes before Fincher had finally reached the end of his silence.

"This is lovely, Mister Victiss, but why are you showing it to us?"

Victiss nodded, and the Ommori pair removed the Prism Gaar from the table and placed it on the ground far from the bonfire. The giants then went back to the shadows from whence they came, returning with another large item that they plopped onto the table.

Another Prism Gaar greeted the children, but this one was a far cry from the wondrous creature that had appeared before. This fish was not thick with fat and meat, but was slender—almost skeletal. Its multicolored scales were dull and lifeless, refusing to throw light back into the air. Many of its teeth were missing, and the entire fish seemed less than, as if it had been rotting away even prior to death.

Victiss allowed the younglings to study the specimen before speaking. "Well? What do you think?"

Ditto was the first to respond. "I think this one's quite a bit less impressive than the last one."

Victiss nodded to Ditto, then to the other two Ommori, who promptly flipped the Prism Gaar over.

"This is why, Young Ditto."

On the opposite side of the Prism Gaar, just below its gills, was a scaleless, elongated, jawless fish with large eyes and a sucker mouth which it had used to latch onto the flesh of the magical creature. Even in death, it refused to release its grip.

"What the fark is that?"

"It is what we call a leecher, Young Fincher, but it is more commonly known as a northern lamprey. They are not indigenous to Crown Lake, but can travel down North Verve or, more often, Crown's Run to infiltrate our home. We have measures in place at the mouths of both major rivers, but even those are not one hundred percent effective."

Sammi shuffled forward, mesmerized. "But what *are* they?"

"They are parasites, Youngtress Sammi. The worst kind of parasite for our lake-dwelling friends. Although they will attach to anything when hungry, they favor the flesh of the Prism Gaar."

"They have good taste in food," remarked Ash.

Victiss could only sigh in agreement. "That they do. They also have a taste for Elder Whale, but their numbers would have to be over-whelming to threaten our Livyatan allies."

Sammi pushed up her glasses as she continued to study the specimen on the table. "But, it only takes one to harm a Prism Gaar?"

"Correct. Now, this Gaar has obviously had this leecher on it for some time, probably since the lamprey was only six inches or so, not the two-foot length that you see here now. But even having a leecher attached to it for a week or so is enough to disrupt a Gaar's eating and mating habits, quickly driving their numbers down."

Fincher's hazel eyes found Victiss in the dark. Firelight danced within them as he spoke.

"And, if you don't get your fill of Prism Gaar meat, you Moon Folk become weak and sickly, just like the farking rest of us?"

Victiss considered the question before responding. "If you think that we will shrivel and shorten, you are incorrect, Young Fincher. But, if you mean that our immunity to things like the Bloat, like the Gloomtide, will fail… I am afraid that you are correct."

Fincher saw an opportunity and jumped. "Then, all the more reason to aid us in our durn quest!"

The Heptorii laughed lightly. "You would make a great Solicitor General, Young Fincher, but we prefer a more proactive approach to the problem."

"You mean ridding Crown Lake of the leechers," said Ditto. "How is that beyond the means of the Ommori?"

"Great question, Young Ditto, and one that forwards our conversation."

Victiss motioned once more to the two Ommori, and they leapt to work, removing the Gaar and its leecher, returning the table to its lean-to, and carrying the healthy Prism Gaar away for later consumption, leaving the giant leader and the four younglings to their private discussion.

When the pair had left, Victiss returned his attention to the children.

"Let us sit around the fire and talk." Everyone followed the Heptorii's suggestion. When everyone had settled, he said, "Leechers find their way through our delta traps at least once a decade. But we are the Keepers of the Lake, and we are good at what we do. For this reason, we are almost always able to clear out the threat before any major damage can be done to the ecosystem. But this time…"

As if he needed more courage to complete his tale, Victiss removed an ornate pipe from his satchel and lit it with a long match. The giant took three long puffs, exhaling smoke rings that expanded and flew off into the night. Still, the giant remained quiet.

"So, what's so farking different about this time?" demanded Fincher, tired of being left hanging.

Victiss took one more puff before answering. "The way to eliminate a leecher infestation is to locate the nest, called a leecher denn. Leecher denns need calm waters to thrive, which is why they are usually found in one of the many underwater caves that dot the edges of Crown Lake. To date, we have been able to find these leecher denns and eradicate the nests, polluting the caves against future incursions. Once the parasites' reproduction has ended, it is just a matter of clearing the lake of the existing lampreys."

Ash's face twisted. "So… you can't find this most recent denn? Is that what you're saying?"

The giant leader took another puff. "I wish it were so simple, Youngtress Ash. Actually, we *have* located the leecher denn. And *that* is what is causing all the trouble."

Ash rubbed the stub of her left arm. "I don't get it."

"Join the farking club," added Fincher.

One last puff and Victiss upended the bejeweled pipe and knocked its ashy contents to the ground. He pocketed the smoking tool before answering.

"We have located the leecher denn, Youngtress Ash. But it is somewhere that not I, nor any Ommori, can go." A pause. "The leechers have made their denn in *Maker's Lament*, or what the younger Ommori call the *Eye of God*."

It took the children a while to digest this new information. As usual, Fincher voiced the collective confusion.

"What the fark does that mean? Just go in there and sweep those buggers out!"

"We cannot, Young Fincher."

"And why the fark not?"

"Because that cave is sacred to the Ommori. Sacred and off limits. According to legend, the Eye of God is where the Grand Maker, upon seeing what his daughters, the Five Sisters, created despite his lack of support and love, went to cry out his indignity, his tears filling the crate that became Crown Lake. Obviously, this was before the Maker's shame was replaced by overwhelming pride.

"Maker's Lament is a lake cave just to the south of the Crown Run Delta. It is said to be the place from where the Grand Maker continues to watch over Quaan, taking special note of how the Ommori treat his children's land. But it is also referred to as the Great Temptation, for its walls are caked in a collection of diamonds and gemstones not found anywhere else in all of Quaan. The songs of old say that any Ommori who steps foot into Maker's Lament is assumed to have given into temptation, causing the Grand Maker to lose faith in all Moon Folk. The Grand Maker's disappointment will reach the Five Sisters, whose sadness will ultimately destroy Vattassav, drying up Crown Lake and withering even the Monarch Browns. All will be lost."

"You don't really believe that, do you, Mister Victiss?" asked Ash skeptically.

The giant leader reached over and tossed another branch onto the large fire. He responded while still staring into the flames. "I do not know what I believe anymore, Youngtress Ash. But enough of the

Ommori *do* believe, and that is all that matters. If one of us were to venture into Maker's Lament and rid it of the leecher denn, anything after that, anything even remotely negative, would be blamed squarely on that action." Victiss swung his amber eyes to the Crimmish kids. "I am not sure of many things anymore. But I am sure of this. If an Ommori were to enter the Eye of God, it would eventually lead to a civil war that would bring finality to our way of life. I know this. And the Primirri knows this."

Ditto leaned forward. "So, where do we fit in?"

Victiss shifted uncomfortably on his backside. "I have spoken in length to Thyccaria the Prime. As you know, she puts the needs of the Ommori above everything else, even her own safety. She has agreed that if one of you were to cross into Maker's Lament and rid us of this leecher denn, she would be willing to breach the Titian Agreement and allow our Tuggers to take you north as far as Cassie's Clutch, providing you with all the protection that we offer other precious cargo."

The children looked to each other doubtfully.

"Uhh, sounds like a really sweet offer," said Fincher sarcastically, "but we're no swimmer folk. There're not a lot of farking places you'd want to swim around Crimmish."

"You can sink, can you not, Young Fincher?"

"Well, yes, but—"

"Then, that is all you need. We are not asking you to swim."

"You know we don't breathe under farking water either, don't you? I don't know what you've heard about the Stenches, but I promise you that we're not freaks."

Victiss flashed another colorful smile. "I know that you cannot breathe under water, Young Fincher. Nor can the Ommori. But we have developed methods for doing just that."

Sammi shot forward, suddenly intrigued. "I would very much like to see this technology, Mister Victiss."

The giant leader chuckled. "I promise you, Youngtress Sammi, it can barely be considered technology." He thought for a moment. "But, I suppose it is interesting. In any case, of course you will see it." Victiss stood with a grunt. "I need to know if this is a deal that interests you. I will not lie to you children; this is no easy task. Any time you travel beneath the surface of Crown Lake, you open yourself up to a host of threats, from a lack of air to a plethora of predators. And although northern lamprey are typically less than four feet in length, the denn mothers can grow to be much larger. You can assume that one will be present in Maker's Lament. In short, it is a dangerous mission."

The crackling of the bonfire was all that could be heard for several minutes as the younglings considered their options.

"What would you rather do, Mister Victiss?" asked Fincher. "Fight off the Famished, face the Worm, go around a group of Berserkers, or enter Maker's Lament?"

Victiss thought it over, wanting to give the boy an honest answer. "Removing the obvious religious and societal implications of the Eye of God?"

"Sure. Removing those."

Victiss thought some more. "I would rather venture into the Eye of God, Young Fincher. Of this, I am sure. And if I could, I most certainly would."

Fincher looked around. Ash nodded, then Ditto, then Sammi. "Well, we've made it this far. But, I don't like our chances of getting much further, of getting across northeast Quaan, without some help. You have a deal, Mister Victiss. We've dealt with one farking parasite already. Time to rid the world of another."

Victiss nodded and tossed another log onto the fire. "Then, I will let the Primirri know. Sleep well, my friends. You will need your rest. I will come for you at the first appearance of Paragon, for there is much to go over before we begin. I will take my leave." Victiss started to leave but stopped at the edge of the firelight. "Oh, and do not eat anything in the morning. It is best to travel beneath Crown Lake on an empty stomach." Victiss continued to walk off, although his voice could be heard from the darkness. "Vomiting under the waves is the fastest route to death…"

Four pairs of yellowed eyes narrowed.

"Why did he feel the need to add that?" wondered Ash aloud.

"Yeah," agreed her little sister. "What was the point of that?"

Fincher kicked angrily at the fire. "I think it was to let us know."

Sammi pushed up her glasses. "Let us know what?"

Fincher kicked at the fire again. "That we made a shite deal." He kicked out once more. "That we're properly farked."

The jellylike sac hit the table with a loud *splat*.

"What the fark is that?"

Victiss smiled under the morning light. "That is an Air Sac, Young Fincher."

Sammi leaned in closer, adjusting her glasses as she did. "But *what* is it?"

"It is the transparent skin of a mushroom jellyfish. We have removed its insides and cleansed it thoroughly. It now barely has a smell."

"I can farking smell it. Smells like shite."

"I said it *barely* has a smell, Young Fincher."

"How does it work?" asked Sammi, intrigued by the clear sac.

"There is a small opening where we removed the tentacles and guts. When stretched over the head, the sac creates an airtight seal around the neck. Then we use the tubular tendrils of the skyreach weed, an emergent aquatic plant that is rooted to the lake bottom but breathes fresh air. We connect several together and fuse one end to the top of the mushroom jelly skin."

Sammi's brown-on-yellow eyes went wide with realization. "Then, you cut a hole in the top of the sac, allowing oxygen from above to fill the Air Sac."

Victiss's jeweled teeth appeared. "You have an engineer's mind, Youngtress Sammi."

"You don't know the half of it," corrected Ash as Fincher and Ditto nodded in agreement.

Sammi ignored the compliments, her mind racing. "But, Mister Victiss, won't the air grow stale as the user exhales."

"Another astute observation, Youngtress Sammi. That is why we connect *two* tendrils to the Air Sac, one on top for fresh air coming in, another on the side to allow stale air to exit and ensure airflow. Each Crown Diver has two Air Chiefs who keep the air flowing and one Ripper."

Ditto's blond-haired head cocked to the side. "What's a Ripper?"

"The Ripper yanks up the Crown Diver by the umbilical cord tied around his or her waist."

"Why would you need that?"

"To rip you free from trouble, Young Ditto."

"What kind of trouble?"

Victiss shrugged. "Megamouth sharks, ogre eels, trapper kelp… too many to name, really."

"Farking heck!"

Victiss held up his hand. "The point is not what is under the water. The point is that you will have ample support from above."

Sammi finally tore her eyes from the Air Sac. "Okay, so when do I go under?"

Victiss's mouth turned down in a frown. The giant leader looked to his right, where the giantess Tufferia stood, having made her own way across the lake before the break of Paragon. She offered Victiss a helpless smile.

Victiss searched for the right words, the right question. "Youngtress Sammi, how well can you see without those glasses of yours?"

"She can't see shite!"

"Shut up, Fincher! I can, too!"

Ash put the stub of her left arm around her little sister. "Sammi, you know you can't see without your glasses." To Victiss, she added, "Why do you ask?"

Victiss pointed to the table. "The Air Sac is quite tight on the head and face. It does not leave room for glasses, I am afraid."

Sammi's face fell in disappointment. Ash worked to comfort her.

"Don't worry, little sis. I'm sure you'll figure out a way to get yourself down there one day. Maybe on our way back. But I promise to explain in detail everything I see down there."

"Uhh," Victiss interrupted, "I'm afraid that being a Crown Diver, especially for this particular mission, will require *two* working arms."

Rage flooded Ash's dark face. "I *have* two working arms! In fact, I'd put these arms up against anyone in Quaan! I will—"

"Hands, Youngtress Ash. I meant two *hands* will be necessary."

Like her sister, Ash looked crestfallen, once again reminded of what the Ghost Puma stole from her not long ago. But, as always, the impossibly strong-willed girl pulled herself together quickly. Her chin shot back up.

"Then, I will assist Ditto from above as best I can."

"Me too," chimed in Sammi.

"Me too," said Fincher. Beautiful Tufferia giggled from the side. Fincher found her with his hazel eyes. "Something I said?"

Victiss took one step closer to Fincher and knelt down, shooting the boy a sympathetic look.

"Young Fincher, Crown Divers always travel in pairs. It is the only way to maximize safety beneath the waves."

As Sammi and Ash laughed at Fincher's shocked face, Ditto approached and delivered a good-natured slap on the back that sent the smaller boy stumbling forward.

"What do you say, Fincher? You and me voyaging underwater to save Crown Lake and the Ommori way of life? Sounds like fun."

Fincher swallowed down the bile that was rising in his throat. "It sounds like a nightmare. Literally like one of my nightmares where I can't breathe."

Ditto placed his forehead against his friend's temple. "But imagine the story you could tell Stella Bugg when we return home as saviors. How could Hylinn Bugg ever compete with someone who's traveled underwater and seen things that no other human has seen?"

Fincher's head cocked to the side and a wry smile perched itself upon the boy's lips. "He couldn't. There's no way that Danglin' Andy could compete with that."

Ditto and Ash shared a look before Ditto spun his green eyes toward the Heptorii.

"He's in."

~

Unlike the Glisser, which was built for speed, the boat on which the children now sat was obviously made for stability and space. Wide, long, and shallow, the vessel—known as a LeekFlatt—was paddled slowly south by a host of Ommori, Victiss and Tufferia sitting comfortably at their head.

Paragon had passed overhead and was now just beginning to creep closer to the Vattassav tree line as it had taken much of the day for Ditto and Fincher to understand their breathing equipment, their weapons, and the more frightening details of their mission.

When Sammi asked why a Livyatan was not pulling the boat, Victiss offered a simple explanation.

"Maker's Lament is just south of here—not far at all. The Eye of God is quite close to the Crown Run Delta, which is, no doubt, why the leechers selected it as their denn. We like to save the Elder Whales for longer, more time-sensitive journeys. They are our siblings in Vattassav, but even the patience of siblings can run short."

"I hear that," said Sammi jokingly and received a punch to the ribs for her attempt at humor.

Less than fifteen minutes later, the LeekFlatt was brought to a stop about fifty feet from the shoreline, which was steep and appeared to drop off precipitously. The younglings looked over the short hull of the vessel to find dark water beneath them, highlighting the depth of the lake here, just a short distance from its edge.

Victiss rose from his seat at the front of the boat as two massive anchors loudly splashed into Crown Lake, one to each side of the LeekFlatt. He knelt once more as he reached the kids from Crimmish.

"We are here. Ditto and Fincher, please join me. It is time to get you suited up and armed. I have brought the best Air Chiefs the

Ommori have to offer, and Tufferia and I will personally serve as your Rippers. In short, you are in the best of hands."

"Farking great. Let's get this over with."

"Of course, Young Fincher. The time for talk has ended. Come."

Ditto and Fincher moved to the center of the vessel, where they stripped down to their pants and were fitted with strange shoes that appeared to be made from the webbed feet of a ridiculously large duck-type creature. Air Sacs, each complete with a pair of skyreach weed tendrils attached to them, were pulled open at the bottom and carefully placed over the heads of the boys by two massive Moon Folk. While the Ommori were helping Ditto carefully let the Air Sac opening close around the large boy's neck, Fincher's giantess assistant simply released the edge of the hole, letting it snap shut with an audible *slap*.

"Fark me," cried Fincher, his voice muffled inside the jelly enclosure.

The female Ommori waved away Fincher's whining and immediately started smearing a thick, dark substance along the edge of the Air Sac, coating the boy's neck in the process but carefully working around their Ghost Puma pendants. Ditto's helper did likewise. Victiss spoke as the Ommori continued their work.

"The gel they are putting along your necks is from the octosatch. It excretes this thick, black substance to blind and repel predators. There is no better sealant in all Vattassav. Feel secure in the fact that your air will remain in your Air Sac."

Fincher grimaced as more of the goo was smeared along his neck. "Oh, yeah, I feel farking great. Really secure."

Victiss turned away so as not to let Fincher see him laugh. Instead, the Heptorii focused his attention on the four Ommori standing on the far sides of the LeekFlatt, one pair to his left and the other to his right.

Two Moon Folk carefully inspected where the skyreach weeds had been joined together to make longer breathing tubes while the other two hung the ends of their respective tendrils, which ended in massive funnels, onto hooks that held them in place. Above these funnels sat two massive circular fans made of thick wooden rods inserted with huge, dried leaves from a plant the children had yet to see. A large crank was attached to each rod.

Sammi poked her sister on the shoulder excitedly. "Oh, wow! So, they're going to turn that crank... and that one, too... and it will force fresh air down the tubes, giving Ditto and Fincher oxygen while pushing the old, stale air out through the other tube." Sammi thought it over. "Still, it seems like it will be hard to expel the bad air as that tube will be climbing up..."

Victiss overheard the young girl and read the concerned expression on Ash's face.

"You are wise beyond your years, Youngtress Sammi. It is no easy task to dispel the bad air from the Air Sac. But keep watching."

The second Air Chiefs, those not managing the air intake, connected unusual pumps to the ends of their skyreach weeds and placed them on the floor of the LeekFlatt. They each placed a giant foot on their respective pump pedals and pushed down a few times. They then looked over to their partner Air Chiefs, who felt along the funnels with their hands before offering nods of approval.

Victiss went on explaining the system to Sammi. "The second tube and its pump certainly help in keeping the air moving, but it is, admittedly, not as efficient as we would like. For this reason, Crown Divers can only stay below for a short period of time. The stale air does build up, no matter how much air we send in and pump out, making every second count."

"What the fark are you saying over there?" asked Fincher loudly as the tether, thick rope made of dried lakkelp, was tied tightly around his waist and small weights were clipped to the boy's pants.

Victiss spun back. "Nothing, Young Fincher, just reminding Youngtress Sammi that time is always of the essence beneath the waves."

"Don't *I* need to know that more than her?!"

"Young Ditto was informed."

"Oh, farking great. Keep me happily in the dark, then."

Victiss held back another laugh as he stood. "Are we ready?" he inquired loudly to the other nine Ommori on the LeekFlatt.

"Ready, Heptorii," came the resounding response.

"Then let us get these boys... nay... these *men,* into the water." Ditto beamed with pride while Fincher simply rolled his eyes. "Everything all set?"

Several Ommori checked the seals, flipper fittings, and, in Ditto's case, that his spearfishing rod was safely attached to his hip and in no danger of puncturing the skin of the boy or his Air Sac.

Eventually, nods were given all around.

"Then, off you go," said Victiss. "May the Five Sisters protect you both."

With that, Ditto stepped off the edge of the LeekFlatt, careful that neither his tether nor air tubes caught anything in the process.

Fincher, standing on the opposite side of the vessel, stared down into Crown Lake, its murky waters hiding an army of creatures that would like nothing more than to feast on young meat. The boy turned back to the boat.

"Perhaps we can go through things one last—"

The female Ommori helper, completely on accident, of course, nailed Fincher's shoulder with her hip as she passed the boy on the boat, sending the child into the water and off onto his aquatic mission.

Fincher offered no poetic last words as he fell into the water. Only a barely audible, "Farrrrrk—"

Fincher sank beneath the water's surface. Although the boy was terrified, he couldn't help but marvel at the scene that came to life before him. The late rays of Paragon shot down at sharp angles from above, lighting up the aquatic world that acted as the heart of Vattassav.

Eagle rays, with pectoral fins easily ten feet across, glided majestically through the water, taking only a passing interest in the two human visitors descending toward the bottom of the lake.

As Fincher continued down, he spun and looked east into the center of Crown Lake. Schools of small fish made sharp turns as larger creatures cut through their groups, mouths open, hoping for an easy meal.

Farther into the distance, the shadows of massive forms could barely be made out, swimming deliberately and without hurry—obviously, the apex animals of Crown Lake.

Fincher prayed to the Five Sisters that they were Elder Whales and not something more carnivorous.

Spinning back, Fincher's eyes went big as he took in the absolute wall that was the western edge of Crown Lake. Unlike the gentle southern shoreline that slowly moved from shallows to deep water, the lake here simply plummeted to a depth of more than one hundred feet, creating breathtaking (and horrifying) underwater cliffs, within which pockets of caves could be discerned. All manner of fish and jellies—and even the grey, happy-looking balls of blubber that could only be reef manatees—drifted in and out of the caves, riding currents of water.

Fincher finally settled gently on the lake bottom, kicking up a small cloud of mud as he did. Ditto was there, waiting for his friend, spearfishing rod already unfastened and ready in the large boy's hand. As the two companions could not hear each other well beneath the surface, they had worked out a series of signals that morning, borrowing much from their experiences as harvesters, needing to remain silent in the realm of Ghost Pumas.

Ditto raised his left hand, thumb out and horizontal, and Fincher "replied" with a thumb up. Ditto offered a supportive slap to Fincher's shoulder, and both began to make their way toward the cliff face, which was slow-moving due to them each dragging three separate lines behind them. As they walked, the boys pulled gently on their tethers and air lines, ensuring they had sufficient slack behind them.

While dozens of dark caves dotted the wall of rock, one resting along Crown Lake's floor clearly stood out from the rest. The interior of the cave was filled with strange light that poured forth, leaking out and creating a halo of color around the mouth of the cavern. The Eye of God certainly seemed a fitting name.

Fincher and Ditto exchanged nods and pushed forward, their Air Sacs expanding and contracting as they did.

Left arms shot up to shield eyes as the boys entered the cave and were immediately assaulted by color. When their pupils had a chance to adjust, they advanced some more, and their jaws dropped within the Air Sacs.

Maker's Lament was a place of unimaginable beauty, something the Ommori didn't bother to cover in their briefing. Instead of rough rock, the sides of the cavern were covered in glowing gem-like deposits that made it appear as if the walls were covered in diamonds and rubies and emeralds and sapphires and moonstones. From fifteen feet above, crystalline stalactites dropped down like the fangs of a god, accepting light from the surrounding gemstones and shooting it back out into Maker's Lament in an incomparable show.

If a god were to come down to Quaan, were to hide away in disgrace, this would surely be the place.

Ditto poked Fincher with a finger, yanking the boy out of his waking dream. Fincher shrugged in apology, and the pair moved deeper into the Eye of God.

Luckily, Maker's Lament was not large, and the leecher denn was not hard to find. In the rear of the cavern, perhaps fifty feet from its entrance, was a clear, round ball sitting atop a bed of mud that had been perfectly shaped into a circular pedestal. Looking eerily like the Air Sacs the boys now wore, the leecher bagg throbbed as tiny, dark forms moved just under its transparent skin.

Fincher leaned forward until he could make out the thousands upon thousands of tiny lampreys wiggling within the arms-wide aquatic cocoon, wanting nothing more than to escape and attach their tiny suckers onto hosts that would feed them for seasons to come—hosts like Prism Gaar and Livyatan.

Fincher's face twisted in disgust, and the boy took a step back, motioning to Ditto as he did. In response, Ditto reached into the belt pack that Victiss had provided and removed two syringes filled with a thick crimson substance, handing them both over plunger-side first.

Fincher wasted no time, removing the needle case of the first syringe before sending its tip deep into the leecher bagg and pushing the dark liquid out to spread throughout the mass of squirming leecher babies. As the crimson poison touched the infant lampreys, it sent them into a brief frenzy before they ceased all movement, quite dead.

Once the first syringe was empty, Fincher went around and replicated his actions, filling the opposite side of the leecher bagg with the Ommori's deadly concoction, a mixture of box jelly toxins, ground flu corral, and trigon newt extract.

Fincher and Ditto watched intently as the leecher bagg writhed and pulled tight under the strain of the dying leecher babies. At one point, both boys scampered backward, afraid that the sac would burst under the pressure. Fortunately, the clear membrane was more durable than it appeared, holding strong as movement within the leecher bagg grew to a crescendo then eventually ceased.

While both Fincher and Ditto exhaled deeply, their relief was short-lived as only half of the mission was complete. Fincher replaced the caps on the needles and pocketed the empty syringes, cognizant of not leaving any trash behind in this most holy of places. He then motioned Ditto to follow him around the lifeless leecher bagg, cautiously peering into the many gaps, crevices, and cavities that interrupted the shining beauty of the Eye of God's back wall.

As his hazel eyes searched the various pits of darkness, Fincher caught a glimpse of something and froze, his small hand shooting up to bring Ditto to a quick stop. Fincher studied one particular round opening for a long while, the pitch black within revealing its depth, and, ultimately, nodded to himself before slowly backing away.

Fincher turned to Ditto, pointed to the round hole, and then raised his index finger, twirling it in a circular motion.

Ditto gave a thumbs up in acknowledgment and darted off to the side of the round hole, careful not to be seen by anything hiding within the tunnel. As Ditto got into position, the large boy placed the elastic loop at the tail-end of his pole spear between his thumb and index finger and pulled the weapon back toward his body with his left hand. Once Ditto's right hand gripped the shaft tightly, it was now cocked back and ready for use. Ditto pulled in a deep breath and exhaled, steadying his nerves. He then signaled to his friend.

Fincher similarly tried to calm his own anxiety, to no avail. The boy's hands shook, and his knees wobbled as he shuffled forward, his gaze firmly fixed on the set of glowing indigo eyes peering out from within the lightless tunnel.

Fincher looked again to Ditto, who moved a little further away from the glowing, gem-covered wall to reposition himself, pole spear still at the ready. Ditto glanced at Fincher, and the boy sensed real doubt in his large friend, perhaps for the first time.

Just like the Timbers, mouthed Fincher within his Air Sac, and those words—that reminder that Ditto Bugg had successfully completed a version of this task dozens of times in the past—seemed to quell some of his fears.

The pole spear immediately felt surer in the large boy's hand. Ditto nodded confidently.

Fincher wished he shared in his friend's faith as he slid forward along the cave's slick bottom, the glowing set of indigo eyes never leaving him.

Closer and closer to the opening Fincher drew, one thought racing in his mind—*Don't miss, Ditto. Don't you farking miss.*

Closer and closer as the indigo eyes seemed to grow wider.

Don't be too early. But don't be farking late, either.

Closer and closer, and Fincher's heart threatened to burst through his small chest. And, still, the indigo eyes remained unmoved.

Closer and—

The indigo blinked out as the denn mother launched herself from the tunnel, her massive, tooth-filled sucker mouth aiming directly for Fincher's bare chest. Fincher froze with fear, waiting for the northern lamprey to pierce his heart with its barbed, too-sharp tongue.

Just as the denn mother was about to make contact, however, she lurched to the side, sending all eight feet of her long body into an absolute frenzy that shot the sea monster toward the far side of Maker's Lament. Just past the denn mother's large indigo eyes, right where Victiss said the creature's heart would exist, was Ditto's pole spear, swinging around the cavern wildly as it hung tight with its own barb.

As always, Fincher thought, there was no one better to trust with his life than Ditto Bugg.

The denn mother continued her frenzy, slamming into the left-hand wall of the Eye of God and knocking off gemstones of various shapes and sizes. She bounced off the color-coded rock and spun away, moving back toward the cave's center in twisting, jerky movements.

The giant lamprey neared Fincher, and the boy had to duck to avoid being clubbed in head by the Ditto's swinging pole spear. Luckily, the boys had pulled enough slack into the cavern behind them that the denn mother flew just above their air tubes and tethers.

The lamprey paused for a moment, leaving the boys hoping that the worst was over, before she sprung again, this time shooting up in a desperate attempt to free her heart of the barb within. This time, her hysteria was short-lived as the denn mother swam directly into a crystalline stalactite, spiking herself onto the natural deposit at about the halfway point of her long, thick body.

Dark, purplish blood poured out of both wounds, dispersing throughout the Eye of God, as the lamprey went limp, its head and back fin pointing to the ground below.

Ditto held his thumb out sideways, and Fincher responded with his own, this one up to show that the boy was alright.

Ditto motioned to the cave entrance and the boys made for it, collecting the slack of their air tube and tethers to prevent them from catching anything in their exit.

Ditto stood on his tiptoes and pulled on his pole spear as he went under the dead denn mother. The weapon held tight, allowing the large boy to slide the carcass free from the crystalline stalactite.

Ditto let the body sink and then began pulling it behind himself, the Ommori demanding proof that the denn mother was no more. As

Fincher exited, his flippers kicked through a small mound of gemstones the injured lamprey had knocked loose in her frenzy. Fincher knelt and collected a few, holding them close as the water was growing murky with leecher blood.

The gems were beyond striking, of a quality never before seen in Crimmish or any other humble village. Fincher's mind raced, thinking of all that he could do for Crimmish with just a handful of these stones. He could—

Fincher looked up to find Ditto's green eyes staring at him from across the now purple-hued cavern. His large friend simply shook his head in the negative, and, with that simple motion, reminded Fincher of where they were, and what this place meant to their new friends.

Wilting under the better judgment of his good-hearted friend, Fincher gently returned the stones to the ground where he found them, back to their rightful place in the Eye of God.

Fincher held out his empty hands to Ditto, and the boy smiled in return, knowing that his small friend's heart was in the right place. The boys met at the center of the cavern, exchanged slaps on shoulders for jobs well done, and exited Maker's Lament.

As soon as Fincher and Ditto had cleared the cavern entrance and pulled out all the remaining slack, they each separated a bit and gently began tugging on their umbilical cords, signaling the Rippers above to slowly start pulling the boys up to safety.

They watched as the umbilical, followed by the air lines, rose to the surface, eventually drawing tight around their waists. Two more soft tugs and the boys were lifted from their flippered feet as they dropped their waist weights to the lake bottom.

Up Fincher went, Ditto joining him twenty feet away, pulling the massive northern lamprey with him by the pole spear. The boys from Crimmish released a collective sigh of relief as the lake bottom drew further away, danger averted once again.

Fincher smiled within his Air Sac, delighted that they had once again—

His smile fell as his hazel eyes narrowed. In the murky distance, highlighted by some of the final rays of Paragon, was the largest creature the boy had ever seen aside from the Livyatan. And it was coming their way. More specifically, it was swimming toward Ditto.

Fincher motioned frantically, catching his large friend's attention, and pointed.

Ditto visibly flinched as the largest fish either had ever envisioned, with a giant mouth that held row upon row of razor-like teeth, advanced on him, a blank death stare painted on its scarred grey face.

It could only be one of Crown Lake's notorious megamouth sharks. And it had found something it wanted.

Simultaneously, both boys reached up and yanked hard on their umbilicals twice, then a third time—the signal for trouble. The signal that said, *Get me the fark out of here now!*

The Rippers reacted almost immediately, and Ditto and Fincher were thrown forward at the waists as they were *ripped* up, flying through lake water impossibly fast.

But not faster than a charging megamouth shark.

Crown Lake's apex predator charged at Ditto with reckless abandon, tearing through water like Alicia Salt's arrows flashed through air. The large boy froze in fear as Fincher released a muted scream, so sure was he that his friend was going to be torn to pieces in front of him. Just before it was his turn.

Ditto remained unmoved as the megamouth closed in, opening its giant maw even further, as if it wanted to swallow its meal whole and not bother with the chewing.

Maybe it will hurt less, thought Fincher darkly.

Just as the megamouth shark prepared for its final push, Ditto finally reacted, quickly swinging his pole spear around and tossing it at his attacker, the denn mother carcass going along for the ride.

When Ditto's aim proved off due to desperation, going just to the right of the megamouth, Fincher groaned loudly, thinking his friend's only chance a failure.

What neither of the boys could have possibly known was that fully grown northern lamprey, and especially denn mothers, were an absolute delicacy to the larger predators of Crown Lake, a rarity that none could pass up.

Including this particular megamouth shark.

The megamouth veered sharply to its left, determined to devour the denn mother as an appetizer before returning to its main course of Cheese-Eyes. The shark darted at the floating lamprey, devouring the uncommon treat in a single too-aggressive bite.

Fincher and Ditto, still soaring to the surface, held their breaths, waiting for the shark to pirouette and renew its charge. Instead, the shark dumbly swam in place, as if it had completely forgotten about the Crimmish boys. Seconds later, blood could be seen leaking from the top of the megamouth's giant head. And then Fincher knew.

"Look," he screamed from under his Air Sac as he pointed excitedly at the languishing monster. "Stupid farker pierced his stupid farking brain with your farking spear!"

Although Ditto could not hear his friend, he recognized what Fincher saw. In its haste for a quick treat of lamprey meat, the megamouth had not noticed the four-foot pole spear latched onto the creature. In an absolute stroke of luck, the monster had clamped down just right, driving the sharp tip of Ditto's spear through the roof of its mouth and into its relatively small brain.

The megamouth shark offered a few more lazy kicks of its massive tail before it slowly began to spin in place, its white belly beginning to show as the boys finally broke free of the water, returning to the world of air.

Fincher and Ditto were flopped down into the LeekFlatt not unlike the hundreds of fish caught by the Ommori daily.

Still freaked out, Fincher pulled anxiously at his Air Sac until Victiss ran over to help.

"Calm now, Young Fincher! Calm now! You'll rip the Air Sac. Here, let me help." The giant leader's massive hands found where the Air Sac met the boy's neck and he widened the hole, allowing Fincher to duck and free himself. Tufferia did the same for Ditto.

When both boys were free of their Air Sacs, they continued to breathe in heavy pants, as if their short time beneath the surface had permanently altered the functioning of their lungs.

The Air Chiefs jumped to attention, removing the oversized dried leaves from their cylinders and using them to fan each boy.

As they did, Sammi went to Fincher and Ash joined Ditto, the sisters offering big hugs before rubbing the bare backs of the boys in attempt to calm their breathing. After a minute of this, Fincher and Ditto's breaths finally began to normalize.

Victiss studied his young friends and nodded.

"There now. That is better. Now tell me—what happened down there?"

Fincher looked to Ditto, and the large boy motioned helplessly back.

"Where do we farking start?"

Victiss and Tufferia shared a look. The Heptorii returned to Fincher. "The leecher denn. Did you find it?"

"We did."

"And did you find the leecher bagg?"

"We did."

"And?"

"And we injected the junk you gave us. Those babies are as dead as farking dead."

"And the denn mother?"

"Ditto got her." Fincher looked over his shoulder to Sammi. "Almost exactly the same as catching a Moon Adder. But Ditto used a spear instead of his giant baby hands."

"I don't have baby hands!"

"I said *giant* farking baby hands!"

"I don't have those either."

Victiss shook his head, unable to follow. "Okay, okay, okay. No one has baby hands! The denn mother? She has been dispatched?"

"I told you that Ditto got her!"

"Then, where is the carcass? I told you that we needed to see the carcass."

"That's gonna be a farking problem."

"What? Why?"

"Because she's currently in the durned gullet of a megamouth shark."

The entire LeekFlatt of Ommori returned stunned looks on too-pale faces.

"What are you talking about, Young Fincher? What megamouth shark?"

"The one that went after Ditto. *That* farking one!"

"Is that why you yanked on the umbilicals?"

"Why else would we?"

Victiss thought Fincher's story over for a moment. "A megamouth shark attacked you?"

"That's what I farking said, didn't I?!"

"How did you manage to get away?"

"We farking couldn't. We farking didn't."

Victiss's eyes narrowed, and his brow furrowed as his mustached mouth twisted. The giant was quickly losing patience. "Then, how are you here before me, Young Fincher?!"

Fincher smiled coyly and followed it with an equally coy shrug. "Ditto killed the bastard."

Ditto started to explain the absolute luck of his kill, but Fincher silenced his large friend with a look.

If the Ommori were stunned before, now they were now furiously skeptical.

"Impossible!"

"You cannot believe this, Victiss!"

"They obviously did not complete the mission at all!"

"This is a clear cover up!"

"I told your we would need an alternative plan!"

"What a tale! It perfectly accounts for their lies!"

This went on for some time, with Victiss limply attempting to defend Fincher and Ditto, although the giant leader, too, had no reason to believe such a farfetched story.

And then…

Something large broke the surface of Crown Lake not far from the LeekFlatt, quieting all the fury.

Fincher smiled smugly as he recognized the mound of flesh for what it was. The Ommori all ran to the side of the LeekFlatt closest to the object.

"What in the Five Sisters is that?!"

As Fincher's smug smile grew larger, Ash and Sammi giggled. The sisters had never doubted their friends for a second.

Fincher stood a bit taller. "*That* is the body of a megamouth shark."

Just as the boy finished his sentence, a geyser of water shot into the air as a Livyatan breached the water right next to the LeekFlatt, sending the boat careening and several of the Ommori tumbling.

Fincher remained on his feet and swelled with pride. "And *that* is the Livyatan who kindly brought Ditto's kill to the surface. And if you all *still* farking doubt us, look in that dead megamouth. In its gullet, *like I said*, you'll find your farking northern lamprey. Your farking denn mother." Fincher paused for dramatic effect. "And when you write poems about two boys from Crimmish saving your arses, remember that Ditto has *two Ts* and Fincher... well, it's just like it sounds."

After almost a minute of silent surprise, the Ommori suddenly erupted in cheers and laughter, Tufferia even bending low to give Ditto a kiss on the lips, which upset Ash to the point that Sammi had to rush to calm her sister amidst the uproar.

Victiss stroked his mustache as a broad smile appeared on the Heptorii's face. The final rays of Paragon caught his gemmed teeth and sent a cascade of color across the crowded boat. He reached down and ruffled Fincher's thick, brown hair.

"I always had faith in you, Young Fincher."

The young boy's hazel eye's shot up. "Really? You could have fooled me."

"Well, perhaps a little doubt."

"And now?"

"None at all. You younglings of Crimmish have proved your worth, which is greater than any set of humans in all Quaan. We will hold a grand banquet in your honor tonight under the Five Sisters. We owe you that."

"You owe us much farking more than that, Mister Victiss. You owe us safe passage north—as far as your people can go."

"I know, Young Fincher. I know. But can we not worry about that right now? And instead focus on celebrating your grand achievement?"

"What kind of celebration?"

Victiss glanced around at the other Ommori, including Tufferia, who not only returned his glance, but returned it with broad grins and heavy nods.

"You will be given Moon Honors, Young Fincher. Reserved for only the grandest of achievements by the most heroic of heroes. How does that strike you?"

"Will there be food?" asked Ditto hopefully.

Victiss laughed. "Of course. The best Vattassav has to offer. What do you say?"

Fincher, as always, made sure to account for Ditto, Ash, and Sammi before responding. Only when their thumbs flew to the darkening sky did Fincher reply.

"We say, fark yes."

Fincher, Ash, Ditto, and Sammi Bugg's four sets of eyes went wide in wonderment as the Moon Lanterns that had been lit and sent flying over Crown Lake suddenly exploded in color, some even making complex shapes.

The younglings called out in joy as each new display lit up the night sky, the Five Sisters serving as the perfect backdrop, as if even the celestials could not help but watch what the residents of Quaan had created. They hugged each other and lamented that their fallen friends Hana and Alicia Salt were not there with them to witness it. They loudly hoped their parents could see such a show just once in their shortened lives.

Beautiful giantess Tufferia wiped a tear from her face as she, too, marveled at the Moon Lanterns. Although she had seen this exact light show numerous times in her life, this evening she was viewing it as if for the first time, taking in the magic through the youthful eyes of her small new friends.

The children screamed in delight as dozens of Livyatan rose to the surface of Crown Lake. It seemed that even the Elder Whales were not too old to enjoy a good show.

After the last Moon Lantern, an especially large one that exploded over Vattassav, creating the distinct outline of a Prism Gaar, the children gathered around a large bonfire that had been built close to the water's edge. They sat on bamboo seats of honor, watching intently as Ommori musicians played unfamiliar songs on unfamiliar instruments. Others of the Moon Folk danced together in circles, pulling Sammi and a reluctant Ditto in with them. It took several minutes, but the bespectacled girl and large boy eventually got the complicated foot movements right, much to the excitement of the Forest People.

Tufferia took a seat next to Ash as Fincher began chatting awkwardly with a young Ommori girl who already towered over him.

The giantess smiled knowingly as she observed the one-armed girl watch Ditto dance. She handed a basket filled with white buns to Ash, startling the girl out of her intent staring.

"What's this?"

"Try it," replied Tufferia. "They are steamed angel wheat buns. But I mix in honey from Vattassav's cyclone bees and place candied butter dates in the center of each. Try it."

After reaching in with her good and only hand, Ash took a bite. The girl's brown-on-yellow eyes closed as she chewed. Only when she had swallowed did she reopen them.

"Well? What do you think? Do not leave me in suspense, Youngtress Ash."

A wide smile broke out on the girl's face. "I think it's the best thing I've ever eaten in my life."

"Well, thank you. But wait until you try grilled northern lamprey."

"Come again?"

"Never mind. Best you see for yourself."

The two new friends fell quiet as the music took over. Ash's eyes, as if pulled by a force she could not control, found Ditto dancing among the Ommori. The girl winced every time another Ommori female took turns in spinning the boy around.

Tufferia grinned once more.

"Your friend Ditto is a handsome one. Ommori tend to only fancy Ommori, but he would catch the eye of any young Ommori girl." Tufferia glanced to her right. "Unlike Young Fincher, perhaps."

The giantess and Ash both looked on as a young Ommori girl scrunched her pale face and walked away, leaving Fincher perplexed.

"What the fark did I say?!"

Tufferia and Ash fell into laughter.

"I should not laugh," said Tufferia. "The boy is only chasing after his heart. I do not mean to mock him or his efforts."

Ash waved the giantess away. "Oh, don't worry about Fincher. He wounds easily but is impossible to kill. Watch."

Fincher, initially crestfallen by the rebuke, had his head snapped to the right as another Ommori girl entered his frame of vision, this one with a thick braids falling over each shoulder, one dyed blue and the other a deep red. The boy inched his way closer until he was elbow to elbow with this new beauty. Fincher said something, and the forest girl covered her mouth in a laugh. As she did, the precocious boy found Ash and offered a discreet thumbs up.

"See. I told you. Impossible to kill."

"And what about you, Youngtress Ash?"

The girl held up the stump of her left arm. "I'm hard to kill, too."

"But what about your heart? Does it rebound so easily like Young Fincher's?" To this the girl had no reply. "I see the way you look at Young Ditto. Does he know how you feel?"

Ash shrugged uncomfortably. "He's Ditto Bugg. He's the kindest, bravest, most generous person in Quaan. And his face is as beautiful as his heart. Any girl would want to be with him. I'm just a friend. What could I possibly offer." She held up her stump once more, but there was no pride in the action this time. "I can't even offer two good arms. Two hands to caress his face."

Tufferia leaned in conspiratorially. "I would not be too sure of yourself in this respect, Ash Bugg." The girl's dark brow furrowed in confusion. "I have seen Young Ditto stealing glances at you, as well. And they are not of the friend variety."

"You're lying."

"Ommori do not lie. Watch."

Ash and Tufferia looked on as Ditto spun from Ommori to Ommori, from female to female. During one such turn, his green eyes floated across the party until they found Ash. The large boy offered a giant smile and an embarrassed, helpless shrug before he was snatched away.

"See, Youngtress Ash? In the ways of sweets and hearts, no one sees more than Tufferia Eleven."

"Then you must see how Mister Victiss looks at you."

"I do."

"And Ashanti Bugg—that's me—also sees a lot. In fact, I've seen the way you look at him, too."

"I do not deny it, Youngtress Ash."

"I know Mister Victiss has children. Does he not have a wife?"

"He did. He lost her during the birth of his second child, Viguss. Childbirth is very difficult on Ommori women. Although our bodies have generally grown, as have our babies, other parts have remained relatively small, making the birthing process not only especially painful, but dangerous."

"Then what is keeping you apart?"

Tufferia let out a long sigh. "Victiss is still in mourning. He blames himself for her death as he pushed for another child. Many Ommori only have one, although we are encouraged to have more to keep our numbers up. Plus, there is a mandatory mourning period for all Ommori."

"How long is that?"

"Five years."

"And how long has it been."

"Twenty-five." Ash stared at Tufferia. "I know, I know. But I think he knows how I feel. He will let me know when the time is right."

There was another long silence before Ash spoke.

"You know, my ma—Jazz Bugg—always told me that most good men know the right thing to do. They are just clueless as to when to do it. And that's where women must help them."

Tufferia's gemmed teeth shone in the light of the bonfire. "Your ma sounds like a smart woman."

"She is."

"And it sounds like both of us, Youngtress Ash, have our work to do in the romance department."

"Yes, ma'am, we sure do."

"Have another angel wheat bun. Even the most monumental task can look like a daily chore with a belly full of sweets."

Turns out, Tufferia didn't have to make the offer, for the girl's cheeks were already as full as a cream-tailed chipmunk's, her eyes once more on Ditto Bugg.

~

The main celebration took place around the unofficial capital of Vattasseer, surrounded by bioluminescent ponds and Astars. Carefully maintained fires roared around the capital, and megamouth shark meat spun slowly on spits.

Ommori dressed in distinct bright orange garb walked around the celebration with platefuls of steaming Prism Gaar, that most enchanted of Moon Folk food.

Fincher fought his way through a crowd to grab a chunk of the Gaar. He swallowed it down without chewing then flexed his unremarkable muscles toward his friends.

"Wait until Stella Bugg sees how big and strong I am when I return." The boy started punching the air. "Stupid Hylinn Bugg won't know what hit him when I get back!"

"Young Fincher," called Victiss from the edge of the group," that is not how the Prism Gaar works. It needs to be consumed regularly over a long period of time."

Fincher's fists dropped in disappointment. "So, no big muscles from just one meal?"

"I'm afraid not."

"What about my Danglin' Andy? Can one meal help me there?"

"Your what?"

"Ugh, never mind." Fincher marched off despondently, muttering to himself. "Stupid farking Prism Gaar…"

At one particularly well-attended fire pit, the denn mother, her thick skin removed along with her head and tail, was laid out on a long wooden board that had been soaked in Crown Lake. The board sat in a rack that secured it over the roaring fire, allowing the flames to tickle the wood, every now and then reaching around to singe the lamprey meat.

Apparently, fully grown Lamprey was a delicacy to more than just megamouths.

The children, initially put off by the idea of consuming leecher, finally drew sticks to see who would try the dark brown meat. Of course, Fincher drew the shortest piece of wood. The boy closed his eyes and held his nose as a giggling Ommori placed a slice of the grilled meat onto his tongue.

Soon after, the fingers came off his nose and a smile filled his face.

"Well?" demanded Ditto, always one wanting to discover a new food.

Fincher's hazel eyes slowly opened, and the boy wobbled as if drunk on honey rice wine.

"It's the best farking thing I've ever tasted."

"What does it taste like?" asked Sammi.

Fincher thought for a moment. "Like Stella Bugg's kiss."

The group collectively rolled their eyes before jumping in line to get their taste of denn mother meat.

The younglings ate their fill of lamprey before moving on to megamouth shark, which was also tasty. Fincher and Ditto took turns seeing how many of Tufferia's angel wheat buns they could fit in their mouths.

The kids danced and danced, both with each other and with the Ommori. They giggled as fireflies collected in mass overhead, creating giant balls of purplish color that further lit the celebration.

When the northern lamprey meat was finished and the shark meat all but gone, the Ommori named Vochus blew into the shell of a king lake conch, sending a deep, loud note across the celebration, drawing a temporary end to the revelry.

All the Ommori made their way toward the main palace of Vattasseer, sweeping the children of Crimmish up with them. As the younglings neared the elegant arches of the palace, they could see that a dais had been erected before its entrance. Atop it stood Thyccaria Prime, looking every bit the part of a queen. The Primirri beckoned the children to join her on the platform, and a path to the dais stairs immediately cleared.

When the friends had finally climbed to the stage, Fincher and Ditto were brought forward just a bit to great applause. While Ditto looked down bashfully, Fincher raised his arms in triumph, soaking in the moment.

The Prime raised one jeweled hand, and a hush fell over the gathering. The striking giantess queen lowered her hand and began to speak in a clear, powerful voice that easily carried across the evening air.

"Ommori! It has been too long since we have been able to join in celebration. We have encountered much hardship over the recent past and have had much to worry about. The world of man outside of Vattassav continues to consume itself, and we all know that its hunger will eventually turn inward toward our home. Within our own borders, we keep on fighting the good fight, eliminating anything that may upset the natural balance of Vattassav. But one threat, however, found a way to thrive outside of even the Ommori's extended reach." Thyccaria paused for effect. "The northern lamprey, always an enemy to our friends beneath Crown Lake, discovered the Eye of the World, the one place that the Moon Folk cannot enter. As scores of Paragons passed, no solution could be found. Until our new friends arrived."

Cheers went back up for the children before the Prime ushered in silence once more. She continued.

"Bravery comes in many forms, large and small. Old and young. And it can require different tasks of all of us, whether that be risking lives or supporting those loved ones that do. The leechers had the Forest People on our heels, at a loss regarding what to do next. But the Five Sisters, ultimately, heard our prayers, as they always do, in time, and delivered to us those joining me here this beautiful evening. It is because of their bravery, their willingness to sacrifice it all, that I can happily announce that our leecher problem is no more. Crown Lake is leecher free once again!"

Another eruption broke out, this one dying down slowly. Thyccaria allowed it to go on.

Finally, she said, "For their heroism, it is my absolute pleasure to present each of the younglings of Crimmish with Moon Honors, something never before bestowed upon those not of Ommori blood." Thyccaria turned her bright amber eyes to the children, offering them a serious look. "You are about to receive the greatest honor that can be given to an Ommori. Even very few of the Moon Folk possess that which I am about to give you." A gemmed smile appeared on the Prime's face. "I could not be more pleased to be the one to give them to you."

Thyccaria snapped her fingers, and an assistant rushed forward with a massive shell plate on which sat four medallions attached to knotted cords. The medallions were round and made of the whitest stone the children had ever seen, the color so intense that they seemed to glow of their own internal light. It truly appeared as if one of the Five Sisters had been shrunk down and flattened to be worn.

Thyccaria removed one, knelt, and placed the cord around Ditto's neck, kissing the boy on the forehead as she did. The Moon Medallion clinked lightly against the Ghost Puma tooth. She repeated the act with Fincher, who immediately looked down to find that the medallion swirled with motion, as if one of the famed storms of the Great Untold had been successfully trapped within.

Thyccaria moved on to Sammi Bugg, who stopped the Prime before the medallion could be put over her small head.

"But Ash and I didn't do anything, Miss Thyccaria. The boys did all the work. We're not worthy of your Moon Honors."

Thyccaria cupped the girl's dark cheek with a ringed hand. "My child, do you think me new to this world? Do you think I do not see where others cannot? I know that there is no Ditto and Fincher Bugg without Sammi and Ash Bugg. Do you think they would agree?"

"You farking know we would," said Fincher, not taking his hazel eyes off the Moon Medallion.

"We most definitely would agree, Miss Thyccaria," added Ditto.

"Then, I would call that settled," said the Prime. "What do you say, Youngtress Sammi?"

Sammi grinned, embarrassed, before pushing her glasses farther up her nose. "I say okay."

"That is more like it."

Thyccaria placed Moon Medallions on Sammi and Ash and then turned to address the Ommori. The gorgeous giantess queen opened her tattooed arms out wide as she spoke.

"Join me in thanking the younglings of Crimmish, forever known as the Child Champions of Crown Lake!"

Vattassav filled with the sounds of cheers, and, this time, the Primirri did not quiet them, letting it continue as she retired to her palace.

When Fincher, Ditto, Ash, and Sammi finally stepped down from the dais, they were greeted with hugs and kisses, shoulder claps and back slaps. The music returned, as did more meat for the fires and moccasin-clad feet for the dancing.

Ommori crowded Ditto, wanting to know how such a small boy could fell a megamouth shark. When Ditto started to lean into the truth, Fincher jumped in.

"Please! My friend is more farking brawn than brain and is without the necessary vocabulary to tell the tale correctly. If I may?"

Ditto nodded, happy to no longer be the center of attention.

Fincher went on to tell how Ditto, faced with certain death, charged at the megamouth shark, throwing off the beast's timing. Before the apex predator could bite down, Ditto was inside its too-large mouth, thrusting his spear up with all his might, piercing the animal's tiny brain with a perfectly aimed strike.

The Ommori howled in delight, referring to the boy as Ditto the Perfect. And although they meant it as a reflection of the boy's aim with a spear, Fincher smiled as his friend tried to dodge the compliments, knowing that it was an even better reflection of the person.

The rest of the evening was spent in dance and laughter. The children ate and drank, even partaking in some watered-down honey rice wine. They played with other Ommori children and swam once more in the waters of Crown Lake. They relished in every moment of being in this strange, wondrous place. They enjoyed every minute of being young and not having a care in the world. They cherished every second of being together, sharing a bond that few others would ever understand.

And they did so knowing that the worst of their journey was still ahead of them. That this might be the last night such as this.

13

GRITSTONE TUGGERS AND HORRORS ALONG CROWN'S RUN

"This is my youngest son, Viguss Three," said Victiss proudly, slapping his boy on his giant shoulder as he did. "Viguss, meet Young Fincher, Youngtress Ash, Young Ditto, and Youngtress Sammi."

Viguss looked very much like his father but without the distinct mustache. However, the young giant did have an unusually large purple feather sticking out from atop the usual Ommori conical hat. Viguss studied the children.

"So, these are the Child Champions of Crown Lake?"

Victiss's head cocked to the side. "You have already heard? I thought you just got in."

Viguss chuckled. "Of course, I have heard. The Delta Receivers were falling over themselves trying to be the first to tell us. It was a real relief to hear that the leecher problem had been solved. The worry was starting to wear on us during our Tugg."

"And how was the Tugg? Any issues?"

Viguss shrugged. "Just the normal stuff from the world of man." The young giant looked to the kids from Crimmish. "No offense meant."

Fincher waved away Viguss's concerns. "None taken. We don't consider ourselves part of those farkers, either."

Viguss shot his father with a look and received an amused smile in return.

"That is just the way that one speaks. You will grow accustomed to it. Then, you will grow to appreciate it. Then, you will grow to like it."

Viguss offered his own smile and nod before continuing. "But, certainly a few things to relay. First, the Gloomtide is running rampant in the towns up and down Crown's Run. Even from the river, there are some real horrors to behold."

Victiss rubbed his mustache absently. "Let us thank the Five Sisters that we have the Prism Gaar to protect us. What else was there to relay?"

"A massive army of Chestnuts has gathered north of Vattassav, the largest since I was a boy. It appears that they are readying for an all-out assault on the Cobalt line. I do not understand the purpose of such a bold move; the timing seems off. The Cobalts have not made any serious movements in a long while, making me question this tactic."

Victiss pondered his son's words. "Thank you for the intel, my son. I wish you could stay and rest a bit—"

"No matter, Father. I heard that I already missed the celebration." Viguss sighed deeply. "The life of a young Tugger, I suppose."

Victiss placed his large hands on his son's shoulders. "Trust me when I say it will all be worth it when you take a place of leadership in the Threes. Anyway, as I was saying, I wish you could stay and rest up, but I need a Tugger crew to take our new friends here north, all the way to Cassie's Clutch." Victiss spun to the younglings. "That is as far north as we can go." The children nodded and Victiss returned to his son. "There is no one else I can entrust with this important task. Will you take them?"

Viguss wasted no time in answering. "Of course, I will take them, Father. They are the Child Champions of Crown Lake. It would be an honor to be even a small part of their tale."

A broad grin broke out under the Heptorii's amber mustache. "It is good to see you, my son. I will make sure you get a much-deserved break upon your return. Now, please go and see to the loading of the Trade Arks. Make sure they leave some open space for the children."

"Of course, Father." Viguss turned to leave.

"And Viguss!"

"Yes, Father?"

"These younglings are under the protection of the Ommori, by order of the Primirri. They fall under the category of "precious cargo" and, therefore, are exempt from any search or seizure."

"And if some Chestnuts insist?"

"Then you show them the difference between giants and men. Understood?"

A dark twinkle appeared in the young Tugger's amber eyes. "Crystal, sir. It has been too long since a Chestnut has given me a reason to send him flying. I quite miss it, actually."

"Good boy."

When Viguss disappeared among the throng of Ommori who were crisscrossing the paths around Crown Lake Delta, Victiss addressed the children once more.

"I am sure you heard. My son Viguss will take you upriver."

Sammi pushed up her glasses. "You called him Viguss Three. Primirri Thyccaria also called you Victiss Three. What does that mean?"

"Always the curious one, are you not, Youngtress Sammi? Although we Ommori are unified, we do divide ourselves into clans— Two, Three, Five, Seven, and so on."

"Why?"

"First, it simplifies governance, allowing us to better manage and organize our people, who are usually spread out across northern Vattassav. Next, it aids in strategic procreation. With our relatively small numbers, we need to ensure that we are not intermarrying. It is against our laws to couple with another from your clan, at least for three generations. In this way, our development is not stagnating nor retarding. Simple logistical reasons, really."

"I see. Thank you."

Victiss's face grew serious. "Now, may I ask you all a question?"

The children nodded. "I did not want to raise this in front of Viguss—the boy will have enough to worry about—but would you happen to know something about this army of Titians to our north? Viguss is correct; none of the dots seem to be connecting in this regard."

When no one immediately spoke up, Victiss knew that the situation was significantly stickier than he had imagined. Finally, Ditto elbowed Fincher in the ribs, drawing a groan from the smaller boy.

"Go on, Fincher. Tell Mister Victiss."

"All right! Fark! The Titian army was to meet up with our original entourage to the north. They were then going to push the Cobalts back in one giant onslaught, clearing the way for us to enter Terminus Grove. Right now, the only way in is behind the Cobalt Insurgence."

Victiss rubbed his mustache. "Okay, that makes sense. Then, let me ask you this. Why would you not simply want to connect with the Chestnuts now, as was the original plan?"

The younglings looked to each other, sharing inaudible opinions, before Fincher responded. "Because fark them, Mister Victiss. Other than Captain Graff, they treated us like shite. I don't trust them. *We* don't trust them to do the right thing. Our mission is to save the people of Quaan from the Gloomtide. We don't give one shite about the Titian Empire or the durned Sluggs. We care about preventing others from suffering how Crimmish suffers and about getting doctors down to our home to save our mas and pas, at least those who are still with us."

"It would be much easier with the army's help, Young Fincher."

"We made a pact to each other, Mister Victiss. We were going to do this ourselves, trusting no adult in the process." Fincher paused. "Not counting you and the Moon Folk, who we obviously trust with our lives." Victiss offered a small bow. "We'll get the durned cure, Mister Victiss. You can be sure of that. And when we do, we'll take it back to Kassimont ourselves and collect what's owed to us. But we won't be used as pawns in some larger game. Not this time."

"I see. In that case, I support you with all my heart. You are now effectively members of the Ommori, and welcome back anytime you wish. When your mission is complete and your families healed, return to Vattassav. You will always have a home here."

"We're banned from leaving Crimmish, Mister Victiss," said Sammi sadly. "Unless we're saving the world."

Victiss knelt before the girl. "Where there is a will, there is always a way, Youngtress Sammi. And I have never seen such will in my life as I see in this group of friends. Now, Ommori touch palms when they say goodbye, but I have always preferred the way humans hug. Shall we hug and not say goodbye but, rather, see you soon?"

Fincher, Ash, Ditto, and Sammi all buried Victiss Three in a giant group hug, and everyone, including the giant leader, was wiping tears when they separated.

Victiss rose to his height. "No matter what happens, younglings, stay true to yourselves and each other. The Five Sisters see all, and they certainly recognize bravery when they see it, now more than ever. You *will* be rewarded for what is in your hearts, in this life or the next. Of this, I am certain."

"Goodbye, Mister Victiss," said Ditto, and he, Fincher, and Sammi made their way toward the Trade Arks filling the Crown Run Delta. Ash Bugg held back, motioning the giant leader to her.

"Yes, Youngtress Ash?"

"As a Child Champion of Crown Lake, what does that give me?"

Victiss looked confused but tried to answer. "Well, I assume that any request within reason would be granted."

"Then, I have a request."

"But you are leaving and—"

"I still have a request."

"Of course. Name it."

"Ask Miss Tufferia out on a proper date?"

The Heptorii fell back a step, causing Ash to giggle. When he had recovered, he managed, "Well, that certainly is an odd request. You see, the thing about that is—"

"Are you denying my one and only request?"

"Well… of course, not. But you see—"

"Then, you'll do it?"

Victiss rubbed his mustache so hard it threatened to come off. "You think she would say yes?"

Ash smiled knowingly. "I'm sure of it."

"But, I have waited so long. I fear I've missed my opportunity."

"Good things come to those who wait. Miss Tufferia knows this. And you, sir, would certainly fall under the grouping of *good things*."

"I thank you for the kind words, Youngtress Sammi."

"Then, you will do it?"

"How could I deny a request from one of the Child Champions of Crown Lake?"

"You can't. That's the beauty of it. Goodbye, Mister Victiss."

"Goodbye, Ash Bugg. And thank you." Ash bowed deeply and moved to follow her friends. "Youngtress Ash!"

The girl turned back. "Yes?"

"The adults of Quaan have a lot to learn from its children."

"We know. Which is why we must do this without their interference."

"May the Five Sisters protect you, Youngtress Ash."

"They will. I am sure of it. And may your first date with Miss Tufferia go well."

"It will. I, too, am sure of it."

The children climbed onto one of the large, flat-bottomed Trade Arks used to transport goods between the worlds of man and Ommori. The Loaders had not only left a large area clear of goods, but they had also laid out straw for bedding and erected a small tent so that the children could escape Paragon's rays or the elements, as needed.

Viguss shouted orders as the children dropped their packs and settled in for the long trip north.

Fincher exhaled deeply as the boy plopped down onto the soft straw and leaned against one of the large boxes containing an assortment of dried fish from Crown Lake.

"Now, this is the way to farking travel. Sure beats hiking through the farking Mutewoods."

"Don't relax yet, Fincher," countered Ditto. "We haven't even left the Delta. Who knows what awaits us out there on Crown's Run."

"Well, are farking Marsh Ghouls gonna be waiting for us? Berserker Bears? Farking Borggos the Worm?"

"No, I guess not…"

"Then, let me farking relax and regale you with tales of my exploits last night with the girls of Vattassav. I—"

"I saw you, Fincher," Ash interrupted. "And it looked like it played out very similarly to Crimmish."

Fincher leaned forward. "I'll have you know that I did very well with one young Ommori lass who found me quite charming."

Sammi jumped in. "Yeah, it seems like a recurring theme, Fincher."

"What recurring theme?"

"You like them big. You like big Ommori. You like Stella Bugg's big ego. And you like Reba Bugg's big horse teeth even more!"

"Fallacious! Fallacious on all accounts," protested Fincher as the other children howled in laughter. "She'll grow into those teeth in a few years and be a real stunner. Then, who will be laughing?!"

"We will! Still!"

Along the southern bank of Crown's Run, Viguss Three could not help but overhear the children. The young giant laughed to himself, immediately understanding why his father had such a fondness for this tight-knit group of friends.

The muscled giant moved to the front of the attached Trade Arks and called out in a booming voice. "Gritstone Tuggers! Are you ready to launch?!"

"Yes, Grand Tugger," came the resounding cry in reply.

"Then grab your ropes and let us be off! May the Five Sisters protect us and our invaluable cargo!"

"Yes, Grand Tugger!"

With that, Viguss and numerous other Ommori bent down to retrieve thick ropes that ran from the Trade Arks to the southern bank of Crown's Run. The giants began to pull the heavy vessels against the current, taking them up Crown's Run and away from their home of Vattassav.

The children stood up and watched in amazement as the powerful Ommori moved thousands of pounds as easily as the younglings carried their packs.

"*Tuggers*, huh?" remarked an awestruck Ditto.

"Yep," agreed Fincher from the side. "Farking Tuggers, they are."

It took the better part of the day for the group to pass through the northwest corner of the Mutewoods. Luckily, towpaths had been cut along the bank, giving the Tuggers few obstacles and good footing for their massive moccasins.

The children took in the beauty of Vattassav, unsure if they would ever see this magical place again, as they passed the final tree and watched it melt into the rest of the Mutewoods behind them. They offered silent, heartfelt goodbyes to the forest that took so much from them, but also gave much in return.

As Paragon began to fall in the west, a large settlement came into focus on the opposite bank of Crown's Run. As they drew closer, however, the town continued to grow, showing that it was not a town at all, but a bustling city of trade.

"This is Woodlow," Viguss called back from his position as Grand Tugger, as if he could read the children's minds. "The place is crawling with Chestnuts. And the Gloomtide."

The kids from Crimmish could feel their eyes grow bigger as they took in the largest city they had ever seen. Truly, the *only* city they had ever seen.

Crown's Run had become significantly wider and deeper as it exited Vattassav, so the city was now a safe distance away, with massive docks dotting the far bank. Goods were being loaded and unloaded at a rapid pace—whether out of efficiency or fear, it was hard to tell.

"Look at them go," remarked Ash.

"Looks like a shite job," commented Fincher.

"Worse than being a harvester?"

Fincher relented. "Fair enough."

"Looks like fun to me," added Ditto. "Paid to exercise all day? Count me in."

Sammi adjusted the glasses on her face. "What's going on over there?"

The other younglings looked to where Sammi was pointing. Rushing down the steps toward one of the few empty docks was a woman carrying a baby, a group of men in hot pursuit, shouting after her.

"What are they trying to do to that poor woman and her baby?" asked Ash.

"She's gonna run out of real estate soon," observed Fincher.

"Look away, younglings," called out Viguss from the front, but the children did not heed his demand.

Small hands went to mouths in a collective gasp as the woman raised her baby over her head upon reaching the end of the dock. The men behind her screamed that she stop, and the woman paused for the slightest of moments, just enough for a speck of hope to form, before tossing the infant into the swirling waters of Crown's Run.

"Oh, no! No, no, no," called out Ash. The others were too stunned to speak at all. Half of the men tackled the blank-faced woman while the other half searched the water with their eyes, desperate for any sign of the baby.

But there was none.

"Why? Why would she do such a thing?" asked Ash.

"It's the Gloomtide," called out Viguss. "I am afraid that you will see more of the same as we continue northwest. Some towns have been hit harder than others."

"So, this is what we're fighting to cure," offered Ditto. "A worthy cause, if you ask me."

"Saving babies from drowning? Fark yeah, it is."

The kids of Crimmish fell into a dark, reflective silence as the Tuggers kept them moving up Crown's Run. Eventually, Woodlow began to shrink in the distance. Unfortunately, another massive grouping began to take shape, this one on *both* sides of the great river.

"Chestnuts," Viguss called out. "Stay calm, younglings. Let me do all the talking."

"That means you, Fincher," Ash clarified.

A half-hour later, as Paragon was nearly behind the Spired Curtains, the situation ahead started to clarify. Parked along the far bank of Crown's Run was a massive encampment of soldiers, just a portion of the Titian army sent to push back the Cobalt line. On the southern bank, along which the children now traveled, was a much smaller contingent of Chestnuts. As the Tuggers approached, a narrow-faced soldier with numerous medals pinned to his chest held up a hand and called for the giants to stop.

"Go no further, you Bloodless laborers," called out the soldier in a grating, high-pitched voice.

"What is the meaning of this?" demanded Viguss Three. "The Ommori have authority to transport between Vattassav and Cassie's Clutch. As a representative of the Titian Empire, you should know this better than any other."

"Oh, I know this," said the soldier slyly. "But I am not looking for *goods*." His beady eyes went around the giant Tuggers and began to search the train of connected Trade Arks. "I am looking for people. *Five* people, to be exact. Five *children*, to be more exact." Tiny eyes narrowed to slits as they fell upon the four Crimmish kids tucked away on the second Trade Ark. A wolfish grin formed. "But four will do. Yes, these four here will do just fine."

"That is *not* going to happen," stated Viguss flatly.

The Titian soldier's hand drifted to the sword at this hip as the wolfish grin transformed into an angry frown.

"Do you know who I am, Bloodless?"

"I do not," answered Viguss. "Nor do I care. You have no jurisdiction here… *Soul-burned*."

The wicked smile returned. "So, it seems we both have cute nicknames for each other. How delightful. And you should care. I am Lieutenant Benson Kruger, on a special directive that has come straight from Imperator Kasspar Rayne. Is that good enough for you, giant?"

"It is not."

"What?!"

"I said, it is not," roared Viguss. "Under the Crown Treatise, the Moon Folk were granted free, uninterrupted trade along Crown's Run and North Verve. We are protected from search and seizure of any kind. *Any* kind!"

"That doesn't apply to *people*, you idiotic oaf!" The dozen other soldiers' hands went to their weapons.

"It applies to *all* cargo, you insignificant mint-weasel of a man! Everything on our Trade Arks is considered *cargo* and is protected as such. Would you like to be the one who brings down two hundred years of peace between the Ommori and the Titian Empire? Do you have authority for *that*!?"

Hearing their Grand Tugger's rage, the other Tuggers dropped their ropes onto the towpath and drew prismatic axes and curved blades, each large enough to cleave two humans in half with one massive swing. The soldiers began to back away under the serious Ommori stares. They looked to the far bank and did the quick math. By the time their backup safely crossed the swift river, there would be nothing left but pieces of Titian-clad humans spread across the towpath.

Kruger took an angry step forward, but another medal-adorned Chestnut whispered desperately in his ear, stopping the narrow-faced lieutenant. The wolf-like smile returned.

"But, of course, you are right, Sergeant. Who am I to break the wonderful Crown Treatise?" Kruger sent a dangerous look toward the Crimmish harvesters. "Let us simply meet up with the rest of my men and head to Cassie's Clutch. There are women and drink for all there. And who knows who else we may run into?" Kruger licked his thin lips. "You all travel safe. Until our paths cross again. Soon."

With that, held breaths were released in relief and shaking hands fell from hilts. Lieutenant Kruger's men all went around the Tugger crew, carefully eyeing the giants and giving them a wide birth as they made their way back toward Woodlow.

Fincher was unable to resist.

"Hey, Lieutenant Kruger! High Captain Graff told us about you! Said you really surprised him!"

Kruger rolled his beady eyes. "And how did I manage to surprise that decrepit warehouse?"

Fincher had to calm his voice, lest he lose it. "Yeah, Captain Graff said that when he first met you, he thought you were a Danglin' Andy. But as he got to know you more, he realized that you're much more. Said you're really a Queefin' Kelly!"

The younglings howled, and even the Titian soldiers were unable to suppress their laughter. Kruger's beady eyes went wide.

"How dare you?!" The Lieutenant turned to his underlings. "And how dare *you*?!"

"Sorry, sir," came the apologies, the words broken apart by more laughter.

"You will regret that, boy! You all will! I'm going to—"

"Keep walking," shouted Viguss. "If you turn around or speak again, I will see if that armor floats."

Kruger, his face red with rage, flailed his arms around several times like a petulant child before angrily spinning on a booted heel and power-walking downstream, his still-chuckling retinue in tow.

When the Titians were out of earshot, Viguss spoke to his crew and the children.

"A pity. I would have enjoyed heaving that rat into the water."

"But I do not think this rat would have swam," added another Tugger.

"No, all those medals surely would have booked him a one-way passage to the river's muddy bottom."

"Where he belongs," said the lone female Tugger of the crew to everyone's agreement.

"Where are they going?" asked Sammi.

Viguss responded as he retrieved his thick rope from the towpath.

"There are boats at Woodlow that will ferry them back across the river. I am sure that is where they are going."

"To join the rest of their battalion?"

"Yes. Then, I assume they will head west with all haste to Cassie's Clutch, where they know our journey with you must end. They will be waiting when you arrive."

"Then why farking go there at all?" asked Fincher. "Let's bail before then, sneak our way through the Contested Zone."

"Lieutenant Kruger is a weasel, but weasels are intelligent and cunning. I am confident that he will have spies placed along the river. And the protection of the Ommori ends once you step foot onto land. Just as Kruger will not break the Crown Treatise, neither will I. There is too much at stake. I am sorry, children."

Ditto spoke up first. "There's no reason to be sorry, Mister Viguss. You are doing what you can for us, and we appreciate it. If we have a fight on our hands once we set down in Cassie's Clutch, so be it. We've fought through worse." Viguss began to laugh. "Something I said?"

"Not at all, Young Ditto. And my apologies for laughing. It was not at your expense, but, rather, Lieutenant Kruger's."

The large boy's brow furrowed. "How's that, Mister Viguss?"

"Well, I can tell that the man has never actually been to Cassie's Clutch. For if he had, he would know that the Chestnuts have less jurisdiction there than even here on Crown's Run. In fact, those who frequent Cassie's Clutch have little love for any kind of authority, especially the Titian kind. They listen only to Cassie Hawkkends, who founded the Clutch as a kind of anti-establishment stronghold."

"And what kind of woman is Cassie Hawkkends?" asked Ash.

"The kind that will not take kindly to a weasel like Lieutenant Benson Kruger making demands."

"But will she take kindly to children?"

"Yeah," added Fincher. "Especially children bringing a host of farking Chestnuts into her home?"

Viguss shouldered his rope and began to pull, the other Gritstone

Tuggers following his lead. The Grand Tugger responded over this shoulder. "Now, *that* is the million chip question, Young Fincher."

Fincher looked to his friends doubtfully. "Well, that's no kind of farking answer."

"No," agreed Ash, "But it's the best we're gonna get, I'm afraid."

The Gritstone Tuggers pulled on well after the Five Sisters had risen in the night sky. Ommori Prime, in particular, cast her ghostly glow against the swift waters of Crown's Run as the river dipped south for a bit before returning to her usual northern tilt. The too-white skin of the Tuggers also stood out in the moonlight, their red tattoos almost shining as they reflected the energy of the Five Sisters.

Finally, the Trade Arks ceased moving against the current as the thick pull-ropes were tied to large metal eyehole anchors placed every now and then along the towpath.

Grand Tugger Viguss visited the children, his amber hair heavy with sweat.

"We should be far enough away from the Chestnuts to get some undisturbed rest. I'm sure that they simply made a straight line for the Clutch, keeping just south of the Contested Zone. You all can stay on the Trade Ark or camp with us along the bank."

The kids from Crimmish didn't need to discuss a preference. Instead, all four quietly grabbed their packs and accepted the Moon Folks' assistance in safely making the small crossing onto land. It felt good to be on solid footing once more.

The Tugger crew sat around a small fire, passing around a meal of dried fish and hot soup made by boiling a tied bag of spices, bones, and crushed nuts. The younglings shared what little remained of Alicia Salt's world-famous jerky and laughed as wide-set amber eyes snapped shut in pure ecstasy.

Eventually, Fincher could keep his own mouth shut no longer.

"How the fark do you all not get tired?"

Viguss chuckled, as did the other Tuggers. "Oh, we get tired,

Young Fincher. But the ride back down keeps us going. The excited faces of Ommori when we arrive at the Delta, packed with all the goods we cannot get in Vattassav—that keeps us going. Coming out into wider Quaan, seeing what men have done to the world, and what the world has done to them—that constant reminder of what the Ommori have in Vattassav and in each other... That keeps us going."

The lone female Gritstone Tugger chimed in. "And knowing that after one hundred tuggs, we never have to do it again—that keeps us farking going!"

"Topporia," exclaimed the other Tuggers in unison, and the children doubled over in laughter, for it was one of the very rare times that they had heard an Ommori curse. Fincher especially appreciated the outburst.

"I farking like her!"

Topporia threw Fincher a wink, ignoring the reproach of her giant companions.

When things had settled, Viguss spoke to the younglings once more.

"I know very little of your mission and do not plan to pry. But is there any other path that you children can take? The Chestnuts are a terrible plague on this land, but you will not find the company much improved in Cassie's Clutch. I fear for your safety and find myself bothered that there's nothing I can do to help once we arrive. Is your mission *that* important?"

"It is," answered Ash.

"And there is no other way to accomplish it? No other direction you can go?"

"There is not."

Viguss let out a massive sigh, and his amber eyes fell in sadness. "Very well. Then, I will put my worry aside and wish you the best. You are the Child Champions of Crown Lake. You are the holders of Moon Medallions and..." Amber eyes squinted in the firelight. "... the teeth of some sort of large predator."

Fincher followed Viguss's stare and looked down to find that this

Ghost Puma tooth had fallen out of his shirt. "That's a farking Ghost Puma tooth."

Viguss smiled broadly, showing gems in his teeth, although far fewer than his father Victiss. "I see. Then perhaps you do not need my well wishes at all. Perhaps it is those who foolishly try to stop you four that truly need all the well wishes."

"You got that farking right, Mister Viguss." Topporia giggled from behind the fire.

The unusual group ate in silence for a bit, staring up at the stars that served as the perfect background for the majesty of the Five Sisters. Until Ditto chimed up.

"Mister Viguss?"

"Yes, Young Ditto?"

"You think I could take a turn pulling the Trade Arks tomorrow?"

"Do you think you are strong enough for that, Ditto?"

The large boy shrugged. "There's only one way to find out. Plus, I don't like not contributing. I feel bad watching you Tuggers do all the work."

Fincher cut in. "For the record, I have no such issues."

Viguss had to swallow a laugh, but otherwise managed to ignore the precocious boy. "If you feel up to the challenge, Young Ditto, I would welcome you to take a turn."

As usual, Ditto didn't need to respond, for Fincher responded for him.

"Of course, he's up to the challenge. Just look at the size of the farker. I wouldn't be surprised to find out that old Link Bugg, may his soul rest in peace, was half Ommori, with Ditto being part Moon Folk. Ditto, tell them about the time you walloped that big farking brute Whyllo Bugg. Why, I tell you, stankin' Whyllo had three stone on Ditto here. And you know what happened? Ditto started by..."

Both human child and Ommori remained silent as Fincher Bugg regaled the group with heroic tales of his friend. They laughed in some places, gasped in others. They waved the large boy away when he tried to protest, which was every minute or so.

The Gritstone Tuggers soaked in the stories, for it was wonderful to experience the love and joy of real friendship. It was something the Ommori valued over all else.

Ash and Sammi also embraced the stories, despite being there for all of them.

For the sisters knew that there was no person in all of Quaan who deserved to be celebrated for his selfless actions and valiant soul more than their friend Ditto Bugg—the heart of what once was the Sour Flower Gang.

As expected, Ditto did exceedingly well during his turn as a Tugger the next morning, especially given the fact that he was young human boy. He received well-earned claps on the back from the Tugger crew before collapsing onto the Trade Ark, completely exhausted.

Ash kindly massaged Ditto's burning shoulders with her lone hand as Fincher and Sammi shared a knowing smile.

The smiles were not to last, however, as the Tugger crew began to pass various riverside towns, where it became immediately apparent that the Gloomtide was on in full.

One man waved to the children and smiled dumbly before kicking a massive bag of stones off the dock and into the swirling waters of Crown's Run. His smile vanished briefly just before the rope that connected the bag to his waist went taut and yanked him over the side, dragging him to the muddy river bottom.

At another small town, two women wept gently on the far bank as they took turns slicing pieces of skin off each other, tossing the chunks of flesh into the river to be gobbled up on the surface by ravenous hinge bass.

Ditto and Ash made Sammi go into the Trade Ark's makeshift tent as a young man waded into the shallows near the riverbank, a toddler in each arm. He drowned each one in turn, holding them under the water with an empty, lost look on his face as an elderly gentleman, obviously the man's father, screamed at him in horror from land.

When the gruesome deed was done, the young man let the bodies of the toddlers simply drift down Crown's Run, waving to them as they disappeared in the distance. As soon as the man waded back to the bank, he was attacked by his father, who slammed a rock against his son's skull over and over again until only an unrecognizable mound of gore remained where a head once stood.

The father knelt by the bludgeoned body and cried for a while before taking the bloody rock in both hands and ramming it into his own temple. The old man wobbled but repeated the act numerous times until he finally collapsed, quite dead, onto the body of his son.

These were just a few of the many terrible images the children encountered over the next day. Eventually, they all retreated into the safety of the tent, fearing there would be no coming back from prolonged exposure to such horror, such madness.

The kids of Crimmish, more than anyone in all of Quaan, understood the Maddening, understood the toll that it took on a community. But this Gloomtide, this was something else entirely, something even more sinister, more hopeless.

"This is what we're fighting to stop," said Ditto to the others in the tent. "When things get hard or scary or painful, remember that *this* is what we're fighting to stop. *This* is why we were chosen."

"*This* is why we're going to see the farking God-Snails."

Ditto's green eyes took in those of his best friends, youthful eyes that had now seen enough awfulness to fill a score of lifetimes.

"So, we're still good?"

"I don't know if I'll ever be good again," said Sammi sadly. Ash put the knob of an arm around her sister.

"Ditto means, are we still willing to go on, sis?"

Sammi reached under her glasses to wipe a tear. "Of course, we are. As long as Ditto's here, I am, too. He'll keep us safe." Ash pulled her little sister in tight and nodded to Ditto. She then pulled the young girl down onto her bedroll, hoping that sleep would help them escape a living nightmare.

As the two sisters slowly drifted off, Fincher looked to his friend, who seemed to have the weight of the world on his large, but still boyish, shoulders.

"No farking pressure, huh?"

"Yeah, none at all."

~

"Red feather sighted!"

"Who is it?!"

"Looks like Tequirra Seven!"

"Oh, this is going to be a good one!"

"I knew I should have brought more chips!"

The loud calling out from the usually quiet Tuggers roused the children from their uncomfortable sleep and drew them out from their tent. Fortunately, there were no towns in sight, meaning no barbarity to witness. At least for the moment.

Fincher scrambled across the Trade Ark and jumped across to the one leading them so he could easily converse with the Tuggers.

"What the fark is going on?" he asked Topporia, his favorite of the crew given her soft spot for colorful language.

The giantess turned to respond, a naughty gleam in her amber eyes. Fincher immediately knew he was going to hear something he liked.

"It is another Tugger crew making their way down the river. They are called the Trinitees—short for the Tireless Titan Tuggers."

Fincher rolled the name over in his mouth a few times. "That's a good farking name. Better than your Gritstone Tuggers… no offense."

"None farking taken," said a laughing Topporia as her giant companions rolled their amber eyes.

"You know, we used to call ourselves the Sour Flower Gang. What do you think of that?"

The giantess considered the name for a moment before answering. "The Sour Flower Gang? I quite like it. It really sticks."

Fincher beamed with pride. "You're farking right it does!"

"Why do you no longer call yourselves that?"

"Because a key member is no longer with us."

"Oh. I see. My apologies."

A heaviness fell over the light conversation and lasted until Fincher finally recovered enough to break it.

"So, what's going on between you all and the farking Trinitees?"

Topporia nodded to the oncoming crew floating down Crown's Run and now slowly making their way to the Gritstone Tuggers' side of the river.

"You see that Ommori sitting at the head of their Trade Ark?"

"The one with the big red feather in her hat? Hey, that's kind of like the one that Viguss wears."

"That is correct. That is Tequirra, and she is the Grand Tugger of the Trinitees. Whenever two Grand Tuggers pass each other on a tugg, they must engage in physical combat to see who is the true River Chief. Right now, Viguss holds the top spot, the Purple Feather. But Tequirra is more than a worthy foe. In fact, she may win."

Fincher's hazel eyes went wide. "Do they farking fight to the death?!"

Topporia belted out a laugh. "Do not be farking ridiculous, Young Fincher. It is more of a wrestling match than anything. These competitions were created soon after the Crown Treatise. They break up the monotony of the tuggs, give the crews something to bet on, and motivate the Grand Tuggers to stay in peak physical form, which trickles down to the rest of the crews."

"So, what do we do?"

"We watch. We cheer. And we bet! Do you have anything to bet with, Young Fincher?"

"I have a whole farking pack full of socks."

"Ommori-sized socks?"

"No."

"Then perhaps it will be best if you simply watch. But trust me, watching will be enough. Especially since…"

"Especially since what?"

The giantess grinned broadly, showing a couple of gems on her perfect teeth. "Especially since these two really like each other."

"You mean farking like-like?"

"Oh, yeah."

"Oh, they're gonna try to farking kill each other!"

"In the best way possible, Young Fincher!"

∽

The two giants faced off on the flat grasslands that sat several hundred feet from Crown's Run.

"You could just hand over the Purple Feather, Viguss," said the gorgeous giantess, her short-cropped, boyish hair standing in stark contrast to her impossibly feminine and sharp-featured face.

"Where would be the fun in that?" answered Viguss as he circled the dangerous female Grand Tugger.

"It would not be fun, Viguss. But it would save you some embarrassment and bruising."

"You know, this is my second tugg in a row with no break."

"Are you making excuses already, *River Chief*?"

"Quite the contrary, Tequirra. As you have been floating lazily down Crown's Run these last days, I have been enhancing my strength."

"You *do* look good, Viguss."

"I have never felt better, Tequirra."

"Should I go ahead and concede now?"

"It might be prudent."

Fincher's face twisted in confusion. The boy looked up at Topporia. "What the fark is going on? I thought they were gonna fight."

Topporia glanced down at the boy and offered a helpless shrug. "I do not know how to explain it, Young Fincher. But one day, you will understand."

Fincher shook his head. "Fark that! And fark this! I've got thirty chips—all that I have—riding on Viguss!" The boy shouted to the River Chief. "You gonna fight her or farking kiss her, Mister Viguss!"

Viguss turned to respond to Fincher and Tequirra took advantage, throwing a massive right hand that caught the Gritstone leader flush on the jaw, sending him sprawling to the ground.

"Whoops," exclaimed Fincher and scrambled back a few feet as Topporia's raging amber eyes met his.

"If Viguss has to relinquish his River Chief title because of you, *Young Fincher*, you are going to lose a lot more than chips on this day."

Fincher swallowed hard. "I'm sure he'll recover." Just as the boy spoke, Tequirra pounced on her downed opponent, landing swift kicks to the ribs and one to the arse as Viguss worked desperately to escape. "I think," Fincher added with a groan, wilting under another of Topporia's dark looks.

Viguss scrambled to his feet and brought his left arm up against his head just in time to block a wild right hook from the aspiring River Chief. Three more strikes were dodged, deflected, and stifled before Victiss's son was able to regain his balance and wits.

"You are not doing so well, Viguss," stated Tequirra amusedly as the giantess circled once more.

"I agree that I could have started stronger," retorted Viguss. "But the battle is far from over, Tequirra."

"Isn't it now?"

Viguss showed his gemmed teeth, already basking in the glory of what was to come. "It is! For Vimmos shared your secret weakness. The one he said that you revealed during a quiet night alone—just the two of you."

Tequirra's amber eyes went wide in absolute rage. "Why, that dirty Ommori clown! That liar! I have never spent time with that side-burned leecher! I would rather—"

As Tequirra raged on about Vimmos, attention ripped from the combatant before her, Viguss shot forward, a grim smile painted on his determined, tattooed face.

The River Chief's massive arms wrapped around the female tugger's legs, lifting her high into the air before slamming her hard onto the grassy field below, blasting the air from the Ommori woman's lungs.

Both tugger crews went wild on the edges of the battle, those of the Gritstone Tuggers bellowing in delight while those of the Trinitees screamed in fear for their leader.

Fincher let out a relieved breath as the giantess next to him screeched her support for Viguss Three.

"You are not off the farking hook yet, Young Fincher," said Topporia, refusing to take her eyes from the two warring Grand Tuggers.

"Fark me," said the boy under his breath as Ash and Sammi giggled next to him. Fincher called over to Ditto, who was entranced by the battling Titans. "Ditto, you got my back if this farking giantess takes a swing at the young king, right?"

"Sorry, Fincher," replied Ditto in between cheers for Viguss. "You're on your own on this one."

"Some farking friends! Let's go, Viguss! I need this more than you know!"

Viguss advanced his position atop his opponent, finally freeing his giant legs from hers and mounting Tequirra, his thick legs now along both sides of the giantess's hips.

Once in mount position, Viguss rose up, his right arm cocked back, threatening to smash a pale elbow into the woman's face.

What a farking pity that would be, thought Fincher from the sidelines.

Tequirra, seeing the threat above, twisted beneath Viguss, turning her shoulders and letting her hips follow, finishing the desperate maneuver on her belly. The giantess didn't stop there, knowing what was next to come. Instead, she immediately attempted to get to her knees, hoping to either toss Viguss off or, even better, stand up to spin back and, ultimately, disengage.

Unfortunately, Viguss also saw this coming. The reigning River Chief knocked the giantess's knees out from under her, flattening her out on the grass. With nowhere to go and more fists coming, the Grand Tugger of the Trinitees bucked hard in a last-ditch attempt for freedom. In doing so, she raised her large head and neck from the grass.

It was all Viguss needed.

Just as Tequirra's chin cleared the ground, the Gritstone leader's right arm slid under it, his hand finding the bicep of his left arm. Then the giant squeezed.

Tequirra's beautiful, pale face went red, and her eyes seemed ready to explode from their sockets. Just when Fincher was about to call out to stop the fight, the giantess tapped her hand three times on the ground and Viguss instantly released her and rolled off.

The fight was over.

"To Viguss Three! Who remains the River Chief on this day," called out one of the Gritstone Tuggers, and Topporia shot Fincher with a look. The boy offered a disarming smile and a complementary shrug.

"Better farking lucky than good, that's what I always say."

"I've never heard you say that," corrected Ash.

"Well, I better farking ought to."

"And to Tequirra Seven! For offering our champion such a memorable battle," continued the Gritstone Tugger. "The fighting heart of your Grand Tugger is a testament to all the Trinitees!"

The Trinitees, dispirited just moments before, cheered loudly for the recognition of their beloved leader. The two groups of Tuggers then came together in massive hugs, with chips changing hands, where necessary.

Tequirra waved away the cheers as Viguss helped her to her moccasin-clad feet.

"One day, I will get you, Viguss Three."

"You almost did on this day, Tequirra Seven."

"I will have the Purple Feather, Viguss."

"I believe you."

"But not today."

"No, not today, I'm afraid."

"And I'm afraid that you look much worse than I, Viguss. I am afraid that I may have permanently damaged that pretty face of yours."

"Ommori women like scars."

"Who told you that? An Ommori woman? Or a man whose face resembles fish netting?"

Viguss's massive shoulders slumped as he recalled from whom he had received that bit of wisdom. He reached up and gingerly touched his face, which was already beginning to swell.

Tequirra smiled. She may have lost the physical battle, but she certainly came out the victor in the war of words. The giantess stepped forward and softly removed Viguss's hand from his face.

"Stop. You are only going to make things worse. I have balm in my pack and some ice in a chest to keep the wind lizard meat. Go sit under the shade of that tree, and I will see to you momentarily."

Both tugger crews unpacked for a celebratory lunch along the southern bank of Crown's Run. As fires were lit and food was laid out, Fincher looked over to find Viguss sitting cross-legged under the shade of a tree he could not identify. The River Chief's amber eyes were closed, and a small, poorly hidden smile perched on his lips as Tequirra held ice to his cheek with one giant hand while rubbing an ointment onto his various cuts with the other.

She, too, wore a poorly hidden smile.

Fincher elbowed Topporia in the hip as the giantess moved to place some meat on a spit above one of the fires. When the boy had her attention, he nodded toward the tree line.

"Like-like, huh?"

Topporia looked over and grinned. "I farking told you."

Fincher continued to watch. "Geez, we're lucky they really didn't farking kill each other."

"There is always next time."

The boy from Crimmish looked shocked. "You really think there's gonna be a next time?"

Topporia hung the meat, another thing unrecognizable to the boy, before she answered.

"Of course, there will be. One is the River Chief. The other wants to be the River Chief."

Fincher kept watching as the tender scene unfolded.

"Well, I hope they have kids before one of them kills the other."

Topporia threw a massive arm around the small boy. "Me, too, Young Fincher. Me farking too." The giantess looked down at Fincher. "Do you have some lucky girl waiting for you back in your home?"

"I do. Her name is Stella Bugg, and she lights up the night when the Five Sisters fail to show up."

Sammi was walking past and couldn't help herself.

"You mean *Reba* Bugg, Fincher. And she lights up the day when Paragon reflects against her horse teeth!"

Fincher's hazel eyes went wide with embarrassment.

"Fallacious! Some teeth simply mature faster than the surrounding face! It's science!"

The surrounding Ommori laughed aloud as they went on with their lunch preparations. Whether Gritstone Tugger or Trinitee, all could agree that they would miss the company of these human children who had brightened up an otherwise tedious and nondescript tugg.

~

The sounds of screams and cries, laughs and howls, denoted the location of Cassie's Clutch long before the trading stronghold came into view.

The Gritstone Tuggers had pulled the entirety of the day and into the early evening to get the children to their destination lest they lose another day. Whether another day mattered or not, the younglings honestly did not know.

A thick layer of smoke and hundreds of torches eventually showed Cassie's Clutch to be on the opposite bank of Crown's Run, at the intersection of where the great river and even larger Crisp Run broke free from one another.

An impossibly tall, fortified wall surrounded Cassie's Clutch, upon which rugged-looking men and women paced with bows in hand. Every dozen feet, a giant freestanding crossbow stood, ready to send its four-foot bolt through any collection of flesh that dared to offer threat.

"It looks farking impenetrable."

"It is," responded a tugger to Fincher's left. "How else do you think it maintains its sovereignty? The Titian Empire would love to have the city under its thumb, but there is nothing it can do. Cassie's Clutch trades with Chestnuts, Titans, and even the Cobalts."

"It looks like a prison," observed Ash.

"To some, it might as well be one." The giant said no more, and the children didn't think to ask.

As the Trade Arks drew even with the walled port city, the Gritstone Tuggers all leapt onto one of the cargo flatboats as Viguss reached down into water and retrieved something—a large hook—from the relatively shallow bottom near the bank. The River Chief connected the hook to the front of the first Trade Ark, joined the other Tuggers on the boat, cupped his large hands around his gemmed mouth, and called out toward Cassie's Clutch.

"Titan tugger delivery! Dock Four!"

An incomprehensible shout echoed across the mist-covered water as the line of Trade Arks jerked forward and began to move across the current, heading directly for the notorious city.

Sammi turned to face her friends, excitement on the young girl's face.

"They're pulling us in using some sort of winch. I wonder what is powering the thing? Couldn't be just manpower, could it?" Sammi pushed up her glasses and began speaking to herself. "Could it? Maybe if there was some way to increase their strength. A pulley system perhaps? But then…"

Fincher, Ash, and Ditto simply shook their heads as their smart friend went on, talking herself through a hundred different possibilities, a dozen different scenarios.

As Sammi continued to muse, Viguss jumped from one Trade Ark to another, joining the children. The Grand Tugger's face still showed the effects of his battle with Tequirra.

"Well, younglings, it looks like we made it. Lucky for us, it was a fairly uneventful trip."

"Is *that* what you call uneventful?" asked Ash, obviously confounded.

"Yeah," agreed Fincher. "What would have made it farking eventful? One of us getting gobbled up by a durned river crokkodile?"

Viguss turned to Fincher, a surprised look on the Ommori's pale face.

"How do you know of the River Wraith, Young Fincher?"

Now it was Fincher's turn to look taken aback.

"What?! They really exist?! I thought I just made the farking thing up! I thought crokkodile's only existed in the Black Bog!"

"The Black Bog. *And* Loch Terminus," Viguss corrected. "*And* in Crown's Run, but only near Ptero Heights, behind the South Cobalt Insurgence." Fincher's jaw fell open at this terrifying news as Viguss continued. "But let us put talk of crokkodiles behind us. I have come back here to tell you that while Cassie's Clutch may be considered *civilization*, it holds just as many dangers as the southern portion of Vattassav."

"With all due respect," said Ditto, "I don't think that Borggos the Many is in there, Mister Viguss."

Viguss's face twisted in confusion. "But... how do you... Why do you know that name?"

The children ignored the giant's befuddlement.

"Yeah, or farking Marsh Ghouls. You know, the farking Famished?"

"The Famished? But, Young Fincher, how do you know—"

"Yeah, or Berserker Bears," cut in Sammi. "There can't be Berserker Bears in there, Mister Viguss."

The River Chief's mind spun like a top.

Finally, he got it. "Wait! Wait! Wait, please! Are you telling me that you younglings faced all these monstrosities in Vattassav?"

"You're farking right we did. And we lost a good friend... No! *Two* good friends in the process."

The giant's amber eyes fell onto the longbow across Fincher's lap.

"Alicia Salt, I presume?" The children nodded. "I thought I recognized the weapon but did not want to pry. She was a great human and a friend of the forest. I will release a Moon Lantern in honor of her soul when I return." A long pause. "So, you are no novices to monsters, and that is good. There are plenty of them behind the walls of Cassie's Clutch. Young Ditto, you are correct. Borggos the Many will not be found within, but there are countless other worms in the forms of men and women. They will try to infect you just as surely as Borggos will."

"Full of good news, this guy," pointed out Fincher as the others shushed the boy.

Ash took the lead. "We would welcome any advice, Mister Viguss."

"Go through the city as fast as you can. Stay to the shadows. Do not draw any attention. If you are lucky, you will exit the main eastern entrance without much trouble. I know very little of your mission, but I do know you are going north. There is much trouble there. Use Ptero Heights to your advantage. Neither Titian nor Cobalt attempts to cross that difficult land. But I have no doubt that you four can make it. From there, you are near the northernmost part of Quaan and, I would assume, the crux of your mission."

"If we do find ourselves in trouble in the city," said Ditto, "can we rely on the help of Cassie Hawkkends? Surely, she will want to help four children tasked with saving the world?"

Viguss let out a deep sigh. "I would not count on that one, Young Ditto. I have only met the woman once, but her reputation certainly precedes her. She is a woman who carved out her own fiefdom in a world of men, meaning she is tough as nails. She gives no favors, and makes only deals. Do you see those ballistae on the walls—they look like great crossbows." The Crimmish kids nodded. "Her family invented those. When it became in vogue for the royalty and rich families of the Titian Empire to wear robes decorated with the feathers of the redcoat starhawk, the teenaged Cassie Keller—as she was known back then—used it as opportunity to separate herself from the pack. She wheeled her weapons all around Quaan, hunting the majestic redcoat starhawks until few remained. She then used this scarcity to raise prices to cosmic levels, selling only to the royal Rayne family. Within a decade, all the redcoat starhawks were gone and Cassie Keller was rich beyond her wildest dreams."

"That sounds awful," stated Sammi flatly.

"It was worse than you think, Youngtress Sammi. With the

starhawks gone, mice ran rampant through the angel wheat flats, destroying entire crops and almost leading to mass hunger."

"And Cassie didn't have to answer for that shite she did?"

"Even worse, Young Fincher; she further profited from it."

The younglings' eyes all went wide at the same time. "How?" they asked in unison.

Viguss turned to check their progress—they were near the dock now—before going on.

"Somehow, the woman saw this coming, so she had a solution ready. One that could be purchased only from her. From secretly trading with the Cobalts, Cassie knew there was a mongrel that was bred in Merriworth—a half-dog, half-fox mix—that loved nothing more than to hunt field mice, going several feet beneath the ground to find their burrows. Even better, other than their bloodlust for mice, the animals were friendly and made lovely pets.

"By the time the Titian's mice problem was evident and widespread, Cassie had been breeding *Graxxora* for years and had inventory to sell... if you could afford it." Viguss let that sink in. "Now with wealth to rival the oldest Titian families, Cassie Keller founded Cassie's Clutch and changed her last name to *Hawkkends*, a reminder that she can make whatever she wants vanish from the face of Quaan. As if it was never more than a dream."

Viguss concluded, and the children sat in stunned silence.

Until Finch blurted, "Give me ten minutes with this farking Cassie. I'll win her over just as I do all the lasses!"

"You mean like Stella Bugg?" asked Sammi.

Ash jumped in. "Or that pretty Ommori girl?"

Thankfully, Ditto did not pile on.

"Fallacious! Those were all girls. I'll have you know that grown women take quite the shine to me."

Viguss looked back to find that the Trade Arks were pulling alongside the dock. He spun back.

"I hope you are right, Young Fincher. But I also hope that you do not have to find out."

Fincher nodded. "Of course, Mister Viguss. Better to slip through without fuss."

"Good boy." Viguss's voice lowered as dockworkers began to surround the Trade Arks. "Trust no one, younglings. Move quiet and quick. Remove yourselves from this cursed city as fast as possible."

Ash matched the giant's volume. "Why do you think we're not just meeting up with the Chestnuts, Mister Viguss? We've already agreed not to trust anyone who's not from Crimmish."

"Good lass."

Viguss stood, leapt onto Dock Four, and immediately began speaking with the assumed dock-manager, identified by his orange vest and clipboard. Viguss ran down the items that were being delivered as the manager made note, checking things off as other dock men unloaded the goods.

In the blink of an eye, the Trade Arks were empty, leaving only the kids of Crimmish aboard.

"And these?" asked the manager through his thick, greasy beard. "I never took you Bloodless as flesh traders, but we'll definitely accept." The man's dark eyes fell upon the sisters. "Especially those two. In fact, if you want to cut a deal right now with me, I'd gladly take—"

The dock-manager was unable to complete his proposition through a closed windpipe as he was lifted into the air by a large Ommori hand. Viguss brought the grotesque man's face close to his own.

"These children are to be considered precious cargo of the Ommori," Viguss said, his voice trembling with rage.

"He's gonna pop his farking head off," whispered Fincher to Ash.

"Good riddance."

Viguss continued. "If they are not given clear passage through the Clutch, I will return with an army of Ommori. I know that we may not be able to take the city, but we *will* take the docks. And I *will* make sure that you, in particular, will have your arms and legs ripped from their sockets. I will then have fire put to your holes to keep you from bleeding out, to keep you alive. I will then—"

The manager tried to talk around the giant's grip. Viguss released the man, who dropped to the wooden decking like a carcass, gasping for air.

"Did you have something to say," demanded Viguss a minute later.

"I said, okay," declared the bearded man, now with a raspy voice. "Shite, you got it! No one touches the durned children!" The manager rose on unsteady legs. "But I can only guarantee safety through the delivery station. After that, I have about as much control as a skeeter on a Bog Behemoth."

Viguss leaned down. "The Ommori have spies everywhere. I will know if you are not a man of your word. And you know I will be back."

"Okay! Okay! Fark, man! I'll bring them across the delivery station myself, okay? I'll even let them know that the kids are some sort of Ommori favorite, not that that will scare off the savages around these parts."

"Just make it happen!"

"It's done! Fark!"

The dock-manager ran off to check the delivery and ensure that the proper goods were placed back on the Trade Arks for travel back to Vattassav. Every now and then, the manager would throw his dark eyes towards Viguss, making sure the giant had not changed his mind, instead deciding it was best to simply pop the head off the offending human.

Thirty minutes later, the children of Crimmish waited on Dock Four, their packs strapped to their small backs and, in Fincher's case, an ornate longbow slung over his shoulder. The Trade Arks were now full of goods from behind the Cobalt Insurgence, across Ptero Heights, and along the northwest corner of the Titian Empire.

After Viguss nodded and signed the dock-manager's transference ticket, he turned and knelt before the younglings. There were tears in the giant's amber eyes.

"I'm afraid that I have done all that I can, my young friends. Although I wish there was more."

Sammi threw her arms around their giant friend.

"You've done quite enough, Viguss, son of Victiss. We are in your debt."

"There are no debts between friends, Youngtress Sammi. Anyway, you are the Child Champions of Crown Lake. It is the Ommori who will always be indebted to you."

"I thought we weren't keeping farking track."

Viguss laughed through his tears. "Father said that I would grow to appreciate your language, Young Fincher. As in all things, he has been proven correct." The River Chief stood. "I hope you complete your mission, younglings. And I hope to see you return one day to Vattassav, a place that is now always your home."

Ash stepped forward and buried the giant's waist in a hug. "And I hope that one day you're free to leave Vattassav, and we're free to leave Crimmish. Then, we can meet anywhere in the world that we'd like."

Viguss softly patted the young girl's braided head. "Yes, that would be something, Youngtress Ash." He separated. "And now, I must bid you all a farewell. You have all made my life significantly richer. If I do not see you again in Vattassav or elsewhere in Quaan, I am sure that we will connect again in the Wellspring."

"You think we'll all reach the Wellspring, Mister Viguss?" asked Ditto.

Gemmed teeth shone in the torchlight. "Of course, you will, Young Ditto. All of you. Your spirits are too bright. And the Wellspring is always greedy for bright souls. See you all soon. In one form or another."

Viguss Three then jumped atop the now-rearmost Trade Ark and waved as the other tuggers pushed away from the dock with long poles. Just as the Titans passed into shadow, the River Chief spoke, offering one last bit of advice.

"Cassie's Clutch is not a city of men. It is a city of demons. Do whatever you need to get out. Even if it means becoming one."

14

UNWANTED ATTENTION IN CASSIE'S CLUTCH

True to his word, out of fear rather than duty, the dock manager personally escorted the children of Crimmish through the massive delivery station that separated the docks from the actual city that was Cassie's Clutch.

The delivery station, which resembled an enormous warehouse, was a hive of activity, with workers pushing carts piled high with goods to and fro, some labeled for pickup and others marked for delivery.

The dock manager, grumbling the entire time, did manage to shoo away several particularly ill-intentioned warehouse workers who began to approach the younglings.

"Not these, you bastard! Unless you're itchin' to see what your insides look like on the floor!"

After numerous near-collisions with rushing carts, several of which required the children to quickly cut to the side to avoid being run over, the dock manager finally reached a door at the far end of the delivery station and pushed through it.

Within was a large office that was warmly decorated with thick, expensive carpets, leather cushion chairs, and paintings representing styles from across the entirety of Quaan. To the right, a fire was raging within a massive hearth, and the children could not help but think of Matilda Hamm and Borggos the Many, who hid within her fleshy folds.

To the left, a small, dark-complexioned man sat behind an ornate wooden desk covered in stacks of documents and maps. He wore thick, round glasses, similar to those of Sammi's, although his frames were made of gold. A heavy mustache sat on the man's upper lip, the ends twisted and greased so that they came to sharp points well past his weak jawline. The little man spoke without looking up.

"You had better have a good reason for A—disturbing me during my reconciliation time, and B—not knocking. I may very well have had a young man in here with me." The man finally looked up at the dock manager with light grey eyes that shone behind thick glass. He smirked. "Unless that is what you were hoping to see."

The dock manager began to stutter. "N-no! It was not! I s-swear!"

The little man waved him away. "How boring. I know you. State your name and why you've decided to bother me."

"I'm Dock-manager Hurly Snoot, Trademaster."

The Trademaster's mouth twisted in disgust under his black mustache. "Hurly *Snoot*? What a dreadful name. No wonder I refused to commit it to memory. What is it you want, *Snoot*?"

"I didn't know where else to go."

"That is not a reason. Why. Are. You. Here?"

"These children were brought to Dock Four by a crew of Bloodless tuggers. Apparently, they're some kind of friends of the Titan freaks. They told me to make sure that they get through the Clutch without harm, or they'd bring an army of god-durned giants up the river to attack. I promised the bastard that I could only guarantee safe passage through the delivery station. So, here we are."

"Yes. Here you are." The Trademaster turned to the children. "Who are you? Where are you from?"

Fincher stepped forward. "I'm Fincher. This is Ash, Sammi, and Ditto. We're from Crimmish."

The little man tapped a pen to his lips as he thought out loud. "Crimmish? Crimmish? Crimmish? Oh, yes, the Stenches! Well, now I see why they call you *Cheese-Eyes*. I never got the nickname before, but it's all too clear. What in the Five Sisters are you doing here in Cassie's Clutch? I thought you lot were forbidden from leaving your toxic home."

"Special farking circumstances. And we're just passing through. We don't mean to stay, and we certainly don't mean any farking harm."

The little man giggled and addressed Snoot. "I like this one." Turning back to the younglings, he said, "Fine. Keep your secrets. One thing you'll soon find out is that the Clutch makes friends of secrets, and we never pry. Well, almost never. My name is Spyrros Milaan, and I am the Trademaster here, which means that there is no one more vital to the city's wellbeing than me, except for Cassie herself. Tell me, how did a group of Cheese-Eyes from the Stenches befriend the Ommori, who are notoriously closed off, particularly when it comes to us normal-sized humans."

Fincher shuffled from one foot to the other, unsure how much to reveal. "Like I said, we were passing through."

"The Mutewoods, you mean? You were just *passing through* the Mutewoods?"

"That's right."

"Just checking. Please continue."

"Anyway, the Moon Folk took a shine to us."

"*Took a shine to you?*"

"Are you a farking brandyback parrot? Repeating everything I say?"

"Just making sure that I understand, young sir. Why did the Ommori take a shine to you?"

"Because the Ommori have pure souls. And they recognize and appreciate this in others. Even in humans. Even in kids."

"And that is the only reason?"

"The only one I'm going to tell you."

"Oh my. Very well, then. Again, the Clutch is nothing if not a protector of secrets." Spyrros removed his glasses. "But we are not the Ommori. We care nothing for the purity of souls or how kind someone is. We care only about one thing—trade. Now, I don't really care what old Snoot here told the Bloodless. If you have something to trade, you can enter the Clutch. If not—"

Dock-manager Snoot cut in. "That tugger was insistent that—"

"You can leave, *Hurly Snoot*. I've heard enough from you. Don't take it personal if your name passes from my memory as soon as you pass through that door. I'm growing old and can only remember those worth remembering."

Snoot was about to fire back a retort but thought better of it. Instead, he simply turned to leave, speaking as he did.

"I've done what I said I'd do. If the Titans come back looking to avenge those little wankers, I'm gonna point them in your direction."

"Of course, you will. Goodbye, Dock-manager!" With that, Snoot exited the office, slamming the door behind him. Spyrros returned to the younglings. "Now, where were we? Yes! Trade. Do you have anything to trade? Any money with which to advance commerce? The Clutch is a business, not a babysitting service."

Fincher looked to his friends, and they all started rummaging through their pockets and packs.

"I have some jerky," said Sammi.

"I've got some shells that I took from Crown Lake," stated Ditto.

"And I've got way too many farking socks. Any use for those?"

The Trademaster's mouth turned down. "I'm afraid not. We're flush with socks and old, dried out meat. How are you for money?"

The children desperately rummaged through shirt pockets. As Ash went to reach into her shirt pocket, she knocked her collar loose, letting the Moon Medallion fall out.

Spyrros's grey eyes went wide as the medallion caught the office light and sent it back in a prismatic show of color.

Meanwhile, all the children placed whatever chips they had into Fincher's cupped hands. The boy quickly counted the coins.

"We have a hundred and fifteen chips, Mister Milaan."

Spyrros shook himself free from the Moon Medallion. "Well, you're poor but certainly not broke, at least." A sinister gleam appeared in the little man's piercing eyes. "And children always have *something* they can trade in the Clutch." A pause. "I suppose I can let you through. In fact, I'll do you one better, in honor of our ongoing partnership with the Titans of Crown Lake. Vassily!"

Several seconds later, the door opposite from where the children entered opened, revealing the bustling nighttime streets of Cassie's Clutch beyond. A large man stepped into the frame, a strange bowl cut sitting above a scarred face that looked to have been chiseled from rock.

"You called, boss?"

"Yes, Vassily, these younglings are new to the Clutch. They have come a long way and retain some very powerful friends. Please see that they are fed. Take them to *Spinner's Tavern* and tell that old crone Joanie to put their meals on my tab. Go on, now. Be a good boy and do as you're told."

Vassily, despite his significant size advantage, bowed before the diminutive Trademaster.

"You got it, boss. I'll be waiting outside when they're ready."

Ditto turned to Spyrros as Vassily left. "Thank you kindly, Mister Milaan. We're most appreciative."

"Think nothing of it, you big, beautiful boy. Friend of a friend and all that. Enjoy the sights of Cassie's Clutch. Vassily is known throughout as my man. No harm should come to you in his presence."

Fincher spoke as the children placed their chips back in their pockets. "Again, thanks a bunch, Mister Milaan. You know, they said the Clutch was full of farkers, but you don't seem a bad sort."

Spyrros returned his gold glasses to his face. "I appreciate that, young man. Now, off you all go! Into the night with you!" The children made for the exterior door. "Hey, girl!" Sammi turned back. "Love the glasses."

Sammi smiled and the children exited, meeting up with Vassily, who began leading them down the busy street. Ash ran back to close the office's front door, calling out as she did.

"Thank you for the hospitality," said the girl as the door closed.

Spyrros waited a few moments before responding into the now-empty office. "Oh, but you haven't seen anything yet, girl."

Spyrros rose with purpose, tossing on his long overcoat and gaudy top hat before grabbing his silver walking cane. He banged the top of his cane onto his desk three times for good measure.

"Looks like I'll be back in her good graces once more," the Trademaster said to himself before giving his mustache a twist and heading out into the night, quickly disappearing into the throng of traders, revelers, thieves, and murderers.

～

"It's not half-bad," stated Ditto happily through mouthfuls of stew. "I mean, it's no Ommori feast, but it sure beats more jerky."

All the tables at *Spinner's Tavern* were full of ruffians, with many of the women looking more intimidating than the men, even with their beards and tattoos and scars. A large fire pit dominated the center of the tavern, and a massive cauldron of bubbling stew hung over the flames.

The other children found that their appetites simply were not there, especially with the dozens of eyes on them in the busy tavern.

One young man, wearing a reddish undershirt common to the Titian Army but no other discernible uniform, studied the Crimmish kids for several minutes before tearing off across the dining room and exiting into the night.

Vassily took notice.

"Eyes cannot hurt you, children. I am the Trademaster's Keeper. None will make a move on you with me here. You should eat."

Fincher, Ash, and Sammi shared a look, shrugged, and then began spooning chunks of meat and potato through their lips, trying their best to focus on their bowls and not the hungry looks surrounding them. Vassily spoke as they ate.

"I know he doesn't look like much, but Spyrros Milaan is one of the most powerful men in the Clutch. If he says you are to be protected, then you'll be protected. I'm not sure what you gave him, but it must have been exceptional. Not that I'm asking you to tell me, mind you."

"We didn't give him anything," countered Fincher. "Like Mister Milaan said, we came here with strong friends. *Very* strong friends. Plus, I think he just wanted to help."

Vassily looked doubtful. "Yes, I'm sure that's precisely it. The goodness of his heart."

The younglings ate their stews in silence, with Ditto ordering a second bowl that he managed to finish before the others polished off their first.

"What's after this, Mister Vassily?" asked Ash. "Are we free to go?"

"Your guess is as good as mine, young miss. You heard what I was told; no other orders were given. I'm not trying to pry, but what is your business here in the Clutch?"

"We have no farking business in the Clutch. We're just passing through. I mean literally *just passing through.*"

Vassily chuckled. "I don't think I've ever met someone *just passing through* the Clutch. But I'll choose to believe you. If you truly do aim to simply leave the city, I'll be happy to escort you to the main eastern entrance. My shift is almost over anyway."

"We'd be grateful, Mister Vassily," said Sammi, and the brutish man simply nodded in return.

"It is settled then. Care for more stew? It's on the Trademaster, after all." The younglings all shook their heads in the negative, although Ditto did seem torn. "Very well. Let us be on our way."

Vassily rose, followed by the children, and all turned to leave. Just as they did, a rough voice cut through the tavern, easily heard over the general din of the establishment.

"How much, Vassily?! How much for the two chocolate ones?!"

Vassily spun back and found the source of the voice, an equally giant man with a heavy gut, crooked yellow teeth, and a long beard that had been tied into two thick braids. The man wore a black fur coat and had three Xs tattooed on his left cheek.

"Watch your words, Fezzin! I don't want to hear shite from the mouth of a flesh trader!"

The rest of the tavern fell silent as the large pair stared each other down from across the room.

Fezzin's eyes scanned *Spinner's Tavern*. There was no going back now lest he lose his hard-earned reputation.

"Settle down, Vassily! I'm only offering a trade! You are the Trademaster's night flower, are you not?" A gasp rose from the enraptured audience.

Fincher leaned into Ditto. "Fark me. I don't even know what that means, but it sounds bad. He's gonna have to fight this guy."

"That's the last thing we need right now," Ditto whispered back.

"Well, what we need and what we get are usually two different things now, aren't they?"

Ditto only shrugged helplessly in return.

Vassily took one dangerous step forward. "What did you call me?" Vassily was no longer yelling back. A cold edge had begun to color the Keeper's words.

Fezzin also took a step forward, his hairy hand falling to the hatchet at his belt.

"I called you a night flower. Now, be a good little night flower and carry my offer back to your master. I'm collecting talent for a wealthy new peddler who's setting up shop west of Crisp Run." Fezzin's eyes went to Ash and Sammi. "And these two would be perfect." The bearded man blew the sisters a kiss. "The peddler caters to all, so I'll take the little boy off your hands, as well, if that sweetens things. Money is no object."

"Seems like you got left out of the farking deal," said Fincher to Ditto jokingly. "Try not to take it personal."

"I'll do my best," responded Ditto, but the large boy was beginning to shake with rage, his hand now on his blade.

But if Ditto was raging, Vassily was absolutely ready to explode. He took two more steps toward Fezzin, and those in attendance not too drunk to notice the danger they were in cleared out of the way.

"Last chance to shut your dirty gob, Fezzin."

"Oh, I have to admit, I don't want them *just* for the peddler, although that's where I'll earn my money. I've only had chocolate quim a couple of times, something I'll never forget. And I've *never* had a one-armed girl. I can't wait to pin that one arm behind her back as the other watches through her thick glasses. I'll try 'em good, I will. In fact, I think I'll—"

Vassily exploded forward, sending bar patrons, chairs, and tables flying sideways in his wake.

Fezzin grinned darkly through his thick beard and quickly drew his hatchet from his belt. The flesh trader readied his weapon and planted his feet, delighted to see that Vassily was too enraged to pull his own blade. He would kill the Keeper and take the younglings for his own. Not only would he get his meat spear wet and make a year's worth of chips, but his reputation would reach untold heights. Not bad for a night's work.

Vassily came on like a man possessed, no weapon in either hand. Fezzin, a veteran of countless battles, cocked back his hatchet and timed Vassily's advance. Best case, Fezzin would bury his weapon in the side of the arrogant Keeper's head. Worst case, Vassily would have to pull up, leaving himself vulnerable to a backswing that would introduce the hammerhead side of Fezzin's hatchet to the bridge of his nose. Either way, the fight would belong to the flesh trader.

Fezzin's grin transformed into a wide smile as he began his strike, putting every bit of strength behind the blow, waiting to see which scenario would play out.

Unfortunately for Fezzin, there was a third possibility he'd failed to consider.

Seeing the slave trader's arm moving forward, Vassily shot forward in a blur, shifting into a gear that Fezzin though impossible for a man his size, especially one who wore the scars of so many wars.

Getting to his opponent much sooner than expected, Vassily was able to get inside the blow, catching Fezzin's wrist in an ironlike grip with his left hand. Vassily's right elbow then came down and across, smashing into the flesh trader's left temple so loudly that faces in the crowd screwed up from the sound.

The hatchet fell from Fezzin's grasp, clanging to the floor, as Vassily grabbed a handful of the wobbled man's black fur, holding him up as he punched the man's face repeatedly, busting open lips, swelling eyes, and ripping skin along the eyebrow.

The fight was over. But Vassily was not.

A storm still raging in his eyes, Vassily dragged the near-unconscious Fezzin toward the fire pit.

"Oh, fark me, what's he gonna do now?" asked Fincher.

When he reached the fire, Vassily pulled Fezzin in close. The man tried mumbling something through broken teeth, but nothing coherent came out. Vassily put his nose to Fezzin's.

"Hungry for children, are you? That appetite of yours knows no end, does it, Fezzin? Here, let me try to fill that belly of yours!"

"Oh, fark," shouted Fincher as Vassily took the flesh trader by the back of his neck and dunked the man's head into the boiling cauldron of stew.

The entire audience recoiled as Vassily held the kicking man down for several seconds before releasing him. The once-excited spectators then screamed in horror as Fezzin came up, howling into the air as several layers of flesh slid from his face and fell with a sickening *plop* into the vat of meat and potato.

Fezzin collapsed onto the tavern floor and began to convulse, staring up through lidless eyes that no longer worked.

"What is the meaning of this?! How dare you disrespect my establishment," cried an enraged old woman who had come in from a back room. "Vassily! How could you?!"

Vassily seemed unconcerned. "Good evening, Joanie. Put all of this on the Trademaster's bill. And add whatever you need to make this right."

The old woman's anger immediately subsided.

"Well, all right, then. As long as there is recompense. I'll get this all cleaned up."

Vassily nodded and made for the exit, patrons literally diving out of the way to avoid the Keeper, who wouldn't find himself the butt of any jokes for a very long time.

Vassily spoke as he reached the younglings. "Have all your belongings?" They nodded dumbly. "Good, then let us finally be off." A pause. "I'm sorry you had to see that."

"Seemed a bit farking much, huh?"

"I do not like flesh traders. Particularly those who enjoy flaunting their dark occupation. Let this be a lesson to all of them. Shall we?"

Vassily led the way out of the still-silent *Spinner's Tavern*, the children in tow.

Ditto addressed Fincher over his shoulder. "Glad he's on our side."

"Know what I'm glad about?"

"What's that?"

"I'm glad we ate the farking stew *before* those two went at it."

Vassily chatted as they walked through the crowded streets, as if he'd had nothing to do with recently melting someone's face off.

"Best we get you all out of here as soon as possible. This place grows increasingly dangerous as the night deepens."

The children of Crimmish looked around at all manner of depravity. Drunkards stumbled down the thoroughfare, shouting at anyone with the nerve to look in their direction. It never took more than a minute to spot a fight underway, whether that be single or group combat, often between women. Elsewhere, teenagers could be seen pouncing upon those traveling alone, swarming the man or woman before running down the closest alley with whatever they were able to pilfer.

"Worse than *this*?" asked Ash.

"Yes, I'm afraid so, young miss."

Soon, the quintet passed a row of buildings where scantily-clad women stood outside, most looking bored, scared, inebriated, or some mixture of all three. Every now and then, a dirt-covered trader would approach and engage in a quiet conversation before being led inside.

"Hey, you! You! Handsome boy!"

Fincher looked over to find a woman wearing a corset three sizes too small for her ample bosom yelling in his direction. She could have been twenty-five or fifty for all the boy knew.

"Me, ma'am?"

"Yes, you! Oh, but you're a handsome one. How about you come inside and let Minnerva make a man out of you? I won't bite… hard!" The woman started cackling but soon fell into a coughing fit. When she finally stopped hacking, Minnerva spat a green loogie to the ground and continued. "You got chips, don't ya, sweetie?"

"As a matter of fact, I do, ma'am. Perhaps I could just—hey!"

Ditto dragged Fincher away as Ash and Sammi rolled their eyes, although Sammi was having a hard time keeping her giggles to herself.

"Unhand me, you big galoot," said Fincher, shaking Ditto loose when they had put some distance between themselves and the woman. "We were just talking. She was taking a real shine to me."

"To your chips, you mean," corrected Ash.

"I didn't hear her calling out for any of you," stated Fincher smugly.

"That's because she knows to only go after the desperate-looking ones," joked Sammi.

"Fallacious!"

Vassily laughed from the head of the group. "That was Minnerva, also known as Minnie the Spike. Minnie likes to spike the drinks of those who pay her a visit. They wake up the next day in a random back alley, naked, and with all their chips and belongings missing. That is, if they wake up at all. Old Minnie's no expert at adjusting the dosages for different body types. Sometimes she gets it wrong."

"And the city just lets her keep operating?" asked a confounded Ash. "They don't arrest her or anything?"

Vassily shook his bowl-cut. "Minnie makes a good living, meaning she can always pay off whoever she needs to. This is Cassie's Clutch. Chips are king, and there is no queen."

"You sure know how to pick 'em, Fincher," said Sammi. "I'm not sure which is worse, getting poisoned by an escort, getting trampled by a giant, or getting cut open by horse teeth!"

Ash, Ditto, and Sammi collapsed into laughter as Fincher raised his chin defiantly.

"Yeah, well, at least I have farking options."

"Night flowers," said Vassily.

"What's that, Mister Vassily?" asked Ash.

"In the Clutch, we call them night flowers. Come, we're almost to the city center. From there, it's not far."

Vassily pushed on, Ash and Sammi on his heels.

Fincher pulled on Ditto as they moved to follow.

"Farking night flower. I told you it was something bad. Calling a man—a man like Mister Vassily—the night flower of another man—a man like Mister Milaan—there was gonna be a fight. No farking doubt about it."

Ditto glanced down at his friend. "Bad enough to melt a man's face off?"

"Hey, we're not in farking Crimmish. I don't know the rules of engagement here. Plus, fark him. You heard what he was saying about Ash and Sammi."

"I certainly did."

"Then, he got what was coming to him. Now, do you think there will be any other night flowers around the city center?"

"Fincher! Haven't you learned your lesson?"

"What?! They all can't be Minnie the farking Spike. Maybe I'll meet a Livvy the Lovely, or Keely the Kind. What do you think?"

"I think you're a lunatic, Fincher."

Fincher threw an arm around his large friend. "Yeah, but that's why you farking love me."

Ditto reciprocated, tossing an arm over Fincher's shoulders. "I know. The Five Sisters help me, but I know."

"Vassily! Vassily! Halt there, man! Do you not see me?!"

The children and their chaperone had just reached the bustling city center, a circular area many times more crowded than any other part of the Clutch, when a high voice cut through the throngs of traders and revelers. Ahead and to the right of the group, masses of people entered and exited the enormous arched entryway, above which hung a heavy metal portcullis.

Far to the north, well past the city gate and adjacent to the city wall, sat a huge, fortified palace, with ballistae atop its towers and armed guards pacing below and along the battlements. Were it any larger, the building would surely be considered a castle.

"Vassily! Are you deaf, or just dumb?!"

Vassily finally pulled the younglings to a stop, a sad look on the man's otherwise face of stone.

"Wait here, children."

Soon, the Trademaster appeared out of the crowd, flanked by ten soldiers wearing white headbands and carrying wicked spears, longswords on their hips. Each of the rough-looking men and women wore bright white vests that had the talons of a hawk embroidered in bright red. They created a protective circle around Spyrros Milaan as the little man finally reached his Keeper.

"Oh, thank the Sisters!" Spyrros swatted Vassily on the big man's chest as he came upon his guardian. "Why did you eat *so* fast?! I almost missed you." The Trademaster leaned in. "And almost missed our chance of getting back in her good graces."

"You mean Cassie?"

"Of course, I mean Cassie, you big brute! Is there any other female in Quaan that I need to impress?"

Vassily glanced back at the children. "What does it have to do with them?"

"Everything."

"I won't be a part of the younglings being harmed. In fact, I'll openly oppose it." Vassily's small eyes, covered in scar tissue from hundreds of fights, swallowed his diminutive boss. "I'll *violently* oppose it."

Spyrros, shocked by his usually obedient employee's angry response, recovered quickly and waved his Keeper away.

"No one said anything about hurting them, you fool! They have something that I think... that I *know* Cassie has been looking for."

Spyrros puffed out his small chest. "I'm going to bring the woman who has everything something she's always lusted after."

Vassily looked doubtful, lines of worry appearing just below his bowl of dark hair.

"Cassie does not have anything that the children need."

Spyrros's grey eyes flashed behind his gold-rimmed glasses. "How do you know that?! Have you asked them? Do you even know *why* a group of children from the Stenches are passing through the Clutch? Do they look well-equipped to you?" Vassily had no response. "See! You don't know shite! Here's what *I* know. Cassie wants to speak with them—to make them an *offer*. Not to enslave them. Not to steal from them. Come on, Vassily, you know the woman! She may have a sack of gold where her heart should be, but she's about making deals, not stealing."

"Sometimes, the two become the same."

"So, you want me to run back to Cassie?! Tell her that my *Keeper* doesn't think it's a hot idea for her to meet the Cheese-Eyes? Tell me, where will you run to after my head is nailed onto the front door of the *ChippHouse?*"

Vassily thought it over, so long and hard that Spyrros could swear to hearing the rusty gears turning in the veteran soldier's head.

"Fine. But if I fear for their safety, it will get ugly fast."

Spyrros let out a relieved sigh. He didn't want to have the best Keeper he'd ever had killed… but he would if he had to.

"Good. I know Cassie is anxious to speak with them. Let's—"

A scream from Sammi turned everyone around. The young girl was in the grips of a Titian soldier in full armor. The other younglings began to pull their blades.

Vassily proved the faster, rushing over to land a straight right against the offending soldier's jaw, laying the man out onto the cobbled street, before pulling the girl and the other children to safety.

For a moment, chaos ensued.

Four other Titian soldiers, including an irate Lieutenant Benson Kruger and an oaf with a heavy brow, drew their army-issued swords while the Clutch Guard, dressed in white, advanced with their spears held high.

Spyrros, showing surprising courage, stepped between the two dangerous groups.

"Whoa! Whoa! Whoa! What is the meaning of this?! We are on important business of Cassandra Hawkkends—maybe you know her as Cassie. You know, of *Cassie's Clutch*! You Titians need to be on your way. Get drunk on honey rice wine and pick a fight with another group!"

Benson Kruger's weasel face took in the scene, the officer doing the basic math. He motioned for his soldiers to return their swords to their scabbards. The man knocked out by Vassily was just starting to rise to his feet, albeit wobbly.

"I will have your name, sir, for mine is Lieutenant Benson Kruger of the Titian Empire!"

Spyrros stepped forward, unwilling to back down, especially with advantageous numbers supporting him.

"I am Spyrros Milaan, Trademaster of Cassie's Clutch. I dare say my title holds much more sway in this place than yours."

Kruger's face twisted in rage, the man unaccustomed to not being openly feared. "I am here on direct orders of Imperator Kasspar Rayne! I am to locate and seize *these* children as they are needed for a mission critical to the Empire. Not allowing me to fulfill my duty is an act of defiance against the crown and will be treated as such. Your Clutch exists because of the good graces of our Imperator. You know this."

The Trademaster snickered. "Actually, I know the opposite to be true. The amount of effort, resources, and lost lives it would take for the Titians to capture the Clutch would weaken the Empire to the point where the Cobalts could take advantage." Spyrros smirked and made a show of looking around. "We maintain a good relationship with our trade partners to the northwest. There might even be some around today..."

Kruger looked as if he had eaten something rotten. As the

Lieutenant pondered his next move, Vassily knelt before the Crimmish kids.

"Children, do you know this man?" They all nodded. "Do you want to go with him?" They all shook their heads. "Fair enough." The giant man rose, his hand going to the mace at his side.

Kruger, however, had decided on a more diplomatic approach, the choice made easier with ten spears pointing in the soldier's direction. Kruger beckoned Spyrros to the side, where Vassily joined them despite a side-eye from the Titian officer.

"Look," said Kruger, attempting his best to sound rational and genuine, two attributes that the narrow-faced man was not known for. "The Titian Empire made a deal with these children, a deal that they and their parents agreed to. We were separated early in the mission but can now get back on track. I wasn't lying when I said that my directive comes straight from the Imperator himself. And he makes demands, not requests."

Spyrros held his ground. "Yes, well, that is good and all, but I am here on a directive straight from Cassandra Hawkkends—who wants to speak with these children. And that woman does not even know what a request is."

"Your Imperator demands it," said Kruger loudly, his patience wearing thin.

"Your Imperator has no jurisdiction here! We are ruled by a matriarch!"

Kruger closed the distance on Spyrros and began speaking in a threatening hiss. Vassily moved in, as well.

"You may only let six soldiers in at a time, but I have the *entire* Titian Army gathered not far from these gates. You have the numbers now, but what happens when I storm the Clutch by the thousands, with men and women well-rested and well-fed and thirsty for blood?! Yes, you may be right. It might be a tactical error with the Sluggs so close, but, with the Five Sisters as my witness, I *will* do it. And before the Cobalts sweep down from their hovels to attack, I'll make sure that your skinless body is hung up while you still live. I'll sell handfuls of salt to spectators so that they may hurl it onto your exposed flesh. Then, we'll all lose. I'm ready for that."

The Trademaster's pointed mustache twitched as the little man considered his options.

Finally, he said, "Heck with this." Spyrros looked up at Vassily. "When faced with two shite options, make up your own." Eyes to Kruger, he added, "You will not stop me from taking these children to see Cassie, but you may join us and make your case to the woman herself. You can both sort it out once my task is complete." A sly grin appeared on Kruger's wolfish face, and the soldier offered an acquiescing bow. "And Lieutenant," continued the Trademaster as the officer drew upright, "I expect to be compensated for any deal made. For putting the two parties together, you understand?"

Kruger's smile vanished. "I would expect nothing less from a man of your… stature."

Spyrros led the way toward the home of Cassie, also known as Hawkkends ChippHouse. Five of the Clutch Guard surrounded the Trademaster while the remaining five brought up the rear, keeping sharp eyes on the untrustworthy group of Titian soldiers.

Grouped between the Clutch Guard was Vassily, Kruger, and the younglings, followed by the other five Titian soldiers, one of whom was nursing a severely bruised jaw.

Any time Vassily's attention was torn elsewhere, Lieutenant Kruger would take the opportunity to shoot vicious glances at the kids from Crimmish, his beady eyes promising payback for their collective insolence.

Ditto walked several steps behind Fincher, Ash, and Sammi, forcing a gap between the Chestnuts and his friends. One of the soldiers, a particularly cruel-looking fellow whose missing chunk of upper lip made him resemble a talking skull, moved up to walk alongside the boy. When Ditto looked up, he noticed that one of man's eyes was clouded over, with a deep scar running from forehead down to cheek.

"Hey! Hey, boy," said the Titian, his one good eye remaining forward. "You know, we were gonna have a little fun with you before dropping you off at Terminus Grove. Well, with your little girlfriends, to be more exact, but we had exciting things planned for you and your boyfriend, as well."

"Oh, yeah?" responded Ditto, attempting to remain calm.

"Yeah, yeah. But we *were* gonna have our fun and then cut you loose. But now, with all this extra trouble, plans have changed. I think we're gonna keep your little girlfriends at our camp, make real women out of them while you and your boyfriend go retrieve what the Imperator wants. You lot have already shown that you'll run off. Now, Lieutenant Kruger says you'll need a reason to bring you back." Ditto's hand began to shake. "But I'd be quick about it. Our encampment holds thousands of men. Their little chocolate bodies will not hold up under the stress for long. Especially the one-armed one. She's a rare temptation that few will be able to resist. In fact—"

Ditto drew his hunting knife and swung it toward the lipless soldier, who just barely managed to leap away from the blade.

"Why, you little shite," spat the soldier as his hand went to his longsword. "I'm gonna gut you like a fish!"

Vassily was there in an instant, one gnarly hand around the Titian loudmouth's throat, lifting him into the air as the other soldiers began to pull their weapons.

"No, no, no," cried Spyrros, whose words were echoed by Kruger. "Everyone, put your weapons away! Vassily, drop that ugly man!" The Keeper did as he was ordered. "Good! Now, all of you shut your gobs and let me do the talking. We're here."

The lipless soldier and Ditto shared one last hate-filled look before the group advanced once more, now approaching the ornate, double-doored entrance of the ChippHouse, where dozens of Clutch Guard stood watch. The white vests that had been accompanying the Trademaster, Crimmish kids, and Titians fell off to the sides, intermingling with their fellow guards.

"What's your business, Trademaster?" called out one of the Clutch Guards, this one bald and wearing a red headband instead of the more common white. "Gambling or trading?"

"Trading, of course."

"Then you know the way to the Trade Hive. May fair deals find you."

"No, no, you misunderstand. I'm here to trade directly with Cassie."

The man in the red headband shook his head violently side to side. "You know very well, Trademaster, that none see the Woman without an appointment. She's no longer willing to—" A member of the Clutch Guard tore out of the ChippHouse and slid to a stop next to the man in the red headband. He whispered into the bald man's ear, who shouted in return. "You know, this is why we have transition meetings during shift changes! Where was this information ten minutes ago, Guardsman Jeffs?!"

The defeated-looking guard backpedaled as he replied.

"I'm sorry, Talon Shellburn! I ate some bad river clamms and was stuck in the latrine the past half-hour!"

"Your need to shite *does not* come before my need for timely information!" The guard bowed strangely, a pained expression on his face. "By the Five Sisters, man, return to the toilet before you sully your reputation further!"

"And your pants," cried out another guard, much to the delight of the others. Poor Jeffs offered an embarrassed laugh before rushing back into the ChippHouse and its many places to relieve oneself.

Talon Shellburn returned to Spyrros. "My apologies, Trademaster. As you can see, I was without the necessary information. The Woman is awaiting you upstairs in the Nest." Shellburn took notice of the entire party. "But she is expecting you and some children. Nothing was said about Titian soldiers." The Talon shouted over his shoulder. "Jeffs, you cur, you better hope that shite kills you!"

"It wasn't his fault, Talon," cut in Spyrros, drawing Shellburn's attention back to him. "This is a very recent addition to the deal. But they *are* necessary stakeholders and, therefore, should be included in the discussion with the Woman."

The baldheaded Talon studied the Titians. "I hate Chestnuts."

"We all do," agreed Spyrros. "But they remain our trade partners, do they not?"

Shellburn spat onto the cobblestone. "They do. Go on, then." He directed his next words to Lieutenant Kruger. "But I'll be joining you."

"Place looks farking amazing," remarked Fincher, his hazel eyes wide as they drank in the sights, sounds, and smells.

The ground floor of Hawkkends ChippHouse was comprised of several cavernous rooms, each full of rows upon rows of tables topped with expensive goods, sparkling trinkets, and rare items. Men and women from across Quaan pored over the items, sometimes handing over gold, silver, chips, or other merchandise in exchange for something that caught their eye.

One massive room emphasized bars of gold and silver alongside raw gemstones while another held vendors offering finished jewelry. A third room contained dresses and outfits made from luxurious materials, and a fourth specialized in weaponry, including both the antique and modern marvels.

One heavily-armed woman hungrily eyed Alicia Salt's longbow as she moved from one room in the Trade Hive into another.

"I think she likes what she sees," bragged Fincher to Ash, who didn't even bother to respond.

At the rear of the ChippHouse, Talon Shellburn led the group up a cascading staircase to the second floor and then immediately cut right, heading back toward the front of the establishment.

"Farking heck! And I thought the bottom floor was grand," exclaimed Fincher, his voice almost drowned out by the rings, shouts, bells, and fist-pounding emanating from the gaming tables that dominated the level's wall-less, open space.

Cards displaying Kassimont royalty and the Five Sisters, among other notable Quaan imagery, flittered back and forth across tables, and chips changed hands from dealer to player and back.

Other games were played with dice while some required no more than a sharp knife and someone willing to put fingers on the line.

Male and female waitstaff wearing just enough to cover their private areas crisscrossed the space, keeping mugs full of mead, wine, and any other spirit available as a potpourri of smoke wafted through the Game Lair.

Just as before, Talon Shellburn guided the group on until they reached another cascading staircase, this one at the front of the palace. A large group of heavily armed Clutch Guards barricaded the stairs.

Shellburn stepped forward as another man in a red headband came out to meet him.

"Fair play, Talon Femmell."

"Well met, Talon Shellburn. An interesting party you currently keep. Is the Woman expecting them?"

Shellburn nodded. "She is. At least, she is expecting the Trademaster, the Keeper, and those children. Apparently, the Chestnuts are a recently added touch." Femmell looked doubtfully at his fellow Talon, who held up his hands innocently. "I know, I know. But, seemingly, it is for a deal that the Woman is desperate to make."

Femmell rubbed the grey hair of his well-kept beard. "There is very little that the Woman still desires."

"Which is why you see my predicament. Do you want to be the one who keeps Cassie from something she covets?"

"I do not."

"And neither do I. Let us pass. If she decides to toss out the Chestnuts, so be it. At least you'll have some fun kicking them across the ChippHouse and down the stairs."

"What are you saying up there?" demanded Kruger from several steps back.

Femmell smiled knowingly at Shellburn. "I do hope it goes remarkably poorly." Shellburn returned a slight nod. "Let them up," called out Femmell to the guards behind them. "But stay ready. And if we have to crack open some Chestnuts, all the better."

The Titians, literally surrounded by enemy blades, kept quiet, each secretly promising that the day would come when Cassie's Clutch was left in smoldering ruins. But not today.

The third floor was much more like the Trade Hive than the Game Lair, with smaller passages breaking off from the main corridor, a heavily decorated and marbled hallway that showcased all of Cassie's wealth in the form of rare paintings, detailed sculptures, and bejeweled weaponry.

Sammi looked up and squealed in delight, discovering the bones of a gigantic serpent hanging high above from the tiled ceiling. The skeleton, with a twisting spine and hundreds of mammoth ribs, went on for what seemed like an eternity, easily over one hundred feet.

Vassily noticed Sammi's wonderment and leaned down as they walked. "The only known complete Bog Behemoth skeleton in all of Quaan. It is said to be the one that Prince Kasstin claimed before he fell."

"No way," said the girl through an open mouth.

"Way," replied Vassily with a grin.

Fincher looked to his right as the group moved forward and found nude and half-naked men and women exiting rooms only to enter others, giggling with red faces.

Soon, the grand hallway gave way to an even grander meeting area, where the Woman sat, the namesake of this twisted city of commerce.

Cassie Keller, now known as Cassie Hawkkends, lounged on a large ornamental chair that compared boldly to a throne. While sitting on the chair of a queen, however, that is where the parallels between Cassie and royalty ended.

With one leg draped lazily over the arm of her throne and a blue drink in one hand, the Woman wore a skintight, black leather pantsuit that would have been just as at home on a burglary as during an evening out on the town. Cassie's long hair was the color of fire, braided in neat rows along each side and pulled back in a loose ponytail.

Cassie's age was indiscernible, with smooth skin and an athletic body sitting in stark contrast to the wisdom and experience that marked her high cheek-boned face.

Fincher elbowed Ditto. "Should I give it a go? Turn on the old charm?"

Ditto looked down. "Please do not."

"What could go wrong?"

"Everything."

"But, other than that?"

The Woman studied the odd group as it entered her chamber, taking in every individual with bright yellow-green eyes that peered over her cocktail glass as she sipped purposely.

Massive Clutch Guardsmen, including several denoted as Talons, looked on with serious faces, praying that someone would step out of line.

When the full group finally reached the dais upon which Cassie's chair was set, they naturally separated, the children going to Spyrros's and Vassily's left while the Titian soldiers took their place to the right.

All remained quiet, waiting for the Woman to speak.

Cassie finished her drink and held out the empty glass to the side, not bothering to look as a handsome young man who had misplaced his shirt shot forward with a crystal pitcher to refill her cup. Cassie brought the now-full drink around, and the young man quickly disappeared into the background.

"You made good time, Trademaster," said Cassie, her voice heavy and powerful. "But I remember asking you to bring me *four younglings*. And yet, standing here before me are four younglings, yes, but also your Keeper and... *six* Chestnuts! I hope you have a good reason for bringing Chestnuts into my personal space."

Spyrros bowed so low to Cassie that Fincher feared the little man's gold glasses would fall to the marble floor and shatter. Luckily, they did not, and Spyrros pushed them back up his nose as he straightened.

"My sincerest apologies, Cassie, but it could not be avoided. Just as I was fetching the children for you, this group of Titians accosted us, making all sorts of wild accusations and aggressive claims. They *did*, however, seem to have a legitimate complaint regarding a broken contract—and I know how much you value agreements, so…"

Cassie leaned forward on her throne. "So, you thought, *just let Cassie deal with it?*"

Spyrros shrugged helplessly. "More or less. I know when I'm out of my depth, Cassie."

Cassie waved the Trademaster away with a manicured, tattooed hand that held more jewels than many frontier towns.

"Fine, fine. A typical solution from a typical man." Cassie's yellow-green eyes drifted to Ash and Sammi. "Keep your wits sharp, ladies, because men will never cease to disappoint and enrage. And then, they will call us crazy for voicing our displeasure, as if *we* forced them to stop growing up at twelve!" Ash and Sammi snickered, and Cassie returned to Spyrros. "Fine, Spyrros, I will bail you out…*again.*" Spyrros offered another slight bow as Cassie turned to the Titians. "You in the front! State your name!"

Kruger's mouth turned down in distaste, unused to being talked to in such a manner, especially by a woman who wasn't the Imperatrix of Quaan.

"I am Lieutenant Benson Kruger of the Titian Army, on a special mission from the Imperator himself. I have five thousand soldiers stationed not far from the entrance to the Clutch and many more a bit farther out. We have been tasked with—"

"Yes, yes, yes," interrupted Cassie. "But I didn't ask for your life history, just your name." Kruger looked as if someone had thrown a drink in his face. "Now, Lieutenant Kruger, I am willing to hear your case as one of the Clutch's Deal Ministers. However, I don't think you'll mind if I conclude my own business with these younglings first, would you? I mean, although I rule over all you see here, I am still just a trader at heart."

Kruger could feel the venom rising from his throat and filling his mouth. Just as he was about to release it onto Cassie, however, he glanced back to see the Clutch Guardsmen, outnumbering his Titians five to one, fingering their axes, swords, and daggers.

In the end, the narrow-faced lieutenant simply nodded in reluctant agreement.

"I really appreciate your patience, Bennie," stated Cassie, her words dripping with sarcasm. The Woman emptied her drink, almost a full glass, and tossed the crystal cup behind her. Just before the goblet shattered against the marble floor, the topless young male attendant dove into view, cupping his hands under the expensive vessel and saving it from certain destruction.

Cassie smirked when the sound of breaking crystal failed to materialize. She then sprung out of her throne and leapt down from the dais in one smooth movement, showing everyone that you underestimated her physical prowess at your own peril.

Cassie sauntered across the empty space separating her from her audience. She approached Spyrros, but not before running a ringed hand across Vassily's chiseled jaw.

"Heard there was some trouble at *Spinner's Tavern*, Vassily."

"Not for me."

"Yes, never for you, you human rock. But the man you hurt—"

"Not a man. A Flesh Trader. No loss."

"Maybe not to you, but Flesh Traders spend a lot of money here. It's one of the few places where they can freely spend their blood-soaked chips. I'd prefer it if you let them spend it. Instead of, you know, melting their faces off."

Vassily started to form a retort, but a sharp elbow from Spyrros stopped him. The scarred warrior recalibrated before answering. "That Flesh Trader threatened the younglings that I was to protect. His flapping mouth gave me no choice."

Spyrros rolled his grey eyes, questioning what Vassily would have said without his interruption.

Cassie smiled at Vassily, showing the nicest set of white teeth the children had ever seen. "I understand, Keeper. I understand that your soft heart is going to get you killed one day. Next time you feel the need to reprimand one of my traders, make sure he has a face left when you finish. In fact, make sure he has everything he needs to keep making and spending chips. Is that clear?" Cassie punctuated her question with a playful yet hard smack to Vassily's face.

Vassily's small eyes closed in anger, but he could still feel Spyrros's grey eyes pleading with him from below. When the Keeper opened them, he found Cassie's gaze still on him.

"Clear, Cassie."

Cassie moved on to Spyrros. "Good! That unpleasantness is out of the way. Now, Spyrros, on to our simplest of business. Please introduce me to my new young friends."

Spyrros silently celebrated that he wasn't dead yet and turned to the younglings. "Cassie, I am pleased to present..." The Trademaster rubbed his too-long mustached furiously as the names refused to come to him. Vassily grinned darkly, letting the little man struggle.

"For fark's sake," said Fincher, stepping forward as Ditto, Ash, and Sammi winced. "I'm Fincher Bugg, and this is Ditto, Ash, and Sammi Bugg."

Cassie's yellow-green eyes burned bright as the Woman side-stepped away from the Trademaster and toward Fincher.

"Well, well, well. I didn't believe Spyrros, but he was right. Children from Crimmish. If the Bugg last names weren't a dead give-away, your yellow eyes certainly are."

"Yours look pretty yellow, too," shot back Fincher, Ditto's hand growing tighter on the crook of his left elbow.

Luckily, the Woman simply laughed. "Yes, young man, our eyes may be different, but they do share a yellow hue. Maybe we can see what else can be shared."

Cassie started to pace before the younglings, with Fincher and Ditto's eyes being drawn to the tightness of the Woman's leather pants. She spoke as she walked, as if her hips could hypnotize coun-terparties into giving her a better deal. Which they usually did.

"As you can see," said Cassie as she marched back and forth, "there is little that I do not have. That which I have not been able to capture myself, I have traded for. That which I have not been able to trade for, I have purchased. And that which I have not been able to purchase...

well, let's just say that I've made alternative offers that have proven most enticing. In short, I have everything I have ever wanted." The Woman stopped. "Except for one thing—a Moon Medallion."

The younglings' hands instinctively went to their chests, where their Moon Medallions rested comfortably under wool shirts. Cassie did not notice, however, for her attention was squarely on Ash. The Woman stepped over to the girl.

"May I see it, young miss? I am not a man, so I can promise to look and not touch."

Under the sharp yellow-green gaze of Cassie Hawkkends, Ash reached under her shirt and pulled out the Moon Medallion, which immediately caught the many lights of Cassie's chamber and incorporated them into the white maelstrom that continually took place within the material.

The Woman's gemmed hand went to her mouth as she stared down at the ultra-rare stone. "May I?"

Ash nodded.

Cassie carefully reached for the medallion, as if frightened that her unworthy touch would cause the trinket to crumble. When she finally made contact with the pendant, it halted its spinning momentarily before twisting in the opposite direction, as if sensing the soul of the person contacting it.

"It is more beautiful than I ever imagined," stated Cassie breathlessly to no one in particular. "You know, I have literally offered the world to the Ommori for one of these Moon Medallions. You would have thought that I'd spat in their faces."

Cassie shook her fiery head to loosen the medallion's grip on her too-bright eyes before dropping the pendant back to Ash's chest. The Woman then snapped her fingers in the air and another male attendant appeared from the ether to present her with a third goblet of blue spirits. Cassie accepted the drink without thanks and took a sip.

"Although I am supremely curious, I will not ask you how this Moon Medallion came into your possession. That is not the Clutch way. However, should you be willing to share your story with me, I could formulate a chip number worthy of such a tale. But I digress."

Cassie finished her newest beverage and tossed the glass behind her. This one was juggled for a moment by an unfamiliar errand boy before it was eventually secured and taken to safety.

The Clutch founder's yellow-green eyes fell upon the children. The Woman's intent stare reminded Fincher of that of a bird-of-prey just before it swooped down from on high to snatch an innocent life.

"I do not care where or how you took hold of that Moon Medallion, young miss. I want it and am willing to pay whatever you ask. You have me over a barrel, which is something that I am quite unaccustomed to, unless I have made special arrangements for it. Name your amount, and it is yours. And then we can cheers as new friends."

Ash looked to her friends, none of whom had answers for the girl.

"I'm sorry, Miss Cassie, but it's not for sale. We were given these Moon Medallions by the Ommori as a show of lifelong friendship. I wouldn't be a very good friend if I sold one off at the nearest chance of trouble."

Cassie's head snapped back as her attention was piqued. "Did you say *we* were given? Did you say *Moon Medallions*?" Ash cursed at herself under her breath as Cassie dropped to her knees before the girl and whispered, "Do you *all* have Moon Medallions?"

With no room to backtrack, Ash put out her chin and nodded. "And none of us are giving them up."

Cassie gently grabbed Ash from behind the girl's braided head and pulled her in close. "We'll see about that."

Cassie rose and addressed the other Crimmish kids.

"So, you *all* have Moon Medallions. That is fantastic news for both me and you. You can make a fortune off one or two while I can finally complete my collection of oddities." Cassie motioned in the direction of Ash. "This girl was unhelpful, but I'm sure that, between the three of you, you can formulate a fair price for just one of those Moon Medallions." Silence. "Look around you! Do you think I cannot manifest anything that you can give voice to? Name it! And watch how I make dreams become reality! Name it!"

After another uncomfortable silence, Fincher finally stepped forward. "I'm sorry, Miss Cassie. You're great and all, but we went through a lot to get these medals and they mean a lot to us. They were given to us by good friends who we may never see again. We don't care about their value, only what they mean to us."

A dark cloud crossed over the otherwise beautiful face of Cassie Hawkkends. "So, there is nothing that you will take in exchange for one of your Moon Medallions?"

Fincher cleared his throat before responding to the Woman, in whose eyes there now swam storms similar to the children's pendants.

"I'm sorry, ma'am, but we're literally just passing through the Clutch. You don't have anything that we need. And we'd like to be on our way now."

"And that is final? *You* are refusing to trade with *me?*"

"I'm afraid so, ma'am."

The storms left Cassie's eyes, replaced by a coldness that was somehow more unsettling.

"Very well, children of Crimmish. I am Cassie Hawkkends, the great trader, not the great thief." A dark smirk found its place on Cassie's drink-stained lips. "But before you go, I must attend to our second bit of business. Let me put my administrative hat on—that of one of the Clutch's few Deal Ministers—and hear what Lieutenant Benson Kruger and his merry band of Chestnuts have to say. *They* say that you broke some kind of contract, some kind of deal. And that is the *one* infraction that we, as an entity, do not tolerate in Cassie's Clutch. Isn't that right, Guardsmen?!"

"Yes, Cassie," came the powerfully unified call of the guards in attendance, a quick reminder of where the power in the room resided.

Cassie flashed one last dangerous look at the Crimmish kids before directing her next words to Kruger.

"Lieutenant Kruger, it's your turn. Tell me your grievance with these children, and please remember that I care not about governance, proclamations, or royal dealings. I care only about deals and whether words were broken or not."

Kruger stepped forward, a confident grin on his wolfish face. "Then you will care about our tale, Cassie. For it is certainly a tale about words being broken by those who only had to gain from a deal. In fact, it is a tale about—"

"No! No preamble! Just the story, Lieutenant. In fact, I don't want to hear the story at all. What was the deal? And give it to me straight! Save your layered meanings for the night flowers."

Kruger bowed before continuing. "It is *very* simple, Cassie. These Cheese-Eyes from Crimmish agreed to be guided north by a contingent of Titian soldiers on a mission of direct import to Imperator and Imperatrix Rayne. The Titians leading them, including the venerable High Captain Gorman Graff, were fallen upon by a group of assassin Sluggs in Salt's Pass. We lost contact with the children, but the plan was always to meet back with them around Woodlow, where we would help them complete their mission for the Crown." Kruger glanced over to the Crimmish kids, rage apparent in the man's beady eyes. "But *they* decided they no longer wanted to uphold their end of the bargain. *They* decided that they were no longer on a mission of the Crown but, rather, on an independent mission of filthy Cheese-Eyes! You see! Now, do you see how they have stabbed the Empire in the back?! Make things right, Cassie! Take what you want from them, Moon Medallions and all, but give the children to us so that we may complete our critical task!"

"We don't simply take things here in the Clutch, Lieutenant. That is something of your Crown's design." A self-satisfied smirk landed on Cassie's face and remained there as she spun to face the younglings. "Tell me, children, is what Lieutenant Kruger says here true?"

Fincher wrung his small hands. "Well, not farking exactly."

"Then, illuminate me, young man."

"First off, have you heard the things that those men and women have said to us? And not just now; this started as soon as they began escorting us north. We were not partners—as agreed. We were property, and they could do what they wanted with us. Captain Graff made sure that we were protected, but this group—"

"That is neither here nor there, child Fincher. What was agreed upon? I will hear it as if from Gorman Graff's lips."

Fincher shuffled from foot to foot before responding. "We were to go north—far, far north—to get something for the Titians. In return, they would send the Empire's best physicians and apothecaries to Crimmish to find a cure for the Maddening. That is—"

"I am quite familiar with the Maddening, child Fincher. This is the Clutch. Do you think I don't operate in the unique offerings of the Stenches? Quite the contrary, dear boy! Goods from your community are among my best sellers. Where would I be without your people?!"

Cassie's ham-handed attempt to connect with Fincher left the boy feeling as if he had sipped sour stonecattle milk.

"Well, Captain Graff had offered to dedicate all Titian resources to finding cures for our mas and pas... if we basically saved the world."

"Save the world?" asked Cassie to herself before realization almost immediately set in. "Ahh, the Gloomtide! Am I wrong? You *can't* tell me I'm wrong! You were hired to go north and find a cure to the Gloomtide!"

"The details of our agreement are under Royal Confidence," roared Kruger. "It is treason to even be discussing such things!"

Cassie waved the weaselly man away. "Oh, calm down, Chestnut. You are only a lieutenant *out there*. Here, you are simply someone begging something from Cassie Hawkkends. Now, shut your mouth and keep it closed. Believe it or not, I need none of your help."

Kruger's hand went to his blade, but Cassie, almost imperceptibly, shook her head at the soldier. Kruger's own head cocked to the side in confusion before he released his sword pommel, nodding to the despised woman who may yet prove an ally.

Cassie paced for a bit longer, that knowing smile remaining on her now-blue lips.

"So, children, was the original plan to connect with the Titian Army around Woodlow, where you would be escorted further north?"

Sammi spoke up, not liking where this line of questioning was leading. "Yes, but that was when Captain Graff was in charge. Once he—"

"Just answer the question, child. Was that the original plan?"

"I suppose."

Cassie stopped before the younglings. "I'll take that as a yes. And when the Titian Army met up with you, as planned, you refused to go along with them?"

"Yes, but—"

"So, you see my dilemma here? It sounds to me like you broke the agreed upon terms of the verbal contract. Sure, your path north took a detour, but it ultimately landed you exactly where you promised to be—to meet Lieutenant Kruger."

"So, what are you saying, Miss Hawkkends?" asked Sammi.

"I'm saying, dear girl, that as one of the Deal Ministers of the Clutch, I must consider all the elements of the case, even those that *may* come to pass. I am inclined to designate you all as Wordless, meaning you have no place in the Clutch. Given that you can't stay here, I'll have to see you placed in the custody of Lieutenant Kruger and the Titian Army."

"You can't!" cried out Fincher, and Ditto looked over to see the one-eyed, lipless soldier licking his teeth in excitement.

"Calm down," insisted Ash, a stoic look on the girl's dark face. "That's not what she's saying." Ash carefully removed her Moon Medallion and held it out before her. "*This* is what she's saying. Give her this Moon Medallion and she'll find in our favor."

"*Even those that may come to pass,*" recalled Sammi, silently applauding her older sister for spotting Cassie's veiled offer.

"This cannot be allowed," shouted Kruger from the opposite side. "Is this what goes for justice here in the Clutch?! Open bribery of an official?! No wonder the Titian Empire wants nothing to do with you!"

Cassie spun to the lieutenant. "Silence, you fool! I am not a bureaucrat, and this is not a government! We only care about fair deals here. And the execution of those deals. I am offering a time-critical service in exchange for a rare item." Turning back to Ash, she said, "Do we have a deal, young miss?"

"Don't do it," argued Fincher. "We'll find another way."

"It's okay," said Ash. "I didn't really earn it anyway." She held the Moon Medallion out to Cassie. "You find in our favor as a Deal Minister, and I hand over this Moon Medallion."

"Agreed," replied Cassie, not missing a beat. The Woman took the medallion from Ash and then spat into her right hand. "Make it official?"

Although hesitant, Ash spat into her lone hand and shook Cassie's. The deal had been made.

"Are we made right, Cassie?" asked Spyrros hopefully as the Woman studied her newest acquisition.

"Yes, Trademaster. All is forgiven. Next time, think twice before setting aside rare items for your own personal dealings. I will not be so merciful if you cross me again."

"A momentary lack of judgment! Nothing more, Cassie! It will never happen again."

Kruger continued to vent his frustration as Cassie slowly made her way back up the dais. As she settled onto her throne, Cassie's yellow-green eyes refused to leave the swirling Moon Medallion. She ran a finger along the edge of the strange material, as if it were the face of an old lover.

When Cassie was finally able to tear her gaze away from the item, she found herself in the middle of a real mess, with Vassily arguing with the Chestnuts as her own guards waited to pounce.

"Lieutenant Kruger!" Cassie's powerful voice demanded silence from the entire chamber. "My task as Deal Minister has ended. The official stance of the Clutch is that the deal was materially broken once Captain Graff was attacked, leaving these children to fend for themselves. Because of this, the Clutch cannot surrender these younglings from Crimmish to you. The Clutch, as Quaan's preeminent trading house, has washed its hands clean of this matter."

Kruger's narrow face was now beet red. "The Imperator will hear about this! You can be sure of it!"

Cassie sat amused atop her throne. "Oh, I am sure of it, Lieutenant Kruger. Now, please leave my chambers, and take your motley band with you. Our business is done here." Kruger attempted to renew his complaints, but Cassie simply spoke over the man. "Of course, if you feel that you have been personally wronged, apart from your dealings, that is something that you can pronounce as a separate issue. There are mechanisms in place to address personal feuds. But not in these chambers."

It took several beats, but Kruger's toothy snarl finally fell away as the officer at last realized what Cassie was proposing. He bowed low to the conniving Clutch founder.

"Of course, you are right, Cassie! Soldiers! Let us be gone from the Woman's chambers."

Despite appearing profoundly confused, the Titian soldiers did as they were told, following Benson Kruger as the narrow-faced man exited Cassie's chambers and moved down the ornate hall toward the staircase. While Kruger refused to look at the children, the lipless man flicked his tongue between dirty fingers as he passed the girls, his ogre-like companion in tow.

"Thank you, Miss Hawkkends," said Sammi.

"Think nothing of it, girl."

"Are we free to go?" asked Fincher.

"You're not a prisoner, dear boy."

"Could have farking fooled me," mumbled Fincher.

"What was that, boy?"

Ash cut in. "He wondered if you had any tips for traveling north."

"As a matter of fact, I do." A pause. "Don't."

Fincher hopped back in. "Didn't you figure out what our mission is? Don't you want us to find a cure? Aren't you afraid of the Gloomtide?"

Cassie made a big show of glancing around the room before placing the Moon Medallion around her neck. "Look around, children. How could I ever feel gloomy?" The Woman snapped her fingers. "I'm afraid our time is up, as well. I hope you feel like you made a good deal. I sure do."

"Come," said Vassily gently, sweeping the kids from Crimmish away from the dais and the dangerous woman who lounged atop it. The Trademaster gave another bow before following.

Sammi spoke to the block of a man as they walked. "Mister Vassily, I feel like we're walking out with the worst deal possible."

Vassily looked down through small eyes. "I've seen worse, young miss. At least you still have your legs to walk out on."

"Farking fair enough."

Sammi giggled. "Yeah, what he said."

Spyrros, Vassily, and the quartet of Crimmish kids descended the elegant staircase, passed more Clutch Guards, and began making their way through the busy Game Lair. A small crowd waited ahead of them, blocking their path.

"Oh, what the fark is it now?"

Lieutenant Benson Kruger stepped out from the group. If the officer usually had the look of a wolf, he now looked like a wolf chasing down its injured, blood-soaked quarry.

"Cassie's Clutch," proclaimed Kruger loudly, drawing the attention of scores of nearby gamers. "I am Lieutenant Benson Kruger, and *these younglings* have spat in the face of the Titian Empire and have personally injured me by showing clear and obvious disdain toward my authority, a dangerous thing for an officer during wartime!"

"What is going on here?" came the powerful, familiar voice from behind. The children turned to find Cassie gliding across the Game Lair floor, surrounded by her Clutch Guard.

Kruger's eyes searched the crowd until they met Cassie's own. A moment passed between them.

"Cassie, these children have inflicted major damage to my reputation, and I demand satisfaction."

Cassie continued to glide closer, finally stopping her entourage several steps behind the children.

"Are you saying, Lieutenant Kruger, that you were personally harmed by the actions of these Crimmish kids?"

Kruger smiled at the setup, like two entertainers falling into an old routine. "Yes, that's right, Cassie! After having a civilized conversation about a breached agreement, this group made some extremely unconscionable remarks, making me look bad in the eyes of my men and women—people I need to follow and fear me!"

"What, exactly, were the remarks, Lieutenant Kruger?" asked Cassie.

Kruger hesitated but soon realized Cassie would not be letting the details go unannounced.

"They called me a Danglin' Andy." Chuckles spread across the Game Lair. "And followed that up by calling me a Queefin' Kelly!" Raucous laughter broke out throughout the growing audience. "It's not funny!"

Cassie spoke over the background noise. "So, you feel personally affronted?"

"I do! By the Five Sisters, I do! This has directly impacted my ability to lead! My ability to advance in my career!"

Fincher leaned into Ditto. "What a farking moaner."

Cassie ignored Fincher, instead opting to shout out loud to no one in particular.

"Clutch Guard! What do we offer if two parties have personal issues with each other, away from the mechanics of any deal?"

"The Pitt, Cassie," came the return call from all the Clutch Guards in attendance.

"Surely, you can't be serious?" stated Vassily flatly, but the Keeper was similarly ignored.

"That's right. Although I deemed the contract voided, there are still personal injuries that must be accounted for. Lieutenant Kruger, do you wish to announce an official grievance against this collection of younglings?"

"I do, Cassie!"

"And are you willing to send one of your representatives into the Pitt to seek retribution?"

"I am, Cassie!"

"What is happening?" asked Ditto.

"We're getting shited on, Ditto. We're getting doubly shited on."

"Very well." Cassie stared down at the children. "Younglings, you have a choice to make. You have been called out publicly for personally injuring another. From what I see, there is a case to be made."

"Funny, that isn't what you said two farking minutes ago!"

Cassie's tone switched to one she would use when speaking with a dog. "Poor boy, these are two very separate issues. I resolved the first in your favor in a Deal Minister capacity. But I'm afraid my hands are tied when it comes to personal grudges and vendettas. All I can do is offer a fair battleground."

Ash, although she had lost the most, remained calm, as if she understood the world of adults better than any, and was not surprised in the least by their lies.

"You mentioned a choice, Miss Hawkkends. What choice do we need to make?"

Cassie glanced down at the Moon Medallion before answering. "When two groups experience irreconcilable differences, they can take their dispute to the Pitt, where one champion representing each side will battle it out."

"To the death?" asked Sammi fearfully.

Cassie shrugged noncommittally. "Oftentimes. Although some do submit before the lights go out permanently."

Ditto watched as the lipless, white-eyed Chestnut stared lustily at Ash. Another soldier leaned in and whispered something that both found humorous. When the man caught Ditto looking at him, he brought his filthy fingers to his nose, making a show out of sniffing them.

"I'm still confused as to what choice we have to make," said Ash.

Cassie played with the many rings on her left hand. "It couldn't be simpler. Elect someone from your little group to fight for resolution in the Pitt, or relinquish your right to a fair, physical trial."

"What happens in that scenario?"

"You are basically admitting guilt, and the opposing side can make whatever demand they want. In your case, I would assume that Lieutenant Kruger would like to take you as captives so that you may conclude your business together under his watchful eye. Would I be correct in that assumption, Lieutenant?"

"The Woman is wise," agreed Kruger.

"And we can keep that massive collection of Chestnuts of yours away from my Clutch?"

"Of course, Cassie. I see no reason for any Titian to enter your domain now... unless it's to spend chips."

The children came together, although Ditto's green eyes remained pasted on the lipless Chestnut.

"She farking screwed us," complained Fincher. "How the fark does any real business get done in this shite hole?"

"Well, we don't really have any choice to make," stated Ash.

"What do you mean, sis?"

"We're just kids. There's no way any of us could fight any of them. We're out of options, I'm afraid. I think we're just gonna have to go with them, maybe find a way to escape during the journey north."

Ditto watched as the lipless man continued to stare at Ash, his hand slowly moving toward his crotch. The scarred Chestnut then began massaging the front of his pants, wetting his teeth with his tongue every few seconds.

"But that would just be farking giving up," declared Fincher.

"Do you want to go into the Pitt with one of those killers, Fincher?" asked Sammi.

"Well… no."

"Then Ash is right. There is no choice to make. We'll—"

"I'll go to the Pitt," declared Ditto loudly, forcing a shroud of silence onto the chamber.

Ash and Sammi wore stunned looks as Fincher's jaw fell to his chest.

"Then, it is decided," stated Cassie, although there was something vibrating beneath the surface of her words, as if this was one turn that she didn't see coming. "Prepare the Pitt! Spread word across the Game Lair. See these two groups downstairs—and keep them away from each other!"

The Clutch Guard then stepped between the Chestnuts and the children, removing the Titian soldiers from the Game Lair first.

Vassily searched the room desperately for help but found none. "Is no one going to stop this madness?! These are children!"

"They are traders, Vassily," corrected Cassie. "And all traders are equal, regardless of age or sex or station. Spyrros, take your Keeper down before he finds himself in the Pitt for insulting the Woman of the Clutch."

"How dare you?" started Vassily, but he was pulled away by the Trademaster, who did everything in his power to talk over his bodyguard so that Cassie might not pick up on the words being thrown her way.

Sammi held Ash as her older sister cried in her arms.

When Fincher was finally able to lift his jaw, he found Ditto standing alone, an unreadable expression on his large friend's face.

"Oh, Ditto, what have you farking done?"

"Just trying to keep our friends safe, Fincher. Just trying to keep *you* safe."

"Oh, Ditto, do you *always* have to be so farking good?"

"I'm not going to be *good* in an hour, Fincher."

"How can you possibly win, Ditto?"

"I don't know, Fincher. Maybe I can't. But I couldn't live with myself if I didn't at least try." Fincher's hazel eyes began to water. "I'm sorry, my friend."

"Me, too, my friend. Me farking too."

15

SACRIFICE IN THE PITT

On the bottom level of the ChippHouse, one floor below the Trade Hive, was the Pitt. Sitting in the middle of a room about one-quarter the size of the Game Lair, the Pitt was a circular area partially sunk into the floor, with walls that rose out to a height of four feet. Bleachers and chairs were placed on three sides of the Pitt while an unsurprising dais dominated the back of the room. The bottom of the Pitt was hard-packed sand with blood (both old and recent) splattered throughout.

An absolute buzz filled the room as excited patrons of the ChippHouse started to fill seats and find spots along the bleachers. Word had obviously spread quickly, and while dice and cards were fun, there was nothing more exciting to gamble on than human life. Men and women in white sashes sped from one spectator to the next, recounting current odds and taking bets, writing everything down in small notebooks.

Between the dais and the Pitt were two open areas along the wall, ostensibly for the two aggrieved parties.

The group once known as the Sour Flower Gang entered the room to guffaws, cackles, and outright disbelief.

"Hey, I was told they was young, not that they was babies," cried out one audience member in protest.

"Yeah, who's gonna bet on this sham of a fight?" shouted another.

Cassie Hawkkends, sitting on another of her presumably many ornate chairs atop the dais, called down to the rowdy crowd.

"Don't like the matchup? There are many bets to make beyond mere victor and loser. Still don't like it? Then get out! If you aren't gambling, then you're not watching!"

The Woman's harsh words quieted the protests as none wanted to miss the show, regardless of whether it was a massacre or not.

Ditto, Ash, Sammi, and Fincher followed Spyrros and Vassily around to the left of the Pitt, taking note of the Chestnuts already waiting within one of the empty areas. The Titian soldiers laughed, pointed, and made crude gestures as the children rounded the sunken area and came to a stop in the other designated preparation space. Benson Kruger appeared particularly excited for the fight, bloodlust apparent on his narrow face.

Fincher, Sammi, and Ash had already spent the last thirty minutes attempting in vain to talk some sense into their large friend. Ash was especially upset, finding it difficult to form coherent sentences through her tears. In the end, Ditto would not budge, stating simply that there was no other way. His friends had no choice but to support their friend.

As the younglings looked around in fear and shock of the scene unfolding around them, Spyrros and Vassily joined Cassie on the dais. While Spyrros quietly took a seat far from the Woman of the Clutch, Vassily elected to sit right next to Cassie, close enough to converse in a low tone.

"This is madness, Cassie," the Keeper angrily whispered. "How could you let such a thing happen?! This is madness!"

"Yes, I heard you the first time, Keeper. And I'm not disputing it."

"Then why?!"

Cassie spun to face Vassily, and the veteran warrior saw things he had never seen in the Woman's yellow-green eyes—fear and doubt. And perhaps a twinge of sadness.

"Do you think I want this?" she hissed. "But what would you have me do? You may not have heard, but the largest Titian army assembled in decades is sitting right outside my door, looking for a reason to burn this place to cinders!"

"The Clutch has always held out," offered Vassily weakly.

"Against the odd contingent of Chestnuts, sure. But against the full might of the Titian Empire? And do not doubt that is what's waiting to the east."

Vassily thought for a moment. "You have never shown anything but contempt and disregard for the Chestnuts."

"Not everyone is built like a rockslide, you fool. Some us have to fake it to make it."

Vassily's arm shot out toward the Pitt. "Fine, but why *this*?"

Spyrros listened in carefully despite the distance, a necessary component of his job as Trademaster. The fact that Cassie was even explaining herself to the Keeper meant that the Woman must be truly torn.

"What was I to do, Keeper?! I could not simply hand over the children to the Chestnuts based on their agreement. I would look as if I was a stooge for the Titians and might as well have the Sluggs kill me now. So, I officially ruled against the Titians."

"That could have been the end of it, Cassie."

"This is why you are a Keeper—dumb muscle—and I founded the greatest trading post in all of Quaan. The Titian Empire, in full, has arrived *for these children*. They were getting them one way or another, whether that be peacefully through the front entrance or violently through the ruins of everything I've sacrificed to build! At least this way, my hands are clean. It was a personal grudge, nothing connecting me to Chestnut politics." Cassie theatrically wiped her hands together and turned away from the Keeper.

Vassily watched Cassie squirm under the weight of her own words, the protector's scar tissue-wrapped eyes boring holes in the Woman's soul.

After several beats, the Woman twisted back heatedly.

"And for the record, you judgmental arse, I never thought the children would accept the fight! I thought they would simply go along with the Titians. That way, I got my medallion, protected my reputation as a Trader, *and* discreetly gave the durned Chestnuts what they wanted. But, no! This... *boy,* has to have more heart than the entire Clutch Guard. Curse him! This is not my fault!"

"Who are you trying to convince, Cassie?"

"Not you, you mound of chatting stone! Now, get away from me before I have you added to the card. You against ten of my guard sound about right?"

Vassily knew he was on thin ice and moved away from the divided Clutch founder. Meanwhile, the Pitt continued to fill with men and women happily discussing the gruesomeness they were about to witness.

Cassie reached over to the silver stand to her left and poured herself an extra-tall glass of honey rice wine with a shaky hand. She downed the alcohol and repeated the exercise until her hand no longer shook.

The Woman had readied herself for the atrocity she was about to commit. She stood.

"Patrons of the ChippHouse," called out Cassie from above as the final spectators entered and began to fill the few remaining seats. "Welcome to the Pitt!" An eruption of applause followed. When it finally began to quiet, she continued. "We are here to settle a grievance between two parties! The details no longer matter, for they have already been deemed worthy of violent resolve. To my right is the offending party—the Children of Crimmish!" A mixture of cheers, jeers, shouts, and curses sprang into the increasingly thick, tense air. Cassie leaned down to address the younglings. "Visitors from Crimmish! Who shall be your champion to resolve this disagreement?"

Ditto raised his hand without hesitation to great applause. His three friends swallowed down the bile that rose up in their throats.

"Your name, young man?"

"Ditto… I mean, Deetarik Bugg!"

Cassie nodded. "Well represented, Deetarik Bugg!" The Woman rotated to the collection of Chestnuts. "To my left is the offended party—soldiers of the Titian Empire!" Many, many more boos than cheers followed. "Titians! Who shall be your champion?"

The white-eyed, lipless soldier stepped forward confidently, but was pushed back by Kruger.

"Not you, Swinley," shouted the Lieutenant as his subordinate's face twisted in rage. "You're good, but I need a sure thing."

"Are you stupid?" demanded the lipless Swinley, forgetting his place. "I'll wear this boy's carcass as a boa! His corpse will be cold before the final bets are in! You have to let me—"

"That's enough, Swinley," shouted Kruger, finally silencing his irate soldier.

As usual, Fincher couldn't resist. "Hey, Swinley, you heard him. He thinks you're too much of a Danglin' Andy to fight a twelve-year-old. And you know what? *We all* think he's right!"

"You little shite," roared Swinley, having to be held back by three other Chestnuts.

"Enough! Enough! Enough," bellowed Cassie from above, effectively quieting the room. "Lieutenant Kruger! Who will be your champion?"

A dark glint shone in Kruger's animal eyes. "Angiss Blatch will be our champion!"

"Oh, fark me," muttered Fincher as the Titian ogre stepped forward and released a primal cry into the air. Closer to seven foot than six, the massive Chestnut named Angiss sported tattoos under thick body hair, a flattened nose, several gaps where teeth should have been, and a chunk of missing scalp that exposed the monster's white skull.

After an initial collective gasp, calls for bets dominated the auditory landscape as spectators threw life savings behind various methods by which the ogre Angiss Blatch might kill the boy Deetarik Bugg.

These wagers doubled as Angiss removed his Titian vest and shirt, revealing mounds of muscle topped with a potpourri of scars, burns, fresh cuts, and ridiculously objectionable tattoos.

"Fark me, Ditto, you've already shown you've got giant cobblers. Let's just go with them and be done with it! What could be worse than seeing our friend beaten to death?"

Ditto's green eyes flared. "Watching my friends be molested and knowing I did nothing to stop it."

"I know, Ditto, but can't you see?"

Ditto's hand on Fincher's shoulder calmed the younger friend. "I can see, Fincher. And it's okay." He bent down to whisper in his friend's ear. "And I'm counting on you to figure things out after."

"Figure out what?!"

Ditto rose to his full height. "I don't know. But you always do!"

"Farking good guy! Why do you have to be so farking good?!"

Sammi opted for a much simpler approach. The small girl wiped tears from under her glasses before standing on her tiptoes to hug her friend.

"Good luck, Ditto. We love you. You concede once you've made your point."

When Sammi stepped aside, Ditto could see that Ash was despondent at the edge of the small clearing. He went to her.

"Wish me luck, Ash?"

The girl spoke in a watery voice. "I don't want to wish you luck, Ditto. I want to take you out of here."

"Maybe you still can."

"You! Not your lifeless body!"

"Maybe you still can."

Ash looked up with tear-soaked cheeks. "You think so?"

"You never know. But a hug from a friend never—"

Ash buried Ditto in a hug, soaking his shoulder in the process. She pulled the boy in tight, desperately hoping that her physical touch could convey the feelings that her mind and mouth had been unable to express. Ditto reciprocated, even placing a gentle kiss atop the girl's forehead.

When they finally separated, Ash was surprised to find a Moon

Medallion around her neck, replacing the one that she had traded away. After studying the swirling white pendant for a moment, the girl looked up with waterlogged brown eyes.

"But why?"

Ditto presented one of the big boy's famous shrugs. "A pretty stone should have a pretty wearer. Plus, despite what you think, you *have* earned it."

Ash began to argue, but Ditto turned away, peeling off his shirt in the process, leaving only the Ghost Puma tooth to touch his scarred, hairless chest. He handed his shirt to Fincher, and the two exchanged knowing nods. Ditto's hunting knife and other valuables had already been packed away in Fincher's sack—along with the too-many socks the boy refused to part with.

Fincher grabbed Ditto as the large boy began to walk away.

"You farking concede when the time comes. Make your point and concede. Let me figure out the rest."

"It'll probably be me who figures it out," said Sammi from the side, attempting to inject some levity into the dark situation.

Fincher shrugged helplessly. "She's probably right."

"I know," said Ditto with a smile. "I gotta go. I love you all. See you in a bit."

With that, Deetarik Bugg, better known by his dear friends as Ditto, followed the ogre Angiss Blatch down the small ladder and into the Pitt, where the two would face off in a violent and potentially deadly exchange.

As soon as his big feet touched down into the Pitt, Angiss moved to the far side, scooping some sand into his hands and rubbing his palms together in the process. The ogre was no novice to pit fighting.

Ditto moved to the opposite side, intensely studying the battlefield for any tactical strategy or potential trickery. Seconds later, the large boy sighed deeply, finding none.

"Stop this now, Cassie," begged Vassily from the side.

"Shut up, fool," the Woman shot back. "It's too late now! Plus, the boy will quit after the first solid blow. I will be quick to stop it once the admission of guilt is given. My guards are already on notice."

"Yes, but what if—"

"One more word and I'll have you barbecued."

Vassily fell silent, knowing the Woman's words were not an empty threat.

Cassie addressed the room. "Angiss Blatch and Deetarik Bugg! You have both been elected as champions of your respective parties. Violence has yet to occur! Either of you can concede now, and the matter will be resolved without bloodshed!" Neither combatant moved. "Very well. You have both been stripped of weapons. No outside assistance is allowed. You battle until one of two things occur. Either one of you surrenders… or one of you dies. Those are the only two options. There is nothing noble in the latter." Cassie seemed to be addressing Ditto. "If the fight is lost, you would be smart to concede."

"Stop swaying the bets," shouted someone from the throng.

"Yeah, I got good chips on a fatality," added another.

"Me, too!"

"Yeah, yeah! I need one of these farkers dead!"

Cassie Hawkkends almost retched onto her dais, wondering what kind of world she had helped build. But the Woman recovered quickly, as she always did, and swept away the unsettling thoughts.

"Very well! Angiss Blatch! Deetarik Bugg! You are foes of the Pitt! Only one can climb out the victor! Do battle! And may the righteous prove the stronger! Engage!"

Ditto Bugg surprised everyone by immediately charging the oafish Chestnut. Angiss laughed as the boy rushed in, tossing out a lazy backhand that Ditto easily slipped under.

When the boy came up, he did so with body and foot, slamming the top of his boot into the Titian's testicles. Angiss doubled over in pain, and Ditto swung a wicked elbow that caught the giant in the temple, sending the man spinning away. Angiss reached out and caught the Pitt's curving wall at the last moment. Had he not, the first knockdown would have certainly gone to Ditto Bugg.

Fincher jumped up and down as he peered over the wall and down into the Pitt. "That's right," he screamed, so loudly that he almost lost his voice. "The cobblers! Even the biggest bastard is soft around the cobblers!"

On the Titian side of things, words were much more tense.

"See," shouted Swinley to Kruger," this is why you should have chosen me!"

"If that was you, *Swinley*, we'd already be on our farking way," called out Fincher. "Danglin' Andys don't last long in the Pitt!"

"You little snot! I'm gonna roast you over a spit! I'm gonna—"

"Enough," roared Kruger. "The fight has just begun, you fools!"

Sadly, the Lieutenant was correct. Angiss Blatch had already recovered from Ditto's flash offense, easily blocking the boy's next three punches before grabbing ahold of both the child's wrists.

Ditto, his arms trapped, attempted to kick out, but Angiss simply lifted him into the air and spun, releasing the large boy after one quick turn. Ditto flew across the Pitt and slammed into the wall on the far side. The audience collectively winced as the dull thud of skull on concrete reverberated throughout the Pitt.

Ditto plummeted to the sandy bottom after the collision, leaving a bright red spot behind.

"Oh, no, he's dead," said Sammi through the hands at her mouth.

"No, he's not! Shut your mouth," spat Ash, the young girl on the brink of hysteria.

"He's farking tougher than that. Look! He's getting up!"

Fincher was correct. After a few seconds, Ditto crawled to his feet and stood on rubbery legs.

Cassie discreetly released a relieved sigh. "Deetarik Bugg! Do you concede?!"

"I do not!"

Fincher shook his head and spoke to himself. "Farking heck, Ditto. Farking heck."

Angiss Blatch did not await further instruction, instead opting to carefully march forward, no longer willing to take the large boy before him lightly. Angiss rubbed the growing knot on his temple. The ogre growled, no longer considering this a dramatic show. If the boy wanted to play for blood, Angiss was willing to oblige him.

Despite still not having his balance, Ditto did well to dodge and duck the first few strikes from Angiss, the man's disfigured knuckles just missing the boy's face.

Unable to land any blows of his own from this range, Ditto was forced to move in close, getting inside the brute's vicious attacks while risking getting grabbed up by the large man. What Ditto didn't anticipate, however, was the massive knee that flew in to greet him, connecting squarely with his chest and launching him backward to land heavily on the Pitt floor.

Ditto immediately spun to his stomach, rose up on his hands and knees, and let out a loud wheezing noise, desperately attempting to get air back into his lungs.

Angiss Blatch gave the boy no such opportunity, rushing forward and kicking Ditto in the side with all his strength, sending the child spinning once more, this time coming to rest on the opposite side of the Pitt, just beneath the other Crimmish kids.

"His ribs have to be shattered," stated Sammi flatly, and Fincher looked over to his bespectacled friend. A blank look had taken over her dark face, and Fincher knew that Sammi had gone somewhere else in her mind, away from the horror that was taking place before them.

Ditto once more tried to rise, so Angiss waded in and delivered a crushing uppercut to the boy's face that left the youngling sprawled out and wearing a crimson mask.

"Deetarik Bugg! Do you yield?" cried out Cassie from above, her voice full with anxiety.

"No," yelled Ditto from his back, spitting up significant blood in the process.

"Ditto, you must," begged Ash from the wall. "Please, give up! You've done enough!"

"His insides are filling with blood," said Sammi, sounding far removed.

"Shut up! Shut up!"

Back in the Pitt, Angiss Blatch looked helplessly to his group of Titians.

Kruger screamed back. "What are you waiting for, you fool?! Finish him! Let them see what happens to those who oppose the Empire!"

Angiss nodded, less than excited about what was to come next. Moving closer to the felled boy, the ogre reached down and collected Ditto by the throat, raising him into the air by his neck.

"Sorry, lad," said Angiss as he squeezed the life from Ditto, whose arms flailed as his bloody face grew even redder and capillaries burst in his green eyes. "But you made a good showing. You can die as a man." The giant's hands tightened.

Darkness began to creep in around the edges of Ditto's vision. Soon, only Angiss's scarred face remained. The cacophony of the Pitt also fell away, and only the sounds of a pleading Ash reached the nearly unconscious boy.

In a final act of defiance, Ditto grabbed at the Ghost Puma tooth at his chest, missing it the first few attempts.

Just as all went black, however, Ditto caught the tooth, ripping it free from its leather chord and swinging it in one smooth motion. Thinking it just a punch, Angiss accepted the blow—and the one after and the one after—only understanding that something was amiss when his mouth began to fill with blood and rivers of red started to stain his chest and arms.

The Chestnut released Ditto, dropping the boy to the ground as he reached up to discover a massive hole in his left cheek. Ditto coughed as he crawled away, forcing air through his bruised windpipe and clutching the blood-soaked Puma tooth.

"What has he done to me?" demanded Angiss as he sprinted over to his Chestnut allies. "Is it bad?! Is it bad?!"

The Titians all grimaced as their colleague's injury became clear. Angiss's entire left cheek looked like undried jerky, with long strands of skin hanging down from his face. The man's rotten teeth could be seen through the meaty drapes.

Swinley giggled at the gruesome scene. "Don't worry, Angiss, the ladies will still take you... It might just take a little more coercing!" Swinley licked his teeth where his upper lip ended. "Take it from me!"

Swinley's callousness further enraged the maimed soldier. "He's dead! He's farking dead!"

Angiss Blatch, blind with fury, spun to find that Ditto had climbed to his feet once more and waited patiently across the Pitt, both hands balled up at his sides.

"Do you yield?" called out Ditto, and raucous laughter filled the room.

In response, Angiss ran forward, oversized fists clenched. No longer would he choke the boy unconscious. No, Angiss now vowed to leave a steaming pile of meat behind, one resembling what was done to his cheek.

Ditto, predicting his opponent's foolish rage, steeled himself, remaining unmoved as Angiss hurriedly advanced.

As soon as the boy was within reach, Angiss leapt into a straight right, meaning to take Ditto's head clean off his shoulders.

Luckily, the boy saw it coming, stepping to his left to avoid the blow. Ditto then ducked and slipped to the right, sliding under the ogre's left hook that was thrown with even worse intentions. As Ditto shot up from the evasive maneuver, the boy's clenched right hand swung around and opened, sending a fistful of sand and dirt into the brute's disfigured cheek.

Angiss roared in pain as the sharp grains lodged themselves against tongue, muscle, gums, and raw nerves, working their way deep into the wound. The Chestnut fell to his knees, one hand to the side of his face as he attempted to spit out a mouthful of sand.

As his opponent tried to recover, Ditto darted back in from behind, using both hands to claw at the exposed skull alongside the top of Angiss's head. The boy's nails found where skull gave way to scalp, and he raked down with all his might, further ripping flesh from bone.

The crowd went into a frenzy as the huge Chestnut roared and twisted violently, sending a left backhand through the air like a scythe. Ditto spotted the strike and tried to back away but was too late, Angiss's agony lending impossible speed to the blow.

The ogre's gnarled hand smashed into Ditto's jaw and the boy collapsed where he stood onto the Pitt floor that was becoming increasingly stained with gore.

"Oh, no," cried Ash, sobbing.

"Fark me," whispered Fincher.

"He's done," stated Sammi.

"Do you yield, Deetarik Bugg?" called out Cassie as Ditto stared up. There was no recognition in the boy's green eyes.

"No," shouted Angiss, still clutching his mangled cheek. "It's too late for that! It's too late!"

Cassie ignored the brute. "Deetarik Bugg! You must concede!"

"Never!"

Fincher and Ash's eyes snapped shut, unable to bear witness to what would come next.

Unable to stand, Ditto crab-walked away for a bit before rolling onto his stomach. As he did, Angiss kicked out with a boot, catching the youngling in the arse and propelling him headfirst into the Pitt wall.

Another *crack* echoed through the room as Ditto's forehead split open, sending more blood to cascade down the boy's sweet face.

Leaning against the wall for support, Ditto tried to face his opponent, but ate a right hook to the jaw just as he attempted to turn. The boy folded to the floor and was greeted with three swift kicks to the side, each of which caused wads of blood to fly from Ditto's mouth.

"That's enough, please," implored Ash through heaving sobs, the girl only hearing the violence being done to her friend.

"You must stop this," demanded Vassily, who had returned to Cassie's side.

"Deetarik Bugg! Concede this instant! This is your last chance!"

"The fark it is," stated a breathless Angiss Blatch coldly. "Last chance done passed. You hear me, boy?! It's done passed!"

To accentuate his point, the Chestnut reared back and kicked out again, his heavy boot getting under the boy's ribs and sending Ditto airborne to crash several feet away.

"Dumb little bastard," shouted one spectator.

"Fark me! Last time I take a long shot," complained another.

"The Reaper's taking this one," cried out a third excitedly.

As Fincher and Ash's heads continued to fall, Sammi's sprang up, as if the girl had been startled awake from a deep slumber.

"That's it," Sammi said to herself. "Of course, that's it!"

Fincher and Ash's eyes popped opened and flashed to their young friend, desperation painted across their faces. Sammi ignored them, sliding the pack from her shoulders and dropping to her knees. When Sammi finally stood up, the girl was holding the Ghost Puma stomach between her hands.

"Yes! Farking yes! Do it!"

Sammi couldn't hear Fincher shouting right next to her, so focused was the girl on untying the stomach knot with shaking fingers.

"Hurry, Sammi," cried Ash as Ditto was again punched in the face, sending the boy stumbling back toward his friends. Ditto managed to stay upright for several seconds before falling to the dirt. The large boy looked up with a swollen eye and through a mask of red, and seemed to say a silent goodbye.

"Not yet," said Sammi as she finally undid the complicated knot and opened the Ghost Puma stomach.

"Come to me, boy! It ends now," bellowed Angiss Blatch from behind Ditto, drawing every eye in the room to the ogre, his missing cheek, and the horrifying chunk of skull peering out from beneath the man's blood-soaked hair.

Just as the Chestnut called out, Sammi Bugg discreetly dropped the dried Reaper Vine over the lip of the wall. The inconspicuous brown tendril blended in perfectly with packed sand, rendering it nearly invisible.

Sammi leaned over the wall and snapped her fingers, trying to catch Ditto's attention. The boy's wandering gaze fell onto the bespectacled girl.

"Ditto! Look down! Here!" She pointed down with a dark finger.

Although he was having difficulty focusing, Ditto eventually spied the Reaper Vine laying against the Pitt wall. A grim smile found its way onto the boy's gnarled face.

"That's right," said Sammi quietly. "You get him, Ditto."

"Farking kill that farker, Ditto!"

Ditto grunted as he crawled forward, his lone eye locked onto the Reaper Vine. Just as he was about to reach it, however, Ditto was ripped backward by Angiss Blatch, who violently twisted the boy over and mounted him.

Sitting heavy on the boy's hips, Angiss laughed maniacally as he slapped Ditto repeatedly, sending rays of blood across the sand. Ditto reached back with everything he had, but it was no use. The Reaper Vine was too far from his grasp.

Angiss raised off Ditto a bit, giving himself the space needed to deliver a killing blow.

"The cobblers," shrieked Fincher. "The farking cobblers!"

Ditto reacted immediately, his left hand shooting up to grab Angiss by the crotch. With the little bit of strength he had left, Ditto squeezed, drawing a squeal from the Chestnut and forcing the soldier back a few steps. As he did, Ditto flopped back onto his stomach and writhed forward.

"Little shite," roared Angiss, snatching Ditto up by the back of his neck, pulling the boy in close, and throwing his massive right arm under the boy's chin and across his throat. Once the Chestnut's right hand gripped his left bicep, Angiss squeezed, ready for this costly battle to be done.

As the ogre compressed the life out of Ditto, the boy reached up weakly, his right hand just barely touching Angiss's face. Several seconds went by, and Ditto's features began to fall.

Just as the contest seemed to be at its end, Ditto plummeted yet again to the Pitt floor as Angiss backpedaled, a strange, wild look on the man's face. The Chestnut's eyes went wide with panic and his mouth opened and closed like fish tossed upon the shore.

"Now, Ditto! Farking now!"

"Go, Ditto, please!"

"Get up! You have to get up!"

His face was red. His eye was shut. His face swollen and bloody beyond recognition. His lungs rattled like an instrument. But Ditto

Bugg willed himself back to his hands, then his knees, then his feet, his right hand holding something in a death grip.

With nothing else to do, Angiss rushed at Ditto, surprised when the boy did not attempt to run or dodge. Ditto simply waited, accepting a swat to the side of his head as he stepped forward, running his right hand down Angiss's bare chest.

Another elbow sent Ditto spinning away and the ogre moved to give chase. He stopped, however, and looked down at his chest. Black lines had appeared under the surface of the veteran soldier's scarred skin. Where they rose, it felt as if fire had been injected into his veins.

Angiss Blatch fell to his knees, swatting at his chest as if there were flames to be extinguished.

"What's this?" demanded Kruger from above the Pitt wall. "Something's wrong! Something's wrong!" His weasel face spun toward Cassie. "Something foul has transpired out there!"

"I see nothing but heart out there, Lieutenant. Now, turn back around before I have yours removed."

As Angiss tore at his chest, Ditto once again shocked the audience by climbing to his feet, cheers from the rowdy crowd now urging him on.

"Fark my wager, let's see the boy win!"

"One in a million, this is! I've never been happier to lose chips!"

Ditto stumbled forward, a monumental achievement given his injuries. Unable to properly breathe and still combating invisible fires, Angiss did not note the boy's approach.

In a seemingly foolish tactic, Ditto timed Angiss's flailing, darted ahead, and open-hand slapped the giant Chestnut, perfectly connecting with the gory hole in his opponent's cheek.

Angiss's thrashing immediately ceased as the man's scarred face adopted a dumb, confused look. As Ditto snuck around behind his challenger, Angiss reached into his mouth and pulled out what looked like a bloody twig.

As the Chestnut studied the object through blurry eyes, Ditto attacked, wrapping his arm across Angiss's thick neck and driving the dying man to the dirt.

Then, it was Ditto's turn to squeeze. And while it was the Reaper Vine that was truly killing Angiss Blatch, Ditto's arms shook with effort, putting every ounce of himself into the choke as time was lost to rage.

Ditto did not know how long he held the choke, or how long the audience had watched him asphyxiate a corpse. Finally, however, the large boy known as Ditto Bugg stood triumphantly over his larger foe as the room exploded in pandemonium.

Cassie Hawkkends, looking beyond relieved, stood and addressed the room.

"Deetarik Bugg! Congratulations, you are the victor! It has been determined by the laws of the Pitt that you and your friends have given no personal offense."

"The fark they haven't," yelled Kruger. "Something happened in that Pitt, and I call for a full investigation!"

"Request denied."

"I'm taking those rotten kids with me! The Clutch be durned!"

"Are you refusing to accept the outcome of the Pitt?"

Kruger's fury was past the point of considering his words. "Fark your Pitt, you wench!"

Cassie grinned wickedly. "The show is over! See the White Sashes to collect your winnings, although I doubt many of you won on today's show of bravery. Clear the room!"

The crowd, still buzzing from the recent display of violence and courage, did as they were told. No one wanted to risk a Pitt banning should the next contest be even remotely as entertaining as what they'd just witnessed.

When the room had emptied, Cassie went on. "Clutch Guard! Lieutenant Benson Kruger has decided that he does not want to abide by the results of the Pitt. Therefore, I find him in contempt of the ChippHouse. His lazy attitude toward arrangements and fair deals makes him and his entourage unsuitable for the Clutch. Please see them through the eastern entrance and do not allow them back in. They have lost their Clutch privileges."

"The Empire will have your head for this, wench! I will personally place your ginger head on a pike in the center of the city as it burns down around me!"

"And Clutch Guard! No need to be gentle."

With that, the butt-end of a halberd flew in from the side, cracking Kruger on the jaw and eliciting a loud curse from the enraged officer.

"You heard the Woman," said Vassily, who had borrowed one of the Guard's weapons. "Move it or you *will* be moved. Conscious or unconscious—your choice."

The Titian soldiers, surrounded and outnumbered, begrudgingly made their way to the Pitt's exit. Lieutenant Kruger hesitated, rubbing his bruised chin, before joining his men. "This isn't over, Cassie. This is just the beginning."

"I have done nothing wrong, Lieutenant. I have followed all the appropriate protocols. Just because your side failed to earn the victory does not mean that I or the Clutch is at fault. I'm sure your Imperator will feel the same way."

Kruger's teeth appeared. "The Imperator may. But the Imperatrix certainly will not. She doesn't care for you; I don't know if you knew that. You just gave her what she's always wanted. A reason."

"What do you want done with the body of your man?"

"You deal with it. Throw it to the pigs if you want. The man was a loser."

"Get out of my sight, Kruger."

Kruger followed the other Titians, his beady eyes locked on the children of Crimmish as he crossed the emptying room.

"Great farking fight, Kruger," mocked Fincher. "Next time, don't pick a farking man to do a kid's job! You Queefin' Kelly!"

Kruger simply pointed to the exit. "I'll see you all *out there*. This changes nothing, it just increases the amount of pain I'm going to inflict as you do our bidding. See you soon, kiddies."

As soon as the Chestnuts had left, Fincher, Ash, and Sammi dove into the Pitt where Ditto now lay several feet from the dead body of Angiss Blatch.

"Ditto, Ditto, Ditto," they all cried in unison as they reached their friend. Ash gently lifted the large boy's bloody head and placed it in her lap, allowing her to wipe his face with a rag.

"How did I do?" asked Ditto quietly, as if the air was being forced through a crimped straw.

"You farking won, Ditto! Who the fark back in Crimmish would dare challenge you now?"

"You did great, Ditto," added Sammi.

"Thanks for the help, Sammi. I'd be dead without you."

The girl's head dropped, sliding her glasses to the end of her nose. "I'm sorry it took so long for me to remember. I didn't even think about using it for—"

"It's okay," said Ditto. "You were there when I needed you."

Cassie's voice ripped through the empty room. "I don't mean to break up this happy moment, but you children also need to be on your way."

Ash looked up with indignation. "You're kicking us out now?! He needs to rest and heal! Look at him!"

"I am, young miss! And do not confuse my callous orders for self-interest. The Chestnuts are gathered at my gate—for you! Kruger will be back within a few hours with an army that we will not be able to turn away, lest we invite all-out war with the Titian Empire. When they reenter the city, they will search every home, flophouse, gaming den, and tavern to find you. And they *will* find you, you can be certain."

"But you can't just cast us out!"

"I am not casting you out!" Cassie looked around before lowering her voice. "This way. Follow me."

Fincher angrily hissed back. "And how the fark are we supposed to get Ditto up there?!"

Cassie thought for a moment before releasing a high-pitched whistle. The two Clutch Guards stationed outside the Pitt ducked their heads in.

"Lift the boy out of the Pitt and bring him up here. Now!"

The two guards jumped at Cassie's orders, leaping into the Pitt as Fincher moved to collect the blood-soaked Ghost Puma tooth from the sandy floor. Within a few moments, the city defenders had gently lifted Ditto into the waiting arms of his friends who had already climbed out via the small ladder. Together, they helped Ditto up the stairs and onto the raised platform.

Meanwhile, the Woman of the Clutch spun on a fashionable heel and moved to the back of the dais. She touched a nondescript area of the wall and stood back as a door swung silently inward. The children approached, Ditto draped between Fincher and Ash, Sammi carrying the large boy's pack. The kids looked at Cassie questioningly.

"What? You think this is the first Pitt contest to go sideways? I didn't get where I am today without having contingencies in place. Stay ready and you don't have to get ready, children. Let's go."

Cassie passed through the secret door and the kids from Crimmish followed. When the door quietly closed and the guards exited, the Pitt was left empty and silent. Other than the metallic taste in the air, there was nothing to show that this had been the site of a great battle between good and evil, right and wrong.

Except for the fast-bloating corpse of Angiss Blatch, who would remain there for some time before being fed to Cassie's collection of award-winning swine.

The younglings struggled to keep up with Cassie as the Woman marched through a labyrinth of small storage rooms. Ditto groaned in pain every time Fincher or Ash tried to reposition themselves under their big friend while Sammi stumbled around hauling two sacks.

Eventually, Cassie reached a massive set of double doors that had been thrown open and sped through.

"We're here," she said as the quintet entered a large loading area that was stacked high with all manner of unusual goods. There was no wall on the far side of the space, allowing teams of carts to pull up and unload their goods. It was pitch black beyond, as if something was blocking the night sky.

The half-dozen Clutch Guards present nodded respectfully toward Cassie as she crossed the room.

"This is the Northern Drop," said Cassie as she walked. "Few know about it. We use it to trade with the Cobalts, who use a small path between the Clutch and the hills."

As the group stepped out into the torch-filled night, heads went up and eyes went wide. The Five Sisters could be seen in the sky above giant, rolling hills. Every now and then, something large passed in front of one of the moons and strange sounds would echo across the uneven landscape.

Cassie's voice stole the children's attention. "Here he is. Finally." She called out to an approaching shadow. "Taking your sweet time?"

Spyrros Milaan's high voice reached the group a few seconds before the Trademaster stepped into the torchlight, two tiny horses in tow.

"Do you realize what you had me do? Given this dreadful time of evening and the list of items you had me collect, I'd say I did pretty durned well."

Cassie waved the small man away as he neared. "Fine. Fine. You did a wonderful job. Now, show me what you were able to secure."

"Well, other than these two beauties," said Spyrros, motioning to the tiny horses, "I got the balm, blankets, coats, fresh water, bandages, and a hodgepodge of food items. It's all stored on the—"

"What are those things?" interrupted Sammi, staring intently at the miniature horses.

Spyrros's grey eyes narrowed behind his gold-framed glasses. "Haven't you ever seen a scrambler before? You know, a donkey?" The children shook their heads. "Well, these are them!" To Cassie, he said, "Like I was saying, all the goods are packed away on the scramblers."

Cassie nodded. "Well done, Trademaster. You have redeemed yourself."

Spyrros shifted uncomfortably. "You know, these items weren't cheap, Cassie. Especially the scramblers. Bastards could see it on my face that I was in dire straits, so they—"

"You will be compensated, Spyrros. Now leave us."

The Trademaster delivered a small bow before turning to the Crimmish kids.

"It has been most... eventful. Good luck, children. I really mean that."

"Please tell Vassily goodbye for us," said Sammi. "And tell him, thank you."

"I will, young miss. Vassily will be delighted to hear that you departed safely. Safe travels north."

And with that, Trademaster Spyrros Milaan disappeared into the shadows, relieved he was back in the Woman's good graces.

Ash adjusted her hold on Ditto, drawing another pained grunt from the boy. "What are we doing, Miss Hawkkends?"

"You are leaving, child. You all are leaving." Cassie pointed north. "You see those hills there?"

"How could we farking miss them?"

"That is Ptero Heights. The terrain is rough and steep, which is why armies avoid it. For every three horses that go into the Heights, two have to be put down for broken legs. No one can stand to lose valuable warhorses."

Fincher looked doubtfully at the two donkeys. "And these little shites are supposed to make it?"

"Those are not mere donkeys, child. Those are scramblers, born and bred for impossible terrain. They can go where horses cannot. This is where you must go. The Titian Army has infiltrated every nook and cranny to the east. I'm afraid there is no other choice if you want to complete your journey north."

"Thank you," stated Ash simply, and she and Fincher worked to get Ditto onto one of the two scramblers. Sammi flinched as the boy cried out before settling onto the back of the donkey, Fincher holding him upright from behind.

Ash and Sammi moved to mount the other scrambler but were stopped by Cassie's raised hand.

"Uh, children, before you leave, there is still the matter of my payment."

"What farking payment?"

"Look around you, child. Who do you think is going to end up footing the bill for all this? Do you have any idea how expensive good scramblers are?"

"You've got to be farking kidding me."

"I assure you that I am not. I have given you an escape route. I have given you a conveyance—*two* conveyances. I have given you provisions. I have given you hope! All these things come with a price and a hefty one, at that. Nothing is free in the Clutch. I thought you would have learned this by now."

"What the fark do you want?"

"There are still three more Moon Medallions, as I recall. I would have just one."

Ash's lone hand shot up to her neck protectively. "But Ditto gave me this one," the girl said desperately. "I can't possibly—"

Sammi's hand on Ash's shoulder quieted her big sister.

"Don't worry, Ash, she can have mine." Sammi removed the Moon Medallion from around her neck, admired it one final time, and handed it over to Cassie. "It's not like I earned mine, either," said the young girl sadly as she climbed atop her scrambler, Ash sliding in behind her.

Cassie slipped her second Moon Medallion over her fiery head and then looked upon the younglings with mournful eyes.

"Go into Ptero Heights, children. If you manage to get through the Heights, Terminus Grove is not far from your reach. I wish you all the best; I really do. Go now, while the Chestnuts are still licking their wounds. They'll be back in full force once Paragon arrives."

Ash nodded, spun her Scrambler around, and kicked its sides, sending the donkey forward into the darkness of the hills.

Fincher, maneuvering around Ditto, spun his own scrambler but took one last look back before speeding off.

"You know, I don't know whether to say *thank you* or *fark you*, Miss Hawkkends."

Cassie smiled. "Then just be off, child."

Fincher did as he was told, spurring his scrambler into the night.

Cassie's hands went to her neck and her long, ringed fingers caressed the *two* Moon Medallions that she now possessed. It was a costly transaction, and one where the final amount was far from being tallied. But, as Cassie Hawkkends learned long ago, no price is too great for something you truly covet.

As Cassie started back toward the Clutch, a young voice tore out from the night.

"I've decided," called out Fincher from the shadows. "Fark you!"

Cassie then let loose a great laugh, admitting to herself that she might miss that loudmouthed boy and his loyal friends.

16

FLIGHTS FROM PTERO HEIGHTS

"What the fark are they?" asked Fincher as another large form flew overhead, blotting out Kori for the briefest of moments.

Sammi adjusted her glasses as she studied the cold, dark night sky. "I read about them in an old book Da had. I think they're called wind lizards. Or pterosaurs."

"Ahh… Ptero Heights," Fincher, Sammi, and Ash said in unison.

Fincher went on. "Well, are they friendly or…"

"Or what?"

"Or… are they gonna try and farking eat us?"

Sammi shrugged, seemingly unconcerned. "I know that they're carnivores. But as to what kind of *carni* they *vore*, I have no idea."

"Great," responded Fincher, slipping Alicia Salt's longbow from his shoulder and notching an arrow as he rode. "Then, I'll just keep this here at the ready."

Ash's head spun back and forth, desperately trying to spy wind lizards in the air above them. "Good idea."

The younglings made their way north for several hours, traveling deep into the night. While the scramblers proved more than capable, trudging up steep inclines and sharp declines without ever losing their footing, the children began to falter, the horrors of the past day finally catching up to them.

Fincher, in particular, struggled in keeping Ditto upright while holding his longbow at the ready. Eventually, he had to admit he was beaten.

"I'm sorry, but we've got to stop," said Fincher, the boy's voice breaking with emotion. "I can't hold him up any longer. I'm afraid he's going to fall off and crack his farking head again. I don't think I can—"

"It's okay, Fincher," cut in Ash. "We all need to rest. Let's camp out in one of the gaps; that way, no one can see our fire."

The younglings all agreed, and camp was made in the relatively flat space between two of Ptero Heights's gigantic hills. As Sammi cooked some of the meat Spyrros had provided over a small fire, Fincher kept his hazel eyes to the Five Sisters, watching for pterosaurs with Alicia Salt's longbow cocked back.

A bit farther back from the fire, Ditto laid flat, whimpering in pain, as Ash hovered over the boy in attendance. After giving him water, she carefully wrapped Ditto's ribs, rubbed balm on his chest and cuts, and bandaged his many open wounds.

Every now and then, the delirious boy would cry out for his ma, and the three others would briefly glance at each other before returning to their duties.

After a silent meal of cooked meat, none of which Ditto would consume, the younglings searched through the items that Spyrros had packed away. Tucked between sets of blankets was a piece of paper folded into a pouch.

"What's this?" asked Fincher before handing it over to Sammi. "It has some chicken-scratch on it but I can't make it out."

Sammi pushed up her glasses before pulling the paper pouch in close. Several seconds of study later, the girl smiled.

"I think it's medicine for Ditto. Something for his pain."

"You *think* or you *know*?" demanded Ash, much more harshly than she intended.

Sammi took no offense, understanding more than anyone in Quaan how her sister was suffering.

"I *know*. Here, it says to mix one punch of powder with a glassful of water for pain relief."

"How much is a farking punch?!"

"We don't have any glasses!"

"I know! I know," shot back Sammi. "Give me a second to think!" A few beats passed. "Here, let's consolidate our water, leaving one skin at about one-quarter full. Then… Well, we'll just have to guess what a punch is."

"Too much could kill him," stated Ash, her voice heavy with concern. As she did, Ditto wailed in pain.

"He might farking prefer that."

Ash was about to lash out at Fincher, but Sammi halted the words before they could escape.

"I can guess the amount, sis. I've watched Widow Till measure out medicine before." Ash's brown-on-yellow eyes rested on Ditto for a while before the girl finally nodded her assent.

Water skins were consolidated, powder was carefully estimated and added to the chosen skin, and Ash slowly poured the resulting mixture down Ditto's throat.

Several tense minutes passed, Ash listening intently to the large boy's chest. Numerous wind lizard sightings later, Ash rose from Ditto, tears welling up in her eyes.

"He's sleeping. He sounds better. And his heart sounds good."

Fincher and Sammi let out grateful sighs.

"Thank the farking Five Sisters. Let's all get some sleep. I'll throw some more of this dry-bush kindling on the fire. That should keep those scaly farkers away."

With cold winds whipping through the Heights, the children made good use of the extra blankets the Trademaster had supplied, holding each other close and piling the layers high on top of themselves.

When they were all tucked away—warm and comfy and together —Sammi spoke up just before sleep gripped her.

"Goodnight, Fincher. Goodnight, Ash. Goodnight, Ditto."

Only Fincher replied, Ditto and Ash already fast asleep. "Goodnight, Sammi."

"I hope tomorrow's better, Fincher."

"How could tomorrow possibly be any farking worse than today, Sammi?"

A pause. "I don't know, Fincher. But it always seems to be."

Fincher tried to reassure his young friend, but the scream of a pterosaur interrupted his thoughts. In the end, the boy simply fell into a dreamless sleep, leaving Sammi alone as a lifetime of worry consumed her nine-year-old spirit.

Fincher woke with a start, as if sensing one hundred sets of eyes on him.

And he wasn't wrong.

"Fark, fark, fark! Everyone up," the boy said urgently, rousing Ash and Sammi as Paragon was climbing in the eastern sky. Ditto remained unmoved.

"Oh, the Five Sisters," exclaimed Sammi, bouncing to her feet. "What do they want?"

"I think I can venture a guess," answered Ash, carefully rising to her feet.

Surrounding the children's small camp, slowly shuffling forward on taloned feet, were scores of pterosaurs. Large lizard eyes were locked on the younglings as strange sounds escaped pointed beaks. Each creature stood around four feet high, with a wingspan more than triple that length. Four on one, the children could take a wind lizard. But four on sixty?

"Go on," shouted Fincher at the encroaching ptero army. "Get farking out of here! Go on!"

The pterosaurs continued to advance.

"I don't think they're afraid of you, Fincher," remarked Sammi.

"Yeah? Well, I'll farking show them." The boy picked up Alicia Salt's longbow and notched an arrow. He lifted the bow, taking aim at the nearest pterosaur. It hissed at the boy through rows of sharp teeth.

"Wait," said Ash just as Fincher pulled back on the magnificent bow.

"Wait for what?" demanded Fincher. "Wait until one of them takes a chunk out of one of us?"

Sammi jumped in. "My sister's right. If you shoot one it might send them all into a frenzy."

Fincher released a bit of tension on the bow. "So, I do nothing and they farking attack us. I shoot one and they farking attack us. You all got any options that don't end with us getting farking attacked?"

"If Hana was here, she could calm them with a song," said Sammi.

"And if Ditto was awake, he could fight them off," added Ash.

Fincher rolled his eyes. "Well, looks like you're farking stuck with me. And this is what I'm gonna do!"

Without warning, Fincher pulled back on Alicia Salt's longbow and fired an arrow into the smoking pile that was last night's campfire, spraying the nearest pterosaurs with hot coals.

The wind lizards that were struck by the scorching assault jumped back as they released ear-splitting shrieks into the air, agitating the other pterosaurs, who began snapping their too-long beaks in the air at the younglings.

"And *that* is what I was afraid of," sighed Sammi.

"Well, I couldn't do farking nothing!"

"No matter, no matter," interrupted Ash as the voice of reason. The girl pulled her blade from her hip. "They're going to attack now. Get your weapons ready and protect your face and neck. Let's surround Ditto so they can't get to him."

As always, the child harvesters once known as the Sour Flower Gang jumped to, ready to fulfill their roles as crew mates and best friends.

Sammi flashed her knife across, forcing one pterosaur to backpedal, while Fincher swung his longbow, just barely missing the beak of an oncoming attacker. And still the creatures pushed forward, closing in tightly around the children.

Fincher shot again into the campfire, momentarily clearing another space.

"All this farking way," said the boy despondently," just to get eaten by a bunch of farking lizards. What a shite way to go!"

"Get ready," shouted Ash as her dagger cut through the air. "They're about to make their move!"

"I love you all," cried out Sammi, panic settling into the young girl's voice. "Don't let them eat me alive, please!"

"Fark this! I'm shooting one in the durned chest!"

"One's flying at me! No!"

Just as the Pterosaurs started their collective attack on the younglings of Crimmish, loud squawking from above stole the attentions of child and lizard alike.

A blur of color fell from the sky like a divine spear, landing on the elongated head of the wind lizard nearest to Sammi. The scaly creature howled in pain as small claws raked at round, reptilian eyes.

"Rashii," hollered all three kids at once, delighted by the return of their dear companion but worried for his safety.

Surrounding pterosaurs bit at the Quilted Raven, but Rashii proved too quick, dodging left then right before soaring into the air, squawking angrily the entire time.

Rashii dove again, hitting three more wind lizards, before flapping to safety once more. This was repeated several times, the Quilted Raven never ceasing his auditory assault.

Soon, the pterosaurs started calling back to the colorful bird, and a cacophony of sound took over that part of Ptero Heights as a conversation took place that only residents of the sky could understand.

After minutes that felt more like an hour, several of the wind lizards shrieked loudly into the crisp Heights air, shook their triangular heads, and flew off to the west. Other pterosaurs followed, then more. Within thirty seconds, the children were alone in the gap, their good friend Rashii back by their side.

"Rashii, you saved us," exclaimed Sammi as the Quilted Raven gently landed on the girl's shoulder.

"Farking heck, Rashii. You're a sight for sore eyes. I thought you would have flown back to Shadowset, for sure." Rashii shot back an angry squawk and Fincher held up his hands in defense. "I know, I know. I won't doubt you again, my friend."

"Is that… Rashii?" came a weak voice from below, and the children all turned to find that Ditto had awakened. The injured boy's green eyes took in the Quilted Raven, then the blades being held by Ash and Sammi, and then Alicia Salt's longbow in Fincher's hands. "What did I miss?"

"Oh, nothing much. We almost got gobbled up by a band of sharp-toothed pterosaurs, but Rashii found us and managed to talk them out of it."

"What's a pterosaur?"

"It's a farking wind lizard, Ditto."

"What's a wind lizard?"

Fincher looked to the sisters helplessly. "Anyone want to help me out here?"

The girls giggled before dropping to Ditto's side, Rashii departing Sammi's shoulder to join Fincher.

"How are you feeling, Ditto?" asked Ash, wearing a mask of concern over her brown face.

The large boy wheezed loudly as he fought through labored breaths. "Never better."

"Do you want something to eat?"

"I don't think I can chew, Ash."

"Can you ride?" asked Fincher.

"Just try and stop me."

Fincher, Ash, and Sammi shared in a much-needed smile.

After packing up their belongings and storing them on the scramblers, Fincher and Ash helped a struggling Ditto onto one of the donkeys while Sammi mixed another painkilling concoction for the large boy. Once Ditto choked down the bitter drink, the younglings were on their way, their mounts easily ascending the next steep incline.

As before, Fincher rode behind Ditto to prevent his injured friend from sliding off their scrambler. When the boys reached the top of the hill, the world opened up, showing Cassie's Clutch to the south and much more of the Heights to the north.

Large, winged creatures swept back and forth—banking and diving through the air in every direction.

Ditto nodded to one of the swooping shadows. "Wind lizard?"

"Yeah, that's one of the farkers. Also called a pterosaur."

"They look scary."

"Wait until you see the farkers up close, Ditto."

The large boy shivered uncontrollably from the front of the scrambler. "No thanks. I've seen more than enough monsters up close, Fincher."

"We all have, my friend. We all have."

From above the Crimmish kids, Rashii squawked in agreement.

For two days, the children trekked north through the western portion of Ptero Heights. Luckily, other than the dozens of wind lizards always hovering around, the Heights didn't have much in the way of large predators the younglings had to worry about.

What they did have to worry about, however, was the bumpy terrain that constantly threatened to toss a rider from their scrambler. Things were infinitely worse for Ditto, who bravely stifled pained moans for hours at a time as his donkey dipped, leapt, and bounced beneath him, shaking broken bones and bruised organs.

"He's looking paler today," remarked a worried Sammi from the other scrambler.

"Shut up! He looks fine! It's just his body healing!"

Sammi frowned as her sister's pain also seemingly grew by the day.

"You're probably right, Ash. He's using a lot of energy in the healing." Sammi's own words rang empty in the young girl's ears.

Every now and then, a small group of wind lizards would drift closer to the children—Ditto, in particular—and would have to be chased off by Rashii, who remained fearless before the flying reptiles.

On the third night, after Ditto had been put to bed for the evening, his head back on Ash's lap, Sammi came around the fire to Fincher, who was absently sharpening his knife.

"That was the last of his medicine. Ditto's going to be in a lot of pain tomorrow."

"I know," sighed the boy, and Sammi had never heard her spirited friend sound so old, so defeated. "But we're almost out of the Heights. When we topped the last hill, I could see the end of this horrid place."

"This horrid place saved our lives."

"For now."

Sammi sat in silence for a bit, unaccustomed to such an attitude from Fincher. After a while, she said, "What do you think we'll find when we exit Ptero Heights? Do you think Kruger will just be waiting for us? Do you think all of this was for nothing?"

It took Fincher several seconds before the boy could answer. "I don't know, Sammi. I really don't. I would like to tell you that the land will be empty, that the path to Terminus Grove will be clear. I'd like to tell you that we'll definitely find some medicine for Ditto and much-needed rest for all of us in that forest. I'd like to tell you that the journey through the Grove will be uneventful and that we'll reach the Northern Goddess in short order. I'd like to tell you that the God-Snails will still be there waiting for us, and that they'll hand over whatever gift they have for mankind, and we'll whisk it back to Kassimont. I'd like to tell you that the Chestnuts will forgive our transgressions, so happy they'll be to have the cure to the Gloomtide. I'd like to tell you that the Titians will live up to their end of the bargain and send doctors to Crimmish. I'd like to tell you that our mas and das will be healed and the Maddening vanquished. I'd like to tell you that we'll all live happily ever after, Sammi."

"But…"

"But, I can't. Not this time. My jar of hope is empty, Sammi. Right now, I just want my friend to make it through another day. I don't dare ask for any more than that."

Sammi wiped a tear from her face. "You should get some rest, Fincher. I'll watch the fire until it dies down."

Fincher simply nodded as he slipped his hunting knife back into its holder. "Thanks, Sammi. I'm gonna go lay down next to Ditto, maybe see if Ash needs anything."

"You do that, Fincher."

Fincher started around the fire but stopped midway and turned back to his young friend.

"I'm sorry, Sammi."

"Sorry for what, Fincher?"

"I don't know. But I am."

"Me, too, Fincher. Me, too."

"Well, it ain't a beautiful sight, but it's a farking sight."

"What is this place?" asked Ash, her words dripping with both awe and fear.

"It's a farking graveyard."

"These aren't graves," corrected Sammi. "This is a boneyard."

"Well, it's a giant farking boneyard then."

"Yes, it is," said Sammi, unable to disagree.

For the first hour of the morning, the children had traversed the lower regions of Ptero Heights, hopping from gap to gap until one spilled out in a great valley filled with the bones and decomposing bodies of wind lizards. Mounds of bones absolutely filled the large space, the remains of millions of pterosaurs from across the decades. While the older specimens were just bones, the dry winds having scraped away any vestiges of meat, the newer ptero bodies still had flaps of skin or leathery wing whipping around in the stiff breeze.

"This must be where they all come to die," said Sammi as the girl studied the scene through round glasses. "Or, at least those that can make it here." A pause. "I guess this is how they spend their eternal rest together."

Ash's brown eyes ran east to west as she took in the ptero boneyard. "It gives me a sense of peace."

"It gives me the farking creeps. Let's keep moving."

Through the ptero boneyard the younglings traveled atop their scramblers, who always managed to find a path through the mountains of hollow, bird-like bones. At the far end of the boneyard, the donkeys began to ascend the next hill, an especially tall one, taking the children away from the ghostly landscape.

"Eww, what the fark is this now?" asked a disgusted Fincher when he and Ditto, who hadn't spoken all morning, topped the giant hill. "Looks like piles of farking lizard skins! Yuck! That one still has an eye on it!"

"That's exactly what it is," agreed Sammi as she and Ash caught up to the boys. "Hold up for a minute, sis."

Ash drew their scrambler to a stop and Sammi hopped off. The young girl pushed up her glasses as she bent low to inspect the discarded skin.

"Check out how stretchy this stuff is," exclaimed Sammi as she pulled on both ends of a piece of skin, giggling as it refused to rip.

"I hope you're going to wash your hands before we eat again," stated Ash dryly, more than used to her little sister's never-ending curiosity for the world.

Sammi ignored her sister. "They must be like snakes or, even better, timber skinks. They shed their first juvenile layer of skin to keep growing." Sammi lifted a massive piece of especially thin skin into the air, marveling at how she could make out Paragon through the membrane. "And look at this old wing skin! I bet you there are tons of applications for this stuff!"

Ash's brown-on-yellow eyes narrowed as the girl focused on the next mound over, another massive hill that was the twin of the one on which they currently sat. "What's that over there?"

Sammi observed for several minutes as wind lizards dove down toward giant piles of woven sticks, dropping meat from their beaks as they passed. High-pitched noises emanated from within the unusual formations.

Eventually, Sammi nodded to herself, another mystery solved. "Those are ptero nests. See them dropping food for the babies? It's a good thing we came up this hill and not that one. I don't think even

Rashii could have scared them off if we threatened their nests." Sammi motioned to the hill under her. "And while they're born and raised *there*, they must use this hill just for molting."

"For farking what?"

"Molting, Fincher. It means peeling away their skin."

"Farking gross."

"Maybe. But fascinating, all the same."

Fincher and Ash shared a knowing look.

"Let's keep moving, sis," said Ash. "Ditto needs to get out of the Heights."

Although disappointed, Sammi climbed onto the scrambler and the quartet was off, riding along the top of the largest hill in all western Ptero Heights.

~

"Well? What farking now?"

"What am I even looking at?" asked Ash, as if the scene below was too much for her brain to comprehend.

Fincher motioned to the ocean of bodies far below, first pointing to the left. "Those are the Cobalts. See the blue flags?" Fincher pointed right. "And *those* are the farking Chestnuts. It's hard to miss that awful rust color."

Sammi adjusted her glasses. "It doesn't look like the Cobalts are just waiting to be pushed back by the Titians."

"No. No, it farking doesn't," agreed Fincher. "There's gonna be battle soon. Right below us. Right where we need to get to. We're farked."

Sammi thought for a moment. "What if we go deeper into Ptero Heights? Further northwest? We can get around both armies. We can—"

Fincher simply shook his head sadly. "He won't make it, Sammi. Without his medicine, he won't make it."

"What then?" asked Ash, panic again setting in.

"I don't know, Ash."

"What do you mean, you don't know?! It's your job to know! You're our leader, aren't you?! It's your job to know, Fincher!"

Fincher had no answer for his dear friend's desperation. "But I don't, Ash."

"Well, you'd better come up with something! You'd better—"

"Enough!" Ash's mouth snapped shut at her little sister's insistence. "Ditto needs to rest, anyway. And now's as good a time for lunch as any. And I need to think!"

Fincher and Ash did not argue, both dropping free from their respective scramblers. Ash immediately went over to help Fincher lower Ditto. Before her mouth could begin to form the words of an apology, Fincher squeezed her lone remaining hand, and the two friends knew that no more was needed.

Ditto's pained cries had become weaker, and he was as white as an Ommori. It looked as if life was slowly leaking out of the large boy.

Ditto was made as comfortable as possible after another liquid lunch.

"I'm cold," the large boy stated flatly, even though he was already covered with every blanket and jacket the children owned. Ash rubbed his head, and Ditto immediately fell asleep in her lap.

Ash's hand ran back and forth across the boy's forehead. "He feels hot. Really hot."

Fincher, not knowing what else to do, made a small fire and began to grill the last of the fresh meat given to them by Spyrros Milaan. As he numbly cooked, Fincher looked over to find Sammi sitting along one of the hill's sharp western edges, staring out into the abyss. Concerned, the boy stoked the fire and walked to his young friend.

The girl did not look away from the empty space before her. "How's Ditto? Honestly."

"I'm not a doctor, Sammi. But he doesn't look good."

"He won't survive more time in Ptero Heights."

"No. He won't."

"And he's dead if either army gets ahold of us."

"Probably."

"Thanks for the truth."

Fincher stood awkwardly for a minute, not sure where to go with his words. "Sammi. Are you okay? The food's almost ready. You want me to—"

"Go away, Fincher. Please. I need to think."

"Okay, Sammi."

Fincher finished grilling the meat, brought Ash some as she tended to Ditto, and set some to the side for Sammi. After packing away the supplies, he joined his two friends, holding Ditto's hand as Ash sang the injured boy songs from Crimmish.

As Fincher, Ash, and Ditto soaked in their time together, Sammi Bugg stared out across Ptero Heights, watching as wind lizards crisscrossed her field of vision. The bespectacled girl watched in amazement as the creatures swooped and dove, banked and rose, using strong currents of air to lift their large bodies into the sky.

Sammi's eyes went wide behind her glasses as one particularly big pterosaur shot up from the gap below and perfectly hovered before her, the crosswinds keeping the flying reptile perfectly in place.

Sammi studied the massive, outstretched wings, taking note of how the wind slid under and kept the animal aloft against all logic and reason. She watched as that same pterosaur dipped its wings a few degrees, sending it speeding down the valley at a sharp angle.

Sammi observed more. Sammi made calculations in her too-bright mind. And Sammi mentally balanced risks versus returns. Finally, the girl got up and walked over to her three companions.

While Ditto did not wake up, Fincher and Ash looked up at their younger friend, both their faces void of optimism.

"I have a crazy idea."

"Those are the only ones worth farking having."

"It's really dangerous."

"We're still listening," said Ash, desperate for any sliver of hope.

"And I don't think I have everything I need."

"What do you farking need, Sammi?"

"Cord. Lashing. Rope. Way more than we have with us. Basically, I need anything that I can tie a tight knot with."

Fincher thought it over before a thought struck him. The boy looked up and smiled.

"Can I interest in you in some socks? Like, way too many farking socks? Will that work?"

Sammi pushed up her glasses and then returned Fincher's smile. "It just might, Fincher. It just might."

~

Ash had no idea what was going on. After helping to collect armfuls of bones from the ptero boneyard—Sammi demanded very specific types, lengths, and thicknesses—she was basically sent away by her little sister and Fincher to simply watch after Ditto and make the boy comfortable.

Which was fine with the girl, for there was nowhere else in the world she would rather be.

Every now and then, between dropping capfuls of water into Ditto's mouth and massaging his head, Ash would look over and find Sammi and Fincher hard at work, never stopping to rest.

Fincher had all his socks laid out before him and was carefully ripping each one into long pieces of material that he would drop onto a pile. After a few minutes, Sammi would walk over from whatever strange work she was doing on the ground to retrieve a handful of strips before returning to her pile of bones.

Sometimes, Sammi would call Fincher over to hold something for her as she tied intricate knots that connected bones in unusual ways.

Ditto moaned in pain and Ash returned her full attention to the ailing boy. Soon, she laid down next to her friend and drifted off to sleep. When she awoke, Fincher and Sammi were still hard at work.

On what, only the Five Sisters knew.

This repeated several times. Ash would awaken to find Fincher and Sammi still working, their bone construction growing larger and odder each iteration. During one such waking period, Fincher joined Ash at the campfire to eat, Sammi refusing to stop as Paragon began to fall toward the Spired Curtains.

"What is my sister making, Fincher?"

"I have no farking idea."

Ash nearly dropped her dried fish. "What do you mean? How could you not know? You've been building that... thing with her for hours."

Fincher shrugged as he popped some jerky into his mouth. "I'm basically just a farking grunt. Fetch Sammi this, bring her that. Hold these bones steady while she binds them together. Cut this, sharpen that."

"And you haven't thought to ask her what the heck she's making?"

Fincher argued between chews. "I farking tried! Your *little* sister waved me away and told me there was no time. She said I wouldn't understand even if she told me. Then she barked at me to get a bunch of those gross wing skins—you know, from the baby pteros. Which I farking did! This whole process has been farking emasculating!"

Ash couldn't help but laugh despite the direness of their situation, something Fincher Bugg was always good for.

After dinner, which Sammi skipped, Fincher went back to work and Ash returned to Ditto. She used her lone hand to rub balm on the boy's chest, hoping it would help him breathe, before curling up next to her hurting friend. For a long while, Ash did not sleep. Rather, she talked.

Ash talked about Crimmish and the things she missed about their home. She talked about their first foray into the Tainted Timbers, and how a star-nosed mole made Fincher say *fark* for the first time. She talked about the first time they heard Hana sing, and how her voice had made Ash cry. She talked about Ditto's da and what a great man he was—a true pillar of the Crimmish community.

She talked about how much she loved Ditto and how he was the best person she would ever know.

Ditto kept still during all of this, offering no clue as to whether he heard Ash's words or not. But Ash still needed to tell him and felt relief when she did.

Unburdened a bit, Ash fell back asleep next to her friend, the eerie glow of Sammi and Fincher furiously working under the light of the

Five Sisters the last thing she saw before her brown-on-yellow eyes slid shut.

Ash woke once in the middle of the night, the campfire now low. A few feet away from her and Ditto, Fincher snored loudly on his back, the boy utterly exhausted.

"Hey," came a harsh whisper from the other side, and Ash jumped.

"Sammi," Ash hissed back. "Are you trying to give me heart attack?! Why are you still up?"

"No time for that. And sorry for scaring you. I need the sleeping bag that Spyrros gave us." A pause. "Actually, I need two of them."

Ash shook her head. "Ditto is shaking and needs both of them."

Sammi stared at her sister in the darkness, the firelight flickering off her round glasses. "I need them more."

"What for?"

"No time."

"Then I can't let you have them."

Another pause. "Do you trust me, sis?"

"You know I do."

"And do you love Ditto?"

A longer pause. "I do."

"Then you need to let me have the bags."

"Take them," said Ash, and this time there was no hesitance.

Sammi grabbed up the thick bags and marched back over to her workspace.

"What can I do to help?" Ash called out in the darkness.

"Go back to sleep. The only help I need right now is the voice in my head."

Ash started to say more but decided it was best to simply trust her brainy sister.

As Ash closed her eyes for the final time that evening, Sammi threw down the sleeping bags next to her project, which had grown significantly. And had gone from one construct to two.

~

"What in the fark are these?" asked Fincher, more to himself than anyone else as Ditto, Ash, and even Sammi were fast asleep under a pile of blankets.

Standing before Fincher were the obvious fruits of Sammi's tireless labor. Two massive triangular fabrications now stood where Sammi had spent every waking hour the day and night previous.

Upon inspection, it looked like Sammi had made both large triangular frames from connected wind lizard bones and then stretched molted wing skin over them like a canvass.

"Ahh," remarked Fincher as he discovered how the many wing skins had been sewn together to create two massive pieces of the flexible material and finally understood why Sammi needed to shred his favorite (and only) extra shirt.

The front points, or noses, of each triangular build were lifted into the air, and Fincher walked around to see that another piece of the frame hung under the canvassed section—another triangle with the bottom piece running parallel to the ground, almost stabilizing the construct.

As Fincher continued to move around open-mouthed, studying his brilliant friend's work, a great roar from far below stole the boy's attention.

Fincher ran to the northernmost edge of the hill, looked down, and felt his hazel-on-yellow eyes go wide as the two massive armies of Cobalts and Chestnuts came together in an explosion of metal, screams, and violence.

Fincher watched in silence for several minutes as the true horror of war assaulted his young senses. Despite his height, Fincher could hear the screams of the wounded, the cries of the terrified, and the roaring laughter of the psychotics.

It looked to Fincher as if the Cobalts had initiated the attack, pushing the larger Titian force back and threatening to break through various lines of defense.

"What's going on?" asked Ash from behind, startling Fincher to the point that the boy almost toppled over the hill's sharp northern edge.

"Farking heck, Ash, if you want me dead a farking knife in the ribs would be a lot more effective. And less farking painful!"

"Sorry, sorry. What's going on down there?"

"War, Ash. War is going on down there."

"Because of us?"

"The war? No. This battle right here? Yeah, maybe."

"That's crazy."

"Yes. Yes, it is, Ash."

Ash moved away, less intrigued by the battle than Fincher. But then, she asked, "What in the Five Sisters are these?"

Fincher ripped himself from the gruesome scene playing out below and joined Ash next to Sammi's bizarre contraptions.

"This is what your sister worked on all day and night."

"But... what *are* they?"

"They're called *Skymmers*," called out Sammi as the girl rolled out from under the piles of blankets, rose on unsteady feet, and slipped on her round glasses. She smirked as she approached her two friends. "That's *Skymmers* with a *'y'*, you know, like *sky*."

Ash rolled her eyes. "Yes, very clever, Sammi. Now, what do they *do*?"

"Yeah, what the fark are they?"

Sammi pushed up her glasses, a proud smile widening. "They're our tickets out of Ptero Heights and away from the mess playing out down there."

Fincher and Ash's faces twisted in confusion at the same time.

"Are they gonna make us farking invisible?"

"No." Sammi let a few beats pass for dramatic effect. "They're going to make us fly."

"Impossible."

"What. The. Fark."

Sammi rushed over to her Skymmers, excited to explain her work. "Wait! Wait! Hear me out! I got the ideas from watching the pterosaurs. They use the wind under their oversized wings to give them lift and allow them to fly on currents of air. So, I thought, well, if I build a big enough pair of wings, it should allow enough wind under them to lift more than a pterosaur—say, a couple of undersized children."

"Ditto ain't farking undersized."

"Which is why he'll ride with me," shot back Sammi. "I've already done the calculations."

"What calculations?" asked Ash.

"Sorry, sis, but you wouldn't understand. You either, Fincher. No offense."

Fincher continued to inspect the Skymmers. "I don't need to understand them, Sammi. But I need to farking trust them."

"No," responded Sammi. "You don't need to trust them. You need to trust me."

"Farking heck, Sammi, I *do* trust you, but I don't even know how these things work!"

"You don't need to know how they work, Fincher. You only need to know how to fly them. Which I'll tell you."

"This is crazy. And dangerous. There has to be another way," stated Ash flatly.

Sammi pushed up her glasses. "I've thought it through, sis. There isn't."

"But Ditto—"

"Ditto is the reason that this is the only way, sis. Go check on him."

Ash rushed over to the sleeping boy, putting a hand to his forehead and her ear to his chest. It only took a few seconds for the girl's head to pop up, worry painted across her face.

"He's burning up. And his breathing sounds… uneven."

Sammi nodded sadly. "I heard it before I passed out this morning. If we don't get him off this hill and into Terminus Grove fast…"

"Don't say that," screamed Ash.

"It's the truth, sis."

"Shut up!"

Fincher cut in. "Sammi's right, Ash. Ditto doesn't have long now. If we can get to Terminus Grove, no one can follow. And who knows what kinds of farking medicines could be found there. There could be daze cherries like in the Timbers. Or lumin trees! The sap from those has been known to heal bones. Not to mention that we can finally make a real camp and let Ditto rest. Maybe all he needs is some farking rest and to not be jostled about on a durned scrambler for days on end!"

Ash looked from Ditto to her friends as a tear ran down her cheek. "What are the chances, Sammi?"

The bespectacled girl shifted from foot to foot. "That they'll fly? High."

"What are the chances that we won't crash land into a sea of Chestnuts and Cobalts, sis?"

More shuffling. "That, I don't know, Ash. I'm sorry."

Ash rose from Ditto and began to walk, pulling the others with her. "We're all dead if these things flop, and most of us are dead if we land in the middle of a war. What are our other options?"

Sammi cleaned her glasses before answering. "We can use the scramblers to travel up Ptero Heights and hope to get around both armies, sneaking into Terminus Grove further north."

"What's the downside?"

"Ditto won't farking make it."

Sammi nodded in agreement. "Fincher's right. Ditto will be dead long before we make it out. But the three of us *will* make it out."

A heaviness fell over the three children as they stood atop the tallest hill in Ptero Heights, only the sounds of the whipping winds and monstrosities of bloody battle filling their young ears.

"Farking vote," asked Fincher, seeing no other alternative.

"Vote," agreed Sammi.

"Vote," echoed Ash.

"I'm willing to farking die for the chance that my friend lives. I vote we try the Skymmers."

"My Skymmers will work. I've done the calculations. Wind shear and direction are the great variables, but I'm willing to take the risk."

Fincher and Sammi then looked to Ash, who was watching Ditto sleep restlessly from across the hill. Ash didn't take her eyes off her unconscious friend as she responded.

"I'm not interested in living in a world without Ditto Bugg." Ash turned back to face Sammi. "Now, tell us how to work your Skymmers."

Sammi's proud smile returned. "I thought you'd never ask."

"No, no, no! I'll ride with Ditto!"

Sammi rolled her eyes at her sister, trying to be sympathetic to her feelings. "I know you do! *We all* know you do, sis! But it just isn't feasible."

"Why?!"

"I've told you!"

"Tell me again!"

Fincher stepped back a bit, knowing better than to be caught in the middle of a rare battle between the two headstrong sisters.

Sammi took a deep breath to calm down, reminding herself of the stakes and emotions involved.

"Very well. Again. We have to get a running start. Otherwise, the Skymmer will just take a nosedive off the hill. Ditto's not going to be any help, so I'll need both you and Fincher to run with me. Once we're in the air, I can slip my legs into those straps there. Then, we're flying."

"What about Ditto?"

Sammi looked unsure for the first time. "We'll have to have him strapped up before we even start running."

"Can the three of us even carry his weight?"

Sammi shrugged at her sister and Ash began to explode. "Then how can you—"

"You won't have to carry my weight," came a weak voice from behind. The trio turned to find Ditto standing on uneasy legs, gingerly holding his side. They ran to their friend, Ash throwing her good arm around the boy for support.

"You shouldn't be up, Ditto. You should be resting," said the concerned girl.

"I've rested and not helped for long enough." Ditto spun his green eyes to Sammi. "It's brilliant, Sammi. And it will work. You're right; I'll need Fincher and Ash's help, but I can make the run with you."

Ash's face went tight. "Ditto, no. Who knows what's loose inside you. What could get worse!"

Ditto smiled as only the large boy could. "I heard you talking... some of the time, at least. You all are taking a big risk for me. It's only fair that I share in that risk." The three others had no counter to Ditto's logic, so they simply nodded in agreement.

Belongings were packed away, with Fincher now having much more space in his sack. Weapons were secured, including Alicia's Salt's longbow, which was tied down directly onto one of the Skymmer frames. The campfire was respectfully buried, and the scramblers were given one last meal before being set free to roam their native land. The saddles and other items that couldn't be adequately stored were put in a neat pile and left for the next escapees in need.

The sounds of raging battle continued to drift up from below, with the Titians starting to recover lost ground, pushing the Cobalt lines west. Fincher watched, noting how they would now be forced to fly directly over the Chestnuts, who executed a quick offensive and had, in a few places, advanced beyond the great lake of poison known as Loch Terminus.

"Fincher!" The boy spun to find Sammi calling to him. "It's time."

Some thirty feet back from the northern edge of the hill sat the two Skymmers. In one, Ditto and Sammi stood holding the Skymmer's central bar, the large boy shouldering the weight of the glider. Both children had straps around their shoulders. Another pair of loose straps hung limply behind for their legs when they were aloft. Ditto's too-white face was already drenched in sweat and the boy grimaced in pain, although he was doing his best not to show it.

"This is it," said Sammi as Fincher reached them, the girl sounding far less confident than earlier that morning. "Fincher, take the right side and, Ash, you obviously take the left. Run with us as fast as you can, giving us a little push at the end. When we're airborne, you strap yourselves in and follow. No matter what happens, we meet just inside the forest. Good?"

"Good," replied Fincher and Ash together.

Sammi took a deep breath and pushed her glasses further up her nose. "Okay, then."

Ditto turned to his friends. "You all don't have to do this. You can go around, still finish the mission."

"Yes, we do, Ditto," said Ash.

"Fark that, Ditto."

The large boy smiled, and the rays of Paragon put a twinkle in his green eyes. "Thank you." A pause. "I love you all."

"Farking love you too, Ditto."

Ash came around, tears running down her cheeks. She cupped Ditto's face with her one hand and kissed the boy gently on the lips. Fincher and Sammi shared a glance and a small smile before looking away.

"See you down there?" Ash asked as she separated from the boy.

Ditto smiled. "Where else could I possibly want to go?"

Ash went to her side and Fincher to his. The four friends locked eyes one last time, conveying more in silence than words ever could.

"Let's go," called out Sammi and the group took off, running toward the edge as fast they their little legs could carry them. "Don't fall off the edge!"

"Now you farking tell us!"

Sammi grunted with effort and Ditto cried out as he ran. Fincher and Ash put their heads down and drove on, determined to reach maximum speed.

Just as the edge of the hill drew near, Ditto stumbled.

"Oh, no," screamed Sammi, knowing it was too late to stop.

Fincher, however, seeing his friend start to fall, braced himself and pushed forward, taking up the additional weight with a massive groan.

"Push! Push now," demanded Sammi as the ground fell away beneath them.

Ash and Fincher gave a mighty shove with all their might before sliding to the ground. Mercifully, both children stopped just before tumbling over edge, two sets of shoes dangling over air.

Ahead of the panting Ash and Fincher, the nose of the Skymmer immediately dropped and the glider began to speed toward the ground.

"No," shrieked Ash.

"We killed them! We farking killed them!"

~

Sammi's eyes watered, cold air rushing behind her glasses as the Skymmer plummeted.

"Come on, come on, come on," the young girl cried out, as the ground rose up to meet them.

Sammi did her best to remain calm, fighting the urge to push out fully on the central control bar. Instead, she steeled herself and slowly pressed forward, feeling the Skymmer's frame start to vibrate as wind began to flow under the nose and not over it.

Just as it appeared too late, like the Skymmer would be smashed against the sharp foothills below, the glider leveled out and then began to rise.

Sammi realized that she'd been holding her breath and exhaled in relief before lifting her feet into the loops in the back. Finally stabilized, the young girl looked over to find Ditto struggling, his legs flailing in the air.

"Use the leg loops, Ditto! Back there!"

The boy's face twisted in agony. "I'm trying!"

Sammi's mind raced. "Here! Keep this central bar steady," she yelled against the wind. "Don't push or pull, just keep her even! I'm gonna try to help!"

Ditto nodded and Sammi went to work, removing her right shoulder harness altogether and hanging from her left strap using only her hand. This allowed her to reach down several feet. "Raise your left leg, Ditto!" The large boy grunted with effort. "Higher!

Higher! There!" Sammi's right hand got under Ditto's left foot. "Now push off, Ditto! Push off and throw your right foot back!"

Ditto followed orders, stepping down with his left foot, using Sammi's hand as a boost, and kicking his right foot out behind him, yelping as he did. Although he failed to get very high, Sammi purposely left his leg straps long, and the boy's toes barely caught the bottom of the loop. Crying out in effort, Ditto slid his right leg further into the loop and then accepted Sammi's aid in bringing his left leg up and back.

"You did it," Sammi exclaimed, and just as she did her left hand gave way and she fell forward.

As he had in the Tainted Timbers and Maker's Lament, Ditto's left arm shot out like an arrow, catching Sammi before she fell out of her leg harness and pulling her up just long enough so that she got both straps back under her arms.

"Now we're even," said Ditto with a smile, and the two laughed as the Skymmer ascended into the air, leaving the world of man behind.

Sammi and Ditto Bugg soared like a wind lizard, the two massive groups of Cobalts and the Titians looking like ant armies far below.

Gone were the screams of the dying and the ringing of steel. Gone was the fear of getting caught, the fear of being subjected to endless torture. From this vantage point, there was only the wind to hear and one thing to see—beauty.

The Spired Curtains greeted the pair to the left, while the many colors of Terminus Grove welcomed them straight ahead.

To their right, Galanis Dawn loomed over Loch Terminus, its red-tinged water looking like a sea of blood. Something gigantic, three times as large as a Livyatan, leapt from the poisonous water, hanging in the air impossibly long before crashing back down, its four tails creating a huge wave that ran to the shore.

As the Skymmer made its way north, six pterosaurs joined the unusual sky visitor, three to each side, falling back a bit to make the glider the head of a V formation.

Sammi could feel the wind on her teeth, such was the wide smile she was wearing. She glanced over to find a similar grin on Ditto's too-pale face.

"What do you think, Ditto?"

"I think I'm flying, Sammi." The boy's head swung left and right, taking in all that Quaan had to offer, all that the Five Sisters had created for mankind. Ditto's green eyes came back to Sammi. "Thank you for this."

"You're most welcome, Ditto. You're always welcome. Now, let's see if I can land this thing."

Ditto looked away. "Just do your best. I'm at peace."

"Farking heck! It farking worked!"

"I knew it would! I never doubted my sister! Not once!"

Fincher's hazel eyes narrowed but he was able to let the fib go. The pair stood for a minute, arms around each other, watching as Sammi and Ditto flew with the pterosaurs, gently gliding out of harm's way and toward Terminus Grove, one more monumental step in completing their mission.

Ash slapped her friend on the shoulder. "Well? Shall we?"

"No time like the farking present."

Desperate to reach Ditto and Sammi, Fincher and Ash wasted no time in checking knots and strapping up. In short order, they were rushing forward as quickly as possible, sucking in air as the hill fell away beneath them and the glider immediately began to tip forward.

"Easy like she told us!" yelled Ash, as her sister had already educated them on what would happen if the nose shot up too quickly. Fincher responded, and the glider fell into a gentle arc that ultimately left the Skymmer even with the ground. Both younglings slid their legs into the rear straps. "Yes! We did it!"

"You're farking right we did!"

"Should we go higher like my sister did?"

A mischievous smile found its way onto Fincher's lips, and Ash immediately grew concerned.

"I have a better idea."

"Fincher?"

"Trust me?"

"I do."

"Then, let's go!"

Instead of rising well above the fray of soldiers as Sammi and Ditto had done, Fincher pulled in on the Skymmer's central control bar, lowering the glider until the individual faces of Sluggs and Chestnuts could be made out. Some stopped mid-swing as the bizarre contraption soared overhead, and at least one Titian caught a spear tip through the neck as attentions were ripped from the fight.

"There's the bastard," said Fincher as his sharp eyes studied the battlefield ahead and continued to drop the glider.

"Fincher?"

"It'll be worth it, Ash. I promise."

As the Skymmer flew closer to the ground, Ash finally saw what Fincher had found. Just ahead, behind several lines of charging Titians, was Lieutenant Benson Kruger on horseback, shouting out orders to his soldiers, spittle flying from his thin lips.

Fincher was already laughing before he even shouted.

"Hey! Kruger! Looking for us?!" Kruger's beady eyes went up and wide as surprise and recognition took hold. "You look like even more of a Queefin' Kelly from up here," shouted Fincher, and many of the soldiers couldn't stifle their laughter, even those actively engaged in combat.

"You little shites," screamed Kruger. "Archers! Shoot *that thing* down! Now! Now! Now!"

Ash looked over with concern. "Archers, Fincher?"

The boy offered a helpless shrug. "Sorry, I didn't think about that."

"Well, you're about to! They're getting ready!"

Arrows were notched and bows cocked back in seconds. Kruger pointed with his sword as the Skymmer flew past. "Fire! Fire! Fire, you fools!"

Fincher could hear the twang of string releases followed immediately by swishes of air as several quarrels just missed their target.

"Are you okay? Are you hit?" Fincher asked Ash, who shook her head in the negative. The boy looked back with another devilish grin. "Missed again, Kruger! Catch ya later, ya Danglin' Andy!"

Just as Fincher completed his insult, a bolt tore through the Skymmer's wing skin canvas, forcing the glider to shake suddenly.

"Fincher!"

"Sorry, sorry," exclaimed the boy as he and Ash worked to regain control of the glider.

"It's hard to handle now!"

"What am I, hard of feeling?! I know, Ash!"

"What can we do?!"

Fincher pointed ahead. "Look! There's the forest. If we run her low and fast, we should just make it!"

"I don't like this!"

"It's our only choice!"

The Skymmer raced on, speeding several dozen feet above the battlefield, bucking wildly each time the hole in the right sail ripped open more. Every now and then, an arrow would fly past, but the glider was moving too quickly and erratically now for any of the archers to get a good shot off.

"We're going too fast, Fincher!"

"I agree! But she's gonna rip apart if we don't hurry!"

"Then let's hurry!"

"We farking are!"

The Skymmer continued to pick up speed as it began to descend. Soon, they had reached the edge of the battle, leaving the last of the Titians behind and only clear ground between them and Terminus Grove.

"Fark," roared Fincher as the back half of the right sail fully tore away, and the glider tilted sharply to the side, almost throwing the boy from the Skymmer.

"Hold on, Fincher!"

"I'm trying!"

Ash desperately worked the central bar with her lone hand. "I'll keep us up as long as I can!"

To her credit, the girl was able to get maximum distance out of the compromised glider, bringing the pair to within several hundred feet of Terminus Grove before there was nothing else to do but land.

"Brace yourself, Fincher!"

"Farrrrrrrk!"

Just like Sammi had taught her, Ash pushed the central bar out as hard as she could just before impact. In theory, this would lift the nose straight up and dramatically slow down the glider, allowing the children to drop softly to their feet.

But they were too low. And they were going too fast. And the damaged sail would only lift the nose so much.

And so, they crashed. Hard. And there was a jumble of arms and legs and bones and wing skin and ground.

And then all went dark.

~

The voice was distant, hollow, as if coming from another dimension, another world.

"Fincher! Fincher! Get up! Ash! Wake up!"

Fincher opened his eyes, unsure of where he was. The boy saw grass and ptero bone and blood on his arms, and awareness slowly crept back. This awareness quickly morphed into panic as Fincher remembered not only what had just happened, but what was coming for him.

Fincher pushed the wreckage of the Skymmer off him as he rose to his feet, his head spinning and hurt running through almost every part of his small body. The boy fought through the blinding pain and dove back into the remnants of the glider.

"Ash! Ash! Ash," cried the boy, desperation taking hold as no answer came. "Ash! Ash!"

"Over here, Fincher," came a call from the side as Ash stumbled toward her friend, her right leg obviously damaged. "Stupid thing threw me way over there."

"Are you okay?!"

"I'll survive," said the girl through gritted teeth. "Hurry, let's get what we need."

Another voice reached the pair, this one from the edge of Terminus Grove. "Fincher! Ash! Hurry! They're coming! Look!"

First, Fincher and Ash spun to find Sammi at the entrance to the forest. Although her Skymmer was still recognizable, it had obviously also endured a rough landing, with the crossbar crushed, the nose snapped off, and both sails ripped to shreds. Ditto laid next to the crash site, as did their packs.

"Hurry! Look," Sammi shouted again, pointing.

Fincher and Ash followed their friend's finger and their breaths caught in their young chests.

A band of Titians on horseback had broken free of the battle and were fast approaching, blades drawn. One Chestnut had a large net in his free hand, and Fincher didn't like what that foretold.

"We gotta farking go. Now!"

Fincher and Ash jumped to, ignoring the searing pain in their muscles and joints. They ripped through the glider, locating their packs and tearing them free from the wreckage.

Ash shouldered her bag. "We got them! Let's go!"

"Miss Salt's longbow," said Fincher. "I have the quiver but where's the bow?"

"No time, Fincher! They're coming!"

"I have to farking find it!"

The sounds of hooves pounding the ground grew louder. The shouts of soldiers could be heard.

"Fincher! Please!"

"Fark, yeah! I've got it!"

At the bottom of the pile, tied tightly to the bone frame, was Alicia Salt's longbow, miraculously undamaged by the crash. In one quick motion, Fincher cut the bow loose and pulled it free. The boy then slung his own sack over both shoulders, keeping the longbow in his hands.

Ash's voice was filled with desperation. "Now?"

"Yes! Let's farking go!"

As faces of individual Chestnuts were starting to come into focus, Fincher and Ash took off in a sprint, although Ash was running with a pronounced limp.

While the distance was only several hundred feet, injuries, combined with panic, had the children breathing hard in no time, fighting to catch their breath as they pushed on to avoid capture.

Sammi urged on her companions from the edge of the woods. "Come on! Come on! You're almost here! Yes!"

When Fincher and Ash finally slid to a stop next to Sammi, the Titian riders still had some distance to cover. Despite this, Sammi was in no mood to greet them.

"Hurry! It's Ditto. I can't move him by myself. He couldn't help me land, so we hit pretty hard. I managed to untie him and drag him out of the Skymmer, but he's too heavy for me…" The young girl's voice broke, and tears ran down from behind her glasses. "My arm hurts so I couldn't get him into the woods. I tried but—"

Fincher buried his friend in a hug. "You did so awesome, Sammi. You made us fly." They separated. "Now, we need to get Ditto into the farking forest, right?"

The sound of hooves grew louder.

The bespectacled girl nodded.

"You get Ditto's pack. Ash and I will pull him in."

As always, the group formerly known as the Sour Flower Gang understood their roles and went to work. Sammi ran over and shouldered Ditto's pack as Fincher and Ash went to the unconscious boy.

"Lazing about again, Ditto?" asked Fincher jokingly. "This is becoming a farking habit, you know." Although Fincher's words were meant to lighten the mood, they fell flat when Ditto didn't respond, the large boy's face looking whiter than ever before.

Ash slid her right arm under Ditto's armpit, and Fincher did the same on the other side, and the pair began to drag their friend to safety. The soldiers were so close now that their words could be made out over the general din of the battlefield.

"We've got you, you little rats!"

"Stop there, and we'll let you keep your eyes!"

"Don't move, you urchins!"

Fincher and Ash's legs pumped as hard they could, every now and then tripping over an odd branch or hole. As they neared the forest, two riders had moved far ahead of their fellow soldiers and were closing fast. Too fast.

"We're not going to make it, Fincher," said Ash through heavy breaths.

Fincher looked to the forest, where Sammi waited within, and then back to the approaching riders, whose swords would reach them in seconds.

"The fark we aren't."

"What?!"

"Keep pulling, Ash!"

Fincher dropped Ditto, drawing a groan from the large boy, and swung Alicia Salt's longbow free. Ash cried out briefly from her increased burden, but swallowed her discomfort, put the stub of her left arm under Ditto's other armpit, and began to backpedal. Although much slower than with Fincher's help, the girl still managed to make good progress.

As Ash and Ditto slid away, Fincher quickly notched an arrow and drew back.

Two horsemen were far in front of the Chestnut group, a few strides away from Fincher. There would only be time for one shot.

"I'm farking sorry," said Fincher softly, hoping that his words reached the Wellspring. He released the longbow.

The arrow flashed through the air, the rays of Paragon catching it for just a moment before it buried itself in the neck of the horse on Fincher's left. The animal screamed out in a mixture of surprise and agony, cutting to the side, directly into the path of its fellow steed.

The two muscled animals collided violently, sending both horses to the ground and both riders flying. One soldier tumbled to stop just as his injured mount rolled atop him, shattering his back. The other Titian was a bit luckier, having been launched free of the twisted mass of animals, actually landing past Fincher. The lucky Chestnut immediately leapt to his feet, ignoring a deep cut on his chin, and threw himself at the boy.

An arrow through his forehead immediately dropped the man, a dumb look pasted on his face for all eternity.

While the paralyzed soldier whimpered, both animals shrieked, one having multiple broken legs and the other having a bolt in its neck.

Sammi's voice flew in from behind. "Fincher! Hurry!"

"I'm sorry, my friends. You didn't deserve this," stated the boy as he quickly put an arrow through the heart of each mortally wounded horse. As he turned to leave, Fincher's hazel eyes caught those of the downed soldier. "Sorry. No farking mercy for you."

Fincher shouldered the longbow once more and dashed to catch up to Ash, who was still struggling to pull Ditto on her own. Together, they managed to drag Ditto into the safety of the forest as Sammi cheered them on.

"Yes! Yes! You did it! You—"

Sammi's mouth snapped shut as her brown-on-yellow eyes went wide with terror. A Titian soldier, realizing that she was too late, had pulled her mount up short and pulled out her crossbow, aiming its razor-sharp tip directly at Sammi's chest. The Chestnut's teeth appeared in a wicked smile.

As the lady soldier's finger began to pull on the crossbow's trigger, a flash of color plummeted from the sky and tore into the woman's face, ruining her shot as the crossbow moved far from its intended target.

"Rashii," called out Sammi in relieved delight as the Quilted Raven continued to peck away at the eyes of her would-be killer. "Rashii, get away from there," screamed the girl as Fincher and Ash sped past with Ditto in tow. "Rashii, we're safe! Come on!"

The Quilted Raven offered one last angry squawk before ascending again, leaving the Chestnut's face a mask of blood. The bird deftly turned in the air and began to speed toward Sammi, its mission accomplished.

Rashii's flight was cut short, however, when an arrow tore through its small chest, dropping the too-smart avian to the ground—dead.

"Rashii! No! Rashii!"

"Sammi! We have to go," demanded her older sister from deeper in the forest. "Don't let his death be for nothing!"

Something in Ash's words, something that tugged at the rational side that comprised most of Sammi Bugg, forced the young girl to say a quick goodbye and follow, just as the next wave of Titian soldiers raced in.

Their horses' hooves carved deep divots into the grass as the animals were viciously yanked to a stop by their riders, bringing them just to the edge of Terminus Grove.

"Whoa! Whoa! Whoa," shouted one of the Chestnuts as the children of Crimmish disappeared into the thick, colorful forest.

"They're right there," complained one of the soldiers. "Let's go in and get them!"

"You fool! You'd be dead within thirty paces! In fact, my skin is already itching being *this* close! We missed them. Nothing to do but tell Lieutenant Kruger."

"He's not going to like it," came a voice from the back.

"Then *he* can farking go in there," shot back the head Chestnut.

"I don't get it," said the youngest soldier of the group. "If we can't go in there, then how can those kids?"

The ranking Chestnut spun his mount around and made his way back to the battlefield, cutting through his fellow Titians.

"*They* can because they're Cheese-Eyes from the Stenches. And for all intents and purposes, they're already dead."

Ten minutes passed before the children finally stopped, breathing in massive gasps as the effects of their adrenaline began to wear off.

Looking around, it was as if Terminus Grove had literally swallowed them whole, for no sign of Chestnut could be seen and no sounds of battle could be heard. Instead, the younglings were surrounded by color and sweet smells and the gentle whispers of nature.

"I think… we're… farking… good."

Fincher and Ash dragged Ditto to a soft, moss-covered space on the forest floor and gently released their friend. Ash remained with the large boy as Fincher stumbled to his feet, walking strangely to Sammi, who was staring back the way they had come, her brown cheeks glistening with salty wetness.

"Rashii," was all the young girl said as Fincher approached. "He saved me. Again. And in the end, I couldn't do anything for him. I haven't been able to do anything for anyone."

"The fark you haven't," objected Fincher, his voice sounding especially strained. "You did the impossible, Sammi. You flew us over certain death. You saved us."

"But not Rashii."

"No, not Rashii."

"I should be dead. That quarrel should be in my chest right now. Rashii made sure it missed everything."

Fincher sucked in. "Well, not everything."

Sammi's sad brown eyes shifted to Fincher. "What do you mean?"

The boy did not answer, instead simply turning around to show the crossbow bolt jutting out from his left shoulder.

"Oh, the Five Sisters! Fincher! Are you okay?"

The boy waved his young friend away. "I'll be fine. Didn't hit my farking heart or brain or chest or Danglin' Andy. But maybe you could…"

"Oh! Of course! Hold still!"

Fortunately, the crossbow bolt had a field tip and not a broadhead point, making it easy for Sammi to pull it free without further damaging Fincher's shoulder. This, of course, didn't prevent the boy from shrieking in pain as Sammi completed the grisly task.

Fincher then gingerly removed his bloodstained shirt and knelt on the soft forest floor as Sammi retrieved bandages from her pack and began to wrap his wound.

As the girl smeared ointment across the hole in Fincher's shoulder and wrapped it tight, the boy's hazel eyes took in his surroundings.

"Look," he said, nodding to where a grouping of Reaper Vines excreted a poisonous mist into the air.

Sammi nodded as she wrapped Fincher's shoulder. "That's irony, I guess. The things that are killing our parents just saved our lives. And Ditto's before that."

Fincher nodded in silent agreement as he continued to look around.

Although both Terminus Grove and the Tainted Timbers contained Reaper Vines, that was where the comparisons ended. While the Timbers were a collection of blacks and greys, as if fire had greeted the woods long before life, Terminus Grove was a kaleidoscope, filled with colorful blossoms of all shapes and sizes. While the Timbers were static, a dark painting devoid of motion, Terminus Grove was movement personified—the plants, trees, and even Reaper Vines swaying to and fro, reaching here and there, spreading out as if they were schools of fish beneath Crown Lake.

"It's actually quite farking beautiful, Sammi."

The girl pushed her glasses up on her nose. "It is. And you're done. I'll wash and change these wrappings tomorrow."

Fincher stood with Sammi's help. "Thanks, Sammi. I don't know how much more progress I can make today. I feel like a pile of shite."

Sammi assisted Fincher with getting his shirt back on, no small task given the boy's injured shoulder.

"Funny," said Fincher when his tunic was on him once more, "I thought it'd be colder up here."

"It was in Ptero Heights, Fincher."

"Yes, it was as cold as a Reba Bugg dirty look. But here… I don't know… It feels… Nice."

Sammi considered Fincher's words. "You're right. It *does* feel nice. I'm neither hot nor cold. But I *am* tired. Let's find a place to make camp and lick our wounds."

Fincher offered his friend a wide smile. "That's the best suggestion I've heard in a long while."

"Better than leaping off a mountain on a kite of skin and bones?"

Fincher laughed and threw an arm, his good one, around his younger friend. "Better than that, even. And, technically, it was a hill."

The friends turned their attentions away from the forest's edge.

"Ash, we're going to go in a bit further, find a place to make camp for the night. What do you need to help move Ditto?" There was no response. "Sis? Did you hear me? We need to move farther in but just a bit. We'll eat and rest and recover as soon as we find a good place." There was no response. "Ash? Sis?"

A wave of nausea hit Fincher and Sammi Bugg as they moved cautiously toward their other two companions. Ash was leaning over Ditto, who remained where they had laid him. The large boy looked peacefully asleep, as if he hadn't a care in the world, as if all was right in the land of Quaan.

"Ash," called out Fincher weakly, the boy terrified of what was to come. "Ash… We need to move Ditto." There was no strength in his voice. "We need to get him somewhere where he can rest. And recover. And stay with us."

Ash's reply came wrapped in a tone that Fincher had never heard from his too-strong friend. Ash had faced prejudice and death and the loss of a limb, and never had the boy detected such sadness, such hopelessness from the one-armed girl.

"He's gone."

"What?" came the disbelieving response from both Fincher and Sammi.

Ash, still on her knees next to Ditto, slowly turned to face her remaining friends. If brown skin could blanche, Ash's would have.

"He's gone. Ditto's gone. My Ditto is dead."

Suddenly, the surrounding forest didn't seem so beautiful.

PART III

THE GOD-SNAILS OF QUAAN

17

PYGMY SCAMPS AND THEIR PSYCHEDELIC FOREST

Working in pained silence, Fincher, Ash, and Sammi gently pulled Ditto's body deeper into Terminus Grove, stopping only when they reached a small clearing of soft, vibrant grass in the middle of the dense forest.

Fincher looked around at the surrounding color—massive flowers, multihued plants, and glimmering insects. The boy looked up and could see Paragon through a clean break in the Grove's canopy.

"Lots of beauty. A clear view of the sky and the Five Sisters. What do you think?"

Sammi nodded. "I think Ditto would like it here." Her older sister did not add anything. "Ash?"

"Let's just get on with it."

The three remaining members of the Sour Flower Gang stood to the side looking down, watching as the sliding rays of Paragon tickled the gentle face of their dear friend.

"Should we remove his Ghost Puma tooth?" asked Sammi.

"And give it to who?" responded Ash. "His ma and da are gone; we were his only family left."

"Let him keep it," said Fincher. "Perhaps he can take it with him to the Wellspring. Maybe he won't forget us if the tooth stays close."

The children knelt in quiet heartbreak. Fincher softly wept. Ash, numbed by overwhelming grief, stared at her forever love with brown-on-yellow eyes. Sammi, as she was wont to do, had gone somewhere else in her mind, to a safer, warmer place away from violence and death and loss.

For over an hour the trio sat in observance, the only thing they could do to honor Deetarik Bugg.

Finally, Sammi spoke. "Do you think Ditto made it to the Wellspring?" she asked, recently returned from her mental sanctuary.

Fincher rose, pulling up Sammi with him. "If anyone in all of Quaan were a shoo-in for the Wellspring, it would be Ditto. He was the best of us. He was the heart of us."

"He was our protector," added Ash from the ground.

"You've never needed protecting, Ash," corrected Fincher.

"That's not true." Ash stood on wobbly legs. "When I lost my arm, I lost a piece of my soul that I thought was gone forever. I thought I would be a burden to everyone. I was ready to walk out into the Timbers alone and be done with it. When I finally mustered the courage to end it all, guess who was waiting for me at the forest entrance?" Tears began to flow. "He didn't try to talk me out of it. He didn't say much of anything really. He just told me—*If you're going, I'm going. Because I failed as a friend if you don't feel loved and needed.*"

Fincher wiped some wetness from his face. "How far into the Timbers did you both go?"

Ash laughed. "Are you kidding me? That's all it took. I melted into his arms right then and there. We went back to town soon after."

Sammi adjusted her glasses. "Ditto always knew the perfect thing to say."

"At the perfect time," agreed Fincher.

"And using the fewest words possible," added Ash. "Something you could learn a thing or two about, Fincher."

"There are lots of ways I should be more like Ditto," replied Fincher sadly.

Ash recognized the hurt on her friend's face. "Sorry, bad joke. I was just kidding, Fincher."

"I'm not."

Several more muted minutes passed before Ash finally broke the spell of silence.

"Our friend is gone. My love is gone. And life will never be the same. Even if we somehow manage to save Quaan from the Gloomtide, what is a world without Ditto Bugg?"

"It's a shite place. That's what it is."

"But there's still good here," said Sammi.

Fincher nodded. "Yes. Yes, there is. Which is why we have to keep going."

Ash angrily wiped her cheeks with her lone hand. "Ditto wouldn't want us to stop."

"Which is why we won't." Fincher went over and hugged his two friends. The three children put their foreheads together and shared in one last heavy moment of grief. "We have to bury him," stated Fincher as they separated. "I'll go find a stick and start digging."

Ash nodded. "I'll join you."

Fincher and Ash went off into the forest, leaving Sammi to stand watch over Ditto. Their search for worthy digging instruments was cut short after only a few minutes.

"Fincher! Ash! Come back! Come quick! Hurry! Hurry!"

Fincher and Ash tore into the clearing from opposite sides, desperate to reach Sammi, who sounded in grave danger.

Ash's head shot back and forth as the girl reached her younger sister. "What?! What is it, Sammi?!"

Fincher slid to a stop. "Yes, what's the matter?!"

Sammi pointed down. "Look!"

The ground around Ditto rippled and the grass surrounding the dead boy stretched up and over, as if determined to make contact with the body. Ditto then sank gently into the soft ground, as if being lowered into Crown Lake. The children watched wide-eyed as Terminus Grove swallowed their friend, leaving only a small mound to denote his existence.

A few beats later, a green shoot sprang up from the mound. It reached for Paragon before ultimately exploding into a hand-sized white blossom tinged with red. More shoots followed, then many more. Within a few minutes, the entire area where Ditto had been returned to the land was covered in a potpourri of flowers, greater than any funeral the children had ever attended.

It was Sammi who was finally able to lend words to what they were seeing.

"Looks like even Quaan is excited to have Ditto around."

"Farking right."

Fincher leaned down and picked that first white-red flower that rose from Ditto's grave. The boy then went to his pack and placed the blossom in a side pocket that also held Hana's Ghost Puma tooth.

Fincher shouldered his pack, quietly prompting the sisters to do the same.

"He's with his ma and da now. Let's keep moving so we can be with ours again. You ready, Ash?"

"I'm ready, Fincher."

Fincher thought for a moment, and a shadow passed across the boy's face. "It's Finch from now on. Call me Finch."

Sammi pushed her glasses farther up her nose. "And I'm Samm."

Ash nodded solemnly. "It should have taken longer for us to reach our short names. A lot longer."

"But here we farking are."

"Yes. Here we are. Ready to go save the world… Finch? Samm?"

"Yes," they both said in unison. But there was very little strength behind their words.

For the strength of the Sour Flower Gang was gone, buried beneath a fitting bouquet of life.

Mentally exhausted and physically depleted but unwilling to rest, the remaining children pressed on through Terminus Grove. Although their hearts were still overflowing with melancholy and anger and disbelief, the forest offered countless sights to keep their young minds occupied.

Glowing, arm-length canker worms ventured out onto low-hanging branches. Every now and then, one of the creatures would shake violently before releasing a shimmering cloud of smoke that coalesced into a variety of shapes. Fincher walked right through one that looked to be an arrow. The boy angrily waved the smoke away.

"Farking thing put a Danglin' Andy in my face! Little shite's lucky I don't roast him over a fire!"

Despite their loss, the sisters giggled at Fincher's predicament.

Elsewhere, other magical shows were being revealed.

Giant blossoms from one plant would fire off purplish balls of pollen that were gobbled up by the writhing, jaw-like flowers of another. Massive bees flew back and forth, uninterested in the children passing through, their bodies coated in sparkling spores, bringing starlight to the daytime forest.

White antelope pranced across Terminus Grove, unafraid of the kids from Crimmish. As their sharp hooves dug into the ground, sweet smells were released, a mix of jasmine, vanilla, and pine.

A brook containing all the colors of the rainbow ran unencumbered through the forest. Small prismatic fish would leap from the flowing waters and fly on makeshift wings before landing next to a plump insect, which was promptly devoured. The fish would then waddle its way back to the stream, dropping into the clear water with a full belly.

While the Monarch Browns of the Mutewoods were living giants, some of the trees of Terminus Grove absolutely dwarfed them in comparison. Taking more than a minute to walk around, these colossuses were covered in multicolored vines that spiraled up their bright orange bark. When one of the children approached, the tree would sing out beautifully in tones that could only be matched by their fallen friend Hana.

"It's too bad the rest of the world can't see the beauty of this place," commented Sammi.

"Is it, Samm?" questioned her older sister. "Perhaps that's why Terminus Grove is the way that it is… to keep the world of man from encroaching. To keep the world of man from ruining everything."

"She's got a good farking point," agreed Fincher.

Sammi shrugged. "Maybe. But, still, it's too bad. Maybe seeing such beauty could quell the rage in men's hearts."

"I wouldn't count on it, sis."

"Me farking either."

The children kept moving, as if frightened of where their minds would travel if their bodies stopped. As Paragon fell, more of Terminus Grove awakened, and if the forest was beautiful by day, it was downright heavenly at night.

All of Terminus Grove's residents, from its moving vines to its bustling insects to its animated blossoms, were bioluminescent, showering the dimming forest with a warm, polychromatic glow.

Fincher, Ash, and Sammi chuckled as they marched on, something new catching their yellow eyes around every tree.

"I can farking see better now than when Paragon was up!"

"Better and more," agreed Sammi excitedly.

"But we still have to stop at some point," cut in Ash.

"You're right," Fincher agreed. "And this looks as good a place as any. I haven't seen one danger or heard one lurking predator since entering this forest. Could we have finally caught a farking break?"

Sammi slipped her pack off with a groan. "Well, let's not jinx it. Do we need a fire?"

A few moments of silence passed as the children thought it over.

"It's strange," said Ash. "I'm not cold in the least."

"Me either," Fincher concurred. "I was freezing my farking cobblers off in Ptero Heights, but here I feel… comfortable."

Sammi looked around through her glasses. "This place must be a complete biosphere all to itself, a self-contained and separate environment. So, do we need a fire?" she asked again.

"Not for warmth, sis."

"I couldn't be farking toastier if I was in the tight embrace of Stella Bugg."

"You mean Reba Bugg," teased Sammi.

Fincher scoffed. "I'd take the farking Widow Till at this point, Samm."

Ash jumped in when she had finished laughing. "Well, we certainly don't need a fire to see. The whole forest is aflame with light."

Sammi nodded. "And we're just eating jerky for dinner… Then, it's settled. No fire and let's just enjoy the beauty."

The children agreed and spread out their bedrolls. Although the Five Sisters could be made out through the thick canopy, for once the real show wasn't the moons overhead but the shifts of colorful flora and sparkling fauna of the world around the younglings.

After a quick meal, the kids of Crimmish laid on their backs and looked up as translucent birds fluttered in the air above. As they shot from branch to branch, the magnificent creatures left rainbow trails in their wake that crisscrossed overhead, creating a better show than any traveling light merchant.

"Rashii would have fit in perfectly here," commented Sammi.

"You said it, sis."

More time passed as Terminus Grove continued to awaken. High above in the giant unnamed trees, swollen fruits previously unseen during the day flared to life, emitting light reminiscent of the Astars of Vattassav.

The children continued to look up in awe, each second bringing new wonders and new questions of what was to come next.

"I wish Ditto and Hana could see this," said Sammi as she swept some salty water from the corner of her eye.

"They don't need to," countered Ash, refusing to look away from the display overhead. "They're in the Wellspring now, and I imagine that puts this place to shame, no matter how beautiful we think this is."

Some time passed before the bespectacled girl responded.

"Good. They deserve it."

"Farking right, they do."

The younglings watched on in astonishment as a show never meant for human consumption played out. Slowly but surely, however, eyelids grew heavy, and the weight of loss began to steal wakefulness. The last image the children had before the world went dark was a magnificent one, filled with color and wonder and life.

It was a poor substitute for the brightness of their beloved Ditto, but it would keep them going. For a while longer, at least.

~

"Someone was here last night. Someone other than us, I mean." Sammi continued to collect her belongings that had been removed from her pack and strewn across the small sleeping area. "It doesn't look like anything has been taken," the young girl said as she pushed the items back into her sack.

"An animal, maybe?" guessed Ash.

"I don't think so, sis. Nothing is torn up or even damaged. And the jerky is still here. What kind of animal wouldn't eat jerky?"

"Perhaps one of those white deer creatures," ventured Fincher.

Sammi shook her head. "Would they really dare to get that close to us?"

"Well, if they don't have any farking predators in this forest, maybe they would."

Sammi considered the boy's rationale. "No. I think it's something else. Something more… human."

Fincher let out a great sigh. Although the boy had slept, he was still exhausted. They all were.

"Farking great. Right when I started to believe that maybe we didn't need to keep watch at night."

Ash helped her sister gather the rest of her stuff. "Well," she said as she bent over to collect a pair of trousers, "better to discover that this way, I guess."

"You mean rather than waking up with our farking guts spilled out across the ground?"

"Yes, Finch, that's what I mean."

"Ugh. Farking grim, that mind of yours."

Ash rolled her eyes and Sammi giggled as the last of her meager belongings were returned to her pack.

Ash hefted her own sack. "Let's get moving."

Fincher slung Alicia Salt's longbow over his shoulder. "I'm ready."

"Me too," responded Sammi as she cleaned her glasses with a handkerchief.

The kids from Crimmish made good progress for the first several hours of Paragon. No longer amazed by the distinct beauty of Terminus Grove, they rarely had to stop and gawk; one exception was when a crystalline ray swept down from the branches above. Smaller than its aquatic cousin from Crown Lake, the eagle ray, this one soared through air, not water. The majestic creature's clear wings would flash in changing colors as it flew low, circling the children.

"Beautiful," remarked Sammi, the girl entranced by the discovery of another new life form.

"Yeah, but watch that farking stinger on its tail."

"Why would it attack us?" wondered Sammi aloud.

Fincher and Ash looked at each other dumbfounded.

"Have you been with us these past weeks, sis?!"

"Yeah, what planet have you been farking living on? On this one, *everything* has attacked us!"

Sammi kept staring up, a big smile on her lips. "Yeah, but this one won't."

The grove ray continued its slow, looping descent, flashing loud colors, almost desperately. Soon, it was only several feet above the younglings, and Fincher and Ash's hands went to the hilts of their blades.

The grove ray executed one final lazy turn and came directly at the kids, soaring so low that Fincher and Ash had to duck.

"Ruuuuuuuuuuuuuuuuuuuuun," the animal hissed as it passed over the younglings, flapped its pectoral fins, and disappeared into the forest.

"Farker hissed at me," said Fincher as he stood upright once more.

"That didn't sound like a hiss to me," disagreed Ash. "I don't know what it was, but it wasn't a hiss."

Sammi pushed up her glasses. "It wasn't a hiss," she stated flatly. "It was a word. *Run.*"

Ash's faced twisted in confusion. "Run? Run from what?"

Sammi shrugged. "I don't know. Hopefully, we don't find out."

Fincher groaned as he readied his bow. "Fark me. Why couldn't it just have been a hiss?"

"Yeah, you're used to those from Stella Bugg. Aren't you, Finch?" Sammi could barely get the words out through the laughs.

Fincher's chin shot up defiantly. "Fallacious! You are confusing *kiss* and *hiss*, I'm afraid."

The sisters doubled over in laughter. When she could breathe, Ash shot back with, "We'll see who's confusing words, Finch. In the meantime, please don't try to *kiss* any Moon Adders that we see, thinking it's making a pass at you."

Sammi roared once more, and Fincher's chin went up even higher.

"Well, seeing how neither of you are currently fit to lead this excursion, I'll take the lead."

The boy stormed forward in anger, leaving the still-giggling girls behind. As soon as he was out of earshot, Fincher's frown transformed into a grin which became a chuckle. Unlike most, Fincher Bugg could appreciate a good joke. Even when he was the butt of it.

The kids from Crimmish pushed north, even as Paragon reached its full height and began to slide off into the Spired Curtains. Every now and then, a rustle could be heard in the forest. First to the east, then to the west. Ash and Sammi kept hands on their weapons. Fincher kept an arrow notched and at the ready.

Something tore through bushes to the right, just beyond their range of vision.

"Animal?" asked Ash hopefully.

Sammi listened so hard that her brown eyes narrowed. "It's an animal, to be sure. But maybe not the one you'd want it to be."

"What the fark that does mean?"

Sammi adjusted her glasses. "Doesn't sound like something with four legs. Doesn't move like them. Sounds like... us."

"Farking great. The one time that fewer legs is a bad thing." A pause as they continued to listen. "What do we do?"

Ash was the first to break the spell. "We keep going. Shoot anything that moves, Finch."

With that, Ash marched on, quickly vanishing into the Grove ahead. As she did, Sammi leaned into Fincher.

"Please don't do that. Most of the things in this forest seem harmless… to us, at least. You shoot the wrong thing and who knows what could happen." Sammi went after her sister.

Fincher thought for a moment. "Then, what should I shoot?"

Sammi called out over her shoulder. "Use your discretion, Finch."

The boy kicked at a root as he moved to follow. "Perfect. The *one* thing I don't farking have."

Fincher, Ash, and Sammi were all fast asleep under Terminus Grove's kaleidoscope night. For some reason, the children had elected to sleep apart, and were laid out on the far edges of the tiny glade they had selected for the evening.

Two sets of oversized purple eyes took in the scene.

"Who sleep at night and travel in the day?" said one creature in the high-pitched, raspy voice of a child who was a lifelong fireplant smoker.

"*They* do. You know that," replied his equally diminutive comrade. "They are ever foolish. But needed. Ever more now than ever. We need them."

"Then, let's gets them."

"In time, fellow. All in time. Let's find out more."

"Nows?"

"Of course, nows! They sleeping tight!"

"Oks, then."

"Oks."

The tiny human-like pair crept out of the bushes and carefully tiptoed on bare feet into the glade. One motioned the other toward Fincher with a light blue hand, and they both silently slid in the boy's direction.

Fincher had foolishly left his pack a few feet from him, making it easy pickings for the intruders.

One of the creatures gently nudged the sleeping boy. When Fincher didn't move, it offered its partner a *thumbs-up* with a freakishly long digit.

Fincher's pack, which was now carrying Ditto's stuff along with his own, was quietly emptied onto the too-brilliant grass. The duo of blue humanoids carefully began rummaging through the items. One would pick up a piece of jerky and smell it with a pug nose while the other studied the boy's lone remaining set of spare socks.

Eventually, one of the little men reached into a side pocket and retrieved a blood-caked object—Hana Bugg's Ghost Puma tooth. He held it up and both creatures shared a curious look.

"I don't think that farking belongs to you," came a voice from the "sleeping" boy, causing the tiny raiders to jump into the air.

When they came down, the would-be thieves immediately turned to flee, running headlong into Ash Bugg, who was now standing with her knife drawn.

"Blasted," cried one, pivoting on blue feet and darting back toward Fincher, who now had Alicia Salt's longbow cocked back, the arrow tip pointing directly at the unwanted visitor's chest. The boy grimaced from the intense pain in his shoulder. The blue man slid to a stop and froze.

His companion, deciding to live to fight another day, slowly backpedaled away, hoping that minimal motion would help him avoid detection. This proved not to be the case, however, as Sammi appeared from behind and placed her own blade under the little creature's chin.

"That's the second pack of ours that you've ransacked," said Sammi into the robber's too-large ears. "What is it you're trying to steal?"

"Steal?" shrieked the miniature human. "Why steal?! What do we need for steal?!"

"Then, what were you looking for?"

"Answers! Answers we need!"

"Answers to what question?" demanded Ash as she waved her knife in the air threateningly.

"How!"

"How the fark what?!"

The little man wiggled in Sammi's grasp. "How you are not dead! Here! In the forest!"

"We could ask you the same farking question."

"No! This *my* home. This *our fellows* home. This not *your* home."

Ash jumped back in. "And so, you would see us dead?"

"Never!"

"But you were following us."

The little man was growing frustrated, his oversized purple eyes shooting back and forth.

"You not belong here! We need to make sure you not bring harm to the Pygmy Scamps."

"The who?"

The blue man puffed out his chest. "The Pygmy Scamps! Us!"

Ash looked to Fincher. "What do you think, Finch?"

Fincher thought for a moment. "It's a good name. It's not as catchy as the Sour Flower Gang, but it sticks."

"Not the stupid name, Finch!"

"Fark me! Sorry! What then?!"

"Do you believe him?"

Fincher removed some of the tension on the bow. "I'd like to, Ash. But I'm a little low on trust at the moment."

Ash nodded her braided head. "As am I."

"I'm not." Fincher and Ash turned together to view Sammi, who had removed her knife from the second blue creature's throat and returned it to her waist. "They could have slit our throats while we slept last night. They could have taken the last of our food. But they didn't. They are looking for something, and it isn't a fight."

"Never," shouted one creature.

"No fights," cried the other.

An uneasy moment passed before Fincher finally lowered Alicia Salt's longbow, wincing as he did.

"Fark me. If Sammi's willing to give the little shites a chance, then I am, too. Plus, I'm too tired for violence and still too sad for killing."

Ash was the last to lower her weapon. "Very well. Who are you and what do you want from us?"

The pair of forest folk ran to each other before responding. Standing at less than four feet, both men wore brown overalls shorts that highlighted blue chests and legs above bare feet. Too-big purple eyes with massive pupils matched oversized ears that twitched in the lukewarm breeze. While one of the Pygmy Scamps had short yellow hair, the other had a mohawk of bright pink. Although lightless when they snuck into the camp, both of their manes now glowed, pulsing with anxiety.

"I am Doona," said the Scamp with the yellow hair. "And this Jaloo. We are scouts, looking for danger. Humans in our forest is danger. We have to check out why here. And how here."

Sammi came around to join Fincher and Ash, theorizing that it would make the Pygmies feel less like trapped animals. Fincher took the lead in the discussion.

"Nice to meet you… Doona and…"

"Jaloo," Sammi finished for him.

"Jaloo," stated Fincher, tossing a thankful look to his younger friend. "My name is Finch. This is Ash and her sister Samm. We're just passing through your beautiful forest on our way to the Northern Goddess. We don't want to stay, and we promise not to hurt anything or anyone." A pause. "Do you believe us? As we believed you?"

Doona and Jaloo glanced at each other, both sets of ears twitching violently in the brightness of Terminus Grove's night. After a while, "Yes," said Doona. "We believe you. But still need to know."

"Need to know what?"

Jaloo replied for his companion. "How. How you are here. Should be dead. Long dead. Any human who comes into forest dead." Jaloo shared a strange look with Doona. "Most human dead, anyway. Why you not dead? How?"

Sammi stepped forward. "I understand." She turned to Fincher and Ash. "They can't understand how we're not dead like everyone else who comes into Terminus Grove." She spun back to the Pygmy Scamps. "Do you know Crimmish? Far to the south?" There was no reaction. "Maybe you've heard it referred to as the Stenches, although we don't care for that term." Still no reaction.

"Farking heck, Samm, they've probably never ever seen a normal human."

"Have, too," argued Doona.

"Many, many," shouted Jaloo.

Sammi moved to calm the little men. "Okay, okay. We believe you again. Crimmish, where we all come from, is very much like your forest. It has Reaper Vines…" Sammi looked around before her eyes went wide behind her round glasses. She dashed over to a tree to her right and pointed out the Reaper Vine wrapped around it. "These! These vines poison the air for normal humans. Our home has these, as well. That's why we're used to them. That's why the air in your forest can't kill us."

"Right away, at least," Ash muttered under her breath.

Doona and Jaloo considered this new information.

Jaloo ran a blue hand through his pink mohawk. "You… are… forest folk?"

Sammi nodded happily. "That's right! We are forest folk. Just like you and Doona."

"Like us," echoed Jaloo.

"No," disagreed Doona. "Not like us. Humans hate us. Humans hunt us. Humans enslave us. We not same."

Fincher stepped forward. "But we are! Other humans hate us, too! Our town is a prison without walls. People only come when they need something from us. They call us names and throw shite at us, even when we're trying to do them a farking solid." A pause. "We are the farking same, my little friends."

Big blue ears quivered for several moments.

"It is decided," said Doona. "You come to Sanctoom Olaroo. Our village. Our gaffer want to meet. Meet new friends of forest."

The children of Crimmish looked at each other doubtfully.

"We appreciate the offer," stated Fincher carefully," but we'd better keep traveling north. We are desperate to complete our mission and get back home."

Jaloo bounced with excitement. "Home! Yes, home! We take you home."

"No, no, you don't understand. We don't want to go to your home. We want to keep going north."

Jaloo nodded dumbly. "Yes, yes! Home is north. Have food. Have water. Have peace. Safe! Very safe!"

Ash looked around. "But we don't need safe. This forest seems safe enough. Not like our Tainted Timbers."

Doona cut in. "Not safe! Not safe! Have many monsters in the forest. Beautiful? Yes! But dangerous? Yes! Can swallow you whole!"

Sammi's voice came in from the side, where the bespectacled girl was quickly running through their packs.

"Actually, I hate to be the bearer of bad news, but we *are* getting low on supplies. We have a few more days of jerky left, but that's it."

"There's has to be food all over this forest," said Ash.

"Sure," Sammi conceded. "But what's edible and what isn't? We don't know this forest. Who's to say that one of those glowing fruits wouldn't turn our insides to jelly?"

"Farking heck, Samm."

"I'm serious! We don't know how long it's going to take us to reach the Northern Goddess and we don't know when we'll be able to find food that won't kill us. We could use a restock."

Ash turned to her sister. "Samm. Do I have to remind you of the last time we accepted a stranger's invitation? Have you already forgotten about Dooley Hamm?"

Sammi waved her older sister away. "First off, how dare you?! And second, Dooley Hamm was not the last invitation! The Ommori opened the doors to Vattassav for us, and *that* turned out pretty well, didn't it!"

An uncomfortable silence fell over the group. Fincher finally turned back to Doona and Jaloo.

"How far is your village?"

"Not far. Not far. Still night when we get there."

"And if we don't come with you?"

The Scamps shared a look before Doona answered. "Up to you. But you will die. Forest kill you."

"Weren't you listening? The Reaper Vines can't farking kill us."

Doona smiled, showing off sharp, crooked, too-white teeth. "Not vines. The forest. You get lost. You starve. You get swallowed."

Fincher, Ash, and Sammi all thought of Ditto's body being consumed by the forest floor.

"And how can you help?" asked Ash.

Jaloo shrugged. "Can guide. If Gaffer Olaroo say oks, can take you north. Can take you to north edge of forest."

Sammi pulled Fincher and Ash to the side. "See?" she whispered. "Now we can get more food *and* a guide north. We don't know what secrets this forest holds. *These* Pygmy Scamps do. We need them." Fincher and Ash thought it over. "Finch?"

The boy released a deep sigh. "Fark it, then. I'm too exhausted to fight you on this. Ash?"

The girl hesitated, but ultimately nodded her braided head. "Fine. But let's keep our hands to our hilts. And keep that bow ready."

Fincher glanced over to where the little blue men patiently waited. "What could those tiny farkers do to us?"

Ash's faced hardened. "I said the same thing about Dooley Hamm. I won't make the same mistake twice. If either of them makes a funny move, I'm going to run my blade across both their throats."

"Farking heck, Ash. What's gotten into you?"

"I'm tired of being the prey. If needed, I'm willing to be the predator."

Fincher smiled. "Looks like these little farkers caught us on the wrong day." The boy spun back to Doona and Jaloo. "Gentlemen! Lead the way!"

There was very little talking in the hours of trekking that followed. Every now and then, Doona or Jaloo would point out a glowing fruit, floating seed, or shimmering plant, simply saying either *not eat* or *can eat*. As the odd quintet went around one of Terminus Grove's mammoth trees, Doona rubbed its bark tenderly, repeating the word *Numinoos*.

As time passed, Sammi regularly looked up through the thick, bioluminescent canopy, making sure the Scamps were taking them north, as promised. From what the girl could ascertain, it seemed they were abiding by their word.

Eventually, as the children's legs were growing tired from the little sleep they received, Doona and Jaloo brought the group to a stop before one especially massive Numinoos Tree. The pink-mohawked Jaloo reached into his small sling bag and retrieved an ornate flute made of a beige material. He placed the instrument to his blue lips and blew, creating a soft, haunting melody that wound its way through the wooded kaleidoscope.

Several seconds passed before a small voice could be heard somewhere in the bright tree above.

"Who comes?" demanded the gravelly, child-like voice.

"Doona and Jaloo," replied the blond Scamp.

"And who?"

"And some humans. Human children."

"Impossible."

"Possible."

"How?"

"They are forest folk."

"Impossible."

"True. Gaffer Olaroo needs to meet them."

"Most gone on a Baashing."

"That's oks."

"Oks, then."

Another haunting tune, this time from high above, cascaded over Terminus Grove, causing insects and animals alike to scatter. Just as the music settled, the younglings watched in absolute shock as the Numinoos Tree quietly split down the middle and separated, creating a natural doorway through which even brighter light leaked out onto the forest floor.

"What the fark is this?" asked Fincher, the boy's hazel eyes the size of saucers.

Jaloo returned his light brown flute to his bag. "Silly humans. This Sanctoom Olaroo. This is home."

~

If Terminus Grove was a kaleidoscope of color when the Five Sisters were overhead, then Sanctoom Olaroo was an absolute prismatic explosion.

The forest floor had been swept clean, leaving a thick layer of softly glowing blue moss to greet bare feet. Bright orange rocks that swam with light outlined the entirety of the village as well as footpaths and circular fire pits.

Within each round pit was an impossibly narrow but tall fire containing all the colors of the spectrum. It was as if a lean man, engulfed in a magical blaze, danced inside each circle, unable to break free.

Above the ground, modest homes of brightly painted wood were built into the thick tree limbs, with bridges of thick vines connecting tree to tree, home to home. These vines, unlike their boring but deadly cousin the Reaper Vine, shone with purplish illumination, making travel in the shadowy trees as easy as possible.

As Pygmy Scamps lounged around their fires, some dancing, some eating, and some playing music, the air around them was heavy with life. Fireflies, crystalline butterflies, and an array of insects crisscrossed Sanctoom Olaroo, making a far greater show beneath the Grove's canopy than above it, even with the Five Sisters and their countless stars in the night sky.

Doona and Jaloo led the children through the village, minding the orange-bordered pathways. Although they drew the eyes of many Pygmy Scamps, Fincher was surprised by the lack of response they received as foreign visitors. The boy leaned into his friends.

"I thought we'd get a bigger reaction."

"Didn't you say that after your big solo dance at the Warming Festival last year?" teased Sammi.

"Fallacious," hissed Fincher. "People came up to me all evening to pay their respects." A pause. "Just none of you were around to hear it."

"Was Stella Bugg around to hear it?"

"Unfortunately, no! Poor thing found herself entangled in another affair."

"You mean a date with Hylinn Bugg?"

"Fallacious!"

Ash shushed them both. "Will you two stop? Something's happening. Look!"

In the middle of the village was the largest Numinoos Tree the children had seen yet, which was saying something given the colossuses they had already passed. Several feet in front of its massive trunk was a large rectangular rock sunk into the mossy ground. Unfamiliar shapes and runes, seemingly etched into the stone, swam across the face of the material, making the children blink heavily in response to the optical confusion.

The Pygmy guides stepped onto the rock and motioned for the Crimmish kids to join them. Jaloo once again pulled out his flute and played a quick tune. The stone vibrated underfoot for a second before launching into the air, sending Fincher, Ash, and Sammi clamoring to each other for balance and support.

From the surrounding fires, Pygmy Scamps watched indifferently as the heavy column of rock exploded from the ground and rose up into the boughs of the Numinoos like a new tooth breaking free from the gum. The stone column shot up sixty feet before slowly coming to a rest where the main trunk of the tree split into eight equal segments. Soon after, the Scamps went back to their conversations, meals, and grating laughter.

High above, the pillar of rock had stopped level with the wooden floor of a giant construct within the Numinoos. Pygmy guards were stationed to either side of the group, each holding hooked blades at the ready. One of the diminutive soldiers waved the visitors on with a curved weapon.

As Doona and Jaloo led the way, tendrils of sweet smoke weaved their way through the group, with the blue men inhaling deeply as any drifted their way. Fincher, seeing this, followed suit, sucking in a fat collection of bright green vapor. The boy's pupils immediately dilated, his shoulders slunk, and the throbbing of his injured shoulder ceased as Sammi and Ash pulled him back.

"What are you doing, Finch? You don't know what you're inhaling," admonished Sammi.

"Yeah, dumb move, Finch," agreed Ash.

Fincher looked to his friends through bleary eyes. He spoke through a stupid grin. "Really? Because I feel great. In fact, I feel better than ever before. In fact—"

"Okay, okay," interrupted Ash. "Samm, you stay clear of that smoke, at least until we figure out what the heck is going on."

Fincher leaned into Sammi on unsteady legs. "Yeah, Samm, you stay away. More for me, and me for more, and me for me, and…"

Ash faced her little sister. "He's worthless for a while. Stay away from that smoke until…"

"Until when?" asked Sammi after Ash didn't compete her sentence.

"Until now, I guess."

Sammi looked up to find that the group had reached their destination. The children stood on a huge circular platform installed next to the trunk of the Numinoos. A cavernous room lay beyond, carved into one of the tree's main stems. Within was empty, save the ever-present faery light and a lone Pygmy Scamp who sat cross-legged on a throne of sprouts that sprung from the tree on all sides to meet in the middle, leaving its occupant to hang ten feet in the air.

After bowing their heads for an extended period, Doona and Jaloo entered the Numinoos hollow, halting several steps before their elevated leader.

Doona stepped to one side as he spoke, with Jaloo moving in the opposite direction. "Gaffer Olaroo. We bring something for you."

The Gaffer was an older Scamp, simultaneously childlike and

elderly. Bright red hair marked the sides of the man's head while the top was bare blue skin. Age lines crossed his cherubic face and dark blue scars marred his light blue bare chest. The Pygmy chieftain, unlike his overalls-wearing brethren, donned pants covered in long animal hair and wore shoes of animal hide. His eyes, while purple and oversized like Doona and Jaloo's, danced lazily, reminding the children of the Crimmish of adults after they had consumed too much honey rice wine.

As if awoken from a long slumber, Olaroo finally peered down from his perch and spoke. "And what you bring me? A baby? A meal?"

Doona and Jaloo chuckled nervously before Jaloo took the lead. "No, my Gaffer. We bring humans. Humans who forest not kill. Humans like us."

"From far south," added Doona. "From far south but like us."

Olaroo's purple eyes looked everywhere but at the younglings. "Like us, you say? Will they be us?"

Doona and Jaloo exchanged glances again.

"They go north, my Gaffer," said Doona, almost as if to a child. "Let them rest in sanctoom before we help through the forest? We can learn much from them. We can gain much. If we have *time*. If you allow *it*."

Fincher shot a concerned look to Ash, who returned it. It sounded strange the way Doona was speaking to his chief, but perhaps that was just the way of things among the Pygmies.

Olaroo sat in silent thought for several minutes, his oversized ears twitching. Ash looked down to find Doona and Jaloo's lobes moving in similar fashion. Finally, a fat, self-satisfied grin settled onto the face of the Gaffer, as if he had released a massive fart into a tub of hot water.

"They are forest folk," came the slurring words from above. "They are us. Let them stay. Let them enjoy. Let them become."

Jaloo, looking concerned, added belatedly, "And take them north once rested, my Gaffer?"

The Gaffer's jaw clenched and ground as his too-purple eyes went wide. "Oh, sure! Sure! Once rested. Anything can happen, once rested. But first, rest. And become. When one becomes, guides not needed."

Fincher, despite the lightness in his head, couldn't help himself. "What the fark is he on about?"

Doona and Jaloo sprung into action, with Doona taking charge.

"Nothing. Nothing at all. The Gaffer has much to think on. Much to worry about. The Gaffer welcomes you. Can stay as long as want. And if want leave, guide north given to you."

"What do you mean, *if?*" exclaimed Ash. "We *will* want to leave. And soon."

Jaloo stepped forward. "Of course. Of course. Wrong words. Pygmy words. You are guests. Stay when want. Leave when want. But first must rest. Edge of forest not close. Far. Too far. Need rest. Need fun."

The Gaffer spoke from above. "You go now. There is no beauty like sanctoom. There is no happiness like Pygmies. There is no world like Terminoos. You welcome. You are family."

And with that, Gaffer Olaroo's purple eyes rolled back into his bald head as another tendril of thick smoke wound its way into his nostrils.

Doona and Jaloo hooked the children by their waists as the Scamps exited the throne room, Doona speaking as they did. "You home now. Now can see."

"See what?" asked Sammi, the young girl much more excited than afraid, which was quite the opposite of Fincher and Ash, despite Fincher's compromised faculties.

Jaloo offered a naughty smile. "See Terminoos as she really is."

Fincher wobbled as he made his way back to the stone column. "She seems a farking war of color, a bloody mess of senses."

Ash and Sammi helped Fincher back onto the etched pillar. Ash held him tight to make sure he didn't tumble off the edge as Sammi embarrassedly faced their Scamp guides.

"He didn't really mean that," the young girl said through nervous laughter.

"No, no," said Doona dismissively. "He know Sanctoom Olaroo well already. He know. And the best to come. You see. You see soon."

~

Fincher danced and danced. The boy danced like he had never danced before, even when doing his best to attract the attention of one Stella Bugg.

He giggled with laughter, his cheeks aching from the strain of a sustained smile, as he circled the tall shoot of magical fire, arm-in-arm with two new Scamp friends.

Sammi howled in approval, shoveling one last delicious spoonful of roasted vegetables into her mouth as she did. Apparently, meat was not regularly on the menu for the Scamps. In fact, much of Sanctoom Olaroo was out that very evening on what they called a *Baashing*, which the children took as another word for a hunt.

With bellies full of unfamiliar root vegetables and the air filled with bioluminescence and warmth, the music of the Pygmy Scamps began to take hold, forcing Ash and her sister to join Fincher in orbiting one of the many campfires littering the sanctoom.

The three friends held hands and shouted gleefully as they spun, temporarily forgetting about Ditto and Hana and Alicia Salt and Captain Graff. They were toddlers once more, playing together on the fringes of the Tainted Timbers, too young to be harvesters and too naive to know what the future held as residents of the Stenches.

At some point, the music faded into a deep thrumming that shook the mossy ground and sent vibrations up the spines of the younglings. The children were sat back down around the fire before all the surrounding Scamps retreated into a rhythmic swaying, their over-sized purple eyes rolling back in their blue heads.

As the Pygmy Scamps oscillated like trapper kelp under Crown Lake, one particular character took center stage.

Stepping out of the forest and moving across the brilliant moss on the balls of tiny blue feet was the first clearly female Pygmy Scamp they'd seen. She had long hair that danced around her head and contained all the colors of the rainbow. She wore a furry robe of white, and runes had been painted across her beautiful face in shimmering ink.

"Moossa! Moossa! Moossa," chanted the swaying Scamps as their priestess approached.

Fincher watched through bleary eyes as the striking blue female sensually strode over to the children. Sitting calmly across the woman's shoulders was the largest caterpillar the kids had ever seen. Glowing a fierce yellow-green, the caterpillar wore a near-human face that appeared perpetually surprised, its oversized mouth shaped in a perfect O.

Moossa stopped before the sitting children.

"Welcome. Sanctoom is home now. Accept gift of the Cattipilloos and join us. You are home."

Moossa held out her right hand, palm up, to the kids from Crimmish. The Cattipilloos, with wild hairs of light sprouting across its back, crawled down the priestess's arm and lifted its harlequin head into the air, taking in each of the seated younglings.

After noting each child, the Cattipilloos's body flashed and swelled, growing to almost double its width, before the creature exhaled loudly, releasing a thick plume of yellow smoke that enveloped the trio, forcing its way into their youthful lungs.

Fincher, Ash, and Sammi all succumbed to violent coughing as their vision was momentarily consumed by the bright vapor. By the time they were able to catch their breaths, the smoke had cleared and Moossa had vanished. Fincher looked to Ash, who looked to Sammi, who looked to Fincher, and all three fell into raucous laughter, their heads swimming.

Pygmy Scamps surrounded the laughing children and gently helped them to their feet, welcoming them home as they did.

When Fincher was finally able to maintain balance on his own, he looked around and saw Sanctoom Olaroo through new eyes, the way that the Scamps must have seen it. The boy glanced over and found similar wonder on Ash and Sammi's faces as the sisters took in their magical surroundings.

The music kicked back up, the deep thrumming giving way to flutes and stringed instruments never before seen.

Fincher could feel his face pulled tight smile. "Well? What farking now?"

Sammi stumbled away, pulling Ash with her.

"I want to dance! Come on, sis! Dance with me!"

Ash could barely speak through her giggles. "Okay, okay! Finch! You want to dance with us?"

Fincher rubbed his arms, sending small jolts of electricity through his body, and his body felt lighter by the second.

"Dance? I can do farking better than dance. I feel like I can farking fly!"

And, so, Fincher Bugg closed his eyes and flew.

Dance and laughter and smoke and color filled the sanctoom. The children spun and jumped, twirled and ran. Although their feet remained firmly on the mossy ground, the younglings felt as if they were floating from fire to fire, receiving snacks and drinks and beautiful jewelry at each stop.

At one point, a basket of bright purple berries called dreampods were passed around, and the Crimmish kids popped several of the sweet, plump treats into their mouths.

Several minutes after they did, everything increased in intensity. Laughter became cackles. The tall fires shifted, seemingly made of flowing liquid. Long streaks in the air appeared overhead, as if a monstrous spider had weaved a web of rainbow over the village.

"Check this out," exclaimed Fincher. "Farking wild!"

The sisters watched as the boy waved his arms through the warm air, creating hypnotizing prismatic trails. Soon, all three were prancing across the sanctoom, their brows wet with sweat as they made a game of who could conjure the most magnificent display.

Through it all, the Pygmy Scamps were there to support the intoxicated children. Sweet drinks were given, when needed. Kind blue hands pulled the younglings away when they played too close to one of the fires. Massages were given between bouts of physicality, bringing dumb, satisfied smiles to innocent faces.

"I could stay here forever," said Sammi as two Scamps rubbed her tired shoulders.

"And you can," replied one of the Scamps. "You home now. All home. Is oks."

"See?" said Ash, her words slurring. "This can be our new home. Who needs the rest of the world?"

"Yeah," agreed Fincher. "They didn't want us until they needed us. Now? Now we don't need them. Good riddance."

The Pygmy Scamps surrounding the children shared big toothy smiles as Fincher's, Sammi's, and Ash's eyes grew heavy.

Sammi went on. "Maybe all this was just a way for us to find this place. And these wonderful creatures. Maybe all the death and pain we experienced was the price we had to pay to get here. Maybe this is the end of our journey. Maybe this is our prize."

"Maybe, playbe, daybe, shaybe, doo," muttered Fincher, the boy sinking deeper and deeper into psychedelic psychosis. "Farking, barking, tarking, sharking, moo!"

Ash ignored Fincher's outburst, her own mind spinning out of control.

"You could be right, sis. I mean, what could be better than this? Surely not stupid Crimmish. Surely not terrible Cassie's Clutch. Surely not freezing Ptero Heights." A long pause. "Quaan stole my love from me. Let the Gloomtide devour it. See if I care."

"Home," repeated the Scamps as they continued massaging, and popping more dreampods into the younglings' drooling mouths. "You home now. You home. Home."

"I think we're home," echoed Fincher, his voice sounding far away, as if the boy's soul was already drifting through the cosmos.

"I think we're home," repeated Sammi.

"This is home," stated Ash, and there was no doubt in the girl's words.

~

"What does it say?! Tell me, durn you, or I'll use your oily skin to feed the castle lanterns!"

The Chancellor jumped at the Imperator's harsh words as the Imperatrix shook her beautiful head in disappointment. Her husband had grown increasingly belligerent over the past few Paragons, with the lack of updates about the younglings of Crimmish beginning to crush his spirits. Kassidy prayed that the Imperial Courier Dove, which had just arrived to the castle balcony, brought good news. She stood with bated breath as Sologar Crimm read the small note aloud.

Crimm cleared his throat and tucked away a growing grin. *"My Imperator, I have collected the children of the Stenches (of which only four now remain), have led the successful pushback of the Sluggs, and have seen the children off into Terminus Grove. They have taken a real shine to me. We now await their return with the Pentad Gift. I will return with utmost haste. Victory is almost ours. Also, Cassandra Hawkkends has proven a real enemy of the Empire. I suggest she be hanged for treason. Signed, Lieutenant Benson Kruger."*

"By god, the weasel-faced man did it!" roared Kasspar Rayne in celebration. "And not a moment too soon, for I had almost given up hope!"

Almost, mouthed Sologar Crimm to the Imperatrix, and she discreetly waved the little man away.

The Imperator went on. "This calls for a drink! Someone join me! Chancellor?"

Crimm bowed slightly. "With all due respect, my Imperator, this wonderful news also brings many tasks—preparations, really—that I must see to."

"Oh, very well, you scoundrel! Kassidy! My lovely wife! A drink to this fantastic and most needed turn of events?"

The Imperatrix bowed slightly to her husband. "Later, my love. I, too, must see to some things in the wake of this most welcome update."

Wetness appeared in the corners of Kasspar Rayne's eyes. "Of course, my heart. You were right all along, weren't you? It looks as if everything you said has come to pass. The God-Snails may be our saviors from the stars, but you are truly my salvation here on Quaan."

"It is my duty and privilege, my husband."

The Imperator leapt down from this throne, goblet and honey rice wine bottle in hand. "You and you," he exclaimed, pointing out two soldiers stationed along the throne room walls. "Join me on the balcony and be ready to drink, durn you!"

The two grizzled veterans looked to each other doubtfully for a moment before rushing after their Imperator, eager but nervous to share a toast with the most powerful man in the world.

As usual, Sologar Crimm slid up next to Kassidy Rayne as soon as the Imperator was out of sight. There was greasy grin on the diminutive advisor's face.

"What are you smiling about, Sologar?"

"Should one not smile when they've been officially resurrected, my Lady?"

"Nothing is official yet, Sologar."

"Perhaps. But the Five Sisters are certainly brighter this evening than they have been in a while, are they not?"

"They are. But there is still much to be done. The younglings still must make their way through Terminus Grove, locate the Supreme Helices (if they are still on Quaan), and be deemed worthy of receiving the Pentad Gift. Don't start counting your chickens before they hatch."

"It's not chickens that I'm counting, Kassidy."

"Then what is it?"

"Favors. Favors that will be owed to me after concocting the plan that saved the Empire."

"And what kinds of favors, pray tell, are you expecting, Sologar?"

The Chancellor waved a soft hand in the air. "Oh, let's not ruin the surprise. But they will be substantial. Something befitting the architect of the Gloomtide's demise."

The Imperatrix snickered at the grotesque Chancellor. "Don't get ahead of yourself. Instead, I want you to start drafting plans for an all-out assault on Cassie's Clutch."

A confused look crossed Crimm's goateed face. "Talk about getting ahead of yourself, my Lady. Shouldn't we first—"

"Of course, you fool. First, we get the Pentad Gift and save the world. But after? Soon after? I want Cassie's Clutch razed to the ground as soon as this business with the Gloomtide is over. For too long that woman has thought herself a queen of Quaan. There is only room for one of those, and that is the one who couples with the Imperator. Within two more Warmings, what is hers will be mine. Those treasures that she surrounds herself with will fill my royal bedroom and personal safe. I will have her head embalmed, shrunken, and encased in crystal. I will wear it like a pendant at the end of a thick chain of twisted gold. This will serve as a constant reminder to any woman who thinks herself my equal." A pause. "Do this for me, Sologar, and some of those *favors* that exist now only in your mind could be made real."

"Which favors?" dared the Chancellor.

"That depends on you, Sologar. And how much Cassandra Hawkkends suffers before her head is brought before me. We may share a nickname, but that is where the comparisons must end."

"I'll get started right away, my Lady."

"Of course, you will."

18

DREAMLAND WARNINGS AND REAL ESCAPES

Ditto and Ash sat on the edge of a cliff overlooking Sanctoom Olaroo, the girl's right hand in the boy's left.

"I love it here, Ditto. Especially with you here."

"But I can't stay."

"I know, silly. But I still love it here. Even without you, this place feels like home. I can't imagine returning to Crimmish without you. In fact, I can't imagine facing any part of Quaan without you."

A long silence followed, with both children quietly enjoying each other's company.

"This isn't your home, Ash," Ditto said finally. "You have a home. A home with a ma and da. And a community that loves you."

"This is just as good. Even better."

The handsome boy shook his head. "It's really not, Ash. It just looks that way now. Try viewing it through eyes that aren't clouded. See this place as it really is, not as you want it to be. And certainly not as *they* want you to see it."

"How do I do that, Ditto?"

The large boy smiled, and Ash could feel her heart melting.

"I don't know. But you'll figure it out."

"I'm not smart like my sister."

"Seeing this place won't take smarts, Ash. It will take resilience. It will take seeing the truth of something hidden in shadow. But mostly, it will take strength. And there's no one in Quaan who has the strength that you possess. Of this, I'm sure."

Ash looked down. "I don't know…"

"Do you trust me, Ash?"

The girl's brown-on-yellow eyes shot up. "With my life."

"Then trust me on this. Keep your mind clear. See what this place really is. See what these creatures really are. And don't forget who you are. Because you are the most spectacular person in the world. And although Quaan doesn't deserve you—any of you—it needs you. And there's still good worth saving."

"But, Ditto, I—"

Ash's words were cut off as Ditto leaned in, pressing his lips against hers, making real a moment she had dreamt about for years. When they finally separated, an eternity had passed and Ash felt complete, as if the last puzzle piece of the girl's soul had been placed where there was once a yawning chasm of regret.

"I have to go now."

"So soon?"

"It's already been too long."

"Will you get in trouble?"

"Who cares? It was worth it."

"It better have been," Ash said jokingly.

Ditto rose to his feet, his hand still holding tightly to Ash's. "I'm sorry, Ash."

"For what?"

"That I couldn't stay. That I left you all. That I failed the mission."

Ash jumped up. "Oh, Ditto. You've never failed at anything in your life. Being a good friend, most of all. We never would have gotten this far without you."

"But you still have further to go. You need to know this."

"I do, now, Ditto. I do, now."

"Good. Then my job is done." The boy placed a gentle kiss on Ash's forehead. "Watch Fincher for me? Sammi doesn't need any help."

"Of course. He's lost without you."

"Not for long."

With that, Ditto turned and began to walk away, his form growing increasingly ghostly as he did.

Ash's heart felt as if it was going to burst from her chest.

"Ditto!" The large boy turned around. "I love you!"

"I love you, too, of course. Always have."

"Always will," cried out the girl.

The boy nodded and faded away, until only his voice could be heard. "Finish the mission. Save Fincher and Sammi."

"I will, Ditto!"

"And don't eat the meat."

"What? Ditto? What does that mean?"

But Ditto was gone.

Ash woke with a start, her head swimming and her mouth dry. She was on a too-soft bed of animal furs, Fincher and Sammi sleeping soundly next to her. Looking up through Terminus Grove's thick canopy, the girl could tell it was late in the day, with Paragon already invisible overhead.

Ash rose to her elbow and then to her knees, placing her hand onto the unconscious Fincher for support against the wave of dizziness that fell upon her.

Pygmy Scamps were laid out across Sanctoom Olaroo, sleeping soundly in groups of five, ten, and even fifteen. All was quiet in the village, and it was obvious that the Scamps truly were nocturnal creatures.

Ash shook her braided head, attempting to clear the thick haze that had taken hold. When that didn't work, she simply laid back down, basking in the wonderful dream of Ditto leaning in to—

Ash sprung back up. What was it Ditto had said? *Complete the mission?* None of that mattered as the girl recalled the most important part of her dream.

She told Ditto that she loved him! And he said it back!

Ash's heart swelled as she fell back into the warm, soft furs, forgetting all about Ditto's warnings and pleas.

She said she loved him! And he said it back!

Ash didn't care if what she experienced was real, or imaginary, or some strange hybrid of the two. The girl felt more alive, more complete than she did the previous day, and she was going to bask in this feeling for a while—everything else be durned.

With a too-wide grin on her dark face, Ash closed her eyes, mentally replacing forest leaves with Ditto's green eyes. Shoving aside the sounds of the Grove's buzzing insects for Ditto's sweet voice. Pushing away the feel of fur on her bare arms for the gentle touch of Ditto's lips on her own. Forgoing what is for what could be…

A shrill but melodic horn blasted across Sanctoom Olaroo, ripping Fincher, Ash, and Sammi from their slumbers. The children rose groggily, all three realizing that they had slept through the entirety of Paragon as Terminus Grove was already awakening with its usual evening color.

"What the fark is going on?" asked Fincher, the boy rubbing his temples as he spoke.

"I don't know, but can they *not* do it," said Sammi, the young girl looking especially worse for wear.

Around the children, the Pygmy Scamps were up and active, restarting fires in the designated stone circles. They jumped with joy and hollered with excitement, running back and forth across the mossy ground.

Fincher reached out and grabbed one of the little blue Scamps as he cartwheeled near their fur-lined bed, making the creature jump.

"Sorry if I scared you," said Fincher. "But what's all the commotion?" The blue face twisted in confusion. Fincher tried again. "What's going on?"

Big purple eyes widened in understanding. "Ahh, everyone back from Baashing. Big celebration to come. Big meal. Special meal. Fun! Fun! Fun!"

"What do you mean by *big celebration*? What was last night?"

The Pygmy Scamp waved Fincher away. "Last night nothing. Regular. Basic. Nothing. Tonight will be real party. Special party. Baashing successful. Must enjoy soon." After a moment, the Scamp continued. "You will see. You home. This home. Tonight real party. Real treats. Real Scamp fun. See you!"

After offering little tangible information, the blue man cartwheeled away from the children, stopping only when he reached the far side of the village.

Sammi cleaned her glasses, hoping it would also clear her head. "What did he say, Finch?"

Fincher shrugged. "Said that the... those involved in the Baashing were back? That there was going to be a big party tonight in celebration? Honestly, I couldn't understand most of it."

Sammi placed her cleaned glasses back onto a confused face. "Big party? What the heck do they call what we attended last night?"

"Not big, I guess," responded the boy. "Farking heck, maybe they didn't even consider that a party."

Sammi pushed her glasses up her nose and let out a tired sigh. "I'm not sure I can do another one of those." She looked over to her sister. "You're awfully quiet, Ash. How did you sleep?"

"Okay... I think."

Fincher stood on unsteady legs. "Yeah, well, good for you. Because I feel like one of Whyllo Bugg's fat turds. It was fun but I don't think—"

Three Scamps approached, cutting off the boy. Each held a V-shaped glass containing a golden concoction with a mass of bubbles racing from the bottom up, creating a foamy lid along the top.

"Here, here," said one. "Drink. Feel better. Much better."

Sammi waved her hand in refusal. "No, thank you. I think once was quite enough. I already have a screaming headache and—"

"Drink! Drink," cried another. "Better! Better!"

Fincher was the first to reach for one of the offerings. "Shite, if this will quiet the pounding in my brain, then I'm trying it." The boy took the nearest drink and downed a quarter of it in a single gulp. "Not bad. Not bad at all." A moment passed. "Wow! I feel better already. Way farking better!"

"Good enough for me," stated Sammi as she took one the golden drinks and put it to her lips. Shortly after the thick liquid had been consumed, her teeth showed in a relieved smile. "He's right, sis. This stuff is amazing. I already feel infinitely better. A big celebration doesn't sound like such a bad idea anymore."

"Farking right on that, Samm," said Fincher just before draining the remainder of his drink, the Scamps excitedly encouraging him. When he'd finished, he handed the strange glass back and looked to Ash questioningly.

"Well, sis?" asked Sammi, giving voice to Fincher's look. "It will make you feel better. Wait, not better. Wonderful."

"Farking wonderful," added Fincher.

Although something in the back of Ash's mind urged her not to, the girl couldn't help but accept the drink, such was her desire to alleviate the ache behind her eyes.

Two sips later and Ash understood. Gone was the pressure at her temples. Gone were her aching joints from jumping. Gone was the tiredness of her muscles from dancing all night.

As Terminus Grove slowly awakened in tandem with the fall of Paragon, the children's spirits continued to lift. After a small "breakfast" of more roasted vegetables, the younglings spent some time investigating the magical forest surrounding Sanctoom Olaroo.

Although they were generally left alone, three Pygmy Scamps were sent to follow at a distance, ensuring the children didn't get lost.

Their young brains humming from the golden drinks they had imbibed, the kids from Crimmish found something new to marvel at around every Numinoos Tree. Fist-sized white spiders spun giant webs in the glowing tree above. Starlight flickered in the webbing, each design containing its own galaxy, its own worlds, its own stories.

A small stream filled with ropes of light contained fish that would crawl out of the water on their front fins to snatch a glowing bug out of the air with foot-long tongues. Mission accomplished, the fish would release a melodic tune before sliding back into their cool, liquid home.

Just as the children started to follow another extraordinary find, a family of emerald rabbits that walked upright on long back legs, they were called back by their trio of Scamp guides.

"Baashers here," cried out a little fellow with one yellow eye and a second red one. "Need go back. Party start! Food here!"

Although disappointed to have to leave behind the wondrous hares, the children did as the Scamps requested, following the diminutive group back to Sanctoom Olaroo.

Stepping back into the village, the younglings found the place a literal hive of activity. Tall fires were already lit, and Scamps were running back and forth to each, placing slabs of skewered meat across the flames, sending the sizzling sounds and aromas of roasted flesh into the warm air.

In the center of the Sanctoom, a large group stood, surrounded by an animated audience of Scamps. Fincher did not recognize any of the Pygmies holding court. They seemed slightly larger and more muscled than the others and earrings of white bone hung from their large ears. Although too far away to hear clearly, the new group seemed to be answering questions from their fellow, excited Scamps.

"I guess those are the farking Baashers."

"Yes, yes," confirmed Doona as the yellow-haired Pygmy appeared next to the younglings. "Good Baashing. Very good Baashing. Everyone happy. We party now! We party! Come! Come!"

As Fincher, Ash, and Sammi drew closer to the collection of Baashers and other Scamps, a hush fell over the group. Two of the earring-wearing Pygmies stepped forward to greet the children. One was clearly a female and had almond-shaped eyes like those of their fallen friend Hana. She spoke as the younglings reached her.

"Ahh, happy for guests. Me Pixxy. This Greezy. This home now, yes?"

"Well, we're really just passing through," said Ash, watching carefully as purple eyes shared odd glances.

Pixxy smiled, showing crooked, too-bright teeth. "Sure, sure. But still home. Come. We party, then feast. Then party, then feast. Then party, yes?"

"Why the fark not?" said Fincher happily before Ash could stop the boy.

Permission given, the younglings were whisked away and seated at the nearest fire as the Baashers moved farther down the Sanctoom to continue answering questions from the other Scamps.

As soon as they were seated, more golden drinks were offered to the younglings. While Fincher and Sammi enjoyed theirs, something held Ash back. The one-armed girl paused as the liquid touched her lips, something echoing from the recesses of her mind.

Keep your mind clear.

With purple eyes watching her, Ash drank a tiny amount, making a big show of swallowing. She handed the glass back with the vast majority of the drink remaining in the V-shaped glass.

"I want to save room for other party fun," Ash exclaimed to address the questioning stares. Her acting seemed to work as the Scamps simply shrugged and went about other party business.

Soon, music began to fill the sanctoom, melding with the smells of cooking meat and the audible pops of rendered fat hitting the coals below. Fincher and Sammi were up and dancing in no time, leaving Ash alone to sit with a fake smile plastered on her face.

After spinning across the village's mossy ground and back, Fincher and Sammi collapsed next to their older friend, panting heavily.

"Why aren't you dancing, sis?"

"Just saving some energy for later, Samm."

Fincher rolled his hazel eyes. "What the fark for? We have drinks and smoke and food! There's no durned way we run out of energy!"

Ash simply shrugged. "Still, what's the rush?"

"I guess you're right. Oh, but here comes the farking good part!"

The Priestess Moossa stepped once more out of the smoky shadows, her rainbow hair dancing around her. The Cattipilloos was again draped across the shoulders of her white-haired robed.

This time, Moossa knelt before the children, letting the Cattipilloos simply raise its harlequin face before blowing thick smoke into their faces.

See this place for what it really is.

As Fincher and Sammi inhaled deeply, Ash opened her mouth but held her breath, allowing the yellow vapors to simply bounce off her face. Moossa didn't seem to notice as the Priestess stared hungrily at the meat sizzling above the fire.

Her job complete, the striking Priestess pranced to the next tall fire, where a group of Scamps welcomed her with large mouths agape.

Fincher and Sammi stood dumbly, giggling and holding each other for balance. Forgetting that Ash even existed, they stumbled off, finding the nearest group of blue creatures to frolic with.

Ash tried to keep up appearances, swaying back and forth to the music as she made her way across the sanctoom. Her mind much clearer than the previous evening, Ash watched as Pygmies staggered around the village, falling drunkenly to the moss-covered ground.

In some of the darker corners of the sanctoom, fights broke out, with one Scamp being viciously beaten by four others until they noticed Ash observing. They quickly picked up the little man they were assaulting, putting their arms around him and laughing as if it was just part of some violent but good-natured game.

On the edge of the village, just inside a shadowy part of the forest, Ash looked on in disgust as two male Scamps held down one of the few females while a third fought to pull down her overalls. The girl Pygmy, donning a thick mane of lime hair, cried out in fear-soaked fury until she spotted Ash in the near-distance. When purple eyes met brown-on-yellow, the lady Scamp's frown twisted into a forced smile and she offered a blue thumbs-up, growing quiet as the twisted little men continued their work.

Her brain unclouded, Ash's mind nonetheless reeled as she wandered back into the heart of Sanctoom Olaroo. As she did, a shrill whistle cut through the music, laughter, and general din of the village. An enthusiastic, unified shout went up as Scamps scurried to the nearest tall fire, taking seats wherever possible, shoving each other aside, if necessary.

"Ash! Ash! Ash!"

The girl spun several times before she found Sammi calling out to her from several fires away.

"We saved you a farking spot," shouted Fincher through intoxicated laughter. "Better hurry! These little shites are serious about their meat!"

Ash took a seat between her two friends. Before them, several Scamps worked furiously, removing the spiked meat from the fire, sliding it from their skewers, and carving the flesh into neat cubes with curved blades.

"Farking heck, that smells good!"

"I'm gonna stuff myself," added Sammi.

Ash rubbed her braided head, but something there, something within, continued to itch, continued to scream out at the girl.

And don't eat the meat.

Ash grabbed her sister and pulled her in close. She whispered desperately into Sammi's ear.

"Samm! Listen to me. You *can't* eat the meat."

"Why not? I'm starving and haven't had warm protein since the Clutch."

"You just can't!"

"That's not a reason, sis." Ash cursed under her breath, something rare for the girl. Her sister took notice despite her compromised faculties. "What is it?"

"You're just going to have to trust me. Do you trust me?"

"Of course, with my life. But that—"

"Then listen to me… please! I'm begging you. Do *not* eat that meat."

The bespectacled girl's face twisted behind her glasses, her stomach at severe odds with her older sister's pleas.

Finally, she said, "Okay, sis. I don't know why… but okay."

Ash repeated the desperate exercise with Fincher as the cubed meat was put into a bowl of woven leaves and began being passed around. It didn't go quite as smoothly with the hungry boy.

"What?! Fark that, I'm starving."

"Finch, please! You *must* listen to me!"

"Why?! You aren't making any sense!"

To their right, the three Scamps seated next to the children wildly attacked the cubed meat before them, scooping it up with blue hands and shoving as much as possible into their eager mouths. Their cheeks puffed out as they shoveled more and more in, growling at each other every time two hands reached for the same morsel.

Within literal seconds, the bowl was empty and sadly given back to the meat carvers, who started refilling it with more carved flesh.

"Finch! Please! I can't explain it, you but must believe me! Don't eat this meat."

The boy's eyes hungrily took in the smoking chunks being placed into the leafy bowl. His words slurred as he spoke.

"But.. I farking want it…"

"I know, Finch. But you can't have it. I'm begging you. For me. Pass on it for me?"

Despite his voracious hunger and muddled mind, Fincher looked into his friend's eyes and saw genuine concern. And that was one of the few things that he could trust as true and pure.

"Okay, Ash. Okay. I won't eat it. But they aren't gonna farking like it."

"You leave that to me."

Seconds later, the woven bowl was presented to the children, purple eyes closely following the steaming pile of meat.

"Thank you so very much," said Ash, putting every bit of gratitude into her words. "But we don't eat meat." Baffled looks encircled the younglings. Ash warily looked around, making sure that Doona and Jaloo were not in earshot, for the pair had seen the dried jerky in their bags. Satisfied that the two Scamps were not around, Ash continued. "I know you might find it strange, but we don't eat meat where we come from." Purple eyes narrowed. "It's against our religion, you see. Our gods don't allow it."

A Pygmy from across the fire voiced the confusion of the group.

"But this special meat. Baasher meat. Number one meat."

As Fincher and Sammi tried to slink lower into the moss, Ash doubled down. "I realize that, and we are thankful. But we cannot." Ash swept her lone hand across to encompass all the Scamps around their fire. "We give our share to all our friends sitting with us now."

A heavy, uncomfortable silence fell over the blue-skinned group before something clicked.

"More! More for us! Gimme! Gimme! Gimme!"

In the fight over the unclaimed meat, the children were quickly forgotten, and Ash pulled her friends from the tall fire in the chaos. Fincher groaned loudly as she did.

"Fark me, Ash! Your reason better have been worth it!" The boy paused. "What was your reason, again?"

Ash hesitated. "Just a feeling. A gut feeling."

"Yeah, well, I've got a feeling in my farking gut, too. Emptiness!" When Ash had no response to his complaining, Fincher grumbled loudly with frustration. "Okay, okay, okay. Everything's fine. I'm going to go find that farking Cattipilloos. And the beautiful girl on whose shoulder he lives. If I can't feed my farking belly, I'll fill my farking eyes!"

Sammi stepped in as Fincher shuffled away. "Don't worry, sis. He won't even remember this tomorrow." Ash didn't respond, her mind still searching for the source of the words that kept echoing in her skull. Sammi gave her sister a moment before going on. "There's something weighing heavy on you, sis. I'll let you sort it out. I'm going after Finch. I don't want that Moossa turning him into a frog for saying the wrong thing." Another pause. "You okay, sis?"

Ash smiled at her little sister. "I'm fine. You go have fun. Just stay away from the meat."

"I promised I will, and I will. I'll see if I can find us some more of those roasted veggies. They were as good as meat, anyway."

Sammi turned to leave. As she did, Ash grabbed her sister's arm.

"Samm."

"Yes?"

"Have fun. But be careful."

"Careful about what?"

"I don't know. Just be careful."

Sammi could have blown off her older sister. She could have offered a snappy retort about who was whose boss and how their ma and da were not around. But that wasn't the relationship between the Bugg sisters. Instead, she said, "You got it, sis. Find you later?"

"Of course. Love you."

"Love you, too."

For the remainder of the night, Fincher and Sammi caroused, dancing and drinking and smoking. But, regardless of their inebriation, the pair followed their friend's cryptic wishes and avoided the celebratory meat, even when it was pushed upon them.

Instead, Fincher and Sammi doubled down on the cooked vegetables when they finally made an appearance and readily accepted the dreampods when offered.

As for Ash, the girl gyrated around, feigning tipsiness, taking everything in with clear vision. When a dreampod was tossed into her mouth, Ash kept it in the corner of her cheek, spitting it out only when finally alone, making sure to stamp it deep into the soft moss when no one was looking.

With the Five Sisters falling overhead, Sammi spun and spun. Fincher somehow found one of the few duos of Pygmy females and spent the night dancing and stealing kisses. The music continued to blare. The fires continued to burn.

And Ash Bugg continued to bear witness.

Finally, when the fires started to die and the Scamps started to fall unconscious in groups like puppies, Fincher and Sammi and Ash found their way back to their fur-lined bed in the far corner of the sanctoom.

There, they held each other closely, giggling with laughter until their eyelids fell, replacing the colorful canvass of Sanctoom Olaroo with the blackness of sleep.

At least, that was the case for two of the three kids from Crimmish.

~

Despite her exhaustion, Ash fought off sleep, slipping into a place between the conscious and unconscious. It was there, not quite awake and not quite asleep, where Ash finally remembered her dream in full. Only, she realized that it wasn't a dream; it was Ditto crossing the cosmos to warn her.

Finish the mission. Save Fincher and Sammi. And most importantly—*I love you.*

Ash summoned her will and forced her eyes open, attempting to clear the last of the golden cocktail she was pressured into drinking. Sitting up carefully to not draw attention, Ash found the sanctoom as she had hoped.

The first rays of Paragon were beginning to pierce Terminus Grove's thick canopy, illuminating the now-quiet forest village. While most of the Pygmy Scamps had made it up into their treetop homes, several piles of the blue creatures could be seen throughout the sanctoom, each mound snoring more loudly than the one next to it.

Even with the loud shrieks of grove birds shattering the silence every few minutes, the Scamps remained unmoved. It quickly became clear to Ash that the Pygmies' nocturnal activities rendered them fairly useless during Paragon. The one-armed girl nodded to herself at this realization and slowly rose to her feet, cognizant of not waking her two companions.

See what these creatures really are.

The sanctoom's mossy ground proved the perfect environment for sneaking around, with Ash crossing the village like a phantom.

As the girl approached the central Numinoos Tree, she could hear talking coming from the Gaffer's quarters above. Unable to use the magical square stone, Ash was relieved to find small stairs spiraling up along the far side of the colossal tree. She crept up, careful to hug the trunk as there was no railing to protect one from a high fall.

When Ash reached the top, she slowly poked her head above the wooden platform. Fortunately, the Scamp guards were no longer stationed in the front area, allowing Ash to crouch-walk her way toward the Gaffer's receiving area.

Ash stopped as soon as she could see the group gathered in Olaroo's quarters, ensuring that she could make out their words as she slid behind a mass of vines to her right.

When she had settled in, she eased open the vines so her brown-on-yellow eyes could take in the scene.

Olaroo sat in his usual throne of sprouts, only, this time, it was lowered so that the Gaffer was eye-level with the other Scamps in attendance. The Pygmy chieftain looked down sourly at a mound of furs on the wooden flooring beneath him.

"Grey, grey, grey. Always grey."

The female Baasher Pixxy shuffled uncomfortably from one foot to the other while the male Greezy pretended to be studying something high in the Numinoos.

"All that's there," said Pixxy, a twinge of fear coating her words. "Young people gone. Gone to fight. Big war going on."

Greezy finally found the courage to jump in. "Yeah, yeah. Big human war. Only old people and babies left."

Olaroo's too-big purple eyes floated back and forth. "And you brought baby?"

"Yes, Gaffer! Many baby!" Pixxy sounded much more confident in this news. "Put with others. Will start feeding soon. Change come soon. Our numbers big soon."

"Well, that something," stated the Gaffer, his voice sounding far away. "War will take half man. Gloomtide take the other. Then sanctooms unite. Take Quaan. The Great Puke come. Our time. Our time. Our time."

"Yes, my Gaffer," stated Greezy reverently, his blue head bowed. "Their babies are our future Baashers. Soon, human gone. Only Scamps. The Great Puke complete."

"No, no, no," corrected the Gaffer as his sprouts lifted him higher into the air. "Must keep some. As pets. As fun. As meat. No sweeter meat. Must keep some around."

Pixxy's chin went into the air as she followed her chieftain with purple eyes. "Of course, my Gaffer! As they force us into forest, we force them into cages. For the fun. For the meat."

Ash's face twisted in confusion, and her eyes fell onto the pile of furs laid out before the sanctoom chieftain. The girl's eye's narrowed before going wide, and her lone hand went to her mouth, where bile had begun to appear.

That was no mound of furs at the feet of Gaffer Olaroo—they were human scalps. Ash looked on in horror as she started to make out strips of bloody skin surrounding the clumps of white and grey hair. The youngling then looked up in disgust, recognizing that the Gaffer's "fur" pants were made from a similar material. Ash's mind flashed back to Priestess Moossa's ornate robe, and she felt her stomach turn.

The Gaffer continued to rise on his sprout throne, speaking as he did. "And the humans? The forest folk?"

Pink-mohawked Jaloo stepped forward, with Ash noticing their former guide for the first time. "Forest not hurt them. They can go forest or village. Very valuable. Very valuable. Soon, they one of us. After enough dreampods, they do what we say. Very valuable. Can go where we cannot. Can unlock doors from inside."

The Gaffer thought over this new information. "Good, good. Feed them more. Sharpen our new weapon." The gathered Scamps looked relieved, but it was only temporary as the Gaffer continued. "But not good enough. Must do better. Need more baby for more Scamp. Need younger meat. Need to ready for war."

"Oks, my Gaffer! Oks," came the unified cry, alerting Ash that it was time to leave.

While the Baashing party was still paying respects to their Gaffer, Ash slipped out from her vine hideaway and sprinted down the Numinoos stairs, taking two at a time to avoid detection.

When she hit the mossy turf, Ash sprinted in a crouch back toward her friends, sliding against Fincher just as a group of Baashers was descending from above on the rune-covered square rock.

Ash kept her eyes shut, feigning a deep slumber, as several Baashers passed by, one commenting that if they wanted younger meat, they didn't have far to look. This was met with several dark chuckles of agreement.

Ash's eyelids remained tightly closed. Two dozen minutes passed before the girl dared to look upon the sanctoom once more. Gone were the Baashers, either into Terminus Grove or back to their homes in the trees.

Ash rose to her feet again, stumbling with the weight of recent discoveries. Doubt crept into her young mind.

Did I hear their words correct? Was I jumping to conclusions? Is this real or am I still in the throes of a dreampod? Am I awake?

Ultimately, Ash Bugg decided that she wasn't dreaming, nor hallucinating, nor hearing things. But perhaps she *was* jumping to conclusions. There was only one way to find out.

Just as she did a half-hour before, Ash lightly crossed Sanctoom Olaroo, passing the central Numinoos and continuing on, eventually exiting the village opposite from where the children had first entered. No guards appeared stationed anywhere, although Ash did pass three sleeping Scamps who may have been shirking their duties.

Soon, Ash found herself surrounded by Terminus Grove. The girl looked up and found Paragon peeking through to her far right. She committed to keeping Paragon there, allowing her to find her way back when her investigation was complete.

Minimal searching was needed. Shortly after crossing a small, melodic stream, Ash heard the familiar cooing of a baby—a human baby. Prior to her harvester days, Ash watched several of Crimmish's newest residents as their parents tended to the day's labors. This was in addition to raising her little sister once she was off Jazz Bugg's bosom. In short, Ash knew a baby when she heard one.

The girl from Crimmish followed the sounds, taking her around one particularly giant Numinoos Tree, across a meadow of massive, wind lizard-sized orange blossoms, up the bank of a raging forest river, and to the mouth of a cave that was hidden by a thick growth of hanging vegetation.

Faint cries could be heard within, followed by the demands of Scamp voices. Ash carefully leaned around the edge of the cave mouth and peered between the mixture of roots and stalks. Her breath caught in her throat.

Inside the cave, placed on woven mats positioned several feet apart, were hundreds of human babies, either asleep or reaching up to claw at their terrifying surroundings.

Pygmy Scamps walked between the rows of infants, placing bottles of a bright red substance into the mouths of those awake. Other Scamps made rounds, looking at each baby before jotting notes onto a large ream of homemade paper.

Some of the infants had the reddish skin of newborns while others were normal shades of peach and brown and white and caramel. But others…

Ash squinted, ensuring she was seeing things correctly. She was. More than half of the babies in the cave were various hues of blue, their mouths and ears growing faster than usual, their eyes becoming an unusual shade of purple.

See these creatures for what they really are.

Ash fell away from the cave mouth, almost tumbling into the swift waters of the forest river. Her young mind spun, and her stomach tried in vain to evict food that simply wasn't there.

Ash stumbled down the steep bank and cut left, trying to put as much space between herself and that awful cave as possible.

In short order, the one-armed girl was lost, tearing through bushes and walls of vines with reckless abandon. Her young mind was a tornado, shifting, from concern for the babies she found, to the horror of the scalp pile placed before the Gaffer, to her unconscious friends who were positioned to become pawns in an evil contest between human and Scamp.

Left. Right. Right. Straight. Straight. Straight. Right.

Ash passed between two modest trees, ripping through the thick vines that connected them, and immediately tripped over something, falling face-first into a heap of jagged whiteness.

Ash scrambled atop the stack, cursing under her breath as her hands and feet failed to find purchase. Finally, she ventured to look at one of the items comprising the pile and recoiled in disgust.

In Ash's right hand, caught between her brown fingers, was a femur—a thighbone undeniably from a human.

"Shite, shite, shite, shite," repeated the youngling as she backpedaled, rib bones and skulls and tailbones and forearms falling in after her as she retreated.

Finally free of the macabre collection, Ash took in the gruesome scene in full, her back against one of the many trees bordering the clearing. Before the young girl stood a mountain of bones—human bones—its zenith almost reaching the lowest surrounding tree limbs.

And don't eat the meat.

"Impossible," said Ash to herself, refusing to acknowledge the hideousness before her.

"Not impossible. True," came a small voice from behind Ash, forcing the girl to jump up and spin around, blade drawn.

Ash's brown-on-yellow eyes went wide with rage, and the tough girl from Crimmish advanced on the female Scamp who stood there. She marched forward with murder on her mind. The girlish Pygmy recoiled in fear.

"Not cut! Not cut! Friend! Partner maybes!" Ash continued to advance. "This not me! Not me! I taken, too! Taken! Want to leave! Can help you! Help you leave!" Ash hesitated.

"Why would you help me?"

"You know me! You see me!" Ash's mind reeled as she noticed the female Scamp's bright lime hair and recalled the image of several males assaulting a female Pygmy the evening before.

Ash stumbled over her words. "I saw you. You were in trouble. I was going to save you, but you gave me a thumbs up." The girl's mind whirled. "Why did you do that?"

The lady Pygmy shrugged. "Do no good. Only hurt you maybes. But you see. You see this place."

Ash's face transformed into a grimace, and she slid toward the lime-haired Scamp, knife-point leading the way. "I see. And you're an active member of this place. And, therefore, no friend of mine."

To her credit, the female Scamp did not run, opting instead to remain where she stood, even jutting her chin out at the approaching human.

"Do what you want," said the Pygmy defiantly. "But I can help. This not my home. Taken from home. Made into Scamp. Most not remember. But I do. I do. I want to leave. Can take you with me."

Ash's eyes narrowed, now used to being lied to. "And why do you need me? Just go! Nothing is stopping you!"

"Not true," protested the Scamp, desperation painting her words. "Cannot just leave. Must be taken. If taken—by you!—can escape to another sanctoom. But cannot just go. Oh no! If just go, will be caught and killed for sure. For sure. You see! You see what they do to lady Scamps here. No good! No good, at all! Want to leave. But need to be taken!"

Ash remained unconvinced. "And where will you go? You can't exactly march into a human town, especially given what it looks like your people have been doing to border towns in Cobalt territory."

The lady Scamp shook her lime hair in frustration. "No, no, no! Not human town. I go to other sanctoom. They nicer to lady Scamps. Have more priestesses than one. Have good Gaffer. Not crazy Gaffer like Olaroo." A pause. "I need go! *You* need go! I can take you. Help you, help me!"

Despite the constant lies, the constant letdowns, Ash found herself trusting this seemingly demoralized female Scamp.

"And what's your name?" asked Ash.

"Dazzy. Dazzy Mae. They hate I remember old name Mae, but I do. I remember all. So, I make them call me Dazzy Mae. Even though it makes them beat me, I don't care. That's my name."

Ash looked down upon the pretty, lime-covered Scamp and felt a strange kinship to the Pygmy girl.

"Why do we need you, Dazzy Mae? I know which way is north. I know Terminus Grove now. What do my friends and I need from Dazzy Mae?"

Dazzy smiled smugly, as if the Scamp knew the location of a hidden treasure. "You can go north. But not fast enough."

"Fast enough for what, Dazzy Mae?"

"Fast enough for Baashers not catch you. Fast enough for Baashers not take you back. Or not take your hair. Or not take your meat. Baashers not care. Just want to catch."

"We've traveled a long way, Dazzy Mae. Farther than you could ever imagine. We can move fast."

Lime hair flashed back and forth. "No. Not fast as Baasher. Will catch you." Dazzy hesitated for dramatic effect. "But I can make faster."

"How?"

A blue finger went up to blue lips. "Cannot say. Must see. Trust me?" Ash offered no response. "Trust me?!"

"I do. I do trust you, Dazzy Mae," Ash finally said.

The lady Scamp nodded. "Meet north end of sanctoom. Bring everyone. Bring everything."

"I will."

Dazzy Mae turned to head back off into the forest.

"Dazzy Mae!" The Pygmy stopped and turned back. "Uh, I don't know where I am. Point me in the right direction?"

Dazzy released a great sigh, and the obvious question hung heavy in the air. She held out a blue elbow. "Take arm. Don't let go."

Ash shoved something large under her shirt and her right hand shot out, finding the crook of Dazzy's elbow. "I'm Ash, by the way."

"I know. Olaroo want eat you because hand missing. But Doona say you still good warrior."

"And what does Dazzy Mae think?"

"I think you my way out. Out of Sanctoom Olaroo. Out of nightmare." Dazzy Mae pulled Ash into the thick forest. "But only if you shut up and stay quiet. And not get us all eaten."

"Is it night again… already?" groaned Fincher as Ash jostled the boy awake.

"No," stated Sammi wearily from the side, the young girl also ripped from a deep slumber. "It's actually still quite early in Paragon," she said, slipping on her glasses as she did. "Which means I have no clue why my sister is waking us."

Ash knelt and spoke in an urgent whisper. "Be quiet, both of you! We have to leave."

"The fark we do," hissed Fincher. "We finally found a place that accepts us! A place where dreams come true every night."

"He's right, sis," agreed Sammi. "This is a magical place. This might be *the* magical place. Who's to say that this whole journey wasn't just to get the three of us *here*? Who's to say that Sanctoom Olaroo isn't where we belong? Isn't our new home?"

Ash hesitated before responding. "Ditto."

Sammi's eyes narrowed behind round frames. "What do you mean?"

Ash paused again, reluctant to share that most intimate of moments. Ultimately, however, it seemed the only way.

"Ditto came to me while we slept this past Paragon. He told me that we couldn't trust the Pygmy Scamps. He told me that we needed to complete our mission. He told me that I had to save the two of you."

"Oh, how farking convenient! Ditto came to *you* to save *us*? In case you didn't notice, Samm and I are doing great here!"

Sammi held out a hand to quiet Fincher before taking a more tactful approach.

"You saw Ditto, sis... in a dream?

"Yes..." Ash shook her head in frustration. "I mean, yes... it was *in* a dream, but Ditto was *real*. He crossed the cosmos to see me. To warn me. To save *us*."

Fincher and Sammi shared a look. Sammi placed her hand on her older sister's left shoulder.

"The dream doesn't mean anything, Ash. It just means that you miss Ditto. We all do."

"No!" Ash looked around before lowering her voice. "No. He told me things. Things that are proving to be true."

"Like what?"

"He told me to see this place for what it really is. So, I didn't partake in any of the Cattipilloos smoke or the dreampods, and do you know what I saw?"

"What did you see, sis?"

"I saw, away from the sparkly things and colorful shows, I saw what really drives this place... violence and hate."

"I haven't seen any of that," shot back Fincher.

"That's because you don't even know where you are half the time, Finch. And the other half of the time your focus is solely on lady Scamps. Who, by the way, are treated awfully here."

Fincher started to argue again, but Sammi cut the boy off.

"What else did Ditto tell you?"

"He told me that we had to finish the mission. I think he was trying to say that this... place... is just a diversion. A dangerous diversion."

Fincher snickered. *"Finish the farking mission.* Are you sure it was Ditto that visited you and not the farking Imperator?"

"I'm sure!"

"How do you farking know?"

"Because he told me he loved me!"

"That means it was all in your head, Ash!"

"No! No, it doesn't!"

"How farking so?"

A pause. "Because I could never dream that! Never in my wildest dreams could I ever dare to imagine Ditto saying that to me! *That!* That's how I know it to be true! That he was real! He was real, and he was warning us!"

Ash's emotional outburst silenced her two companions. When it was obvious that they had nothing more to add, Ash went on, pushing her embarrassment aside.

"Ditto said one last thing."

"What's that, sis?"

"He told me not to eat the meat."

Fincher rolled his hazel eyes. "That's why I couldn't enjoy that delicious meat?! Because dream Ditto told you not to?!"

"That's right. And I'm glad we didn't."

"And why the fark is that?"

"Because of this," stated Ash, removing the item from under her shirt and letting it roll toward Fincher on the mossy ground.

"Fark, fark, fark," exclaimed the boy as he scampered away from the human skull that came to rest at his feet. "Where the fark did you get that, Ash?"

"Oh, there's a whole mountain of them off in the forest, not too far from here. And it's not just skulls, either. There are leg bones and arms and hips... every part of the human body. At least, every part that you can't eat."

Fincher's face turned green and Sammi's hand went to her mouth.

"You mean, sis..."

"That's right. Now, are you ready to listen to me?"

Fincher and Sammi looked to one another before nodding sadly, upset that their paradise may have been hiding nightmares. Fincher kicked at the human skull, sending it rolling away.

"You could have picked a less shocking way to break the farking news to us, ya know."

Ash rose to her feet. "Oh, I did, Finch. The other way would have been to point out what our bedding was made from."

Fincher sprung to his feet and looked down at his blankets in horror, the reality of the long grey and white "fur" finally coming into focus.

"Oh, fark me! Fark me! This place is a durned freak show."

Ash helped her sister up. "Oh, you haven't heard the half of it. You both pack as I talk."

This time, there were no arguments.

Fincher and Sammi shoved their items into their packs, moving quickly but quietly as Ash recounted what she had discovered and what she had overheard.

Fincher and Sammi's eyes went wide upon hearing that Baashing parties were raiding villages along Terminus Grove, butchering the adults and absconding with infants. Bile had to be swallowed back when Ash shared that Olaroo complained about the age of the most recent meat. Fincher's mouth fell open and Sammi wiped a tear after learning of the cavern of stolen babies and how they were being transformed into the next crop of Pygmy Scamps.

"Farking bastards," spat Fincher. "And to think that I shared kisses with some of these monsters!"

"I hope you didn't get any of that meat in your mouth, Finch," teased Sammi, and the boy immediately rinsed his mouth with water. Again. And again.

Eventually, bags were packed and hefted, weapons were secured, and the younglings were ready to sneak out of Sanctoom Olaroo.

"We'll go out the northern exit," whispered Ash as the children crossed the mossy village, giving a wide birth to the sleeping piles of Pygmy Scamps.

"Did Ditto tell you that, as well?" asked Sammi.

"No, someone else gave me that bit of advice."

"I hope this someone is more farking real," said Fincher under his breath.

Sammi leaned into her older sister as they tiptoed through the sanctoom. "Sis, how are we going to find our way through Terminus Grove? I mean, the whole point of going with Doona and Jaloo was to find a guide to the Northern Goddess. We're right back where we started."

"Not quite, Samm."

"How so?"

"You'll see."

The trio passed the last group of slumbering Scamps and approached the hanging vines between two Numinoos Trees that marked the northern entrance of the settlement.

Fincher's hunting knife came out in a flash.

"And who the fark is this?!"

Dazzy Mae jumped, sending her lime hair flying as Fincher advanced with his blade drawn.

"Friend. Friend. I help you." Dazzy Mae looked to Ash for help. "She tell. She tell."

"Finch," hissed Ash as loudly as she dared. "Put your weapon away. This is Dazzy Mae. She's gonna guide us to the Northern Goddess."

Fincher's knife stayed at the ready. "In case you didn't notice, Ash, these Scamps are the ones we're running from."

"Me too," protested Dazzy Mae.

"I don't farking trust her."

"Well, I do, Finch."

"Why? Why do you trust her?"

Ash looked to Dazzy, and the two simultaneously recalled the evening prior, when the female Pygmy was attacked by a group of male Scamps.

"I just do! And I need you to, as well!"

Fincher refused to move. "I don't think that you should. Or that I can."

A voice from above plucked at the tension, forcing the three children and female Scamp to visibly flinch.

"Stay there! Not move!"

The odd quartet looked up just as a Pygmy Scamp rappelled from the treetop living quarters toward the ground.

"Fark me," was all that Fincher could muster as the Baasher known as Greezy touched down lightly onto the spongy turf. Greezy wore a wicked-looking curved blade at his hip and held a golden, spiral trumpet in his blue right hand.

"Here they are," said Dazzy Mae excitedly. "I catch for you. I trick them for Olaroo. Take them! Take them!"

"Farking heck! You sure know how to pick them, Ash." The one-armed girl had no response, Dazzy's betrayal having left her mute.

"Go on! Take them, Greezy," begged Dazzy Mae, determined to cover up her own involvement in the potential escape.

Sammi fingered the dagger at her hip and Fincher remained frozen but coiled, ready to strike out. Greezy, a veteran of countless Scamp battles and raids, took in the scene, ran through several scenarios in his head, and offered a crooked, too-white smile.

"*I* not need to take. Not when *we* can take." Greezy slowly placed the end of the trumpet to his blue lips. He spoke around the mouthpiece. "We tell you this home now. Before? As guest. Now? As prisoner. You are Scamp. You just not know it yet. Let me show you."

Greezy's lips engulfed the trumpet's end and the Pygmy's cheeks began to inflate with air. Fincher did a quick calculation and realized he would never reach the Baasher in time. That soon they would be surrounded by Pygmy Scamps. That their soft beds of human hair would be replaced with bars. That they would be turned into something terrible, something not quite human.

Fincher closed his eyes, waiting for the inevitable note that would wake the entirety of Sanctoom Olaroo, shackling the kids from Crimmish to their fate.

But instead of the sharp tone of a trumpet, Fincher only heard a dull *thud* followed by a low wheezing.

The boy's eyelids sprung open, and Fincher looked upon the shocked face of Greezy, a curved knife buried in the right side of his neck.

The Baasher dropped his trumpet to the cushioned ground and reached up to gingerly touch the handle of the blade that was there, as if making sure it was real and not some terrible trick of a dreampod.

As realization set in, Greezy fell to his knees and attempted to pull at the hilt of the blade. His blue hand was knocked to the side, however, as Dazzy Mae stepped forward, a cold look in her oversized purple eyes. The lady scamp took hold of her cherished weapon and viciously ran it across Greezy's throat, sending a river of blood to pour down the Baasher's overalls.

As Greezy's life force pooled under him, staining the bright moss, he looked to Dazzy Mae, perhaps searching for some kind of mercy.

But there was none to be found.

Instead, Dazzy Mae ripped the bone earrings from Greezy's large right ear before plunging her curved blade repeatedly into the Baasher's chest, cursing under her breath the entire time.

When her grisly attack finally ended, Dazzy Mae deliberately wiped her blade clean on the deceased Greezy's clothes and returned it to the sheath at her hip. She then grunted with effort as she pulled the corpse into the thick collection of hanging vines, essentially hiding the body.

"We ready?" Dazzy asked cheerily after returning from the dangling vegetation. The younglings barely moved. "Well?"

Ash shook off her paralysis and smiled. "Well, Finch? Can you trust her now?"

Fincher matched Ash's smile with a naughty grin of his own.

"*Trust* her? Farking heck, she's my new hero!"

"Then, we can go?"

Fincher made a big show of sweeping his arm toward the sanctoom entrance.

"Of course! After you, my lime-haired beauty."

Dazzy Mae tossed Fincher a purple wink as the lady Scamp led the way. She spoke as she passed from village to surrounding forest. "Now know why human tongue taste best. Not careful with sweet words. Maybe same as honey?" Dazzy Mae shot Ash and Sammi a toothy smile before turning back to Fincher. "Only way to find out."

With that, Dazzy Mae moved deeper into Terminus Grove, Ash and Sammi Bugg following closely behind, leaving a stunned Fincher to take up the rear.

"I don't think I can trust her anymore," Fincher called out to the sisters.

"Too late, Finch. She's yours now," giggled Sammi.

"Farking heck!"

"Still early. Guards not out yet. Forest sleep."

Dazzy Mae's whispered declaration was in direct response to Fincher, Ash, and Sammi looking around nervously, examining the trees overhead for any sign of Scamp sentries.

After an hour of walking through the dense, melodic Grove in silence, curiosity finally started to get the best of the children. Fincher, obviously, was the first to lend voice to his questions.

"Uh… Dazzy Mae?"

"Yes?"

"Not to sound ungrateful or anything, but why, exactly, are you helping us again?"

"She already explained it to me, Finch," interrupted Ash.

"Well, I'd like to hear it for myself. And I'm sure Samm would, as well." The bespectacled girl nodded in agreement.

Dazzy answered without taking her purple eyes off the small, almost imperceptible animal trail ahead.

"Sanctoom Olaroo no good. Not good for lady. Only good for Baashers and Moossa and Olaroo."

Fincher thought for a moment. "So, where will you go?"

Dazzy Mae did not hesitate. "Will go to another sanctoom. Farther west. Have good sanctoom there."

Sammi jumped in with a question. "What makes you think it will be any different, Dazzy?"

Dazzy Mae shrugged from the front of the line. "No Moossa. No Olaroo."

"I would think that Moossa would want to help other lady Pygmies," said Ash.

Dazzy Mae shook her head violently in the negative, sending her lime hair side to side.

"Moossa the worst. She couple with Olaroo and use him to make sure there only one priestess. Make sure other lady Scamps are nothing. Make sure that we just fun for males. No good."

"And other sanctooms are different?" inquired Sammi.

"Sure, sure. Most sanctooms have many priestess. Only Olaroo just allow one. I am good priestess. Better than Moossa. But she not like me. She scared of me. That why they hurt me."

The younglings marched on despite the discomforting news.

"I'm sorry that happened to you, Dazzy Mae," offered Fincher. "But that didn't really answer my question. Why are you helping us? What's stopping you from sneaking out on your own?"

Dazzy Mae stopped and turned around, bringing the children to a halt.

"No good. No good. Cannot simply leave sanctoom. Cannot switch. But if taken?"

The boy's jaw fell a bit. "Taken? We did no such thing. If anything, you were the one who—"

"Finch," interrupted Sammi. "I think what she's saying is that it needs to look like she was kidnapped and forced to go with us." Dazzy nodded.

"Okay," Fincher responded, thinking things through. "But then wouldn't she be expected to return to Sanctoom Olaroo after?"

"No, no," stated Dazzy Mae flatly. "After taken I will be Pygmy Waif. Can go to any sanctoom that will adopt me."

"And… you're sure that they're gonna want you?"

"Finch!"

"What the heck, Finch?!"

Fincher held his palms up defensively. "Hey, I'm just asking questions here. Our lives are in her blue hands, after all!"

Dazzy Mae, instead of growing upset by the boy's words, presented a genuine too-white smile.

"It oks. It oks." Oversized purple eyes found hazel-on-yellow orbs. "I am *very* good priestess. They will want."

"See! That's all I was farking asking."

Ash shifted uncomfortably. "That does still beg the question, Dazzy. You're out of Sanctoom Olaroo now. Why keep helping us?"

Dazzy Mae thought it over, attempting to find the words with her limited vocabulary.

"Humans bad to us long ago. They push us into forest, make us Pygmy Scamps. Many, many die. Others change. Adapt. Now, we bad to humans. Very, very bad. Too bad. I not like. Want to help. Want to make right. Even if little."

"And these other sanctooms? Do they…" Fincher paused but pushed forward. "Do they… eat… the meat?"

Purple eyes went wide. "No! Not do! Well… most not do. Place I go not do." Dazzy spat onto the forest floor. "I never do! Never do!"

Fincher finally relented. "Okay, okay. Thank you for answering my questions, Dazzy. We're really happy to have you as our guide."

"For sure," added Sammi.

"No doubt about it," concurred Ash. "Please lead on, Dazzy Mae!"

The lady Scamp grinned at the last bit and plowed ahead once more, passing between thick, multicolored bushes and making sharp turns to avoid things that the younglings were unable to detect.

During their march north, Dazzy would point out fruits that could be eaten, and those that would lead to certain death. The aspiring priestess picked one particularly delicious-looking fruit and held it out for the Crimmish kids to study. It was a brilliant yellow color and shaped like a diamond. Fincher thought that it must taste like Widow Till's sugared red bean squares.

"This one," said Dazzy, rotating the natural diamond for all to see, "taste like honey—"

"I knew it," exclaimed Fincher, reaching for the yellow fruit. Dazzy pulled it back.

"But turn your inside jelly."

A smug look crossed Sammi's face. "I told you, Finch."

"Yeah, yeah, yeah. Jelly guts. I farking got it."

After a quick lunch of fruit and some of the remaining dried jerky, the quartet moved on, their small legs growing heavy as Paragon rose and then began to fall. Sammi tripped on an upraised root but was caught at the last moment by her sister's lone good hand. Fincher's foot slipped off a lichen-covered rock, twisting his ankle.

"Faaaark!"

Ash stumbled while traversing a shallow stream, almost dumping her full pack into the water.

"Hey, Dazzy Mae," Fincher called out to their lime-haired guide. "When are we going to stop to camp for the evening? I think we're all getting tired, and someone's bound to get hurt."

"Cannot stop."

"Come again?"

"Cannot stop."

"And why the fark not?"

Dazzy refused to turn around, her little legs still pumping away.

"Scamps start wake now. See you gone. See me gone. See Greezy dead. They hunt soon. Come for us."

"Surely, we have a big enough lead—"

"Not safe. They come. They come fast."

"Well, we can't farking keep on like this!"

"Not have to."

"So, we'll stop?"

"No."

Fincher looked to Ash and Sammi for support. "Can someone farking help me out here?!"

The sisters shared in a giggle at Fincher's expense before realizing that their friend was right. Ash spoke up. "Hey, Dazzy Mae! Can you please stop for a minute?" Dazzy Mae did as requested, although the lady Scamp appeared annoyed and a little worried as she spun to face the younglings. "Thank you. Dazzy, Finch is right. We're exhausted and need to rest soon." Ash shifted the large pack on her shoulders. "These bags aren't light."

"Can rest soon."

Ash sighed in relief. "Oh good. How long before we can stop, you think?"

"Cannot stop."

Ash looked perplexed while Fincher offered a smirk of his own.

"Uhh... Dazzy... we can't rest if we can't stop."

"Can."

"Uhh... cannot."

"I'm dying to see where this farking goes."

"Shut up, Finch," demanded Sammi as the boy rolled his eyes.

Dazzy Mae's blue mouth formed a small O, finally understanding the children's confusion.

"Can rest but not stop. I show you. But must go farther."

"But Dazzy..."

"Trust me?" The Scamp's purple eyes seemed to swallow the one-armed girl.

Ash paused, but only for the briefest of moments. "I do, Dazzy Mae."

"Then come. I show why I good priestess." The Pygmy Scamp began walking away but stopped momentarily to talk over one blue shoulder. "Best priestess."

Within seconds, the lady Scamp had disappeared, forcing the children to hurry along after her.

"Well, that didn't farking accomplish anything."

Ash shot Fincher a dangerous look. "She said that we can rest, Finch."

"Without stopping, Ash."

"I don't get it, either. But I trust her."

"Farking great. The last guy to trust her ended up with a farking knife in his neck."

Sammi chuckled, already laughing at her upcoming joke. "Afraid of a girl hurting you, Finch?"

"Always, Samm. Farking always."

The girl pushed her glasses farther up her nose, hooked her friend and older sister by the elbows, and pulled them after Dazzy Mae. "Come on, Finch! Aren't you dying to see what rest without stopping looks like?"

"Shite choice of words, Samm. Shite choice of words."

The children stumbled forward, tripping every few steps, their little legs no longer able to support their weight. Ahead, Dazzy Mae marched on, paying little attention to the struggling younglings behind her.

Around the temporary quartet, the forest was awakening as the Five Sisters took over from Paragon, which had disappeared behind the tree line. Fincher, Ash, and Sammi attempted to enjoy the wondrous spectacle playing out once more, but their fatigue stole any potential enjoyment.

"Hey, Dazzy Mae," called out Fincher. "We're farking dying back here. How about a rest? Just for a bit?" There was no response. "Dazzy!"

"Not talk to me," spat the lady Scamp without turning around. "Looking."

"Looking for what?" asked Sammi. "Maybe we can help."

"Cannot. Not know what you see."

Sammi pushed her glasses farther up a nose beaded with sweat. "But, maybe if you explained it to us, we could—"

"There," shouted Dazzy Mae, her little blue legs leaving the ground as she leapt into the air in excitement. "There he is! There my lord!" Dazzy shot off to the right, leaving the thin trail on which they had been traveling and going deeper into the dense Grove.

Fincher looked to Ash and Sammi, a concerned look on the boy's face as he mouthed the word *lord*.

In seconds, Dazzy Mae had vanished into the thick brush that was coming alive with bioluminescent color.

"Where did she go?" asked Ash.

"Did she farking leave us behind?"

"She wouldn't do that," stated Ash, a bit less confidently than she would have liked.

"Why the fark not? She got what she needed out of us. Now she can bail, leaving those shite Baashers to hunt us while she slithers away to another durn sanctoom. I'm telling you—"

Dazzy Mae's soft voice cut through the now-glowing forest. "Over here! Over here! Come, come!"

Ash shot Fincher with a look. "You were saying?"

Fincher shrugged and smiled. "Happy to be wrong."

"Then you must be happy a lot, Finch," joked Sammi.

"Come on," Ash cut in before Fincher could reply. "She sounded like she's over here, through these bushes."

The kids from Crimmish fought their way through a small thicket, nearly tumbling out as they cleared the final sharp-tipped branches.

"Fark that hurt," complained Fincher, rubbing the scratches that now ran across his forearms. "This better be worth—"

Fincher's words fell off as the younglings took note of what lay before them.

They were in a tiny clearing, no more than several feet across and surrounded by a wall of thorn-covered shrubbery. In the center of the clearing, Dazzy Mae sat cross-legged, a giant smile pasted on the Pygmy Scamp's too-big mouth.

Before her, in the middle of the empty space, a single mushroom sprung up from the forest soil. It rose two feet into the air and released a bluish light like that of Ommori Prime.

"This is it," said Dazzy Mae, her words dripping with awe. "This Terro. This the Buried God. My god."

The younglings shared in a doubtful look, afraid that their guide had completely lost her mind.

"Uhh, Dazzy Mae," said Ash carefully, "that's just a mushroom. It's a beautiful mushroom. Maybe the prettiest I've ever seen. But it's just a mushroom."

"Mushroom," snickered Dazzy Mae, her purple eyes never leaving the gently pulsing fungus. "This not mushroom." A pause. "It *is* mushroom. But more. Much more."

"What else is it?" prodded Ash.

"It ear. Ear of God. Ear of the Buried God. Ear of Terro."

Fincher rolled his hazel eyes. Sammi pushed her glasses up as she scrunched her face. But Ash kept the faith.

"If that mushroom is the ear, Dazzy Mae, then where is this Terro?"

"Under. Under the forest. Terro is the Buried God." The lady Scamp spread her blue arms out. "He everywhere under Terminoos."

While Fincher and even Ash remained confused, Sammi began to understand. The bespectacled girl stepped forward.

"Dazzy Mae, is this Terro's only ear?"

A blue hand waved dismissively in the air. "The Buried God everywhere. Have many ears. And many eyes. And many hands."

"Hands?" Fincher asked Ash, but his one-armed friend could only shake her braided head.

Sammi's quick mind continued to process Dazzy's words. After a few beats, her brown-on-yellow eyes went wide behind round lenses.

"Dazzy Mae, are you saying that there is a giant fungal network under Terminus Grove? Like one giant thinking organism?"

The lady Scamp twisted to face Sammi, a toothy grin showing. "Not organism. Terro. The Buried God."

"And you can… talk to it?"

"Oh, this is rich," whispered Fincher to Ash and was promptly hushed.

Dazzy Mae turned back and gently stroked the top of the blue mushroom. "Can talk. Can listen. Can ask for help."

Sammi thought over her words before speaking again. "And Terro… the Buried God… he can help us get to the Northern Goddess?"

"Sure. If I ask nice."

"Do you know how to ask nice, Dazzy Mae?"

"Sure."

Ash was also beginning to understand. "Do the other Pygmy Scamps know about the Buried God, Dazzy Mae?"

Blue lips twitched as Dazzy mulled the question over. "They know something there. But they not know Terro. They not know how to talk to him."

"And you do? How?"

Dazzy Mae presented a smug smile. "I am good priestess. Best priestess."

A strange shriek rang out from the forest, not close but also not far away enough for comfort.

"Uhh… Dazzy Mae. You said the Baashers are farking fast, right?"

"Baashers move fast."

"Then maybe we should get a farking move on?"

"Baashers fast. The Buried God faster. Now, no more talk!"

The younglings moved around their new Scamp friend, taking up silent positions around the glowing mushroom. Dazzy Mae motioned, and the children sat down on the ground, boxing in the "ear" of Terro.

Dazzy Mae reached into her sling sack, speaking as she fished around. "Only Dazzy Mae know this the ear of Terro. Only Dazzy Mae know what he like." A blue hand removed a small flute-like instrument carved from an old, twisted root. "Only Dazzy Mae friend to Terro."

The unusual instrument went to blue lips and a haunting melody escaped its hollow end, with notes foreign to human ears reaching the children, pulling them into a deep trance. As Dazzy Mae played, the Ear of Terro swayed back and forth, every now then shooting starlight spores high into the air, as if applauding the priestess's efforts. The kids from Crimmish could not help but think of fallen Hana, and how their young friend's singing could have a similar effect on animals.

After several minutes, the mushroom halted its motion and began to pulse dramatically. Dazzy Mae nodded and put her magical flute away.

"The Buried God want treat," she said, pulling an item out from another pocket. "Want favor, must give favor. Here, Terro. This for you. Your favorite."

Fincher, Ash, and Sammi watched on as Dazzy Mae placed a chunk of red meat on the ground before the blue mushroom.

"What is that?" Sammi dared to ask.

"Tongue. Greezy tongue. I take before I leave."

"Dazzy!" exclaimed Ash. "Why would you do that?"

The priestess shrugged. "Terro favorite. Favorite treat. Pygmy Scamps burn our dead. Eat other dead. Give nothing to Terro. I give him."

"Well, that took a dark farking turn," said Fincher to himself, although Sammi nodded in agreement.

All four sat cross-legged and stared down as Greezy's tongue, much like their dear friend Ditto, sank gently into the forest floor, a coin-sized grouping of yellow flowers springing up from where the meat once rested.

The Ear of Terro pulsed even more violently for several seconds before eventually slowing down. Dazzy Mae celebrated with a self-satisfied look.

"The Buried God happy. Can ask for help now."

Fincher leaned into Sammi. "I'd like to farking see how a farking dancing mushroom can get us to the farking Northern Goddess."

"Terro farking show you," echoed Dazzy Mae upon overhearing the boy's words.

Dazzy Mae bent forward and placed her forehead against the Ear of Terro. The priestess spoke in unfamiliar words, delivered quietly, as if speaking in bed to a secret lover.

In short order, the lady Scamp stood, signaling that the younglings do the same. The quartet stood in silence for several moments, which ultimately proved too much for Fincher to bear.

"Well? What now?"

"Can rest."

"How can we rest, Dazzy? The farking Baashers are coming. We have to keep moving!"

"Can rest while move."

Fincher looked around helplessly. "This farking again?!" To Ash and Sammi, he said, "This was a waste of farking time! They're coming for us, and we've lost valuable time! We need to—"

Fincher flew up, one of the many glowing blue vines seen throughout Terminus Grove wrapped around the boy's waist.

"Faaaaaaaark," he cried as he was swung through the air by the shining tendril, which took Fincher to the end of its reach, where it handed him off to another vine that had climbed down from the canopy above to make the exchange.

"Oh, the Five Sisters! Finch," called out Sammi in concern, but her worry proved to be unfounded, for the hazel-eyed lad had never felt more secure.

The blue vines were tight but gentle, keeping the boy secure without harming him. As Fincher was launched from vine to vine, his mind fell back to a simpler, happier time, when Gill Bugg and Link Bugg used to toss him and Ditto to each other as toddlers. Fincher recalled the exhilaration that he and Ditto felt as they soared through the air, fully confident that one of their fathers would pluck them out of the sky before any harm could come to either boy.

There was trust in the danger, and that made it unbelievably fun.

Fincher felt the same now, laughing hysterically as he was flung from vine to vine, soaring through the kaleidoscope forest, easily passing over obstacles that would have taken hours to cross or circumvent, shooting past bizarre, fanged predators before they even had a chance to mark the boy's location.

Fincher was moving. But he was also resting. And he was having the time of his life.

"Who next?" asked Dazzy Mae as Fincher's thunderous laughter faded in the distance.

Two brown hands shot into the air simultaneously.

The three Cheese-Eyes from the Stenches giggled with delight as they cut through the prismatic landscape of Terminus Grove, taking in sights and sounds and smells that neither human nor even Scamp had ever experienced.

In more open areas, they moved as a blur, the Buried God's "hands" sending them speeding over vast spaces. When passing through the Grove's denser areas, Terro took his time, ensuring the children and their priestess guide were carefully maneuvered under thick branches of Numinoos Trees or above lower parts of the massive forest canopy.

Although thrilling, after an hour the younglings were lulled into a restful state, the swinging of the Hands of Terro reminiscent of being swayed in their mothers' arms, the wind in their ears bringing up memories of Crimmish lullabies.

And in that movement, the children found much-needed rest and enjoyed a much-needed break from reality. If only for a short time, the kids from Crimmish were literally above the madness.

And they found sleep within the eye of the storm.

Fincher woke with a start, as he always seemed now to do. His hazel eyes looked up at a beautiful morning sky, Paragon still far on the edge of the horizon, meaning he was no longer in the arms of the

Buried God, no longer soaring through the dangerous beauty of Terminus Grove.

The boy sat up and spun around desperately, his panic subsiding when he saw both Ash and Sammi waking alongside him. Dazzy Mae stood behind the rising trio smiling, but gone were any signs of Terro.

"Good trip?" asked the priestess Scamp, already knowing the answer.

"The best," responded Sammi.

"And I thought the Tuggers were cool," added Ash.

"Farking awesome."

Several seconds later, the children each turned in a tight circle, taking in their new surroundings.

"Dazzy Mae? Where are we?" asked Ash.

The Scamp's face twisted in confusion. "Where you want. Northern Goddess. You here."

Three jaws dropped in disbelief as the younglings put their backs against the forest's edge and looked north, Paragon peeking out over Sierra Dawn to their right.

The Northern Goddess was a great plain of knee-high flowers broken up by large rolling hills of lush green. Like Terminus Grove, the air was not cold, despite being this far north, but was rather crisp and clean, with a gentle breeze that gave color to one's cheeks. A series of knolls sat in the distance, preventing the children from seeing what lay beyond.

"Happy?" The younglings turned back to the forest, where Dazzy Mae stood waiting. "Happy?" the Pygmy asked again.

Fincher hurried over and took one blue hand in his.

"Oh, Dazzy Mae, you've saved our farking lives. Truly! This is exactly what we needed. How can we possibly repay you?"

The lady Scamp kissed Fincher's hand before dropping it.

"Dazzy Mae free." A pause. "But need one thing."

"Farking name it."

"Need you hit me."

"What?"

"Need bruises. Need scars. Need look taken."

Fincher looked horrified. "Well, I can't help you. There's no way any of us could—"

A dark fist flashed past Fincher's face, slamming into one of Dazzy Mae's purple eyes, dropping the Pygmy Scamp to the forest floor.

"Farking heck! Farking heck! What are you doing, Ash?!"

"She's right," said the one-armed girl, opening and closing her now-sore hand. "She needs to have physical evidence that we made her come along with us."

Fincher remained confounded. "Okay, but we can't just farking—"

A glint of metal filled the air as Sammi thrust down with her dagger, slicing a neat cut along Dazzy Mae's blue cheek, sending a river of blood running across the Scamp's face.

"Sammi! Farking heck!"

The bespectacled girl wiped the blade on her shirt before returning it to her hip. "She's right, Finch. The wounds have to be real. And better us than someone or something else, right?"

"No! Not farking right!"

Ash waved him away. "Oh, calm down, Finch. She's tougher than she looks. Tougher than you can possibly know. Isn't that right, Dazzy?"

On cue, the Pygmy Scamp crawled to her feet, one eye swollen shut and a nasty gash leaking blood down her chin.

"That right. How I look?"

"You look farked up, that's how you look!"

Dazzy Mae's remaining open eye flashed with excitement. "Good. Then ready to go."

Ash knelt next to her Scamp friend. "Can you make it, Dazzy? With the Baashers coming?"

Dazzy Mae patted Ash on the shoulder. "Will make it. Have Terro to move me. Baasher not catch."

"And what about us?"

"Finch!" cried out both sisters in unison.

"Selfish much?" added Ash.

Fincher pushed back. "Sorry about worrying about us and our mission to, you know, *save the farking world!*"

"Not worry," said Dazzy Mae. "Baashers not enter Northern Goddess. Cursed place. Dead place."

"Well, that's not farking encouraging."

"Finch!"

"Must go now," said Dazzy Mae, stopping further arguments before they could begin. "Will miss you. I think the Buried God send you. Send you to free Dazzy Mae."

"Are you sure you'll be ok, Dazzy?" asked Sammi from the side. "You can come with us, you know? We'd love to have you. Don't you want to see the God-Snails? That's who we're going to see, you know?"

The lime-haired priestess shook her head. "Go find your god. I go to mine now. You go to yours."

"We'll never forget you, Dazzy," whispered Ash as she hugged her blue-skinned friend.

"And I not you," replied the Scamp, patting the girl on her braided head. "Now you go. And I go."

Dazzy Mae headed back into Terminus Grove, pausing momentarily when Fincher spoke.

"Hey, Dazzy Mae!"

"Yes."

"You're not a good priestess. You're a farking great one!"

Dazzy nodded in appreciation. "And you not oks dancer, Finch. You good one."

With those parting words, Dazzy Mae, the greatest priestess of the Pygmy Scamps, walked south several steps and was quickly swallowed by the toxic forest known as Terminus Grove.

"For the record, I'm a farking *great* dancer, not just a good one."

"That's not what Dazzy Mae said, Finch," shot back Sammi.

"The woman has an obviously limited vocabulary. She probably couldn't put into words how farking great my dancing was."

"Or she was just being nice."

"Fallacious! You know I'm a fantastic dancer!"

"I know you *think* you are!"

"Fallacious! If I were to survey—"

"Enough," shouted Ash, in no mood for one of Fincher and Sammi's good-natured back-and-forths. "We're here. Let's finish this thing. Are you two with me?"

"Of course, sis."

"Always."

Ash repositioned her pack as Fincher moved Alicia Salt's longbow from one shoulder to the other. She looked out onto the Northern Goddess with her brown-on-yellow eyes.

"I sure hope they're out there. And that they're worth the sacrifice."

"Only one farking way to find out."

"Agreed. Let's go."

19

ON THE TRAIL OF THE SUPREME HELICES

The Northern Goddess was a sight to behold.

Fincher, Ash, and Sammi Bugg walked through the massive meadow with smiles on their small faces as Paragon dripped warmth and light onto each of the children. They breathed in the fresh, crisp air and ran their hands across the tops of the endless rows of blossoms.

Sammi adjusted her glasses as she looked around, taking in the surrounding scene. "I don't know if it's magical, but it certainly is lovely."

"It sure is, sis."

"Farking right. I feel less..."

"Nervous. Nervous about the future," answered Sammi for her friend.

Fincher nodded in appreciation. "Yeah, I suppose that's it, Samm."

"Me too, Finch."

"Let's see what's past those hills," said Ash, bringing the group back to the mission at hand.

It took the better part of an hour, but the younglings finally reached and began passing through the series of hills blocking their view of the rest of the Northern Goddess. They considered climbing one mound to gain a better vantage point, but their experience at Ptero Heights left wounds that still had long to heal.

As the children slipped between a gap that wound its way between two of the larger knolls, Fincher began to talk, more to himself than to his two companions.

"We're gonna march back into Crimmish as farking champions. Nay! Conquerors! We took everything that Quaan could throw at us. Took it on the farking chin a few times but fought on. We'll be undeniable when we get back! There's no way Stella Bugg will pick that Danglin' Andy Hylinn once she sees the man I've become…"

This went on for several minutes, with Sammi and Ash simply sharing a silent laugh with their eyes. No matter how high the risk involved, nor how dire things may look, they could always count on their friend Fincher to be a light, constantly pushing against the encroaching darkness. And they loved him for it.

"… and you know what? If Hylinn or Whyllo or anyone else does get in my face, let's see how they react when I take Alicia Salt's longbow off my farking shoulder. Let's see how farking tough they are then. I bet they shake in their shite-covered boots at the man I've become. Heck, I've got—"

"Finch."

Fincher looked to Sammi. "What? I was on a farking roll!"

"Shut up and look."

Fincher did as his friend asked, ripping his mind from the clouds and looking forward, realizing that they had cleared the hills. The boy's breath caught in his throat as he, Ash, and Sammi stared down in absolute shock at what lay before them.

The ground descended quite a bit before flattening out, allowing the younglings to look down upon the landscape in full, soaking in the alien environment laid bare before them.

"But fark me, what am I looking at? Samm?"

"Why are you asking me?

"Because you're the smartest one here."

"Smart has nothing to do with this, Finch. This… makes no sense."

Ash took the first step forward. "Well, we're not gonna solve this mystery up here, now are we?"

"Are you sure we farking can't? Because that would really be preferable."

Ash ignored Fincher, knowing he would follow her into the Great Untold, if asked. "You ready to solve one final riddle, sis?"

"You know I can't stay away from a puzzle. And this looks to be the most confusing yet."

"Then let's go. Finch?"

"Right behind you."

"Ready your bow?"

The boy already had Alicia Salt's longbow in his hands and was reaching for an arrow from his quiver. "Way ahead of you. Anything moves down there, and I'll put a bolt through its dome."

"Finch."

"Yes?"

"Please be careful with that thing."

The trio from Crimmish slowly exited the darkness of one colossus only to enter the shadow of another shortly thereafter. Child heads swung back and forth in both fear and amazement, taking in the bones of a once-thriving civilization.

"Look at the size of these farking buildings," remarked Fincher through a gaping jaw. "I can't even imagine Kassimont having castles and structures like this."

"They don't," responded Sammi. "I read a book on Kassimont architecture last Freezing. There's nothing there even remotely close to what these things used to be... to what they still are."

Surrounding the younglings were remnants of grand fortresses, massive defensive constructs, and at least half a dozen truly gigantic castles, all abandoned and partially digested by the natural world.

Heavy, dark green vines encased all the buildings, ripping precisely cut stones from their foundations, forcing walls to slope at odd angles, and filling in spaces left by holes and collapsed areas. In the few places where the vines did not hide the stonework beneath, scorch marks, deep fissures, and projectile impacts could be seen, evidence of a great battle that had taken place long ago.

Between these dead sentinels, flowers continued to bloom in abundance, as if attempting to erase the ugliness that once marred the Northern Goddess.

Three sets of eyes narrowed, searching every nook, every empty window, every doorway for signs of movement or life.

There were none.

"This place is a tomb," concluded Sammi as they continued through the ancient city. "And don't you doubt that we didn't do this to ourselves."

"*We*, Samm? What do you mean, sis?"

The girl pushed her glasses farther up her nose. "We, as in humans. We did this to each other. Look at these markings, this proof of a great battle. This wasn't beast or sickness that did this. This was *us* who did this."

Fincher's hazel eyes studied the crumbling parapets and citadels as he spoke. "Chill out, Samm. Remember, we're kids from Crimmish. They don't consider us as one of them and, personally, I'm farking delighted not to be included."

"I don't think that's what Samm means, Finch."

"You're right, Finch," corrected Sammi. "But what I mean is that humanity, as a whole, is responsible for this... this... this decay. Maybe we deserve the Gloomtide, after all."

The companions walked in tense silence for a bit before Finch blurted, "Nah, fark that. No matter what our forebears did to the stupid Titian Empire, we don't deserve to see our families and friends die early from the Maddening. And no matter what these people did to each other, that doesn't farking mean that moms now should lose their minds and toss their babies into Crown's Run. I refuse to buy that. And neither would Ditto, and neither would Hana. And neither should you, Samm. Otherwise, what the fark are we doing out here?! I mean, really?!"

Several more minutes passed.

"You're right, Finch."

"He really is, Samm."

"Sorry for losing it for a moment there."

Fincher waved away his young friend's concern with the tip of his longbow. "We all have our times of doubt." A pause. "Women, especially, must be forgiven for brief lapses in judgment. I mean, take Stella Bugg, for example. The poor girl was obviously having some sort of mental break when she decided to dance with that shite-breathed Hylinn Bugg over yours truly. You know, I bet…"

The sisters did their best to hold in their laughter, but it eventually escaped, sending Fincher into another rant that brought on even more howling.

Paragon had peaked in the sky and was starting to fall when the younglings were able to put the ghost of the great settlement behind them for good.

Once clear of shadow and vine, the Northern Goddess continued to reveal itself to the children, ushering in further questions and surprise.

The land beyond the skeletal city sat in stark contrast to what the younglings encountered upon first exiting Terminus Grove. While wildflowers still dominated the landscape, as if the Northern Goddess continued to celebrate the disappearance of man, sheer cliffs could be seen to either side and straight ahead. The rocky terrain rolled in from the east and west before diving to the blossom-covered ground below.

"There must have been a massive river, or lake, or both here at some time," guessed Sammi. "I don't know what else could create such faces in the rock."

Ash pushed on. "Well, whatever caused it, it looks like we have a path forward. Let's keep moving."

If the walls of the empty city were stifling, the cliff faces that loomed over the younglings were truly suffocating, drowning Fincher, Ash, and Sammi in wind and dimness. The younglings pulled their arms in tight as a constant, chilly breeze cut through the canyon, Paragon no longer able to reach them to offer its warmth.

Eventually, as shadow transformed into total darkness, the friends were forced to camp for the evening, using some long-dead roots found scattered throughout the ancient riverbed as kindling.

A sour look crossed over all three children's faces as they removed items from their packs. Sammi sighed audibly as she handed jerky to Ash and then Fincher, but the boy refused.

"You take it, Samm. I'm not hungry."

"Finch…"

"I'm serious. I'm too excited to eat."

"Finch…"

"What's going on?" asked Ash. Sammi continued to stare at Fincher through her round-shaped glasses. "Sis?"

"Finch knows that we don't have enough food for the trip back. So, he's trying to be a martyr."

"Farking heck! Can't a person just not be hungry?!"

"You know you're hungry!"

"Do not!"

"Do, too!"

Ash stepped between her two companions. "Okay, okay. Look, we're all tired and beat up and thirsty and hungry. Finch, you have to eat. I'm sure we'll find food once we get out of this stupid canyon."

"I'm not farking eating."

"Fine. Suit yourself. Samm, you eat. If Finch wants to die and be a permanent fixture here, so be it."

"I do!"

"Well, good then!"

"Farking great!"

"Fantastic!"

With that, Fincher collapsed onto his bedroll, placing his back to the fire and his best friends. When it was clear that madness boy had nothing more to say, the sisters slowly ate some of the meager jerky that remained, enjoying none of it.

As their teeth fought against the dry meat, the weight of their journey began to press down on the sisters. The pain of loss. The constant fear of violence. The never-ending physical exertion. The missing of loved ones. The longing for those never to return.

Ash and Sammi Bugg ate without speaking, every now and then wiping a tear from a brown cheek. Eventually, each girl fell back on her roll and stared up at the Five Sisters, asking questions that they dared not voice aloud.

The trio from Crimmish did not converse for the rest of the night, but not because they were upset at each other. Rather, they were scared. Scared that their food would soon run out. Scared that fresh water may start to become an issue. Scared that they might not be able to find the God-Snails in the vast, unexplored country known as the Northern Goddess. Scared that the Supreme Helices may have already left the world, tired of waiting for Quaan's ambassadors to arrive.

But most of all, the children feared what would happen if they *did* locate the Divine Pentad. Of how they would be received. Of how they would be judged.

The children remained quiet, only the crackling of the fire filling the cold canyon air, until each finally succumbed to exhaustion and drifted off into uncomfortable slumbers.

The younglings had never been closer to their goal. And, yet, they had never felt worse.

～

Fincher brought Alicia Salt's longbow up in an instant, arrow notched.

"What the fark is that?!"

The children had walked along the canyon floor for most of the morning after an evening of restless sleep. As Paragon began to peer over the eastern edge of the cliffs, the younglings exhaled in relief, the northern mouth of the gorge finally coming into focus as they rounded a sharp bend.

The younglings' pace picked up as soon as the exit was spotted, so desperate were they to be free from the weight of the suffocating walls around them. As they began to close the distance, the world of the Northern Goddess slowly began to reveal itself once more, the cliffs to their left and right shrinking with every dozen steps.

The trio was quickly approaching the gorge's mouth, where the rock faces simply fell off into the land below, when the sisters were brought to a sudden halt by Fincher, the boy's weapon down and ready.

Ash narrowed her brown-on-yellow eyes and Sammi adjusted her glasses as a form entered the mouth of the canyon from the west and began creeping its way toward the children, who looked on in fear.

"It's walking this way," said Sammi, her hand going to her dagger.

"Not walking," corrected Ash. "Floating. It's floating this way."

"Fark. You're right."

And Ash *was* right. As the round form drew closer, the children could better make out what they were witnessing.

A large, magenta bubble, twice Ash's height in diameter, danced in the air one hundred feet before the kids from Crimmish, riding the chilled currents of air that constantly ran through the gorge.

Ash squinted harder, as if that would reveal the true nature of the strange anomaly. "What is it, Samm?"

"How would I know?"

"You're supposed to be the farking smart one," replied Fincher, his wounded shoulder and hands starting to ache from keeping tension on Alicia Salt's longbow.

"Well, giant floating bubbles of the Northern Goddess were never a topic of discussion in the books I've read!"

"Sounds like you need some new farking books."

"Or maybe you need—"

"Quiet, both of you," snapped Ash. "Just watch."

The magenta bubble continued its advance, forcing the children to the side of the canyon to give it room to pass.

Ultimately, the space was not needed as the wind shifted directions suddenly, forcing the bright bubble to swing wildly to the west and smash into the cliff face.

The younglings jerked to cover their eyes from the explosion of light and color that followed as the magenta bubble burst upon the ragged rock.

Ash was the first to recover and realized she had been thrown to the canyon floor. She stumbled to her feet, stars still crossing her vision, and moved to help her sister and then Fincher up.

"Well, that was... something," said Fincher as he accepted Ash's hand and rose. "I don't know what I thought would happen, but—"

"Guys, guys, guys," said Sammi excitedly. "Look."

All three jaws fell, a common occurrence on their journey, as six eyes discovered what remained where pink bubble had met rock.

Growing out of the side of the cliff face was a translucent tree that swam with light and color within. The narrow trunk dipped low, almost reaching the ground, before twisting in on itself and heading toward Paragon above. Halfway up the gorge wall, the magical stem mushroomed into a triangular spread of clear branches, each of which was covered in wide, magenta blossoms that drummed with energy.

"So... what farking happened?"

"It's beautiful," remarked a breathless Sammi as the girl pushed her glasses farther up her nose and made her way to the crystal tree.

"Careful," warned Ash. "Don't touch it, sis! It looks like it's full of power."

"Agreed! You'll get a nasty shock if you farking touch it!"

Sammi waved her companions away as she neared the throbbing, rainbow-filled sapling. "I just want to look." Spectacle-covered eyes studied the threads of red, orange, yellow, blue, and violet that undulated within. They took in the wide blossoms and noticed how waves of energy rippled from the base of each magenta flower to the tips of each petal. They watched in awe as small fingers of lightning flashed from one blossom to its neighbor, energizing the latter while offering release to the former.

"What do you see?" asked Ash from a safe distance back.

Sammi looked back, a toothy smile showing. "I thought Vattassav and Crown Lake were the most wondrous things that I'd ever seen. And then Terminus Grove showed me things I couldn't even dream of. But this... This is something else entirely. Something... divine."

Fincher moved the longbow from one shoulder to the other.

"Good. Then we must be getting close. I assume that where there are divine trees, there will be farking gods. Particularly of the snail variety."

"Say goodbye to the... sacred lightning pine, sis. The sooner we put this canyon behind us, the better."

"No farking disagreement here, Ash."

Sammi sighed in disappointment. "I guess you're right." The young girl slowly backed away from the sacred lightning pine and joined her friends. "I hope we get a chance to see it again on our trip back."

Fincher threw an arm around the bespectacled girl. "And I just hope there is a trip back, Samm."

"Me, too, Finch," echoed Ash.

Sammi nodded, and the kids from Crimmish, marching shoulder to shoulder for support, made their way out of the great canyon of the Northern Goddess.

"Still," said Sammi as they stepped out into the wider world, "it'd be nice to see such unimaginable beauty again."

"Perhaps you won't have long to wait, sis."

"Whoa."

For the longest time, this was the only word to escape the lips of the three children. It was silently agreed upon that no other language could accurately describe what lay in front of the journeying younglings.

After exiting the winding canyon, Fincher, Ash, and Sammi had marched north, gently ascending an inclined path until they reached the top of one of the Goddess's many hills.

It was there, looking down at the rolling, rocky land below, that the children were forced to pause.

Magenta bubbles by the hundreds floated above thousands of the lightning pines that filled the spaces between hills both smooth and jagged. Pink petals pulsed and bolts of energy lit up the air as trees reached out to connect with appendages of lightning.

Wherever one of the bubbles would touch the ground or glance a hillock, a flash would follow, leaving behind another of the sacred trees and further adding to the impossibly colorful canvas of the Northern Goddess.

"Looks like you got your farking wish, Samm," remarked Fincher when ample time had been given to digest the scene below them. He looked over and smiled at the look of pure elation that he found on Sammi's face. "Shall we, Samm?"

"Yes. Let's," she replied, her legs already churning before she completed the two-word response.

Stomachs growled, but the younglings ignored them as they entered a forest of sacred pines, staring up in wonder as lightning streaked overhead and watching intently as ropes of color swam through the crystalline trunks.

Every now and then, the kids from Crimmish had to sidestep one of the magenta bubbles that had floated down, missing the increasingly thick canopy of pulsing pink.

On occasion, when a magenta bubble made contact with a sacred pine, an especially large flash would occur, leaving behind a massive lightning tree that was three times the size of its predecessor, almost a quarter of the size of Terminus Grove's Numinoos Trees.

"What do you think these are for?" asked Sammi, the young girl's head swiveling as she attempted to take in every detail of the swelling magical forest.

"Maybe the God-Snails just like pretty things?" ventured Ash.

"Or they're farking gone and this is what they left behind."

Sammi pushed up her glasses. "I don't think so. There's too much power in these trees. It has be for something."

"Like blowing up this shithole world?"

"Now, that would be *something*," laughed Ash, accustomed to her friend's dark humor despite his generally positive outlook.

Sammi shook her head, still studying each crystal tree they passed, squinting as lightning appeared overhead, temporarily linking a sacred tree on her left to one on her right. "I don't think so. But they're definitely energizing each other."

"Well, let's keep farking moving. I can't see shite ahead between these trees and this craggy terrain. The durned Pentad could be right in front of me, and I wouldn't know it."

"Sure, sure," responded Sammi, although her attention was elsewhere. "I'm curious to see how far this forest goes."

"And what's at the end of it," added Ash.

The children sped up through the sacred forest. And like anything, what was once unimaginable and wondrous soon grew commonplace with time. Bellies began to rumble, and legs quickly grew sore as Paragon rose to its full height.

Sammi passed around the very last scraps of their food as they marched, with Fincher once again lying about not being hungry. This time, however, the sisters didn't have the spirit to argue and were actually appreciative of the sacrifice.

The younglings continued to make their way northwest as Paragon fell, the dimming light making the sacred forest even more luminescent and affecting. The kids finished off the final skin of fresh water as darkness tried to take hold but was shoved aside by the glowing forest and shining balls of magenta that swung through the air like untethered, weightless chandeliers.

"Anyone want to stop?" asked Fincher.

"I can see," replied Ash.

"Me, too," echoed her sister.

And, so, the children forewent rest, opting to push on, desperate to learn if the pot of gold at the end of their journey was worth it—or existed at all.

The Five Sisters joined them, a streaking red star making an appearance alongside the celestial siblings.

As the Sisters observed from above, the children struggled below. Feet grew heavy, causing someone to trip or stumble every few minutes. Mouths became dry and tongues thickened. Sharp pains ran through midsections and cramps formed in muscles.

The kids from Crimmish pushed on in silence.

Eventually, as the Five Sisters moved toward the Spired Curtains, the Sacred Forest began to thin, giving way to an increasingly rocky landscape that forced the younglings to zig-zag around obstacles. Although their path darkened as the sacred trees shrunk in number, there was still ample light to see, driving the children on well past the point of safety and exhaustion.

Every time they rounded a hill, the younglings prayed for a sign, any sign, that they were nearing their goal, that they were not simply walking toward their own graves.

And, each time, their prayers went unanswered as all that could be seen were more hills, and more rocks, and more sacred trees, and more magenta bubbles. Even the Five Sisters became tired of waiting and seemed to hasten their descent.

To get around one particularly gnarly looking crag, the children were driven far to the east, climbing over sharp rock outcroppings and scrambling across fallen boulders to minimize the distance off-path. When they finally cleared the edge of the angry rock and turned north once more, they were met with more hills, more sacred trees, and dwindling hope.

Sammi, her glasses balanced precariously on the tip of her nose, plowed forward, as if denying the unwanted scene before her. In her haste, the young girl tripped over a stone and fell with a hefty thud onto the hard-packed turf. She cried out as she hit, and a *clinking* sound could be heard as she tumbled.

"Samm," cried out Ash, rushing over to help her sister. "Are you okay?" She hooked her lone hand under Samm to lift her up.

"My glasses! My glasses fell! I have to find them!"

"Okay, okay," said Ash through grunts as she yanked her little sister upright. "Just get to your feet; I'll find them."

Sammi limped to the side, her knees obviously in pain from the fall, as Ash searched the ground.

"Here they are! I've got them! They're..." A pause.

"What is it? Here! Hand them over!"

Ash did as Sammi commanded and passed along the glasses.

Sammi immediately put them on and wailed in agony as she did. Both lenses were shattered, with the right one especially spiderwebbed.

The brilliant young girl, never one to give up or surrender, slunk to the ground, tears streaming down both cheeks. Seconds later, heaving sobs assaulted Sammi, a lifetime of fear, sadness, grief, and anger all catching up to the girl in that moment of monumental loss.

"I can't see," moaned Sammi as she bawled. "What good am I now? What good am I to anyone?"

Ash dropped next to her younger sister, sweeping her up into her arm, quiet whimpers joining the loud howls.

"It's okay," consoled Ash, but there was no strength in those words and no consolation would be found. "It's okay. We're done. We're done."

Ash turned her water-filled, brown-on-yellow eyes to Fincher, who was standing strangely silent as he stared out into the Northern Goddess.

"Do you hear me, Finch?" called out Ash, her voice quivering with emotion. "We're done! The God-Snails are gone! Or maybe they were never here! But we're done! We must turn back now! We've lost Ditto and Hana. We've lost Alicia Salt and Captain Graff. And I'm expected to give up my sister, too?! And you?! And my own life?! *How much more do we have to sacrifice?!*" The last sentence came out in a primal scream, sapping the one-armed girl of her remaining energy. Her next words were barely audible. "I have such little left to give, Finch." The boy offered no response. "Finchius Bugg! Do you hear me?! Answer me!"

Fincher remained where he stood but spun his hazel eyes toward his despondent friends. There was a strange, lost look on his soft face, and Fincher appeared as if he were far away, on a plane of existence that didn't include Ash and Sammi Bugg.

"Do you hear that?"

"Hear what, Finch?"

"That voice. Those voices. It's like they're right here among us."

Ash tilted her head to the side but heard nothing. "There's no one here, Finch. It's just me and Samm. And we're ready to be done with this mission. Maybe Quaan isn't worth saving. Maybe this is the way it has to be. Finch?"

The boy ignored Ash's words. Instead, he looked north again, nodding as he did.

"They're not far now. Not far at all." Turning back to Ash and Sammi, he said, "They're waiting for us."

Ash released a great sigh. "Where, Finch?"

"Out there."

"We won't make it, Finch."

"We may."

Ash shook her braided head. "I can't. Look at Sammi. She's finished. I'm finished. *We're* finished, Finch. It's over."

Then, Fincher did something that rocked the one-armed girl. He smiled.

It wasn't any ordinary smile; it was a Fincher Bugg special, one delivered only when the notoriously mischievous boy knew something that others did not, when he had a surprise notched like one of Alicia Salt's arrows.

"Please," was all that Fincher would offer. Another long pause.

And then, "I can go a bit farther," said Sammi weakly, the young girl all cried out for the moment. "I'll just need someone to hold my hand."

Ash looked down at her little sister and started to protest but something held her tongue. Instead, she turned her attention back to Fincher.

"I hope this is worth it, Finch."

"Me, too," replied Fincher, his gaze having already returned north. "Me. Farking. Too."

More walking. More falling.

More hills. More sacred trees. More magenta bubbles.

And no sign of the Supreme Helices.

Ash swore under her breath every time Sammi tripped, the poor girl's broken glasses rendering her all but blind.

The next hill, Ash repeated to herself, valiantly attempting to keep despair at bay for as long as possible.

"How much longer, Finch?" asked Sammi, her feet now merely sliding across the uneven ground.

"They say we're close," responded Fincher, the boy's hazel eyes remaining pointed north, his voice still sounding far away.

"They've *been* saying that," muttered Ash as she maneuvered her sister over the broken terrain.

The trio skirted the edge of a particularly sharp-looking hillock.

The next hill.

The kids rounded a massive boulder that jutted from the dirt like a molar.

The next hill.

When the younglings passed the next set of crags only to be faced with more hills beyond, Ash Bugg decided that she'd had enough.

"Finch!" The boy turned slowly to face his friend. "Finch, that's it. Sammi can't go any farther—and neither can I. If we have any chance at all of living, we must turn back now."

The boy looked confused, as if he had forgotten where they were, or how dire their situation had become.

"But the voices…"

"What voices, Finch? We can't hear them!"

"But I can."

Rage filled Ash's eyes as she marched toward. Fincher, leaving Sammi behind. "Can you?! Are you sure, Finch?! Or are you so famished and dehydrated that you're hearing things?! You haven't eaten in days! You haven't had water for hours and hours! You're losing it! And you're going to kill us!"

"Please stop fighting," pleaded Sammi from the side, but she was ignored.

Fincher mulled over Ash's words, his unreadable, blank face staying constant. "No."

Ash's eyes went even wider. "What do you mean, no?"

"No. The voices are real. They're talking to me. They know things they shouldn't."

"Because it's all in *your own head*, Finch!"

Sammi cut in again. "Come on, guys! No fighting! Please."

"It's not in my head, Ash," stated Fincher calmly. "And they won't wait much longer."

"Well, that's too bad! Because they will be waiting! Because Samm and I are turning back!"

"Guys, please."

"And you, Finch, are coming with us! I don't care if I have to knock you out and carry you out of here myself!"

"I have to follow them, Ash."

"You don't! You won't!"

With that declaration, Ash launched herself forward, tackling Fincher to the ground. The two rolled around, struggling with each other, fighting without trying to hurt one another.

"Stop, stop, stop," screamed Sammi from the side. "I'll leave you both here if you don't stop! I swear, I will!" Fincher and Ash continued to jostle for control. "That's it!"

Sammi, despite barely being able to see, sprinted north into the night.

Both Fincher and Ash froze at seeing their poor-sighted companion take off into the darkness of an area void of sacred trees.

"Samm!" they both screamed in unison, watching in horror as the young girl's shadow grew smaller before disappearing completely in an instant.

"She fell," Ash exclaimed in a panic, quickly climbing off Fincher and helping him up. "I don't see her. I don't see her!" Ash's tired legs became a blur as she chased after her little sister. "Samm! Samm! Samm!"

"Ugh. I'm here."

Ash exhaled in relief as she slid to a stop next to the mound that was Sammi. "Why would you do such a foolish thing?! Are you hurt?"

"I'm fine," came the voice from below. "I didn't trip on anything. I slipped."

"Slipped on what?"

"Yuck! Something slimy. I'm covered in it." Sammi looked up and could clearly see the strange look on Ash's face. "What? It's not poop, is it? Please tell me it's not poop."

"It's not poop, Samm. Look."

Sammi lifted her hands to her face and watched as starlight danced within the thick, clear substance that coated her palms. The girl slid around on her bottom and found more of the substance—a trail of it, in fact, leading north through the next grouping of hills.

"What is it?" asked Sammi, scooping up more of the goo and staring in wonder as the stars flickered within.

"It's them," said Fincher plainly from behind. "They were here. Recently. This will lead us to them."

Ash turned back to her friend, their fight already forgiven and forgotten. "How do you know, Finch?"

"They told me."

Sammi carefully rose, her feet sliding around in the God-Snail mucus. Ash grabbed hold of her sister to offer support.

"Are you hurt anywhere, sis?"

Sammi shook her head. "I'm fine." Her face twisted in thought. "In fact, I'm better than fine. My stomach doesn't hurt anymore, and my mouth isn't so dry. I also think…"

Sammi reached up, the starlit substance lighting her small face, and remembered that her glasses had shattered and were no longer on her nose. Her eyes shot up as realization set in. "I can see, Ash. I mean, I can really see." Sammi scanned left and right, north and south, her brown eyes growing wider by the second. "You know, I think…" Sammi paused, recognizing that Ash was staring at her open-mouthed. "What is it?"

Ash's lone hand went up and she ran a finger across her sister's brow. "Your eyes, Samm."

"Yeah, they actually work now."

"No, not that."

"What, then?"

"They're clear. The yellow is gone."

"Really?"

"Really."

Sammi thought for a moment. Without warning, she smeared some of the God-Snail mucus onto Ash's face.

"Gross! What are you doing?!"

As Ash worked furiously to wipe the goop off with her sleeve, Sammi stepped over and repeated the act on Fincher. The boy did not move to stop her.

Several seconds passed, and then Sammi shrieked in delight. "Yours, too! Yours, too! Both your eyes are clear now. No more Cheese-Eyes!"

Ash's hand went to her face. "Really? And you're right. I feel much better. Great, in fact! This stuff is magic!"

"We can save Ma and Da with this, no matter what happens with the Titians," exclaimed Sammi, dropping the pack from her shoulders. The young girl dug through its contents, eventually pulling out a single glass vial. She sighed sadly. "This one is all I have. The others I brought are broken."

"Hey," called Ash, hoping to keep up her sister's spirits. "It won't be enough for everyone, but we can still help our parents with that. Get what you can."

Sammi did as she was told, collecting as much of the mucus as possible in the vial.

"They cannot wait much longer," said Fincher, his now-clear eyes glued once more ahead.

"Then, let's not keep them waiting," stated Ash, feeling better than she had in a long time.

Sammi hooked one arm around Fincher, another around Ash.

"No matter what we find out there, we stick together."

Ash offered a nod and a reassuring smile. Fincher simply looked out into the distance.

Fincher, Ash, and Sammi Bugg followed the star-filled trail around and through several more series of rises before it took them straight over one of the gentler hills in the area.

As the trio crested the top of the smooth hillock, their eyes went wide, just before growing wet.

"We farking did it," said Fincher breathlessly.

"S-so, th-this is them," stammered Sammi.

"They're… They're more glorious than I ever imagined," commented Ash.

Below the children from Crimmish, on the northern side of the rolling hill, was a level field covered in wildflowers. Sacred trees ran in straight lines to the left and right, in stark contrast to the chaotic nature of their planting further south. Between them, magenta bubbles hovered in place, as if held steady by invisible leashes.

The starlit trail ran down the hill and across the blossom-filled meadow. At some point, the singular trail split into five, leaving a quintet of sparkling lines to run north, ending in—

"The farking God-Snails of Quaan."

The God-Snails lived up to their reputation, each the size of a mansion belonging to Kassimont's wealthiest class. Their helix shells danced with prismatic light and lines of power coursed through their spirals.

The God-Snails were traveling north in a V, with the Supreme Helix closest to the younglings at the tip of the formation.

At the far end of the meadow, in a neat, horizontal line, were five massive pyramids of startling white. They shone brightly in the deepest part of night, that window of time where the Five Sisters were falling behind the Spired Curtains and Paragon had yet to make its appearance over Sierra Dawn.

Each God-Snail was making its way toward one of the ivory monuments, with those on far left and right having almost reached their destination.

"We must go," said Fincher, unusually relaxed, especially given the gravity of the situation. "They are leaving soon. Very soon."

Fincher started down the hill, forcing Ash and Sammi to chase after their friend. They made it down without incident and began their trek across the magical meadow.

The sacred lightning trees flashed their pink blossoms as the younglings passed, and the magenta bubbles rose to just above the treetops, an odd bow to the Child Champions of Quaan.

After ten minutes of walking, the trio began to quickly close the distance to the nearest God-Snail. As the other Supreme Helices continued their slow but inevitable crawl toward their respective pyramids, the one at the tip of the V turned its head to meet the children, bringing them to an abrupt stop.

Its head, along with the rest of the God-Snail's flesh, was a bright blue that glowed gently in the dimness. The creature's massive foot waffled under the mammoth shell, turning its body perpendicular to the younglings.

As the God-Snail faced the approaching trio, an audible gasp escaped the children. Silver, twirling, hurricane eyes balanced on the end of long tentacles. They absorbed each child, in turn, reading each book of life in an instant.

The lower blue tentacles of its mouth twitched silently, as if speaking a language that no human was worthy to hear, much less understand.

"I don't hear anything," said Ash.

"Me either, sis."

"I hear it."

Ash and Sammi turned to Fincher.

"You do?" asked Ash.

"I do."

"What is it saying?" prodded Sammi.

"I need to go speak with them."

"Of course," agreed Ash. "Let's go."

Fincher shook his head. "No. They said I must come alone."

"No way," argued Sammi. "We're in this together, Finch."

Hazel irises, now on a white canvas, stared down at Sammi with startling calm. "Not this time, Samm. You both wait here. Please."

"But Finch—"

Ash placed a hand on her sister's shoulder to stop further resistance. She didn't know why she did this, but she did. Instead, she nodded to her friend. Fincher dropped his head in appreciation before marching forward.

Ash and Sammi's hearts leapt into their throats as their dearest friend entered the shadow of the godly gastropod. Although they could not hear his words, Fincher appeared to be speaking with the God-Snail.

"I hope he's not cussing too much," said Sammi.

"Me, too, sis. Me, too."

After several minutes, during which neither sister could vouch for whether she breathed or not, the God-Snail lowered its blueish head, bringing it to Fincher's level. The sisters gasped as the Supreme Helix placed the space between its upper tentacles gently against Fincher's forehead, the whirlwind eyes above spinning with increased energy.

As the God-Snail's eyes rotated with power, the boy held out his hands, palms up, as if expecting a reward.

Meanwhile, the sacred lightning trees outlining the holy meadow began to flash in unison. Ash and Sammi Bugg looked to their left and right, the hairs on their arms rising to meet the electricity that was building across the field.

The magenta bubbles pulsed, the sacred trees flashed, and the other four God-Snails spun to face south, their silver eyes appearing as the mouths of tornadoes.

Just then, pink lightning reached out from the points of the ivory pyramids to the far east and west. They each linked to the nearest sacred tree on their side, setting off a chain reaction, with thick ropes of electricity racing from neighbor to neighbor, connecting the trees of both lines. The remaining three pyramids shot bolts of pink-tinted power into the sky.

Moments later, a surge of energy ran down from the cosmos, conducted by the trio of pyramids and passed along across the sacred trees, which now absolutely roared with pink light. The magenta bubbles exploded in rainbow-like cascades.

The Bugg Sisters narrowed their now-clear eyes but refused to shield them, for the pain was worth the show playing out before them.

The air hummed with power. Time seemed to slow. An alien pull could be felt in the hearts of each of the younglings.

And then, the world exploded in a release of color.

When Ash and Sammi's vision had finally cleared, they were on the ground, and Paragon had peeked its head over Sierra Dawn, ushering forth another day.

Where each magenta bubble had exploded, impossibly large mushrooms now grew, their caps hanging heavy over the entirety of the holy meadow.

Two of the God-Snails had disappeared, having completed their journeys to their respective pyramids. Two others were drawing close to their monuments, with cavernous entrances having appeared to welcome each divine creature.

Only the God-Snail that Fincher spoke with remained where it was, and the sisters soon realized that Fincher was walking toward them, an object held in his arms. Before long, the boy was reunited with his closest friends.

"Finch," ventured Ash. "Are you okay?"

The boy offered a soft smile. "Never better, Ash."

"What did they give you?"

Fincher looked down and jumped a bit, as if he had already forgotten the object in his grasp. As if he had more pressing, more interesting matters on his young mind.

"Oh, this?" He held it out to the girls.

In Fincher's hands was a small, wooden box—only it wasn't.

The wood was a glossy cognac that swam like quicksilver, appearing as if it would simply melt around anyone foolish enough to grab it.

When no other explanation was given, Ash prodded her friend. "Yes, *that*. What is it, Finch?"

The boy looked down and thought for a while, as if his mind wanted to be somewhere else, somewhere grander. "This is it, Ash," he finally responded. "This is the Gift. This is what Quaan needs to heal."

"In this box is the cure for the Gloomtide?"

"The cure for Quaan," corrected Fincher.

"Then we've done it?" asked Sammi, the girl hesitant to let hope creep back into her young life.

"We've done what's needed," offered Fincher mysteriously. "We've played our roles. And played them well."

"Then we can go?" dared Ash, the one-armed girl desperate for closure, desperate to see her ma and da again.

"You can."

Ash's chest shrunk with relief. "Finally. Come on then. I don't know how long this mucus stuff works, so let's get going and hope that—"

"Ash," Sammi interrupted.

"Yeah?"

"He said that *you* can go. Not *we* can go."

Ash's brown face fell. "Finch? Fincher?"

"Yes?"

"You're coming with us, right?"

Fincher smiled warmly at his friend. "The Gift is never free, Ash. Sometimes, the cost is the eruption of Mount Ghaal and Galanis Dawn. Sometimes, the fee is the Tainted Timbers." A pause. "And, sometimes, someone has to stay behind."

"So… you're staying behind?" asked Ash, the girl's voice breaking.

Fincher cupped his friend's face in his hand. "*Staying behind* are the wrong words. *Going with* would be more accurate."

"But why?" demanded Ash between sobs as Sammi buried her face in her sister's chest.

Fincher shrugged lightly. "They want to learn more about us. They want to show me things and see how I react. They want to know whether we're worth the effort."

"And they've chosen you?"

Fincher chuckled lightly. "No accounting for taste, I guess."

"No," shouted Sammi as she freed her face from her sister's shirt. "No," she repeated more evenly. "You're the perfect choice, Finch. After all, you're the soul of the Sour Flower Gang."

Ash kissed Sammi atop her head. "Well said, sis. Well said."

Fincher pushed the Pentad Gift into Ash's arm. "Take this, Ash. And please listen." Both girls leaned into Fincher, for the boy was speaking in a low, calm tone. "There are rules to this Gift, rules that must be followed for it to have its intended effect." The sisters nodded. "No one must touch this box other than you two and those of the Rayne bloodline. Should anyone other than the Imperator try to take it from you… well, it wouldn't be good. The Gift should be opened with great ceremony, before all of Kassimont, with all the ruling Titians in attendance. And the Bugg Sisters should be guests of honor."

"They'll never allow that," stated Ash flatly.

"They better," was all Fincher said in reply.

Sammi wept quietly next to her sister. "I don't want you to leave, Finch. I don't want to lose another friend."

Fincher looked at his young companion, the only person who could verbally joust with the fast-talking boy, and offered a knowing grin as he kissed her forehead. "I'll always be with you, Samm."

"It's not fair."

"Maybe not, Samm. But life's not fair. And Quaan's not fair. And maybe that's why it took a group of kids from the Stenches to save the world. Because no one understands how unfair things are like we do." Fincher looked up at the morning-licked sky. "I think I have to go now."

Ash and Sammi buried Fincher in a hug, their young minds working overtime as they tried to memorize every detail of this moment—the last with their dear, dear friend.

When they separated, Fincher removed Alicia Salt's longbow and handed it to Sammi, along with the quiver of arrows. "This is yours now. Don't let people forget about her. Or Rashii."

"I won't."

Ash wiped the tears from her face. "Anything you want us to tell your da, Finch?"

The precocious boy offered one final, naughty smile. "Tell him I'm off on another adventure." The boy's voice cracked. "Far from any muddy prison." A pause. "Tell him that."

"I will, Finch. I promise."

The boy nodded, placed one last kiss on the forehead of each girl, and headed back toward the God-Snail.

Ash and Sammi collapsed to the ground in grief, watching through tears as Fincher closed the distance.

As the boy drew closer, the helix shell shook and an entryway folded open, allowing for a view of the cosmos within. Fincher did not hesitate, ascending the natural ramp and stopping at the threshold, where he turned around.

With the swirling of the universe behind him, hazel eyes shone brightly, meeting the brown orbs of Ash and Sammi Bugg. Fincher raised his right hand in a wave goodbye, and the Bugg Sisters bid farewell by blowing kisses to their fellow harvester.

The opening folded closed, and the lone remaining God-Snail rotated on a blue foot and pushed forward, its partners having already entered their ivory pyramids.

Ash and Sammi sat on the soft, flowery ground, holding each other, weeping softly, as the God-Snail containing the last of their party was welcomed into its ivory pyramid with a blinding flash of light.

A few beats later, the ground shook as the quintet of pyramids lifted from the ground and ascended, leaving behind streaks of bright red, eventually vanishing into the sky above.

"Look," cried Sammi, pointing at the red comet as she did. The rose-colored streak in the morning sky flared briefly before fading away, taking Fincher Bugg to places even the most fanciful dared not dream.

It took a long time before Ash and Sammi found the strength to rise again, now under the shade of colossal mushrooms. They collected their belongings, shifted items on shoulders, and turned back toward the south.

"We lost Hana. We lost Ditto. We lost Fincher," said Sammi as the sisters made their way back up the hillock. "Not to mention all the others… even stupid Dooley Hamm. I really hope Quaan is worth it."

Ash helped her younger sister up the hill. "It isn't, sis. It never was."

"Then what was this all for, Ash?"

"Because life is about trying. And doing your best. And attempting to make sacrifices worth it, even if we never get equal value back."

"I don't care what's given, Ash. Nothing will equal Hana and Ditto and Fincher. Nothing."

Ash squeezed her little sister. "I know, Samm. But Quaan's not fair, and we're not fools. So, we press on. And we do our best. And we…" Ash faded off.

"We what, Ash?"

Ash grasped the Ghost Puma tooth that hung at her chest. "We hope that one day our sacrifices are rewarded."

The sisters reached the top of the hill. Sammi spun her sister to face her. "Do you think they will, Ash?" she asked hopefully. "Do you think they'll be rewarded?"

Ash wanted nothing more than to lie to her sister. She wanted nothing more than to make her younger sibling feel like all had been worth it, that the world would break its back in appreciation. But Ash Bugg knew better. And she could lie to her sister no more.

"No, Samm, I don't think they will. But we're used to that, which made us the perfect pawns for their game. Now, let's get going. My body feels great, but my heart is heavy. And I don't want to be here anymore."

"I never thought I would miss Crimmish, sis. But I do."

The Bugg Sisters topped the hill and immediately began to descend.

"Because the world of Quaan is putrid, Samm. And, ironically, the place known as the Stenches stinks the least. Now, let's drop off this Gift and get home. What do you say?"

"Fark yeah."

Both girls shared in a much-needed laugh.

20

THE BUGG SISTERS VS. THE SCHEMES OF ADULTS

There was no anger. There was no relief. There was no joy. There was no fear.

There was only sadness as Ash and Sammi Bugg trekked south across the Northern Goddess. They did not stop to admire the beauty of the sacred forest one last time, nor did they look upon the cliffs of the Great Gorge with worry or concern.

They did not pause for anything.

The Bugg Sisters felt no hunger or thirst. Their muscles did not tire, and their eyelids refused to grow heavy.

They passed through the dead city like two wraiths, paying no mind to their surroundings. They rounded craggy hills and entered Terminus Grove without the slightest hesitation.

The Pentad Gift swirled in Ash's lone hand, and the box dully pulsed, as if it were a heart, its beats providing all the nourishment the sisters would need for the long voyage to Kassimont.

Terminus Grove slept during the day and awakened with bioluminescent color at night. Ash and Sammi kept a steady pace during both.

Every now and then, the glowing eyes of a predator could be seen high in a tree or within a bush adjacent to the small trail on which the girls traveled. The younglings ignored them, somehow certain that no animal would harm them with the Pentad Gift in their possession.

One evening, with the Five Sisters directly overhead, Ash and Sammi surprised a group of Pygmy Baashers, none of whom looked familiar. The warrior Scamps immediately pulled out their curved blades and approached the children, dark intentions evident. When oversized purple eyes finally fell on the Pentad Gift, however, they immediately halted their advance and elected to back away, quickly vanishing into the kaleidoscope forest.

The hoots and hollers of Pygmy Scamps could be heard the next day as the Bugg Sisters sped through Terminus Grove. But none came close enough to be seen.

Eventually, daylight could be seen ahead, marking the end of the toxic forest. Ash and Sammi paused, but only for a moment. They shared in a brief hug and pushed forward, ready to put this part of their adventure behind them.

Clear, brown eyes squinted as Paragon raged at its full height. The remnants of a great battle were evident, with weapons, shields, and the decomposing corpses of men, women, and horses left strewn throughout the level terrain.

Sammi hit her sister on the shoulder and motioned up the tree line, where the broken remains of two Skymmers had been left to the elements.

"You think anyone will believe me when I tell them that we flew?"

Ash nudged her little sister. "They will when you build the next one." Sammi smiled at the thought. "Let's keep moving. I still don't know how we're going to reach Kassimont on our own."

Sammi's now-sharp eyes caught something in the distance. "We're not going to be alone for long."

Ash found what Sammi was looking at—a massive group of riders approaching will all haste from the east.

"Friend or foe, you think?" There was no fear in the one-armed girl's words.

"Does it matter, sis?"

"No. No, I suppose it doesn't."

~

"Do not move," came the high-pitched call as the horsemen closed in.

Ash and Sammi rolled their eyes as the familiar voice of Lieutenant Benson Kruger cut through the chill air. The narrow-faced soldier brought his mount to a sliding stop as the other Chestnuts encircled the two kids from Crimmish. A cold smirk landed on the officer's rodent face.

"I told you I would find you," Kruger said darkly. "And I did. I suffered many losses because of you girls… but nothing you can't pay back in full." Several of the Titians laughed, understanding that the Lieutenant's words were more promise than crude joke.

Kruger then seemed to realize something, and his beady eyes turned to and fro, taking in the edges of Terminus Grove. "Where are the others?! There were four of you who fled into the forest. Where are the boys?! Are they still in the Grove?! They would be making a grave mistake if they think to sneak attack us." Kruger inched his horse closer to the poisonous forest and directed his next shouts to the trees. "You hear that, boys?! If I even smell you nearby, I'll begin leaving a trail for you to follow! A brown finger here, a brown toe there! Keep it up, and you'll start finding more substantial pieces, like arms and heads!" Kruger looked down at Ash with a wolfish grin. "Well, maybe not so many arms!" More laughter. "You hear me, boys?! I'll—"

"They're gone," interrupted Ash.

"Gone where?" demanded Kruger.

"Gone, gone. Dead." Ash saw no reason to clarify Fincher's unthinkable fate.

The Lieutenant danced his horse away from Terminus Grove. "Well, isn't that a heartbreaker. I hope they died like the coward oath-breakers they were." Neither sister dignified the callous statement with a response. When Kruger did not get the reaction he had hoped, the weaselly officer switched gears. "I hope you at least managed to accomplish the one task that you were set out to do. The one task you were commanded to do."

Ash held up the Pentad Gift with her right hand and nub of her left arm. "This is it. This is the Gift of the Supreme Helices. This is what will save Quaan."

Beady eyes swam with greed and ambition as they landed on the swirling box. "Very good, ladies." To his soldiers, he said, "Someone seize the box!"

Two men and a female soldier dropped from their mounts and started to advance on the girls.

"I wouldn't do that if I were you," said Ash coldly, clutching the Gift to her chest.

"But you're not me, are you Cheese-Eyes," shot back the unobservant Lieutenant as the Chestnuts continued to draw close.

"The God-Snails had very specific instructions that had to be followed," stated Sammi with all the calmness and poise her older sister had shown.

"Did they now?" came the doubtful reply as the trio of warriors arrived at the younglings, the female Titian reaching out for the Pentad Gift.

"They did," asserted Ash wearing a cold, determined grin. "And rule one is that if anyone touches this box other than me, my sister, or the Imperator… well, it wouldn't be good."

The female soldier's hand stopped mid-reach. She looked up at her Lieutenant questioningly.

Kruger let out a sigh. "What exactly does that mean?"

Ash offered a casual shrug. "Honestly, I don't know; they didn't go into detail. But I assume that either the Gift will implode or explode, or melt, or something. Either way, your Imperator won't have his prize. And you'll be solely responsible for the Gloomtide destroying this world."

Benson Kruger thought it over for a moment before sending a wad of spit to the ground below. "I think you're bluffing. Take it!"

The lady soldier moved once more to grab the Pentad Gift but froze again when the swirling of the box paused and switched direction, pulsing as it did.

Ash sent her next words to the soldiers surrounding her and

Sammi. "If you have families that you hope to see again, I wouldn't do that. If you're not immediately incinerated, which I'm inclined to believe will happen, you'll return to Kassimont without this cure. I suspect that Kassimont is now sick with the Gloomtide. Are your children safe?"

The woman's fierce green eyes, reminiscent of Ditto's, studied Ash and her steady demeanor. "You don't seem afraid. You would be afraid if this were true. Your voice would shake with the thought of me grabbing that box from you. If this were true."

Ash sent a knowing smirk the soldier's way, further unsettling the lady Chestnut. "Our friends are gone, our parents are dying, our home is toxic, and we've seen the worst that this world has to offer. We have nothing left to give, and even less to care about. So, here..." Ash held out the Pentad Gift. "Take it if you don't care, either."

Green eyes took in the unnatural box for a second, and the woman began to back away from the sisters, the other two Titians following suit.

"I believe them, sir," said the lady Chestnut to Lieutenant Kruger. "Something's not right about that box. I'd rather not handle it."

"Me neither," agreed to man to her right.

"Not touching it," echoed the soldier to her left.

Kruger's face twisted in anger, but the officer swallowed it down. "You girls want to carry it yourselves? Fine by me. I will still get the credit and praise that I deserve, no matter who actually hands the Gift over. But know this. If you try to escape, if you even think about running, I'll put an arrow into each your girlish backs before feeding your bodies to the nearest pack of wild dogs. Do we understand each other?"

"Dear Lieutenant Kruger," said Ash as if she were speaking with a child. "We don't consider ourselves prisoners of yours, so why would we try to leave? We are aligned in our goal, are we not?"

Kruger did not like the tone of the girl's voice. "We are aligned in *nothing* you filthy Cheese-Eyes! Yellish!"

"Sir," replied one of the soldiers who donned the badges of an officer.

"Give them the extra mount. We don't want anyone accidentally touching that box, now do we? Or the dirty skin of a Stench whore, for that matter. The Imperator awaits his prize! Let's ride!"

With that, Lieutenant Benson Kruger spun his warhorse around and kicked the beast into a gallop. The Chestnut known as Yellish brought around a riderless horse and marched it carefully up to the younglings.

"Do you need help climbing on?" asked the bearded man in a deep, gruff voice.

"You mean, you're not afraid to touch us?" questioned Sammi. "And our filthy skin?"

Yellish snorted in response. "I fear touching that devilish-looking box, I admit. But your skin? I have daughters your age." The hairy Titian climbed off his own steed, kneeled beside the riderless horse, and cupped his scar-covered hands, creating a step for the sisters. He looked over at the children with amusement in his tired eyes. "If you prefer, I could simply toss you onto the animal."

The Bugg Sisters shared in a smile before stepping into Yellish's hands and then into the stirrups, finally throwing their short legs over the saddle.

"His name is *Commett*," stated Yellish as he stood and rubbed the stallion's nose. "He's a good horse. And his previous owner was a good woman and even better soldier. I'm happy to see that he will have good-hearted riders."

"How do you know that we're good-hearted?" inquired Ash from the saddle.

Yellish offered a playful slap to the animal's thick neck for good measure. "Ahh, well, you live in this world long enough, it becomes easier and easier to separate the good from the bad."

"Speaking of bad, your commander is a hard guy to like."

Yellish laughed as he remounted. "Wait 'till you get to know him. Then you'll see what kind of rare prick he really is."

~

The contingent of Titians, along with their "captives," drove the horses all Paragon, stopping only when it became too dark for the mounts to see the road beneath them.

As the soldiers made camp, Ash and Sammi sat together to the side, the Pentad Gift nestled between them.

While the fires cooked meat over rotating spits, a small group of male Chestnuts stared hungrily at the sisters, making obscene gestures and even more grotesque comments.

"Cut it out," snapped Yellish dangerously.

"Oh, they're just having a bit of fun, Sergeant Yellish," said a laughing Kruger.

"Well, tell them to have it at someone else's expense," roared the veteran. "Or we'll be entering Kassimont with far fewer numbers!"

Benson Kruger rolled his beady black eyes. "Fine." To the group of men, he said, "No more conversing with the detainees! It seems to injure Sergeant Yellish's more delicate sensibilities." Back to Yellish, he added, "You may want to get ahold of those *delicate sensibilities*, Martinn. After all, aren't they the reason that you've been knocked back to sergeant three… or is it four times now?"

Martinn Yellish's eyes flashed with anger. "Better than being a lapdog and whore of the crown!" Yellish stormed away and Kruger giggled at his ability to upset the too-kind killer.

"Attack dog! Not lapdog, Martinn! Attack dog!"

When the Five Sisters began to rise, lending more of their soft light to the encampment, the meat was removed from skewers and distributed to the Chestnuts. The woman with green eyes brought a plate over to Ash and Sammi, who shook their heads in refusal.

"You have to eat," said the lady soldier.

"We're not hungry," countered Ash. "And we're not thirsty, either."

"But you must eat!"

"No. We mustn't."

"What's going on over there?" shouted Kruger.

"They won't eat, Lieutenant. They say they're not hungry. Or thirsty for that matter."

"Oh, what the fark?" growled Kruger as he stomped over to the children. "What's the meaning of this?!"

"My sister already said," replied Sammi coolly. "We're not hungry."

"Or thirsty," added Ash.

"Or thirsty," repeated Sammi.

Kruger's narrow face twisted in confusion. "What's this about? Some kind of nonviolent resistance? Some kind of shot at my authority?"

"No. We're just not hungry. And don't plan to be," answered Ash.

The Lieutenant angrily dropped to a knee, keeping a wary eye on the ever-flowing box. "Now listen here, you little shites. You're no good to me dead. If I'd wanted you dead, I'd have let my men have their way with you before tossing your naked, battered little bodies back into Terminus Grove with the rest of the toxic filth. But this loathsome assignment seems as if it will go smoother with you alive, so here we are. Now eat."

"Not hungry."

"Or thirsty."

Kruger showed his teeth in a mirthless grin. "So be it." He sprung to his feet. "They want to be rebels, let them starve like rebels. They'll be begging for morsels this time tomorrow. Maybe I'll give some to them. Maybe not."

Now it was Benson Krueger's turn to storm away, leaving the Bugg Sisters alone with the vulgar Titians. The men waited in silence, stuffing greasy cooked flesh into their mouths, until both Kruger and the green-eyed woman were out of earshot. One especially lumpy and hairy soldier leaned forward, the campfire reflecting off his eyes—one brown and one milky white.

"Youse don't have to eat, and youse don't have to drink. But youse girls do have to sleep. And when youse do, one of youse is getting yanked away and dragged into the bushes for some fun. At least, fun for one of us." The other grizzly Titians cackled.

"But we don't have to sleep," said Ash matter-of-factly. "And if I see you come anywhere near me or my sister, I'll open this box and vaporize your Danglin' Andy. How about that for fun?"

Several of the Chestnuts instinctively reached for their crotches. The white-eyed brute spat on the ground.

"I've been on the battlefield my entire life, youse little night flowers. We'll see who can go longer without sleep."

"Yes, I suppose we will," said Ash, putting the veteran soldier back on his heels. For the girl truly sounded unconcerned. She even managed to toss a wink at the would-be rapist.

~

"The wench didn't sleep! Not a farking wink! She or her sister! I stayed up the whole night watching them, and they didn't move or nap or nothing. They just stared out with those dead tart eyes of theirs!"

The white-eyed Titian, his lone good eye red from exhaustion, launched into his tirade as soon as the first of his fellow soldiers started to stir with Paragon rising in the east.

"And why were you staying awake to watch them, *Specialist* Ullmer?" asked Sergeant Yellish, a serious threat buried in the question.

Ullmer stammered in response, obviously intimidated by both Yellish's reputation as a fighter and the officer's superior rank.

"I-I... I had to! I, mean, someone had to!"

"We had sentries posted last night. As we always do."

"Yeah, well, maybe I forgot. But youse is missing the point, Yellish! They. Did. Not. Sleep."

Although Martinn Yellish found Olaff Ullmer to be the worst kind of Chestnut, he found himself unable to sweep aside the brute's claim, especially seeing how worked up the experienced soldier was. Yellish looked over to the Bugg Sisters, who sat cross-legged on the grass, the Pentad Gift sitting between them, appearing as if they had not a care in the world.

"Is this true, girls?"

Ash shrugged lightly. "I told him we didn't need to sleep."

"And why is that?"

Another light shrug. "I suppose it's the Gift. It… gives us strength. I think it wants to be in Kassimont even more than the Imperator wants it there."

"What's this about?" came the familiar high-pitched voice of Lieutenant Kruger. "It looks like a meeting of the minds, only there's no farking minds here."

Ullmer saw his opportunity and jumped at it. "These witches don't sleep! They aren't human! We need to kill them now and take the durned box!"

"That would be extraordinarily foolish," responded Sammi without emotion.

"No one asked youse, wench," snapped back Ullmer.

Kruger ignored the loathsome Specialist. "Why do you not need to sleep?"

Ash put on the face Jazz Bugg wore when explaining something to her daughter for the thousandth time. "We don't get hungry. Or thirsty. Or tired. I think we've been over this before."

"But why, durn you?!"

Sammi cut in. "The Pentad Gift nourishes us. It's desperate to get to Kassimont."

To his credit, Kruger did not explode in a fit as he was ought to do. Instead, he mulled over the younglings' words, his weasel brain churning.

"So, you don't need rest? And you don't need to stop to eat? And you don't even need farking water?"

"Correct."

"Fine." Kruger spun to Yellish. "We'll use this to our advantage. Tell the team to eat a hearty breakfast. We no longer need to worry about our captives' ability to travel. We'll push our mounts to the brink, switch them out at one of the towns along North Verve if we have to. We will drive late into the night, halving our camp time. Eat in your saddle, whenever possible. These little girls from the Stenches don't need to take it slow… well, neither do we." Kruger stomped away, calling out over his shoulder. "Eat! Pack! Mount up! The race to Kassimont begins now!"

Martinn Yellish looked down at the siblings. "You're good now, but if you need anything, you let me know." Ash and Sammi nodded in turn.

Olaff Ullmer appeared gobsmacked by the whole encounter. "So, we're just gonna let these devil-twats lead us to certain doom?!"

All the other Titians paid the white-eyed soldier no mind as they raced to eat and break camp.

Ash watched as Ullmer's complaints fell on deaf ears. "You look tired, Specialist," she finally said. "It's too bad you didn't get much rest last night; it looks like there won't be much to be had from this point on."

"Youse don't talk to me with your forked tongue! She-devil!"

The green-eyed female Chestnut walked by carrying a saddle. "Give it a rest, Ullmer. Thanks to you, the Lieutenant is going to try to reach Kassimont in record time. I think you've done enough for one day, and Paragon just showed up."

Ullmer's hairy jaw fell open in anger, and he began to formulate the bumbling beginnings of a retort. Unfortunately for him, Sammi Bugg beat him to it.

"Yeah, give it a rest, *Olaff*. Cause it's the only rest you'll find for a very, very long time."

True to his word, Lieutenant Benson Kruger pushed his men and women as if they were transporting a haul of priceless perishables—because as far as he knew, they might have been.

They drove their horses the duration of Paragon, stopping only to water the horses and shovel meager lunches of nuts and dried berries into their mouths.

They pressed on as the Five Sisters rose overhead, slowing down a bit to minimize the chances of a mount stepping into a hole and breaking a leg.

The moons of Quaan were already reaching for the Spired Curtains when Kruger finally decided to make camp, promising they would be back at it at the first sign of Paragon. When grumbles started to reach the Lieutenant's ears, he quashed them by promising triple pay should they make it to Kassimont in three days, something he was confident he could make happen.

As the overly tired soldiers collapsed onto their bedrolls, some with unchewed food still in their cheeks, Ash and Sammi Bugg simply resumed their position at the campfire's edge, sitting cross-legged and staring out with eyes far wiser than their ages should allow.

While all the other Titians slept soundly, the drone of snores evidence of the general exhaustion of the group, Olaff Ullmer did his best to fend off unconsciousness, opting instead to keep his good eye on the child sisters, whenever possible. The brute would drift off, only to rip himself awake, always finding Ash and Sammi in the same position, with the same looks on their brown faces, and the same knowing smiles on their lips, as if they knew a secret that the world did not.

When the first rays of Paragon shot over Sierra Dawn, Kruger and Yellish were up, walking through the camp and kicking soldiers awake. Ullmer cursed aloud when Yellish delivered an unnecessarily swift boot to his ribs, tearing the oaf from a slumber that had begun in full only an hour prior.

Specialist Ullmer immediately looked over to the Bugg Sisters, who remained exactly where they were when his heavy eyelids finally closed.

The two girls looked as rested and relaxed as a vacationing Quaan noble. Ullmer rose on rubbery, weak legs and spat onto the ground in silent disapproval.

No one cared.

As the Chestnut regiment left the Contested Zone behind and entered the more civilized parts of the Titian Empire, the expansion of the Gloomtide became painfully apparent.

Some villages they passed were no more than cinders, with those still alive weeping uncontrollably as their former lives smoldered around them. In other towns, chaos reigned as men chased each other with blades, their snarling faces flush with mania. Children could be seen hiding under overturned carts and on top of thatched roofs, terrified of the monsters into which their families had transformed. Even the detestable Lieutenant Kruger seemed moved by the scene.

"This is why we must press on," he told the troops as several wept softly under their helmets. "This is why time is of the essence."

Luckily, they found a town along North Verve, just south of one of several massive bridges that spanned the raging river, that had yet to experience the worst of the Gloomtide.

"We can trade out the horses here," stated Kruger after determining the village was fairly safe from the sickness. "This day makes me want to redouble our efforts."

"Uhh, sir," said the green-eyed woman.

"What is it, Corporal Ridlee?" The woman started to respond but hesitated. "Speak your mind, woman!"

"Uhh, I'm not sure they need it, sir."

"Who needs what, Corporal? Use your farking words, durn it!"

Ridlee jumped in her saddle. "I'm not sure the horses need to be switched out. Mine seems fine. Better than fine."

"Actually, mine does, as well," agreed Yellish as several other confirmations regarding the health of horses came flying in.

Kruger thought for a moment and then twisted in his saddle to look at Ash and Sammi, who rode several columns back. "What is going on?"

"We told you," Ash answered. "The Pentad Gift wants to reach Kassimont. It's probably feeding the horses just as it's feeding us."

"Hey, we could use some of that shite, too, you know," said a soldier from the back, which was met with a combination of laughs and serious agreement.

Kruger continued to study the children, attempting in vain to discern any clues of deception. When he didn't, he said, "Very well." To the group, he added, "We're not stopping here!" The officer disregarded the groans. "We cross the bridge north of here and head across the angel wheat flats! Kassimont—and your prizes—await!"

~

Another ride deep into the night. Another short camp. Eyes grew red with fatigue. Tempers shortened.

But the horses remained strong. And the Bugg Sisters remained at peace.

"They're marching us straight to our deaths! I'm telling youse!"

"Shut your gob, Ullmer," came the unified response.

More villages came and went. Some were dead. For others, death would have been a welcome reprieve. Every now and then, a lunatic would run, screaming, at the Titians with an upraised sword or sickle, only to fall well short of the object of their Gloomtide-induced rage, the feathered shafts of arrows jutting from their chest.

One last short night of rest, only this one offered even less respite.

With the Five Sisters low in the western sky, Specialist Olaff Ullmer, his one good eye wild with hysteria, tip-toed quietly across the camp, careful not to disturb any of his resting comrades.

Ash and Sammi watched his approach, their expressions never changing, even when Ullmer pulled a knife from his belt. The crazed man spoke in a furious growl.

"Youse thinks you can drag me to the dark end without me kicking and screaming? Well, I ain't screaming, night flowers, but this is me kicking. Kicking back hard, youse wenches from the abyss!"

"We're sorry you feel that way," stated Ash calmly, even as the blade went up.

Sammi grinned softly in agreement. "Yeah, we know what it's like to be scared. To not know what's coming next. We understand you, Olaff Ullmer."

"The fark you do!"

"Kill us if it will make you feel better," said Ash, and neither girl moved.

"But it rarely does, sis."

"No, Samm, it almost never does."

"Enough," spat Ullmer. "Enough of youse's poison. Youse may have them all fooled, but not me. Not me!"

Ullmer moved forward to strike.

"Don't take another step!" Ullmer, Ash, and Sammi looked over to find Corporal Ridlee wading in, sword drawn. "I'll not have you shite on all the work we've done, Ullmer. All the good people we've lost. Everything we've sacrificed has been to get this box to Kassimont, and now that the end is near you want to fark it all up? Well, I won't let you!"

"Youse as blind as the rest of them," said Ullmer, spittle flying from his mouth. "And it's my job to make youse see."

"Don't do it, Ullmer. I'm warning you."

Ullmer's white eye danced with the reflection of fire. "Oh, no, Ridlee. It is *I* who am warning *youse*. But youse obviously don't appreciate my efforts."

"I said put it down," repeated Ridlee. "Or I'll run you through. This, I swear."

Ullmer stared down Ridlee for a moment before holding his gnarled hands out wide. "Have it youse own way, Ridlee. Wenches will always stay together, I see. In fact, perhaps youse can—"

Ullmer lunged at the sitting girls, his blade leading the way. When Corporal Ridlee went to intercept, however, Ullmer pivoted impossibly fast for a man his size, rotating in a backhand that put his blade in line with the green-eyed woman's throat.

Ridlee, showcasing her own skills, back-stepped just in time. Instead of her throat, Ullmer's knife sliced neatly across the woman's cheek, sending a river of blood to flow across her chin.

While most would have retreated from such a wound, the Corporal slid forward, behind the brute's strike, and her arm shot ahead, sending her sword out like a lance. The tip of her cutlass found Ullmer's exposed chest, and the oaf cried out briefly as metal touched heart, dropping the specialist dead where he stood.

"What's going on here?" demanded Yellish, flying in from the shadows, his broadsword drawn and ready. The grizzled veteran took in the scene, including the unmoving body of Olaff Ullmer at his feet. He dropped to his knees. "Are you girls all right?"

"Fine, Sergeant."

"Never better, Mister Martinn."

Corporal Ridlee clutched her bleeding face as she spoke. "The bastard went for the younglings. I had a feeling he might try something, so I was ready when he attacked."

Yellish, after checking on the sisters from a safe distance, ran to the woman, pushing a handkerchief against her open wound.

"Foolish woman," he reprimanded as he pressed the cloth against her face, concern thick in his voice. Ash and Sammi shared a knowing look. "Why did you not wake everyone? What made you think you could best a savage like Ullmer? Were you not scared?"

Ridlee took the makeshift bandage from Yellish and pushed the Sergeant away.

"Of course, I was scared!"

"Then why?!"

"Because I might have feared Ullmer, but I'm absolutely terrified of these children. And what might happen should harm come to them."

Yellish nodded in understanding, his fear and anger starting to subside. "Fair enough, then. And good job."

"What now?" came the tired voice of Benson Kruger, the man doing his best to clear the sleep from his beady eyes. "Don't we have enough to deal with?" The Lieutenant found Ullmer's corpse in the firelight. "He dead?"

"He is," replied Yellish.

"And why, pray tell?"

Ridlee slid her cutlass back into its scabbard, not bothering to wipe off Ullmer's blood. "He went for the… captives. I had no choice."

Kruger took a moment. "Very well. He won't be missed. You and Yellish toss his body into the flats; the wheat could use the food. We'll split his share evenly among the troops." Kruger aimed his next words at the camp. "You hear that?! An extra share for everyone! Compliments of Benson Kruger!"

Unfortunately, no one reacted to Kruger's announcement. They were all still fast asleep.

Despite the weariness of the group, Lieutenant Kruger sent two riders streaking ahead as soon as the Chestnuts traversed Rayne Crossing, the massive, ornate bridge that spanned South Verve and represented the final push into the Titian capital of Kassimont.

Ash and Sammi Bugg, despite the wonders they had witnessed in Shadowset, Vattassav, Terminus Grove, and the Northern Goddess, could still feel their brown eyes widen a bit as they rode into Kassimont as Paragon inched closer to the Spired Curtains.

Before even entering the fortressed heart of the capital city, the sisters were forced to crane their necks to look up at the top floors of mansions that rested on the large estates of the Titian elite. Dirt-covered landscapers and gardeners glanced up from their labors as the troops passed, their faces perpetually tired and without hope.

After trotting through Kassimont's affluent suburban areas, Ash and Sammi's jaws opened a bit to match their eyes as they approached an impossibly colossal wall that marked the main part of the capital. Soldiers dressed in their finest rust-colored uniforms marched along the battlements and filled the looming towers. In the distance, the great construct known as Kass Keep hung heavy over the land, a stone sentinel that kept track of every slight, every whisper of revolt, every potential threat.

The younglings looked at each other, silently agreeing that the place was as terrifying as it was impressive. Some would call the castle beautiful, especially those who spent most of their lives toiling away in country soil, but the Bugg Sisters could not, for they had witnessed true magnificence.

A large contingent of Titians awaited the group's arrival, alongside the two horsemen Benson Kruger had sent ahead. At the head of the meeting party was a familiar face, that of Second Lieutenant Tobias Vale, the yellow-eyed soldier who had accompanied Gorman Graff to Crimmish and the only Titian to escape the Slugg assault at Salt's Pass.

Vale shot a sour look at Benson Kruger as the weasel-faced Lieutenant drew near, reminding Ash and Sammi of how much they liked the young, handsome officer.

"I have returned, a conquering hero," declared Kruger as the two groups met. "First, I vanquished the Azure Sluggs..." Various looks between soldiers hinted that this wasn't entirely factual, but the arrogant Lieutenant continued. "And then I captured the Empire's most notorious scofflaws. And, with them, the greatest gift Quaan has ever known!"

Tobias Vale did his best to ignore Kruger, instead opting to swing his unusual yellow eyes toward Ash and Sammi.

"Ash and Sammi Bugg—"

"It's just Samm now," interrupted Sammi.

It took Vale a moment to pick up on the meaning of the change, the heaviness of the act. The thoughtful officer's face fell a little.

"Apologies, young miss." He restarted. "Ash and Samm Bugg. It is truly good to see you again, all in one piece. Where, pray tell, are your —" The shadow that passed over each girl's face told the tale in full. "I see... I will say a prayer for them."

"Yes, yes," cut in Kruger in his usual grating voice. "Prayers for the fallen but, better yet, rewards for the victors. As you can see, *Second Lieutenant*, the children have the Gift of the Helices in their possession. And they are ready to deliver it to the Imperator and Imperatrix... with me at their lead, of course."

"Yes, of course," muttered Vale. Back facing the Bugg Sisters, he said, "Can I relieve you of that burden, younglings?"

"You cannot," shot back Kruger, answering for the girls. "*Apparently*, only the Imperator can receive the Gift, just as only he can open it. Trust me, I have my doubts about this, and it's proven one big pain in the arse. But better safe than sorry, I suppose. I'll receive my accolades and rewards all the same."

Vale simply nodded and returned his attention back to Ash and Sammi. "You have done the Empire a great service, young ladies. Songs will be written and sung in your honor for generations to come. We will not forget your service. Or your sacrifice."

"They merely fetched a box! I'm the one who stared down the Slugg army and pushed those devils back into their frozen holes! Oh, enough of this! Lead us to the Imperator, Vale, or are you unable to complete the most basic of tasks? I mean, you obviously failed horribly at keeping that old shite stain Graff alive, didn't you?"

To his credit, Vale was able to ignore Kruger's jabs. "You're right. The Imperator and Imperatrix, as you can imagine, are eager to receive you all. When the Rose Comet reappeared and then disappeared in the sky several nights ago, they feared that all hope was lost." Vale made sure his next words were clearly aimed at the remaining kids from Crimmish. "Your arrival has swollen hearts and renewed our spirits. Come, let us complete your arduous journey."

"We'd have been there already if you'd shut your gob," snarled Kruger.

Vale refused to take his yellow eyes from the siblings. "It's time for you to meet the Imperator Kasspar Rayne. And collect your prize." Vale spun his horse toward the giant open portcullis guarding the city but turned back to face the younglings once more. "Keep your eyes ahead. The Gloomtide has come to Kassimont, and there is much horror to witness, despite our best efforts to restrict it to the fringes of the capital. Had your arrival come many more Paragons later, there may not have been a city to return to."

There would have been a time when Ash and Sammi Bugg would have been overwhelmed by the colorful tapestries, the jewel-encrusted vases, the golden sculptures, and the thick, heavily patterned carpets that lined Kass Keep. But now, all the sisters noticed was the unnecessary opulence, the waste, and the general inequity of the place.

Ash hugged the Pentad Gift tighter, praying it would cure more than the Gloomtide.

The sound of the large throne room doors opening ripped the sisters from their wandering thoughts.

The Imperator, sitting on his gilded throne, jumped excitedly when the party entered. "Ho, ho! The young champions of the Stench... of Crimmish, have returned! And they have brought the Gift! Long live the Supreme Helices!"

"Long live the Helices," came the cry from all the uniformed soldiers, sharply dressed bureaucrats, and sharp-eyed advisors in attendance.

Imperator Kasspar Rayne chugged the rest of the wine in his gem-studded goblet and tossed the cup into the waiting hands of a servant before rising on unsteady legs and stumbling a bit toward the arriving group. Kassidy Rayne shared a glance with Chancellor Sologar Crimm, both of their too-sharp minds racing with possibility.

As the Imperator marched across the room, the few Chestnuts who had accompanied the sisters in, including Second Lieutenant Tobias Vale, fell to the side, their heads bowed in appropriate fealty. Benson Kruger proved the exception.

"My Imperator! I have traveled far and wide, have battled the Azure Sluggs, and driven my troops beyond the point of exhaustion, to bring you the greatest of prizes—the Gift of the Divine Pentad!"

Kasspar Rayne looked at Kruger through blurry eyes. "Who are you?"

Benson Kruger fell back a step, obviously disheartened, and the Bugg Sisters did their best not to laugh aloud.

"Well, I... I'm Lieutenant Benson Kruger, my liege. It is I that has delivered the..."

The Imperator waved away the weaselly Lieutenant with a jeweled, manicured hand that, alone, cost more than the total value of Crimmish's yearly exports.

"Yes, yes! See the Chancellor for your recompense!"

Kruger's beady eyes flashed to Crimm, who subtly bade the man to calm down, the promise of reward evident in the Chancellor's nonverbal cues. The Lieutenant joined the others along the side, and Vale refused to hide his gleeful smile.

Only Ash and Sammi Bugg remained on the extravagantly woven carpet that ran from the throne of the Imperator to the room's entrance. Kasspar Rayne closed the distance, his eyes dancing with a touch of mania. The Imperator lowered his voice.

"You have done us a great service. I'll have your names, and they will be recorded in the annals of our Empire's vast history—as heroes of the land."

"I am Ashanti Bugg. And this is my sister Sammira Bugg. Our dearest friends who did not make it to complete the journey were Hanako Bugg, Deetarik Bugg, and Finchius Bugg."

Imperator Rayne called out over his shoulder. "Chancellor! Have you taken permanent note of these champions?!"

"I have, my lord," declared Sologar Crimm, without the slightest memory of the children's names.

"Good." Kasspar's wild eyes fell on the swirling box in the cradle of Ash's lone good arm. The drunken king spoke in a whisper. "Is that it? Is that what was given by the Supreme Helices?"

"It is," answered Ash.

Kasspar licked his dry lips. "And it will clear the world of the Gloomtide?"

Ash looked to her sister before responding. "They said that it will heal Quaan of its ailments."

The Imperator's eyes leapt from the Gift to Ash. "So, you spoke to them?"

"We did," the girl replied, seeing no reason to delve into the particulars.

"And what were they like?"

A pause. "They were... not of this world."

"But what did they look like?"

"Like... snails. Like really, really big snails."

"How glorious! Oh, how I would have loved to meet them. After all, they are the greatest supporters of the Rayne Dynasty, are they not? And I would have made the trek, if it weren't for Terminus Grove and my duties here in Kassimont." Sologar Crimm hid a smirk with a pale hand. "They tell me that only I may accept the Gift. Is this true?"

"It is."

"Then I am ready to receive the Gift of the Divine Pentad as evidence of my rightful claim as the supreme leader of Quaan and the Titian Empire's jurisdiction over the land." Kasspar Rayne reached for the swirling box.

"There are rules to follow," stated Sammi Bugg, freezing the Imperator. "For the Gift to work."

Rayne licked his lips once more, almost demanding that more wine be brought to him. "I am the Imperator."

"But there are still rules." Sammi did not flinch under the uneven stare of the most powerful man in Quaan.

"Name them. Name them quickly."

Ash stepped in for her sister. "First, as you know, only you or another of the Rayne bloodline can receive the Gift."

"Yes, yes, we know this. Go on!"

"Second, the Gift should only be opened with great ceremony, with all of the key figures of the Titian Empire in attendance."

Imperator Rayne's face twisted in frustration. "Yes, but the Gloomtide has already reached Kassimont! Every day it creeps closer to these walls, to—"

"That is the rule," declared Sammi, leaving no room for argument or interpretation.

Kasspar rubbed his dry lips with a finger. "Fine, fine. Is that all?"

"No," said Ash flatly. "The God-Snails also stated that *we* should be included in the ceremony. And given places of great honor."

At this, Imperatrix Kassidy Rayne choked on her wine as Sologar Crimm aggressively smoothed his carefully trimmed goatee.

"Yes, yes, this is all perfectly fine," rushed the Imperator, desperate to hold the magical box.

"Then you agree?" asked Sammi.

"Of course! Now, hand over the Gift! I will fulfill my duty as Imperator and save my people from the scourge that is the Gloomtide. And I will be remembered as the greatest member of the Rayne dynasty, finally putting to bed all memories of Prince Kasstin Rayne."

Kasspar Rayne reached for the Pentad Gift again, and Ash Bugg placed it in his soft hands.

The throne room held its collective breath as she did, fearful that this was perhaps some sort of ingenious trick. Fearful that the walls would explode around them, leaving a crater where Kassimont once stood.

But these fears proved unfounded.

Imperator Kasspar Rayne grinned from ear to ear as the Gift of the Helices entered his possession. He spun to face Kassidy Rayne, already forgetting about Ash and Sammi, and offered his wife a jubilant smile, as if he had accomplished something that the rest of the world could not. The Imperatrix offered a supportive nod in return.

"I can feel it, my love," the delirious Kasspar said to his better half. "I can feel the power of the Gift. I can feel it making me greater than I ever could have imagined. Making me more than I ever could have dreamed. Making me the vessel through which the world will be renewed!"

Kassidy Rayne offered a wide smile that touched her too-blue eyes. "And you have earned it, my husband! And we are all in your debt!"

"Long live the Imperator," came the cry from around the throne room.

The small voice of Ash Bugg sliced through the celebration. "Remember, it must be opened with great ceremony. And with all in attendance."

"Yes, yes," replied the Imperator absently. "We heard you the first time." To the Chancellor he said, "Light Kass Keep's tower flames! And toss all the lithium chloride you can acquire into them. I want them burning bright! And red! And launch all the signal flares that we have in stock into the night sky! I want all the nobles, governors, and magistrates from here to Nordessia to see them and know that they are called upon! They have four days before we open the Gift of the God-Snails!"

Tobias Vale spoke up, well out of place. "But, my lord! It was said that *all* need to be in attendance."

"And all will," shouted back the Imperator, unable to take his eyes from the whirlwind taking place within the unusual wood of the box in his jeweled palms. "All that matter, anyway. All that can make it here in time."

Kassidy Rayne stepped forward, urged on by a look from Chancellor Crimm.

"My husband, perhaps we can give it some more time. This is a big moment for us… for you… and I want all of those of sufficient import to be here to witness your glory and pay the appropriate respect."

Kasspar Rayne slowly marched back to his throne, his eyes still firmly held by the Gift at his chest.

"My wife, I spoil you, but this is one wish that I cannot grant." The Imperatrix's impossibly beautiful face twitched in a rare bout of uncontrolled emotion.

Kasspar sat upon his golden throne, the Pentad Gift on his silk-covered lap. His fingers ran across the smooth contours of the box as if it were one of his royal pets. After taking in his prize for several more seconds, the Imperator went on.

"Today, I watched from the safety of the castle walls as a man below—a man of means, by the way—sat on the cobblestone and cut off the fingers of his left hand one by one. He was laughing the entire time." Kasspar gave the ghastly image time to sink in. "That story is just one of many from inside Kassimont these past few days. The Gloomtide is here, ladies and gentlemen, and it is tearing through our people with the hunger and ferocity of a Bog Behemoth. I will not let it go on any longer than necessary." The Imperator's eyes found the striking blue orbs of his wife. "No matter who is left out." A pause, then, "Four days! Do you hear me?!"

"Yes, my lord," came the thunderous reply from all.

"Good! Then begin the preparations!" The Imperator returned his gaze to the Pentad Gift and its stormy surface. He spoke next without looking up. "And make sure that those girls are justly rewarded. Everything that we promised and more!"

"I'll take care of that, my husband," said Kassidy Rayne, slipping in next to the golden throne. "You already have much on your plate. And a world to save."

"Of course, my heart," replied Kasspar absently. "That would be exquisite of you…" His voice faded, as if the box had already taken him to a far-off place, at least in his mind.

Sologar Crimm smoothed his goatee and stepped forward. "You all heard the Imperator! There is much to do! Light the fires! Launch the flares! And prepare the Grand Hall! This will be the most momentous occasion in the history of the Titian Empire and its surroundings need to reflect that. There will be no sleep tonight. I'll be making rounds in a few hours, and I had better see significant progress. Do you understand?"

"Yes, Chancellor," came the cry, and guards, head servants, and dignitaries scattered, desperate to please their demanding leaders.

Ash and Sammi Bugg remained where they stood amidst the cyclone of bodies, their arms hooked at the elbows. The Imperatrix noted the girls and drifted over to Crimm.

"What are they waiting for?" she asked the Chancellor.

"I'm not sure," said Crimm quietly. "They already received their thanks, whereas, I have yet to receive mine. This entire plan—you know, the one that just saved our entire Empire—was my conception, after all. At no minor risk, may I add."

"And you'll be justly compensated, Sologar. As you always are."

Crimm breathed in heavily, drinking in the perfume and beauty of the Imperatrix. "Perhaps I desire more than mere chips and titles this time. Perhaps I desire something… more carnal."

Kassidy Rayne understood her Chancellor's meaning, and she was unsurprised by his gall. She had been around powerful men all her life, and they always got around to this behavior soon or later. If they lived that long.

"Your plan has not been seen through to its conclusion, Chancellor. That is a conversation for *after* the Empire is saved. A conversation I may, or may not, be willing to have." Crimm smiled darkly, for that was markedly *not* an outright denial. The Imperatrix continued. "Now, answer my question. What are those Stench rats waiting for?"

Sologar Crimm leaned in close. "I guess to be brought to their chambers, my Lady. After all, they are, *apparently*, supposed to be guests of great honor."

Kassidy looked as if she had smelled something rotten. "Well, that is just absurd. And who promised them that? Not I, certainly. And not the Imperator."

Sologar played with one of his many rings. "I suppose the God-Snails made the promise," he said snidely.

"Oh, please. What's more likely? That the Divine Pentad promised two dirt-covered urchins a place of honor at the Imperial Reveal? I mean, why would celestial beings even care? Or that those two girls simply tacked that *rule* onto the others in an attempt to infiltrate a royal ceremony?"

Crimm giggled under a soft hand. "But it seems like your husband has taken a real shine to them."

"Oh, please. He has already forgotten that they even exist. Look at him." The conspiring pair glanced over to find Kasspar Rayne staring deeply into the box on his lap, completely oblivious to the world around him. "As usual, it will come down to us to do the heavy lifting." Bright blue eyes caught the Chancellor. "And make the tough decisions."

"So, they will not have places of honor. Where would you have me put the younglings?"

Kassidy's flawless face twisted in rage. "I will not have two mud-skinned miscreants from the Stenches anywhere near this occasion. Imagine the looks. Imagine the questions. No, no, no. There must be no distractions. All eyes and thoughts must be on the Imperator."

"And his Imperatrix," added the Chancellor slyly.

"Well, of course." A long moment of quiet passed, two calculating minds spinning webs of possibility. "Tell me, Sologar. What story will you paint of the Imperator and the Gift of the Helices?"

"I have given it thought. Very few know of how the Pentad Gift was obtained, and most of those are soldiers loyal to the Empire—easy to control, bribe, or dispose of, as needed. I could even have them all sent south to serve on Black Bog patrols for the rest of their lives. No one would hear from them again."

"And the story?" prodded Kassidy.

Crimm shrugged. "Simple is always best. Simple stories for simple minds. Perhaps Imperator Kasspar Rayne, showing his Imperial courage, secreted out under the cover night with a small contingent of men and met with the God-Snails where few men reside. Perhaps the God-Snails landed not far from here, along the black shores of the Great Untold, where they delivered their holy Gift directly to our Imperator. The trip there and back could, theoretically, be made in a single evening."

Kassidy Rayne thought it over. "I don't know, Sologar. There were various individuals in this room just now. And more than simple soldiers."

"Only the most trusted advisors and dignitaries were allowed in."

"Is there really such a thing as a *trusted* advisor or dignitary?"

"Fair point, my Lady. But we have kept larger secrets within larger groups. It just takes more creativity. And more resolve."

"There is no larger secret."

"Of course, you are correct, my Lady."

The Imperatrix's next words were more to herself than to her Chancellor. "If what you say is true, then these filthy girls represent the only loose ends that will remain outside of our control once they are sent away."

Crimm leaned in even more, soaking in the closeness. "Allow me a few hours of consideration. There could be a way that I could—"

Heavily decorated nails waved in the air. "No. You have enough to do. I'll take care of this. In this case, your plausible deniability might best serve me."

The Chancellor grinned wickedly. "And in Kassimont, that is all that really matters, is it not? Best serving you?"

Kassidy shot Sologar with a dangerous look. "Yes. And you'd do well to remember that."

"I'm still alive, aren't I?"

"For now."

With those parting words, that veiled threat, the Imperatrix floated away from Crimm. It was now the Chancellor's turn to look as if the smell of rotten fruit was in his nose.

"My dear, dear girls," said Kassidy as she approached Ash and Sammi, using an affectionate tone perfected through years of high-risk politicking. "The Empire owes you a great debt, one that can never be fully repaid."

"Just send your Imperial physicians and apothecaries to Crimmish to cure our people of the Maddening, and we'll call it even," responded Ash. "You know, as was our bargain."

Kassidy could feel her smile dip a bit before she was able to pull it taut once more.

"Of course, my dear. I will personally see them sent off right after the Imperial Reveal. I'll also make sure that your pockets and packs are full of chips before you leave."

From their time as harvesters, the Bugg Sisters knew a snake when they saw one, no matter what skin it wore, no matter how beautiful it appeared. But the Imperatrix seemed willing to pay the Empire's debt, and that was all that the younglings could ask.

Despite the commotion and excitement, Sammi leaned against her older sister for support. As soon as the Pentad Gift had left their possession, both girls could feel the energy instantaneously drained from their young bodies. Their stomachs rumbled loudly, and their mouths grew dry. The power of the God-Snails was gone, and all that was left were two children who were tired beyond comprehension, having just lived several lives in a few turns of Paragon. Lives filled with pain and suffering and loss.

Sammi spoke from her sister's shoulder. "Could we please be taken to our room, Imperatrix? As you can imagine, our road was a long one and full of much hardship."

Kassidy pretended to think it over. "You know, I can't even begin to imagine how much you must miss your family and friends."

"Our friends are all gone," cut in Ash, and Kassidy's friendly facade fell again, but only for the slightest of beats.

"Your family, then. I would think that you'd want to be on your way as soon as possible. This place is going to be absolute chaos over the next four days and will not be very conducive to rest. Plus, with all the governors, officials, nobles, and dignitaries coming in, some probably as soon as this evening, I'm not even sure that we have available quarters."

The sisters looked around the cavernous throne room, just one of the hundreds of rooms in Kass Keep, the largest manmade structure in Quaan.

Ash looked down at her weary sibling. "So, you... want us to leave Kassimont? Tonight?"

The Imperatrix nodded, and Ash could have sworn that reptilian pupils flashed for a moment within those blue orbs. Or maybe she, too, was weary to the point of hallucination.

"If it were up to me, I'd have you stay here forever. But logistically, I'm afraid things are a bit convoluted. A bit messy. But not to fret, for you'll be leaving with heavy packs and all the food and water and wine... are you old enough to drink wine? Anyhow, I'll make sure that you set off with whatever you may need for the journey home."

"But what about the opening of the Pentad Gift?" asked an increasingly tired-sounding Sammi. "We're supposed to be at it."

"We're supposed to be guests of honor," corrected Ash. "As per the rules set by the God-Snails."

Striking blue eyes narrowed. "And who else heard these rules?"

"Well, no one, of course. But—"

"Then perhaps you simply imagined it, hmm? I'm sure it was a stressful, bizarre situation—talking to literal gods. I would think that the human brain would conjure all sorts of things that weren't there. Would hear things that may not have been said."

"They said it," Sammi protested weakly.

Kassidy waved a hand in the air, her many bracelets clinking loudly. "Well, nevertheless, the last place you sweet girls would want to be at would be a stuffy Imperial ceremony filled with old nobles. Personally, I would love nothing more than to skip it myself. Maybe I'll travel to Crimmish with you!" The Imperatrix's joke fell flat. "Anyway, I hope you see that it's best that you leave this evening. With our most sincere gratitude. And all the chips you can carry. And a promise to heal that town of yours of its terrible affliction."

"But the God-Snails *did* say—"

"It's okay, Samm," interrupted Ash, who sounded infinitely older than her years. "I knew they wouldn't want us here."

"It's not a matter of *want*, dear girl."

"Yes, it is. But that's okay. We're used to it."

Kassidy's fake smile broadened. "Wonderful! Then, it's settled!" She snapped a ringed finger. "Lieutenant Kruger! A word!"

Benson Kruger, who had been standing silently along the throne room wall, a self-satisfied smiled pasted on his weasel face, hurried toward Imperatrix Rayne.

"Yes, my Lady."

"Lieutenant Kruger, you did well to shepherd these girls from Terminus Grove to Kassimont. I'm sure you three have developed quite the rapport."

"We have grown quite fond of each other, my Lady."

Had their stomachs not been empty, Ash and Sammi would have emptied their contents onto the throne room floor.

Kassidy went on. "Fantastic! Then I'd like you to be the one in charge of seeing that these girls are outfitted for their trip home—all the food, drink, and chips they can carry." Blue eyes met beady black and unspoken words were exchanged. "I want you to see that they are *properly* rewarded. Do this for me, Lieutenant, and I will see you handsomely compensated for your service."

A wolfish grin appeared on Kruger's narrow face. He bowed deeply.

"It would be my great honor, my Imperatrix." The loathsome officer rose and swept his arm out toward the throne room entrance. "It has been a long road, children. You must be antsy to see your family. This way, please, and we'll get you to them in due course."

Ash and Sammi, drained of their strength and will to argue, simply nodded, turned, and began shuffling away.

Kruger started to follow.

"Lieutenant." The officer raised an eyebrow. "There was no command."

"Of course not, my Lady. There never is."

~

"This way," stated Kruger flatly, the faux warmness gone from his voice.

The girls looked worriedly at the small door but pushed though without argument.

After a small landing, concrete steps spiraled down the castle with only a few torches to light the way.

"What is this?" asked Ash nervously.

"It's a service flight, used by attendants and maids," replied Kruger coldly. "It will get us there quicker. And more discreetly. We don't want a bunch of wealthy regents making callous comments toward you girls as we exit the Keep, now do we?"

"I guess not."

"Good. Now keep moving."

The mismatched trio passed several more landings and numerous doors before the tight stairwell finally corkscrewed to an end, opening onto a massive chamber under the castle that housed a stockpile of armaments and barrels of grain. Given the time of night, no others occupied the massive space.

"This is the undercroft," explained Kruger as he carefully looked around. "Or storage room for those living under a rock."

Ash and Sammi walked on for a bit, eventually coming upon a large waterway running across the storage basement, neatly cutting the undercroft in half. A small bridge that looked like it could be lifted, when needed, appeared to their right. The girls angled toward it.

The sound of a sword being freed from its sheath stopped both younglings in their tracks. Their small shoulders slumped.

"That's quite far enough," declared Kruger, the man's words like ice. "I've been waiting for this moment for a long, long time. It's only too bad that I couldn't personally give each of you filthy Cheese-Eyes your much-deserved rewards. Now, on your knees in front of the water." The girls didn't move. "Do it!"

The wild rage in Kruger's voice sent both girls to their knees. Sammi began to weep quietly. Ash was too dehydrated to cry. And too used to the schemes of adults.

"Why?" was all that Ash asked, although the too-mature girl already knew the answer.

"Why? Because we can. And because your value has run its course. And because trash needs to be disposed of. And because your little shite friend called me a Queefin' Kelly!"

Both girls, facing imminent death, giggled at the memory.

"Bow your filthy heads! I'll try to make it quick. But no promises."

"All this for nothing," bemoaned Sammi.

Ash held her sister tight and whispered to her. "Not for nothing, sis. We've saved Quaan from the Gloomtide. We've earned our ticket to the Wellspring."

"You think we'll see Ditto and Hana there?"

"I don't think. I know. And maybe Finch, too."

"Then it was worth it?"

"It was."

"Ma and Da will be sad."

"They're used to that. Everyone in Crimmish is."

"No more words," shouted Kruger from behind. "You've said your goodbyes, yes? Now, let me offer mine."

Two pairs of clear, brown eyes stared down at the swirling liquid of the waterway, smiling as it reminded them of the rivulets that crossed the Salt compound, where they splashed and played with their dear friend Hana.

Two pairs of clear, brown eyes closed as the *swoosh* of a descending blade could be heard, followed by the wet *thwack* of metal carving through meat and bone, and punctuated by a dull *thud*.

When the world didn't collapse into oblivion around them, when the cosmos didn't jump forward to welcome them, and when the echoey sounds of the undercroft failed to go silent, Ash and Sammi opened their eyes to find crimson ropes fleeing down the waterway. The girls looked down in tandem to find the head of Benson Kruger rolling to a stop between their knees, a stupid, shocked look permanently etched onto the hateful officer's face.

"Please get up, girls. It's time to go," came a familiar voice from behind Ash and Sammi. They turned to find Tobias Vale there, wiping his bloody longsword off on the body of the recently deceased Kruger.

Second Lieutenant Vale returned his blade to his hip and held out a hand, his yellow eyes shining in the torchlight. He helped up Sammi and then Ash, accepting a massive hug from the sisters when both were upright.

"Thank you," said Ash into the man's uniform.

"No," responded Vale, patting each girl on the back as he did. "It is *I* who should be thanking you. It is *all of us* who owe you a debt of gratitude. Now, let's get out of here. There is an exit on the far side, across the waterway."

When the girls separated, their gazes naturally fell to the body at their feet.

"And what about him?" asked Ash.

"Fark him," replied Vale, and he kicked at the corpse with all his might, sending the body rolling into the waterway, where it drifted away for a moment before sinking, Kruger's gauntleted hands, chain-mail, and many medals forcing him below the water's surface.

The sisters eyed the head of Kruger before looking back to Vale.

"I said, *fark him,*" he stated with a grim smile.

Ash and Sammi snickered as they both kicked at the head, sending it flying to drop into the swirling waterway. The girls spun back to face Tobias Vale.

"I like the way you talk," said Sammi. "It reminds me of my friend, Finch."

"I remember the lad. I liked him. I know Captain Graff liked him. I'm sorry he is no longer with us."

"He's in a better place now," said Ash warmly.

Vale nodded, not understanding the full meaning of the one-armed girl's words. "I'm happy you think that. Now, let's get you two out of this cursed keep. To a better place."

21

OVERDUE REUNIONS—AND THE JOY AND SORROW THEY BRING

illy Graff rolled out of bed with a grunt and stood on legs that had felt increasingly weak since the news of her beloved husband's passing. She grabbed a dagger off the dining room table as she made her way to the front door—a front door that had been disturbed by heavy knuckles.

Have they finally come for me, then? thought the aged woman. *What secret do they think I possess that I need to be silenced forever?* And finally, she conceded, *So be it.*

Hilly ripped open the front door, dagger at the ready, but was immediately taken aback by the two dark-skinned girls who appeared before her. Behind the young girls, a soldier stood, his yellow eyes darting back and forth.

"Apologies, Widow Graff," said the youthful officer, "both for the intrusion and the awful time of night. You may not remember me, but my name is—"

"Tobias Vale," cut in Hilly. "You were the young man that was with my Gorman when he fell. And you were the young man who stepped up to inform me when others—others that owed my husband much more—were too cowardly to do so. And, as I recall, you did so with an empathy and warmness I was very thankful for. Now, then, tell me why you are here and who these two beautiful girls are."

~

Second Lieutenant Tobias Vale and Hilly Graff sat at the dining room table drinking tea as Ash and Sammi Bugg snored softly in the widow's soft bed.

"As you can see," said Vale through sips of delicious tea, "they were in no condition to travel. They have survived unspeakable trials and the loss of three close friends. The soldiers who accompanied them from Terminus Grove claimed that they have not slept nor drank nor ate since they picked them up."

"You mean, since they captured them?"

"Yes. That is what I mean."

"How is that possible?"

"They had the Gift of the God-Snails with them."

"Which was promptly taken from them, no doubt."

"It was."

"And their prize for traversing all of Quaan, entering Terminus Grove, and meeting the Divine Pentad on behalf of all humanity?"

"Assassination, Widow Graff."

The old woman pushed her tea away, as if everything in Kassimont had been tainted.

"Kasspar is too shortsighted, too weak for such an order. This reeks of the Imperatrix and her lapdog Chancellor."

"My thoughts exactly."

"Well? What are we to do, Tobias? What is your plan?"

The young officer took a long while before he was able to answer. "Honestly, I don't have much of one. I just saw that rat Benson Kruger lead the girls down a service flight and knew that nothing good would come of that trip. I wanted to simply set them on the road to Crimmish and be done with it, but as I reflect on what has transpired—"

"You want nothing more to do with this rotten empire. With this unjust tyranny."

"Yes. Even were I to stay, to remain perfectly loyal, I fear that I would be sent down to the Black Bog to keep their secret safe. To bury the key role that the Stenches played in saving this world."

The Widow Graff slammed her hand down onto the table and then immediately winced, fearing that she had awoken the kids from Crimmish. Neither sister stirred.

"Then it is settled." The old woman looked around her comfortable, relatively lavish country home, tears welling in her soft eyes. "This place, this farm, no longer has meaning for me. It hasn't since Gorman passed. It was built not with chips but with blood. I will stay here no longer. I hate to wake them, but, at first light, I will rouse the girls and we will leave this capital of greed and cold ambition behind. I will accompany the children back to Crimmish and then head north. I have one last thing to do before I pass from this world, and that is to see where my Gorman fell." The widow's voice began to break. "And to say goodbye properly." The proud woman quickly wiped the wetness from her cheeks. "Of course, we wouldn't turn down the company of a strong man who knows how to handle a weapon."

Tobias Vale chuckled into his tea. "What a relief. And here I thought that I was to be sent away. After all, it seems I would only slow down three powerful women."

Widow Graff shared in a much-needed laugh. "Oh, Tobias, haven't you learned? Flattery will only get you everywhere here in Quaan. Now, can I top off that tea?"

Vale looked down at his empty cup. "Actually, do you have something a bit stronger? I don't think that sleep is in the cards for me, having abandoned my empire and all."

Hilly Graff feigned surprise. "Well, well, Tobias Vale. I think I know now why Gorman took a shine to you. Not only will I get you the finest honey rice wine I own... but I'll join you."

❧

"Are you sure you will not postpone, my husband? Just another three days? By then, almost all of your most ardent supporters—and, more importantly, most troublesome detractors—will be able to reach Kassimont. In time to honor *you*."

Imperator Kasspar Rayne looked down at the Pentad Gift from his perch atop the Imperial Dais. It sat in the center of the Grand Hall, on a crystalline support, placed there carefully by Kasspar himself.

Without taking his eyes from the swirling box, the Imperator swept his arm across, encompassing the thousands in attendance to witness their world be saved.

"It is too late, my love. Look at all who have come to watch me reclaim the land. I could not postpone at this late stage."

Kassidy leaned in, whispering angrily. "You are the *Imperator*! You *can* postpone! You can do anything you want!"

Kasspar still refused to look at his beautiful wife. "Fine. I can postpone, but I do not wish to. I wish to open my Gift. I wish to end the suffering of my empire. And I wish to write my name in the history books—as one of the heroes of Quaan."

Kassidy looked over to Chancellor Sologar Crimm for support, but the extravagantly decorated man could only shrug helplessly from the far side of the platform.

The Imperatrix returned to her husband. "Please, Kasspar, I know you think this right but—"

Imperator Rayne simply held up a soft hand between himself and his wife. "It is time," he said simply before descending the Imperial Dais. As he did, the crowd exploded—hooting and hollering and screaming rising out above the general applause.

Kasspar Rayne basked in the attention and adulation as he marched forward, head held high. His name would ring out across the ages—the Imperator who faced down humanity's greatest foe and struck it down with a gift from the Gods.

Imperator Rayne reached the crystalline support, his eyes glued to the box within which swam the spinning of a thousand storms. Although he dared not look away, Kasspar could feel the faces of the

Titian elite upon him, eager to see their champion ascend to greatness.

The Imperator reached for the Pentad Gift, and a hush fell over the enthralled crowd of thousands. The air thickened around the Grand Hall, and Kasspar Rayne felt his breath quicken, as if the tension had removed oxygen from the cavernous room.

"Claim your prize, my Imperator, my hero, my husband," cried out Kassidy Rayne in the silence, seizing the perfect opportunity to become part of history. "And save our world. Long live the Imperator!" The crowd echoed their Imperatrix. "Long live Kasspar Rayne!"

"Long live Kasspar Rayne!"

"Love live the Titian Empire," called out the Imperator as his lacquered nails touched the warm box. "And long live my rule," he whispered to himself as he gently lifted the top of the box.

An impossibly bright light, like a star fallen from the night sky, shot forth from the open container, filling the giant chamber. It lit up the Imperator's face for all to see, highlighting a wonderstruck look that had consumed the man's face. Despite the light hurting their eyes, the crowd leaned forward.

As they did, Kassidy Rayne turned to the Chancellor, who had slithered behind the woman as her husband left the dais. She spoke under her breath to her confidante.

"The world is ours now, Sologar. We can do with it what we wish. We can right many wrongs."

"And punish many enemies."

Kassidy offered a menacing smile. "And some friends." Crimm grinned wickedly.

Back in the center of the Grand Hall, Kasspar Rayne soaked in the warm light, feeling the power it provided. And the promise of so much more. His mind raced with possibility. His thoughts ran wild. He would be a king of kings. A god among men. None would dare oppose him. All would fall to their knees in worship.

"At last, I have gotten what I deserve. What the Titian Empire deserves."

∿

The Five Sisters had been in the sky for a couple of hours, but the quartet of Ash Bugg, Sammi Bugg, Tobias Vale, and Hilly Graff pushed on through the night. Although they had been on the road for four days, the group still felt the shadow of Kassimont in the near distance and wanted to put more steps between them and that accursed city.

They maintained a strong but steady pace, respecting the mounts that Hilly had given them from her and Gorman's private stable. With no one missing them, they were able to travel along the Kassimedes Thoroughfare without attracting much attention.

The quartet did, however, find themselves often pulling their mounts quickly off the Thoroughfare as Titian elites in horse-drawn carriages accompanied by regiments of guards and soldiers tore north along the busy road, no doubt racing to reach the capital before the Imperial Reveal. These dignitaries, nobles, lords, and ladies cared not for who else was on the Thoroughfare, and several unlucky merchants and travelers found themselves trampled under hoof and wheel. No one even stopped to help the fallen.

On a few occasions, men and women from a settlement bordering the Mutewoods, driven wild by the Gloomtide, would tear out of the shadows and attack. Fortunately, they were easily dispatched by Vale's longsword, Hilly's dagger, or Alicia Salt's longbow, with Sammi becoming surprisingly proficient with the masterfully crafted weapon.

The group, who had grown quite close in their few days of travel, now walked in silence, enjoying the solitude with no others in sight. Hilly looked up from her horse as they rode along at a canter, admiring the stars above and hoping that her Gorman was up there among the celestials. No, she didn't hope. She knew.

"Toby, I think that's enough for the day," said the old woman, not wanting to put undue stress on her beloved horses, or the young sisters who had already survived ten lifetimes of pain.

Vale looked around. "I think you're right, ma'am. There's a break in the trees to the west where we can make camp."

"Great, then let us get off this cobble. I'm sure the horses would like the feel of grass under their hooves. In fact, why don't we—"

"What's that?!"

Everyone turned in their saddles to face Sammi, the girl's brown eyes wide.

"What, sis?"

"That! That! That! Look!"

They spun as one to the north, where a thick ray of light had reached down from Ommori Prime and touched down on Quaan in the distance.

"By the Five Sisters, that's Kassimont! I'm sure of it," said a slack-jawed Vale.

"They must have opened the Pentad Gift," concluded Ash.

"Without us," added Sammi.

The one-armed girl rubbed her stump, which had started to tingle. "I just hope they use it for good," said Ash. "Use it to cure the sick. Use it to heal the injured. Use it to—"

Ash's words were chopped off as Ommori Prime's beam of energy abruptly ceased to exist. The quartet held their collective breath.

A moment later, an explosion of prismatic light filled the air over the capital, temporarily transforming night into day as Kassimont was vaporized in an instant.

A circular shockwave of warmth and color and energy and life rippled out from where the capital city once stood, running in all directions, cascading over Quaan like a tidal wave from the Great Untold.

Ash, Sammi, Hilly, and Tobias sat dumbly on their mounts staring openmouthed through too-wide eyes, unable to move as the shock-wave raced toward them. They all bowed their heads as it hit, thinking that their times had also come to an end.

Instead, the four unusual friends were swallowed by an over-whelming sense of love, a warmth and understanding that could only be felt in the arms of a sister or husband or parent or friend.

It took several minutes after the shockwave had passed for heads to raise once more. All seemed as it was before. And yet, everything felt different.

~

There was little conversation to be had that evening or on the road the next day. The riders rode in silence, contented smiles pasted on each of their faces. They didn't know why, but things felt *right*. For perhaps the first time ever.

Later in the day, the quartet came across another woodland settlement. A man from the town sat just off the Kassimedes Thoroughfare, softly weeping, his head buried in his hands.

"Whoa, whoa," said Hilly Graff to her mount, bringing the horse to a stop. The old woman climbed down from her saddle and went to the man, placing a weathered hand onto his shoulder.

"Are you all right, lad? What's wrong?"

When the young man looked up, it was not the face of loss or sadness that met the group of friends, but, rather, a look of pure relief.

The man sniffled and wiped his cheeks before standing. "I'm sorry, I didn't even hear your approach. I only came out here so that my children would not see their father cry."

"But what's wrong?" Hilly repeated.

The young man shook his head emphatically. "Nothing's wrong. Nothing's ever been so right." He took a second to compose himself. "My wife… she fell sick with the Gloomtide several Paragons ago. I caught her trying to hang our youngest—just an infant—from the rafters by her tiny neck… oh, what a sight to behold!" Hilly rubbed the man's back while he recovered. "I had to lock her away in the basement lest she try to harm another of our daughters. She scratched at the door like a wild beast, ripping all the nails from her fingers. She would slam her head into the wall until she fell unconscious, only to wake and do it again." Ash and Sammi exchanged knowing looks. "Today… today I was going to go down in the basement and do the unthinkable… I was going to end her suffering… and my own." The young man's face brightened. "But when I went down there, cudgel in hand, you know what I found?"

"Tell me," begged Hilly, tears welling in her eyes.

"I found Susann. *My* Susann. Not a crazed monster sick with the Gloomtide but *my* Susann. She was confused and sad. She was injured and scared. But she was *Susann*. The Gloomtide has gone from her, and my life has been returned to me."

"What about others in the settlement?" inquired Tobias Vale from above.

"Same," answered the man. "All those who were sick are better this morning. I should be dubious. I should worry that this is just a small reprieve. But I'm not. For some reason, I feel confident that the Gloomtide is gone from our home. And I feel wonderful about the future. About what will be waiting for my girls."

Hilly Graff offered the young man a hug and some kind words before sending him back to his family, who no doubt still had much more healing to do.

The old woman pulled herself onto her saddle with a grunt and turned her mount back south. "Come," she said to the group. "Let us see what other magic is at work."

"You don't have to take us in," said Ash as the group left Salvation Outpost in the distance. "I don't want you two to get sick. Some say just an hour in Crimmish is enough to make them ill for weeks."

Hilly Graff waved away the girl's suggestion. "Nonsense. We've come this far, and I will see you returned to your home—not *close* to your home. And for selfish reasons, I will witness the look on your parents' faces when they see their daughters. It will be a scene that will bring this old woman much joy."

"And you forget," said Tobias Vale, "I have already been to Crimmish. I picked you up alongside Captain Graff. I felt no residual sickness after I left." A pause. "And I, too, will see your family reunited. I have enough memories of violence and death.

Time to start replacing them with something better. Something wholly good."

Ash nodded in silent thanks and spurred her horse along toward Crimmish, Sammi, Hilly, and Tobias in tow.

Hours later, with Paragon high in the sky, the Bugg Sisters returned to Crimmish, once referred to as the Stenches. The buildings still looked humble and mismatched, made from whatever materials could be found, traded for, or recycled. Mud still covered the ground and coated the walls. A cold chill whipped through the town as air was funneled between the Spired Curtains and the Fringe.

Crimmish was exactly the same and, yet, it looked entirely different. But it was not the town that had been altered, it was Ash and Sammi Bugg who had changed. It was the young sisters who were now viewing the world through new eyes.

As usual, it was Simple Edd who took note of the visitors, for the slow-witted man had dedicated his life to doing just that. Typically, Simple Edd would run off to fetch Mayor Dann Bugg at the first sight of newcomers. But a pair of dark faces held the sweet man back for a moment, making him curious. And a missing left arm made that same kind-hearted man sure.

"Ash," Simple Edd called out, tentative at first, but gaining confidence as the quartet drew closer. "Ash! Ash Bugg! And Sammi! Sammi Bugg!" The watchman began dancing a jig in the street as the riders approached. "It is! It is! By the Five Sisters, it is!"

"How are you, Edd?" yelled Sammi through fits of laughter as the man continued his jubilant dance. "You look in good health, at least from your moves!"

"Good, good, good, good," exclaimed Simple Edd through heavy pants as he ceased his celebration. "And better soon! I go get the Mayor! I go get your parents! I go get everyone!"

"Okay, but Edd—" shouted Ash, but it was too late. Edd had already rushed off, screaming at the top of his lungs as he did.

Ash smiled warmly at her sister, and all four riders dismounted and began walking their mounts into the town.

It should have come as no surprise that Jazz Bugg rounded the town square before anyone else, for the woman had been the fastest in Crimmish in her day. Despite being past her prime, Ash and Sammi had never seen their ma run so fast, the woman closing the distance at a full sprint.

There were no words. There was no greeting. There was simply a mother sliding to a stop to embrace her daughters with all her might, three sets of shoulders growing immediately wet with tears.

"I thought I'd lost you. I thought I'd lost you. I thought I'd lost you." Jazz Bugg repeated the phrase over and over, refusing to release those closest to her heart.

"Ash! Sammi! Oh, thank the Five Sisters," wailed Taff Bugg as the man entered the square, a group of residents on his heels. In short order, Taff slammed into the group, finally reuniting his family, swallowing everyone in a massive hug.

After a lifetime of love had filled a few minutes, parents separated from children.

"Let me look at you," said Jazz, holding both girls at arm's length to examine her daughters. Finally, she said, "You look different. You both look different. Still my darling children, but… different." Jazz's head cocked to the side. "Sammi! Where are your glasses?"

The girl could only offer a shrug. "I don't need them anymore, Ma."

"Why not?"

Ash cut in. "There's plenty of time for stories, Ma. And that's a long one." Now, it was Ash's turn to cock her head to side. "Ma?"

"Yes, my love?"

"Your eyes…"

Jazz Bugg's hands reflexively went to her face. "Oh, this? Yes, we got hit by… something a few nights back."

"A surge," clarified Taff. "Some kind of energy surge."

Jazz continued. "Yes, well, the next Paragon, the yellow was gone from my eyes."

"And mine," said Taff. "And everyone's." The father's now-clear eyes narrowed. "Say, it looks like your eyes… both your and your sister's eyes cleared up, as well. Did you get hit with the surge, too?"

"We all did," answered Hilly Graff from the rear, the old woman wiping her cheeks with a handkerchief. "The whole world did."

"Ma. Da. This is Hilly Graff, widow of High Captain Gorman Graff."

"Widow?" asked Taff, confused, but Jazz shushed her husband and motioned for Sammi to continue.

"And this is Tobias Vale of the Titian Empire."

"*Formerly* of the Titian Empire," corrected Vale. "I'm done giving my allegiance to those who don't deserve it."

Sammi continued. "We wouldn't have made it back without their help."

Jazz Bugg gave each an appreciative nod. "Then they will be guests of honor. We don't have much here, but you are welcome to anything we have. Anything at all."

The collection of townsfolk had continued to grow, although they kept a respectable distance away from the rejoined family.

Jazz Bugg returned her attention to her daughters, pulling them in close. "And you know what else? Do you know what's even more wonderful? Gill Bugg. He seems to be better from the Maddening. Six Paragons ago, the poor man was ramming his head into walls. But since the surge..."

Taff Bugg took up where his wife had finished. "And not just Gill. Anyone sick with the Maddening is now back to normal. Let us just pray to the Five Sisters that it stays that way."

"Oh, but it will, Taff," reprimanded his wife. "Negative thoughts breed negative results. But, oh, how I can't wait to see the look on Fincher's face when the boy sees his father all better." Jazz looked behind the quartet into the distance. "Where is Fincher? And Ditto? And Hana? Are they far behind? Don't tell me they're nobles now and have decided against returning to our little hovel!"

Instead of laughter as Jazz Bugg had hoped, she was met with dejected looks from her daughters during what should have been this most joyous of occasions.

Jazz's now-clear eyes filled with new tears, as did her husband's. Both winced as familiar voices sliced through the reunion like a cutlass, neatly cutting free what happiness the pair could feel from the return of their own children.

"Hana? Hana?! Where's our Hana?" cried out Joon Bugg, with Kenn Bugg holding her upright for support. "Is she back *there*? Is she on her way?"

Ash thought of a million things to say. The girl mentally reached out into the ether, trying to grasp the perfect words to soothe the frantic parents. She came back with nothing.

Instead, Ash simply shook her head, the girl's fallen face telling the story that her lips could not.

"Nooooooo," howled Joon Bugg, collapsing into Kenn's arms, and the heads of all fell toward the muddy ground.

Before Ash could begin to offer condolences, before she could even begin to vocalize how brave and true their daughter had been, Kenn and Joon Bugg dragged each other back to their permanently empty home, where they could begin the impossibly long grieving process in privacy.

A heavy silence fell over Crimmish then as the cost of things started to fall into view. This worsened as the group of residents suddenly split in half, allowing Gill Bugg to pass between, hat in hand.

The tired-looking man, his head heavily bandaged and fresh scars covering his body, shuffled forward as if on his way to the Imperial headsman.

When he finally reached Ash and Sammi, Gill looked up with sad, clear eyes. Although the man knew the answer, he also knew that the question had to be asked. Some things simply had to be done, no matter how much they hurt.

"Where's Fincher? Where's my boy?"

Although Crimmish and its inhabitants had been given a new, better future to look forward to, although they had been granted new life, everyone in the town died a bit when they heard those words.

22

JUST REWARDS

"Still nothing?" asked Ash.

"I'm telling you, sis, we're heading into the end of the Heating and nothing. Zilch. Nada. This is usually when the Reaper Vines are most active. And they simply are not there."

Ash took a moment to consider her little sister's words. "Alright, then. I think enough time has passed to make it scientifically significant."

Sammi's face soured. "With all due respect, *sis*, I think I'm more qualified to make a scientific conclusion."

Ash rolled her clear, brown eyes. "Fine. And your conclusion, my impossibly brilliant and wise, *little* sister?"

Sammi pretended to think it over. "I think the Reaper Vines are gone. And maybe gone for good."

"Excellent. You should write that up in one of those pretend papers of yours. You'll—"

"They're not pretend papers," Sammi shot back. "One day, they'll be foundational to our technological advancement! One day—"

"Riders! Riders! Riders!" Simple Edd came rushing through the town, crying out to anyone who would listen.

"Edd," Ash screamed, bringing the man to a sudden stop, forcing him to slide and almost fall to the muddy ground. Simple Edd looked over but said nothing more. Ash sighed and asked, "Who are they? What do they want?"

"Don't know! Don't know! But looks like soldiers! Definitely soldiers! Must find the Mayor! Must tell the Mayor!" With that, Simple Edd took off once more, leaving Ash and Sammi with more questions than answers.

"I guess we had better take a look," said Ash. "Come on, sis!"

Both girls sped off at a sprint that would have made Jazz Bugg proud.

A sea of blue greeted the Bugg Sisters when they arrived at the town entrance.

"Well met," came a familiar call from the crowd of horses, soldiers, armor, and gleaming weapons.

Several warhorses stepped to the side, allowing a lone rider to pass between. He removed his blue-plumed helmet to reveal the kind face of Byronn Paxxis, Commander of the Cobalt Army. The handsome man's smile threatened to touch both ears.

"Commander Paxxis!" exclaimed Ash, relieved to find a friendly face at the head of so much firepower. "What brings you to our muddy corner of the world?"

"Yes! Yes, indeed," shouted Mayor Dann Bugg as he hurried to the front of the growing crowd of onlookers. "Welcoming visitors is *my* job," he reminded Ash as he pulled even with the girl.

Paxxis ignored the bumbling mayor, keeping his turquoise eyes locked onto Ash and Sammi. "You never told me!"

"Told you what?" called back Ash, playing coy.

"Ha, ha!" The Cobalt commander dismounted and approached the Bugg Sisters as the other women of Crimmish swooned. "You never told me that your mission was to save the world."

"We did," argued Sammi. "In our own way."

"Had I the full information, perhaps I could have helped more."

"I think we did pretty well, regardless."

Paxxis roared in laughter. When he had recovered, he said, "You certainly did! In fact, I don't think you have any idea of how well you have done!"

"What do you mean, General?"

"I'll show you. Pack up your belongings. Only what can't be replaced. You don't need to rush, but please don't dawdle, either. We'll make camp between here and that shite hole Salvation Outpost, which I may burn down on my way out."

The sisters looked to each other with apprehension.

"But Commander," said Ash carefully. "We've only been back a few months. Many here are still grieving for loved ones lost. We can't leave them again. Not soon, anyway."

The handsome officer's bluish eyes flashed. "Leave? Who said anything about leave?" Paxxis called out to the entire town of Crimmish. "You are *all* coming with us!"

"Have we done something wrong?" came a concerned voice from the back.

"Quite the contrary," exclaimed Paxxis. "You are all being rewarded. And handsomely!"

"For what?" came another cry.

The young commander thought for a moment. "For the deeds of your children!"

"But we cannot leave!"

"Yeah, Crimmish is our prison! The Titian Empire has banished us here!"

"They'll never let us go!"

Byronn Paxxis held up his gauntleted hand, quieting the worried crowd. "You're right, good people! The Titian Empire would *never* let you go!" He waited for dramatic effect. "But the Titian Empire is no more!" He took in the audible gasp. "The Titian Empire is no more! Owed in great part to the efforts of Ashanti Bugg, Sammira Bugg,

Deetarik Bugg, Hanako Bugg, and Finchius Bugg!" Paxxis lowered his voice and spoke directly to Ash and Sammi. "Of course, I've had to piece much of that together over the past few months, through bribery, threats, and, in some cases, torture. Only the Moon Folk spoke freely of their *Child Champions of Crown Lake*."

"You met with the Ommori?" asked Sammi excitedly.

"Of course. We had to make friends with our new trading partners." Paxxis threw in a wink for good measure.

Mayor Bugg stepped forward. "I still don't understand. You want us to abandon our homes? Abandon the lives we know?"

The commander put a reassuring hand on the Mayor's shoulder. "Think of it not as leaving something behind. Think of it as rushing toward something new. And better. And more deserving of your people's hearts and minds... and their contributions to this world that we call Quaan."

Mayor Dann Bugg smiled dumbly, finding himself lost in Byron Paxxis's hypnotic eyes.

"Well, when you put it that way..."

The people of Crimmish, a town formerly referred to as the Stenches, traveled northeast at a slow, constant pace, all their meager worldly belongings strapped to the surrounding horses, mules, carts, and carriages. The collection of townsfolk and Cobalt soldiers eventually met up with the Kassimedes Thoroughfare and followed it, tracing the same line that Ash, Sammi, Hilly, and Tobias took during their exodus.

The trip was long but uneventful. This was unsurprising, for who in their right minds would dare threaten such a large contingent of Cobalt warriors?

Any time Ash or Sammy asked Commander Paxxis where they were going, or how much longer the journey would be, the man offered one simple (and increasingly annoying) response.

"Let us not ruin the surprise."

On the twentieth Paragon since the group had set out from Crimmish, the convoy summited a small hill that overlooked South Verve.

Ash and Sammi were brought to the head of the line, and the sisters' breaths caught in their throats as they looked past the singing waters of the massive river.

There, where the Titian capital city of Kassimont once stood, were thousands of acres of resource-rich, even ground dotted with colorful meadows, masses of fruit tree groves, and lush green forests.

"What is this?" asked Ash breathlessly.

Commander Paxxis leaned forward in his saddle and breathed in deeply. "This is where the old and vile was made new and vibrant. This is where the God-Snails hit the reset button on Quaan. They could have simply let us rot away from the Gloomtide, but they did not." Paxxis looked over at Ash and Sammi. "Because of you. And your brave friends. This is now where we will begin anew." Paxxis pointed to the northwest. "Merriworth will always be the heart of the Cobalt Republic." He returned to the scene below. "But we will need a capital in the east to service all our new citizens. This will be that place. This will be Coballis."

Sammi's finger went to her nose to push up glasses that weren't there, a habit she found difficult to break. "What are those buildings going up over there?"

Ash narrowed her eyes and found that her sister was correct. Around a massive area that had been sectioned off with large, painted posts driven into the fertile ground, teams of men and women scrambled back and forth, hammering nails into timber and raising walls with complex pulleys.

Byronn Paxxis presented one of his patented warm smiles. "Those are your homes, Mistress Sammi. And yours, Mistress Ash. They are homes for all of you. And not just homes, but homes befitting your new stations. You are lords and ladies. And this is your land."

Ash and Sammi Bugg looked down at the richest land they had

ever seen. They watched in awe as the bones of great houses, with deeds that bore their names, went up in rapid succession.

"But why?" is all Ash Bugg could ask, her mind terrified to believe what her eyes were relaying.

Commander Byronn Paxxis shifted in his saddle, considering his words carefully. "Because you have earned it. You all have. Your fore-bears were banished to Crimmish for resisting the tyranny of the Titian Empire. Your people then sacrificed their sanity, and then, ulti-mately, their lives to cure the world of the Bloat. And most recently, your people sacrificed something unimaginable to find a cure for the Gloomtide, a plague that had yet to touch your own town. Crimmish sacrificed its greatest children." Ash and Sammi then wept openly. Paxxis rode over and put a supportive arm around the girls. "Yes, cry. But do not cry for what you have lost, but for what you—and Fincher, and Ditto, and Hana—have earned. Not only for *your* people, but for *all* the people of Quaan. This is your reward. It is great, but I fear that it will never cover the costs that it required."

Ash and Sammi Bugg dismounted from their horses and walked forward along the grassy hill, leaving their ma and da and Paxxis and Cobalt soldiers behind.

Sammi put her freshly braided head against her older sister's shoulder, and Ash put the stub of an arm around her sibling's neck.

"It's beautiful," said Sammi, and there were no lies in the girl's words.

"It is, sis. It is all that I imagined and so much more."

"But…"

"But it will never be home, will it? It will never be home because we can't share it with Fincher and Ditto and Hana."

"So, what do we do?"

Ash pulled her sister in tight. "We move on and create a new life. And we love those still with us even harder. And we take solace in the fact that Fincher and Ditto and Hana are looking down on us from the Wellspring. And they're smiling, knowing that we finished what we all started. Knowing that we never gave up. And knowing that we've built lives that they can be proud of. Lives that were worth their sacrifices."

Sammi looked up at her big sister. "You really believe that, sis? You really believe that they're in the Wellspring, looking down on us?"

Ash looked down and smiled. "Fark, yeah. I do."

Sammi hugged her sister tighter.

"Good. Because so do I."

EPILOGUE

Samm Buggsly, formerly known as Sammi Bugg, pored over the stack of engineering schematics that covered her ornate work-table. As she examined the designs, her finger rose to push up glasses that were not there, a habit that the woman had been unable to break, even after twenty years.

A gentle breeze crept in from the open window of her office, ushering in the salty sweetness of the Great Untold. As her manor had been built onto a bluff, one look out of that same window showed Paragon slowly rising above the beautiful, endless ocean that marked the eastern edge of the Cobalt Republic.

A woman, approximately the same age, entered the office carrying a tray of tea. She placed the serving plate at the far end of the desk, on one of the few spots not littered with papers, and walked behind Samm, who barely acknowledged her presence. She rubbed Samm's shoulders and placed a soft kiss on top of her braided head. Samm turned her head and smiled.

"Ahh," said the woman. "So, that's what it takes to get your attention."

"Sorry, love," replied Samm with a heavy sigh.

"Isn't it a little early to be calculating torque and leverage and all that other stuff that I don't understand? You haven't even had your morning tea." The woman leaned forward to get a close look at the documents on the table. "What is this stuff, anyway?"

Samm exhaled loudly once more. "Plans for a series of automated angel wheat harvesters." She paused for a moment, as she always did after speaking that word aloud. "If we can build them and get them to run properly, it should increase production by up to fifty percent."

"Well, that certainly sounds like a worthwhile endeavor."

"It is."

"But, in case you've forgotten, you are the Ministress of Science—for the entire Republic. Surely, there are other brilliant minds, those that call you *boss*, that could look at these and double-check their accuracy."

Samm grabbed a cup of tea and placed it to her mouth. She sipped the hot liquid, closing her eyes as she did. It was made just the way she liked it.

After opening her eyes, Samm turned to the woman, placing a brown hand over the tan one on her shoulder, and offered a nod of thanks before responding.

"Of course, I could. But it needs to be done fast. If we can get the design nailed down quickly, we can go into production and, hopefully, have working prototypes ready for next year's Cooling. Plus, it needs to be done right. Just one mistake could throw everything off and render the machines useless. And, lastly—"

"She doesn't want anyone stealing her fun," came a youthful voice from the doorway, a voice that Samm Buggsly had only heard in dreams and memories for the last two decades. It was a voice that the woman would have gladly given over her title, lands, and home to hear again in person.

Samm Buggsly looked up and the teacup fell to her table, cracking in half and spilling its hot contents across the schematics.

"Oh, my! How did that happen?" exclaimed the tan-skinned woman, rushing to run a towel across the mess.

Samm did not move.

Instead, the Cobalt Minister of Science stared open-mouthed at the boy standing at the entrance to her office. But it wasn't just any hazel-eyed boy.

It was Fincher Bugg.

"Impossible," was all Samm could say as the woman cleaned around her. After several beats, she muttered, "Can it really be you?"

The woman cleaning finally realized something odd was going on. "Be who? Do you know this boy?" As Ministress, Samm Bugsly maintained an open-door policy during Paragon, meaning it was not unusual for her to receive uninvited guests.

"Yes. I grew up with him," Samm replied under her breath, such that the woman could barely hear.

"What was that?"

Fincher, sensing the mounting confusion, stepped into the room, the boy's hazel eyes sparkling. "Fincher. At your service, Miss…"

"Larissa. Larissa Buggsly," answered Samm for the woman. "Larissa is my wife."

Fincher delivered a wink and a smile to Samm before returning to Larissa. "It is an absolute pleasure to meet you, Miss Larissa. And might I say that you look lovely."

Larissa laughed lightly and touched her hair, which had been pulled into a loose bun. "Oh, well, if I'd known we had a young gentleman coming over, I would have made myself up a bit more."

"One cannot improve upon natural beauty, Miss Larissa."

Larissa giggled like a schoolgirl, and Samm chuckled through welling tears and a tightness in her chest.

She stood and faced her wife. "My love, can you excuse us? I'll take care of this spill."

Larissa looked from Samm to Fincher, a mixture of curiosity and concern on the handsome woman's face. "Are you sure?"

Samm smiled as wetness appeared on her cheek, and she squeezed her partner's hand. "Very."

Larissa nodded, trusting her wife, and began to exit the office. "It was nice to meet you, Fincher."

The boy delivered a deep bow. "The pleasure was all mine, Miss Larissa." Fincher watched the woman descend the manor's cascading staircase before turning back to his old friend.

"You've done well, Samm." Fincher looked around the massive office. "In more ways than one."

Samm came around the work desk on legs of rubber, holding onto its corner for support. "But how?"

"Not the right question, Samm. At least, not for now. That's something that we can chat about, in time."

"Where have you been, Fincher?"

The boy's eyes, still full of innocence and compassion and love, now held something much greater, a wisdom and understanding that was not present when her friend was taken.

"You know where."

"The Wellspring," Samm whispered.

"And everywhere else. Some could say—"

Fincher didn't get a chance to complete his sentence, for the boy was knocked back two steps by a rushing Samm Buggsly, who buried her old friend in a tight embrace.

And they remained like that for several minutes, for Samm was terrified that if she let go, her friend would vanish once more, leaving her as cold and sad as the time they'd had to say goodbye.

Eventually, however, the two did separate. Samm smoothed down the boy's hair as she spoke. "You saw things no one could ever imagine. You traveled with gods. You found the Wellspring. Why did you come back to Quaan, Fincher?"

"I missed my friends."

Sammi scoffed at the boy's reasoning. "We're not the Wellspring, Fincher."

"No. You're better. You're the Sour Flower Gang. And never before has the universe seen such a force. Trust me."

Sammi wiped more tears. "Okay, okay, I believe you. Did you at least bring me something back from your trip through the cosmos?"

The boy offered one of Fincher Bugg's patented sly grins and reached into his pocket. When he revealed what he had retrieved, Samm could feel her brow furrow in confusion.

In Fincher's hand were two objects. One was a Ghost Puma tooth, still covered in dried blood. The other was a large, flattened white blossom tinged with bright red.

Samm studied the objects for a moment. "Is that the Ghost Puma tooth you took off Hana?" Fincher nodded. "And is that…"

"The flower that sprouted from Ditto's grave in Terminus Grove," the boy finished.

Samm nodded sadly. "You know, my sister never married. Never even dated much. She's the Ministress of Chips now and a great one, at that. Suitors from across the Republic have tried to win her heart, but none have even come close. I think she walled it off when Ditto died."

"I'm sorry to hear that."

"Yes, well…" Samm shook the melancholy thoughts free. "But let us not sully this joyous occasion with sad memories. What would you have us do, Fincher? Deliver the tooth to Hana's parents and the flower to Ash?"

Fincher's knowing grin transformed into a toothy smile. "Oh, I think we can do better than that, Samm. Much better."

Kenn Buggabe, formerly known as Kenn Bugg, chopped onions in his lovely kitchen while his wife Joon, Head of Education for the capital of Coballis, considered a proposal to build a new school closer to the Mutewoods to accommodate the children of smaller settlements.

As she read the detailed supporting evidence, her husband's chopping kept her going at a steady pace, the perfect human metronome.

Until it stopped. And the sound of a cleaver hitting wood rang out across the villa.

Joon Buggabe looked up from her work and froze, her mind and heart unable to comprehend what her clear eyes were seeing.

Hana Bugg shuffled into the kitchen, the young girl's sweet face filled with a smile. She looked the same as did the day she was stolen from them by the Titian Empire.

"Hi Ma. Hi Da. Did you miss me?"

Joon could not find the strength to stand as an uncomfortable mix of hope and terror filled the woman. The Head of Education had survived one heartbreak. She would not make it through another.

"If this is a dream, let me never wake," said the woman as tears began to fall. She reached out with a shaky hand. "If this is a dream…"

"That is no dream," shouted Kenn Buggabe as he flashed past his wife and dropped to his knees before their daughter. He hesitated for a moment before touching Hana's shoulders, afraid that his hands might pass through what would prove to be only an apparition.

But Kenn's hands didn't pass through. They were met with the solid resistance of soft flesh, and the father pulled his long-lost daughter in for a desperate hug.

They were soon joined by Joon Buggabe, who had finally dared to let her heart believe the miracle that stood before her.

"Where have you been, my darling?" cried Joon. "Where have you been?"

"Quaan has gotten so much better, but our lives have remained empty," added Kenn. "Nothing could fill the hole left by our Hana."

"Nothing," agreed a weeping Joon.

Hana gently pushed her parents to arm's length. "I was gone. And then Fincher brought me back. But can I fill you in on the details later? I'm starving."

Joon Buggabe kissed her daughter on her forehead, breathing in a scent that she hadn't experienced in twenty years. A smell that meant more to her than life itself.

"You know, even though they're hard to find this far east, I always keep some tart ice berries on hand. I don't know why I did that. I guess, just in case. Would you like some added to Da's stir fry?"

Hana pressed her forehead against her ma's. "That sounds yummy."

"Kenn? Kenn!"

Kenn snapped out of his trance. "Yes, yes! Of course! I'll get right on it."

Kenn raced to the kitchen and, within seconds, the chopping of vegetables could be heard, faster than ever before.

Joon sat her beautiful daughter down at the kitchen table, refusing to let go of the young girl's hand.

"Hana, would you like to sing us a song while Da cooks? Oh, how we've missed your voice."

Hana squeezed her Ma's hand in return. "Of course, Ma. What would you like to hear?"

"Anything. Anything at all."

Ash Buggsly tended to one of her many gardens, having taken the morning off from her duties as Ministress of Chips. There were several gardeners under the woman's employ, but she had given them the day off.

Sometimes, one needed to feel connected to that which they owned.

As she finished planting the last of a series of plants that would one day soon yield white blossoms—her favorite—the powerful woman rose, rubbing the stump of her arm as she did.

"Stupid thing," Ash bemoaned. "Why are you itching this time?"

"Perhaps it senses the approach of a friend," came a deep voice from across the lush garden.

Ash spun at the words, bringing her trowel around, the brave woman always ready to defend herself and those around her. The garden tool immediately fell from her grasp.

Marching down one of the many garden aisles was a striking, muscular man of about Ash's age. He had the blond hair and chiseled jaw of many of the wealthy suitors who had visited over the years to win the heart of one of the most influential women in the Cobalt Republic.

But his eyes… His bright green eyes marked the man as more—so much more.

"Ditto?" Ash dared as the man neared, the familiar details of his face becoming increasingly evident. "It… it can't be." She started to cry.

"But it is," Ditto said simply as he reached the woman. "I don't how, either. But it is."

"How?"

"Fincher."

Ash chuckled between sobs. "I should have known. That one had probably won over the God-Snails before they reached Ommori Prime."

Ditto began to lean in closer. "He did."

"And why did he bring you back?" asked Ash, her heart racing.

"Because I asked." Ditto inched closer.

"You asked to return to Quaan?" Ash's voice came out in a whisper.

"No. I asked to return to you."

"But you were a boy when you died."

Ditto shrugged. "What would the neighbors think if you had to couple with a boy?"

Ash inched forward. "Who cares what the neighbors think? Who cares what anyone thinks? Nothing matters, not anymore. Only you. Only you, Ditto. It was always you. I waited for you. I don't know why, but I did."

"How can I thank you?"

"You already did."

Ash's lips met Ditto's, and the world melted around them, the woman once known as Ashanti Bugg embracing her own personal Wellspring.

~

Gill Bugg, still known as Gill Bugg, sat on his rocking chair on the porch of his modest but elegant home just outside of Coballis.

As he had for two decades, the aging man rocked back and forth as Paragon fell behind the Spired Curtains. He looked out into the distance, willing his son to return. Nothing ever came of this ritual, but it brought some strange solace to the father's permanently bruised heart.

Soon, when it was too dark to see beyond the gate of his front yard, Gill Bugg would shuffle back into his lonely home and drink expensive honey rice wine until he fell into unconsciousness.

At least the clout that came with Bugg-based names was good for something.

Just as the old man rose and began to retreat into his too-empty home, a figure appeared by the gate, cloaked in shadow.

"Do you have an appointment?" called out Gill to the stranger, knowing that no such arrangement had been made.

"I didn't know that I needed one." Gill's heavy heart dropped, and the old man dared not move as the figure passed into the light emanating from the house. "Not one for my own home, at least."

Fincher Bugg crossed the cobbled pathway that cut through the manicured front lawn and ascended the porch stairs. The old man fell back in his chair, his son's appearance sapping him of his limited strength.

Fincher smiled warmly and slid into the second chair that rested next to Gill's—one that had never been used but had been reserved for twenty years.

"I never gave up hope, my son. I want you to know that. When Ash and Sammi—sorry, I still call her Sammi—told me what happened, I said that if there was anyone who could return from the heavens, it would be my boy Fincher."

Fincher took hold of his father's hand. "I did it, Da. I came back to tell you. I escaped the mud and rock, not only of Crimmish, but of all Quaan. I saw magnificent worlds. I soared through the cosmos. I swam in the light and warmth and life of the Wellspring. I can't show these things to you and, for that, I'm sorry. But I can tell you about them, Da. I can describe them in vivid, magical detail. Would you like to hear about them? Would you like to hear about my adventures, Da?"

Gill Bugg reached over and cupped Fincher's youthful face in his calloused hand, something he had wished to do for longer than he cared to remember. He leaned back in his rocker, a satisfied look on his weathered face.

"Fark, yeah."

THE END

ABOUT THE AUTHOR

Jarrett Brandon Early lives in Virginia Beach, VA with his wife Natthicha and daughter Alexandra Beam. Children of Madness is his fourth novel. His other three books comprise The Station Trilogy.

ALSO BY JARRETT BRANDON EARLY

The Station Trilogy

Station

The Rott Inertia

Ill Messiah

The Station Trilogy - The Complete Collection